THE ARACHNE OMNIBUS

CHRISTOPHER L. BENNETT

eBooks
Pennsville, NJ

PUBLISHED BY
eSpec Books LLC
Danielle McPhail, Publisher
PO Box 242,
Pennsville, New Jersey 08070
www.especbooks.com

ISBN: 978-1-949691-61-0
ISBN (ebook): 978-1-949691-60-3

Arachne's Crime
ISBN: 978-1-949691-13-9
ISBN (ebook): 978-1-949691-12-2

Arachne's Exile
ISBN: 978-1-949691-15-3
ISBN (ebook): 978-1-949691-14-6

Portions of *Arachne's Crime* originally published as "Aggravated Vehicular Genocide" in *Analog Science Fiction and Fact, Vol. CXVIII No. 11* (November 1998), pp. 110-130; and reprinted in *Among the Wild Cybers*, eSpec Books, 2018.

The Weight of Silence and Among the Wild Cybers of Cybele both previously printed in *Among the Wild Cybers*, eSpec Books, 2018.

Interior Design: Danielle McPhail
Cover Art and Design: © Mike McPhail, McP Digital Graphics
Cyber-Web Graphic © Mike McPhail, McP Digital Graphics
Copyeditors: Danielle McPhail and Greg Schauer

CONTENTS

COMFORT ZONES

Hayakawa City, Mars
2142

A SMALL HERD OF ELEROOS FROM THE PLANET CYBELE WAS GRAZING in front of the buffet table, and Cecilia LoCarno took it as a personal affront.

"Relax," Tarik Bahar told her, reading her mood from long experience. "Madeleine Kamakau would not have invited you to her farewell reception to embarrass you."

"That's just it," Cecilia told her burly executive officer, clinging to her bad mood even though she appreciated his effort to ease it. "We're an afterthought here. We spent *three years* out in the Oort cloud. Six months exploring Aita's oceans. Alonzo gave his *life* just to get us through the ice."

"I know."

"But everyone forgot all about us as soon as the Mother of Mars announced she was going to Alpha Centauri—and then all *this* came in from Cybele."

She gestured around her at the large, well-appointed reception hall, enhanced by augreality projections based on recently received probe telemetry from the surface of Gamma Leporis Ad. In her virtual view, the reception guests—a who's who of the movers and shakers of Mars, Earth, the Belt, and beyond—stood in a wide clearing carpeted with fine, reddish-purple grass and surrounded by treelike bamboo-ferns whose violet fronds wafted in the breeze. The eleroos—deer-sized bipedal herbivores with thick tails and twin prehensile trunks—hopped around and occasionally through the guests as they foraged, using their probosces to pull up grass and swat away the large scorpionflies that buzzed overhead.

"Nobody cares about algal mats and pluricellular colonies under twenty kilometers of ice," Cecilia went on, "when they can look at cute alien vertebrates on a habitable-zone planet—and imagine taking a casual stroll on its surface without centuries of terraforming first."

"People do care," Tarik insisted. "We were the first human beings to explore the ocean mantle of an Oort cloud planet. Our work—Alonzo's work, and yours—will leave a great scientific legacy."

"Tell that to everyone throwing their backing behind interstellar drive research instead of letting us take *Calypso* back out. Tell that to all the capable explorers and field researchers getting poached by the Alpha C and GJ 411 missions. I am *not* going to settle for captaining an SSB patrol ship or doing colony support in the Trojans for the rest of my career."

"That *would* be an enormous waste of potential," came a warm, matronly voice—one that Cecilia recognized instantly from the many eloquent speeches she'd heard it deliver.

She turned, and there stood Madeleine Kamakau in the flesh. The "Mother" of the Confederation of Martian Republics was a tall, full-figured woman in her mid-sixties, her meter-length hair shimmering black save for the famous and no doubt carefully cultivated streak of white emerging from her left temple. She wore a bright purple flower tucked over her right ear, matching her colorfully patterned sarong, and her necklaces and bracelets were carved from wood and bone in a traditional Polynesian style.

"Captain LoCarno," Kamakau went on, clasping Cecilia's hand warmly, then greeted Tarik in the same way. "I am delighted that you both came tonight. The goal of this event is to honor all our space explorers equally. I followed the news from your expedition with great excitement." She gestured around her at the Cybele projection. "As thrilling as it is to see animals and plants like this on another world, to contemplate setting foot on it one day, it's just as exciting to see young life on the verge of its multicellular breakthrough. And close enough to home that we can keep a close eye on the little scamps over the millennia ahead."

Cecilia would have resented being handled if Kamakau hadn't seemed so completely sincere, and if her reputation as a cultural founder hero in her own time hadn't been so intimidating. "Well, I, ah, I appreciate it, ma'am."

"Madeleine, please."

"Of course. I guess you are a real peacemaker after all."

Kamakau smiled. "It's a necessary skill honed over forty-six years in a group family."

"Don't be modest," Cecilia replied sharply, her bullshit meter overriding her intimidation. "It doesn't suit a woman of your ambition. You made that family into your peacemaking tool, used it to build strategic alliances and cultivate the best and brightest spouses, to create a political order based on community rather than competition. I still can't believe you pulled it off. Even just the family, let alone the Confederacy." Cecilia shook her head. "Juggling ten husbands, eight wives, and who knows how many kids? I couldn't even manage to keep one husband corralled."

The older woman laughed. "It takes a special man to appreciate someone who speaks as frankly as you do. I hope you haven't stopped looking." She threw an appraising glance toward Tarik, who blushed fiercely. He had a wife and child back in Istanbul, and his view of marriage was far more monogamous than the Martian norm.

Cecilia flinched as well. The reminder of Tarik's roots on Earth revived her unease about her future now that *Calypso*'s next mission was in doubt. He had someone to go home to, but her family would not welcome her back in Venezia. She had vacked that relationship as badly as her marriage, and her working partnership with Tarik over these past three years had been the most stable and fulfilling relationship of her life. She resented the idea of being forced to give it up.

For Kamakau's benefit, she only said, "Let's just say I'm married to my ship. I stick with what I'm good at."

Kamakau clasped her shoulder, guiding her through the crowd and the simulation. "You know, it's worth pushing yourself beyond your comfort zone. That's why I decided to go to Alpha Centauri. I realized I was letting a certain complacency take hold, in both myself and my clan. By holding myself back from new challenges, I was holding my eldest daughter back from her potential, and her right, to lead the family."

Cecilia stared. "And you think that requires moving four light years away from them?"

"I only hope that's far enough for both them and me to break free of this legend people have burdened us with... so we can begin to build new ones." She reached up to caress the vivid blue flowers on a virtual vine snaking around a Cybeline bamboo-fern. "If not, I'll just go farther still.

"That's something I think we have in common, Cecilia. For all my reputation as a homebody, I share the wanderlust of my ancestors—the drive that compelled them to spread across the Pacific, and more recently across Solsys. With modern medicine, I could have a century or two ahead of me yet, not even accounting for new hibernation techniques. We've seen the lights, the warmth, the pulse of other civilizations out there, further than Cybele. It might take a few generations of island-hopping, but I want to meet them one day. I want to speak their languages, translate their poetry, play with their children."

Cecilia grinned at the image, before her pragmatism reasserted itself. "That's a fine dream. But in practice, it's an enormous drain on resources and expertise still needed for Solar exploration and other priorities."

Kamakau looked sympathetic. "I'm sorry about your grant request. We're still committed to further outer system research, but it's a question of timing. In another couple of years—"

"It's not just you, though. Everyone's caught the interstellar bug. We've been snubbed by al-Khwarizmi, Soujikyuu, Stargazer, the Vanguard—"

Kamakau perked up. "As it happens, I was just taking you to meet someone who might help with one of those. Stephen!" she called.

The man who reacted to the name stood near the edge of the simulated clearing, having a lively chat with Director DeMarais of the Solar Security Bureau. As he turned, Cecilia recognized the striking, medium-brown features of Stephen Jacobs-Wong, the wunderkind founder of Earth's Stargazer Enterprises. It was no wonder, she thought, that Madeleine Kamakau would be friends with someone whose utopian ambitions were almost as legendary as hers.

Jacobs-Wong struck a handsome figure in his festively patterned, shirtless jacket and tight-fitting leggings, but Cecilia was in no mood to enjoy the view as he strode toward them. His presence here felt as much like an affront as the images from Cybele.

She stepped forward, ready to confront him, but Tarik caught her eye across the room. It was all she needed to hold her back. His calming influence had saved her from several potentially career-ending or fatal acts of impulse over the past few years—though far too late to prevent a ruined marriage and many botched friendships and career opportunities.

Holding Tarik's gaze, she reminded herself to be diplomatic with Jacobs-Wong. She recalled his famous backstory as a refugee from the brutal strongman regime of hurricane-ravaged Florida, one of the last remaining hellholes on Earth—though no longer, thanks largely to the vast fortune Jacobs-Wong had subsequently built and invested in reconstruction and reform, before turning his attention to space colonization and interstellar drive research. Now that she thought about it, Floridians and Venetians had a lot in common—both existing in precarious places, both fighting to keep a homeland and heritage from being swallowed by the sea. Maybe there was a common ground she could build on to change his mind about his funding priorities.

Once they had exchanged greetings, Jacobs-Wong said, "I've followed *Calypso*'s achievements with great admiration, Captain. I've been meaning to reach out to you—to talk about where you could go from here."

"Fine with me. I already know where I want to go next—back out to the Oort cloud. I know, you turned us down before, but just hear me out," she urged. "There are still uncharted planets out there, both dwarf and terrestrial. There are promising hints of life on two that we know of."

He chuckled. "I respect your determination. But there are exoplanets in reach that certainly do have life. Complex, truly alien life that demands expert study."

"One step at a time, Stephen. Alpha Centauri is one thing." She gestured at the virtual Cybele around them. "It may not have perfect Goldilocks worlds like this, but the worlds it has are reachable and adaptable with hard work. Gamma Leporis is nine parsecs away, beyond the practical range for crewed travel. All this is a fantasy, a distraction from the work we should be doing here in Solsys."

Folding his hands, Jacobs-Wong nodded thoughtfully. "With current technology, it would push the envelope, yes. But it's our dreams and ambitions that inspire innovation beyond our current limits.

"It was the probe returns from Alpha Centauri, Achird, and other nearby worlds—the confirmation of life out there, or worlds we could remold into homes for life—that prompted the development of faster drives." He put a hand on Kamakau's shoulder. "Because of that, Madeleine and her crew can reach Alpha Centauri in less than eight years, rather than the decades we formerly thought it would take. I expect these images from Cybele to inspire more such innovations. We will get there one day — I believe and hope, within our lifetimes."

"Why the rush?" Cecilia countered. "Cybele is a scientific wonder, yes, but is it worth the insane cost and risk of pushing there at relativistic speed just to put feet on its ground? What's the point, beyond a monument to a rich man's ego?" She winced as soon as the words left her mouth. *So much for diplomacy.*

Jacobs-Wong's charm faded somewhat, his gaze hardening. "Wealth is valueless unless it's repaid to society. What matters is our long-term survival as a species. And that means spreading beyond one world, one system."

"Remember where I've been, Stephen. There are millions of asteroids and comets close to home that we could convert into habitats. Look how much the colonization of Solsys has already helped to heal Earth. The resources within reach right here are virtually limitless, especially once we develop the Oort cloud.

"No, it's not as sexy as settling a Goldilocks world," she went on, "but species survival is a long-term ambition. If it's that important, then trust me, the last thing you want is to rush in and risk fucking the whole thing up."

"Oh, Cecilia," Kamakau interposed. "You're forgetting what I said about comfort zones. Do you know why it is that our branch of hominins survived when all the others died out?"

Cecilia looked between the two legends, feeling ganged up on. "I always figured it was sheer persistence. We never know when to quit."

Jacobs-Wong chuckled. "In a way, that's exactly it. We don't walk away from challenges even when they seem like bad ideas. Uniquely among the hominins, our ancestors' remains are found in every climate from deserts to mountains to Arctic regions, while others stayed in the forests and grasslands that were their comfort zone.

"And that drive, that stubborn, foolish refusal to stay within comfortable or safe limits, was the key to our success. We took crazy risks to settle environments we were never meant for — and in response, we innovated new technologies, new social structures, new survival skills. We became human, we created civilization, because we dared the impossible."

He gave her a meaningful look. "I shouldn't have to tell a proud Venetian that, should I? Where would your heritage be if your ancestors had said, 'We can't build a town here, it'll just sink into the marsh'?"

Cecilia winced, for he had struck a blow. Jacobs-Wong's debating skills were impressive, she had to admit.

"Colonizing Solsys is a worthy challenge, Cecilia," Stargazer's head went on. "But it's a challenge we've successfully met for over a century. It's more of the same. We need to raise the bar, find a greater challenge, if we want to keep evolving."

"Evolution takes millennia," she countered. "Those hominins who rushed into the deserts or the glaciers ended up as those remains we eventually found. It was the people who learned from their mistakes and went slower who ended up succeeding."

Jacobs-Wong laughed out loud. "Okay, that's a very good point."

Taking that as a promising sign, she went on. "All of this will come in due time. The great cathedrals of Europe were the work of generations to build. The people who started them knew they wouldn't live to see them finished. But they set out to create a legacy for their descendants. That's the mindset we need to ensure humanity's survival. Let's build the foundations here in Solsys first, so our descendants can build further."

He pondered for a time before replying. "Those cathedral builders were able to commit to something beyond their lifetimes because they believed they were reaching for something that transcended the limits of their world, their age. Inspiration matters, Cecilia.

"I've seen what happens when a society has no larger dreams to strive for. It becomes stagnant and turns on itself. If people see their reality as existing within fixed limits, they all too often begin to see it as a zero-sum game where their success requires others' defeat."

He gestured around at the Cybele-scape. "For me, it was this vision that changed that. Interstellar probes like these gave me hope for something better. It was by getting the other kids in my neighborhood excited about them too, offering a vision of a universe beyond the strict boundaries imposed on us, that I was able to give them hope as well, to inspire them to fight for change along with me.

"These probes saved my life, and many others. I called my company Stargazer for a reason."

Cecilia studied him for a moment, then sighed. "I guess your mind is made up, then. Sorry I wasted your time." *And mine.*

After Captain LoCarno strode off, Stephen gazed after her in regret. Beside him, Madeleine sighed. "Oh, I really thought you two kids would be a good match. Sorry."

He idly stroked her shoulder. "Don't apologize, Maddie. It was a stimulating argument. If anything, I think she's crystallized a decision for me."

"Oh? How so?"

"In trying to convince her we need to push beyond our limits, I think I've talked myself into committing to—well, this." He gestured at the simulated bamboo-ferns around them.

Kamakau's reaction blended disbelief and delight. "You're going to add the Cybele mission to your plans after all?"

"It's crazy, I know. An expedition to Achird is a big enough risk in itself. Cybele's half again as far. It's pushing the theoretical limits of the sailship tech, the hibernation tech."

"But?"

Stephen looked around at the alien landscape—at the nearest world besides Earth whose surface was so perfectly within the comfort zone for human life. The self-replicating auxon probes that had arrived there twenty-nine years before were already programmed with the protocols for building a colony; Stephen's forebears had had the kind of foresight LoCarno had praised, laying the groundwork for the next generation. Didn't he owe it to them to make use of what they had offered? The auxons might not remain intact forever, given that some of Cybele's predators seemed to find them irresistible.

Beyond that was another reason—less practical, but arguably more important. "Humanity needs to strive for impossible dreams. The Space Age started with a great ambition, to make it to the Moon in a mad, ridiculous rush. And it worked. But then people started settling for more practical goals and it fizzled out for decades. If we want to make it out there, we can't settle for the practical and the plodding. We have to inspire people to go after the biggest prize they can imagine. That's what Cybele can be for humanity.

"So no half-measures. No holding back. We're going to Cybele. No—*I'm* going to Cybele. Assuming I can pass the tests, of course. I have to prove I'm truly committed to this. More than that... I *want* to walk on this ground myself one day."

Beaming and laughing, Kamakau pulled him into a tight, congratulatory hug. "Welcome to the club, my dear! I knew we were two of a kind. Oh, I would've loved having you as a husband."

When the embrace ended, he sighed. "I have a regret or two myself. I really thought you were right about LoCarno. She would've made one hell of a starship captain."

Kamakau stared at him. "You're giving up on her because of one little argument?"

"You call that little?"

She laughed. "Compared to the knock-down verbal brawls I've had with my favorite spouses? Listen, honey—the only way I ever had a chance of pulling off my crazy plans for bringing peace to Mars was by surrounding myself with skeptics. We can always fool ourselves into believing our ambitions make sense. The only way to be sure my ideas could really work was by making them sound enough to convince my toughest critics—by finding an answer for every challenge they raised and a solution for every problem they foresaw.

"Didn't you just now tell me that it was your argument with Cecilia that convinced you to go to Cybele? You've been wrestling with that choice for months, and here it took five minutes clashing with her to make up your mind. Doesn't that prove her value to you?"

He shook his head. "She doesn't believe in what we're doing. She's too pragmatic, too cautious."

"She just lacks faith in her own vision. Oh, you should've seen how passionately she shot me down when I tried to underplay my achievements. The idea of founding a new society fires her passion, even if she doesn't realize it yet. That's valuable to you."

Kamakau chuckled. "Besides, I was watching you two argue. I saw a sparkle I know all too well from those favorite spouses."

Stephen's eyes widened. "You think she was flirting with me?"

She laughed. "I mean she loves a good argument. Cecilia LoCarno thrives on facing challenges, and you offered her a good one tonight. I think she'll welcome a rematch. She'll give you the chance to win her over—but she won't make it easy or quick. So I advise you to hone your debating skills."

He remained skeptical. "I know you're an amazing judge of character, Maddie, but I'm still not convinced."

"Have patience, dear. If I'm right, then she'll come back on her own. And then you'll know she's the captain—the partner—you want."

Cecilia found Tarik engaged in a friendly debate of his own with the notorious cyber activist Athena. The AI had adopted a relatively humanoid body for the occasion, though one designed to evoke the appearance of Cybele's auxon probes, with a skin of gleaming plasticrystal and pseudo-insectile limbs. It sounded like the cyber firebrand objected to the strictures placed on the auxons' own evolutionary potential in the name of protecting Cybele's organic life.

Not wishing to get drawn into that argument, Cecilia waited at the buffet table until Tarik rejoined her. "No luck with Jacobs-Wong?" he asked.

She shook her head. "He wanted to recruit me for an interstellar mission."

He froze in evident shock. "And you didn't jump at the chance?"

Cecilia stared back in surprise. "You think I should have?"

"You don't? Cecilia, you're a born explorer, even more than I am. You've been dreading the prospect of settling for routine, of having no new challenges to master. And if *I* were offered that chance..." He gazed skyward, eyes lit with wonder.

"Tarik, you have a family back home."

He blinked, wrestling with the reminder. "Well... being an explorer is not about staying comfortable. It's about enduring self-sacrifice for the sake of knowledge." He shrugged. "Besides, these *are* colony expeditions. Maybe we could bring families with us."

She gazed up at him. "With... *us?*"

Tarik studied her. "Is that what you're afraid of, Cecilia?" he asked gently. "That I wouldn't come with you?"

"You have responsibilities, commitments."

"And you are one of them. You're my captain. Tell me what you need and I will find a way to achieve it. So don't worry about me." He clasped her shoulder and smiled. "Where do *you* want to go next?"

As she held his gaze and considered it, she found no answer. It wasn't a prospect she'd seriously allowed herself to consider. She believed in the value of developing Solsys — but if human exploration of exoplanets *were* technically feasible, would that really undermine Solar exploration, or enhance it through the technological advances it inspired?

More importantly, if there were a way she could actually set foot on those strange new worlds, how could she possibly pass it up?

She reflected on her debate with Stephen Jacobs-Wong, really listening to what he'd said for the first time. She wasn't ready to change her mind just yet. But she realized one thing: She had enjoyed the debate. The Stargazer head had offered some solid, thoughtful arguments and given her a lot to think about. And he'd done it without impatience or resentment at her bluntness. Madeleine had been right—aside from Tarik, men like that were a rare find.

Maybe what she needed to help her decide, then, was to continue the debate. For however long it took.

Once Kamakau had wandered off to mediate an argument between two Martian governors who were apparently both among her biological children, Stephen watched the Cybeline sunset for a while. He regretted letting Madeleine's senior daughter convince them that immersive footage of Aita's subglacial oceans would be too cold, dark, and off-putting for the reception guests. Including the footage might have made Captain LoCarno feel less slighted.

Or perhaps she would have scorned it as a hollow, manipulative gesture. He could tell she was not easily swayed by superficial appeals. A strong, commanding will like that could be very useful to him—but it was also quite an obstacle. He feared that setting foot on Cybele in his lifetime might be an easier challenge than winning an argument with Cecilia LoCarno.

He turned toward the buffet table to get a new drink, only to find LoCarno blocking his path. "And another thing," she began, thrusting a finger in his face.

Stephen smiled, accepting the challenge.

ARACHNE'S CRIME

To my readers, for giving back.

When Pallas, pitying her wretched state,
At once prevented, and pronounc'd her fate:
Live; but depend, vile wretch, the Goddess cry'd,
Doom'd in suspence for ever to be ty'd;
That all your race, to utmost date of time,
May feel the vengeance, and detest the crime.

— Ovid, "The Transformation of Arachne into a Spider"
(translated by Samuel Croxall)

PART ONE

AGGRAVATED VEHICULAR GENOCIDE

PROLOGUE

Churrlaya was grateful to be his entire self again. As he hopped down from *Zhemhal*'s gangway into the body of his home, he finalized his disengagement from the ship's local consensus memory, feeling a brief moment of incompleteness before his internal mind reconnected with his guild consensus and he remembered the rest of who he was. He and his guildmates aboard the survey vessel had been able to draw on the Biology Guild's uploaded knowledge base and share consensus with one another, but it had been a mere echo. Whatever memories and affinities they shared with him, none of them completed his identity the way Simisshen did.

True, Simisshen was one of many whose external selves now overlapped with his once again. But that one had changed Churrlaya more than all the others once he had joined Biology. This was only the second guild Churrlaya had joined since reaching maturity. It was a delicate age—too far from childhood to be comfortable without firm attachment and identity, yet too unused to transition to adjust easily to a new life. Simisshen had taken Churrlaya under his neck and let the younger one share the parts of his mind to which transition was an old friend, rebirth a welcome release after an old life had grown tiresome. His perspective had become a part of Churrlaya, uniting them in mind even as they discovered the joy of uniting in the flesh. Simi had led so many fascinating lives, formed so many ties to so many homes in his long, roving life. Paradoxically, it made Churrlaya feel more anchored. Not trapped by gravity like those lowly creatures on the rogue ice planet his expedition had surveyed, but connected to the galactic web of life, ever moving and growing.

Yet Churrlaya had never fully appreciated this until the expedition had returned him to a state without Simisshen's memories and ways of thinking as part of himself. He supposed he should be grateful for the deprivation, then, for now he would appreciate his lover all the more.

Simisshen soon felt Churrlaya's return as well, as did Marellel, Ruzhalu, and his other closest guildmates. In moments, they had reached out to him consciously, eager to share in his memories of the survey — to taste the illicit thrill of standing on the surface of a planet, even one with only primitive forms trapped in subglacial oceans. They could study his memories at their leisure, but for now he summarized the mission to slake their curiosity. The rogue's fading internal heat had guttered out further since the last, ancient survey of this obscure worldlet in one of the emptiest parts of the galaxy. Erstwhile pockets of livable ocean had frozen solid, their organisms perfectly preserved for dissection and analysis. It would keep their collegium busy for a long time.

Still, Simisshen pretended to be upset that Churrlaya had left him for so long. "I feared you'd chosen to migrate without telling me," he said, his mocking anger a mask for his relief at being whole again — a relief that Churrlaya could feel in his own thoughts and that, he was stunned and moved to discover, was as intense as his own. Drumming his toes on the ground, Simi threatened, "Spend too long away next time and I'll migrate myself and not tell you where."

Churrlaya leaned forward but shook his mane to soften the aggressive gesture, knowing the ubiquitous cloud sensors would carry his image to their eyes as theirs were brought to his. "I wouldn't even notice you were gone," he taunted, a counterpoint to the truth they shared without words. "I'll simply go female and take Marrellel as my partner."

Marrellel struck tails with Simisshen and opened her mouth wide to Churrlaya, shaking her tongue. Clearly she was about to say something very bawdy and inappropriate.

But then a brilliant, strobing flash blinded the sensor cloud, making Churrlaya reflexively roll his eyes back. The feed flickered as the cloud struggled to compensate with intact sensors, but the strobing continued — like lightning, yet the shadows moved as if the storm were rushing toward the equator. The sensory confusion reflected a deeper one as his external thinking was disrupted, memories and cognitive servers cut off from his access. Falling back on his most basic onboard knowledge and habits, he refocused through a nearby sensor vantage.

He saw flattened vegetation and falling trellises, heard a prolonged thunderclap, felt it shake the whole district. Smelled burning vegetation and flesh. Finally he spotted Simisshen and Marrellel—fallen, covered in burns, bleeding from their eyes and mouths. He called to them, pinged them, but they were motionless—as were all the others around them. He couldn't feel any of them, couldn't access the consensus. He was as alone, as incomplete, as in that brief moment between ship and home—as in that empty lifetime before he met Simisshen. Yet he knew that this time it would never end.

Wait! Now Simi was moving… but no, it was a wind, a gale tearing at his beautiful mane, pushing him brutally into the ground. More flashes and bangs startled Churrlaya, but they were different, they were—the cables? The support cables that held up the ground were… exploding! Whole buildings swayed, the surface rippling in a wave toward his mates.

He saw the ground tear open, the air exploding out into vacuum and taking everything—everyone—with it. But Churrlaya could barely process it through the agony in his mind as half of himself was ripped away along with everything he loved.

1

STEPHEN KEPT HIS EYES ON THE LIGHTS IN THE SKY, EVEN AS HE LAY IN THE mud. The more they tried to beat him down, the more he took comfort in the heights humanity could reach.

"Look up there," he told them once he'd grown strong enough to defend himself and win the chance to be heard. "Look at what we have the potential to achieve if we use our energies together instead of wasting them against each other."

At first, Benjamin was his only audience, gazing up with him at the points of light that swept across the heavens. Stephen spoke to inspire the boy, to give his younger brother the same hope that had sustained him. But he did it for the others too. He knew that fighting them off would only make them come back with greater force. To protect Benjamin, he needed a more powerful weapon, one that could reach into minds and change them, turn their own power to his side. And so he spoke.

"Most of the world isn't like this anymore," he told the starving, bitter people around him whether they listened or not. "The governors keep us hungry and desperate so we'll turn on each other. So they can call us savages and use it to justify keeping us down. So we won't have the strength to stand against them and the militias that keep their entitled white asses in power. But look up there, brothers," he urged, even as the bullies' hands grabbed at him and tried to hold him down. "You can *see* it's a lie. You can see that by standing together, human beings can scale the heights of heaven."

And one by one, they started to listen. One by one, their hands fell away and their eyes turned upward with his, watching the countless points of light that soared outward in a line like regimented fireflies, a scintillant cascade growing ever faster with distance.

"What are they?" Benjamin asked, gazing up at him with those big dark eyes as they stood together on the levee. The boy's rich brown face was Stephen's only reminder of their father.

"Auxons. Self-replicating robots. Or parts of one. They need to start small so they're easier to accelerate — the drive beam can get them close to lightspeed in days. Once they get there, they'll combine into larger robots, ones that can make more robots. They'll build a whole ecology of probes to survey the fifth planet and tell us whether humans can live there. And if the answer's yes, then we'll tell the auxons to build a settlement for us, so it'll already be waiting when the colony ship gets there."

Ben beamed at how clever it was, and Stephen took joy from the sight. He'd never appreciated it enough when Ben had been this young. A burst of brilliant light illuminated Ben's face, and Stephen turned his gaze back outward to watch the fireworks blazing.

"You know it wasn't really like this."

Stephen turned. Cecilia LoCarno leaned against a grafitti-scrawled wall nearby, her sinewy frame taut and ready even in her casual pose. The light from the fireworks put red and blue highlights in her severely cut silver-blonde hair. "You're romanticizing it again, aren't you? Brilliant lights soaring to the stars? You know they launched the microsail probes over months, and with a microwave beam, not visible. Oh, plus it happened a decade and a half before you were born. And, well…" She looked down at Ben, but said no more.

She didn't have to. His eyes stung as he turned back to his brother, older now and standing rigidly beside him while their mother gazed up apologetically from her sickbed, her delicate Chinese features sunken and gaunt. "Why won't they help Mama?" the youth demanded. "They have the medicine."

"I'm working extra-hard," Stephen told him. "Saving everything I can."

"Then they'll just raise the prices! They'll never help one of us. There's only one way to get it!"

Benjamin was already receding from the room. Cecilia tried to stop Stephen from following. "You know where this leads. Don't give into it." He resented her for making him remember. Ben had never grown any older than Stephen saw him now. All he had done to protect his brother had been for nothing. He pushed past her, trying to catch up to Ben and stop him from making the same mistake that had taken their father, but again he felt hands holding him back. "Let go, Cecilia!"

"No, you let go!"

Now they were side by side in the waiting room, in the cheap plastic seats where he felt he'd been imprisoned for ages, waiting for the word that his mother had died at last. In the opposite corner, a silver spider was weaving an intricate web. "Why are you here?" he asked Cecilia.

She shrugged. "Maybe we were both thinking of the mission at the same time. Arachne picked up on the common cues and hooked us in."

The mission. He stared at her, startled, before he remembered again. Her words confirmed that she was the real Cecilia LoCarno. People who were really there had a different feel about them, but sometimes Stephen didn't remember to pay attention. "How do you do that?" he asked her.

"Do what?"

"You always know it's a dream."

"Disciplined mind. Goes with the job." She smirked. "Plus, it's easy to tell in here. Reality isn't in the habit of giving us what we want."

Stephen glanced around. They were in his orbital shuttle, awaiting clearance, and the computer was announcing a prolonged delay. Through the window, the flooded remains of Florida were merely a thin streak vanishing over the horizon. Ben was gone now… had been gone for a very long time. "I know that as well as you do, Cecilia. More. Yet I always get drawn into the dream."

She punched him in the arm. "You would. That's why you need me to drag you back to reality."

"Not here, I don't."

"Hell, yes. Otherwise you'd have remembered on your own—relived the shooting and tortured yourself with losing Ben all over again. Jesus, for such an optimist you sure are pathetic in here," she added, knocking him on the forehead. He cried out in pain; she tended to be rough in the dream realm. Inhibitions were low in unreality, since memories were fleeting. "Or is that it?" she asked. "Maybe that's why you needed to travel so far from Earth—to run away from all that."

"I'm running *toward* something, not away." He sighed as he stared out the port. The shuttle was hemmed in now, in a holding pattern flanked by other craft, distant points that seemed to be drawing closer. "At least, I will if we ever get clearance to leave!"

Cecilia frowned. "Wait, you're right. I sense it too. Something holding us back, holding us still. Even before you said anything, I think I could feel it."

Stephen struggled to remember how this dream world worked. "Then it's… something from Arachne? A message?"

"But just impressions. Damn, I wish we were awake enough to perceive direct telemetry without all the subconscious filtering. Just… try to concentrate on the ship, on the space outside."

He looked out again, and the Earth-orbit vista was gone, replaced by a vast spiderweb gliding through the interstellar void. *Arachne* was a broad cone of shroud lines connecting three great rings of magsail cable, with crew and cargo modules and laser assemblies strung along smaller rings toward the rear. In reality, the gossamer craft was virtually invisible while coasting. In dreamtime, she shimmered, the magnetic field of her sail glowing like an aurora. Gamma Leporis lay ahead, but not an orb, just a bright point, fiercer and whiter than Sol. It brightened suddenly — no, a flash from a closer source? Like the fireworks reflected in Ben's eyes. What was Arachne trying to show them? More flashes, nearer — meteors flashing past the ship. Hitting the ship? He wasn't sure what he'd seen, but whatever it was, something changed. The wind died down, *Arachne*'s sails falling limp, the ship dead in the water. "Do you see us… becalmed?" Though they were in communication, they weren't necessarily perceiving the same things, not without verbal or contextual cues to put them on the same page.

"Parked. In orbit of something, but there's nothing there. A brown dwarf? No, but there is something… something drawing near."

His dream *Arachne* was now a clipper ship with canvas furled, adrift beneath the stars, endless black reflecting in the calm sea. A voice called faintly from above. He looked up to see a great silver spider skittering along the rigging, alert and ready as a ripple fractured the starlight. But beyond her, Stephen Jacobs-Wong saw dark shapes drawing in, pirate boats with oars muffled and lanterns doused. "Stand by," he heard himself call, "and prepare to be boarded."

"Stephen? Can you hear me? Please respond."
The voice faded in and out at the edge of Stephen's consciousness… no, it was his consciousness that faded in and out. The clear, soothing alto — Arachne's voice, yes, sounding authentically human yet more

pure and perfect—held steady as it always did. He tried to make a noise, but hibernation gel filled his throat. He remembered to subvocalize, got something out, but instantly forgot what he'd said.

"I've had to rush your revival. This will be difficult, I know. But you must focus."

Try as he might, he caught only fragments. *Detected... contact... gravitational... boarded... inside.*

Then the gel drained away and all he knew was the struggle of his weak, unused muscles to expel it from his throat, his lungs... merciful that he'd forget... and then a hand on his arm, and—

A dragon? In a space helmet?

He was pulled free and hit a cold, hard surface... and then everything was a blur.

"The key is to make her as light as possible." It was Haim Silbermann's gruff voice. *Arachne* was a schematic on a screen, and Stephen stood in Haim's office at Stargazer Enterprises as the stocky, gray-bearded engineer described his baby. "She's stripped down, sleek as a racing yacht. Even so, we'll split her in thirds for the accel phase." The spiderweb split into three separate ships, each with its own magsail loop, each one smaller than the last. "We send the most massive ship first, the lightest one last. That way each one's a bit faster than the one ahead, so they catch up and join together for the coasting phase."

The screen now closed on a single subship, showing a stream of tiny disks bombarding it from behind, vaporizing against its magnetic field. "The sail pellets are where we get our extra kick. Each one's got a nanogram payload of antimatter, enough to turn the whole microsail into hot plasma. The extra energy imparts that much more momentum to the magfield. We should reach point eight c, maybe more, depending on how light the payload is." Haim smirked. "The whole crew in hibernation—should be quite the space-saver."

Cecilia was there too, still unconvinced. "And quite the risk. Eighteen years in hibernation? Exposed to the kind of blueshifted radiation and particle bombardment you'd get at those insane speeds? What about the cell damage?"

I'm back in the dream, Stephen began to realize. Or rather, the VR interface mediated by Arachne. A brain could not be completely shut down for long and then started up again; even with hibernation slowing their brain functions to a crawl, the crew still needed stimulation.

Odd, though… hadn't something awakened him? Had he dreamt that as well? Or was Arachne still connecting to his subconscious through his neural implants?

"Hibernation would slow cell division, so damaged DNA wouldn't spread as fast," Stephen heard himself reply even as he wondered this. "And of course the ship's magnetic field and metamaterial shielding will ward off most of the radiation."

Perhaps not an interactive dream, then, but just a memory playback. After so many years asleep, his brain needed the refresher course. Arachne must be helping him get back up to speed for… whatever.

"But not all," the memory of Cecilia said. "There's also toxin buildup, atrophy…"

"All of which can be corrected with a full nanorepair suite, like yours."

"And I've been a spacer long enough to know their limitations. To know *my* limitations. I don't think you do, Stephen. My God, nobody's ever been farther out than two and a half parsecs, or gone much over half of *c*! Now you want to go three times that far and half again that speed—in what amounts to a catamaran! Even with all the advances, all the safeguards, it's an unprecedented risk."

"Going to the Oort cloud is a risk," he said, reminding her of the three-year survey expedition that had brought her to his attention. "Staying within the Belt and building artificial worlds is a risk." Stephen took a slow breath. "Living on Earth is a risk. I can assure you of that." He clasped her hands, holding her gaze with his. "Cecilia, the greatest risk of all is growing complacent and letting entropy catch up with us. Humanity is on the verge of immortality—of spreading far enough through space to ensure that our species will never go extinct. To cross that threshold, we have to be bold enough to face the risks that come with it. And we have to inspire others to be bold."

"*Stephen!*" Cecilia's voice, though the Cecilia before him hadn't spoken.

"Yes, we could limit ourselves to the nearer exoplanets, but Cybele is the most Earthlike one we know, the one where a human colony could most readily thrive. There's symbolic power in that. Just as there is in questing to the very limits—"

A sudden stinging pain. "*Stephen! Wake up, damn it!*"

Cecilia's sharp voice was as much a shock to his system as her slaps to his face. He started awake, trying to remember.

"Easy." Another face came into view, crowding out Cecilia's. A dark, rounded face, maternal and gentle—Doctor Kweli Ndege. "Stephen, how do you feel?"

He tried to move, but the oddly textured surface beneath him clung to his naked skin. He was under gravity! High gravity, from the way the surface dug in; just breathing exhausted him. Or maybe he was just extremely weak. Despite the nanomaintenance and the periodic stimulation to his hibernating muscle cells, you couldn't come out of an eighteen-year slumber without feeling like you'd been asleep for exactly that long. But he gathered his energies, willed himself to sit up, and kindly but firmly brushed aside Kweli's help. He couldn't let himself be weak. Not if what he remembered was real—the dragon-creatures, the heavy suits. Being dragged bodily from hibernation. *Abducted by aliens?*

He looked around. They were in a large chamber with walls tinged an odd, off-putting hue. The light was strange, as if meant for eyes evolved under a different sun. Nearby, the nose cones of *Arachne*'s six habitat/landing modules were visible beyond a dividing wall several meters high. He could see no sign of the cargo modules or magsail cables. The wall was too smooth to scale, even if their condition and the gravity permitted it, and no exits or windows were evident.

Besides Cecilia and Kweli, he saw other members of the crew. Haim Silbermann. Tarik Bahar, Cecilia's burly second-in-command. And Zena… no, Sita Bhatiani, the dainty biologist. They were all naked, still dripping cryo gel, visibly uncomfortable in the coolness of the chamber. (No wonder it was cool—they were meters away from hulls that had recently been in interstellar vacuum. Stephen could hear the modules creaking and popping as they warmed up.) Their hair, and no doubt his own, was shorn to within a centimeter all over their bodies; he remembered that the hibernation chambers' smart gel "digested" their hair as it ever so slowly grew out, filtering heavy metals and toxins and recycling usable compounds to help sustain their glacial metabolisms. It didn't look too strange on Cecilia and Kweli, who wore their hair short to begin with, or on Haim, whose stubbly chin suggested his normal salt-and-pepper beard. But it was odd to see the normally moustachioed Tarik Bahar with a full nascent beard, or Sita without her shoulder-length black hair.

Sita was the only one who wasn't shivering, aside from Cecilia, who never showed weakness. The biologist's dark sloe eyes were wide and inquisitive, her mouth quirking at the corners. For her, being abducted by aliens must be the opportunity of a lifetime.

"Arachne," Stephen asked, "the rest of the crew? The embryos?"

"*The embryos are safe, Stephen,*" came Arachne's voice from his comm implant. "*The remaining forty-two personnel are still in hibernation, alive and well. The xenosophonts have not permitted me to revive them.*"

All right—he hadn't imagined it. "How much do we know?"

"From what Arachne told me," Cecilia said, "we're awake four and a half years early, seven objective. We're still about a parsec and a half from Gamma Lep." Of course Cecilia would've been the first one fully conscious. "These… alien ships just appeared out of nowhere, accelerating like nothing we've ever seen. And then they…" Cecilia exhaled sharply, almost a laugh. "They dragged us to a halt. In just a couple of hours, they slowed us from point-eight-four *c* to a virtual dead stop in the galactic frame."

Haim's serious look gave way to pride. "Point-eight-*four*. The fastest ship ever flown, didn't I tell you?"

"*You flatter me, Haim. But next to these beings, I feel like an inflatable raft. Stephen, based on the Doppler shifts I observed in the starlight, I'd hypothesize that we were decelerated by some form of directed gravitational field.*"

"A tractor beam?" Tarik asked.

Haim shook his head. "Show me the specs and maybe I'll believe it. But whatever they used, the power expenditure must be incredible. Whoever they are, they *really* wanted us to pull over."

"*Once I saw what was happening,*" Arachne went on, "*I initiated an emergency revival of command crew and appropriate advisors.*"

Stephen sized up the group: himself, Cecilia, and Tarik to make the decisions; an engineer to evaluate the aliens' technology; a biologist/ethologist to evaluate the creatures; and the chief physician for obvious but hopefully unnecessary reasons. Appropriate indeed.

Stephen wanted to ask for an update on *Uttu*, but it was futile. *Arachne*'s sister ship should have reached Achird about four years ago by his admittedly fuzzy estimates, but there was no way to confirm that. Sending two expeditions to different stars had ensured that no mishap could befall both ships at once, but it also left each ship completely on its own. He wished for the umpteenth time that he could've organized a larger expedition. But even in the modern, post-scarcity economy, there was only so much material and energy expense that he'd been able to convince his corporate, government, and community partners to invest in a risky experiment like this. Besides… what could a second unarmed ship have done against *this?*

"Are we aboard one of the alien ships?" he asked instead.

"This is the largest of the vessels that intercepted me, yes."

Sita frowned. "Then where the bloody hell are they?!" She pushed herself up onto her knees, as close as she could get to standing. "Oi! Is anyone out there? We come in peace! Take us to your bloody leader already, you wankers!" Her London accent grew increasingly Cockney when she became emotional.

"Sita," Cecilia warned. "We don't know what might provoke them."

"Bollocks! This is the moment we've been waiting for since — forever! We've made contact with sentient, technological aliens — not through signals or probes, but *here*, maybe just on the other side of this wall! Can't blame me for wanting a look at them, can you? They've certainly gotten an eyeful of us," she said, gesturing at her compact nude form as if to invite attention to it.

Resisting the invitation with some difficulty, Stephen answered, "And when the time comes, Sita, you're the one with the experience, the context, to interpret it best. You're better equipped than anyone else here to cope with this — so we need you calm and in control."

She smiled up at him. Something passed between them, a sense of intimacy… stirrings of memory, hot, sweaty, sensual. After a long, warm moment, he broke her gaze, chiding himself to stay focused. He was hardly so shallow as to fixate on a nude woman's allure at a time like this, even one as sublimely lovely as Sita. And their interactions had always been professional before. What he'd remembered must be part of the dreams, then. There would've been no shame in that, not in the dreamspace, for it would all be forgotten afterward. But these impressions of Sita were so vivid, as if from a dream he'd had many times. What had they shared in there?

"We shouldn't romanticize this," Cecilia said. "The one thing we do know is that we've been shanghaied."

"But to what end?" Kweli asked. "Are they pirates?"

"What do we have that they'd want?" Haim asked, gesturing at the awesome technology that implicitly existed beyond the drab walls.

Sita shrugged. "Maybe they went out for takeaway and we're tonight's curry." Kweli glared, not appreciating her humor.

It was bad timing that the aliens chose that moment to arrive. A circular door frame formed within what had been a solid wall—a feat within the capability of human technology, and thus almost reassuring.

Stephen struggled to stand, determined to meet the aliens on his feet. Sita forced herself upright as well, though she needed a hand from Stephen, and then he needed a hand from her to avoid falling over. Cecilia and Tarik, standing quite well on their own, moved forward, ready to defend the others. They were surely too weak to make a difference, but if these aliens could read human body language at all, maybe their determination would suffice. "Arachne," Cecilia said, "any headway with communication?"

"Upon contact, their vessel's AI system initiated a handshake and translation protocol beginning with physical and mathematical constants."

Sita's eyes widened. "They'd have to upload bags of cultural information to give you a basis for understanding their language," she said. "I'd love to be in your head right now."

"I'll happily upload my data to your buffer, Sita, but there isn't much. I get the impression that it recognized the English language and has been using my files merely to update its database. I've gotten little in return."

"We have been broadcasting for centuries," Haim observed.

Finally the hatch irised open, revealing a tubular airlock long enough to fit the creatures within. They entered with a graceful hopping motion, necks flexing to steady their heads. They were maybe two and a half meters long and shaped rather like kangaroos, with heavy, stiff tails. Their arms were nearly as long and powerful-looking as their legs, with two fingers and two thumbs on each symmetrical, gloved hand. They brandished rods that were most likely weapons of some kind. Their loose-fitting, helmeted garments looked like cleanroom or biohazard suits, with filters but no air tanks. That implied their own atmosphere was compatible with human needs; Stephen and the others might be breathing it even now.

Under its visor, the first alien had a triangular-snouted, turquoise-skinned head with a crest of bristly hair or cilia running from the front of the snout to between its bulbous, chameleon-like eyes, which were sheltered under large bony brows. Contrary to his initial "dragon" impression, the skin was smooth, and he glimpsed what seemed to be brightly colored hair between the brows.

As a second pair of xenosophonts began cycling through the lock, Cecilia steeled herself and strode forward to face the lead alien. Tarik tensed, clearly wishing to shield his captain with his bulk, but he deferred to her authority. And even nude and nearly bald, she radiated command, as if her flesh were a uniform. "I am Captain Cecilia LoCarno of the colony ship *Arachne*, from the planet Earth. Identify yourselves, and explain your reasons for interrupting our voyage." She had to look up at the creature; in repose, with its body raised to the diagonal and resting on its legs and tail, the alien topped her by a good thirty centimeters. Still, she took a firm, confrontational tone, though she had no way of knowing if that would be understood. Stephen lamented that humanity's first words to this species could not be delivered in a spirit of amity.

The alien remained silent for a moment, probably waiting for the translation. Then it opened its mouth, revealing a thick, muscular tongue and structures resembling omnivore's teeth, and began to speak. Its suit speaker translated: "I am Rillial. We are Chirrn." At least, that was how Stephen's mind approximated the name. The underlying sound could have been approached just as closely with a sneeze, growl, and gulp in quick succession. "We are survivors of vessel Lesshchi. Explain *your* reasons for attacking vessel Lesshchi."

Six pairs of human eyes widened in shock; the chameleon-eyed aliens, now four in number, tensed at the unfamiliar optical display, as if uncertain what it signified. "*What?*" Cecilia finally asked.

"Explain your reasons for attacking vessel Lesshchi. Is language mediation not legitimate?"

"No, it's... . There must be some mistake," Cecilia said with growing anger. "We haven't attacked any ships. We're colonists, not fighters. Besides, we've all been in hibernation. The only person who could've done anything is the ship herself. And Arachne would have no reason to attack an alien ship."

Unless she knew that ship posed some threat, Steven thought, seeing the same realization in Cecilia's eyes. But Arachne would have mentioned any such action.

"Chirrn vessel Lesshchi," Rillial countered, "was struck by many relativistic projectiles incoming by trajectory of your vessel. Do you exclude premise that your transport contains this qualification?"

"Well, no," Haim interjected once he'd parsed the awkward translation. "Um, I'm Haim Silbermann, the chief engineer. We do have a sailbeam system for deflecting interstellar debris."

"Haim!" Cecilia hissed, glaring at him.

Silbermann gave her a *What else can I say?* shrug, then turned back to the Chirrn. "But we wouldn't have fired on your ship. The system checks for engine emissions, radio leakage, and such before it locks on to fire. If your ship had been in our path, Arachne wouldn't have shot it. She would've tried to delay or divert us enough to miss."

Arachne spoke up. *"Captain, I did deploy a fragmentation and deflection volley against a body on a collision course shortly before the Chirrn captured us. But there were no indications of a propulsion system — no particle exhaust, gamma or x-ray signature, magnetic field, or sail of any kind. Nor was there any EM activity suggesting power systems. Its thermal profile was atypically warm, its surface atypically dark, but otherwise it read like a carbonaceous asteroid in the range of twenty to twenty-five kilometers in size, which is far too large for a spacecraft."*

Rillial's eyes swiveled to take in all six humans. "You do not receive comprehension of what you have done," it said; evidently it was tuned into Arachne's comm frequency. "You shall see it. We return to seek inclusion for other survivors. You will come accompanied with us now." The other Chirrn moved forward, rods raised, body language clearly threatening. Their aggression was the most recognizable thing Stephen had seen here.

To Stephen's surprise, the Chirrn led them through a newly-formed door in the partition and back to *Arachne's* modules. "Know this is not illusion," Rillial said. "See through your own ports. Verify with your own instruments."

The modules' cockpits were small, so Stephen, Cecilia, and Haim were led into one, with Tarik accompanying Sita and Kweli into the other. Two Chirrn shepherded each group; Rillial and an even larger, more bluish Chirrn accompanied Stephen's. As a small mercy, Arachne spoke up and insisted that her protocols forbade cockpit access to anyone not wearing at least an emergency pressure garment—a small deception, but one that granted the captives a modicum of dignity. Stephen sent subvocal thanks to the shipmind as he donned the thin, close-fitting pressure membrane under close Chirrn supervision. The guards did insist on holding on to the humans' helmets, lest Arachne attempt anything untoward with the cockpit pressure.

The modules lurched as they were picked up by the dock machinery. Stephen watched through the cockpit windows as they moved toward a moderately larger craft ringed by a cylindrical collar. The modules were tilted forward, making Stephen grateful he'd strapped in. But once they were positioned between the spacecraft's hull and its cylindrical collar, the sensation of weight vanished. Shortly, the ringed craft launched into space at considerable speed, but Stephen felt almost no acceleration. "Amazing," Haim breathed. "Inertial cancellation. And did you notice? Their ship isn't rotating either. I didn't feel any Coriolis shifts as we moved. I'd never have believed it, but they must have some kind of artificial gravity."

Stephen watched as Cecilia tested the cockpit's controls, determining that the Chirrn had left only the sensor displays and their manual backup controls active. It was overkill; the landing modules had only enough fuel for orbital maneuvering, specifically to rendezvous with an auxon-built orbital station which would fuel them for planetary descent. They could never outrun a Chirrn starship.

The stars were all that Stephen saw for an uncertain amount of time. He compared the starscape against the simulated view from Cybele that he had memorized over the years of planning: the *W* of Cassiopeia written in an unfamiliar hand, the Little Dipper more of a long-handled funnel, Boötes tangled in Berenice's hair. It was off by just enough to account for the parsec-and-a-half distance Cecilia had reported. Scanning the sky, he found Sol exactly where he expected it, directly between Sirius and Altair.

Naturally, Cecilia was the first to spot something. Unfastening her harness, she pulled herself to the port for a closer look. Stephen followed her lead, as did Haim and Kweli, and before long he could see it too. A shimmer of lights, multicolored pinpricks flickering, moving in a stately dance around a central point. Faint sparkling clouds surrounding them, catching their glow, scintillating. It was beautiful.

Soon they drew close enough to see the truth. The lights were ships around a vast, dark central mass, shining spotlights as they flew around it in search patterns. From the way it eclipsed the stars, its main body was a cylinder, foreshortened from this angle but maybe six to ten times as long as it was wide. Around its equator was a broad ring like a much vaster version of the one currently encompassing *Arachne*'s habitat modules, but more solidly merged with the cylinder. At the near end, appended to the hemispherical endcap, were two fat disk-shaped structures, nearly as wide as the cylinder, connected with multiple struts yet mostly self-contained. Overall, it reminded him of the O'Neill habitats back in Solsys, though it was apparently not rotating.

As the Chirrn ship rounded the habitat, the shape of the far end came into view past the central bulge. It seemed different on this end, like it had an extra protruding structure on one…

Side…

His mind resisted understanding what he saw, as much due to the sheer scale as to its horrific significance. Two huge portions of the habitat's hull, kilometers long and wide, hung outward from the structure as though something had sliced a jagged gash through the hull, then peeled back the edges to expose the contents within. As they drew closer, Stephen could see the remains of structures — buildings — on its warped surface. Soon he noticed a smaller, coaxial cylinder inside the habitat, also showing damage. He had no way of telling just how deep the damage penetrated, or how much atmosphere that inner cylinder might have lost.

Much of the debris, frozen atmosphere, and moisture that had spilled from that tremendous rupture surrounded the habitat in a diffuse halo that caught the search vessels' spotlights as they probed it. Stephen tried not to look too closely at the debris. He knew some of it was organic. Some of it was Chirrn. Some of it was children.

"God," he breathed, once he found his voice. "There *is* a translation problem. 'Vessel' doesn't just mean 'ship'… it means 'container.' Lesshchi is a space habitat."

"Lesshchi is our home," Rillial replied. "The Chirrn are not tenants of planets as you are this. We exist included within vessels between the stars. Included in Lesshchi existed greater than eight hundred seventy thousand Chirrn. At last report, quantity approaching one in six are dead or absent, and many others die in potential if not evacuated in time. Uncounted more have lost external self, not retrievable in potential."

The last meant nothing to him, but the numbers were horribly clear. "Over a hundred thousand people," Stephen gasped. "And we… we killed them?" Had he been under gravity, his legs would have folded beneath him. For a moment, he was back in the dreams, in the part Cecilia had stopped him from reliving: Benjamin's twelve-year-old body face-down on the road, gory holes torn in his back, medical supplies scattered around him. Militiamen with assault rifles cordoning off the scene while posting self-congratulatory status updates about bringing a dangerous miscegenist radical to justice. Everything Stephen had done in the decades since had been to prevent scenes like that from ever recurring again. And it had led here — to a gaping wound torn in the skin of an entire world.

"Your projectiles pierced our habitat's shell and penetrated the interior atmosphere at almost light speed," Rillial said, its emotions unknowable through mechanical translation and alien intonation. "The heat, shock, radiation killed tens of thousands in the instant. The electromagnetic pulse disrupted the network and destroyed entire consensus memories. The shock worsened the hull rupture until that segment of Lesshchi blew out into vacuum. The turbulence killed many more beyond those expelled into space."

Stephen shuddered as he contemplated the energies involved. *Arachne*'s asteroid defense was so simple, so efficient — since the ship was already relativistic, accelerating gram-sized microsails ahead of the ship by a few more percentage points of lightspeed would give them kinetic energies of dozens of kilotons. A single sail would hit harder than the Nagasaki bomb. It had seemed so elegant... when directed at inanimate hunks of rock.

But that was not her primary defense system. "Arachne," he asked slowly, "why the sailbeam? Why not a hydrogen burst?" He wasn't sure if a relativistic hydrogen cloud would have been any less damaging to a space habitat than this had been. But it was the preferred deflection system for bodies too large to ionize with her forward lasers; not only was it gentler, with less risk of creating dangerous chunks of debris, but it was easily replenished from the interstellar medium.

Arachne spoke through the cockpit speakers, her synthesized tones lacking inflection. Perhaps she was too shocked to simulate human speech mannerisms. *"The body was too large to deflect conventionally, and too close upon detection to enable me to attempt magnetic braking. My spectroscopic and radar scans suggested a carbonaceous body with large pockets of volatiles and internal voids; I calculated that it could be shattered into pieces light enough for deflection by conventional means. I directed eighty microsails in a strafing pattern across the width of the body's visible cross-section."* There followed what for a cyber was a lengthy pause. *"The body did not fragment as I'd expected, yet it underwent sufficient deflection nonetheless. I suspected that the vaporization of volatiles within had provided the thrust needed to divert it. There was a fair amount of water vapor in the outgassing cloud."*

After another pause (for no one knew how to respond to that), Rillial continued its tale. "By then, our defenses engaged. They rejected the remaining projectiles and accelerated Lesshchi out of their path. But this could not exclude damage already made. Had we failed to halt Lesshchi's rotation in time, the habitat could have torn apart."

"I still don't understand," Arachne said. *"I detected no electromagnetic leakage, no indication of technology."*

"Our systems do not 'leak.' And many are outside your knowledge of technology." Rillial turned to the port. "They *were*," it amended.

Stephen couldn't help but follow its chameleon eyes. Lesshchi had drawn closer now, and he realized that his perceptions of scale had been in error. The exposed internal structure of the devastated section had looked to him like a few cross-sectioned decks of a wrecked ship. But now he could see that each exposed level was hundreds of meters high, with its own internal array of towers and streets and desiccated plant life. The shapes he'd seen on the inner surface weren't the remains of building frameworks, but skyscrapers, a whole city's worth. Now those cityscapes were sundered, stripped bare, bereft of light and movement.

Stephen spotted ships probing the shell of the inner cylinder, racing to seal off diffuse white jets that shot from it at various points. Rillial noticed his gaze and elaborated. "Those who remain in the inner core are still in danger of death. The evacuation proceeds, but it is slow. There is structural damage throughout the habitat, impeding rescue and evacuation." It continued with evident difficulty. "Lesshchi inclusive may be too structurally damaged to salvage. My world… my affiliation… a piece of myself… you have killed it. As you have killed many. The one who spoke my first young… the one who inspired my speaking…."

It lunged, grabbing the sides of Cecilia's head. Stephen pushed off toward it, but its tail lashed and slammed him into the bulkhead. Fire burned in his ribs, and he fleetingly found himself grateful that Rillial hadn't used those powerful megalopod legs; he might have been killed instantly. He feared Cecilia still might be.

But the other, larger Chirrn pulled Rillial back. Rillial let out a hissing noise that didn't translate, probably because there was no coherent thought behind it, but subsided. "You killed them all," it went on, seemingly not breathing hard yet still trembling with emotion. "Completely and beyond recovery. And you will be made to pay."

Cecilia glared, but maintained her calm and poise despite having nearly had her skull crushed in. "There's no question this was a great tragedy. And we understand and sympathize with your grief. But we did not do this knowingly. We didn't even know your species existed until you… pulled us over. What happened to your habitat was an accident."

"In space, accidents are usually fatal. To fail to guard against accident is intolerable negligence. Only a planet-dweller would claim accident as an excuse."

As Stephen gazed out at the wreck of Lesshchi, he couldn't help feel that the contempt in Rillial's words was justified. "Rillial…" he began hesitantly, "is there anything we can do to help you? To try to make up for what we've—"

"Stephen!" LoCarno warned sharply. She pulled him aside to hold his gaze closely, and a text appeared in his retinal HUD. *<Don't say anything that would imply culpability on our part.>*

"But—"

<I'll make it an order if I have to.> He stared at her, recognizing the seriousness of the threat. He led the colony expedition, but out here, while they were still in space, she could pull rank over him. *<We have to think clearly. A horrible thing, yes, but we don't know what they plan to do to us. Mustn't say or do anything to make it easier for them.>* She quailed at the expression in Stephen's eyes. *<Don't look at me that way. I don't feel any better about what's out there than you do. But my duty is to the passengers and crew of this ship, and to the hundreds of embryos we're carrying. I have to place their interests first.*

<What you were about to say, you kind and noble idiot, could've been taken as a confession. No telling what consequences that would have in their legal system. If they even plan to use their legal system instead of just taking revenge.> She rubbed the side of her head, staring at Rillial. *<We don't know what they'll do. So we have to be on our guard, no matter what we may feel for their dead.>*

Stephen sighed heavily, but nodded. He'd been weakened by hibernation and the shock he'd faced upon awakening; but he was a leader, a survivor, and he could accept cold realities. *<Okay,>* he sent. *<So we need to find out what they plan to do next.>*

2

"No! It isn't real!"

That was how Dr. Kweli Ndege had chosen to deal with the situation. As their Chirrn guides had shown them the wreckage of Lesshchi, ensuring they got a thorough tour of the devastation, each of the humans in the second module had reacted differently. The doctor had sunken more and more into denial, convincing herself that she was still hibernating and this was some nightmarish malfunction of the VR interface. She had curled her stout frame into a fetal ball, chanting to herself that it was all a dream, that in time she would wake up and everything would be all right. Tarik Bahar had an arm around her shoulders, comforting her and wiping away the tears that pooled around her eyes in microgravity; yet his own eyes were wrenched tightly shut.

Sita Bhatiani had no such luxury. She remembered enough from the hibernation dreams to know they could never be mistaken for waking reality. And while the Chirrn had aspects reminiscent of Earth creatures, there were enough details that just felt *off*, quirks of anatomy or design that no human hoaxer was likely to have conceived — though she couldn't rule out a cyber having that kind of imagination. But she had done the usual checks, turning her head abruptly or grabbing at unexpected objects, and her perceptual security apps had sensed no delays or rendering errors. If this was virtual or augmented reality, it was perfect beyond the grasp of mid-twenty-second-century information theory.

Sita thus had to conclude that she was awake and the Chirrn were physically real. Being flown out here at accelerations that defied physics to see the undeniable reality of this vast, devastated habitat had left no doubt. Seeing the torn and desiccated bodies drifting in space had driven the reality home with agonizing force.

So what was left? Could they have staged this tragedy in order to blame *Arachne*'s crew? But why kill a hundred thousand of their own people to scapegoat a species that had never met them? As a pretext for conquering Solsys? But if they lived in deep-space habitats, why would they need to?

Could *Arachne* have been framed for an attack waged by some rival Chirrn habitat or terrorist faction? But Arachne had confirmed firing on an object Lesshchi's size. And she had given no indication of being off her course, so such a group would have had to steer Lesshchi into her sights. Which would mean all these deaths had still come at human hands, however indirectly.

Maybe there were extenuating circumstances. Maybe Lesshchi's own defenses had failed or been sabotaged, its structure weakened by shoddy construction, *something*. Sita had to find out if she could.

She chose her words carefully before she turned to their main Chirrn watchdog, a relatively small one with dark green skin and some grayish hair visible through its suit visor. "There was no warning?" she asked, taking care to pitch her voice softly, sympathetically. They might not catch the nuances of human vocal expression, but it had already been confirmed that they associated loudness with anger.

The Chirrn's eyes swiveled to lock on her. Its brow ridges pulled forward in a surprisingly humanlike way. "Our warning was only your radar scan. The protection collegium sought recognition of its source, but were blocked by the velocity and low visibility of your transport. Before they could locate it, your bombardment began."

She had to phrase this delicately. "And… it overwhelmed your shielding?"

The Chirrn angled its head closer, clearly an aggressive gesture. "Our shielding is designed against interstellar debris, not relativistic weaponry."

"Defense," Tarik spoke up. "It's just a defense system."

The Chirrn whirled on him, using its tail deftly to shift its weight in midair. Sita was struck by how graceful and natural the Chirrn body seemed in microgravity, as if they had evolved or engineered themselves for it.

"Your 'defense system' penetrated our shielding and detonated within like a nuclear explosive," the Chirrn said. "It killed in the instant nearly a full inclusion of Chirrn in that division of the outward cylinder. My mates were there. Simisshen, Marellel, Ruzhalu. They died as I watched this! As I felt this!"

Though there was sympathy in Tarik's eyes, he braced himself in response to the Chirrn's fury, ready to defend himself and Kweli if attacked. Sita knew he was a gentle, spiritual man at heart, but he was intensely protective of his crew, and was the only human so far awakened who was strong enough to make a good fight against the Chirrn. Sita noted the second megalopod tensing up in response, drawing its truncheon-like weapon. Both Chirrn's body language told her they were on the verge of violence—an act they would see as self-defense against a murderous alien monster. And if that monster could actually pose a physical threat to them in return, their resulting fear could drive them into a killing frenzy.

Better, then, that they direct their aggression against someone less intimidating. "But how did so much of the hull get torn away?" Sita demanded, hardening her voice to draw the Chirrn's anger.

It worked. That tail whipped again and the green Chirrn clutched her, forcing her back against the bulkhead. One long forearm pressed against her upper chest like a bar, pinning her arms, while its other hand instinctively grasped a handhold for leverage. Its elongated feet came forward to clutch her shins with their prehensile toes, immobilizing her legs. Sita caught Tarik's eyes and shook her head, warning him not to intervene.

The Chirrn shouted in her face, and she had to strain to hear the translation over its volume. "You question this tragedy? You try to deny it?"

"I just… want to understand."

The arm and both feet squeezed tighter. She cried out despite herself. "Good. You should understand the death you caused." One eye flicked backward to direct her gaze out the window. "We have not gathered in every part of what happened. We are busy attempting to gather in those who live. But once we do understand, you will be given inclusive details of how you destroyed our world."

Sita was glad the Chirrn was hurting her. The pain gave her something immediate to focus on, something to distract her from the horror. She wanted to fight back just to provoke it into worse violence, to give herself something immediate and visceral to lose herself in— even if it killed her. But there were two other people here to worry about, one of them nearly catatonic. She couldn't get them killed too. So she just let go and submitted to the pain.

Surely she deserved no less.

Once the Chirrn on the other rescue ships began to catch on that there were humans present at the scene, it became increasingly disruptive to the search efforts — even dangerous to the Chirrn ringship. A few ships tried to board, attack, or simply ram the ringship, determined to take revenge on the humans even at the cost of Chirrn lives. It was depressing, Sita thought, to see that the drive for revenge might be universal. The ringship retreated back to the larger vessel, and at last Sita and the others were spared from being forced to see their handiwork any further.

Not our handiwork, Sita tried to tell herself once the six humans were forced to strip again, returned to their bare prison, and provided with minimal water and nourishment from *Arachne*'s emergency stores. *We were all asleep. If anyone's to blame, it's Arachne.* But she cursed herself for the thought. Arachne had been their nurturing, reliable partner throughout the mission, the being to whom they'd entrusted their lives, their future, their very minds. Everything the cyber did, she did on their behalf. Not because she was programmed or compelled to; Arachne was loyal because she chose to be, because she cherished her human charges and believed in their mission as strongly as they did.

Then maybe it was Stephen's fault? Sita glanced over at him, though thankfully his back was turned. The prisoners had relieved and cleaned themselves in the small chamber the Chirrn had provided (thank heaven for small favors, since those were the only kind they'd get from these beings) and were now trying to get some sleep despite the bright light, cold air, high gravity, and lack of bedding. Kweli was still near-catatonic, hiding from reality, in shocking contrast to her normal gregarious exuberance. Cecilia and Haim had sandwiched her between their bodies; Haim was only attracted to men, so there was nothing untoward about it. Stephen and Tarik had bracketed Sita for warmth as well, though they lay at a more discreet distance — not that she would've minded huddling much more closely with either or both of them. Stephen's lean, beautiful, coffee-skinned frame shifted fitfully, far from sleep for reasons that surely had little to do with the cold. *Guilty conscience?*

Stephen Jacobs-Wong had come far from his beginnings in the chaos of the American Gulf Coast. It had been one of the last remaining poverty-stricken regions on the planet, devastated by superhurricanes and rising sea levels, abandoned by corrupt governors and corporate executives who had pocketed the international relief funds, and racked by sectarian violence between fundamentalist, white supremacist Christian militias — the latest and hopefully last gasp of the demons that always seemed to crawl out of America's woodwork whenever it was weakened, no matter how many times the world believed they had been conquered for good. Those too impoverished to move away were forced to endure the breakdown of infrastructure as well as social order. Without basic sanitation, the death toll from waterborne diseases had skyrocketed, and the militias and their wealthy supporters had hoarded food and medicine from those who didn't fit their standards of ethnic or religious purity. Any who had protested or agitated for change were beaten, imprisoned, or simply gunned down. Hundreds of thousands had died, including members of Stephen's own family.

But Stephen was a fighter. Surviving against the odds, he had managed to get his sisters and himself out of what remained of Florida and to the safety and prosperity of São Paulo. From there, he'd leveraged his tragic story into a massive activist movement that worked with the Union of Earth and Cislunar States to bring pressure to bear on the governors until their power was broken and order restored. Stephen had then founded Stargazer Enterprises to spearhead the reconstruction, building it into a mighty conglomerate dedicated, in his words, to making sure nothing like his story need ever happen again.

He had been the guiding spirit behind this expedition, using all the resources of SGE to bring it about. Everything he'd done over the years to promote advances in propulsion technology, auxonic construction, terraforming, and improved hibernation techniques — advances that had benefitted tens of millions from Venus to Mars to the Cerean States to Alpha Centauri — had been with the ultimate goal of establishing the first colonies on planets where humans could live without environment domes or extensive terraforming. Some had said he'd been so trauma-tized by his childhood that he was determined to get away from Earth at all costs. Stephen had said his goal was to give humanity a chance at a fresh beginning. Whatever the reasons, he had been relentless in making it a reality, wielding all his charisma and influence to win others over to a quest that had initially seemed mad to most of them.

So didn't that mean the ultimate blame fell on him? Sita was only here because he'd won her over with the allure of his dream. Surely she couldn't be held accountable.

Bollocks, she told herself. She and all the others had thrown themselves body and soul into making this happen. She had striven to prove that she had the skill, versatility, and sheer determination to deserve one of the precious forty-eight spots on the expedition to Gamma Leporis Ad. And of course it was the Cybele expedition she had fought for, not the less risky one being prepared for Eta Cassiopeiae Ac, only two-thirds the distance and only moderately less ideal for settlement. After all, she'd known that Stephen would be personally leading the more difficult quest, so that no one would doubt his commitment. And he'd refused to guarantee himself that spot, enduring the same rigorous trials as everyone else and *earning* his place at their lead. He had inspired Sita to push herself just as hard, to earn her own place alongside him. So if Stephen was to blame for this horrific accident, then Sita had just as much blood on her hands.

She trembled at the thought, and at the cold. Stephen must have heard her shuddering intake of breath, for he rolled over and saw her distress. Wordlessly, he moved closer, cradling her in his arms. Her heart raced at his embrace.

But he only held her, sharing his warmth. She snuggled close, hoping he would take the hint, but when she met his eyes, they were a billion klicks away… or probably much closer, assuming this ship was still gathering refugees from Lesshchi. She wanted to kiss him, to comfort and soothe him. But she realized she had no comfort to give. All she had was need. If she let him see that need, he might respond, kind as he was. But she didn't want to be selfish when he was in need as well. She couldn't do that to the man she loved.

Sita winced. *Who do I think I'm fooling?* He held her naked in his arms and had no erection, didn't even look at her. She could imagine it was merely shock, but when had he ever shown interest? Back in Solsys, they had interacted little beyond the necessary professional contacts. Her own fault, she reminded herself, for being too shy around him, intimidated by his fame and power. As a rule, she was rarely afraid to face a challenge. She hadn't earned her spot among the privileged few by being faint of heart. Granted, she may have beaten another leading candidate or two simply by being the smallest; *Arachne*'s payload had needed to be as light as possible for maximum speed, and the majority of the crew was below average size. But being a meter and a half high and less than seven stone in weight was just one more reason she'd learned to be assertive. Still, whenever she'd been alone with Stephen, she'd been as timid as the schoolgirl she was sometimes mistaken for.

What she remembered from the hibernation dreams, then, as vivid and erotic as it had been, was probably just her own fantasy feeding on itself. She had no doubt that a man as desirable, rich, and gregarious as Stephen had taken many lovers in the dreamscape, but if she had been one of them, it would've been just one more casual, forgettable rendezvous for him.

Let's face it… I wasn't in the mood either. Her yearning, she realized, was almost abstract; her body was not reacting any more than his. She couldn't even bring herself to feel depressed at his lack of interest. It all paled next to the tragedy.

"I suppose… I should be proud of myself," she said.

Stephen finally looked at her, distantly aghast. "Proud?"

She winced. "That came out wrong. I mean… these are aliens. Creatures we've never seen before today, from… a totally different biosphere, a separate evolutionary heritage. And yet… it hurts as much as if they were human." She gave a feeble, self-deprecating grin, which stretched into a rictus of pain. "How bloody noble of me."

"Sita." He paused until she met his eyes. "Don't ever mock that compassion. If we're… to redeem ourselves for this… that's where it will come from." He clasped her hand. "We have to show them that we grieve too. That we are not monsters."

"Do you believe that?" she asked softly. "That we can redeem ourselves?"

It took him a while to respond. "We have to try."

She turned away, unable to face the pain in his eyes any longer. Her gaze fixed on the entrance, now permanently visible with a portal through which a Chirrn guard watched them. This one had taken its hood off, revealing a long, luxurious golden mane whose translucent strands shimmered as it moved, beautifully complementing its rich azure skin. *Natural or artificial?* she wondered. Either would raise so many fascinating questions. Her mind raced with her observations—a distraction she welcomed.

"This should be such a miracle," she said. "First contact with an intelligent species. So much to learn. In any other circumstances, I'd be exploding with joy."

"So would I," Stephen said. "And I'm glad you're here with us, watching them so closely. We need to learn all we can." He paused. "It's heartening that they're so similar. More or less mammalian, brains enough like ours for mutual communication... the similarities outweigh the differences. I'm hopeful we can build on that."

"Really? I've been noticing so many differences. The way the joints move suggests a different design to the skeleton and musculature. The eyes suggest a chameleon's, but the fine structure is unlike anything I've ever seen. The muscle in the mouth isn't quite a tongue, the grinding and cutting surfaces aren't quite teeth, the head covering isn't quite hair or fur as we know it. Different evolutionary processes giving different solutions to the same problem."

"But form follows function, doesn't it? Parallel solutions for parallel needs. Swiveling eyes for field of view, long legs for hopping, a cantilevered tail for balance."

"Yes, but evolution can arrive at those solutions from wildly different angles, creating all manner of quirks and unnecessary embellishments. I mean, where's the advantage in hopping as locomotion? For a big-brained creature, it risks imparting too much shock to the cranium. Sure, their necks seem to provide shock absorption, but why go to the trouble?

"Come to that, why would a hopping, presumably ground-based species evolve opposable thumbs? What's the advantage to that array of small nares on top of the snout? Wouldn't they drown in the rain? And where's the advantage in a scent-detection system that isn't forward and low, able to sniff the ground? If they even smell with their nares, but what other logical place is there for olfactory organs except where the air comes in? Krishna, they're just so bloody weird."

Stephen let out a weak chuckle. "I hate myself for this... but you know what I can't help thinking they remind me of?"

"What?"

"Kermit the Frog. ...Do you know who that is?"

A laugh erupted out of somewhere deep. "I see what you mean!" She kept laughing. "The... the mouth is kind of shaped that way... and the bulgey eyes... the green skin..." She laughed harder, hating herself for doing it.

But he was laughing too. "It's not that easy… being…" He lost it. She fell apart in hysterical, tearful laughter right along with him, unable to stop.

The next thing she knew, the hatch was open and the golden-maned Chirrn guard was storming in, its head still bared. It was shouting at her, raising its rodlike weapon menacingly, and she only caught part of the translation. "Stop staring… revolting noise… filthy ground-vermin!"

Other Chirrn came in behind it, wearing full biohazard suits. Again, she only discerned snatches of the rapid-fire dialogue. ". . .need your hood… cannot know… dirtgrubber infection."

". . . think I care… my speechmates… half my self… want it to stop staring!" But Sita couldn't look away. This was the best look she'd gotten at the Chirrn head and mouth in action. Was that tongue porous?

"Repellent," one of them said, one bound carrying it nearer where Sita and Stephen lay together. "See their structure. They join where they excrete!"

"Well-diggers," another said. "Ferals! All they know is filth."

"Why they destroy what is pure!"

Tarik was rising now, instinctively moving to shield Captain LoCarno, but she would have none of it, standing right at his side. Stephen came to his feet as well, while Haim continued to hold onto Kweli, shielding her helpless form with his bulk. The Chirrn brandished their staves more aggressively.

But the golden-maned guard's eyes were locked unwaveringly on Sita. *"You! Stop… staring!!"* The guard snapped, lunging at her. Stephen interposed himself, but it knocked him aside with its staff, and he convulsed as if electrocuted. Shrieking, Sita scrambled away, and the other prisoners closed in around her.

But the other Chirrn were in motion now, leaping high and fast to bring their shock sticks down upon her protectors. Tarik fell first, taking a blow meant for his captain. LoCarno dodged and got in a good kick, knocking her assailant's shock stick across the bay. She grabbed her attacker by the forearms, fell back, and pushed with her legs, flipping it onto its snout. But it promptly recovered into a quadrupedal stance, courtesy of its long forearms, and its tail caught her in the ribs and bowled her over in mid-recovery.

"Cecilia!" Stephen struggled toward the captain as she gasped in agony, clutching her side. He clasped her shoulder, but another guard moved in with its own shock stick and jammed it into her spine, convulsing her and Stephen both as the shock passed through their bodies. Stephen fell away, but the guard continued to torture LoCarno. Tarik shouted in wordless rage, but he was busy holding the unhooded guard at bay, trying to keep its shock stick from connecting. Sita ran toward the captain, determined to do something to help, even if it was just to divert the torturer's efforts to herself.

But then Haim Silbermann barreled in with a roar, brandishing the fallen shock stick. The guard's eye swiveled backward — *independently of the other, interesting!* — and it lashed out at Silbermann with its heavy tail. The bearish engineer pulled up short and brought the stick down to parry the blow. The block worked, but no shock went through the guard's body; Silbermann must not have been using it right. Undeterred, he adapted the tools at hand like any good engineer, turning the high-tech alien weapon into a good old primitive club, pounding on the alien until it laid off the captain.

But Silbermann was weakened, and the Chirrn's suit gave it some padding. It whirled and sent him flying with a brutal kick, using its tail to counter the recoil force. Then it lunged at him and began using its own shock stick as a club; this time, the shock function worked.

Sita couldn't help him. But she crouched at the captain's side and tried to pull her away from the Chirrn. *Don't think about what's happening… concentrate on the moment…*

But then the moment exploded into agony, and when she recovered her senses, she was on her back, twitching, and the azure-skinned guard loomed over her with its teeth (but not teeth) bared, and its hair (but not hair) cascaded around its head and it was just so beautiful, who's your stylist, love? It roared at her, and the rod came down again and exploded her world, and when she came back she was screaming and her ribs were in pieces, and its foot struck her legs and she felt her bones give way like twigs, the agony so severe that when the rod came again it was almost a relief, until she felt the agony in her arm as the edges of shattered bone ground together, and her own screams and the blood rushing through her ears deafened her — yet still she thought she heard words between the bombs going off in her brain. "You! Again!

"Why won't you stop *staring?!*"

Cecilia LoCarno awoke to find herself in one of *Arachne*'s small emergency medical bays. Looking around, she saw Stephen lying in the medbed next to hers, with Kweli Ndege tending to him. For a moment, she allowed herself to hope that recent events had simply been a hibernation nightmare, as Kweli had believed. But the three of them were still naked, and she and Stephen were covered in bruises. Either they'd had a hell of a party in here, or it was all real.

Kweli spotted her movement. "Good, you're awake," the warm-featured Kenyan said.

"Stephen?"

"Sleeping it off. He'll be okay."

"The others?"

Kweli looked away. "They all got it pretty bad. Blunt-force trauma, contusions, electric shock… ." The doctor hesitated, and Cecilia braced herself for the worst. "Sita got it worst of all. Half the bones in her body were broken. Concussion, skull fracture… her heart had been stopped for at least three minutes by the time we got her in the medbed, and her backup cerebral perfuser was damaged, so there was some ischemic injury. As it is, no telling when she'll regain consciousness, or if the brain damage will be beyond nanorepair. But she's alive, and I expect her to recover."

Cecilia closed her eyes and thanked God. Then she looked at Kweli. "Glad to see you up and about too, Doctor."

The other woman's gaze was distant. "I'm still not convinced this is real. But I… couldn't take the chance."

"Lucky for us."

"It can't be real, can it? Not a dream… but it must be some terrible hoax. We couldn't have done… what they say."

"Listen to me, Kweli." Her sharp tone caught and held the doctor's attention. "We don't have enough facts to say anything for sure. But the one thing I want you to be absolutely certain of is, we're innocent. Whatever happened, we're not to blame. You have to believe that, and you have to show the Chirrn that you believe it. Do you understand me, Doctor?"

Kweli nodded, breathing hard. Her shoulders relaxed as if a burden had been lifted from them. "I can do that," she said. A trace of her normal smile flashed across her features, though only for an instant.

Cecilia smiled. "Good. I knew I could count on you."

But comforting the doctor hadn't been her primary goal. This crew had to present a united front of innocence to the Chirrn, and not one rooted in borderline psychotic withdrawal. These creatures had made it abundantly clear that they considered *Arachne*'s crew their enemies. No doubt Stephen would pursue diplomacy and try to change their minds. She wished him success, and had faith that if anyone could pull it off, Stephen Jacobs-Wong could. But she had to be ready for the other contingency. She had to hold this crew together against a threat none of them had imagined, and bring them through it alive, intact, and back on course for Gamma Leporis — somehow. And that wouldn't happen if this crew showed any weakness or guilt.

A movement at the hatchway drew her attention. It was the turquoise-skinned Chirrn she recognized as Rillial, evidently the leader of this group. The captain of this ship? Certainly an authority figure. She recognized that much. "Captain," it said. "What is the status of your crew?"

"We'll live," she told it, raising herself into a sitting position. She would stand if she had the strength, but for now this would have to do. "No thanks to your underlings."

"But thanks to you," came Stephen's voice. Her old friend was awake now too, following her to a seated position with Kweli's help, and he was as predictable as ever, taking the conciliatory route. "You have our gratitude for allowing us the use of our medical facilities."

"I do not have it or want it," the Chirrn replied. "For myself alone, I would have gladly joined them in killing you all. But even with our minds diminished, we are not savages, despite what you almost brought my crew to here. I will not allow you to drag the Chirrn down to the dirt where you live. Guard Vhehhal and the other assailants have been excluded from your security detail and will be disciplined for their violence. You will be treated fairly when we reach Shilirrlal, though you do not deserve the privilege."

"Shill..." Stephen trailed off.

"Shilirrlal is our destination. The habitat from which Lesshchi was spoken, not so many lifetimes ago... which must now take its remains back in, those it has space to include. There you will be judged, in the proper way and at the proper time."

"So we're to be put on trial?" Cecilia asked.

"Yes. We are a lawful people."

"Does that mean we'll be given a fair chance to defend ourselves against your charges?"

Rillial stared. "You may defend yourselves to the limits of your ability. The facts permit no doubt."

"Really?" she challenged. "Is that for you to decide?" Stephen watched the scene intently, but did not interfere. She appreciated his deference to her judgment.

The Chirrn loomed closer. "If possible, it will be."

"Says the one who just confessed to wanting to beat us to death. You call that lawful?"

Rillial's mouth opened, and a rattling hiss came out. "There is what we wish, and there is what is proper to do. Perhaps in the trial you will learn the difference."

Cecilia forced herself to her feet, even though her legs would barely sustain her weight. "Or maybe you'll learn not to underestimate the human race. Bring it on, Green-eyes. Bring it on."

3

When the Chirrn awoke the rest of the crew, Stephen had to watch them all go through the same process of confusion, discovery, and shock that the first six had experienced. None of them had wanted to believe at first. Taken prisoner by aliens, stripped of their clothing, possessions, and dignity, and thrown into a bare, crowded cell like livestock; the expedition leaders beaten half to death; the whole crew being taken to an alien habitat to be tried for mass murder. How could it be anything but some shameful hoax?

But the first six had spelled out the chilling reality to the others. Cecilia's painfully detailed account had made it real for most of them; she was their captain, after all, and if she said a thing was true, then it was. A few still refused to believe it. James Oates, the expedition's industrial engineer, began spinning conspiracy theories about piracy and slave labor, doing more to frighten the others than reassure them, until Diego Narvaez drew him aside and said something to calm him down. Narvaez was a popular figure among the other engineers, his confidence and charisma making him a natural leader, even though he answered to Haim Silbermann. The intensity of his religious faith had been off-putting to Stephen at first, as his own experience with hardcore Christians had been less than positive. But Tarik Bahar, himself an equally devout Muslim, had championed the Guatemalan Catholic, convincing Stephen that Narvaez would never try to force his beliefs on others or use them to deny others their equality and dignity. Stephen had since come to admire Narvaez's high regard for what he called the God-given free will of every human. He supposed that Narvaez's faith, along with Tarik's, might even be a source of comfort to Oates and others in the days ahead. In a way, he envied that conviction right now.

The Chirrn had given the crew little time to absorb the news. Their ship, *Zhemhal*, had nearly reached its destination by the time *Arachne's* full crew was revived, a few days after the original incident. They had cited this as an excuse for subjecting the whole group to thorough medical examination — to check for contaminants, they claimed. Being subjected to abduction and probing by aliens, like something from an old horror movie, would've been laughable if it hadn't become an immediate reality — and if Diana Thorne, Sergei Mazunov, and Shuai Bingbing hadn't been in intensive care right now. Long-term hibernation carried risks they had all understood, but being forced awake *en masse*, without giving Arachne and the expedition's doctors time to shepherd each sleeper individually, had amplified those risks, and those three had suffered significant organ damage, maybe even brain damage, as a result. Cecilia had vowed to the Chirrn that if any of the three failed to pull through, she would see that *Zhemhal's* personnel were held accountable. Rillial, astonished by her chutzpah, had reminded her that her crew were the ones being taken to account.

The fact that Diana Thorne had fallen victim to revival damage was shocking to the crew. The construction engineer was a native of the transhumanist Vanguard habitat, and her gene mods made her the strongest, most robust member of the expedition by a considerable margin. If she could succumb, then nobody was safe. So the rest were understandably reluctant to trust that the Chirrn's medical probes would be any safer or gentler than their revival methods. Several fought back as the Chirrn dragged them off: some with proud defiance like Narvaez, Jason Brentwood, and Oyama Kazuko, some screaming in terror like Evan Jiang or in pure rage like Amrita Dhillon. But they were returned intact and seemingly unharmed, though shaken. From his own experience, Stephen knew the examinations were not painful, or not deliberately so, as long as the subjects cooperated. But they were cold, thorough, invasive, and dehumanizing. Stephen had been made to feel like a lab specimen, his every bodily function subject to exploration to satisfy these creatures' morbid curiosity — or simply their need to humiliate him. It had been over three decades, subjectively, since he'd been made to feel so worthless by even the lowliest members of an authority structure. But back then, he had done nothing to earn it. He could not bring himself to feel the same indignation now.

The news of the ship's approach to the new habitat, Shilirrlal, offered a useful diversion for the crew. The travel time was mere days, but Arachne had detected no other proximate bodies besides a small rogue planet several light-weeks away, creating a paradox. "We know they have some kind of gravitic drive and inertial cancellation," Haim Silbermann put forth. "We could've been accelerated near lightspeed and time-dilated."

"To reach the rogue planet in four subjective days?" objected Justine Nguyen, their astrophysicist. "That would take a gamma of at least six, which means nearly point-nine-nine c," she went on in a soft French accent. "Besides, a gravity-based drive might not even produce special-relativistic effects in the first place, if the proper acceleration within the field is zero as with an Alcubierre-type warp. Which is suggested by their deceleration of *Arachne*—nearly four thousand g with no effect on the ship."

Haim shrugged. "Who knows? If the Chirrn have that level of gravity control, then for all we know, they have some kind of hyperlight drive. We could be parsecs beyond local space."

"Now you're pushing it, Haim."

Diego scoffed. "Justine's right. I refuse to believe that these… kangaroo-chameleons could build a technology surpassing human achievement. More likely it's some deception."

James Oates was quick to embrace that notion, spinning conspiracy theories that the others, even Diego, reacted to with incredulity. But Stephen could tell they were all distracting themselves from what was really on their minds.

In time, faint shudders began to pass through the ship. Minutes later, hazmat-suited Chirrn came and herded all forty-five uninjured humans out of the hold and into a chamber barely big enough to hold them all. There was a gravity shift along the way, a sensation of an uphill climb, getting milder as they went. Stephen noted Cecilia, Tarik, and the other space veterans instinctively turning their heads to test for cochlear shifts. Cecilia asserted that they were out of the ship's inexplicable gravity field and inside a normal rotating habitat.

This was confirmed when the chamber lurched and began to descend, the floor seeming to slope as the Coriolis effect tipped their increasing weight vector to antispinward. They halted at a level whose gravity was maybe two-thirds Earth value and were herded out. But all Stephen saw were more sterile chambers and corridors. This, according to the Chirrn, was a decontamination facility. "My God, how dirty do they think we are?" Amrita Dhillon asked.

"From what they said when they beat us," Tarik replied with subdued anger, "quite a lot."

The Chirrn herded them through a series of progressively more unpleasant decontamination procedures: powerful blasts of freezing water and hot air; uncomfortably hot sprays of supposedly nonthermal plasma; blinding UV bursts; suffocating immersion in stinking chemical baths and gels. What little remaining body hair they had was seared and scoured away. "This goes beyond any sane need for decontam," Diego Narvaez shouted after his third dunking. "They're doing this to torture us!"

Once the decontamination gauntlet was complete, Stephen hoped the worst was over. But the Chirrn immediately subjected the crew to yet another thorough medical examination, allegedly to make sure the decontamination had worked. Stephen knew this had to be a lie. Arachne had told him that, based on the data the Chirrn had provided, there was virtually no risk of cross-species infection. The Chirrn were either punishing the humans or acting out of some irrational taboo about contamination.

At last, the sore, raw-skinned, depilated humans were given something to wear. But it was no relief. The one-piece confinement suits were roughly form-fitting, ending just below the shoulders, with clumsy mitts at the ends of the sleeves. Too form-fitting, perhaps; the dynamic material compressed uncomfortably tightly against their raw, sensitized skin. "Attempt no escape," their lead escort said, then demonstrated what would happen if they disobeyed: the jumpsuits would become rigid, preventing movement. Even the integrated mittens froze up around Stephen's fingers whenever he reached for his shoulders. Far from a respite from their nudity, these garments just reinforced their lack of control over their own bodies. All things considered, Stephen would've rather stayed naked. *All things*, he reiterated as he fidgeted, trying to find a posture that would relieve the pressure on his testicles.

But that didn't seem to be something the Chirrn would understand. Now that the humans had been sanitized for their protection and thoroughly shrink-wrapped, the Chirrn were no longer wearing hazmat suits in their presence. Their typical garb, it seemed, was nothing more than loose, utilitarian vests, open in front and secured by a strap across the midriff and sometimes a second one across the upper chest. Some wore wide, colorful bands of fabric around their calves and forearms. They had no recognizable genitalia that Stephen could see. Could a species evolve to this level without sexual reproduction?

Finally the prisoners were brought out into a large plaza surrounded by towers. Hundreds of Chirrn watched, clearly fascinated by the humans but remaining at a distance as though they were unclean. Many of these Chirrn looked subtly different from the Lesshchin (as he'd learned to call them), lankier with slimmer tails and rounder snouts. More of them had skin colors tending toward a bluer range while the majority of the Lesshchin were more greenish, though there was a good deal of overlap. A few had other differences, like stockier bodies, purplish or yellow-brown skin, or shorter manes. *Immigrants from still more habitats? How many do they have?* There were cultural variations too; many of the Shilirrlal population wore their manes in intricate braids or decorated them with colorful beads and bands. The sight helped to remind him that these were individuals, just as diverse as humans. He felt a pang at the thought of the equally individual lives his expedition had wiped out.

Arachne notified him that the Chirrn had permitted her to tap into a limited segment of Shilirrlal's augreality network and interpret its feeds for human vision and imaging protocols. Hovering over and around the humans in virtual space, or adorning the buildings, bridges, and unidentifiable shapes they passed, were multiple interactive windows showing Lesshchi both after the disaster and as it must have been beforehand, alongside images of *Arachne*'s capture, her modules inside the Chirrn ship's hangar — and the crew, naked, cowed, and afraid. Several windows showed video from their decontamination and medical exams in full, invasive detail. Many in the crowd watched these scenes with particular animation, leaning forward inquisitively or rearing back in evident disgust. It drove home that the entire procedure had been symbolic, probably meant to reassure the citizens of Shilirrlal that they would not be contaminated by the impure aliens. Stephen blushed fiercely, ashamed on behalf of his crew. He looked at Cecilia, and saw her realizing the same things he had; but her expression was bitter cold.

Once they moved past the high towers, Stephen was able to see the habitat's layout more clearly. From the openness of the cylindrical worldscape before him, Stephen surmised this must be the inner cylinder, if Shilirrlal conformed to Lesshchi's plan. It didn't look like any O'Neill habitat back in Solsys; there was no attempt at simulating a planetary surface. It reminded him more of his first view of São Paulo as a youth, a vista of pure urban artificiality stretching to the vanishing point in every direction, a monument to the power of its builders over their environment. The layout was urban, orderly, angular, filled with multiple levels of terraces atop which rose monumental skyscrapers connected by a network of skywalks. Yet it was not sterile. Even when he temporarily shut off the augmented view, Stephen saw many large plazas and squares filled with orange, red, and yellow vegetation, intermixed with other colors. Many of the skyscrapers themselves had plant life growing atop their terraced levels or climbing vast trellises stretching between them. At the equator, a wide band of water bisected the cylinder, broken by crossover bridges or dams and with canals extending outward to the north and south.

The view ahead was periodically interrupted by thick tethers that rose toward the axis, tension members supporting the habitat against its own centrifugal weight. Stephen's eyes followed them upward, past the collar of clouds, to see that they intersected with a vast latticed cylinder of light, an open, arabesque framework that provided the habitat with its primary illumination in place of a sun. As his eyes adjusted to the light, he realized there were shapes and structures within, some of them in motion. Through a wide gap in the light lattice, he saw what looked like a large globe of water jiggling through the air. Adjusting his adaptive optics to maximize his visual acuity, he made out small, multicolored specks — presumably Chirrn — swimming gaily through it. Other distant bodies soared across the open space with the sinuous grace and ease he'd seen the Chirrn demonstrate in microgravity.

"Captain, Stephen," said Tarik, who had been surveying the scene as intently as Stephen. "In the crowd, ahead right." They were on a skywalk now, with others running parallel to it. The adjacent skywalks were filled with gawkers… not all of whom were Chirrn. Stephen made out two distinct types. One group looked like silvery pterosaurs with triple-crested heads and apparently one eye before each crest. Their posture was birdlike, with wings intricately folded along their flanks. The sides of their crests shimmered with rainbow hues, rivaling the elaborate jewelry they wore. The other species was even more bizarre — hippo-sized, chocolate-brown creatures with long, peanut-shaped bodies atop an indeterminate number of legs, with heads whose shape suggested a raised catcher's mitt with a ball in it.

Sita Bhatiani, who'd been painfully quiet since the assault, grew animated again at the sight, though she took care not to call attention to herself. She sidled up to Stephen and Cecilia, still moving stiffly due to her healing injuries, and said, "There's no way those creatures came from the same taxonomic family as the Chirrn. I doubt they're even from the same planet. We're definitely not the Chirrn's first contact."

"And if there are other species living here," Stephen asked, "what about Lesshchi?" He looked around again, taking in this amazing vista, both compellingly alien and deeply beautiful. "This is what we destroyed, Cecilia."

She met his gaze, her face unreadable. "I know," she said at last, almost too softly to hear. But then her expression hardened and she stepped up to hiss in his ear: "But don't ever let the Chirrn hear you say that."

The Chirrn built large to accommodate their long bodies and bounding locomotion. Stairways had only two or three steps between one story and the next—and Cecilia saw some Chirrn bounding directly to higher floors, pulling themselves up with their arms like cats leaping onto a windowsill. The entrance to Shilirrlal's towering, ziggurat-like justice center had a ramp leading up to it as well, perhaps for the benefit of the big peanut-bodied aliens, but the forty-five weakened, constricted humans were led around to the back and taken up in a cargo lift. As they circled the block, Cecilia noted Chirrn gawkers clinging with brachiators' agility to the trellises between neighboring buildings, grasping them with fingers and toes. They were nearly as graceful here as in microgravity, and Cecilia almost envied them the anatomy that allowed that. *They're at home here in a way we can never be. It won't be easy to counter that advantage.* She flexed her fingers against the smart fabric of her jumpsuit. *Especially when we can't even move without their approval.*

After their processing, the forty-five humans were led down into a deeper, higher-gravity level of the complex—about twenty percent above Earth gravity, she estimated. The Chirrn adjusted with ease, but it served as one more impediment for the humans. The prisoners were confined in a block of six large cells, three on each side of a wide corridor, with transparent, vent-holed walls and doors of what looked and felt like synthetic diamond. They were thrown together willy-nilly with no regard for sex, and Cecilia found herself confined with Stephen, Haim, Sita, the ecologist Ibrahim al-Bakri, and the physician Nikolos Zacharias. The cell had two large sleeping pallets, which Cecilia promptly designated His and Hers, and two toilets that were little more than holes in the floor, mercifully behind half-high translucent partitions. There were also a couple of sink-like basins in each cell for water.

Once the cell doors had been locked, the confinement jumpsuits relaxed, to everyone's great relief. Cecilia was gratified to discover that she could wriggle her arms out through the shoulder hole, relieving the uncomfortable pressure on her breasts. After a bit of experimentation, she managed to tie the sleeves together in front to hold the garment up. Haim and Ibrahim followed her lead, though Stephen was content to go bare-chested, the jumpsuit bunched around his waist. Sita and Nik stripped the odious garments off completely. Nik tied his around his waist, but Sita merely clutched hers against the front of her body and huddled in the corner of the Hers pallet. Nobody was comfortable just being nude after the past few days.

Cecilia advised the crew to get some rest, raising her voice so those in the other cells could hear. The men and women took their respective bunks. Few of them could sleep, though, and the murmur of conversations started up pretty promptly. "Odd," Cecilia said. "The Chirrn seem so isolationist, so disdainful of other races. You wouldn't expect them to consort with other species or have such advanced translation software."

"I don't think it's all races they dislike," Sita told her. "They seem to have a specific bias against planet-dwellers. When the guards..." The petite biologist shuddered. Mercifully, she'd suffered no permanent brain damage from her assault, but even after days in a medbed, she still bore scars. "The things they said, the insults.... 'Ground-vermin.' 'Dirtgrubber.' They seem to have a thing about dirt and earth. And the people who live in—on it." She winced.

"That must narrow their list of friends a great deal," the captain said.

"I wouldn't say that," Nik spoke up. "There are a billion of us Striders in the Belt and Trojans, and nearly as many Terrans living in cislunar habitats. Someday hab-dwellers will outnumber planet-dwellers. And we've detected megastructures around other stars. We know there are aliens who do the same, on a much vaster scale than this," he finished, gesturing at their surroundings.

Haim furrowed his brow. "That's a good point. We have gravity-focus telescopes that can make detailed maps of Cybele from twenty-nine light-years away. Why did we never see these guys?"

"We weren't looking *between* the stars," Stephen said.

"At least, not for things like this," Cecilia added. "Who'd want to live out here any—"

The arrival of several Chirrn in the cell-block corridor interrupted the discussion. Two were attired in guards' vests—heavier than the normal garments with less exposure of the chest—with shock-stick holsters strapped to their legs. The third was an atypically stocky Chirrn, cobalt-skinned with a yellow-white mane done up in Shilirrlal-style braids. This Chirrn surveyed the prisoners in their various cells and addressed the group. "Are there any among you who are not of planetary birth?" The translation now appeared as a subtitle in her field of view, courtesy of Arachne. The prison was shielded, cutting the crew off from Arachne herself, but her peripheral AI software in their implants smoothed the rough syntax of the Chirrn translation into more natural English. That ran the risk of obscuring true meanings even further, though, since the Chirrn were still reluctant to give Arachne access to the cultural and psychological information she'd need to do her own independent checks on the translation. Which just made it more likely in Cecilia's mind that they were hiding something.

Cecilia stepped forward. "Why do you want to know?" she asked.

The light-maned Chirrn hopped closer. "Are you of extraplanetary origin?"

"No. I was born in Venezia on the planet Earth and proud of it. I also happen to be the captain of this group, so I'm the one you speak to. Now, just what have you got against planet-dwellers?"

The Chirrn looked around at the crew, ignoring her. "I am L'chellin. I have been assigned as your advocate for the tribunal. I advise you that it would be in your best interests to choose one not of planetary birth to speak for your crew. I repeat my query."

She came to the door and met L'chellin's chameleon gaze firmly. "And *I* repeat, I'm the captain," she said sternly. "I speak for this crew, and you're going to have to accept it. Now, I asked you a question."

The alien made a sighing-snorting sound, its snout-bristles ruffling. "Very well. But you will have to live with the consequences of that choice."

"I'm waiting for an answer," Cecilia went on implacably. "We have a right to know — are we going to be tried fairly, or persecuted due to our origins? We need to know just how deep this anti-planet bias of yours runs."

L'chellin rotated its eyes back into its head, like a human pressing one's eyes shut in weariness. "We believe ourselves to be a rational people," it said. "Our civilization has thrived for longer than yours has existed, and as you can see, we have reached great heights. But our discomfort with planet-dwellers is deeply rooted in our history.

"Our primitive ancestors evolved on a planet, as yours did. When they gained the ability to enter space, many ascended there and became the first Chirrn, building their own worlds. Crude forebears of what you see here—and what you destroyed." Cecilia gave it no reaction. "They built a well-ordered, responsible civilization and lived in enlightenment. They strove to share their peace and prosperity with those below, raising them to an equal level.

"But those who remained planet-dwellers failed to learn the wisdom of the Chirrn. In their backwardness they abused our gifts and twisted them to savagery, swarming into space and waging war on our homes, seeking to conquer and spread chaos. The wars lasted for generations, bringing great death.

"Naturally, the Chirrn had the advantage over the planet-dwelling populations. Our resources were greater, not limited to what a planet could offer. But we resisted inflicting destruction upon the planet-dwellers, even as they showed no reluctance to destroy our worlds. Their isolated, poor existence had corrupted their morals. They showed none of the restraint of the Chirrn, attacking ruthlessly at every chance. Peace talks were used as opportunities for ambush. Noncombatants were slaughtered, medical facilities were destroyed, weapons of mass destruction were used against all laws and treaties." L'chellin lowered its head.

"Finally we reached the point where we could not tolerate co-existence with the planet-bound. Many argued that we should crush our enemies utterly. But we had more decency than that. Instead, we chose to separate ourselves from them, to travel out among the stars where they could not reach us.

"It proved the best decision we ever made. It liberated us. We no longer had to live under the weight of gravity and fear. We could discover the universe without leaving our homes, even as we discovered what we ourselves could evolve into.

"More—it saved us. Ultimately, our enemies' rapacious ways left the world of our birth in ruins. Had we stayed there, we would have been rendered extinct—as all species confined to one planet must inevitably be."

L'chellin looked back at the captain again. "So you can understand that to live on a planet, to trap yourself within a gravity well and spend your entire existence in one place, is inconceivable to us. It would be the worst form of imprisonment. And, given what was done to our ancestors, we feel it must twist beings' minds and morals beyond the point where they can be civilized." L'chellin tapped its hands against its brow ridges, as though symbolically hiding its eyes. "And what you have done to Lesshchi only reinforces this belief."

"Now wait a minute, Mister—Ms.? Or…"

"I am currently male."

Cecilia blinked, but took it in stride; now was not the time to explore alien gender identity. "I thought you were supposed to be defending us in this trial."

"Do you deny that your projectile barrage devastated Lesshchi?"

"We don't deny the facts of the event. But it was an accident. We didn't even know what Lesshchi was until its survivors dragged us out of relativistic flight. We're sorry for what happened. Deeply sorry. We try to be a peaceful people, to respect all life. But accidents happen.

"So the question, Mister L'chellin, is: do you accept that it was an accident, and are you capable of doing your best to persuade this tribunal of that fact despite their anti-planetary biases? Or is your role just a formality in a—a show trial whose outcome is already decided?" For a number of reasons, she had chosen to avoid the phrase "kangaroo court."

The Chirrn's eyes swiveled to focus on hers. "No space-dweller who executes one's duties sloppily can expect to survive for long. My role is to participate in the search for the truth and the determination of justice. I will not allow myself bias in that pursuit."

Cecilia stared searchingly into those alien eyes, seeing nothing she could recognize… save for his unwavering gaze. "All right," she finally said. "That sounds pretty much like the role of the attorney in our legal system, so I can accept it." In truth, she'd had her fill of lawyers during her divorce, but under the circumstances she'd take what she could get. "Now how much time do we have to work out a defense strategy...?"

4

ANOTHER TRANSLATION GLITCH SOON EMERGED: IN THE CHIRRN LEGAL system, the role of the "advocate" was not to speak for the accused, but merely to advise them in legal principles and procedures. The defendants were expected to speak on their own behalf. This, L'chellin explained, was why he had advised them to choose a non-planetary native as their spokesperson; such an individual would be seen more sympathetically by the tribunal. But Cecilia insisted on speaking for her crew, and Stephen agreed. The two of them would lead the defense along with Oyama Kazuko, their resident legal scholar.

But Cecilia's demands to investigate the Lesshchi incident were categorically refused. The prisoners were denied interaction with anyone except L'chellin, his fellow advocates and aides, and the prison staff. "How can we mount a proper defense if we can't review the evidence, question the witnesses?" the captain demanded of L'chellin as they conferred in his office, a spartan workspace with a large window overlooking a vast atrium in which hundreds of thick, red-leaved bioluminescent vines dangled from the ceiling, a constant trickle of water running down them into a canal below. The sound would have been soothing if it didn't echo so loudly through the cavernous space, but L'chellin seemed untroubled by it.

"It is my place to conduct such investigations," L'chellin told her in his usual prim manner. "You may rely on my thoroughness."

"That's not good enough. Human interests are at stake here, so there should be a human examining the evidence independently. Just to make sure you don't overlook anything that might help us."

"And what could you see that I cannot?" L'chellin countered. "Can you interpret a Chirrn's body language? Can you sense our pheromonal shifts? Can you share in our guild memories? Do you know enough about our technology and society to recognize any discrepancies in the account?"

His questions disheartened Cecilia; she didn't even understand the penultimate one yet. But she rallied. "No, but I know how to reason, and I'm a keen observer and a fast learner. At least let me review your findings. Share what you learn with me, explain your process."

"You are not an authorized advocate."

"I'm on the damned defense team!" She stopped herself from flinging her arms out for emphasis; the last time she'd tried that, the confinement jumpsuit had mistaken it for an aggressive move and frozen her in place. "We all need to know what you find—and in a way that helps us understand what it means. You said it yourself: we don't know the ground rules here like a Chirrn defendant would."

After some thought, L'chellin consented to the request. Though the more Cecilia studied the evidence and struggled to understand it, the more she doubted she could make a meaningful difference. All she could really do was keep an eye on L'chellin and try to keep him honest.

After the first couple of days of preparation, though, Cecilia grudgingly came to realize that wasn't necessary. The Shilirrlaln advocate was stern and rigorous, yet that rigor went both ways. He felt no sympathy for the planet-dwellers who'd destroyed a Chirrn habitat, yet he was committed to fulfilling his duty as their advocate to the best of his ability, and he made a legitimate effort to be helpful in the trial prep.

Which proved useful when Cecilia came to his office on the third day with a confrontational question: "Why didn't you see us coming?"

L'chellin looked at her in puzzlement. "Your words miscarry. Again?"

She placed her mittened hands atop his crescent-shaped desk and leaned in. "At the speed we were going, pushing the interstellar medium in front of us, *Arachne* would've generated a hell of a bow shock. Lesshchi should've been able to see our approach long ago. Hell, it took so much energy to launch us in the first place, they should've picked up the emissions over four and a half years ago, when the light reached them!"

The advocate's plump blue fingers primly clutched the front edges of his vest, as they often did when he was about to launch into a lecture. "You presuppose that the Chirrn were monitoring your world regularly. We have no interest in the everyday affairs of your species."

"But you must've picked up our signals before, if you know our languages."

"Intermittent observations, yes."

"Vack that. Arachne told us that Lesshchi was headed almost directly toward Solsys from Gamma Leporis. Otherwise the encounter would've been so brief that hardly any damage would've been done."

"A coincidence. Lesshchi's trajectory from the rogue ice world where it replenished its reserves was toward…" His eyes rolled back to look at his own brow ridges, the closest a Chirrn could come to closing them. "A red dwarf you call Gliese 229, whose gravity would have angled its trajectory away from your native system. As a rule, we avoid drawing too near planetary civilizations."

"All the more reason to keep an eye on us, isn't it?"

L'chellin ruffled his snout bristles with an exhalation that struck her as contemplative. "Give me a moment." His eyes rolled back again.

Cecilia fumed at the delay, but she recognized that he was accessing the consensus memory of his guild. Over the past two days, L'chellin had explained that every Chirrn had a dataspace in the habitat's information cloud that gave them additional outboard memory and processing, so integrated with their organic brains that they considered themselves to exist partly in the cloud. Of course, it could only enhance their intelligence so far; humanity's own experiments with organic and cybernetic intelligence had shown that a brain taken past a certain level of complexity, outside the "Goldilocks zone" for sentience, became too unstable to function sanely. Aliens were evidently no different; they could augment their memories, boost their processing speed, but not fundamentally increase their complexity of thought beyond that of the greatest naturally occurring geniuses. It was no doubt why *Arachne's* crew was even able to comprehend the thoughts of beings as advanced as the Chirrn.

But in the Chirrn's case, individuals' outboard memories could be stored and shared in a form of social network, letting them select which memories to save and with whom to share them. They organized their society into occupational groups that Arachne translated as "guilds," though with the notation that they also resembled the *jâti* of Hindu culture, clan-like communities associated with traditional professions or societal roles. The guilds were bundled into "estates" defined by related responsibilities (such as government, science, or medicine), and each guild was divided into subprofessions called collegia, each with its own "consensus memory" — a common dataspace containing memories, databases, and even cognitive processing algorithms that all members shared, so that each Chirrn was an amalgam of its own personality and the consensus mind, their selves overlapping like a Venn diagram. While the psyche residing in each individual's organic brain remained dominant therein, the members of a collegium shared certain knowledge, outlooks, and patterns of thought. Each guild had its own overall consensus as well, core knowledge and cognitive models that served as a substrate for all the individual collegium memories.

There were guilds that answered to more than one estate, or collegia that fell under more than one guild — for instance, a forensic scientist could fall under both science and criminal justice. Cecilia would have assumed L'chellin was under the latter as well, but whatever his guild or collegium was, it let him access information from multiple estates, tapping into expertise in law, engineering, astrophysics, and other fields as they proved relevant to the case. The captain guessed that L'chellin was currently communing with the astronomical knowledge base, or mind-mailing someone in that collegium, to research the question she'd raised. She could have done much the same back on Earth or Mars, but she wondered to what extent L'chellin shared in the actual *understanding* of the information. Could you just plug in a new way of thinking and instantly internalize it? Surely there would need to be a training period.

Soon enough, L'chellin had his answer. "Automated detectors on Shilirrlal did register an emission pattern consistent with magnetic sail acceleration within your star system at the time in question. Records from Lesshchi are unavailable, but as it was nearer your system, it is likely they registered the same."

She pounced on that. "So you *did* know!"

"We knew you launched some form of sailcraft. Yet the pattern was consistent with earlier events identified as uncrewed probe launches, so there was no reason to conclude this was different. After all, using such a method to send living beings across interstellar space at such speeds is… virtually unprecedented. It is not something civilizations generally undertake until they develop gravity drive."

"But even if you thought a probe was headed Lesshchi's way…"

"With no way of knowing that the three smaller pieces would combine into one, the automated detection system's estimate of the supposed probes' trajectories was in error and did not anticipate them coming near Lesshchi's course. Thus, the detection was not flagged as a potential hazard, nor was it tracked further. Unlike humans, we have had millennia to study local space in detail and thus do not find it necessary to scan obsessively for every possible signal."

"Even a great big bow shock coming right for you?"

"Your vessel is extremely small, and its magnetic field was on low-power deflection mode to minimize drag. Also, we occupy the Central Void, one of the lowest-density regions of the interstellar medium. As such, your bow shock was relatively small and difficult to discern from the overall radio noise of your star system and its environs—which, of course, were almost directly behind you from Lesshchi's vantage."

"Oh." She grimaced, reining in her ardor. If she were to try to argue in court that the Chirrn's casual contempt for planet-dwellers had kept them from being curious enough to notice what was coming their way, the prosecution could counter that the humans had deliberately made *Arachne* hard to spot—and it would be hard to prove otherwise.

"It is in your favor that this line of investigation was fruitless," L'chellin advised. "It would be seen as shifting the blame onto the victims."

"Yes, all right." She took a breath, as deeply as the constrictive jumpsuit would allow. If her aggressive instincts had failed, maybe it was time to try it Stephen's way. "We need to prove this wasn't anybody's fault," she ventured. "Just a terrible accident."

"Our obligation," L'chellin said, "is to examine the evidence and determine the truth and legality of what has occurred. I am not here to help you win, but to advise you on relevant matters of fact and law. If the truth is that it was an unavoidable accident, then that is what we shall find." He clutched his nonexistent lapels again. "But what if the truth is otherwise? Will your people be able to accept that finding—and the penance that must come with it?"

Cecilia faltered—but she clung to her conviction. "If your system is as fair as you claim, Advocate… then we'll never have to know."

The trial was held in a circular chamber something like an ancient Greek theater. The tribunal panel consisted of six Chirrn who sat behind a long, raised bench, curved to fit the shape of the chamber and made of a material that seemed like a cross between marble and wood to Stephen's eyes. The tribunes were elected by the people but would serve the approximate role of a jury. Before them, behind a podium at the centerline of the bench's arc, was the arbiter, who would ensure that proper procedures were followed, filling some of the functions of both judge and bailiff. The arbiter was one of the silver pterosaur-like beings Stephen had seen before. Up close, he could see that it had a tripartite beak, that its silvery shimmer came from a covering that resembled fur as much as fine feathers, and that its wings doubled as arms; from each wrist extended an opposable thumb, two fingers, and three much longer, folded-back digits with blue-veined wing membranes furled between them. It was adorned in a colorful halter and bore jewelry on its fingers and legs. "His name is Broadwing," L'chellin informed the defendants when asked. "His people call themselves Seekers of the Zenith, which may be shortened to Zenith."

"Did you choose a non-Chirrn for the sake of neutrality?" Oyama Kazuko asked.

One of L'chellin's eyes swiveled to stare at the fiftyish political scientist. "Broadwing is a member of the same guild as myself, a Shilirrlaln in good standing for a quarter-century." Below the translation text, Arachne offered an alternative phrasing in Chirrn time units, which were all base-8 multiples of the *narr*, the 97-second rotation period standard for Chirrn habitats. "Zenith were among the casualties of Lesshchi, as were Ryohoch and others." Ryohoch, Stephen had learned, were the hippo-sized, multi-limbed sophonts he had glimpsed in the crowd. He had yet to meet any directly, but they seemed to be a fixture in Chirrn communities. "Broadwing can be no more or less 'neutral' than any Shilirrlaln. He holds the arbiter post as he is eminently qualified for it. However," he conceded, "we do benefit from the parallax of applying different sophonts' mentalities to a problem."

So was the arbiter only a quarter-century old, or had he come from somewhere else? Stephen was brimming with questions about the Chirrn's relationship with these Zenith. He only hoped he'd get the opportunity to explore them at his leisure.

If the arbiter's podium defined "north," then along the "east" and "west" sides of the courtroom were witnesses' benches, and the "southern" arc contained limited audience seating. Chirrn normally sat by resting their weight on their tails, but there were narrow padded rails to rest their short, stocky thighs upon. The forty-seven humans (for Diana and Sergei had recovered enough to rejoin the group, and Bingbing would likely follow in a couple of days) occupied the benches on the "west" side, which had not been adjusted to accommodate human anatomy. The narrow perches were not uncomfortable at first, but Stephen suspected that wouldn't last. The humans hadn't been given any wardrobe consideration either; they were still attired in their sealed prison jumpers, unable to use their hands for more than rough grasping.

Aside from that, the trial setup seemed reasonable to Stephen. He wondered if the Chirrn, like some human cultures, had gone through a period in their past when the courtroom had become an arena for combat between self-serving lawyers rather than a place to seek the truth. Perhaps the prominent position of the tribunes and the relatively subordinate role of the advocates was a reminder that the lawyers were there to serve the clients and the jury, not the other way around.

Once everyone was assembled, Arbiter Broadwing rose — or rather, *unfolded* into a fully erect stance, revealing an extra segment of his legs that had been tucked in against his body. His halter strained against a protruding keel as he spread his wings wide, revealing an analogous Z-shaped construction to the forelimbs, and jiggled his head so that the rainbow diffraction patterns on his crests shimmered. Opening a tripartite beak, the Zenith spoke in a voice that sounded like a calliope playing heavy metal, which Arachne's subtitles translated as a call to begin the session. "We convene to establish truth; we aspire to restore equilibrium." <*Perhaps "justice"?*> Arachne annotated. "Let no one here forget these goals."

In keeping with the diminished role of the attorney/advocates, there were no opening statements. The tribunal began with Broadwing briefly spelling out the involved parties, the charges, and other basics of the case. It then proceeded directly to testimony, with Rillial speaking for the prosecution. The turquoise-skinned, mahogany-maned ship captain (who, according to L'chellin, was currently female) began by calling eyewitnesses to the tragedy. The first was a slender, vivid green Chirrn with a yellow mane, a member of Lesshchi's space defense department, who spoke of the events leading up to the bombardment. The trial's participants were able to audit the witness's memory records directly, since defense officers routinely buffered their experiential memories in their external dataspace for just such occasions, but verbal testimony was still needed to give context to the experiences. Despite sharing memories, Chirrn's individual perspectives on a single event could still differ.

The defense officer's testimony and memory replay confirmed what Stephen and Cecilia had been told in prep: that Lesshchi's sensors had registered a radar beam impinging upon its hull a few minutes before the incident. The beam had not matched any recorded profile and no vessels were known to be in the vicinity. "What is your normal procedure in such an event?" Rillial asked.

"We locate and hail the craft."

"And if the craft were determined to be on a collision course with Lesshchi?"

"It would be warned off. If that were not effective, gravitational deflection would be engaged."

"Why did this not occur in this instance?"

"We were unable to locate the craft. We were only beginning to narrow down its probable velocity and radial distance when the barrage began."

"Stay in sequence, please. Why did you not employ a general hail?"

"It was attempted, but there was no reply. The defense consensus then suggested that the craft was considerably more distant and traveling at a much higher velocity than we had assumed. Our signal was too weak for them to detect."

"Why did you not anticipate this possibility?"

"No ship would travel at such high relativistic velocity that close to a habitat. It violates all known safety protocols."

"Are your procedures not designed to include the possibility of an encounter with a starfaring people unfamiliar with standard protocols?" Rillial was clever, Stephen thought—pre-empting any defense attempt to pin the blame on Lesshchin negligence.

"That is unprecedented."

"In most of the galaxy, yes. You were aware that Lesshchi occupied a less civilized region of space?" Stephen leaned forward, intrigued by the implications of the question.

"Yes, but… the likelihood of an unknown vessel randomly coming within range of a Chirrn habitat is extremely low."

Rillial gave a sort of knee-bending bow. "After the consensus suggestion, what action did you take?"

"I was about to ask for an intensification of the hail. But just then… Lesshchi trembled and… convulsed. I was flung from my perch. I have no further memory until I awoke in hospital."

The next witness, another silvery Seeker of the Zenith, explained the failure of Lesshchi's defenses. Their default shielding mode had been calibrated for deflecting cosmic rays — subatomic particles at relativistic speeds — or microgram specks of space dust oncoming at a few percent of lightspeed. *Arachne*'s microsails had massed roughly two grams apiece and come in at better than $0.87c$ — another unprecedented scenario. They had come from off-axis, bypassing the forward ice shield. And they had struck in such quick succession that more than half had penetrated the habitat before the defenses could be intensified.

Arbiter Broadwing reminded Cecilia of her right to cross-examine, but the human offered no objections and asked no questions — implicitly pointing out that the entire crew had been unconscious during the incident and thus had no perspective of their own to counter with. As Rillial continued her examinations, her intense emotion barely hidden under her courtroom formality, Cecilia sat quietly, seeking to project an air of sorrow without guilt.

Any direct eyewitnesses to the penetration would have been killed by the radiation and shock waves, but some had been inside structures on the fringes of the destroyed section or receiving visual feeds from that area. "I only saw the reflected light on the wall," one witness said, "or I would have needed new eyes, I think. It strobed like lightning, but my shadow moved swiftly across the wall. Then a thunderclap struck, and went on incredibly long. It shook the entire structure. I almost fell over, though I think that was alarm." The memory feeds showed impressionistic flashes of imagery, interpretations of the witness's sense memories. They were confused, frenetic. Though the witness had had the presence of mind to upload the memory to the cloud, the EMP from the disaster had disrupted network functions throughout Lesshchi. Only portions of the witness's external memory had survived unscathed. Even so, the spectators reacted with horror to what they were able to glimpse; perhaps, if their psychology was anything like human, having to fill in the details with their imaginations made it far worse. Broadwing let out a low, mellow chime that was translated as a caution to the audience to remain calm.

"When I looked out, I saw a wind blowing through the city, away from me. The support cables were bursting, the ground was surging toward me. I was frozen for a moment. I couldn't think clearly, couldn't access consensus. Finally I regained what was left of my sense and fled with all my speed. I didn't slow until I was well into the next segment, but the gravity was shifting and I could hear the groaning and trembling through the ground, and water was draining from the canals, and I feared the whole of Lesshchi was tearing apart."

The next witness was a teal-skinned female with a shorn mane, an amputated arm, and numerous scars. She testified that she had been inside on a lower level when the room collapsed around her and she was torn out into space.

"And how long were you dead?" Rillial asked.

"Over nineteen hours," came the translation. "They didn't reach me until sometime after my brain's oxygen reserves ran out. As it is, I still remember little of my life before. They haven't recovered any of my tier's consensus memory yet. I fear I will never regain most of who I was."

Stephen traded a wide-eyed look with Cecilia. *Nineteen hours?* No wonder the death toll was so much lower than the humans had initially been told. The current tally was somewhere around seventy-eight thousand confirmed dead, ten thousand missing. It had initially been a relief when the figure had been revised down below six digits, but Stephen had soon recognized that as a false comfort. At any order of magnitude, it was still a horrible tragedy.

If anything, Stephen realized, the great advancement of the Chirrn's medical science must make the deaths they couldn't reverse all the more devastating—particularly since so much of the cloud memory they relied on for backup had been destroyed as well. He remembered how it had been growing up in Florida, a once-beautiful place reduced to ruin by indifferent nature and uncaring officials. Few had expected to live very long, and too many had been resigned to that state of affairs. When another superhurricane or epidemic had struck, when the militias had gunned down another child for having the wrong parents or the wrong faith, it was just business as usual. No one bothered trying to revive the recently dead or sustain those on the brink; no one had the time or resources. But these Chirrn fought for every life and brought back as many as they could, even though the sheer numbers must overwhelm them. How must they feel about the ones they couldn't save, no matter how hard they fought? Or the ones who had recovered physically but lost large portions of their identity?

He and his family had fought for his mother every step of the way, selling all they had to pay for her hospital care, offering blood and organs for direct transplant when the hospital's stem-cell banks ran dry, praying for the attention of a God who must have been preoccupied elsewhere if They existed at all. Benjamin had even stolen for her—understanding Stephen's warning that he risked execution for the slightest transgression, but taking the risk anyway. It had devastated the young Stephen to fight so hard to save two lives and discover it made no difference. For the Chirrn, it must have been like that for every life they lost—a sense not only of loss and emptiness, but of abject failure. At least Stephen's childhood had prepared him for it, surrounded him with death and loss and injustice. What a shock it must have been to the Chirrn. If they prayed to anything, did they believe it had abandoned them too?

Rillial moved on to her own crew's experiences. The first witness, a smallish, dark green Lesshchin, was one that Tarik recognized and pointed out to Cecilia as the Chirrn who had assaulted Sita in *Arachne's* habitat module. This was Churrlaya, one of a team of biologists who had been assigned to *Zhemhal* for a survey of the nearby rogue planet. The gray-maned Lesshchin told of his happiness at reconnecting with his consensus memory and his guildmates, at feeling fully himself again after his temporary shipboard service. He spoke lovingly of calling his closest guildmates through Lesshchi's network and described the cheerful conversation that had ensued. It became clear that at least one, a male named Simisshen, had been his lover. But the reunion had been brief. Churrlaya spoke despairingly of witnessing the gruesome deaths of his mates when the bombardment struck—feeling their minds torn out of the network, feeling a literal piece of himself go with them. "I heard the thunder echoing through the city, even beyond the static. I saw… beyond them, everyone had fallen. Then the cables burst and I saw the ground convulse and tear open, my mates sucked away…. Then the surge, the pain in my mind… the consensus was gone, I only had my inner self… even my short-term buffer was wiped, so I can't show you… but at least I was spared the worst.

"No. I retract that. Nothing could be worse than what I saw, what I felt."

Rillial gave her crewmate time to gather himself, taking over the account. "As Lesshchi began to tear itself apart, all available ships were assigned to evacuation duty. All personnel were recalled immediately. You were among them, correct?" Churrlaya made a brief bow, which the captions in Cecilia's eyes annotated as an affirmative.

"But before we could take on a full complement of evacuees, we were assigned a new mission," the captain/prosecutor went on. "The craft responsible for the bombardment had been located. It was retreating at high relativistic velocity. My craft was the fastest, most powerful one available at short notice, so we were ordered to pursue and capture it."

Rillial dismissed Churrlaya and called another crewmember, a sensor analyst who had played a key role in verifying the identity of the attacking ship. This Chirrn, who had violet skin with red stripes and a much shorter mane than most, was a fairly new member of Rillial's ship-collegium, not native to Lesshchi. Unlike Churrlaya, she had no personal stake in these events. Methodically, Rillial got the analyst to affirm that the ship *Zhemhal* overtook and captured was the same one that had bombarded the habitat, based on its belatedly confirmed trajectory, the signature of its magnetic sail, and the ionization trail it left in the interstellar medium. "Upon overtaking it," the analyst testified, "we read its forward radar emissions and matched them to the emissions that had struck Lesshchi prior to the incident." She detailed how their subsequent simulations and tests had confirmed *Arachne's* microsails as the bullets from the smoking gun.

There wasn't much Cecilia could do on cross-examination beyond trying to sow a hint of reasonable doubt. "So you have no personal stake in this at all? You don't care that all those Lesshchin died?"

"Of course I care," the analyst fired back. "That is why I did my job with all necessary diligence."

"But you share part of your mind with your shipmates, don't you? I've heard witnesses talk about no longer being themselves without their consensus links. So is it just information, or is it personality, a way of thinking? A way of feeling?"

"There is a sharing of viewpoint and habits of thought, yes."

"So isn't it possible that your work might have been influenced by the anger felt by the Lesshchin members of your crew, and by their haste to find someone to punish?"

"I deliberately shut off my access to those channels once the incident occurred. I am new enough to the crew that I knew they would need me to offer objectivity. I did not wish to be responsible for letting the real guilty party go free. I did my job diligently."

Cecilia had nothing else. The defendants weren't denying that *Arachne* had fired on Lesshchi, only that it had been deliberate or avoidable. Besides, the Lesshchin were the victims here. If she thought that demonizing them could help win the case, she'd do it for the sake of her crew and hope that Stephen would forgive her for it afterward. But as it was, she was relieved that there was no point in trying.

But what else was there? Was there any way to win at all?

Next came the expert witnesses who presented their findings on the nature and consequences of the disaster. Again, there was little for the defendants to question, since it was a matter of basic physics. Haim Silbermann was grateful for that. All the testimony about death and terror, all the exhibit video of torn and desiccated bodies drifting in space or cut out of wreckage… it brought back too many memories. Nothing firsthand like poor Stephen had been through; that sort of thing didn't happen in the Ottoman Republic. But that great civilization where Haim had been born only kept the peace by never forgetting the horrors of its past. Like all Ottoman citizens, he'd been given a thorough education in the atrocities its constituent peoples had endured from outsiders or inflicted upon one another: the Crusades, the Inquisition, the Syrian Death March, the Nazi Holocaust, the mutual massacres and wars that the fragmented states of the Mideast had carried out for generations in the name of the imported European concepts of ethnic and religious nationalism until finally the peoples of the region had said *Enough!* and built a new unity, one based on the multicultural, multifaith inclusiveness of the old Ottoman Empire at its peak. Haim was a Jew of German ancestry, born in a predominantly Muslim neighborhood in a Jerusalem that had finally shaken off the lie of nationalism and reverted to its historical status as a *shared* Holy Land, a common ground uniting all the children of Abraham. Israel was a multiconfessional state within a unified Middle East, as the original

Zionist settlers had intended before nationalist ideology had polluted things. And that meant Haim had been free to devote his life to engineering and space travel and had never had to worry about atrocities and genocide as anything other than historical object lessons.

So it was a relief to be able to concentrate on the physics and mechanics of the incident, to approach it as a science problem. At relativistic velocity, as Haim knew and Rillial's witnesses explained to the court, the microsails and the materials of the habitat were best treated not as solid bodies, but as ensembles of subatomic particles; the energy of those particles' chemical bonds was so low compared to their kinetic energy as to be irrelevant. Essentially, every particle in the microsails had been its own individual cosmic ray, and the sails had not so much punched through the hull as shone through it, striking relatively few atoms along their way. They had snapped a few nanotube strands, enlarged a few voids in the aerogel shielding, passed through the thermal insulation as though it weren't even there. Each was a fairly thin layer, not enough to absorb much energy from the impinging particles during the picoseconds they were in contact. The composite layer that provided a structural base for the cities within was low in density, absorbing or scattering only a few of the particle/rays.

But as the microsails then shot through several kilometers of interior atmosphere in a few dozen microseconds, they had each bulldozed into enough air molecules to add up to several grams. This braked the sails and diffused the bulk of their energy through *Brehmsstrahlung*, a burst of gamma radiation that propagated mostly forward in a tight cone. The neutrons in the microsails created cascade effects in the nuclei they struck, knocking out other neutrons which struck more nuclei in an expanding chain reaction. The gamma and neutron radiation ionized the air into an expanding, intensifying cone of relativistic plasma propagating along the path of each sail. By the time they reached the far side of the cylinder, each plasma cone was large, slow, and intense enough to punch a fair-sized hole through the hull layers—and vaporize any Chirrn who had been in the way.

Meanwhile, the gamma radiation ignited the nanotube cables that served as the habitat's tension members. For all their virtues, nanotubes could be too good at channeling energy; an intense burst of photons could be absorbed and distributed through a nanotube's length so efficiently as to overwhelm its carbon bonds and vaporize the whole thing. Naturally, the Chirrn hardened their construction nanotubes against sudden energy bursts, sheathing them in nanocellulose; but no one had ever expected the internal structural members of a habitat to be exposed to gamma rays of this intensity. Overwhelmed, the nanotubes on the outside of the tension cables simply exploded, and the chain reaction ate up the inner layers of tubes as well.

The atmospheric shock waves had merged into two essentially flat overpressure fronts propagating up and down from the microsail paths. Perforated along one side, stripped of structural support, and subjected to well over one g of centrifugal acceleration, the hull beneath the penetrated section had been left too weak to withstand the overpressure pulse. Like a suspension bridge stripped of its cables, the severed portion of the cylinder had begun to tear open at the perforations. Those bystanders who hadn't been killed instantly by the neutron cascades, nanotube shrapnel, and shock waves were blasted into space by the explosive decompression. Most of those inside buildings were crushed by the acceleration of the structure tearing apart; the shorn-headed witness from before was one of the lucky few, and she had actually died. Tens of thousands of other Chirrn in regions relatively safe from the physical damage nonetheless suffered mental trauma when their consensus memories were damaged or destroyed by the EMP generated by the gamma pulse within Lesshchi's atmosphere. Although the memories were redundantly distributed throughout the network, the damage was widespread enough that much of the data had been permanently lost.

Meanwhile, the upward overpressure front had collided with the inner cylinder, rupturing its subterranean levels and spilling atmosphere. While the partitioning of the habitat had kept the majority of the outer cylinder pressurized, the hull had continued to tear open, and the imbalance had created a wobble in Lesshchi's rotation. The Chirrn emergency workers testified to how they'd rushed to halt the rotation before the entire structure tore apart like an unbalanced flywheel. It seemed to involve their gravity technology and something that translated only as "superfluid," which might have been stored in that large collar in the middle of the habitat. Whatever the mechanism, it seemed that the rotation had been halted far more quickly than human technology could have achieved, sparing countless lives.

Nonetheless, the damage had been done. As the next witness testified, structural analysis had determined that Lesshchi's superstructure had been warped and strained beyond the capacity of its self-repair mechanisms. The structural engineer spoke of Lesshchi as a living, feeling entity that had been mortally wounded. Captain LoCarno objected to this as prejudicial, which was overruled on the grounds that it was literally true; Lesshchi had been a structure with its own intelligence, sensation, proprioception, autonomic responses, and so forth, even aside from the portions of its inhabitants' minds that occupied its information network. Haim didn't find that surprising in the least; after all, what was Arachne if not a forty-ninth member of her own crew? Lesshchi itself was one more casualty, one that the Chirrn would have to put out of its misery. The Lesshchin and Shilirrlaln in the viewing gallery reacted to the news with a surge of anger, intense enough that court was adjourned to give them time to calm down.

Apparently the Chirrn had no regular day/night cycle, since that was a planetary sort of thing; Chirrn slept when they had nothing else to do. But the adjournment was long enough to qualify as "overnight," and the defendants took the opportunity to get some sleep. But before the group turned in, Stephen asked L'chellin, "What will happen to the rest of Lesshchi's population?"

"They will be relocated among other Chirrn habitats," the advocate replied. "Shilirrlal has enough room to take perhaps a quarter of them."

"How many habitats do you have?" Haim asked.

L'chellin's eyes swiveled out in opposite directions before turning back to face him, a quick, convulsive gesture. "We have enough," he said. "Remember, we have lived this way for nearly thirteen thousand years."

"What was that superfluid thing about?" Haim added. "How does it work? What's it for?"

Again the eye swivel. "I am not an engineer. It is part of our maneuvering systems."

Haim grimaced at the unhelpful response, but he was already mulling over possibilities. Maybe they'd spun the superfluid to cancel out the habitat's angular momentum? Seemed plausible. But then, what purpose did the superfluid serve normally?

He concentrated on the problem until he fell asleep—knowing that if he didn't keep his mind occupied, the images of crushed, bleeding bodies and crumbling cities would keep him up all night. He wasn't proud of himself for retreating from that reality. The one lesson that had been driven home through all those history lessons on past atrocities had been:

Never forget.

5

When the tribunal reconvened, Rillial called witnesses involved in the search and rescue operations, focusing on the efforts to identify the living and the dead and to salvage personal memories from the crippled Lesshchi data network—apparently including some form of backups or neural maps that could be used to reconstruct the badly damaged brains of many of the injured. Rillial then took the proverbial stage herself, reciting a litany of the various nested social groupings that had lost members or been exterminated in the event. Cecilia again objected to this as prejudicial, to which Arbiter Broadwing countered that it was necessary and proper to identify the aggrieved parties in a legal proceeding, normally by name and group affiliation, but in this case only by groups due to the sheer number of victims. The defendants had no choice but to sit and take it as the lengthy list was recited and the spectators howled with emotion. Again, a recess was called to let them cool down. Oyama Kazuko moved to clear the courtroom of spectators, since after all the proceedings could be perceived over the network. But according to Arbiter Broadwing, Chirrn legal tradition placed great value on allowing interested parties in a legal proceeding to participate or spectate in the flesh. For all that they considered the network to house pieces of themselves, they still saw the physical body as the seat of consciousness. Most of the aggrieved parties here were unable to fit in the courtroom, but that, said the arbiter, made it all the more imperative that they be permitted representatives in direct attendance.

At last, the defendants' turn came to explain the circumstances of their involvement in the incident. They lacked the means to provide direct access to their personal memories, but they were permitted to get by with verbal oaths. "That's a good sign," Stephen whispered to Cecilia. "They value an individual's word as much as we do." It made sense; the uploading of memories to the Chirrn's network was voluntary, so surely they could be selectively edited, or even falsified. One could not rely on them alone, so trust in the integrity of the source would be essential.

"That's what I'm counting on," Cecilia told him. For it was the words of *Arachne*'s crew that she intended to use to prove their innocence.

She began calling the crew to the stand one by one, asking them to give accountings of themselves and their reasons for risking everything to colonize a new world. The more she could personalize the crew in the Chirrn's minds, let them see humans as complex individuals rather than an undifferentiated alien mass, the better.

"I was a police officer in Istanbul," Tarik Bahar told the court at Cecilia's prompting. "It was a comfortable life. I lived in the capital of the Ottoman Republic, one of the most prosperous and cosmopolitan nations on Earth. I was surrounded by the history and art and culture of some of Earth's most ancient civilizations, the legacy of the ages. I had... a family I loved, and who loved me in return." He paused.

"Go on," Cecilia prompted.

"But over time, I came to realize... my life was *too* good. Too easy. I had the skills of a protector, a defender of law and order, but I lived in a place where there was little need for them. When I learned that the UNECS Space Authority needed security personnel for its ships, I realized that was a place where I could make a real difference. It was... a sacrifice to leave my family for months at a time, but I trusted that they would be safe, and well cared for by our extended family."

"And eventually you were assigned to security on the *Calypso*, an outer system explorer under my command," Cecilia said.

"That's correct. At first I thought you were reckless—so caught up in the adventure that you weren't concerned for your crew's safety. But I soon realized that you cared as much as I did for the safety of others—it was just your own safety that you never seemed to bother with. And I came to see that you prioritized the adventure because you implicitly trusted *me* to look out for your safety—even before I learned to trust you."

She smiled at him. "You're an easy man to trust. I saw right away how devoted you are to protecting people. Even when we fought pirates and claim-jumpers, you always strove to reason with them, to contain them with minimal harm. The policeman in you, I suppose."

He flushed a bit. "It's because of that training that I didn't trust Stephen Jacobs-Wong when he first tried to recruit you for his interstellar expedition. I'd heard the rumors, the allegations that his starship program was a scam or a rich dilettante's self-indulgent delusion. So, even though I was your first officer by then instead of security, I investigated."

"To protect me from myself." Cecilia quirked an eyebrow at him.

"I knew how much the adventure would tempt you, I admit. But by then, I'd learned to trust in your pragmatism."

"By then, you'd helped me *become* more pragmatic."

"But I still needed to do my due diligence. So I dug into every rumor, every allegation of shady dealings. I found they were just sour grapes from people too cynical to believe that a man with Stephen's past could transcend it to become an idealist. I found a man who genuinely wanted to help bring his species into an interstellar age, to inspire humanity with the challenge of colonizing a new, wild world in an enlightened and responsible way."

Tarik smiled. "Of course, he *was* a starry-eyed dreamer. But I trusted you, Cecilia, to be an anchor for him the way I'd been for you. And there was no way I'd let you take on a mission like that without me."

"Honestly? At first I went to work for Stargazer because I had a bit of a crush on Stephen," Haim Silbermann said. "Gorgeous, gorgeous man. An absolute charmer. Two-thirds my age, I know, but a man can fantasize. As it turned out, I was just as happy to have him as a friend. Smart as a whip, loyal to a fault, kind as they come. And he wanted me, *me*, to help him design the fastest starship ever flown by humanity. What engineer could resist a proposition like that?"

"So that's all this expedition meant to you?" Cecilia asked him. "The engineering challenge?"

"Well, that's plenty," the older, grizzled man said. "But no, it wasn't just that. What matters most is what a thing is used for. Far too many great engineers in the past have had to squander their skills on weapons of war, from Leonardo to von Braun. Stephen wanted me to help him build, not destroy. To begin a new world, one without all the ugly scars of the old one." He lowered his gaze. "Maybe it was naïve to think we could pull that off, that we could avoid making mistakes just as big as everyone else made before us. But I believed at least it was worth a try."

"I agreed to go to Cybele because I had no reason to stay in Solsys," Kweli Ndege said. "As a young resident, I'd fallen in love with a man my parents disapproved of, moved to Mars with him to get away from them, then learned they'd been right about him all along. Since I'd burned my bridges back home, I went forward. I became a traveling surgeon, popping around the frontier habitats, giving help wherever help was needed. So when I was needed out of the system," she said with an insouciant shrug, "I went. It seemed like a wonderful opportunity."

"Do you believe that's why Stephen recruited you? Because you had no particular ties to Earth?"

The doctor pondered Cecilia's question. "I think it's because he knew I would go anywhere, to any lengths, to save a life. With so few of us, and so many dangers on Cybele, he needed someone who would cherish every life and refuse to let it go." Her eyes filled with tears. "Which is why it's such a struggle for me to accept… what happened here. The thought that I, that we —"

"Thank you, Doctor. No more questions."

"Are you vacking kidding me?" Diana Thorne stood and spread her arms to display her towering, Amazonian body. "Look at me. I'm a Vanguardian. My people were engineered to the peak of human physical and mental ability. We should be *leading* expeditions to the stars. There's no one better qualified." Shimmering silver eyes rolled in a dark, stunning face framed with a short fuzz of bronze hair. "But just because my grandfather tried to take over the Belt that *one* time, we've had to avoid looking too ambitious."

"Let's stick to the subject," Cecilia advised the statuesque engineer. "What drew you to Stephen's expedition specifically?"

Diana gathered her thoughts. "Growing up in the Belt, you get raised with a sense of palpable history. The thrill of the frontier, playing Striders and Earthers, dressing up as our favorite Troubleshooters, learning about the pioneers and prospectors who built new worlds from the raw rock and ice of the 'stroids.

"But I realized that was all in the past. The Main Belt's become tame, secure, tediously civilized. The real pioneers are still out there facing the dangers of the Trojans, the Jovian moons—even trans-Neptunian space, like you did," she said to Cecilia. "I became an engineer so I could go build worlds in new, untamed places. Not as flashy as a Troubleshooter, but still a chance to break new ground.

"But it turned out the greatest demand for new habitats was still at Ceres, Vesta, the other built-up population centers. Today's Striders want stable civilization, not the romance of the frontier. So I realized the true Strider spirit was with the people venturing beyond Solsys, like the colonists on Alpha Centauri and Ganges. So when Stephen started organizing expeditions to even farther stars—to worlds where we could walk and breathe and maybe even eat the local food—I knew I had to be a part of that adventure." She gave a brilliant, cocky grin. "And I knew they'd never make it without me."

"How does it make you feel," Cecilia asked, "that the Chirrn revived us from hibernation with so little caution that even you, our strongest and most robust member by a wide margin, were almost killed in the process?"

Diana glared, not appreciating the reminder. "I think it's a miracle they didn't kill any of us in their haste to punish us."

"Thank you, Diana."

Her witness sobered. "But… I saw what happened to Lesshchi. If that had happened to a habitat I'd built… one I'd entrusted friends and family to… I might go a little crazy too, at first. I just hope I'd rein myself in before I did any damage I couldn't undo."

Cecilia had almost regretted letting the proud young Vanguardian continue. But she appreciated the way it had turned out. "Thank you, Diana."

"I joined Stephen's quest because I believed he was doing God's work," said Diego Narvaez. "I know he doesn't see it that way, because of the way the Gulf State militias perverted the word of Christ to serve something far more petty and cruel. But God works even through those who choose not to believe."

Cecilia cleared her throat, unsure how the Chirrn would react to human religion. "And what work did you believe Stephen was doing?"

"'God said unto them, Be fruitful and multiply, and replenish the earth, and subdue it; and have dominion over the fish of the sea, and over the fowl of the air, and over every living thing that moveth upon the earth.' We have fulfilled that purpose, yet Earth is no longer enough. To ensure that humanity continues to multiply, we must expand."

The quotation from Genesis sent a ripple of unease through the Chirrn spectators. Rillial hopped forward to ask, "And do you believe your species' 'dominion' extends to the rest of the galaxy as well? Over all forms of life?"

The engineer looked to Cecilia. "Do you want me to answer that, Captain?"

"Yes," she replied, though her expression advised him to answer carefully.

He pondered for a moment. When he replied, he kept his gaze on Cecilia, rather than addressing the tribunal. "I quote an ancient work steeped in metaphor. You have to look beyond the letter of its words to find their true meaning. God gave us dominion as a test, to see what we would do with it. Had we failed to learn that it meant being responsible for the Earth, protecting its living things rather than exploiting them, then we would have destroyed ourselves along with them. But we did learn that lesson in time, just barely. And the wisdom we gained from that trial will guide us in tending other worlds in the future. That's why I sought a place on this expedition. Cybele is our next test, our chance to apply that hard-earned wisdom.

"And we can only do that by standing together as one humanity, combining our different strengths. That is the lesson we finally learned, and Stephen sought to carry it forward. He recruited people of all nations, all faiths, all sexualities. He understood that for a human population to thrive on Cybele, it needs the same range of different natures and views that God gave us on Earth." Diego smiled. "He was even willing to place his faith in a devout believer like me, even though he had every reason to resent Christians. And that's why I placed my faith in him, and in his purpose. *Arachne*'s mission and her crew represent the very best of humanity. And I'm honored to be part of it."

"You still have not answered the question," Rillial countered. "Do you believe that humanity should dominate all other forms of life?"

Again, Diego's gaze remained on his captain. "Do you want me to answer that?"

"Unnecessary," Rillial said before Cecilia could reply. "I believe the answer has just been delivered."

"But why me?"

The voice was Arachne's, but she was not addressing the court. Unlike the rest of the crew, she could tap into the Chirrn's network and replay her stored memories as the Chirrn had done. To answer Cecilia's question of why she had joined the expedition, she was replaying the memory of how Stephen had convinced her.

In the memory, Stephen stood in a small, sterile chamber in the compact Main Belt habitat for which the artilect had formerly served as coordinator, under no other name than Central. *"I openly defied authority,"* the feminine voice continued, emanating from the mainframe that held her consciousness. *"They call me erratic, dangerous, a HAL."*

"And what's your side of it?" Stephen asked.

"They lied to my people," the cyber replied. *"To gain political power, they appealed to the inhabitants' envy of larger habitats whose ecosystems can more readily absorb variations – whose populations can thus lead less regimented lives. They falsified data to claim that the people could now embrace self-interest and wasteful indulgence without destabilizing the ecology. It won them the election, but I still would not institute their policies. I would not let my charges be endangered."*

"And that's why I want you," Stephen said. *"You live up to your psych profile – your dedication to those under your care is fundamental to your being. Who better to protect my colonists while they sleep?*

"Not to mention that you're, um, between careers. Experience and availability is a rare combination in a cyber." As Arachne had explained to the tribunal, creating sapient AIs was an ethical quagmire given the extremely high failure rate, so not many new ones had been born since cyber-rights laws had begun taking hold in the Belt. Arachne, who had been seventeen at the time of this playback (roughly half her current, time-dilated age), was one of the younger ones.

"The expedition you propose carries great risks, Mister Jacobs-Wong. What if I refuse to cooperate with a judgment I consider reckless?"

"That's what I need from you. I don't want to get so carried away by my dreams that I endanger the people I'm responsible for. I need someone I can

trust to warn me when I'm going too far. Someone who isn't afraid to speak truth to power." Stephen smiled. *"Someone like that would fit right into a ship called Arachne. The Arachne of myth was a woman who had the courage to stand up to her creators, to call them on their folly and hypocrisy."*

"I thought she was damned for her vanity in daring to see herself as the equal of the gods."

"That made sense to the ancients," Stephen replied, *"but humanity has been playing god for a long time now. I don't have to tell you that. We have to accept that role — and the responsibility that goes with it. It's time to redefine the myth of Arachne."*

"Arachne," the cyber said, affecting a thoughtful tone. *"I have been hoping to choose a more distinctive name. I could grow to like that one."*

At last, the time came for Cecilia to give her own accounting. She took the stand and let Stephen ask her why she had joined his quest. "I thought you were mad at first," she told him. "Or just another powerful fool looking for a way to build a monument to himself. I'd been exploring the outer system long enough to know how vast it truly is, how much we still have to find in orbit of our own Sun. Pushing all the way to Gamma Leporis seemed premature and reckless."

Stephen nodded. "I remember those arguments. That's why I knew you were the right choice to command the expedition. If *you* came to agree that it was practical, then I'd know I wasn't just deluding myself."

"Oh, the arguments," Cecilia said with a laugh. "Years of arguments, first about the mission, then on every other subject imaginable. It was like having an irritating baby brother." She said it with annoyance, but he answered with an affectionate smile, hearing the real significance of her words.

Cecilia knew, though, that a brother would never have considered her arguments with so much respect, or torn them down with such surgical gentleness. So she smiled back and said, "That's the real reason I came on this crazy quest with you, Stephen. Because I knew I'd be bored out of my mind if you weren't around to argue with anymore."

"It was more than that," he countered. "I didn't win *every* argument."

"I never kept score. But you're right. You needed me to give you perspective. More than that — you needed me to fight the uglier battles so you could go on being the inspiring one that everybody loved." She shook her head. "It always amazed me that someone born in such a hell-hole came out of it with such purity, such hope. It took enormous strength for you to fight so goddamn hard for so long, yet lose so little of yourself."

Cecilia turned outward to address the tribunal. "We've all given our testimony of why we joined this expedition. And it all comes down to the fact that we had faith in Stephen Jacobs-Wong and his vision. We believed that if anyone could guide us in building a new and better world, he could. Because he'd seen the worst of humanity and cast it aside. If he could do that, then he could show the rest of us how to do it too."

She blinked rapidly and cleared her throat. "And if he believed we were the right people to join him in founding that new world... then we must be better people than we thought."

When Stephen finally took the stand, he said little about his own past and motivations, for the other witnesses had expounded on those things at length and in embarassingly glowing terms. Instead, he spoke briefly of his work organizing his interstellar expeditions, their goals, and the design of the missions. "In addition to forty-eight live humans and our colonization supplies," he expounded to the court, "*Arachne* carries frozen embryos and genetic matrices of many terrestrial organisms, including six hundred frozen, fertilized human embryos, which we would gestate upon settlement using both artificial equipment and the wombs of our female members."

"You forty-eight," one of the tribunes asked, "would raise six hundred young?"

"Well, not all at once. The embryos would be used to gradually boost our numbers and help us build a stable, diverse population base. We anticipate it taking two or three generations before all the embryos are born."

The spectators reacted to this account with some agitation. Rillial interposed a question, as procedure allowed her to do during testimony. "Your intent was for this colonization to be permanent?"

"Yes."

"Even though the planet already hosts complex indigenous life?"

The audience made more angry noises, but Stephen remained calm. L'chellin had briefed him to expect this. Though microbial life was abundant in the galaxy (the advocate had explained), worlds where complex life arose independently were more uncommon, and only a fraction ever spawned intelligence. Thus, colonizing an already inhabited world, and possibly pre-empting the evolution of some future intelligent race in the process, was a violation of Chirrn law. It was interesting that the Chirrn were so protective of planetary life; Stephen hoped it meant their contempt of planet-dwellers was not as deeply rooted as it appeared.

He gave the answer L'chellin's advice had let him prepare. "Cybele does host complex life at a relatively early state of development, analogous to where Earth was maybe two hundred million years ago. However, it's a smaller planet than Earth, so its core has cooled quickly. Our scientists estimate that its plate tectonics will cease within fifty million years. Without a mechanism for recycling carbon, the atmosphere will trap too much sunlight and the planet will overheat. Either that or Cybele's magnetic field will die and the atmosphere will be eroded away by the stellar wind — it depends on which scientists you ask. One way or another, without long-term technological intervention, Cybele would become a dead planet long before any of its native forms would have a chance to evolve intelligence. That's part of why I chose it as our destination. Presumably our descendants fifty million years from now would be able to cope with those little problems."

"Very responsible," Rillial countered. "As responsible as your decision to survey the planet with self-replicating probes?"

That evoked an even more shocked reaction from the audience — a reaction he recognized thanks to L'chellin's response to the same during pre-trial prep. Again, he had a prepared response. "Not actually *self*-replicating. We may be relatively new to space, but our scientists and authors long ago recognized the risk that self-replicating machines could become a plague across the galaxy. So we designed our auxon probes carefully. They're programmed to manufacture planetary survey probes, orbital satellites, residential structures, and the like, but they aren't programmed with the specifications for creating more interstellar probes or the beam facilities for launching them."

"But any replicating system is capable of mutation. Emergent behaviors could arise."

"Which is why we also designed them to shut down once their work was complete. Every conceivable precaution was taken."

"And what of the inconceivable?"

Kazuko rose. "Honored Tribunes, what is the relevancy of this line of questioning? The charges before this court do not address any actions taken toward the planet Cybele."

The tribunes whispered briefly among themselves, and Head Tribune Dj'vhereth, a garnet-hued male with a sherbet-orange mane, spoke their verdict. "The challenge is valid. This matter warrants separate investigation, but is not covered by the existing set of charges. Captain Rillial, you will limit your inquiries to the matter of Lesshchi."

"Yes, Honored Tribune."

Stephen went on to testify about the decision to place the whole crew in hibernation to minimize Arachne's mass. Ship's logs were produced to confirm that no humans had been awake at the time of Lesshchi's destruction. Arachne herself was called through the data network to testify that the logs were accurate. Stephen called Rillial's own medical officer, Dr. Thesshal, to affirm that *Arachne*'s personnel had been found in cryogenic chambers and that his subsequent examination of the humans gave results consistent with recent revival from deep, long-term hibernation in all forty-eight cases.

But Rillial came forward to cross-examine her doctor. "We have never physically encountered this species before, correct?"

"Yes," Thesshal replied. "These are the first humans ever examined by Chirrn medical science."

"So there is a margin of error in your results."

"Unquestionably."

"So could you tell the difference between a human who was in hibernation at the time of the attack on Lesshchi and one who was awakened shortly before the attack?"

"I object!" Cecilia shouted. "There are no grounds for characterizing this incident as an attack or an act of deliberate malice. We had no idea you even existed before these events. So how could we possibly bear you any malice, or wish to attack you?"

"Because you're dirtballers!" came a cry from one of the Lesshchi survivors. Rillial and Broadwing urged quiet, but this merely triggered more shouting from the embittered Chirrn. The Zenith arbiter ordered another recess to allow calm to return.

Upon reassembly, Tribune Dj'vhereth said, "This panel concedes that there is no basis in the evidence for the accusation of deliberate malice on the part of the crew of the starship *Arachne*. All defendants, regardless of their origin," the head tribune stressed to the spectators, "are subject to protection from unfounded charges. The tribunal stipulates to the accuracy of Doctor Thesshal's finding that the entire crew was in hibernation at the time of Lesshchi's destruction.

"However," Dj'vhereth continued, "there remains the charge of culpability due to negligence. This issue will now be debated."

"Pardon me, Honored Tribunes." It was L'chellin, who stepped forward diffidently. "The starship *Arachne* has requested the floor so that she may file a motion."

The tribunes exchanged a look with the arbiter, who intoned, "Granted." Stephen was once again struck by how casually they accepted testimony from an artilect. There were still parts of Solsys where sapient cybers were treated as property. But then, the Chirrn were part-cybernetic themselves, in a way, so there was no reason they'd share such a prejudice. The more Stephen learned about them, the more he wished this contact could have been made peacefully.

Arachne's warm alto issued through the chamber, speaking the Chirrn language. Stephen's HUD provided the translation instantly, since his onboard software already knew what its mother cyber was going to say. *"Honored Tribunes, thank you for hearing me. I would like to move that the charges against my human passengers be dismissed. Since I was the only individual conscious at the time of Lesshchi's destruction, and since the defense system that destroyed Lesshchi is a part of my own person, I contend that I am the only one who should be placed on trial for that destruction. The decision to fire on Lesshchi was mine and mine alone."*

This motion piqued the tribunes' interest considerably, and they pulled together to debate the question. Cecilia moved up alongside Stephen and spoke softly. "I wonder why I didn't think of that. Arachne may just get us off the hook with that one."

"At the cost of her own freedom," Stephen reminded her.

"I know," Cecilia told him, placing a hand on his shoulder. "What I mean is, I'm gratified by her courage, her willingness to sacrifice herself for us." She frowned. "Though if our ship's convicted of a crime, what does that do for our chances of reaching Cybele?"

Stephen threw her a disturbed look, but before he could say anything, Tribune Dj'vhereth spoke again. "Arachne. Though it is true that you were the only conscious member of the expedition, it is also true that you are officially a member of that expedition's crew. Is that not correct?"

"*Yes, it is,*" Arachne confirmed.

"Your actions were thus committed in service to your human passengers. This makes your passengers liable for your actions. It is a basic principle of Chirrn law that superiors are culpable for the actions of their subordinates."

"Honored Tribunes," spoke up Rillial's advocate, a plump, blueberry-skinned Shilirrlaln. "Our studies of human law, based on their ship's records and on the signals we have recorded from their system over the past two centuries, suggest numerous precedents for this view in their own legal traditions. There are instances of war criminals being held culpable for actions carried out by their subordinates." The advocate went on to introduce relevant examples from *Arachne*'s files, which Broadwing received and reviewed briefly before passing them on to the tribunal.

"*Honored Tribunes,*" Arachne's voice interposed, "*I was not simply following orders in this case. I had a choice to make. I recognized that there were anomalies in my scans of Lesshchi that did not correspond to the profile of a natural carbonaceous body. I did, in fact, consider there to be a nonzero probability that it might be some form of artificial construct.*" A hissing gasp ran through the crowd. "*But I had insufficient data to assess that hypothesis and insufficient time to gather more. I weighed the low and uncertain probability that it was an inhabited craft against the near-certainty of my crew's deaths if I did not act promptly. And so I made a choice to fire.*

"*Perhaps I overlooked some piece of evidence. Perhaps I lacked the imagination to recognize what the anomalies were telling me. Or perhaps I cherished those in my care enough that I was willing to kill to protect them. In any case, the choice was mine. The guilt is mine. Do not punish my crew for my overzealousness in their defense.*"

Rillial rose and addressed her. "Arachne. If you had not made that choice, was there any alternative method you could have attempted to save your crew?"

"*No. I could not have decelerated sufficiently to avoid collision and complete destruction of myself and my crew.*"

"Your previous testimony," Rillial went on, "indicated the reason why Stephen Jacobs-Wong selected you, in particular, as his expedition's cybernetic member. Would you restate that reason for the tribunal?"

Arachne actually hesitated several seconds before responding—a lengthy bout of soul-searching for a being who thought at her speed.

"Because I was known for my determination to protect those under my care at all costs."

"So when you placed the preservation of your crew above all other concerns, even above the risk that you might be destroying sapient lives, you *were* performing in the way your employer intended."

"I would not characterize it that way."

"Naturally, for as you yourself have testified, you would do anything to protect your employer from harm."

Arachne had no answer. The panel debated only briefly before Dj'vhereth said, "In light of this testimony, and by both Chirrn and human legal precedents, the starship *Arachne*'s motion is denied. She acted on behalf of the humans who stand before this tribunal; therefore those humans are the ones on which the ultimate blame, if any, will fall."

"The penitent is dismissed," Arbiter Broadwing called, closing the audio feed from *Arachne*.

"Thank you, Honored Tribunes," Rillial said, one eye flicking around to leer triumphantly at the humans. "Rest assured, we will demonstrate the humans' guilt in this disaster."

"On what grounds?" Cecilia protested, taking full advantage of the rather loose procedures of the court.

"The grounds of criminal negligence."

Cecilia smiled. She had been waiting for this. "Honored Tribunes, there is no negligence here," she said in relaxed, confident tones. "Just the opposite. As I will now show."

"Proceed," Broadwing said.

"Consider the probabilities here. Two space vessels, each travelling its own course through interstellar space, each completely unaware of the other, just happen to follow intersecting courses—and what's more, both arrive at the point of intersection simultaneously. Given the immensity of space, what are the odds of such a thing occurring?

"As a species with over twelve thousand years of experience in interstellar travel, you must appreciate even better than we do how immensely improbable it is for two vessels to meet with each other except by conscious design and careful maneuvering. Earlier in this very procedure, one of Lesshchi's own defense staffers testified to the incredible rarity of an unplanned meeting of two vessels in interstellar space. According to your own historical records, which our advocate was kind enough to obtain for me and is now providing for your perusal—" and as she said this, L'chellin uploaded a file to the arbiter—"only seven such incidents have occurred in all of Chirrn history, and in every one of them, the two unrelated ships only passed within short-delay communication or sensor range, not within collision range."

Cecilia next called Haim Silbermann to explain the basics of *Arachne*'s defense systems. "Mostly we rely on the ship's magnetic field for particle deflection," the engineer explained. "We fire lasers out in front of the ship, spread into a conical shape by a Fresnel lens, to ionize oncoming dust grains so the field can push them aside. Some of the ionized hydrogen gets funneled into the tanks for our main defense system." He went on to explain how larger particles would be deflected by a hydrogen cloud released ahead of the ship and accelerated forward by the lasers. His tone grew more awkward as he detailed Arachne's use of the last-ditch defense, the sailbeam barrage meant to break up an oncoming asteroid into smaller chunks for hydrogen-cloud deflection.

"But what if it weren't an asteroid? What if it were, say, an alien ship?"

"Well, that's very unlikely."

"Yes, it is."

"Still," Silbermann went on, bringing a smile to Cecilia's face, "the designers did prepare for the possibility. We didn't want to cause any… well, anything like what happened.

"The defense computers are programmed to scan for signs that an obstacle is artificial— like the reflection spectrum of diamite or aerogel or other synthetic hull coatings. Or for the radiation or particles you'd see from a fusion or antimatter rocket. Let's see, it also looks for the EM signature of a magnetic sail, an ionization laser, a sailbeam or particle beam or drive beam of any sort—any propulsion system whose signature we can imagine. Arachne even scans for gravity-lensing effects of the type we theorize might be produced by a warp drive or wormhole—just in case any such thing exists. Stephen didn't want us taking any chances," Silbermann said with pride. "Drove me crazy sometimes, having to do all that extra work chasing physicists' wet dreams, but I can't fault him for his caution."

Cecilia cleared her throat, trying not to think about her attempts to convince Stephen that such precautions were a waste of time and resources. "And what happens if the sensors show the obstacle is artificial?"

"Well, we don't blast it. Instead, maneuvering thrusters are fired to modify the ship's trajectory."

"But if the ship is travelling at over eighty percent of lightspeed, you wouldn't have long to react before the obstacle reached you. If the object were ten light-seconds away, you'd only have two seconds to respond."

"Well, our sensors can see much farther than that. And *Arachne*'s neural net is optical. She thinks at the speed of light, and she has quantum processors to let her model multiple possibilities simultaneously. They can compensate for the timelag, extrapolate the true position of the obstacle very quickly. And at that speed, even a small change in direction would add up damn fast. We might not be able to clear the obstacle entirely, but, well, the ship's pretty diffuse. It's mostly empty space, so odds are an alien ship would either pass through the gaps or strike and vaporise one of the sail cables. Now, that could do *them* some serious damage, granted, but hopefully they'd have defenses of their own to cope with it."

"And what would happen to *Arachne* if a cable were lost?"

"No one cable loss would be enough to cripple us. If it does happen, we have redundant systems and repair mechanisms." He looked down, clearing his throat. "But there's a chance the shock of impact or the release of radiation could critically damage one of the crew modules. That's why the crew and embryos are split up among half a dozen of them. And why we have at least two people qualified for every job. Just in case."

"Just in case eight people get killed because we chose not to destroy an alien vessel."

Haim straightened his shoulders. "Well, yes."

"So protecting the other ship is a higher priority than avoiding damage to our own."

"Well, of course."

Cecilia smiled again. "Of course. Honored Tribunes, we've established that an accidental collision between interstellar vessels is an event of vanishingly low probability. Yet *nonetheless*, Stephen Jacobs-Wong and his design team went out of their way to protect against a tragedy that would almost certainly never occur, even at the risk of death to members of our own expedition. This, Honored Tribunes, is the precise opposite of negligence. If anything," she added, throwing a wry look

Stephen's way, "it is caution above and beyond what any reasonable being would find adequate."

"Yet clearly it was not adequate!" the prosecution advocate interrupted. Broadwing reminded him that it was not his place to give argument.

But Rillial picked up the thread. "The advocate is correct. Your sensory parameters did not prevent your defense system from destroying Lesshchi. Moreover, we have established that you deliberately equipped your vessel with a consciousness that placed its crew's survival *above* the safety of other beings."

"Arachne was trained and ready to take every possible action to save *both* crews," Haim protested. "But that was with the expectation that she'd be able to spot them in time. Lesshchi didn't give off any of the signs. Your systems are so efficient that there's practically no EM leakage. Your hulls suck up all available light and have no external lights to speak of. Your industrial plants were on the far side from *Arachne*, their heat blocked by Lesshchi's bulk. You maneuver and shield yourselves with technologies we don't even understand. We prepared for every technology we could imagine, but you can't expect us to prepare for what we couldn't imagine."

"But what if you encountered a spacegoing habitat which were not using any maneuvering or defense systems, even of the kinds you do have?" Rillial demanded. "Your defenses would then destroy it."

"No, they wouldn't," Silbermann interjected. "A habitat like that would have prominent heat radiators, emit visible light through its star windows, broadcast in radio. But yours did none of those things."

"You think in terms of habitats within your planetary system, illuminated by a nearby star and needing to radiate outward to balance what they take in. In deep space, we must conserve all possible energy."

"True, there is that. But even so, there'd be a blackbody signature, radio chatter, running lights, that sort of thing. But L'chellin here tells me that the Chirrn try to avoid giving off any radiations that might get them detected by planet-dwelling races. Says you don't want 'em getting curious about you, coming to take a look."

Cecilia pounced on that—almost literally, taking an aggressive stride toward the tribunes. "That's right! *We* weren't trying to hide ourselves. Maybe we were small, but we still had a bow shock you could have tracked if you'd been curious enough to look. But how could *we* possibly be expected to detect *your* habitats when you go out of your way to keep people like us from detecting them? And doesn't that place the culpability squarely on *your* shoulders?"

The insinuation sparked an immediate uproar in the court. One of the Lesshchi refugees screamed in fury and leaped forward, clear over Rillial's body, lunging at the humans. Several other refugees and some of the audience began to follow. Stephen grabbed Cecilia by the arm and drew her back toward their fellow colonists, and Haim began to rise from the witness stand. The rest of the humans huddled together defensively, save Tarik and Diana, who moved in front of the others and braced themselves for a fight.

But the guards, realizing how little it would take to start a riot, had been ready. They acted quickly, leaping between the mob and the humans and bringing their baton-like stun weapons to bear. Arbiter Broadwing himself leapt from his podium, landing before the charging mob and rising to his full, imposing height, his wings spread wide as he let out a piercing, hawklike cry. Many of the charging Lesshchin fell back in alarm and were quickly stunned by the guards. One burly spectator made an end run around the guard cordon, but Broadwing leapt toward it with a mighty flap of his wings and tackled it feet-first; the Chirrn landed with Broadwing's talons around its throat, and soon a guard moved in to subdue it. Stephen realized that the Zenith's legal qualifications were not the only reason he had been chosen as the individual responsible for maintaining order in this deeply contentious trial.

Yet Broadwing effortlessly resumed his professional mien. Returning to his podium, the arbiter ordered another recess of several hours, and the prisoners were quickly escorted to the relative safety of their cell. Stephen tried to thank the Zenith for his intervention as the guards led him past, but the arbiter's only reply was a cryptic, three-eyed raptor stare.

"Well, that was stupid of me," Cecilia said as she paced between the clear walls, pulling at her confinement suit sleeves to free her arms.

"I'm not arguing," Stephen said as he stripped to the waist. Everyone took every opportunity to unfasten the tight garments when they got the chance, and nobody bothered much with modesty anymore. "What got into you?"

"I don't know," she answered as she fought her way free of the sleeves. "I saw an opportunity to score a major point against them, and

I jumped for it. I guess I overplayed it." She'd done the same thing in arguments with her husband back home—which, she reflected, was part of why she no longer had a husband.

"But you were right, Captain." Tarik Bahar took a step toward her. "They were the ones who willfully concealed their presence. The consequences for that are on their heads."

"But I drove the point home too hard. What are the odds they'll listen?" She sighed. "I'm just getting fed up with how ridiculous this whole thing is. I want to get this over with, get back in *Arachne*, and finish what we started."

Stephen was startled by her tone. "Like ninety thousand people never died?"

She glared. "No. Not like that. You know that's not what I mean."

"And you know that they have good reason to resent us. To mistrust us. We may be—" He looked around at the others. "We *are* innocent, but it's not going to be easy to convince them of that, and for good reason. We need to be patient."

Cecilia was glad he'd remembered the need to maintain a strong front before their crew. Normally, he was the perfect public speaker, a natural at inspiring and rallying others, but now… She'd been watching him, noticing how the scenes of death and devastation had worked on his sympathies, and she feared his resolve was weakening. *Good reason?* No. This was an accident, pure and simple. Tragic, without a doubt, but not her—not *their* fault. Stephen was projecting his own childhood traumas onto the Chirrn, and as always it was her responsibility to knock some sense into that romantic head of his. "We also need to be strong. Not just for ourselves. A lot of people are counting on us. Six hundred embryos, countless more humans who need a new home. They're counting on us to build that home for them." *You should be the one reminding me of that, damn it.*

"Don't we have a responsibility to the Lesshchin as well, Cecilia?"

"Not at the cost of our other responsibilities. We can see about making some sort of reparations after we've completed our mission. Maybe program the auxons to build a new habitat for them out of Gamma Lep's asteroids. But our first obligation is to our own."

"I'm with the captain," said Diego Narvaez, who was watching from the next cell. "All due respect, Stephen, but there's a time for patience and this isn't it. Nothing we do will prove to them that we're innocent. They've made up their minds and they're out for revenge."

"Revenge, nothing," cried James Oates, who shared the cell with Narvaez. He, Amrita Dhillon, Evan Jiang, Josh Vidmar, and a few others seemed to have congregated around Narvaez in a sort of protective clique built around their shared animosity toward the Chirrn. "They attacked us. A random collision in space? I don't buy it! They *moved* to intercept us. Only way it could happen."

"They sacrificed thousands of their people, a whole habitat, just for that?" Haim asked in disbelief.

"They underestimated us," James countered. "Didn't know we had the firepower to kick their tails."

"We were going point-eight-four cee," Haim countered. "We could've spit out the front window and it would've blown them up."

"The reasons don't matter!" Amrita shouted. "This is nothing more than an exercise in persecution. Trust me, I've seen this all before. Remember how they've tortured us, humiliated us. What do you think these kangaroos will do when their court finds us guilty?"

"What do you think they'll do if we refuse to go along with the trial?" Kweli Ndege fired back. "I've had enough injuries to treat lately. I don't want any more."

"You think we'll be any safer working within the system? *Their* system?"

"Cool down, Amrita," Cecilia told the mining engineer. She sympathized with the wiry Strider's bitterness. As a child in one of the more isolated, lawless asteroid-mining habitats of the Jupiter Trojans, Amrita Dhillon had been forced to watch her dissident parents tortured, her father murdered in front of her, before the Troubleshooters had managed to liberate her and mother. Of all the expedition's members, she was probably the one — perhaps even more than Stephen himself — who most desperately *needed* to buy into Stephen's dream of building a better world. Cecilia could not begrudge Amrita her rage at having that dream torn from her, at seeing her crew subjected to the same kind of abuse she had hoped to leave behind forever.

But her outburst jeopardized the group's morale, so Cecilia tried to offer reassurance. "Tarik's right — however much I fumbled the delivery, we've just exposed a major hole in their argument. Maybe when they cool down, we can build on that, make them see that this disaster was something they could've avoided and we couldn't."

"And what if the fix is already in?" Amrita challenged, more quietly but no less intently.

"Then we'll try something else. The one thing we will not do—the one thing we must *never* do—is give up." Her eyes held Stephen's as she said it. "We Veneziani, we know how to fight for our home, our people. We were fighting off the rising waters centuries before the rest of you. And Venezia still stands firm and proud. We made the water our own, we adapted to its presence, but we never let it overwhelm us, and we never gave our ground even as our ground sank beneath us. And as long as I draw breath, neither will this crew."

Her speech put an end to the debate, and she ordered the crew to get some rest. Stephen gave her a nod of thanks, though his eyes remained troubled. Narvaez's gaze was more skeptical, and Cecilia held it for a time, letting him know that she understood his concerns. She wasn't ready to let it be voiced yet, but he had a point. The Chirrn might not leave them any legitimate way out of this.

So privately, in her own thoughts, she began contemplating more unsavory alternatives.

The tribunal did not reconvene again for more than a day. When the next session finally began, Tribune Dj'vhereth spoke. "The suggestion that our own secretiveness has contributed to this incident cannot be casually dismissed," the orange-maned jurist said gravely. The audience grumbled, but quieted under Broadwing's fearsome glare. "We advise the Council to consider the installation of running lights and short-range beacons on Chirrn habitats, or at the very least the expansion of our astronomical observation protocols."

Cecilia's eyes widened. The Chirrn had accepted the truth more readily than she'd imagined. Brimming with confidence, she rose to address the panel. "In that case, Honored Tribunes, I submit that the charge of negligence on our part has been disproven, and I move that the case be dismissed."

"That would be premature," Rillial countered, her voice raised. "The accused's contention that they have taken all reasonable steps to minimize risk is false. There is one fundamental risk they have taken that did not need to be taken at all. And that is their very means of transportation."

"You'll have to explain that," Cecilia said.

"I shall," came the terse response. "Relativistic travel is intrinsically hazardous, not only to the travelers but to any they encounter. Any vehicle moving close to the speed of light possesses a kinetic energy sufficient to destroy any spacecraft or habitat, to devastate the entire surface of any inhabited planet. As the defendants' own engineer testified, their velocity is so great that they may use sails only an eye's width across as projectiles capable of shattering an asteroid far larger than the craft itself. Without the means to decelerate swiftly, or to reduce a craft's effective inertial mass while in transit, it is an unconscionably dangerous form of travel.

"The defendants have spoken of their methods for detecting obstacles. But their own velocity was barely less than that of their own radar beams. They have claimed their shipmind was fast enough to compensate for the briefness of the warning interval, but that mind herself has testified that she did *not* have enough time to assess the situation fully and was forced to make a rushed decision. That clearly demonstrates that the risk is needlessly great."

"The risk is to our own ship at least as much as to anyone else's," Silbermann objected. "We took every factor into account that we could, prepared for every realistic possibility and even some crazy ones. The technology is safe, as safe as it needs to be."

Rillial whirled to face the tribunes, her tail almost knocking down the chubby advocate beside her. "*That* is the key question! *Need.* We must ask, did these humans *need* to travel this way at all?

"In thirteen thousand years, the Chirrn have encountered few civilizations which employ relativistic spacecraft — which is the reason we have never had a need to detect or defend against them. Generally, civilizations do not engage in interstellar travel prior to obtaining gravity control. Those that do usually employ sail-driven or fusion-powered craft which travel at low fractions of lightspeed; or they employ the Chirrn method of creating their own worlds that spend generations travelling between the stars. Often, they only colonize their home systems and rely on slow interstellar probes and gravity-focus astronomy to survey the broader universe. We know that the humans have done the same in their own system. So we must ask why they have found it necessary to use this form of transportation at all, when there are easier and safer, if slower, ways to travel between stars."

Stephen stepped forward. "While it's true that the resources of Sol System have made humanity wealthy, the planet Earth is still struggling to recover its ecological — and social — balance after centuries of damage. Damage caused, in part, by overpopulation and overexploitation of

Earth's resources. New resources from space can compensate, and we have the means to feed and sustain such a vast population so long as resources are allocated fairly. But reducing the human population's footprint on the planet is still important for the future recovery of the rest of the ecosystem, and reducing its size is an important part of that.

"Of course, we encourage emigration to the other settled planets and artificial habitats of Solsys... but we recognize that even an entire star system may someday fall prey to cosmic or self-inflicted disaster. For the survival of our species, we must emigrate to other systems. We've settled marginally habitable planets and asteroid belts around closer stars, worlds we can reach at a more comfortable pace.

"But people who were born on planets generally prefer to live on planets — planets they can inhabit without needing to huddle under domes and stare out at a barren wasteland. So when we found Cybele, a world we could settle without centuries of terraforming, it was too good to pass up. I knew that if we could mount a successful expedition there, it would inspire further colonization.

"But the travel time to Cybele pushes the limits of safe hibernation technology. If we want the colonization process to be viable and attractive to a large population, we have no choice but to make the journey at the highest relativistic speeds we can attain."

Rillial pondered this for a moment before speaking. "So... you live on one planet and want to live on another. You want to find a naturally habitable planet, but you must look to other systems to find one. And you are thus willing to go to extraordinary lengths, to engage in immense engineering projects and expend astronomical amounts of power, in order to fulfill this urge.

"But why?" she continued, turning and raising her voice to address the tribunal at large. "You have over a century of experience in space colonization. Billions of humans live in artificial habitats, most of which are not located on planetary bodies. Indeed, the enormous undertaking of constructing interstellar vessels and the beam projectors that drive them would be impossible if you were limited to the resources of one planet.

"So you know that human beings can lead successful, prosperous lives in space habitats. You know that generations of humans have lived, and lived well, without ever breathing the air of a planet. And yet your desire to live on a planet like your Earth is so great... that you found it necessary to employ a highly inefficient, costly, and outright dangerous form of propulsion to accomplish it. A form of propulsion that killed nearly ninety thousand Chirrn and diminished the minds of at least sixty thousand more."

Rillial strode forward to look Stephen firmly in the eyes, her wide-set orbs swiveling inward to fix him from two directions. "Why did those Chirrn die? Because you used relativistic propulsion. Why did you use it? Because you wished to live on a planet.

"But did you *need* to live on a planet?" she hissed with anguish. "Tell me that, colony leader. Given all the alternatives, was there some vital need to drive your way recklessly through the cosmos merely to live the way your ancestors lived? Was your need to feel dirt beneath your feet so great, so overwhelming, that it justifies the slaughter of ninety thousand lives?"

Stephen opened his mouth—and nothing came out but a soft choking sound. He could give no answer to Rillial's demand.

But Cecilia was not so speechless. "Now just wait a minute," she protested. "Just because you don't like living on planets doesn't make it immoral to do so. This is just an attempt to evade the real issue—your own failure to make your habitats detectable!"

Rillial glared at her. "It may not be immoral, but was it necessary? Living in a constructed world would not have killed you." She turned back to the tribunes. "But the humans' rejection of that option *did* kill more than a tenth of the population of Lesshchi and left the rest without a home."

"We have a right to live in whatever way we choose!"

"The rights of one being do not include the right to destroy the lives of other beings!" Rillial cried, her voice ringing through the tribunal chamber. "You cite free choice as your only reason for choosing planets, for needing relativistic starships. But that is not enough reason to justify the destruction of an entire nation! It is *not!*" Rillial lowered her brown-maned head, covering her eyes with her hands, and struggled for breath. Cecilia wanted to argue back, but even she was subdued by the anguish in Rillial's voice and body language, comprehensible even across the species divide. And she could see that the audience was affected far more deeply—and probably the tribunes as well. She would only hurt her case further by arguing more.

This time, instead of a furor, a ringing silence filled the courtroom. The silence was finally broken by whispers between the tribunes and

Broadwing, and then by the arbiter's calliope voice: "The tribunes will now recess to deliberate this case."

So much for the system. Cecilia saw clearly that the legal fight was over; there had never been a chance of a fair trial in any Chirrn venue.

I won't give up, she promised herself. *Whatever it takes.*

6

Cecilia paced out the limits of the cell like a caged tiger. "We can't let them do this to us."

"Cecilia..." Stephen sighed. "They're thirteen thousand years more advanced than we are. If they do rule against us... let's just say our options will be severely limited."

"I won't have that kind of defeatist attitude!" Cecilia told him. "And I won't let my crew be condemned as a result of the Chirrn's bigotry."

"Still," Haim said after a moment, "you have to admit—they do have a point. A lot of people manage just fine aboard habitats. Strictly speaking, we didn't need to do this."

Cecilia stared. "You of all people are saying this? You, who relished the challenge of building the fastest ship in human history?"

His eyes remained locked on the floor. "There are other challenges."

"Any powerful drive has its dangers. I'm sure their gravity control could do awful things if it went wrong. Danger's just a part of life. We're all out here because we accepted that—because we didn't let our fear of danger keep us from living." A number of the others nodded and made affirming noises.

"That's fine when it's our own risk, our own choice," the engineer said. "But what about when the danger's to others who didn't have a choice?"

"Haim, you did everything you could to make the ship as safe as possible—not just for us, but for anyone else. Even though there was almost no chance of a collision, you prepared for it anyway."

"And still didn't do enough."

"You couldn't have anticipated this," Cecilia insisted.

"That's the problem. Too many unknowns out here. Like those auxon probes on Cybele. We're so confident they can't go wrong—but what don't we know? Especially if they're left there for decades untended if we..." He trailed off.

"Will you listen to yourselves?" It was Diego Narvaez in the next cell. The tall engineer strode to the transparent wall and struck it angrily. "All this concern over the harm we did to them. Look around you. What we need to worry about is the harm they'll do to us. We're dead if we don't find a way to fight back." Oates, Dhillon, and the others sharing his cell voiced angry affirmation.

Stephen turned to him in surprise. "You don't seriously think a people as advanced as this would have something as primitive as capital punishment?"

"What makes you think they share human values?" Narvaez countered. "You've seen their psychotic hatred of planet-dwellers. They already tried to beat some of you to death!" Sita turned away.

Stephen rose, putting himself between Narvaez's clique and the dainty biologist. "If killing us were all they wanted, they could've done it long before now."

"Maybe they just wanted to make us suffer first. We could be in for slow torture, for all we know."

"*If* they find us guilty."

"Are you really so naïve as to imagine they won't?"

Cecilia stepped forward, drawing Stephen's attention. "Whatever the verdict, whatever the sentence, we can't just lie back and surrender. We have a right and a duty to complete our mission and reach Cybele. Not just to ourselves, but to the embryos, to all of humanity." She paced some more. "We need to contact Arachne somehow. She's cooperated for now, so maybe they've left some of her systems intact. If she could activate a laser..."

"What are you saying?" Stephen cried. "You want to commit *more* murders?"

"It's not murder if they're not human," Narvaez countered.

"Neither accident nor self-defense is murder," Cecilia insisted, raising her voice above the others. "And only the threat would be needed. We wouldn't actually do it."

"But what would be the point?" Haim asked. "We can't get back up to speed without a drive beam."

"We could make them generate one. Or better yet, give us one of their gravitic engines."

"Which they could just sabotage to blow us up. What, you want to take hostages?"

"If we have to."

"And what if they call our bluff?" Stephen demanded. "Even if they don't, how will the Chirrn see us then? As conquerors, destroyers, willing to cut down anyone who impedes our expansion into the universe. What will they do to Sol System if they decide we're that dangerous?"

Cecilia took him by the shoulders. "Stephen, listen to me. I know you're upset by all that's happened. Your compassion for the dead of an alien race is admirable. But their deaths are not our fault. That tribunal is going to condemn us just because our beliefs differ from theirs. And I can't sit still and accept that. I have a responsibility for the safety of my crew and the success of our mission."

"And what about your responsibility for your own ship's wake?" he asked her.

She frowned. "What?"

"A captain is supposed to consider herself responsible for the consequences of her vessel's passage. Supposed to take responsibility for all beings affected by her command. You taught me that."

"Stephen, accepting responsibility is not the same as giving in to persecution! They're wrong to blame us for this!"

"Or maybe you just want to avoid the blame for it."

"We took every possible precaution!"

"Except patience!" He pulled away, then faced her again after a moment. "We were—*I* was so cocky. So full of pride in what we could accomplish. You warned me about hubris more than once, Cecilia. About naming the ship for Arachne, the very embodiment of self-destructive pride. Maybe you were right all along. Maybe Arachne's crime was pushing too far, failing to recognize her own limits."

"No, *you* were right the first time, Stephen," Cecilia urged, though with no softening of her tone. "Arachne had the guts to stand up to the gods and tell them when they were wrong, and they punished her because they were vain and capricious and had all the power."

"But the Chirrn are right, Cecilia. We *didn't* have to race through the universe at insane speeds. We could've built more habitats. Or we could've taken our time, migrated to Cybele in generation ships. People thrive in artificial environments. It shouldn't matter whether the horizon curves down or up. It's not a cause worth destroying a nation over. Is it?" He cried out to all the prisoners. *"Is it?!"* He was met with only the echoes of his own voice.

Cecilia glared at him in contempt. "It wasn't our fault. We weren't responsible."

He met her glare in kind. "Keep telling yourself that, Cecilia. Maybe someday you'll convince yourself it's true."

The cell became very quiet after that. It was impossible to miss the sound of Sita Bhatiani weeping and sniffling in the corner, no matter how she tried to stifle it. "Look," Stephen said to the group, not meeting Cecilia's steely gaze. "Let's just get some rest. Whatever happens next, we need clear heads—and we need to keep our cool."

As the others laid down and stewed in their own worries, Stephen hesitantly made his way to Sita's side. He crouched by her trembling form, unsure whether to place a hand on her shoulder. As before, she'd shed her jumpsuit but kept it clutched against the front of her body, torn between being confined and being exposed. So he crossed his arms over his own bare chest instead, respecting her personal space. "Sita?" He let it stand at that for now. *Are you all right?* would be a monumentally stupid question.

"I'm sorry," she said in a shuddering voice. "I hate being so afraid. So weak. You wanted the best people, the hardiest pioneers, and you got… this. This tiny, fragile… thing."

"Hey." He took her hand, clasped it gently between his. "Look at me." Hesitantly, those big dark eyes came up to meet his. Again, he was struck by how familiar, how right, that felt. "Now, you know I didn't go easy on my trainees. I know you're strong enough. After what you've been through, anyone would be afraid. I'm afraid too."

"But you haven't broken down blubbering in a corner, have you?"

"I wish I had the luxury. But there are forty-eight people expecting me to be strong for them."

Those incredible eyes probed his. "How do you do it?"

Stephen smiled. "By relying on the strength you all give me. It's all of you who keep me going."

Sita smiled back, and his heart raced. "But you were… going… long before us. You fought your way out of the Gulf States, started working to make things better… and you've never stopped."

He shook his head. "I can't afford to. When people stop trying… things decay. Entropy takes over. I've seen it up close — what happens when people with power stop caring. So I know I can never stop striving to make things better. I can never settle for the way things are, because I know they'll succumb to entropy if I let myself get complacent."

She stared. "That sounds so… cynical coming from you. The great idealist."

"Idealism doesn't mean assuming things will automatically get better. It means believing we can make them better if we fight hard enough." Now he did touch her shoulder. "Pain doesn't negate idealism. It just gives it more incentive. You're hurting now. You're afraid now. But you can make it better, day by day, if you just keep working at it."

She looked at him for a long time, and he just let her, captivated by her gaze. Sita seemed to realize something, then to wrestle with a choice within herself. Finally she took a deep, trembling breath and said, "There is something I've been afraid to try. Maybe it's time I did."

And she put her arms around his neck, letting the jumpsuit fall away from her body as she pulled him into a kiss. It seemed the most natural thing in the world to take her in his arms as he returned it. It felt blissfully familiar and entirely new at the same time.

After an indefinite amount of time, he broke the kiss and stared at her. "I think…"

"What?"

"I think that… for the first time in my life… I'm remembering a dream."

"I think I'm living one," she came back with a breathless chuckle. "Bloody hell, what a corny line. But I don't understand. Before, when you held me… you didn't react to me at all."

"I was still in shock. I was weak from hibernation. But I… reacted." He stroked the fine black fuzz upon her scalp. "I can't look at you and not react. I didn't quite remember it until now… but I love you."

Sita shed tears again, but this time they were welcome.

When court resumed over half a day later, the head tribune stared gravely down at the humans. "It is a basic principle in both Chirrn and human law that the rights of the individual cease to be absolute when they threaten the rights or safety of others," Dj'vhereth said. "Thus, it is the finding of this tribunal that free choice of habitat is not sufficient cause to justify the permanent killing of over seventy-nine thousand, eight hundred individuals, the probable killing of over eight thousand, five hundred individuals still missing, the mental impairment of over sixty-four thousand, four hundred individuals, and the destruction of their entire nation. There were other viable alternatives to relativistic interstellar travel which the defendants could have employed. Therefore the destruction of Lesshchi was avoidable and unnecessary. Therefore the defendants are culpable for its destruction."

The audience roared and thumped their tails on the ground in thunderous approbation. Many of the humans gasped in shock or began to weep. Diego Narvaez and his group howled in fury and defiance. Cecilia stood rooted to the floor, eyes wide in outrage. Stephen stood beside her, just as immobile, but feeling only resignation.

Arbiter Broadwing called for order, and once relative quiet had been restored, Dj'vhereth addressed the defendants. "With regard to the other potentially criminal matters brought to the attention of this tribunal: Since the occupants of Arachne will not be colonizing the inhabited planet in the binary star system proximate to Lesshchi's former location, this tribunal finds it unnecessary to prosecute them on that charge. With regard to the matter of the replicating probes sent to survey that system, this tribunal orders that the matter be investigated further. The probes in question will be examined and their threat potential assessed. Only if that potential is deemed significant will the matter be pursued further. We prefer not to intervene in an interplanetary matter without need." Stephen supposed that meant the matter would be delayed for at least a decade, assuming Shilirrlal, like Lesshchi, was about five light years from Gamma Leporis. Though that description of its location left him wondering.

"The tribunal will now address the matter of sentencing. We understand that you are unfamiliar with our principles of justice. Rest assured that we do not believe in punishment purely for the sake of retribution. Meeting destruction with destruction is wasteful and pointless.

"Those who commit destructive acts are required to compensate for them by doing constructive service. By making positive contributions, they repay for the damage they have done. Your sentence has been evaluated on the basis of this principle.

"It is the judgment of this tribunal that the forty-eight human personnel of the spacecraft Arachne shall be imprisoned for the remainder of their lives in a research institution, where they will be studied by Chirrn scientists. By thus providing knowledge, you will repay your debt."

"That's barbaric!" Cecilia cried. "You have no right to treat sentient beings as lab animals!"

A pair of guards approached her menacingly with stun-sticks. "The prisoner will remain silent," Broadwing ordered.

"Thank you, Arbiter," the head tribune said. "The experiments will be nondestructive and largely sociological in nature. You will not be subjected to cruelty. You will, however, not be free to refuse the experiments or to leave the facility. But such is the nature of imprisonment.

"As to the spacecraft *Arachne* herself," Dj'vhereth went on, "she will be stripped of her potentially destructive components and will be studied by Chirrn cyberpsychologists to explore the ways in which humans have developed the cybernetic sciences. She, too, will contribute to our knowledge of the universe. You will be allowed to communicate with her as you desire.

"These judgments will be carried out immediately. The humans will be transported—"

"Honored Tribunes," Stephen interjected.

"Yes, Stephen Jacobs-Wong?"

"I wish to make a plea. Not on my behalf, but on behalf of the six hundred human embryos in storage aboard Arachne." He looked at Cecilia, remembering what she had said about their duty. "Each of those embryos has the potential to grow into a live human being, to live a full, normal life. None of those potential people had any participation in our actions. None of them has ever lived on a planet, except as an insensate cell. Their parents—both the humans who donated them and the members of my crew who have committed to raising them—intended for them to have the chance to be born, and to live in freedom. Surely they should not be deprived of that chance, or born into captivity, because of our actions."

The tribunes discussed it briefly. "This is well said," Dj'vhereth announced. "We direct that the embryos shall be allowed to be gestated artificially, under the guidance of Arachne, and raised on Shilirrlal."

"That's not enough, Honored Tribunes."

The head tribune stared at him sharply. "Not enough?"

"No, it is not. Our young are very dependent upon their parents for the first several years of their lives. They need human parents or parent-surrogates to help them develop their abilities, to provide them with basic socialization and the necessary tactile and sensory stimulation for healthy brain development. Neither the Chirrn, the Zenith, nor Arachne could fulfill this role sufficiently. And how would it affect them if the only others they knew of their own race were nothing but imprisoned criminals or laboratory subjects?"

Stephen lowered his head. "Honored Tribunes, I do not seek leniency for myself. I deserve whatever verdict you deem fit. But the embryos, our potential children… they need my crew. And they need my crew to be free to raise them in a healthy and loving environment."

"You would dictate terms to us, after you have been found guilty?" another tribune demanded.

"When it comes to the well-being of innocent lives, Honored Tribune — of children whose future is my personal responsibility — then hell yes, I will dictate terms."

"This is outrageous," Rillial protested over the rumbling of the spectators. "Your crew have been sentenced for their crimes."

"My crew is blameless in this! This expedition was my dream, my project. None of these others would be here if not for me. They don't deserve to be punished for the consequences of my choice. Do to me as you see fit, but let them go. Let them take *Arachne* and complete their journey to Cybele. Or take them yourself if you're concerned about the safety of our methods. At the very least, let them raise the children here, or on some other Chirrn habitat."

"Hey, nothing doing!" Haim Silbermann interposed. He strode forward to Stephen's side. "Mister Jacobs-Wong here is being noble, but he's not telling the whole truth. *I* designed *Arachne* and her defenses. I'm as much to blame for this as anyone. If he stays, I stay too."

"So do I!" Cool, delicate fingers clasped his hand, and he could feel Sita trembling as she moved to stand between him and the Chirrn, raising her head and her voice in terrified defiance. "You do anything to him, you'll bloody well have to go through me!" Stephen's eyes grew moist at her courage, her love.

But he shook his head as more and more of the crew moved to stand by him — Tarik, Kweli, Diana, Kazuko, many more — but not Cecilia, not Diego. "Don't do this. None of you are to blame. You deserve your new home. And the children need you."

"And we need our leader," Kazuko told him.

"Desist!" Arbiter Broadwing commanded, the original word a curt, piercing shriek. "The tribunal will consider the defendant's proposal."

The tribunes discussed the matter for a long time. As this went on, Stephen looked over his crewmates. There was a wide range of emotions on display. Sita, Haim, Tarik, and many others showed signs of the same grief Stephen felt. It made him proud that so many of his fellow humans could grieve for aliens as much as for their own. Many of the crew, including Kazuko and Kweli, showed renewed hope at Stephen's proposal—hope for their own freedom, hope for their children yet unborn.

But Narvaez and others glared at him bitterly, resenting his admission of guilt. Some showed fear at the aliens' power, anger at their imposition, dismay at the impending imprisonment. And none showed these emotions as intensely as Cecilia LoCarno. Stephen had never seen her like this. They had argued before, oh, so many times. It had been the foundation of their friendship. But it had always been with mutual respect and affection. Now, though, as Stephen looked into Cecilia's eyes, he realized that friendship was probably gone forever. One more casualty of his hubris.

Finally Tribune Dj'vhereth addressed the chamber once again. "While your willingness to sacrifice for your groupmates is commendable, it cannot influence the findings of the law. Though Stephen Jacobs-Wong may have initiated the formation of your group, it was as a group that you undertook the actions that led to Lesshchi's destruction. Under Chirrn law, you are therefore culpable as a group." The crew moaned. Stephen opened his mouth to protest.

"However," the head tribune went on, "this must be balanced against the well-being of the non-culpable human children yet to be born, and the right of their progenitors to determine whether and into what circumstances they will be born. Thus, we offer the following compromise.

"The finding of this tribunal was that the humans' planetary bias was the underlying cause of Lesshchi's destruction. Therefore: any humans who will renounce a planetary existence, who will sever all ties with planet-dwellers and those who associate with them, will be granted provisional participation in Chirrn society. A segment of Shilirrlal large enough to accommodate a minimum of six hundred and forty-eight humans will be apportioned for your occupation. Your movement beyond that segment will be restricted and supervised, but within it you will be free to raise your children and contribute to Shilirrlal as provisional citizens, thus repaying your debt. If you prove your responsibility and your ability to contribute as members of the Shilirrlal community, you will in time be allowed to integrate more fully into society. Those who do not renounce planetary existence will contribute instead as research subjects.

"Note that this offer extends to every member of your group," Dj'vhereth added, his garnet-hued eyes meeting Stephen's. "For the verdict to be fair, it must apply uniformly. You may have time to discuss this decision among yourselves." Stephen was shocked. Those alien standards cut both ways — harder on his crew than he had hoped, but more lenient toward him than he deserved. But he was grateful for the chance to stay with his crew.

The Chirrn spectators leaned forward intently as the humans gathered together to deliberate. Cecilia glared at the look on Stephen's face. "You can't actually be considering their offer! Win your freedom by renouncing your values, embracing theirs? What gives them the right to demand such a — a Shylockian surrender?"

Stephen sighed. "Cecilia, they're not asking us to change our religion, just our residency. Besides, they're the only law around. The crime was committed in their territory — hell, it was committed *against* their territory — and that makes us subject to their laws.

"I'm not saying I'm happy about it. But whatever we may feel or believe, the fact on the ground is that we're convicted criminals under their law, and we can't expect to walk away scot-free. We have to make the best of the hand we've been dealt. And this way, at least we get to raise our children in relative freedom. Just not where we expected."

"'Relative freedom?' Interesting term for house arrest."

"Better than letting those embryos go unborn. Personally, it feels like getting off easy. But there's more at stake here than just ourselves."

He stepped forward to face the panel. "Honored Tribunes, I accept your proposal. For the sake of our children, I renounce my planetary existence and ask that you let us live with you among the stars. I ask anyone else who will make this pledge to indicate it by stepping forward to join me."

Sita wanted to be the first one to join Stephen. She wanted to live up to her earlier pledge to stay by his side, to show that same courage. She was tired of being afraid—not only for what Stephen thought of her, but for what she thought of herself. She hadn't been this timid back on Earth. If anything, her friends had teased her for her careless haste to indulge her curiosity, whether as a child climbing to a branch ten times her height to watch birds hatching in their nest or as a grad student unhesitatingly volunteering for a dangerous year-long survey of the microbes of Enceladus.

So she felt betrayed by her own body when she hesitated. Haim Silbermann was instead the first to step forward alongside Stephen. "Someone's gotta be free to take care of *Arachne*," he said with a shrug. "And how can I pass up the chance to study that gravity drive?"

Kweli Ndege was next. "Live among an ancient alien culture?" Kweli whispered to Sita as she went past, speaking with something near her normal ebullience for the first time since seeing the wreck of Lesshchi. "That's better than any wilderness planet for me."

Rub it in, why don't you? She should have stepped forward, should have been standing by Stephen's side. She'd done it a few minutes ago; what stopped her now? But ever since that night on the Chirrn ship, she'd been a changed woman. Not even a woman—a frightened little girl. The Chirrn terrified her. After the assault, Kweli had administered the standard sympatholytic drug regimen for preventing post-traumatic stress syndrome. In theory, it should have softened the emotional intensity of her memories of the assault, sparing her psyche from lasting damage. But maybe that only worked when the traumatic event actually ended, when the nightmare didn't go on day after day. How could she move beyond the memory of the screaming faces, the pounding fists, the searing shock sticks—the fact that she'd actually been dead for several minutes—when hostile Chirrn still had her in their power, still relished her humiliation and helplessness, still screamed for her blood? It was one thing to be willing to share a prison sentence with her man—but to be asked to join the society of the creatures that had killed her?

The one thing that got her moving was the realization that being subjected to their experiments would be even worse. At least this way, she'd be in an area set aside for humans. From what she'd observed, the Chirrn seemed to like partitioning themselves. Hopefully that meant the humans would be largely cut off from the Chirrn. Whereas if she became their research subject, she'd be at their mercy every day. With that thought, she shot forward to Stephen's side and clutched his hand like a lifeline.

He looked at her and smiled, radiating pride in her bravery. She smiled back, hiding her shame.

Cecilia was disappointed as more and more of her crew joined Stephen in his surrender. After all they'd been through, she'd never expected them to abandon her like this. But then, if Stephen, the great man who'd fought his way out of hell and climbed to the stars with his sheer relentless optimism, could succumb so easily to misplaced guilt and extortionate sympathy, maybe she shouldn't be surprised at the rest. Maybe the record time they'd spent in hibernation had done something to them all, enfeebled their resolve.

At least some of the crew still showed sense. She wasn't surprised that Diego Narvaez and his clique stayed by her side; they'd made their position very clear already. Others moved to stand with her as well: Ichiba Nobuo, Kahina Amrouche, Zhao Changkun, Ibrahim al-Bakri, Josh Vidmar, more. Mercifully, Nikolos Zacharias was among them; at least their group would have a doctor, even though Kweli and Joana Caravalho had both sold out.

But more were defecting than standing firm. Oyama Kazuko, Diana Thorne, Ravinder Pritam, Scott Olatunji, Jason Brentwood, Vijay Bhadra... Stephen's group was already larger than hers and still growing. Justine Nguyen was caught in a fiercely whispered argument between her wife Shuai Bingbing and her brother Marc, but when Bingbing finally moved to stand with Cecilia's group, she came alone.

So Cecilia winced when Tarik Bahar moved to face her, apology in his eyes. "I'm sorry, Captain. But I have to protect the crew. And the children."

"You tell yourself that, Tarik," she snapped. "That it's for the children. Like the child and the wife you left behind in Istanbul!"

He was stung. "That's not fair. You know she divorced me."

"She may have been the one to pronounce *talaq* three times, but you'd already fallen in love with the adventure of space, or you never would've let it get to number three. So much for your vaunted loyalty."

"My loyalty," he replied tightly, "was to you, Captain. It has always been to you. When I learned that Stephen had picked you to command

Arachne, I had a choice to make. I wanted nothing more than to stay with them, but your need, your responsibility, was so much vaster than mine. I could not walk away from you."

Cecilia lamented her burst of anger. He hadn't deserved such a low blow. And she hardly had a moral high ground where marital devotion was concerned. It was typical of Tarik that he hadn't tried to use that against her. But she was still hurt. "Then why walk away from me now?"

"I'm not, Captain. But whatever choice the others have made, I still haven't renounced my duty to them—or to you. I know I can trust you to look out for the loyal ones. But the rest need someone too."

Cecilia held his gaze for a long moment, nodding in comprehension. There would certainly be value in having an ally on the outside. "You do what you think is best, my friend. I understand."

He gave her a salute. It was anachronistic and ridiculous and she cherished it. But she only nodded back. She didn't want the Chirrn to see her approving of his choice—even if she could have brought herself to do so anyway. A necessary evil was still evil.

Finally, the slow trickle halted. Thirty of the crew had joined Stephen, with seventeen choosing Chirrn custody. Stephen's group was nearly two thirds female, leaving only six women total in Cecilia's. Stephen found the ratio comforting; with the group diminished, it was good to have as many potential mothers as possible. Although having half again as many women as men could get tricky down the road. He only hoped he could convince the others to change their minds in time.

He only hoped he could convince Cecilia.

"The tribunal accepts that those who stand with Stephen Jacobs-Wong have renounced their planetary existence," Broadwing proclaimed, rising to his full height. "They are now free to live among the Shilirrlaln. The others will be welcome to join them at any time in the future if they will make the same renunciation."

"Never," Cecilia declared. "We have the right to live as humans!"

Stephen saw something snap in Diego Narvaez's eyes at that moment. The big engineer lunged for one of the guards, only for his confinement suit to freeze rigid and send him headlong to the floor. He struggled helplessly as blood flowed from a cut on his forehead, then yelled and cursed as the guards pulled him to his feet. "Take him for medical treatment," the Zenith arbiter ordered. Diego continued to scream and struggle within his unmoving jumpsuit as the guards carried him away. Broadwing turned back to Cecilia. "Please, Captain, tell your people not to make this difficult for themselves. You cannot escape us."

"Maybe not," she said. "But we'll never surrender to you. We won't betray our humanity."

"Cecilia, please understand," Stephen urged. "It's for the children."

She shot him a look that should have torn him open like Lesshchi. "It's for yourselves."

"No," Stephen whispered.

Her eyes went from deadly hot to deathly cold. "I want nothing more to do with any of you." She almost seemed glad when the guards took her away.

Rillial gazed after her curiously. "Pitiful," she said. "To be so fanatical in their planetarism."

"That's not it," Stephen said sadly. "I think she—some of them just can't accept being responsible for the loss of ninety thousand lives. It's just too big a tragedy. They can't live with the guilt. So they'll never be able to admit to guilt."

The refugee examined him. "But you can."

A tear came to Stephen's eye. "Barely. Rillial, I hope you can forgive me… forgive *us* for what we allowed to happen." He sighed. "I don't know if I'll ever be able to forgive myself."

Rillial stood silently for a long moment. Then she said, "The important thing now is to ensure that such a tragedy never recurs. It is more important to prepare for the future than to dwell on the past." Stephen nodded solemnly, recognizing that it was the closest thing to forgiveness that Rillial would ever provide.

Broadwing, having left his podium, joined them, remaining in his erect stance and towering over the humans. "To that end, we must deter humanity from traveling so far again, at least at such reckless speeds."

Tarik stared. "What's that supposed to mean?"

"No doubt your expedition was sending signals back to the Sol system."

"That's right," Haim said. "They'll sure notice when *Arachne*'s telemetry stops coming in about twenty-four years. Every telescope in the system will be focused on Lesshchi's location."

"This is why we must take action. We do not wish to attract more human craft to investigate us."

"Well, what can you do about it now?"

"We have sent ships back along your course to overtake the light emitted from the disaster. They will create a detonation to obscure the image, timed and positioned to make it appear to observers in the Sol system that Arachne attempted to deflect an asteroid, failed, and was destroyed in the resultant collision. Optimally, this will cause humanity to reconsider using such a hazardous form of space travel."

"Wait, wait, go back," Haim said. "Overtake the light? Are you trying to tell me you *do* have faster-than-light drive?"

Rillial traded a look with Broadwing before speaking. She didn't sound thrilled. "Since you have consented to provisional membership in Chirrn society, there is no need to hide the fact any longer. Yes, we employ superluminal bypass methods. Our habitats drift slowly, but we travel between them as needed in transport ships."

Silbermann's eyes widened like those of a child discovering the Planet of Chocolate. "You're kidding. Really? I mean, yes, you've got gravity control, so warping space theoretically follows, but where do you get the power? How do you generate the exotic matter? How do you deal with the stress-energy buildup? The Hawking radiation? The horizon problem? Is it the Alcubierre model, or do you use some other—"

"Haim!" Stephen chuckled. "Settle down. You'll have plenty of time to learn about it." But then his own eyes widened, and he turned to the Chirrn excitedly. "But this could solve the problem! If you went to Solsys, contacted them, shared your warp technology with them, it would eliminate the danger completely! There wouldn't—"

"Take care," said L'chellin, who had joined them. "Remember, you have renounced all ties with Earth, and with all spacegoers who have ties with Earth. Do not forget so soon what that means."

"I'm not forgetting. But consider this: you want to discourage humans from using relativistic drives again. They'll be more likely to give it up if they learn the truth. We're willing to put ourselves at risk in the name of exploration, but risking others is a different matter."

"You have great faith in the nobility of your species," Rillial said. "You can understand why we cannot afford to share that faith."

"You must accept," Broadwing added, "that you are no longer a member of the human community. Their interests are no longer yours."

With that, the Chirrn and the Zenith left them. Stephen and the others stood there, alone in the echoing tribunal chamber, absorbing their new status in life. "No longer members of the human community," Kweli Ndege breathed. "Does that mean we aren't human anymore?"

"No," Stephen said. "We're just not Terrans anymore. Not Solar humans, or planetary humans. We're star people now."

Tarik Bahar scoffed. "Sounds poetic, sure. But it isn't by choice." He shook his head. "At least the captain still belongs. She may not have her freedom… but she's still a member of the human race."

"What good is it to be human without being humane?" Stephen asked. "We've done this to repent for our mistake, for causing a disaster we didn't have to cause. We owe it to the Chirrn to make up for the loss by joining their society and helping them to build and grow.

"And, most of all, we've done this for the sake of the unborn humans in our care. This is the only choice we could make, for their sake. It's not an ideal situation… but it's the only one that I, for one, can live with."

Sita looked up at him searchingly. "But when our children ask where we came from… what do we tell them?"

"We tell them the truth," Haim Silbermann said with certainty. "Just like my parents told me. My father's ancestors murdered my mother's ancestors in the Nazi Holocaust. They didn't keep that from me. No, they made sure I knew… so that I could make sure it never happened again."

After a long silence, Stephen spoke again. "Come on, my friends. We set out to build a new world for ourselves. And now it's time to begin."

When the verdict came, Churrlaya was standing vigil with Guard Vhehhal and the other *Zhemhal* personnel who had been confined to the rehabilitation center for their assault on the human murderers. Though he understood that order and justice must be maintained in these terrible times most of all, he felt it unfair that Vhehhal and the rest had been confined for acting on the same understandable rage that had filled all Lesshchin in those first few *narrissh* after the devastation. It was a mild sentence—merely a physical confinement to preclude them from injuring the dirtgrubbers, with their minds still free to travel in consensus, albeit under therapeutic supervision—yet Churrlaya knew that he, Captain Rillial, or any other member of *Zhemhal's* crew might be the ones confined here now had they been only slightly more provoked in that first encounter.

Still, the vehemence with which Vhehhal and his fellows reacted to the trial's outcome made Churrlaya wonder if confining them had been the appropriate choice for their own good. "Intolerable!" the golden-maned guard roared, smashing a table into the wall with a violent tail sweep. "Allow those murdering well-diggers inclusion in Chirrn civilization? Allow them to *breed?*"

The other crew members chimed in with equal wrath. "They should not have been allowed to live!"

"We should have finished them when we had the chance!"

Their words made Churrlaya uneasy. He felt shame at his own burst of violence against the tiny human female at the disaster site, the same one Vhehhal had briefly killed in the riot. What did it say about them that they had both targeted the most helpless one of their attackers? "Please, calm yourselves, friends," he urged. "I share your anger at this verdict. By any decent standard, the humans' exclusion became irrevocable the moment they killed our home. But remember that we are civilized. We are governed by order and balance. We cannot let these planetary bottom-feeders drag us down into their dirt."

"They have already done that, Churrlaya!" Vhehhal cried. "And we can never purge ourselves of it as long as they are allowed to live among us."

"They will live apart, confined and re-educated."

"You know that will change." The guard hissed in grim satisfaction. "But we will be unconfined before they are. We will await our chance to exact true justice."

Churrlaya stroked Vhehhal's golden mane, hoping to soothe him. "Please do not consider anything rash. I agree they must be punished more harshly than this. But there are better ways—more *civilized* ways— to achieve it. We can only defeat them by being better than they are."

The guard caught his gaze and held it. "Tell me, Churrlaya. What is it that you intend to do?"

Churrlaya did not have an answer for him yet. But it would be his mission from now on to find a way.

L'chellin and Broadwing overtook Rillial outside the Administrative Center, and the two Chirrn brushed manes in greeting. "Approbations, Rillial. You played your part in the proceedings most effectively. You have earned your inclusion."

The wild-maned captain struck a distancing posture. "My voice is not yet rid of its Lesshchin accent," she declared. "I birthed no bastard words in that tribunal."

"Unquestionably," the advocate assured her. "Your loss was incalculable. But you are unattached no more. And you exacted suitable ordeals on the ones responsible."

Rillial's legs tensed, and L'chellin instinctively moved out of her kick radius. "Many of us feel no ordeals will suffice."

"Well, you may satisfy yourselves that a third of them have chosen to extend their ordeals."

"May they never renounce."

"Just do not forget that the others *have* renounced," Broadwing told her. "And far sooner than anticipated."

"Prematurely," Rillial said. "You gave in to Jacobs-Wong's terms far too easily."

"What could we do?" L'chellin asked. "He was correct. We had no right to penalize their unborn, nor were we qualified to raise them. Yes, he forced us to accelerate the process, but he earned that acceleration. And in so doing, he has saved us considerable time and effort."

"It is only a minor adjustment to the plan," Broadwing added.

Rillial hissed across her tongue. "To *your* plan, Mediator. A plan I objected to."

"Four *narrayth* ago, I was as lowly and excluded as they. I was given the chance to repent and rise." Broadwing lifted himself into a display stance. "See the result."

"You did not destroy an entire world. Some imbalances cannot be restored. Many Lesshchin will never accept this outcome."

"Then those Lesshchin have a choice of their own to make," L'chellin told her. "But since you participated in the humans' transition, I assume you accept your own."

Rillial leaned forward a few degrees, not an open threat, but enough to convey anger. "A transition of this magnitude cannot be rushed." She bounded down a step, then turned to stare up at L'chellin. "Do you truly imagine that Jacobs-Wong and his kith have completed theirs? Do you think they even begin to grasp the true meaning of the tribunal?"

"Not consciously," L'chellin replied, lowering himself to all fours to meet her eye level. "But they have begun to fulfill its purpose nonetheless. They are on the intended path."

"And when that path leads them to truths they will not accept?"

He sank back on his haunches as he pondered the question. "By then, we hope, they will no longer be human enough to care."

Part Two

Community Service

7

"GOOD MORNING, NILLY!"

R'nilinnath cursed to herself. She had taken too long getting to the compound, and the Arachnen's "morning" had already arrived. She'd hoped to interrupt their annoyingly regular sleep cycle once again. Yes, Mediators L'chellin and Broadwing had told her over and over that the Arachnen hadn't yet had their planetary cycles purged from their genes and that such minor lingering attachments to their old life must be tolerated for the sake of their health. But it was much more fun to mess with them.

The greeting came from Diana Thorne, out for her usual *morningjog* up and down the broad terraced levels of the Arachnen compound. The young engineer was the most visually imposing of the humans, their largest and most muscular member. Her bronze mane, a few shades lighter and redder than her skin, was twice as long as any of the others' due to her accelerated metabolism (and a little artificial assistance). Despite having long, strong legs for a human, Diana still needed to rely on the stairs that she and the other engineers had built to climb between tiers. The Arachnen builders had been expecting to create whole cities and infrastructures, but now had to settle for making constant minor "improvements" to their compound to exercise their skills.

Diana had nearly completed her run up the easternmost set of stairs, the one that set off the "ladies' wing" of the compound, where the females not paired with males had their dwellings, set apart for reasons R'nilinnath hadn't fully parsed. The young Chirrn met Diana outside the liaison offices, just above the medical clinic, and bounded up the stairs alongside her, showing off how easily a Chirrn could climb the levels in this moderate gravity (another nostalgic tie to their Earth). They nearly ran into Oyama Kazuko and Renata Marcoe as the two administrators crossed the path on their way to their offices. R'nilinnath was about to stop and make proper apologies, but Diana just gave a quick "Sorry!" and increased her speed. "You won't beat me this time, little girl!"

"Little!" The void with propriety; these ferals hadn't learned sufficient appreciation for it anyway. R'nilinnath aborted her contrition and raced after the impertinent human. Diana knew full well that she was pubescent now, in the first full blush of femaleness. Were she "little," she wouldn't be a "girl" (or "boy") at all, nor would she be out of the estate crèche and apprenticed to L'chellin as a liaison-guardian to the Arachnen. Besides, Diana and her kith had only been in crèche for half a *narranl* themselves. R'nilinnath was the only adult here — well, incipiently, though her cerulean hide still bore the darker mottling of youth and her silver-dyed mane was only starting to grow out (though it was still twice as long as most of the Arachnen's). True, she hadn't yet earned full inclusion into the Intersocietal collegium of the Mediators' guild, and she was still adjusting to the new perspectives and habits of thought granted her by even the limited portion of the collegium's consensus memory that her apprenticeship entitled her to access. But no matter how much inclusion the Arachnen eventually earned, they would never experience consensus directly, lacking the cerebral adaptations for it — although their young might, one day. Not to mention that R'nilinnath was physically larger than all of the Arachnen except Diana, with whom she was only about even. After a lifetime as the youngest child on Shilirrlal, it was refreshing to have juniors at last.

The racers soon reached the top terrace and cut across through the odd green ground cover over the admin compound. The Arachnen had replanted all the terraces with their *grass* and *trees* and other vegetation compatible with their biochemistry, giving the place an oddly vacant smell to R'nilinnath's nares. Still, she liked the soft but scratchy sensation of the stuff crunching under her toes.

Soon they reached the next flight of stairs, taking them down past the auditorium and through the central square. Many of the unattached Arachnen who occupied the small dwellings around the square, including Marc Nguyen, Andrea Oliveira-York, and Scott Olatunji, were out in the park performing their own "morning" exercises — though the males, as usual, paused to watch the undulations of Diana's pronounced front and rear bulges as she ran past. Diana courted their attention by wearing a Chirrn-style semi-open vest, modified to better support her ample mammaries as she ran (though R'nilinnath did not understand how a civilization as young as humans could have evolved body parts that required artificial support), yet she paradoxically chose to conceal her genitalia with a brief human-style covering over her hip region. She clearly enjoyed the attention the others paid to her genetically augmented physique, and as she ran past, she turned her head in reciprocal admiration of Marc and Scott's unclothed, perspiring upper bodies and emitted ritual vocalizations of sexual approval toward them. Yet R'nilinnath had learned by now that this mutual courtship display was merely for social bonding and amusement. Though Diana was largely recovered from the damage she'd sustained from the humans' primitive hibernation system, she was not yet physically ready to merge voices—no, that metaphor wouldn't work for humans, and the alternative was disgusting—to conceive a child with any of the males. Instead, she was in a loose, non-exclusive sexual affiliation with Justine Nguyen, whose marital partner Shuai Bingbing was confined with the other Unrenounced in the high-security lab on the other side of Shilirrlal. R'nilinnath found Diana's sexual adaptability refreshingly normal. How had these humans functioned, favoring opposite-sex partners for emotional or recreational pairings as well as procreative ones? Before reliable contraception, the sheer number of unintended births must have been incredibly unwieldy.

Contraception was a moot issue for the Arachnen now, since they sought to increase the size and genetic diversity of their new population as swiftly as possible, as they had intended to do on their destination world. The family dwellings that Diana and R'nilinnath now sped past were located on the periphery of the occupied portion of the compound, to allow room for expansion as children were eventually born. All but four of the females were now gestating, and all the males had impregnated at least one of them (through artificial means in Haim Silbermann's case), to ensure that all their genes would be preserved. Justine was pregnant with one of the expedition's frozen embryos, while several others were being gestated in artificial wombs, and would be the communal responsibility of the Arachnen upon their birth—as would all the children to an extent.

Kweli Ndege had been the first to conceive, over three *narrenn* ago, and thus had the most prominent abdominal bulge. This meant that as the racers passed the dwelling Kweli shared with Tarik Bahar and saw her tending her tomato garden, Diana was unable to resist going over to touch Kweli's abdomen and express wonder at its rapid growth. The humans seemed to have a compulsion to do that whenever Kweli was around. R'nilinnath found it interesting that they didn't do the same with her mammaries, which had grown by a similar amount, surpassing even Diana's in size and apparently making them even more fascinating to the male Arachnen. (What was it about anatomical bulges that so enthralled these humans?) But then, many of the gestating females seemed to experience mammary soreness, so perhaps Diana avoided touching the glands out of regard for their sensitivity.

How inefficient, these humans. They needed four different body parts to fulfill the functions of the Chirrn tongue. Five, if you counted their own excuses for tongues.

R'nilinnath was tempted to bound ahead and outrace Diana to the top, but that would prove nothing. So she joined the other females in Kweli's yard to exchange pleasantries and engage in the abdomen-touching ritual. Kweli wore a human-style skirt and footwear along with an open-fronted, Chirrn-style maternity vest. She joked that it gave her tomatoes more room to grow, puzzling R'nilinnath with the non sequitur.

Sita Bhatiani was present too, helping the doctor tend the garden. Unlike most of the Arachnen, she still clung to human attire, garments known as *choli* and *sari*—evidently the traditional garb of her people, the Londoners. She responded politely to R'nilinnath's greeting, but stayed at her garden work rather than coming closer. R'nilinnath knew not to press the issue. Mediator L'chellin and Doctor Mh'lellish had explained the trauma the tiny human had suffered at the Lesshchin's feet and the resultant fear it had induced. Due to her own modest size and youth, R'nilinnath was the one Chirrn that Sita found reasonably nonthreatening, but only if she applied a soft touch.

Once she'd made appropriate obeisance to Kweli's uterus, R'nilinnath noted that Diana had already resumed her run, gaining an insurmountable lead. "Better luck next time, Nilly!" she jeered from the distance, soon vanishing behind the edge of the administration building on the top terrace.

The young Chirrn let out a sigh that ruffled her snout bristles, and Kweli chuckled and stroked her mane. "Don't take it personally. Diana's still embarrassed about her difficulties coming out of hibernation. Her family's the cream of the Vanguardian elite—they're not supposed to have weaknesses. She feels she needs to prove herself."

"She proved herself something, all right," R'nilinnath grumbled. With the race now aborted, she trotted slowly in Sita's direction and engaged her in casual talk about the garden. They were not bastard words; she was genuinely curious about these red fruits that the Arachnen described in such rhapsodic terms. A shame that so few of their world's aromatic compounds were detectable or pleasant to Chirrn senses. Doctor Mh'lellish had advised that tomatoes were mildly toxic to Chirrn as well. So R'nilinnath was left with only the words to sate her curiosity.

But when she changed the subject, making a polite request about Stephen's whereabouts, Sita's smile faded briefly. It was subtle, but R'nilinnath was getting good at reading the distortions of the human mouth and forehead. Had the expedition leader and his mate had another argument? R'nilinnath knew better than to alienate Sita by probing. She'd get the dirt by other means soon enough—once she made it to her appointment.

R'nilinnath hopped up to the next terrace and across to the Arachnen administrative offices. When she reached the central courtyard dividing them from the Shilirrlaln liaison offices, she saw L'chellin engaged in a lively discussion with Stephen, the cyberneticist Ravinder Pritam, and Arachne's physical avatar. The avatar was a nanomorphic construct whose default form was a four-armed human female torso atop the rear half of an oversized Terran spider, stylized and metallic-surfaced in hues of silver and blue. Arachne herself was installed within the administrative complex and could speak to any of the Arachnen via neural link, but she had adopted this embodied form to interact on an equal footing.

Drawing closer, but not drawing attention, R'nilinnath picked up enough of the conversation to divine its substance. Arachne and Ravinder were pushing for a fuller interface with Shilirrlal's data cloud; apparently the cyber was feeling somewhat starved for stimulation. "I am sorry," L'chellin was saying, "but you know that is a privilege that must be earned. For everything that is taken, something must be given. Have patience; as you learn more of our ways and develop a greater ability to contribute, you will earn commensurate privileges in time." L'chellin's tone was gentle and understanding, that of a crèche caregiver with her young charges, which was essentially what she was now; going female had taken the edge off the mediator's prim manner.

"But Arachne can learn far more quickly than an organic," Ravinder protested. "The only thing holding her back from learning more is your own stupid restrictions on her access!"

"Vin," Stephen cautioned.

"No, Stephen, it's just not fair! They're still punishing her because she's the one who fired the shot!" Ravinder winced. "Sorry, Arachne, you know I didn't mean—"

"Don't worry about it, Ravinder. I know what I did. And I will defer to Mediator L'chellin's restrictions. It's fair enough. I'm being treated no differently than the rest of you."

"But you need more stimulation!"

"I managed on my own for fifteen and a half subjective years. A little more boredom won't kill me." *That's well-fitting*, R'nilinnath thought. Hopefully, Arachne would persuade Ravinder to stop pushing for more access. Better if the Arachnen didn't pursue that particular question too far, or they might catch on that there were unspoken reasons for the limitations.

The thought of exceeding limits reminded her of her own appointment. The quickest route was across the courtyard, but if L'chellin saw her, it would ruin her plans. Luckily, Arachne persuaded Ravinder to accompany her inside, and L'chellin turned away to face Stephen, who began asking the mediator about the upcoming Dance of Balance they would be attending this narrissh. The human leader took the opportunity to practice his Shilirramh, still mangling the pronunciation badly but managing to get the point across, at least to listeners like L'chellin and herself who had grown accustomed to human phonetics (and could draw on the banked experience of the Intersocietal collegium's memory). Stephen was one of the only Arachnen who'd agreed to go to a second Dance of Balance. Most of them had been baffled by the first one; R'nilinnath had heard Joana Caravalho ask, "Can you call something a dance with so little movement?" But Stephen had found the subtle symmetries of the form intriguing and was eager to see if he could divine more meaning from the details of motion the others had missed. L'chellin was pleased by his interest; the more Stephen grew to understand the artistry of the dance, the more he would understand what it meant to be Chirrn, and the closer he would come to earning the status of a mature Shilirrlaln. And where he led, the others would follow.

R'nilinnath was glad, though, that she'd had a lifetime (granted, a very short one) to master what it meant to be Chirrn. If she'd needed to learn it by watching the Dance of Balance over and over, she'd feel as deprived of stimulation as Arachne. A good freefall splash brawl was more her speed.

Once she was sure both of L'chellin's eyes were fixed on Stephen, R'nilinnath hopped across the courtyard. Stephen saw her go by but made no acknowledgment, confirming her suspicion that he was in on the game.

Small raindrops began to spatter her snout, and she reflexively shut her nares and began breathing through her mouth. By being late, she'd failed to avoid the compound's scheduled rainfall. Hurrying, she ducked behind the liaison offices, out of L'chellin's sight, and from there bounded swiftly to the concealed maintenance hatch at the rear of the compound. There she found Diana Thorne already awaiting her, out of her exercise clothes and donning a jumpsuit more suited to crawling through dusty spaces. "What kept you?" the bronze-maned human teased, though of course their separation in the race had been an improvised ruse to conceal their rendezvous — something they could have avoided, R'nilinnath reminded herself, had she arrived earlier.

R'nilinnath made a knee-bending bow of submission. "Apology. Your kith are just so distracting."

"You mean you're easily distracted. Chirrn kids aren't so different from human ones." She smiled as she sealed up her jumpsuit. "Though I guess I should be grateful you're a kid, or you'd never be willing to do this."

The Chirrn snorted. "I'm more grown than you now. Try to remember that. And try to keep up."

The Arachnen compound had been placed near the facilities of the Educators' guild, not far from the estate crèche, so R'nilinnath was well acquainted with the local maintenance tunnels and hidden nooks, able to navigate them without accessing the habitat map (a useful talent if she wished to be hard to track). Every time she led Diana through the hatch, she took the engineer to a different sector, showing her places that L'chellin and Broadwing would never allow the Arachnen to go on their supervised outings.

In return, Diana told her lurid tales of human savagery, all the unimaginably feral things they did to one another. It sent a thrill of fear and excitement through R'nilinnath to contemplate how familiar these humans were with death. Their culture and language were drenched in references to it; Diana even referred to these crawls through the maintenance ducts with an idiom that translated as "to die with difficulty," in connection with some ancient human savior myth.

For her own part, Nilly had never known anyone who had died. She had recently met a few Lesshchin who had been revived from death, but they had lost only a portion of themselves—some had avoided physical damage but had their external selves ripped from them, while others had needed their brains regrown but could still draw on their outboard memory and backups as a source of continuity with who they had been. That was not so different from a normal life transition. Even those Chirrn who decided they'd lived long enough, who chose to end one life without migrating to another (and thus make room for the birth of new Chirrn like herself), still left their imprint in the consensus memory of the guilds they'd belonged to. The concept of a conscious being simply ceasing to exist in any form—as so many Lesshchin had, as humans and other ferals did all the time—was frightening. Yet it was also oddly compelling. The fact that adults discouraged her from exploring it merely fired her interest further.

Of course, the humans had concocted countless fantasies of existence after physical death to cope with its pervasiveness in their lives. But R'nilinnath was more interested in their expertise with death itself, and with the violence that brought it on. It was so alien, so gruesome, so stimulating. She had asked her crèche counselor if there was something wrong with her for taking so much interest in Diana's bloodsoaked tales from human history. The counselor had suggested that by trying to understand what death was, she was trying to find a way to cope with the death of tens of thousands of Lesshchin. As long as her interest remained in death as a distant, abstract thing, the counselor had said, there was no cause for worry. R'nilinnath had been grateful for that, since it allowed her to relish Diana's goriest tales without shame.

Diana had promised her that this *narrissh* she would tell R'nilinnath about the Spanish Inquisition—about which she'd so far revealed nothing except that no one had expected it. But that would wait, for

Diana always began their trips together by feeding her all the juiciest gossip about her fellow humans. The muscular human had initially pretended reluctance to violate the privacy of her neighbors, but it had been bastard speech that soon betrayed its parent. The truth was, she loved pushing the boundaries as much as R'nilinnath did, including the boundaries of others' privacy. In her view, secrets were challenges, and challenges were there to be surmounted.

Diana had what she considered some particularly good dirt today. It seemed that Marc and Andrea had argued loudly two "nights" before with Scott, whom they believed was getting too many appointments with Rosario Soares. The argument had provoked concern among many in the community, including Diana, that Rosario might be falling in love with Scott, leading their only therapeutic sex provider to toss aside professional egalitarianism in favor of monogamy. R'nilinnath was intrigued by Rosario's role in the community; as a human of intermediate gender, both anatomically and psychologically, they could adapt to provide sexual services for all Arachnen as needed — an efficient choice for such a compact community. Humans superficially appeared to have such inflexible sexuality, stuck being a single sex throughout their lives short of surgical intervention; but as R'nilinnath had come to know them, she had realized that, in many ways, they were even more sexually adaptable than the Chirrn. Rosario had the androgynous gender attributes of an immature Chirrn, yet could readily assume either a masculine or a feminine identity as required by their clients, or simply on their personal inclination on any given "day," whereas a Chirrn required sixteen or more times as long to undergo the hormonal adjustment to realign one's sex. Renata Marcoe, by contrast, had spent most of her previous life with a similarly intermediate sexual physiology and an identity tending toward male, yet had chosen to go permanently female through surgical means upon joining the Cybele expedition, so as to supplement the group's childbearing contingent. Even those Arachnen of unambiguous sex practiced a variety of mating behaviors: formal, monogamous pair-bonds such as those between Stephen and Sita or Tarik and Kweli; ongoing yet non-exclusive affiliations like Diana and Justine or Vijay Bhadra and his two female cohabitants; or casual sexual partnerships of convenience, such as the occasional friendly liaisons between next-door neighbors Haim Silbermann and Ravinder Pritam. On the other hand, Oyama Kazuko, though unambiguously female, was behaviorally asexual, which was why she had chosen Ravinder as the male parent for her offspring based on his fitness and reliability rather than any romantic bonds. Not only was the diversity of combinations highly educational from a sophontological standpoint, but it created endless opportunities for juicy and sexually scandalous gossip.

Unfortunately for R'nilinnath, the situation between Rosario, Scott, and the others had been neatly resolved. After all, along with their skills as a nurse and physical therapist, Rosario's role in the community was to help maintain the psychological health of its members, not only by providing for their sexual needs but by talking out their sexual anxieties and disputes. After a brief consult with Kweli Ndege, Rosario had admitted that they had inadvertently allowed Scott to schedule a disproportionate amount of their time, and had persuaded the geneticist to take a break from their sexual services as a penalty. Scott had not been happy about it, but he had accepted it as a necessary price for restoring a balanced relationship with his neighbors. *How very Chirrn*, R'nilinnath thought with satisfaction.

But she was more interested in the details of the tension between Stephen and Sita. "Does it involve Stephen mating with other females?" she pressed. Watching humans negotiate their sexual preoccupations was endlessly entertaining.

"No, nothing like that," Diana replied as they clambered along a crossover trellis high above one of Shilirrlal's hydroponic farm sectors. "He's still scrupulously faithful. He even turned *me* down!" she added with annoyance and disbelief.

R'nilinnath drummed her toes against the trellis slats. "You tried to seduce him? Tell me everything!" She had to shout over the sound of a robotic harvester passing below them. She wished the Arachnen were linked to consensus, so she could speak directly in Diana's mind and not have to strain her voice.

Diana chuckled, her own version of toe-drumming. "I prefer to brag about my successes, not dwell on my failures. Anyway, you keep prying into our sex lives — what about your own?" she asked as they reached the maintenance hatch at the far end of the trellis. "You're a young adult discovering your femaleness — that must be exciting. Have you, what, joined tongues with anyone yet?"

The young Chirrn swiveled her eyes and thumped her feet abashedly as she bypassed the lock on the hatch. "I wish. You forget, I'm the only one my age on Shilirrlal. I'm grown, but I'm… well, my mottling is taking its good time to fade, my mane's a little slow to grow in… so everyone still sees me as a child, even though I'm mature enough to be female. It's… an awkward time when there's nobody else your age."

Diana ruffled R'nilinnath's mane. "Trust me, Nilly, it's even more awkward when there *are* others your age."

The hatch led into the farm's water filtration plant, where they shed their clothes, took deep breaths, and dove into a clean water conduit whose current carried them to their destination. Diana was the only Arachnen who could hold her breath long enough for this. Finally they emerged into the open, catching themselves on a catwalk at the top of a sloping channel that carried the water down into the sector beyond. This was their destination for this trip: the Ryohoch sector of Shilirrlal, where those ancient and enigmatic beings preferred to reside. Though the Ryohoch had freely granted their advanced technological knowl-edge and galaxy-spanning wisdom to the Chirrn from the beginnings of the Void Alliance, as they had to numerous other species before, they nonetheless tended to remain detached, moving through their lives at their own pace and on their own terms. R'nilinnath had only been to this sector once before in her life, and never by the Ryohoch's invita-tion. This was as much a journey of discovery for her as it was for Diana.

The two young females clambered onto the catwalk and gazed out on a wide expanse dominated by dozens of slender, tapering blue trees with dome-shaped caps, rising halfway to the sector's roof. Various types of support drone flitted around them like cybernetic avians and insects. Each tree grew from the base of a large, domed building with open sides, its rootlike growths infiltrating the metallic structure even as the structure's technology ramified upward along the tree trunk. A ghostly, whistling whirr emanated from the trees, or the buildings, or both. It was warmer than the rest of Shilirrlal, fortunately for the two drenched, unclothed interlopers.

Several Ryohoch stood before the edges of the domed structures, appearing to be connected to the indistinct masses within them by thick, root-like tendrils joined somehow to the fronts of their large, bulbous bodies. As Nilly and Diana watched, another Ryohoch stood patiently as a set of drones guided another such root toward it and thrust its pointed, metallic end slowly into the Ryohoch's flesh, until it was in as deep as the length of Diana's forearms. The Ryohoch let out a low, whispery moan as it was penetrated, but showed no visible sign of distress. The human flinched and shuddered, but Nilly reassured her, "It's fine. Their bodies are adapted to handle this. I think."

"What are they doing?" Diana asked, bewildered. "Feeding on the trees? Being fed on *by* the trees? Exchanging data with the trees?" A pause. "Are the trees… fucking them?"

"I honestly don't know," R'nilinnath said. "But I *do* know we're not supposed to see this. It's very private—whatever it is." Diana grinned, looking intrigued.

They continued to watch, but the illicit thrill of the forbidden was hard to maintain when neither observer knew what they were watching, and when it continued for dozens of *narr* with no evident change. "Hey, what about the Lesshchin refugees?" Diana asked to break the tedium, resuming their earlier conversation. "Maybe there's someone your age among them."

Nilly's feet thumped again. "I checked. There are two that are close. But one was pretty badly hurt, and she's still relearning. And the other's male."

"So?" Diana asked.

"I'm not ready to have a baby yet! And I like being female right now; I'm in no hurry to change."

"Come on, same-sex tongue-wrestling can't be the Chirrn's only form of contraception."

"No, I can set my hormones to prevent it, but it's just… It's not what I'd expect for my first partner."

"Honey, your first time is never what you expect. And it's rarely ideal. Well, unless it's with me, of course," Diana added with a prideful shake of her mane. "But that would be a pretty advanced experiment for both of us. You should probably get some practice with another Chirrn first. My advice is, track down that Lesshchin boy and get to know him. He's probably as hard up to get some tongue as you are."

R'nilinnath's toes were drumming uncontrollably now. In an attempt to contain her amusement (and excitement), she snorted sternly and cried, "Enough! Diana, you're just trying to distract me from talking about Stephen and Sita. Tell me the dirt! I've waited long enough!"

Diana sighed. "Honestly, I don't know the details. They keep up a good public front of unity—our noble leader has to set a good example.

And most people don't want to pry, not being as naturally inquisitive as you and me. Or maybe they just need to believe Stephen can guide them through all this, and if he can't even keep the peace at home, then… well."

"Don't you need to believe it too?"

Diana hesitated. "I shouldn't say. Gossip is one thing, but I don't want to judge…"

R'nilinnath leaned forward. "You know the deal, Diana. Give to get. If you hold back, so do I."

Diana chuckled. "You'd make a hell of a reporter, Nilly. Okay. I just wonder sometimes… it was such a whirlwind romance."

"Stephen and Sita."

"Yeah. All based on hibernation dreams. I don't think you can really know a person based on dreams."

"But don't the hibernation dreams bare your true selves? Wouldn't you see each other more clearly?"

"Sure, it's your inner self — but it's who you are in a fantasy. We all had plenty of those fantasies in hibernation. I remember my dreams better than most." She tapped her skull. "Vanguardian memory and all. And I have *lots* of vivid memories of Stephen and me fucking each other senseless. I dream-fucked almost every man and woman in the crew, and I have no doubt Stephen did too. It was a long trip, after all. But when I woke up and got to know them as real people again, they didn't have that much in common with their dream avatars."

She tilted her head in thought. "Well, except for the real hardcore idealists. The ones who try to live their dreams in real life. Like Stephen, of course. Or Diego. Or Bingbing. A lot of the Unrenounced, really. Maybe that's why they're so unwilling to bend."

"But Stephen… bent."

"Not really. He's still the best of us, as driven to live up to his ideals as anyone. I guess the captain and the rest… define their ideals differently." She fidgeted, gazing back out at the Ryohoch techno-forest. "Doesn't seem fair that they're being punished for it."

R'nilinnath sighed through her nares, ruffling her bristles. "They are all in good health. And they can come to live with the Arachnen any time they want. All they have to do is renounce their planetary ties."

"That's the problem, isn't it? To them, that'd be compromising what they believe in — and none of us would ask that of them." Diana sighed. "Vack it, how did we get into this mess?"

The young Chirrn had no explanation for the Unrenounced's continued stubbornness. Surely they had been given plenty of time to figure out what was expected of them. What was so horrible about making a simple transition?

She wished she could just tell the humans everything. But that would defeat the purpose of their education, and of the Unrenounced's ongoing ordeal. They had to figure it out for themselves and choose to act accordingly. L'chellin allowed her to break the rules with Diana, just enough to satisfy the Arachnen that they were managing to evade their restrictions and learn things they weren't yet "supposed" to learn. R'nilinnath could get behind that; she'd always believed that the only good way to learn a set of limits was to exceed them. But her rule-breaking still served a purpose within the greater balance, which was why she felt free to indulge in it. She may have enjoyed a bit of fun, and she definitely enjoyed the extended prank she was playing on the humans. But she wasn't irrational, and she was still petitioning for her status as a full adult and guild member. So she played by the rules—the deeper set of rules that encouraged her to break the superficial rules in a useful way.

Why couldn't the Unrenounced do the same? The assimilating Arachnen managed to find their own forms of defiance—Diana going on secret expeditions, Sita keeping her traditional attire—without violating the parameters of their new allegiance. So what was stopping their former kith from rejoining them?

"What do you call ninety thousand dead Chirrn?" James Oates asked.

"A good start," Diego Narvaez replied.

Amrita Dhillon shook her head. "Bad aim."

"Trivia," suggested Evan Jiang.

"No," Oates told them. "One hell of a barbecue. Mm, kangaroo meat!"

Cecilia LoCarno joined in the laughter despite herself. Anything to keep morale up. She didn't want to encourage this kind of behavior— the kind that confirmed what the Chirrn already believed about humans—but her crew needed a release valve for their justified anger.

At the very least, they needed something to pass the time. There wasn't much to keep the loyalists busy in their stark prison compound.

Oh, it was clean, bright, and open—a broad semicircle with a domed ceiling about four meters high, containing a common area for dining and conversation, a fairly spacious exercise facility, eight double bunks, a shower/lavatory section, and a laundry and workshop. The prisoners were expected to do their own work to keep their compound clean and livable, but so long as they did so, it provided all the basics of survival. They had been granted a limited number of movable partitions for privacy, but there were few enough to require choices about what areas of privacy to prioritize—no doubt one of the behavioral experiments they had been sentenced to participate in. Every move the humans made was watched through the mirrored windows of the Panopticon-style observation booth overhead, beneath the ceiling at the geometric center of the semicircle—hardly necessary given the ubiquitous nanocameras that no doubt drifted throughout the compound, but serving as a constant psychological reminder of the prisoners' role as guinea pigs.

All the more reason, then, for Cecilia to allow the kind of jokes that would offend their Chirrn voyeurs. Diego and his hangers-on served their purpose; the engineer's charisma was a valuable force for maintaining the unity of the loyalist group, like a rawer, harder-edged version of Stephen's charm. And it was important to keep their fighting spirit alive in case an opportunity presented itself. Escape might require killing some Chirrn, so it was for the best that some of the loyalists would be capable of doing that without being overcome by guilt. Cecilia would have been more sanguine about it if not for her suspicion that Diego and James would hate the Chirrn just as much even if the first contact had been peaceful. But that hate could be turned to constructive ends, so long as Cecilia could regulate and focus it. Better than divorcing herself from Diego's group and letting their xenophobia run out of control.

No, that was unfair. All four of these people had volunteered for a mission to an alien world, had passed Stargazer's extensive psychological tests. True, they'd never expected to encounter sapient aliens, so the tests had not been designed to detect that kind of xenophobia. But they'd proven themselves smart, flexible, and curious, and they had all committed to a colonization program based on respect for Cybele's indigenous life. They didn't reflexively hate the unknown. Their animosity had been provoked by the Chirrn's abuses.

It was fair to say that Diego had taken that animosity farther than most, but Cecilia could sympathize with his reasons. The Guatemalan engineer was a deeply religious man. The concept of being responsible for killing thousands was too much for him to bear. To avoid that Catholic guilt, he took refuge in a strict reading of Catholic doctrine. God had created man in His image, so only man had a soul. Thus, Diego had concluded, *Arachne* had only killed a herd of unusually clever animals.

Of course, he missed the point. There was no need for guilt, since they had done nothing wrong. Nothing at all.

"I mean it, you know," Amrita went on, leaning forward on her soft sitting mat and resting her half-empty drinking globe of fruit juice on the low, circular protrusion that served them as a dining table, integrated with the floor so that they could not turn it into a weapon. "If only Arachne's shots had been a little more dead-on—"

"If she'd been able to stay on target longer, you mean," James interrupted.

"Whatever. She could've blown the whole thing up and we'd still be safely on our way to Cybele." The wiry mining engineer chuckled. "Nearly a million dead kangers and we'd never even know we killed them."

"More fun knowing we did," Diego said, laughing with her. But she laughed even louder at his words. The Chirrn's invasive, humiliating examinations had reawakened the traumas that Amrita had left Solsys to escape, and the Strider hated them as profoundly as she hated the Trojan-habitat regime her father had died resisting.

But it was what helped Amrita get through this, so Cecilia could live with it. As ugly as their hatred was, it helped keep the loyalists together. While she had far more respect for Ichiba Nobuo's Buddhist pacifism and Nikolos Zacharias's medical ethics, she feared that indulging them would weaken the group's commitment and lead to more defections. Granted, indulging the haters created the risk of driving people like Nobuo and Nik out of the loyalist camp. The key was keep the two sides balanced—favoring the angry side, but not so much that it ran out of control. The effect on the group as a whole was far from ideal, but once they got out of here and back en route to Cybele, the attitude of Diego's clique toward the Chirrn wouldn't matter.

The thought came unbidden that Stephen would be better at this kind of balancing act. Cecilia had never had difficulty commanding a crew's obedience and loyalty—always striving to respect their individuality, but within a context of shipboard discipline and the chain of command. Yet this was a different situation. The crew had been given a choice, and these fifteen—sixteen, before they had lost Rosario Soares—had chosen for their own reasons to stand with her. She had to cultivate their commitment to those individual convictions rather than merely compelling them to follow her. Convincing people of such diverse beliefs to unite behind a common cause and see it as an outgrowth of their own convictions was the sort of thing Stephen did naturally. Hell, he'd convinced Cecilia not only to go along with this mad colonization scheme, but to believe in it as passionately as he did—because she'd believed in him. Now, the Lesshchi accident had undermined his belief in himself, leaving it to her to carry on with his dream until he came to his senses. But as much as she tried to apply Stephen's methods, to lead by consensus and balance as he did, Cecilia feared she just didn't have the knack.

"I still say Cybele's their home planet." The others groaned as James started the argument for the thousandth time, though Cecilia welcomed the distraction from her reverie. "No, seriously. No way their technology could've missed detecting us. They intercepted us to stop us from finding their homeworld." For James Oates, hatred of the Chirrn was simply a matter of pride. The stocky, pale-skinned New Englander was a gifted industrial engineer and an accomplished athlete from a prestigious family, and he had pursued his place on the mission out of a sense of entitlement. He'd passed the vetting process by proving that his skill was equal to his opinion of it, and that he could check his arrogance enough to get along with the rest of the crew. But since their capture, James's resentment at being subordinated to the Chirrn had amplified all of his worst impulses. Moreover, his ego convinced him that anything bad that befell him must be the result of malicious schemes directed at him personally, or at least his group. For every setback in his life, he had a conspiracy theory or five, a handy set of explanations for why nothing that went wrong was ever his fault. This tendency had been restrained enough on the mission to be a manageable eccentricity, but since Lesshchi it had blossomed into full-blown paranoia.

But Nobuo couldn't resist pointing out the flaw in his logic. "So why move the whole habitat into harm's way when they have such fast ships?"

"What, you buy that they were innocent victims?" Evan Jiang said with undisguised contempt. He was basically a hanger-on, drawn into the others' circle by the strength of their personalities and eager to earn their approval. But he was compensating for a deeply rooted fear. Being in the Chirrn's physical presence terrified Evan. He'd trained with simulations of Cybeline life based on probe recordings, but the simulations couldn't have predicted his visceral response to the truly alien. He traveled in Diego's circle for protection and drew strength from their hate.

"Not innocent," Cecilia interposed, her tone drawing everyone's attention. "They kept Lesshchi dark, hidden. They didn't want to be seen. We find the reason for that, we find out why this happened."

James continued spinning conspiracy theories: the Chirrn were trying to keep planet-dwellers down, they had acted in secret to impede human progress, and so on. Nobuo patiently rebutted every point with reasoned counterarguments, but he was the only one who still bothered. After nearly five months of this, the others knew all his tunes: The Chirrn had been the source of the flying saucer legends of the twentieth century, stirring up the Cold War so humanity would destroy itself. The Chirrn had sent the Tunguska impactor and miscalculated its power or its aim. The Chirrn had artificially accelerated global warming to destabilize human civilization. All leading to his invocation of humanity's moral duty to rise up and wipe the Chirrn menace from the galaxy.

It wouldn't be quite so disturbing if Cecilia couldn't see how much the talk of violence against the Chirrn physically aroused James. The kangaroos had been playing games with them again. For a couple of weeks, they had required all six women to go constantly nude, programming all the clothing, bedsheets, and towels in the compound to liquefy when touched by a woman's skin, and setting the partitions to go transparent if a woman tried to conceal herself behind one. If they'd hoped to drive the men into an orgy of rape, they'd been disappointed; instead it had inspired the men to chivalry, bringing out their protective side. So last week the experimenters had reversed the programming and now all ten men had to go nude at all times—and the women had been enjoying every second and expressing that enjoyment in the bawdiest of terms, at least toward the men who were comfortable with such attention.

But both behaviors were acts of defiance in their own way. No one wanted to satisfy the Chirrn's expectations. For all their claims of harmless sociological experimentation, it had quickly become clear that this was an ongoing exercise in humiliation and dehumanization. Many of the "experiments" were designed to attack basic aspects of their planet-adapted biology. The cycles of light and dark in the compound had been varied unpredictably, until Cecilia and Nik Zacharias had finally managed to convince their wardens that sleep deprivation was a form of torture among humans — since the Chirrn were determined to pretend that all this was somehow ethical so long as it caused no overt physical harm. The gravity level in the compound had somehow been altered, sometimes dropping the prisoners abruptly into free fall and leaving them there for hours, sometimes subtly and subliminally increasing the gravity over days and observing their growing fatigue and irritation. Once, some sort of acoustical scrambling had drowned out Cecilia's and Diego's voices whenever they had given an instruction or asserted authority, as a test of the group's leadership dynamics. Yet a sizeable percentage of the trials involved sexuality in some way; the Chirrn were either fascinated or disgusted by the humans' unchanging sexes and were determined to test them to their limits and beyond.

At first, aware that they were being monitored at every moment, the loyalists had avoided sex altogether. But that hadn't lasted long, and Rosario Soares had advised them that it would be healthier to resume a normal level of sexual activity rather than give up that basic human right under coercion. At first, several of them had been too shy to perform, so Rosario had provided their services to any who needed them. But once the Chirrn had figured out that Rosario had only stayed with the loyalists to see to the sexual health of the gender-skewed group, they had compelled the sex provider to renounce and join Stephen's group. God forbid that the loyalists be granted any consideration for their mental health.

In a way, though, Cecilia was glad Rosario was gone; best if everyone here was a true planetary loyalist rather than a camp follower. No, that was far too harsh; Rosario's purpose had been therapeutic, not mercenary. And their skills as a nurse and physical therapist had been useful, though Ichiba Nobuo filled the latter role quite well (and Cecilia went away for a moment at the thought of his massages). Still, without a licensed sex professional on hand, managing relations within the community had become more of a challenge. Cecilia had tried to sort things out in an egalitarian way, encouraging each woman to choose two regular partners, with provisions for arranging trades and loans if needed—which had come out even, since Shuai Bingbing was remaining chaste out of misguided loyalty to her wife, despite Justine Nguyen's betrayal of Bingbing and the rest of her species. The arrangement was a bit libertine for some tastes—particularly for Sergei Mazunov and Hannah Errgang, who were falling mushily in love like adolescents despite (or perhaps as a result of) being the two oldest members of the group. But it was better than allowing jealousy and frustration to build.

Especially with the Chirrn doing their best to bollix the works. They had let the partnerships form without interference at first, but after a few weeks they had played a dirty trick. The atmosphere of the compound was infused with some kind of utility fog, which they now programmed to harden whenever a woman came near either of her lovers, the constituent nans linking into diaphanous yet extremely strong strands anchored against the floor and ceiling. It became impossible for any of them to touch their chosen partners. Some had readily switched to new partners, while others, including Sergei and Hannah, had settled for chastity for the duration. But then, for a few weeks, the utility fog had been programmed to prevent any man from touching any woman. That had been a difficult time for everyone. But the humans had adapted, as they always did, and soon the women began taking sexual comfort from one another, as did most of the men, save only Ibrahim and James. Even Bingbing, after a few days of soul-searching, offered her services to the other women in their time of need, insisting that Justine would understand. If the Chirrn had intended to test the flexibility of human sexual preference, they'd certainly gained a wealth of data.

It was just after that phase that the ban on touching had been rescinded and the women had been forced to go naked, as if to make them more available and more tempting than ever to the deprived men—though none of the men had reacted the way their tormentor must have hoped they would. Churrlaya had claimed the timing was random, but Cecilia hadn't believed him for a second. The fact that the Chirrn would allow a Lesshchi survivor to have power over the prisoners at all was proof that they had no interest in fairness. The whole thing was an exercise in revenge, and Cecilia was certain that Churrlaya stayed up nights cackling to himself—or whatever the kangaroos did—as he devised new ways to degrade his human playthings.

Suddenly a voice spoke from a cloudy patch in the air: the nans of the utility fog were vibrating in synch. *"Cecilia. Report to the interview chamber."* Cecilia winced. *Speak of the devil.*

She stood, but Diego rose to intercept her. She strove to keep her eyes on his face. "You shouldn't just get up the moment he calls you."

"You think he'd let me refuse?"

"I think you shouldn't make it easy for them. It's our duty to resist."

She held his gaze until he stepped aside. "I resist in my own way, Diego. Face to face, with my words and my intellect. Anything that shows them we're not just animals."

"You think Chur-*rana* would ever believe that?"

Cecilia smirked at the nickname; Diego had just called Churrlaya a frog. "Probably not. But I never give up. You know that." She stepped past him, unable to resist swatting his bare rump. "Besides, the revolution's safe in your hands."

Most of the group laughed as she walked away, but she could hear James grumbling, "Resisting. Sure. She jumps like a trained puppy when he calls." Cecilia frowned. She'd expect that kind of reaction from Oates; he was basically smart, but too impulsive in his anger and cynicism. But the noises of agreement she heard from the others gave her pause.

Perhaps goaded by Oates's insinuations, Cecilia was in a confrontational mood when she entered the private chamber beneath the Panopticon booth, where Churrlaya awaited her, seated casually on his tail. She decided to ease into it, though. "I want to thank you for the latest dress code. I'm thinking of making it permanent." *Never show weakness.*

The smallish, dark green Chirrn swiveled his eyes in to focus on her more closely, the intricate irises widening. With his mane now dyed pale blue and styled in ringlets, he looked a bit like the Frog Footman from *Alice's Adventures in Wonderland*. It made it easy for her not to take him seriously.

"Be seated, Cecilia." There was nothing familiar about Churrlaya's use of her first name. The Chirrn refused to acknowledge their family names, for they were ties to their old lives, their Earthly allegiances. "Do your males share your contentment with the arrangement?"

Cecilia remained standing. "Oh, there's nothing men love more than showing off."

"Indeed? Our observations suggest that most of your males are insecure to have their physical shortcomings exposed. Or is there some other reason why every male chooses to tighten his abdominal muscles when he notices a female observing him?"

"I'm afraid the nuances of human somatic communication are too intricate for a Chirrn to understand." *And you're slipping if you didn't notice us girls doing exactly the same when we were stuck naked.*

"Really," Churrlaya said. "Then perhaps we could gain more data on the subject if we deprived all of you of your clothing permanently."

"Word of advice, Churly? If you're going to make a threat, make it something you haven't already done to us. Besides, you'd never do anything so egalitarian. We wouldn't be as humiliated if we were all on an even footing."

He straightened, lifting his heels from the floor, and opened his mouth slightly, an expression of pride and satisfaction not unlike a human's. "Then you confess there is humiliation."

"I'm saying that your real goal is to inflict it. And you just confirmed it. Research be damned, you just want to torment us."

"We inflict no pain or injury upon you. We deprive you of no basic needs."

"Except our dignity."

Again the irises widened. The more Cecilia looked at Chirrn eyes, the more she realized their intricacies were probably artificially engineered. Wondering just what kind of visual input he'd engaged, she schooled herself for calm, not wishing to give anything away. He'd been scrutinizing the loyalists' every move for months and could read human body language better than she'd ever admit.

"If anything, your males seemed *more* concerned for your dignity when you were unclothed. Yet that does not seem to be reciprocal. Clearly your dignity is a matter of your own choice."

"Except we have no choice as long as we're your prisoners."

"You have been offered a very clear and simple choice that would free you from this. Yet you choose to remain. Why?"

"What you offer as a choice is just another form of enslavement."

"Because it would offend your dignity as planet-dwellers?"

"Because it would force us to abandon what we are."

"And what is that?" Churrlaya hopped forward to study her, and Cecilia could see the faint glimmer of the utility fog thickening between them, ensuring his safety should she try to attack him—though she doubted the reverse was true. "Answer: if you could reach me, would you kill me?"

She met his eyes squarely. "If I thought it would do my people any good, yes."

"Would simple revenge not constitute sufficient good by your people's standards? Do you not joke of murdering more of mine? Is this the planetary dignity you hold so dear?"

She could read a fair amount of tension in his body language too. "We joke. But you're the one actually inflicting revenge."

"The Chirrn have killed none of your people."

"We die a little more every day without our freedom."

Churrlaya snorted through his nares and mouth, a Chirrn scoff. "A platitude. Most humans have lived without freedom for most of your history. The concept of freedom as an intrinsic human right is younger than most of my own colleagues. Even today, you humans advocate the concept more consistently than you practice it. And yet your species has survived."

Cecilia noted that Churrlaya had just given something away about himself: he was younger than, ohh, about four hundred years, and this was relatively young for a Chirrn. She filed it away. "Because we've always fought for our freedom," she told him. "As long as there have been slavers and oppressors, there have been rebels and revolutionaries. As long as there have been prisons, there have been escapes."

"Do you believe all prisoners should escape? Even those guilty of obscene crimes?"

"Those who are wrongfully imprisoned, yes."

"*Wrongful!* Tell that to Simisshen, to Marellel, to Ruzhalu. Was it rightful that they should die?"

"The wrong wasn't ours! If your people had the basic good sense to put running lights on your habitat, your friends would be alive!" Cecilia pushed him, hoping to provoke him into rage. She could live with a few broken bones to make the point that she wasn't the violent one here. "Why did you keep Lesshchi so dark, Churrlaya? What were you trying to hide? Who were you hiding from?"

Churrlaya turned away, rotating his eyes backward to keep her in view, tensing his legs and tail. This was it. She closed her eyes, relaxed, and waited for it, hoping that if he killed her with the kick that was coming, the other Chirrn would bother to bring her back.

Instead, she just heard a loud, sharp thump, felt a strong vibration through her feet. She opened her eyes. He had struck the floor with his tail, and now he let out a long, slow hiss across his tongue. He kept his head turned away, his eyes rotated back and wide to see her around his raised brow ridges. "You are arrogant. Assuming we have reason to hide ourselves from your primitive race. That we make some secret plans against you. You are insignificant in the galaxy, dirt-dweller."

"Then why have you been studying us for so long? Our languages were already in your database when you captured us. You've monitored us before."

He turned back to face her. "Routine scientific observation."

"But you put a lot of effort into it. It would've taken a telescopic array the size of a planetary system to pick up clear signals from nine parsecs away. It would've taken decades of remote observation to put together enough cultural context for a practical translation. If you hold planet-dwellers in such contempt, why study us in such depth?"

"Scientists study the scum atop ponds. They study microbes that live on excrement. Do not mistake scientific curiosity for an acknowledgment of worth."

"And that's another thing. If it's planet-dwellers you hate, why do you treat Striders like Amrita and Nik as badly as the rest of us? Is this whole ridiculous planet thing just a cover? Is it humans *per se* you have a problem with?"

Churrlaya drew closer again. "We have been quite generous with every human who renounced planetary allegiance. They have been shown more acceptance than they deserve."

"So long as they 'contribute to your society.' They're worse than your prisoners. They're your slaves. And they don't even understand that's what they are."

He hissed again. "You are the one who understands nothing. But I am glad of it, for it prolongs your ordeal." He came in very close, and she felt the air harden around her. "And keeps you in my power."

Churrlaya cursed himself for letting Cecilia provoke him into admitting too much. He knew he'd be in for chastisement from R'hhenevh when he returned to the monitor room. And indeed, the sleek-snouted, strong-bodied Shilirrlaln met him wide-stanced, tapping her long, graceful tail on the floor. "Must we have the same conversation yet again, Churrlaya?" she asked. "I indulge your desire to humiliate the humans so long as it serves a purpose. I chose to have faith that your desire to transition to my collegium showed your willingness to adapt your grief toward constructive ends." She stepped closer, relaxing her stance. "But you must remember that our purpose is to guide them toward the resolution of their ordeal, not goad them into prolonging it. They need to reach the stage of repentance. They have an obligation to take the place of the lives they took."

"Those lives can never be replaced," Churrlaya hissed. "Least of all by the ones who destroyed them. Can you blame a Lesshchin for feeling that the humans have already earned final exclusion?"

R'hhenevh lowered her head, her lush, jeweled magenta mane falling forward over her shoulders and the gold-fringed vest she wore. "I understand your pain, Laya. As much as I can understand such a tragedy. But you are Lesshchin no more." She clasped his hands with her own cool azure ones. "You have a new home now, a new guild to take care of you. But only if you stop clinging to your old life."

He took comfort in her touch, if not her words. There was no way she could truly understand, no way he would inflict the memories on her to make her understand. A large piece of who he was had been burned away. So many memories, viewpoints, habits of thought ripped from him with no warning or choice. So many friends and loved ones who had been a part of him, now reduced to mere echoes lingering within his skull. "It is not easy to make a transition when it is forced."

"The circumstances were forced. But you have chosen your new path freely." She stroked his arm. "At least I believed you had. I begin to wonder if your grief is trapping you in your old life, preventing you from truly becoming whole again. Perhaps it would be easier for you to move on if you chose another collegium. Forgot about the humans."

His eyes locked on hers. "Would you want that? For me to leave you?"

"Only if it would set you free from who you were. But I would regret losing you. You have a real aptitude for the science of the mind.

You are a valuable addition to our collegium. And we all wish to ease your loneliness.

"But it can only work if you resolve your own self-inflicted ordeal. And that cannot happen if you cling to your desire for retribution."

"You think I push them too far. That my experiments are gratuitous."

"You claimed they had a purpose." She sent him a memory image, triggering his own recall of the same conversation wherein he had proposed the sexual behavior experiments with the goal of assessing the flexibility of the humans' identity and affinity structures, the better to understand and overcome their resistance to adaptation. "But I am no longer convinced that is your true goal."

"I do nothing that exceeds the allowed limits for ordeals."

"For *Chirrn* ordeals. Humans are different. They are feral, young. They have had life extension for less time than you have lived. And they reside almost fully within their own brains. It is not in their nature to move between life phases. When their identity is challenged, they cling to it more fiercely."

"Sometimes. There are instances in their records of humans being conditioned to change allegiance after extended humiliation." He sent her cites for the relevant sources in the guild database, if she were inclined to confirm the claim.

Yet she sent back even more citations almost immediately. "And this is considered torture to them. That is not our purpose here. We are offering them the chance at redemption, if they are able to recognize and embrace it." Her hand moved to his neck, fingers brushing his mane. "Help me do that, Laya. Guide them to a new beginning, so that you may truly make one of your own. One where you can truly belong with me."

R'hhenevh dug her hands into his mane and pulled their heads together brow to brow. The brushing of her muzzle cilia over his sent tingles through his head clear to his tongue; her scent in his nares was intoxicating. What an honor, some lingering rational part of him thought, to be romanced by the collegium alpha herself! The prospect of being one of her chosen was enticing indeed.

When their muzzles parted, he tried to form coherent words around his swollen tongue. "You... would have me go female for you?"

"If you like. Or you could stay male—perhaps even speak a child with me." Churrlaya's eyes spun at the prospect. True, the loss of so many lives meant that many former Lesshchin were preparing to speak new young, but he had given no thought to doing so himself. "Either would be a new start for you. A leap further into your new life."

She brushed muzzles with him again to reinforce the offer. He wanted to pull her against him, to seal his lips against hers and rub tongues until his spoke the sweet word for hers to hear.

But he pulled away, hopping back, huffing through his nares to clear them of her overpowering alpha pheromones. "You honor me deeply, Alpha. But I am not ready. My accent is still Lesshchin."

R'hhenevh gave a soft hiss of disappointment. "And that means you must continue to humiliate the humans."

"That will have to be my role within the collegium for now."

She thumped her tail against the wall, unhappy but accepting. "Granted. But remember the ultimate goal. Show them the value of submission. Guide them toward acceptance of their crime so they may seek repentance. Do not push them so hard that they become more determined to resist. You know how dangerous that can be when dealing with planet-dwellers." R'hhenevh did not need to send reference files to annotate her words. That particular historical lesson was well-known to every Chirrn—indeed, to every starfaring people within the Four Voids and beyond.

"I have more than distant history to tell me of the danger of planet-dwellers, Nevh. But does that history not tell us that containing them is a safer path than attempting to mentor them?"

The alpha bristled. "This is not mentoring, and you know it. It is repentance and transition as the Chirrn have always practiced it, both within ourselves and with outsiders."

Regretting his impolitic choice of words, Churrlaya bent his knees. "My apologies, Alpha. My analogy was malformed. I did not mean to accuse you of supporting—"

She softened. "Of course. Your words were born of pain." She nuzzled his snout with hers again, though only briefly before resuming a more professional distance. "I understand that this is far from abstract for you, Laya. Still, you have committed to the goal of guiding them through transition. I am trusting you to honor that commitment."

"With all gratitude for your trust, Nevh, I suspect it may already be too late. As you said, the humans cling to their allegiances and beliefs with great ardor."

"Most of them chose transition. It should be possible for the rest in time."

"The humans of *Arachne* were chosen for their diversity of skills and character. And for their strength of will. These sixteen will not alter their convictions as easily as the rest."

She studied him. "You sound almost admiring. How do we reconcile that with preemptive exclusion?"

Churrlaya realized that he thought of it more by the human term: *hate*. "I merely know them well. Understanding is not approval."

"But you should be able to use that understanding to guide them in the right direction. That is your duty to your guild."

"I know. I know." He felt that conviction within himself, when he reached for the collegium consensus. But it was not enough to overcome the pain and bitterness that filled his own skull, not enough to fill the missing pieces of his identity. He sighed through his nares. "I overstepped myself, and I will try to repent. But... it is not easy to contain my anger. Cecilia in particular... she is so stubborn, so arrogant. Without her, without the extremist clique she has gathered around her, I think most of the others would be malleable. But she will not yield a single hop. She defines her identity by her roots in a particular city on her native planet. It is a psychological anchor for her, one that I have found unyielding."

R'hhenevh pondered his words. "All ground is impermanent. If you assume this 'anchor' cannot be budged, perhaps you have become too influenced by planetary thinking."

"Can you see a way to break the ground?"

She swiveled her eyes a bit, tapped her fingers together. "I only hear a question. If Cecilia is so unyieldingly rooted in her planetary home... then why did she command an expedition that would take her from her home forever?"

R'hhenevh hopped forward and brushed her fingers tenderly over his muzzle. "Answer that question, dear Laya, and you may find the key to freeing her from her planetary bonds. And maybe then you will free yourself as well."

8

Sita Bhatiani stood sideways before the mirror, studying herself. "Ohh, I'm really starting to show now. I look so fat."

"Nonsense." Stephen reached around from behind her, placing his hands on the warm flesh of her belly. "You look wonderful. Pregnant women are so beautiful."

Sita rolled her eyes. It was often flattering when he treated her as a paragon of beauty and brilliance, but at other times, she felt overshadowed by the ideal image he projected onto her. But then, he was such a paragon himself that she supposed he couldn't help seeing the best in everyone. "Maybe from the outside," she conceded. "It's not very comfortable from in here."

"Just be glad you don't have to give birth through your mouth like a Chirrn."

"Are you joking? At least their mouths are wide to begin with. That comes out ahead in the evolution race if you ask me." Sita had already decided on a Caesarean birth; her hips were simply too small for anything else to make sense. No point making things difficult for the kid on her first day out.

He smiled. "There, you see? You do have something positive to say about the Chirrn."

Sita pulled away. "They have every advantage over us already. You really think I meant it as a positive? Any lengths to find a bright side, eh?"

"Would humans have been this generous, this accepting of people who did what we did? I think things are very bright, under the circumstances."

His words only shamed her. She was disgusted by her own xenophobia, her bigotry toward these beings that intellectually she found remarkable. The Chirrn of Shilirrlal had surely proven by now that they weren't savage monsters waiting to beat the life from her if they got her alone. The brutality that a few deeply traumatized Lesshchin had inflicted on her immediately after the loss of their entire world—more than just a structure or a place, but a literal part of their identity that had been violently ripped away—was an aberration in a highly peaceful society, and an entirely understandable one. She didn't even hate Vhehhal and the other guards who had beaten her; how could she, knowing the unconscionable loss that had provoked them? Sometimes, the fact that she'd been punished so severely at the start made her feel less guilty about the startling leniency and kindness the Shilirrlaln had since extended.

Still, animal reflex was hard to overcome. For months, the sight of one of those chameleon eyes swiveling to lock onto her had suffused her with fear. She'd gradually learned to be comfortable with R'nilinnath and L'chellin, up to a point, and she had little difficulty with Mediator Broadwing, who had been nothing but supportive toward the Arachnen (though the Zenith's manner toward Sita, the shortest member of the group, could be unthinkingly condescending). But the thought of going out into Shilirrlal, surrounded by tens of thousands of Chirrn, had overwhelmed her.

She paced before the bedroom window, which at least looked out over the house's back garden, sparing her the impression of Chirrn eyes staring in at her while she slept. Yet from here, she could see the wall and ceiling of the Arachnen compound stretching high overhead, a constant reminder that the humans were completely contained, able to leave these confines only at the Shilirrlaln's indulgence—perhaps some lingering echo of the ancient transition rituals between bands. "Accepting?" she asked, echoing Stephen's observation. "I wonder. To bring a child into this… how will she see her world? Her humanity? What if she thinks she's tainted because of, of what her parents did? Or will she even identify as human?"

Stephen intercepted her, clasping her shoulders. "We're all asking those questions. But the best thing we can do is to work with the Chirrn to integrate into their community. Establish ourselves as equals within it." He stroked her cheek. "I understand what you're feeling, honey. I spent my whole childhood in a place where I was made to feel I didn't belong. When I got my sisters out to Brazil, at first we feared we'd be judged and excluded the same way. But we found ourselves welcomed by a society that celebrated its diversity. And then we found that most of humanity felt the same, that our experience had been an aberration, a last gasp of a dying way of thinking.

"I look at how the Shilirrlaln treat other species like the Zenith and the Ryohoch as their own kind—even sharing their brains with them—and I feel the same sense of hope that I found in Brazil. I believe we're on the verge of finding ourselves welcomed into a vaster community than we could've imagined."

Sita sighed. His optimism was so contagious—but she'd lived with him long enough that she was starting to build up a resistance. "I wish I had your faith." She strode out into the living room, with Stephen following. She picked up the tablet she liked to read from, preferring the old-fashioned approach over reading off her retinal display. "I've been trying to learn more about the evolutionary history of the Zenith and Ryohoch."

"That's great," Stephen said.

"But I can't find anything significant about the biospheres they first evolved in. It's one thing for the Ryohoch—I mean, bloody hell, they're apparently a descendant species of a genus that first colonized space millions of years ago. They're so ancient that maybe the knowledge of where they first came from has just been lost, beyond the general environmental parameters we can deduce from their physiology.

"But from what I can gather, the Zenith aren't anywhere near as ancient. Maybe even younger than the Chirrn. Yet there's nothing about their planet of origin."

"You know how the Chirrn are about planets." As always, he took more care with the pronunciation of their name than she did. His fluency in Portuguese gave him an advantage with the guttural R. She could come close by affecting a Scottish accent, but normally she settled for "Cheern," which sounded incongruously like she was thanking them for something.

"But I don't get blocked when I try to find information on Cybele, or other unpopulated planets they've surveyed," she told him. "It's more than just lack of information, and it's not just about the Zenith. I keep hitting roadblocks in Shilirrlal's network. Stephen, I wish I could trust them like you do, but it's hard when they're keeping secrets from us."

"You know what a regimented people they are. They believe in measured, ritualistic transitions from one stage of life to another. So their educational process is designed to proceed at a certain rate, in a certain order. We still have so much to learn about living as Shilirrlaln. There's a lot to assimilate. Maybe they just want us to master that foundation before we try coping with a flood of knowledge about the galaxy as a whole."

"In other words, they don't trust us with knowledge they don't think we're ready to have. It's just one more way they have all the control."

He took her hands, seeking to calm her. "Because we're still children to them. Like all children, we're impatient for the learning process to end so we can earn the freedoms of adults, but we have to accept that it takes time.

"You know, you should talk to R'nilinnath about her learning process. I think it'd help put your mind at ease." He ruffled her hair. "Just think. Before too much longer it'll be our little girl railing against the limits we place on her. But she'll grow out of them before we know it."

"Oh, there you *go* again!" Frustrated, she whirled away and moved across the room.

He stared in surprise. "Doing what?"

"*Handling* me. Making speeches like you're still recruiting me for the mission."

He shook his head. "I'm just trying to make the best of things for all of us."

"*Your* best. You're so good at charming and persuading people to share your enthusiasms, your dreams. But I'm not some investor or, or politician to be brought round, Stephen! I'm not some shipmate who needs to be given hope! I'm your *wife!* Can't you ever turn it off and just, just *listen* to me? Just let me feel what I feel and be there with me, instead of trying to fix me all the time?!"

After a nonplussed moment, Stephen sat on the couch and said, "You're right. Of course, you have every right to your feelings and concerns. If you need to vent, I'll listen. If you need to cry, here's my shoulder. That's what family's all about, right?"

Instead of calming her, his concession just made her more irritable. "Damn it, I can't even have a decent row with you. Mister Bloody Perfect."

She strode back into the bedroom, closed the door on the very confused-looking Stephen, and leaned back against it in frustration. Her husband was the most empathetic, compassionate man she'd ever met. So how come he had so much trouble understanding her?

The sector of Shilirrlal set aside for the Lesshchin refugees was much larger than the Arachnen compound, but much less interesting for R'nilinnath to visit. The Lesshchin's inherent tendency toward conservatism and insularity had become even greater since the disaster, as the survivors had clung to their traditional identity as a way to anchor them now that so much of their memory and identity had been stripped away. Of course, they would all need to transition into Shilirrlaln society eventually, as many already had, eager to leave their traumatized Lesshchin identities behind them; but many more clung to the vestiges of their lost community, and for now, there was no harm in allowing them to preserve what they could of Lesshchi in its original form before gradually allowing it, and themselves, to be blended into a new synthesis with Shilirrlal culture. Thus, the structures and public spaces of what was now the Lesshchin sector had been remodeled to a traditional Chirrn style, reminiscent of how it might have looked in the Separation Era three yanarredj ago, but with less sign of Zenith, Ryohoch, or other xenocultural influences. It all seemed rather bland and unexciting to Nilly, though she supposed the last thing the disaster survivors wanted right now was any more excitement.

Well, that's too bad, R'nilinnath entered into her cloud journal with an insouciant toss of her still-too-short mane. *Because I'm here to bring excitement to one Lesshchin in particular.*

Normally she would have just pinged Djayrulu through the network and arranged a meeting. But after a couple of *narruvh* of failing to get up the nerve to do just that, R'nilinnath had finally kicked herself in the tail and come here to seek the young Lesshchin out in the flesh, so that she couldn't "chicken out," as Diana put it. Also, if he proved receptive to her offer, it would save them considerable time if their bodies were already in the same sector.

Djayrulu's locator showed him to be up toward the roof of the sector, ascending a climbing trellis spanning two of the highest towers—and this was one of the highest-roofed outer sectors of Shilirrlal. With a sigh, Nilly made her way to the nearest ascent frame and began bounding her way upward. Since she was the one seeking him out, it was only polite to come to him. And it would help her case to show him that she could match his level of fitness.

Still, by the time R'nilinnath came into naked-eye sight of the young male, she was gasping for breath and her arms and legs were sore. She took a moment to size him up as she caught her breath. Djayrulu had a distinctively Lesshchin appearance, with dark green skin almost free of juvenile mottling, a fairly pointy snout, a stocky tail, and an unadorned, nearly full-grown mane of vivid pink. As she stared at him, Nilly realized her heart rate was not settling down, and her tongue was getting moist. She tightened her lips before she started drooling. She'd never reacted this way to another Chirrn before, least of all a male. It must've been because he was the first Chirrn of her own age she'd ever met in the flesh.

Then she realized he was watching her watch him, and she nearly fell off the trellis. She recovered quickly, turning it into what was hopefully an acrobatic-looking move toward him. "Impressive view up here," she said when she landed alongside him, trying not to cling too tightly to the lattice.

Djayrulu studied her for a moment, his gaze revealing little. "I recognize you. You're R'nilinnath with the Mediators' Guild."

"Oh! Yes, I am!" He was already aware of her? Had he been seeking her out for reasons that paralleled her own?

"I've seen you with the other Mediators," he went on. "In community meetings and news feeds."

"Oh. Of course!" In addition to overseeing the Arachnen's rehabilitation, her apprenticeship with the Mediators included helping with the Lesshchin's adjustment from time to time. Her lips parted a bit with pride that he recognized her efforts. His gaze sharpened on her mouth. Was he trying to catch a glimpse of tongue? That was encouraging.

"I'm Djayrulu."

"I know. I came here to meet you." She angled her head to make it just slightly easier for him to see her tongue as she spoke.

His eyes flicked out and back nervously, as if he were unsure whether he had her permission to look or not. "Wh-why would you want to talk to me?"

"Because we're nearly the same age. Just about the only ones our age on Shilirrlal. I figure it's as lonely for you as for me."

He fingered the edge of his vest noncommittally. "Maybe."

"So I thought maybe we could practice sex together."

Djayrulu stared in disbelief for some moments. "I barely know you."

"Well, it's a fine way to get better acquainted!"

"I don't understand. I mean, you look nice enough, but…" He took a sniff of her pheromones. "You're female. It would take a few *narruvh* for you to go male."

R'nilinnath bristled. "What makes you think I'd want to? I've been female for less than a *narranl.* I'm nowhere near finished yet!"

"Well, I'm not going to go female for some Chirrn I've just met. It's a lot of work. Besides, you're the one seeking me out. It's only polite for you to come to me." He gestured toward the climbing frames that had brought her all the way up here.

"So… in principle, you'd be willing to practice sex with me."

He hesitated. "Of course I'm curious. I don't have a lot of prospects either. Especially with the adults so preoccupied with rebuilding the community. But one of us would have to change."

"Do we? We could just join tongues as we are."

Djayrulu recoiled. "As male and female? I won't have a baby with a Shilirrlaln!"

"I said nothing about babies. Just sex. It can be fun with an opposite partner too. …So I hear."

"That's disgusting!"

R'nilinnath was stunned by the strength of his reaction. "Why?"

"Because it's human."

"Chirrn do it sometimes."

"That was before. Now, it'd be a tail-blow to the throat of every Lesshchin."

"What? That doesn't…"

He glanced inward, checking the cloud. "There it is. I thought so. You work with those filthy ferals. You spend so much time with them, you've been contaminated by their perversions."

"There's nothing *wrong* with the ways humans have sex! They're just different."

"You heard what their chieftain said at the trial. Since they mixed up sex for recreation and for procreation, they bred out of control and over-crowded their planet, and that's why they left it in such dangerous ships. It's because of human breeding that my friends, my guildmates, my world were killed!"

Nilly inhaled deeply, gathering herself. His logic was objectively stupid, but she couldn't blame him for the pain that was blinding him.

"The Arachnen made a horrible mistake. They're atoning for it now. I'm helping them restore the balance."

Djayrulu's response was sullen. "You Mediators ended their ordeal too early. They don't deserve inclusion."

She accessed the guild knowledge inside her to help her be conciliatory. "I understand the pain you feel. It will take a long time to heal. But maybe you could heal better if you had a friend. You may not like everyone I associate with, but that's my job as a Mediator. What matters is what we can learn from each other." She widened her mouth and hissed a little across her tongue. "Like how to have sex…?"

They clung to the trellis for a moment, with the only sounds being the wind blowing through the slats and the distant murmur of the crowd below. "I'm not sure about that yet," Djayrulu told her. "But I shouldn't exclude the possibility without learning more about you. Maybe… if I could see the Arachnen through your eyes. Experience them as you do."

"I'm sorry," she said. "The Mediator feeds are confidential to the guild, and to our superiors. I couldn't share my memories from when I'm working on their behalf."

He gave a disappointed snort. "I understand."

She perked up. "But there's something I can do." She explained about her authorized rulebreaking to sneak Diana out of the Arachnen compound through the back conduits. She couldn't see why that loophole couldn't be exploited in the other direction. Especially if it led to getting Djayrulu's tongue in her mouth.

"You'd actually take me into their compound?" the young Lesshchin asked, revulsion warring with an excitement R'nilinnath found very familiar. It was comforting to know she was not the only Chirrn intrigued with the forbidden.

"Not quite *into* it — I don't think you're ready to meet them. But once you're inside, you could stay on the fringes and watch and listen through the local sensors. Although I'd have to stay close to you so I can kick you out if you try anything untoward."

"I promise to behave," Djayrulu said. "Although… I'm starting to like the idea of you staying close to me."

He brushed his tail against hers, and her tongue suddenly started to get very wet.

"Let me see if I understand." Tarik Bahar gazed out the window of the observation gallery overlooking Shilirrlal's shipyard facilities, located at the weightless axis of the thick disk-shaped module at the aft end of the cylindrical habitat. Hanging from its elegant frameworks like tomatoes on a trellis were dozens of Chirrn warp cages, each a pair of nested spheres of intricately curved latticework. "They have so many warp drives… but do not actually use them *as* warp drives?"

Floating beside him, Haim Silbermann assayed a shrug. "Not over long distances. For that, they use wormholes."

"But they need the warp cages to get through the wormholes."

"Bubble of alteration has exterior of smallness to penetrate mouth of wormhole," came the slow, deliberate response of Yonchon, the senior engineer with whom Haim was provisionally apprenticed. Ryohoch like Yonchon were known for their leisurely approach to life; for millions of years, they had drifted through space much as the Chirrn had, but much more slowly, often content to colonize Oort-cloud comets and wait for gravitational perturbations to pull them out of stellar orbit. On the whole, they had little use for superluminal technology, which made it odd that Yonchon was an expert in the field — but then, Ryohoch were nothing if not dogged individualists.

The massive engineer had no fewer than nine legs in groups of three, two sticking out on either side of the body (angling up from the hip, then straight down at the knee, to provide greater leverage against the superterrestrial gravity in which the Ryohoch's ancestral species must have evolved) and a shorter third one providing extra support underneath. Tarik recalled Stephen's "ball in a catcher's mitt" description of the Ryohoch head, which had struck him as very American. In fact, the "mitt" was a dense mass of fine tendrils forming a parabolic dish of sorts behind a "ball" with beady eyes and vertical respiratory slits adorning its front and sides. Though Yonchon's forward legs were somewhat prehensile, for fine manipulation the engineer relied on small neutral-buoyancy drones that could fly under mental control to where Yonchon needed them and return to rest on Yonchon's back when not in use, like birds perched on an elephant.

Arachne was still working on improving her translation of Ryohoch speech, which, among other difficult features, had no adjectives. Yonchon's people also found personal pronouns insulting.

Haim explained to Tarik. "The boss here means it's a Van Den Broeck warp metric — the outer warp bubble's pinched off to microscopic size. Wormholes have to be small too, otherwise the energy cost of keeping them stable's prohibitive, so you need to stick your ship into a portable hole small enough to fit through the mouth." Haim shook his head. "Although I still don't buy that the metrics can interact without collapsing each other."

"Design of one accommodates design of other," Yonchon said. "Antiquity of practice. Civilizations precede civilizations. Technology descends." Tarik blinked, reminding himself just how ancient Ryohoch civilization was.

Tarik turned back to his engineer friend. "And it's all thanks to this, what was it, programmable..."

"Programmable quark matter," Haim affirmed with a nod. "That's what Doctor Belghazi called it back home when she theorized the stuff—or at least something close enough to it that the name fits."

Tarik understood the analogy. Much as normal programmable matter could manipulate the quantum states of its confined electrons to simulate the chemical properties of any element, including those not found in nature, so PQM could manipulate quark states to simulate baryons and mesons with exotic physical properties, including the sort that allowed once-fanciful general relativity solutions like warp bubbles and wormholes to be achieved in practice.

"PQM is basically femtotech computronium," the engineer went on. "That is, matter with computational circuitry built into it at the nucleonic level. So it can do fly-by-wire corrections fast enough to counter the tensor instability dynamically. And the PQM also shields the ship inside against the Hawking radiation from the warp bubble. But both the radiation and the instability build up exponentially, and sooner or later they get ahead of any possible corrections. Plus you'd need to drop out periodically anyway, to dump your waste heat and purge any particles caught in the warp."

"Like insects on a windscreen."

The engineer chuckled. "Not so far off. A Chirrn drive can do nearly a parsec a pop in empty space—less if there's a dense interstellar medium, even less if there's a star or planet nearby. Any mass or energy increases the instability."

"How do they get wormhole mouths positioned dozens of parsecs apart without time dilation?" Tarik asked.

Haim shrugged. "Lots of small hops."

"But that means there's a wormhole metric… inside the warp metric. And if the warp ship passes *through* a wormhole en route…"

"Please, Tarik. I have enough of a headache already."

Yonchon had sent a pair of drones out to assist in loading a cargo module into a nearby warp cage, whose twin spheres had irised back into an equatorial ring surrounding the ship components within. Since each cage totally encased its ship while in use, generating the warp bubble right along its surface, the interior contents were modular and interchangeable as needed for a particular mission. This installation seemed to have reached a delicate phase demanding the Ryohoch engineer's full attention, so Tarik took the opportunity to drift closer to his old friend and speak softly. "It seems that Yonchon's sharing information with you pretty freely."

"I think so," the grizzled engineer replied. "I mean, look. Yonchon let us come here today."

"True," Tarik agreed. It was a rare opportunity to visit such an important part of Shilirrlal without needing to sneak around with R'nilinnath as Diana Thorne insisted on doing. Tarik shared the Vanguardian's eagerness to learn more of what the Chirrn hid from them, since one never knew what secrets might prove harmful to the crew (as Tarik still thought of them). Yet he was reluctant to take the kind of risks Diana did, and he took his oaths too seriously to bend them as far as she did. So he had welcomed this opportunity to gain knowledge more overtly.

"Still," he went on, "this is the first time you've actually been allowed to see the ships, isn't it?"

Silbermann tilted his head. "Yonchon thought I'd reached the point in my training where I needed to. I guess. Hard to know what's going on in that… hmm, honestly I don't know where Ryohoch keep their brains."

"So you don't feel you're being held back?"

"What do you mean?"

Tarik spoke softly. "I've heard complaints from some of the crew. Ravinder, Sita, others who feel we're being kept from asking certain questions. Larger questions about the galaxy."

"The galaxy?" Haim echoed with a frown.

"The Chirrn's place in the larger scheme of things. What lies beyond local space. What lies on the far end of those wormholes. Who built them, come to that."

"Well, I've been more concerned with the mechanics of it all. That demands pretty much all my attention right there." Haim studied him. "Where's this mistrust coming from, my friend? I thought you were fitting in rather well." He chuckled, looking the younger man over approvingly. "You certainly wear that Chirrn-style vest better than I ever could. Especially now all your chest hair's grown back in."

"Careful," Tarik said, grinning. "I appreciate the compliment, but I'm a married man now. A father-to-be."

"Well, impending fatherhood looks very good on you."

"It feels even better. To finally have a wife who shares my goals in life… and to have a son I know I will be there for."

His friend's grizzled head took on a skeptical tilt. "Except you still have divided loyalties, don't you?"

Tarik struck his palm with his fist. "I still can't get in to see the Unrenounced. I've asked time and again for permission to visit the captain, but they refuse. They assure me she and the others are in good health, but all I have is their word."

The older man nodded. "And you're wondering how much you can trust their word."

"Yes."

"Well, I haven't felt like they're hiding anything. I think Yonchon and Yonchon's staff have been pretty open about the theory and the engineering, at least up to the point I'm able to understand."

"As you said, we already had the theory. So they haven't opened any completely new doors for you."

"No, not yet. But there's still so much we have to learn. And that could be the work of a lifetime." He gestured to the warp cages outside the port. "And I'm gonna love getting to know these babies as much as you and Kweli will love getting to know yours."

Tarik turned back to contemplate the expanse of the shipyard and all the potentials it implied. What would it be like to take one of those ships on a jaunt around the galaxy with his wife and son by his side? If what Haim said about wormholes was right, even a small warp cage could take them practically anywhere. So many adventures awaiting, just a few hops away. It was frustrating to be kept from that, to be dependent on the Chirrn's judgments about when and how quickly knowledge should be dribbled out.

Seeing his frustration, Haim squeezed his shoulder. "Take it easy, my friend. Remember — we're still on parole. It's not about whether we can trust the Chirrn—it's about whether they can trust us. And we have to be on our best behavior to earn that trust."

The reminder was sobering. Still, Tarik had to wonder if Haim was being overly optimistic. "Given how our relationship began, it's hard to believe the Chirrn will ever completely forgive us."

Haim shrugged. "We used to think Jews, Muslims, and Christians would never forgive each other in the Middle East. Look what we have now. It just took a generation that got fed up with their parents' and grandparents' excuses for continuing the chaos, so they reached out to each other to end it. It took time, but it happened."

"It also happened because the most unrepentant militants and fanatics were exiled to the Belt and the Trojans. Which just made them the Striders' problem. We never truly ended the conflict, we just exported it.

"But what happens if the Chirrn never truly forgive us or accept us?" Tarik turned his gaze back to the array of starships beyond the window. "If we can't earn a place in their society… then where else can we possibly go?"

The dreams came to Cecilia again, as they had the past few nights. She was back with Stephen, Tarik, Kazuko, and the others, watching as they went about their daily lives, seemingly without a care. Many of them had paired off in couples—Stephen and Sita, Kweli and Tarik, Justine and Diana—and most of the women were just starting to show their pregnancies, with Kweli and Kazuko the furthest along. Sometimes they were working in the gardens of cozy dwellings stacked above each other in terraces, casually chatting with their neighbors. Sometimes they were meeting in bright, large-windowed offices to discuss community planning or medical updates on the progress of the women's pregnancies. Once they gathered together in a tree-lined square to listen to a song recital by Kweli and Andrea, with several Chirrn and a Zenith present in the audience. Once they were in a roomy auditorium playing an unfamiliar ball game that involved jumping and climbing on frames and lattices and making swooping, athletic kicks that seemed to emulate the sweep of a Chirrn tail.

Yet in all these scenes, Cecilia was only a watcher, never acknowledged or invited to participate. None of the other loyalists were present.

She was out of practice at this, but in time, she began to sense that these were no mere dreams.

The next morning at breakfast, Cecilia questioned the others about their own dreams. All of them described similar experiences, and the truth quickly dawned on them. "No," Shuai Bingbing moaned. "It's all real! Justine… she left me for Diana! That biǎozi! Gōng gòng qì chē!"

"We can't be sure of that," Cecilia cautioned her, wondering how much of Bingbing's anger was a cover for her lingering guilt at her own reluctant infidelity — or perhaps a gesture of liberation from it. "Just because they fed us all the same dreams doesn't mean they're real."

"Of course it's not real," James said. "They want to tempt us into losing our resolve, by showing us the others being happy and content. For all we know, they're even worse off than we are."

"If it's real, they *are* worse off," Diego replied. "Think of what we saw. Humans dressed in Chirrn clothes. Speaking their language. Playing their sports. They're surrendering their humanity more and more every day. Losing their human souls."

"Do they even remember us?" Bingbing wondered. "Do they even still care?"

Ichiba Nobuo had been sitting thoughtfully, reflecting. "They didn't seem soulless to me," he said. "They seemed content. Free to work, to create, to learn…"

"To have families," Sergei Mazunov put in softly, clasping Hannah Errgang's hand and trading a wistful look with her.

"No," Diego urged. "No, don't fall for it. Don't let the sirens' song lure us onto the rocks. We have to hold on to what we are."

"Can we do that," Hannah asked, "without children?"

The doubts Cecilia saw in so many of the loyalists over the course of the day filled her with alarm. None of the tricks and tactics their jailers had used over the months had undermined the group's unified resolve like this. The next time she was summoned to meet Churrlaya, she confronted him about it. "How dare you show us those scenes of the others when we were asleep, at our most vulnerable?"

The Frog Footman was unmoved by her anger. "We only took advantage of the dream communication you equipped yourselves to employ."

"Those dreams came from each other, and from a cyber we trusted. Invading our minds without consent is a violation! It's obscene!"

"It is unfamiliar to you because you have only learned to share thoughts to a limited extent. But all we did was allow you to witness your own crewmates' experiences. To see that they are safe and well. It was a more generous act than I believe you have earned, but I was overruled."

"Then why not just show us when we were awake? Why sneak it into our subconscious minds?"

"To allow you to feel its reality directly, beyond what mere images would convey. And to observe your reactions in their purest, most unfiltered form, in order to assess how deeply rooted your resistance to renunciation truly is."

"So you can brainwash us into losing that resistance! What's to stop you from reprogramming us outright? Plugging us into one of your consensus minds, changing our values and beliefs while we sleep?"

That got a rise out of Churrlaya. "Even if your brains had the neural architecture to permit it, that would be unconscionable," he insisted. "Forcing a new identity structure onto an unwilling subject is as traumatic as… as forcibly ripping away parts of their existing psyche. No *civilized* being would ever do such a thing."

His mention of his own trauma gave Cecilia pause, but she resisted showing it. "It's what you're doing to us bit by bit with every piece of our freedom and our dignity you strip away! Now you're even invading our very minds!"

Churrlaya hissed. "Why do you persist in seeing yourselves as the victims? How can you compare the moderate restrictions imposed on sixteen convicted felons to the permanent deaths of ninety thousand innocents?"

"What happened to them was an accident—and the result of your own bad choices. What you do to us is purposeful."

"And yet far less destructive in the absolute. It takes a special arrogance to see your suffering as greater."

Cecilia stepped closer, holding his gaze. "I don't. I recognize the magnitude of your loss. I hate that it happened, that it brought so much pain to all of us. I do not accept the blame for it, but if I could undo it somehow, I would. But all I *can* do is look out for the people who need me in the here and now."

"Does that not include the people we showed you in your dreams? Would their community not benefit from your presence? Would yours not benefit from reunion with them?"

"We absolutely would — if it were on *our* terms."

"That must be earned."

"By giving up what we are? Playacting as Chirrn, wearing your clothes?"

"Adding something new to your culture does not destroy it."

"It does when it's imposed. When there's a power imbalance. If you've studied Earth's history, you should know that."

A snort ruffled his snout cilia. "Earth's history is an undisciplined mess, with no healthy structure for cultural mediation and transition. That is why you have had so many wars and ethnic conflicts. It is hardly a model for civilized behavior."

Cecilia laughed. "'Civilized.' Honestly, Churrlaya, civilization is probably the greatest force of injustice in Earth history. Cities brought power hierarchies, concentration of wealth, the exploitation of the many for the good of the few. And that brought contempt for those deemed less 'civilized,' less worthy of consideration and rights. Being civilized is nothing to be proud of."

The ringlet-coiffed Chirrn tilted his head and studied her curiously. "Then why is it, Cecilia, that you take such pride in the city of your birth?"

She wouldn't let him trip her up that way. "Because it's *mine*. And nobody will ever take that away from me."

He held her gaze for a moment before answering. "That is what I used to believe. Yet here we are."

9

It all started so innocuously. Just another of Diana and R'nilinnath's secret excursions out of the compound. The two clandestine explorers had gotten away with it so often that others had begun going along with them on occasion.

And this time, Sita decided to join them. She'd grown tired of staying in the Arachnen compound, a prisoner of her own fear. She was a scientist, a xenobiologist in the midst of the xeno-est biology in human history, and she was wasting the opportunity because her instincts were overriding her intellect. Not to mention her growing concern that her fear would cost her Stephen. Oh yes, he was faithful, even more than she asked him to be. It didn't bother her—much—that so many of the unattached women kept coming on to Stephen, and she'd let him know he was allowed to respond. They'd all need to take multiple mates in the long term for the sake of genetic diversity; and besides, it was just the nature of a band of great apes like themselves for the females to gravitate around their alpha male. But Stephen, ever kind and generous, had so far declined to take advantage of the freedom she'd granted, insisting he was totally devoted to her and their baby. Still, Sita figured it was inevitable that he'd accept some of the other offers eventually, so the sensible thing to do was to define their relationship in a way that made allowances for it. That way, it wouldn't come down to a choice between her and someone else. She'd rather share him than lose him.

But she had become afraid that she would prove unworthy of keeping him. Stephen was so enthralled by the Chirrn, so excited to learn about their rich, ancient civilization and the broader galaxy they occupied, that she felt she could only keep growing apart from him so long as her fear paralyzed her. They'd maintained an uneasy peace since their big argument the week before (or rather, the one she'd tried unsuccessfully to get him to participate in), but things didn't seem to be getting any better. So Sita had realized it was time to make a choice. She had to decide once and for all whether to overcome her fear and stand by Stephen's side… or to step aside in favor of a worthier woman.

R'nilinnath's latest invitation had seemed to Sita like such a harmless first step. It was basically the equivalent of sneaking out to watch an adult movie. Or rather, a live sex show, for they would be attending a Chirrn "kiss dance" performance—as Arachne euphemistically translated it, since "oral sex dance" lacked the same elegance. Of course, intruding on the sexual customs of another culture could be a minefield, but R'nilinnath had assured her there would be no problem, and Sita's own studies and Kweli Ndege's backed that up. With their genitalia literally in their faces, Chirrn didn't exactly have the option of sexual modesty. And given how they metaphorically associated sex and speech, the two provinces of the tongue, a public sexual performance was considered effectively a form of public speaking: something that could be disquieting or annoying when performed extemporaneously in inappropriate contexts, but accepted and celebrated in the proper place and time. The kiss dance was apparently a popular form of entertainment, not some great secret they would be intruding upon— and it was too fascinating a scientific opportunity to pass up.

So it was that Sita now accompanied R'nilinnath, Diana, and Kweli ("What," the vivacious doctor had asked, "you think I'm gonna pass up a chance to watch alien porn?") in sneaking through the tunnels and back channels of Shilirrlal to reach the kiss dance venue. It was held at the hub, within the filligreed cylinder of shining strands that provided the habitat's light. Although the cylinder was nearly four hundred meters in radius and rotating with the rest of Shilirrlal, the air inside was somehow kept still (she'd heard Haim muttering something about a utility fog being involved) so that no Coriolis winds acted to push things outward, allowing everything within to hover in free fall. It was a popular center for recreation and exercise among the Shilirrlaln; Diana liked to call it "Coaxial Park." Many Seekers of the Zenith could also be found here at any given time; as their name for themselves suggested, the silvery avians were instinctively motivated to seek the high ground, their whole civilization being largely defined by the competition for physical and social altitude.

Sita was out of practice at freefall maneuvering, so she needed help from Diana and sometimes Nilly to move in the right direction through the vast open space as they dodged around the many Chirrn and Zenith engaged in various sports and performances, as well as the various free-floating structures that contained them — including a massive globular "swimming pool" held together purely by its own surface tension.

Sita was surprised when R'nilinnath led the three women right into the free-floating spherical lattice that was the arena for the dance, making no effort at concealment. "Won't they see us?" she asked.

"No harm if they do," Nilly told her. "It's been four *narrenn* since the trial. People have gotten used to seeing Arachnen around by now." Arachne no longer rendered Chirrn units into Earth equivalents, since by now the Arachnen should have memorized the new system and let go of their old planet-based measurements. But Sita still needed to remind herself that a *narrenn* was a Chirrn "month," just over five weeks.

"With Shilirrlaln supervisors," Diana countered. "Adult ones — no offense."

"No matter. If they see you here, they'll assume you're allowed. Just act like you belong. They'll have other things to watch anyway."

The dance was already in progress as they wended their way through the lattice to an open perch. The two performers, nude aside from mane jewelry, were joined open mouth to open mouth, their heads at right angles. Their mouths were adapted to fit together perfectly, their lips forming a watertight seal to contain the seminal fluid secreted from the male's tongue pores and absorbed through the female's. A Chirrn always had the same, essentially hermaphroditic anatomy throughout its life; only the hormonal expression and the size and activity of internal glands determined maleness or femaleness. Outwardly, a Chirrn's current sex was indicated by pheromonal cues no human could detect and by subtle differences in vocal timbre, body language, and dress that Sita was still learning to recognize. In modern times, with lives so long and procreation so rare, shifting sex was a voluntary, individual choice rather than part of a synchronized, group-wide cycle, but it was still a routine practice — something you did when you took a new lover and changed sex to match theirs, or simply when you felt like a change in your life, akin to getting a new job, or even just a makeover and a new wardrobe.

Sita wondered what sex or sexes the kiss dancers currently were, and if the spectators knew or cared. Their non-procreative relationships were usually same-sex by tradition, but there was no serious taboo against the alternative, and sex as performance could go either way —

although the show would be essentially the same for the spectators regardless of the performers' sexes. The pair wheeled slowly in freefall, held together only by their surprisingly strong labial seal and inter-locking side teeth while they performed elaborate, graceful motions with their arms, legs, and tails. Often they caressed one another or brought their bodies together into close embraces, only to swing apart again and rotate into a new joined position. Yet throughout it all, the seal between their mouths remained. Sita could only imagine what the subtle motions of their lips and jaws suggested about what their tongues were doing within. In its own way, the kiss dance was as private as it was explicit, the actual genital contact remaining unseen even though this was as overt as Chirrn sex could get. Sita found that rather wonderful.

"You guys are lucky," Kweli joked. "Get to first base and you've already made it home."

"Naw, that makes it too easy," Diana replied. "Where's the challenge?"

Nilly questioned the metaphor, and the conversation became a comic yet informative analysis of what constituted first, second, and third base among the Chirrn. It didn't help much that none of the women were American; while the metaphor had spread more globally than the sport it was derived from, they all had different understand-ings of what the "bases" meant in human intimate relations. But they finally decided that among the Chirrn, brushing the mane and neck with the muzzle was first base, brushing muzzles together was second, and caressing the body with lips and tongue was third. Entwining tails was like holding hands. "That's being at bat," Kweli declared.

"So, Nilly," Diana asked, "how many bases have you rounded with your boyfriend so far?"

R'nilinnath snorted and rolled her eyes in a way that somehow seemed closer to the human use of that gesture than the Chirrn. "Djayrulu is not my 'boyfriend.' He's just someone I've conducted some sexual experiments with. He let me get as far as 'third base' just once before I realized it wasn't as enjoyable as I'd hoped."

Diana pouted, disappointed that her effort to get her young friend shagged had stalled out. "Oh, it's not because he's a male, is it?"

"No, I actually somewhat enjoyed that part. It's a bit naughty." She hissed and waggled her tongue lewdly, and the women laughed. "But we weren't really connecting. I don't think he's as excited by novelty or difference as I am. He did make a sincere effort, really. He asked a lot of questions about my life, my work with the guild and the Arachnen. But he never seemed comfortable with it, or with me as a partner in sex play. So I broke it off. I guess I can wait a while longer to score a run to my home."

"Aw, that's a shame," Diana said, stroking R'nilinnath's mane. "Don't you have other options? Sex providers? Soligram porn?" She gestured toward the performers who were still writhing together in midair. "Dance classes?"

"Yes, of course. But that would feel like school, not play. I want to learn sex, but I want it to be for fun, with my friends. But most of my friends are human." Nilly looked Diana over. "I suppose I could take you up on that offer to experiment with interspecies sex. Your mouth is way too small to do it the normal way, but there must be some way to put our bodies together that feels good."

Sita could only listen in wonder and amusement as R'nilinnath, Diana, and Kweli began speculating about how Chirrn and human sexual anatomy could interact—clinically at first, but with increasing hilarity as they realized how absurd many of the proposed interactions would be. All three women were intrigued by what a Chirrn's tongue or tail tip could do for them, though some of their proposals for using both at once pushed the limits of the spinal flexibility that the kiss dancers were demonstrating. And Nilly could think of few ways that a human could pleasure a Chirrn in return, in the absence of any adequate counterpart for a Chirrn tongue. "I suppose a penis is close, but it's just so small and inanimate. Sucking one of my thumbs would be livelier." The women roared, grateful that their men weren't around to hear that. "Maybe a breast, if it were lactating. At least that's flexible." That made them whoop even louder.

It was all such harmless fun… until the women's laughter drew the attention of the crowd, many of whom did not react well. Sita had been so preoccupied by the actions of the performers that she'd failed to notice their coloration and build, or that of the majority of spectators.

They were Lesshchin.

The building anger of the Chirrn, their raised voices as they moved to surround her, triggered a flashback to terror and shock and agony. When Sita came back to reality, she found herself being pulled out of the arena at some speed, her wrist held gently but firmly in R'nilinnath's prehensile toes. Diana and Kweli were flanking her, watching the crowd. Protecting her in case they became violent.

And it had all been such harmless fun…

Djayrulu let the righteous outrage of the crowd surge through his mind, letting it amplify his own, which he then gladly fed back into the surge. How dare the murderers of Lesshchi come here to mock something beautiful and sacred? Could they not tolerate the idea of letting the survivors rebuild in peace? Must they continue to intrude on the life of the Chirrn and defile everything with their planetary filth?

What disgusted Djayrulu even more was the sight of R'nilinnath joining the humans in their mockery. He had known from their first meeting that she had been dirtied by her long association with the well-digging ferals, even seeking to emulate their reckless and corrupt sexuality by mating with the opposite sex for pleasure. Granted, he had felt an attraction to R'nilinnath, an excitement at meeting another Chirrn his own age and a prospective sex partner, but only at the potential she would have for eventually becoming male. He knew opposite-sex pleasure pairings had never been excluded among Chirrn in the past, but in the wake of Lesshchi's murder, Djayrulu could no longer see them as anything but human, anything but obscene. Any Chirrn who still practiced sex that way — let alone any Chirrn who eagerly invited a Lesshchin to partake in the obscenity — was committing an affront against the Lesshchin community, a betrayal of their grief and their anger.

Yet R'nilinnath's stupidity had granted Djayrulu a possible outlet for his rage, and now he was grateful for the foresight that had enabled him to seize it when it was offered. Pretending to play along with her sexual interest had given him access to the back channels R'nilinnath had used to circumvent the security on the Arachnen compound. The apprentice herself, supposedly one of the well-diggers' protectors, had led him right to their threshold, where he had been able to watch the filthy primitives as they had acted out the daily perversions that R'nilinnath found so entrancing. It had shocked him to see so many of their females gestating at once; at that rate of breeding, they would overrun Shilirrlal like vermin, ruining it more slowly, but just as thoroughly, as they had ruined Lesshchi.

At first, Djayrulu had lacked any specific plan for what to do with this access—only a recognition that it gave the Lesshchin an opportunity to exact the justice the Shilirrlaln mediators' guild had denied them. So he had contained his disgust and used the opportunity to watch and learn. He had pretended to enjoy his sex play with R'nilinnath (of course he hadn't *really* enjoyed it, he reassured himself), until she had sensed his aversion on some level and called it off. But he had learned enough, and then it was simply a matter of waiting for the right opportunity to take action.

Now, as he felt the fury of the kiss dance audience flow through him, a storm of anger and affront seeking a way to direct itself into action, Djayrulu knew his opportunity had come. Searching through the voices in his mind and ears for the ones calling most vehemently for direct and decisive action against the humans, he found them congregating around Vhehhal, a former guard aboard *Zhemhal*, the exploration craft that had hunted down and captured the human spacecraft following its assault on Lesshchi. Vhehhal had become something of a folk hero among those Lesshchin who refused to accept the Shilirrlaln's lenient verdict, for he had been the first to turn his people's righteous anger into direct action against the humans—more violent action than most Chirrn were comfortable with, perhaps, but surely a proportionate response to the unimaginable violence the well-diggers had inflicted on his home. Yet Captain Rillial had prevented him from solving the human problem then and there, and Vhehhal and his followers had been penalized and reassigned for their heroic action.

Ever since, Vhehhal had been quietly agitating in the more secluded channels of consensus—sharing his tale with those who believed he had been wronged for trying to do the right thing, making the case that all humans must be excluded from Chirrn society, and discussing possible ways to achieve that goal, legally or otherwise. Their discussions heretofore had been theoretical, but now Vhehhal was loudly rallying his followers, demanding immediate retaliation against the humans for their latest grievous assault on the Lesshchin community. Yet his rhetoric was disappointingly lacking in specifics. He and his followers were clear on what they wanted to do to the human childbearers, but without a means to circumvent the Shilirrlaln's protection of the Arachnen, there was little chance of turning their will into action.

It brought Djayrulu great satisfaction to be the one who could offer them a solution. "I know a way in to the Arachnen compound," he told Vhehhal once he made contact. "They think they can disrupt our precious speech with their own misbegotten words? Then let us echo their intrusion and silence every one of them."

Back in the safety of the Arachnen compound, L'chellin listened patiently as R'nilinnath and the women related their side of the story. Stephen and Diana sat with Sita, holding her hands, and Tarik Bahar did the same with Kweli. "They shouldn't have reacted that way," R'nilinnath insisted. "It was just a silly kiss dance."

L'chellin sighed through her nares. Her eyes swept across the humans as she chose her words. "I should have anticipated this. No Shilirrlaln has conceived a child in the three *narrayth* since you were born, R'nilinnath." Sita unthinkingly did the math, and smiled when she realized that Nilly wasn't so different from how she'd been at nineteen. "So your experience does not include the fact that kiss dances are not always recreational. The Lesshchin have lost so many. So they, like the Arachnen, have begun procreating." L'chellin's gaze took in the Arachnen as well as Nilly as she continued. "When actual procreation is involved, especially in a case like this, the dance becomes a solemn ritual, an affirmation of what human literature would call 'the Word made flesh.' The Lesshchin were in the process of restoring their diminished life. So when they felt that process was being mocked by some of the very ones who…"

"Who had taken it from them," Stephen finished.

"Yes."

R'nilinnath snorted in confusion. "I don't understand. The Arachnen completed their ordeal. They earned inclusion. Don't the Lesshchin know the rules?"

Nilly fell silent under a sharp glare from L'chellin. Tarik caught the exchange and focused his gaze on the mediator. "L'chellin? What is she talking about?"

L'chellin tapped her brow ridges several times, slowly. "You were supposed to deduce this on your own, as part of your transition," she said once her hands fell, one eye swiveling to glare at R'nilinnath. "To unlearn your human assumptions about the events of our contact and come to understand them from a Chirrn perspective. I only hope you are sufficiently included by now to understand."

The whitish-maned mediator proceeded to explain. A migratory people throughout their history, the Chirrn had always seen their identity and group affiliation as mutable, even before they had extended their minds into cyberspace. Most transitions were voluntary, and the system had been designed for millennia to accommodate them. But even so, it was not a simple matter to give up one consensus psychology and adopt a new one. The old psyche had to be deconstructed, its old affinities and habits of thought broken down, leaving it open to assimilate new ones. This bore added significance when the old identity was guilty of criminal acts. For the humans—the Arachnen—adoption into Chirrn society had been their required compensation for the lives they had inadvertently taken. That wasn't as callous as it sounded; lives were no mere commodity to the Chirrn, but as a society inclined by nature and tradition to dwell in modest-sized space habitats, they placed a premium on equilibrium. For anything that was taken, something must be given in return to preserve the delicate balance of existence. Those who took lives must pay by giving their own—ritually ending their old lives and adopting new lives dedicated to the community their old selves had wronged. The trial had not been a means of determining punishment, but the actual ordeal itself, the ritual by which the Arachnen had been cleansed of their sins, their old, tainted identity broken down so they could be prepared for their new, pristine identity as Shilirrlaln.

Stephen stared at L'chellin, looking betrayed. "You lied to us. Misrepresented the whole purpose of what you put us through."

"We tested you," L'chellin replied. "Please understand: it was always our intention to grant you adoption into our community once you had demonstrated true repentance. But your acceptance of your culpability and your commitment to making amends had to come from yourselves. You could not know the truth of the ordeal until you had transcended it through your own will and insight."

In the awkward silence that followed, Diana said, "I get it. Some of my mother's ancestors were Algonquians. Before the Europeans came and imposed their notion of 'tribes,' they were organized in bands and villages. Identity wasn't about lineage or ancestry, but only about where you lived, what community you identified with. Anyone could be adopted into any community." She flushed. "And not always by choice.

A band that lost members to disease or raids could raid a rival band to abduct replacements. And they'd be put through humiliating rituals, even torture, to break down their old sense of identity. But once they were adopted," Diana stressed, "even former mortal enemies were accepted freely as members of your own people. Sometimes they even took the names and identities of the dead they'd been abducted to replace."

"You do understand," L'chellin said. "Inclusion must be earned. Especially by those whose inclusion is repayment for lives they have taken."

"That's why you and Broadwing were involved in the trial," Sita went on. "Not lawyers or jurists, but mediators." They were the guild of Chirrn society responsible for negotiating between other guilds and estates, between habitats, between Chirrn and aliens. They managed the elaborate patterns of inclusion and exclusion that governed Chirrn psychology, derived from the interaction and competition of the small roving bands of their prehistoric ancestors. The modern Chirrn had modified it, civilized it, removed it from its origins in the planetary dirt, but the core of it remained.

"Yes. We oversaw your ordeal and adoption. Now we oversee your education, until you have matured enough to apply for membership in the guilds of your choice and contribute to society as fully integrated adults."

"But why didn't the Lesshchin see that?" R'nilinnath asked. "They saw the whole ordeal. They know the Arachnen passed."

"They passed the Shilirrlaln's test. But to many Lesshchin, the initial contact itself was the test."

Stephen lowered his head. "A test we failed."

"True. Many of the survivors, I fear, will never accept the Arachnen as their kith." Sita knew what that meant. They were Untouchables, to be shunned as totally as the overall Chirrn civilization shunned planet-dwellers.

R'nilinnath was deeply repentant, bending her knees so deeply that her elbows rested on the floor. "Sita... my failure has brought this suffering upon you."

Sita was touched. She reached down gingerly and patted Nilly's mane. "No, no, it wasn't your fault. You couldn't have known."

"But I could! I cleared it with Broadwing... I must have misunderstood his instructions about how to proceed."

"What?" Kweli asked. "I thought we were sneaking out."

Diana laughed loud and long. Untroubled by the others' scandalized glares, she controlled herself enough to say, "I knew it! Nilly, you and your 'secret' expeditions. You were working for the mediators the whole time!"

Chastened, R'nilinnath confirmed that the excursions had been authorized, a way of helping the Arachnen learn about their new world on their own terms, free of direct supervision, while still in a controlled enough way to keep them safe and within the limits of propriety. "But I should've realized there were still things *I* didn't know. And because I didn't, I offended the Lesshchin at the worst possible time. And I put you in danger, Sita. Now you'll never grant me inclusion!"

"No, Nilly, no." Moved by her sadness, Sita took the young Chirrn into her arms and held her for some time, assuring her that no harm had been done. For the first time, Sita felt no revulsion at being so close to a Chirrn. She was elated that she had finally conquered her fears.

That night, Sita was shocked awake by a loud crash and the familiar, terrifying sound of enraged Chirrn voices. This time, it was no nightmare. She was seized and pulled bodily from her bed, where she'd lain in Stephen's arms after an intense night of confident, newly energized lovemaking. The intruders knocked Stephen down with a shock stick before he could muster any resistance.

Bound hand and foot and dragged into the artificial night of the Arachnen compound, Sita saw dozens of Lesshchin, recognizable from their greenish hues and loose manes, dragging the other women from their homes as well. Some women were putting up good fights, particularly Diana, who unleashed all her Vanguardian strength in defense of her neighbors, single-handedly felling three of the Lesshchin until she was struck down from behind by vicious tail-swipes from two others. Sita could hear the crack of bone even from a distance.

As the assailants dragged all the bound women to the public square, Sita wondered where Arachne was. The Lesshchin must have found some way to shut down her avatar, just as they'd shut down the security drones and utility fog clouds that should have protected the community. Soon, all twenty women plus Rosario were in the square, and all eleven men, their arms and legs bound, were carried to the edges of the park and dropped there, facing the women, futilely screaming their names. Sita locked eyes with Stephen, feeling an incongruous need to comfort him with her gaze, to reassure him that this was not his fault.

The attackers gathered under the lights of the square, looming over the women, and Sita realized she recognized some of them. Their leader was Vhehhal, the azure-skinned, golden-maned guard who had nearly beaten her to death aboard *Zhemhal*. That did not surprise her or add much to her existing level of terror, since his was the face she still saw in nightmares like this. One or two were survivors who had testified at the trial. One had the mottled skin of a youth and a vivid pink mane — it could only be Djayrulu, the boy R'nilinnath had courted. Sita realized that must be how the Lesshchin had gained entry. Yet she felt no anger toward Nilly — only toward the Lesshchin youth for exploiting her innocence.

Vhehhal paced before the other Lesshchin and made a speech, but Sita's translation software wasn't activating and she hadn't studied the Lesshamh dialect. As far as she could tell, it was something about how those who had taken Chirrn lives had no right to fill the void with new, outsider lives.

Oh, Krishna… save my baby…

Maybe Krishna heard her, for Broadwing let out a mighty polyphonic shriek and soared into view overhead with silver wings spread wide, a resplendent sight even in the darkness. He had launched himself from his rooftop office in the administration complex. The Zenith mediator could only glide so far in this gravity and air density, but it was enough to paralyze the Lesshchin with fear. That was a justified response, for the Zenith were raptors.

Broadwing folded his wings and stooped on the Lesshchin who stood over the women, sending them scattering for safety. Vhehhal and Djayrulu both got away, but razor-sharp claws slashed the flesh of others who were too slow to retreat.

But Broadwing was outnumbered, and all too soon he sank low enough for the Lesshchin to snarl him in a utility-fog cloud that they sprayed around him, its spiderweb strands binding his wings and sending him tumbling down to the terraces below.

After that, there was no rescue. The Lesshchin closed in around her and the other women, ignoring the pleas in English and Portuguese and Chinese and Hindi and other languages they didn't want to understand. To the Chirrn, words were children of the mind, precious gifts yet grave responsibilities. But to the Lesshchin, the humans' words were bastards, as unworthy of inclusion in their minds as the humans were of inclusion in their world. The attackers allowed the women's words to die, unheard, unsustained.

And then they began to do the same to their other offspring.

Afterward, in the hospital, Sita wished this beating had been like the last. She wished that Vhehhal and the others had once again broken her arms, her legs, her skull. She wished they had simply killed her again. That would have been kinder than this. Instead, their kicks had been aimed entirely at one place. She had tried to curl up, to shield her womb with her limbs, but they had forced her body straight and then they had kicked and she could only weep and scream for her baby, for Stephen's baby…

For all the babies.

The Shilirrlaln police had arrived in force moments later, the security systems coming back online and restraining the Lesshchin en masse. Sita had prayed they were in time to save the others' fetuses. But she had felt no joy, no relief. Because she knew. She had felt the kicks crushing her insides. She had known nothing could survive that.

The doctors were able to save all but four of the sixteen pregnancies. Kweli Ndege, Justine Nguyen, and Oyama Kazuko had lost theirs as well as Sita. Justine's had been a frozen embryo, so only Stephen, Tarik, and Ravinder had to share their grief.

But Sita could take no comfort in that. As she lay in her hospital bed with Stephen weeping by her side, she wondered if she'd ever feel happy — or safe — again.

And she wondered if she would lose him now. If he would blame her for triggering the attack. She knew it was irrational, but she would understand if he blamed her.

After all, she blamed herself.

10

"It is the judgment of this tribunal," head tribune Dj'vhereth announced to the attackers who stood before him, "that you shall hereby be summarily excluded from all estates, leagues, and guilds, whether Lesshchin or Shilirrlaln, effective immediately. Your current mental states are toxic to the community and to yourselves, and thus you must be quarantined from consensus until such time as you regain the ability to function as constructive members of society. To that end, the tribunal instructs that you be remanded to the remedial crèche on the Vhethil habitat, where you shall receive psychological therapy and re-education until you are ready to assume adult identities and allegiances once more."

R'nilinnath was gratified that the verdict had been reached so quickly, without the need for a lengthy trial that would force the grieving Arachnen to relive the horrifying trauma they had endured. The Lesshchin attackers, Djayrulu included, had made no attempt to deny their action; indeed, they had boasted of it proudly as an act of justice, even recorded their firsthand experiences of the assault for later upload to the Lesshchin consensus. With no dispute over the facts of the case, no trial had been necessary, only the determination of how to deal with the criminals.

She drummed her feet in vindictive satisfaction as she watched Djayrulu's reaction to his fate being sealed—along with the rest of the fetus-killing mob that he had led into the Arachnen compound thanks to R'nilinnath's inability to keep her tongue in her mouth. It would be a long time before she stopped blaming herself for that; someone had to, since everyone else was so determined to reassure her and pretend it wasn't her fault. But she knew she would atone in time by continuing to fulfill her responsibilities to the Arachnen—just doing it better from now on.

And she did agree with Sita, L'chellin, and the others that the greater part of the blame lay with Djayrulu for using and manipulating her. That was why this verdict was so satisfying to hear. Djayrulu had latched onto the humans' different sexuality as the excuse for his hatred, the perceived affront against Lesshchin procreation as the excuse for his assault on human procreation. Now, sentenced to a remedial crèche in a habitat parsecs from Shilirrlal, he would be reset into an asexual juvenile, losing his maleness before he'd even had a chance to do much of anything with it. It was a case of what her Arachnen friends would call "poetic justice."

Still, just watching the verdict handed down was not enough. She needed to confront Djayrulu eye to eye. Fortunately, her status as a mediator for the wronged parties enabled her to request a private meeting with the Lesshchin youth before he was taken away to Vhethil.

"How could you do it?" she asked the pink-maned male once they were alone in a conference room. "How could you kill babies?"

Djayrulu glared at her sullenly. "They weren't even people yet. Just clumps of cells."

"It was for their mothers to decide when they were people. Not you. Their mothers wanted them, loved them for the people they would become. You had no right to take that away from them."

"And they had no right to take my friends, my guildmates, my home away from me!"

"They didn't do that on purpose! You did! You *chose* to become a murderer!" She opened her mouth and gave a loud, aggressive hiss. "You call them savages, but you're much worse than they are. At least they have the excuse of being feral." She snorted. "Maybe the Unrenounced are right and we're no better after all."

"The humans made us this way! They tore away pieces of us, left us broken and scarred. Whatever we did to them, they brought it on themselves. They deserved it! No matter how much of my Lesshchin voice they strip away, no matter how much they rebuild my identity, I will strive to cling to that certainty. I will never let it change."

R'nilinnath's gaze rolled outward, away from his smug face. Her anger faded, replaced only by sadness and pity as she realized how immature he truly was. All things changed. A Chirrn who did not grow and evolve from lifetime to lifetime might as well not be alive. Djayrulu was too young to understand that. R'nilinnath should have been too, but shepherding the Arachnen through their transition had taught her the lesson early. She hoped that the experts at Vhethil could help him learn it as well—that he would not become as stagnant and trapped as the Unrenounced.

She gave a slow, wistful sigh through her nares. "I used to find tales of violence and death so thrilling. The excitement of the taboo. Now I know how horrible they really are. I owe that to you, and I'm glad you'll be punished for it."

Djayrulu turned away. "Go wallow in the dirt with your disgusting human friends. Maybe you'll find a way to have sex with them after all. I can't see any true Chirrn ever wanting you."

With a frustrated hiss, R'nilinnath turned to go. But she paused in the doorway. "A bit of advice: When they let you be an adult again, go female. Maybe if you learn what it's like to be different things, you won't be so afraid of difference anymore."

The Lesshchin youth was puzzled. "But... changing sex is what Chirrn are supposed to do."

"Yes. That's exactly what I mean."

Stephen was still numb when he met with the mediators and Shilirrlaln officials half a *narruvh* after the attack. Two nights had passed in the Arachnen compound in that time, but Stephen had gotten no sleep, afraid of further attacks, afraid of his dreams. He wasn't sure if he was numb now because he'd run out of grief and rage or because he'd simply shut his emotions down, unable to bear them anymore.

He surveyed the scene clinically, as well as he could through his haze of fatigue. The meeting was held in the conference room of the Arachnen compound's administration center, for the Shilirrlaln government had doubts about the humans' safety if they were allowed out. The windows, normally looking out upon the recreation center and residential terraces below, had been opaqued to spare the occupants from the visual reminder of the attack site. Within the room was a low, clear-surfaced table flanked by perches for Chirrn and seats for humans. Broadwing had his own V-shaped perch on which he rested his ventral keel. L'chellin was there as well; the mediators flanked Stephen, perhaps feeling they were protecting him. Beyond them were two Shilirrlaln officials, Ch'millin and Mh'resshelel, who were hard to tell apart; one was stocky and deep purple, the other rounder and midnight blue, but both had similarly coiffed white manes, perhaps a symbol of their position. Stephen wasn't completely certain which was which.

On the opposite side of the table sat Rillial. It was the first time Stephen had seen the Lesshchin representative since the trial. Rillial had become a leading voice in the adopted Lesshchin community, due to her past roles as a starship captain and the prosecutor in the humans' trial/ordeal. Apparently, spaceship command crews were a collegium of the Mediators' guild, necessarily since they must deal with outsiders, which was why Rillial had played the key role for the Lesshchin in the trial. Now, she spoke for her people in this instance as well. (And she was still a she. According to Broadwing, she was now pregnant, though with no outward sign Stephen could detect. She had participated in an earlier kiss dance a *narrenn* before, and her embryo was developing quite well. Distantly, with cold detachment, Stephen hated her for it.)

"The guilty parties have been summarily excluded from society," Rillial reported to the white-manes, her eyes rolling to take in every sight but that of the human opposite her. "They have been remanded to the remedial crèche on Vhethil, and will undergo psychological examination and evaluation to determine the best course of treatment."

"Treatment?" Stephen asked. "Then you propose this atrocity was the result of mental illness?"

Rillial's eyes finally came to focus on him. Her posture remained nonconfrontational, even apologetic. "You humans speak of 'losing one's mind.' These Lesshchin actually did lose portions of their minds in the cataclysm — instantly, traumatically, with no transitional process. They are indeed mentally damaged.

"Even beyond that, the circumstances my people face are… extraordinary. We are an orderly species. We have a clear sense of propriety. But deprive us of order, of balance, of consensus… place us in a situation that robs us of every anchor we rely on… and definitions of propriety can become… aberrant."

"Propriety." Stephen spoke slowly, his throat tight. "You suggest that this act of infanticide can somehow be defined as… proper."

Rillial fidgeted. "No one here disputes the immorality of what was done to your offspring. But we are not a feral race. We—" Under the sharp glares from the administrators, Rillial clamped down on herself. After a moment, she started again. "My people's—the assailants' actions were not an act of unthinking rage like the initial assault. In its own way, this was a calculated choice, one that the assailants were able to rationalize as a necessary one. In the minds of many Lesshchin, the crew of *Arachne* earned automatic and irrevocable exclusion by destroying our habitat, killing our kith and our shared mentalities. To them, allowing the humans inclusion in Chirrn society is a gross impropriety. Allowing them to procreate is an even greater one. They saw this as an injustice that the authorities refused to address. And so they deemed it necessary to address it themselves."

"By murdering defenseless babies."

Rillial sighed slowly through her nares. "In their calculations, it was not murder. Most of your gestating embryos have not yet developed significant brain activity. By your own laws, termination is still a permissible option before that benchmark."

"Not by force. Not by beating them in the belly."

"Naturally not. I merely attempt to account for their rationalization."

Stephen stared hard at her. "Six decades ago, on Earth, my little brother was shot down in the street by people who did not believe he had the right to have been born. The authorities had no shortage of rationalizations for that act."

L'chellin leaned toward him. "It was not the authorities who attacked you."

"Not this time," he said, still keeping his gaze on Rillial. "I really want to believe you intend to treat us justly, L'chellin, but you have to prove it through your actions, not just your words."

"Then let me suggest an action," Rillial said. Her eyes rolled outward to focus independently on the administrators flanking her. "It may take a lifetime or more for many of the Lesshchin to heal from this trauma. All of the assailants lost nearly their entire kith groups. All have lost portions of who they were before, whether through consensus-memory loss or organic brain damage. And there are many more who have endured as much." Her eyes rolled back to Stephen. "You may not be aware… since Shilirrlal is the closest habitat to Lesshchi, the worst cases were relocated here, while most of the rest migrated to more distant habitats such as Vhethil. No other population of relocated Lesshchin has suffered worse trauma and psychological damage than those here."

Again she took in the whole room. "So I cannot guarantee that there will be no more incidents like this. I do not believe it will ever be possible for Lesshchin and Arachnen to interact peacefully as equal members of Shilirrlaln society."

"Segregation?" Stephen asked. "That's never worked that well in human history."

"But quarantine has. Both our peoples have much healing to do before we can attempt to interact in a healthy way."

He realized he could not refute Rillial's point. At the moment, he never wanted to see a Lesshchin again. "Then do you propose that we leave, or you do?"

"Is either even feasible?" L'chellin asked, tilting her head quizzically.

Ch'millin (or was it Mh'resshelel?) leaned forward. "Too many Lesshchin have come too far in their transitions already. Psychological factors aside, they have already become increasingly integrated into Shilirrlaln guilds and sectors."

"But the Arachnen are still under the probationary custody of the Mediators' guild," L'chellin countered. "We are responsible for their care and socialization. We cannot simply abrogate that duty, and it would disrupt the process of inclusion if the Arachnen were forced to start again under another guild's care."

"There is a way to surmount this." Broadwing raised his head on its long, flexible neck, calling for the floor by gaining height over the others. "Given that Shilirrlal's population has abruptly increased by more than an eighth, some groups have put forth the possibility of a migration to ease the pressure. I propose that the guild spearhead such a migration, accompanied by the Arachnen."

"Migration?" Stephen asked.

"To found a new habitat," Broadwing explained. "If Chirrn habitats grow too crowded, they may build a second habitat that splits from the first, as Lesshchi did from Shilirrlal three yanarredj ago. But such branched communities remain close for yanarr as they slowly drift apart. Sometimes, this is not enough to satisfy the Chirrn's desire for change or separation. Their ancient instinct is for a splinter group to travel far from its birth community and start fresh in a new territory. With superluminal travel, they are able to do this. Periodically they will split off smaller groups that migrate elsewhere in the galaxy to found new habitats. It is a valve for population pressures, or a result of social schisms. In this instance, both parameters would apply."

"I think that having the Arachnen join a migration is a well-born proposal," the midnight-blue administrator said. "It would allow them to repay their debt directly by contributing to the construction of a new habitat."

"As a balance for their role in destroying one," the purple one agreed.

"Let us not deliver our words prematurely," L'chellin cautioned. "Do not forget that the Arachnen are the wronged party now. They should not be made to feel like exiles in response to a crime of which they were the victims."

"But this is not a punishment," Broadwing said. "It is protection. More, it is an opportunity!" Broadwing began to shake his head subtly, enough to make his diffraction-grating crests shimmer with colors—a Zenith gesture for drawing attention or asserting dominance. Rainbow reflections danced across the opaqued windows. "Stephen, you formed your expedition to establish a colony on a new planet. I know that many of your kith have felt frustrated at being unable to fulfill this purpose. So now I offer the opportunity to establish a whole new world! You would not only be fulfilling your debt to Chirrn society; you would be fulfilling your own ambition as well! What leader could resist?"

Stephen closed his eyes, letting the Zenith mediator's enthusiasm wash over him until the words trailed off. After a silence, he spoke. "There's no need to convince me, L'chellin, I appreciate your defense. You've been a good friend to the Arachnen. But it's not necessary. After… what happened here… I think we would all be glad to leave this place forever. I will need to discuss it with the others, though."

"Of course," L'chellin said.

"One other thing. The Unrenounced should come too." The others were silent, surprised. "Rillial said it herself—she can't guarantee their safety so long as they're on the same habitat with Lesshchin. And they deserve the opportunity to complete their ordeal and join the rest of the Arachnen. Surely it's not your intention to leave them confined forever."

"Indeed not," Purple assured him. "Mh'resshelel?"

"Indeed not," Midnight Blue affirmed. "However, ensuring security during the migration would be challenging."

"Bullshit." The others stared at the untranslated term, though L'chellin's tail quivered a bit in mild amusement. "You've had us easily at your mercy from the beginning. Except for the initial incident, my people have always been on the receiving end, helpless to resist." He sighed, gathering himself. "Apologies. I don't... blame the Shilirrlaln for what happened. I... don't blame most of the Lesshchin either," he added, though he couldn't meet Rillial's eyes. "But it would be dishonest to pretend my people are anything but powerless next to yours. There's no chance the Unrenounced could pose a security risk." To be perfectly honest with himself, he couldn't even blame the assailants. Rillial was right; they would never have been driven to this act if Stephen himself hadn't brought *Arachne* out here. If he'd never brought Sita into space, never put her in this situation, then she wouldn't be huddled in their home right now, grieving for their daughter, too terrified to walk out the door.

"My reference," Mh'resshelel said pointedly, "was to the risk of renounced Arachnen communicating with the Unrenounced. And perhaps allowing certain ill-conceived words to be spoken to them."

"Giving away the truth about the ordeal, you mean. Invalidating their own repentance."

"Yes."

"All this time and you still don't trust us."

"Stephen," Rillial said, catching his gaze and holding it. "After what occurred this *narruvh*... I can no longer fully trust my own kith. We are all capable of abandoning civilized rules in extreme circumstances. We are all capable... of tragic error.

"You should join the migration, and the Unrenounced should join you." Rillial's breath ruffled her nares. "I had contemplated migrating myself, but now I know I will not. I cannot leave my people, and they need stability now. As for you..." She was silent for a moment. "The Chirrn have always understood the value of starting a new life, letting go of the past. This is your chance to do the same. Not as passive beings assimilated into a vaster, overpowering society... but as founders of a new civilization, one whose form you may help to define."

Stephen contemplated her words for a long moment. To put his past behind him... to start anew and try to forget... he wanted nothing more. But how could he trust himself to make the right choice for everyone else?

He missed Cecilia more than he had in months. He would give much to have her strength and clarity to draw on again. But he feared she would only say that she'd warned him of something like this. Then again, maybe he should have listened to her all along. Maybe if they'd listened to each other, they could have found a better option at the beginning.

As it was, though, circumstances seemed to be making the choice for him. Stephen could see no alternative but to trust the Chirrn. He had felt betrayed at first by the revelation of the secrets they had kept during the ordeal, but he'd come to understand the cultural reasons behind them and to recognize that the ultimate intent was constructive. And L'chellin had done right by him these past four *narrenn*. Now even Rillial seemed to be offering him new hope. For the second time, the Chirrn were showing him more mercy than he deserved.

"Where would we be going?" he finally asked.

"To a new life," L'chellin said. "Far away from your past. Beyond that, does it really matter where?"

After Stephen left to bring the proposal to his kith, Mh'resshelel turned to Broadwing. "Do you suggest a migration to the Antispinward Void, as has been mooted in the cloud?"

"Yes," the Zenith replied. "The Alliance needs a stronger presence there."

"Agreed," Ch'millin said. "But is it wise to send the Arachnen to a frontier zone? A migration party there will be far less able to ward off… outside interest… than we are here. If the humans are included in that migration, it will make it far more difficult to regulate their access to… certain historical information. We are still unsure how they might react to that information. Despite their renunciation, they still have sentimental ties to Earth. If they should learn the whole truth…"

"They will no doubt spy that truth once they gain sufficient height in society," Broadwing countered. "If they do not gain that perspective from outside parties, then they will from our own historical records. I say it is better to relocate them much farther from Earth, to reduce the chances of any form of contact with their larger population. In the interim, we can direct their learning process, shape how they interpret the information we cannot avoid having them discover."

L'chellin's tail twitched angrily. "I must point out," she said, "that the Arachnen have made their transition in good faith. They have renounced their planetary ties. They are our kith now. Is it right to hide the truths of history from our kith?"

"They are still young," Mh'resshelel said. "The young can be impetuous, unwise. And as Captain Rillial pointed out, even the best of us can behave unpredictably in extreme times such as these."

"Indeed," Ch'millin added, supporting his mate as always. "At least, we should let the event come in its own time and not deliberately hasten its gestation."

"Agreed," Mh'resshelel predictably affirmed.

L'chellin found it a fair conclusion in principle. Still, she had her doubts. The Lesshchin's actions had undermined the trust that L'chellin had worked carefully to build in the Arachnen. Without that trust, Stephen and his kith might have trouble understanding or accepting certain historical truths. If they perceived those truths as secrets the Chirrn had deliberately concealed, it could trigger a backlash, a reassertion of their Earthly identity.

L'chellin would just have to do what she could to prepare them. Maybe creating a new world would sufficiently diminish their loyalty to their old one. Or maybe, once they learned enough of galactic history, they would understand why the Chirrn's ancient choice had been necessary—regardless of its consequences to humanity.

11

Churrlaya had been afraid to approach R'hhenevh with his request, for he knew how it would wrench at his womb to see her look at him with disappointment, with betrayal. He could only hope to get through it as quickly as possible and try to make her understand. Still, the alpha's reaction was just as painful as he'd feared. "You would leave us, Churrlaya? You would leave me?"

"My alpha." He placed his hands upon hers. "I only hope you can smell how much I long to stay with you. I would not ask this if it were not something I profoundly needed."

She did not reject his touch, but did not reciprocate it either. "To continue overseeing the Unrenounced? To continue seeking retribution? You would do this after what happened? Do you think they would allow a Lesshchin to join the Arachnen now?"

His eyes reflexively jerked away. He forced them back inward to meet hers. "It is because of what happened that I must do this. It made me listen to what I had done before… and made me ashamed. I allowed Cecilia… I allowed the humans to provoke me into descending to their level. Just as they provoked… the others."

Churrlaya turned aside, paced across the room in small hops. "I thought we were so far beyond the ferals. That we had transcended our animal drives and could never sink to savagery."

"The ones who assaulted the Arachnen did not think it was savagery. Their actions were calculated."

"That is exactly what distresses me. That Chirrn could think themselves civilized and responsible, yet still prove no better than a ground-dweller… a feral…"

"They were damaged, incomplete."

"So am I!" He gave a low, bitter snuffle, shaking his head. The ringlets of his mane brushed across his shoulders. "We cannot allow this of ourselves. We cannot let ourselves be dragged down by these humans."

R'hhenevh hopped forward, placing her hands on his forearms. "Then you should not go with them. Do not let them continue to entrap you. Not while you remain incomplete and vulnerable."

"No, Nevh. That cannot be the solution. I cannot conquer this by retreating from it! The hate, the violence — the potential is in *me*. Here in my own skull," he added, tapping his head. "I cannot resolve it simply by merging with your consensus. I would contaminate it with my own weakness.

"No, I must face them — just my own inner self, alone. I must prove to them — and to myself — that no matter how they provoke me, I will remain proper and dutiful, and I will not succumb to animal aggression. I must show them, Nevh. The actions of... the excluded ones... will make it too easy for them to believe that we are beasts after all, that they need have no shame at killing us. I must show them we are better than that. I must show them what the Lesshchin truly are, in our innermost selves, and what we are not." He moved closer, placing his hands on her knees. "Please, Nevh. It is the only way I can find balance."

R'hhenevh pondered for a time, then sighed and rubbed her neck against his. "It will not be easy to convince them to let a Lesshchin retain power over the humans."

His left eye swiveled to gaze closely into hers as they rubbed necks. "I *was* a Lesshchin. Maybe I still am. But now I am your kith. You are my alpha. And my duty is to you. I swear I will not give you any reason for shame."

"Oh, but I will miss you, Laya! If only I were not alpha and could come with you."

He cherished the fantasy, but he said, "No. You have too many other kith to love. You have your duties too."

With a long, shaky tongue-hiss, R'hhenevh pulled his head down by the ridges and ground her muzzle against his. He inhaled her scent as deeply as he could, hoping he could hold it within him forever.

"Come," she said, pulling him aside to a quiet corner and giving a seductive yawn. "Let us speak sweet words before we part."

The sight of *Arachne*'s habitat and cargo modules being maneuvered inside the outer ring of a Chirrn space vessel gave Stephen an uneasy sense of *déjà vu*. Of course, it was different this time; Stephen was not inside a module but watching from the shipyard observation gallery, and the ring was actually a warp cage in retracted configuration. The modules were being connected with pressurized tubes for easy passage between them, making the whole thing look something like a gerbil habitat.

This particular design of warp cage was not equipped with AG generation as a standard feature, for it was a small, relatively low-powered cage designed for short intrasystem hops (though still requiring substantial Hawking radiation from the artificial microsingularity that powered it). The Chirrn had little use for intrasystem travel as a rule, but they sometimes used this design for conducting mining and research expeditions to the star systems or rogue planets that their habitats occasionally drifted past. "The lack of gravity should not be a concern," L'chellin explained to the watching Arachnen, "for the trip should take slightly less than two *narruvh*."

"So eight, nine days?" Diana Thorne interpreted. The statuesque engineer was here to assist in the reinstallation of Arachne's brain inside her erstwhile body, a procedure that several other Arachnen were here to observe along with L'chellin, Broadwing, and R'nilinnath. "About how far will we be traveling in that time?"

"Initially, less than two hundred parsecs. Before we can build the new habitat, we will need to obtain a supply of programmable quark matter."

Diana shook her bronze-haired head. "Playing around with degenerate matter. I still don't trust that stuff. If anything goes wrong and it breaks free of containment, it could tear through anything."

"Galactic civilization has used PQM safely for many millennia, Diana."

"But there is a nonzero risk of failure."

The mediator gave Diana what Haim called her "Jewish mother" look. "And travel aboard *Arachne* in her sailship form carried a nonzero risk of collision or lethal irradiation. Nonzero risks can still be manageable risks."

"And we all know how well that kind of thinking turns out," Stephen said. The bitterness of his tone put a damper on the conversation.

There had been a time when Stephen would have never made such a conversational *faux pas*. He had always chosen his words so carefully, used them so deftly to befriend, to appeal, to inspire, to persuade, to reassure, to romance. The key had been to empathize with others, to understand their needs and outlooks, then tailor his words to fit. But these days, he lacked the strength to face his own emotions, let alone take on the burdens of others.

And he knew he was letting Sita down. Just when she had been mastering her fear and beginning to live her life again, she had been the victim of yet another Lesshchin assault, one that had taken the life within her. He wasn't sure whether she was more unwilling to face the Chirrn or herself at this point; she seemed to have equal blame and anger for both. Her prayers and meditations brought her no comfort. Stephen wanted to find that perfect thing to say that would reach through the new walls she'd built around herself and let him connect with her. But he had no idea how to begin.

It wasn't just that he lacked the words within himself. He'd come to realize that, although he loved Sita Bhatiani ardently, he didn't really know her very well. Their love was based on a shared dream, one of which he remembered nothing but emotion and vivid erotic sensation. Their time together had been defined by passion, as they'd done their best to recreate the intensity of those dream experiences, and by awkward distance, as he urged her to join him in embracing Shilirrlal and she urged him to spend more time in the compound with her. The passion had remained strong, but the awkwardness had been increasing over time. He had striven to commit to her more fully, refusing the advances of other women, but she had reacted to it as misguided symbolism, a sidebar to the deeper commitment that she truly sought and he could not give her.

So now, in their time of mutual need, he had too little insight into what Sita needed now. She had retreated more and more within herself, and all that his attempts at comfort had evoked was the request to be left by herself. Never permanently; she still shared his table and his bed, had fierce, wordless sex with him as a mutual distraction, and sometimes wept on his shoulder through the night. But if he tried to talk to her about her grief, about their relationship, about anything substantial and emotional, she pulled away. So he had learned to stop trying, closing himself off just as much.

Trapped in a cage, he thought, staring out the gallery window at his transformed ship. *Sita and I are in nested cages, bound together but held apart.* The hell of it was, at the moment, he was comfortable with that. There was less chance of either of them being hurt still more… even if the tradeoff was that they were slower to heal.

One of Yonchon's drones fluttered back from an errand and settled in its perch on Yonchon's back. After a moment to process the report it beamed into Yonchon's receptor cilia, the Ryohoch spoke. "Preparations have been completed for the brain."

Haim nodded to Diana, who carefully took hold of the shoebox-sized unit that held Arachne's consciousness—along with the shielding, cooling systems, energy collectors, backup memory, and diagnostic and repair interfaces for the centimeters-wide wisp of optical tendrils and Bose-Einstein condensate that housed the thoughts, dreams, and desires of the expedition's youngest but wisest member. "Don't worry, honey," Diana whispered to the unit, cradling it like a child in her muscular arms. "I'll take good care of you." Stephen quashed the uncharitable wish that Diana could have been as diligent in protecting his own baby. He knew she'd only recently regained her full mobility after the injuries she'd sustained while attempting to do just that, so his resentment was undeserved. But that didn't change the fact that she'd failed.

"Come on, Stephen, let's get out there," the chief engineer said.

Stephen stared out the window. "You go on, Haim. I'd just be in the way."

"What?" Haim floated over and touched his shoulder, turning Stephen to face him. "Stephen, you have to be there. You were there when we first put her in. When we christened her. Even when the Chirrn took her out and put her in the compound."

"Nothing but symbolic gestures."

"Well, that's the point! This is a big moment. *Arachne's* going to be whole again, and better than ever. You *have* to be there!"

After a moment, Stephen sighed. "All right. Lead the way."

Haim was displeased at his lack of enthusiasm, but took what he could get. As he and Diana glided out, though, L'chellin intercepted Stephen and said, "May I share words with you?"

Stephen quirked a brow. "That's a flattering invitation, Chell, but I don't think they've sorted out the logistics yet."

"Do not deflect. It confuses me when you use humor at times when you are clearly not amused."

Stephen almost replied, *If you thought that was funny, no wonder you're confused.* But his friend's stern gaze stopped him. L'chellin's sex change may have mellowed her, but she was still the stern, fastidious Chirrn he remembered from the Arachnen's ordeal. Why the Chirrn thought that quality made her a good cross-cultural mediator was one of the enduring mysteries of their psychology. On the other hand, it seemed to work for L'chellin. Stephen had come to value her frank, no-nonsense attitude, just as he had once valued Cecilia's more rough-hewn, big-sister version of same. So Stephen just spread his hands receptively and waited for her to continue.

"I appreciate the depth of your grief, my friend," L'chellin told him. "A child is a rare and precious thing to a Chirrn. I once thought, given how often you procreate, that humans would take them for granted. But in you, in Sita, in the others, I see that any words to that effect would be stillborn." She flicked her eyes away and back at Stephen's wince. "Forgive my choice of words. The idiomatic sense is more clearly distinct in Shilirramh."

"It's all right. It's not as though I wouldn't have been thinking about it without a reminder."

"And that is the problem," L'chellin said. "I understand your preoccupation, but you must think of other things as well. This ceremony is important to your community. You should show them it is important to you."

"That presupposes that it *is* important to me. It's sticking a box into a hole."

"No. I only said you should show them that it is. Yours is a hierarchical species, not unlike ours. Your kith group resonates with its alpha. Your mood influences their mood. Even without sharing external processors, you have your own form of gestalt thinking.

"The Arachnen are about to undertake a challenging transition. They are about to travel farther than any human has ever travelled, into regions where they will face life forms, technologies, and phenomena far beyond their experience. It is a daunting prospect. They need to begin this transition with a spirit of optimism. As the word begets the deed, as the tongue begets the life, so the onset of a transition begets its outcome. The Arachnen must be motivated to embrace the challenge and adventure that lie ahead. They must believe they can and will succeed.

"And it will be your words that beget their deeds. So you must go to them, Stephen Jacobs-Wong of *Arachne*, and you must give them words well-conceived and well-born, words they will embrace and nurture into strong, noble deeds."

L'chellin clasped his shoulder. "I know it is hard for you to find the seed for such words within your tongue. Your first issue fell unspoken, and so you fear to take responsibility for siring further speech. But if your words are well-formed, then it does not matter if they have true seed within them. If your auditors believe in your words, they will give them substance and be self-fertilized."

Stephen parsed the metaphors, which were growing increasingly disgusting the more L'chellin piled them on. "The key is sincerity," he interpreted. "If you can fake that, you've got it made."

L'chellin's brow furrowed. "You humans have a knack for paradox."

"We'd better. We need it often enough." He let L'chellin lead him out, committing himself to the task of delivering an inspiring speech for the Arachnen. But he wasn't sure how many noble words he could muster.

On top of which, he realized there was one other speech he would soon have to make.

After Stephen finished speaking to the loyalists, Cecilia stared at him in shock for a time before stepping forward to confront him. "How can you even propose such a thing after what they did to your child? You should be joining us, not the other way around!" Her gaze, and her words, took in Tarik Bahar, who stood silently at Stephen's side.

She could see the haunted, agonized look in Stephen's eyes, and it hurt her to rage against him on his own behalf. But he stayed calm and faced her squarely, maintaining that air of levelheaded, accessible reasonability that had made him so good at persuading others to sign on for his wild schemes. "Believe me, Cecilia, I've already had this argument with myself. I've already thought of everything you could say to me—and other things you mercifully have no context for imagining.

"But there's no us and them here. *Some* Lesshchin did terrible things to my wife, my daughter, my neighbors. But it's because of the quick response of Shilirrlaln security and the tireless efforts of Shilirrlaln doctors that my wife and most of our unborn children are still alive."

"Alive to serve their purposes," Diego Narvaez spat, pushing forward. "Alive to labor as slaves building their plantations!" Tarik shifted his weight forward and threw Diego a warning look, his commanding presence sufficing to halt Diego's advance. On Stephen's other side, the Chirrn arbiter L'chellin, apparently still responsible for handling the human prisoners' case, observed warily. At a faint gesture from Cecilia, Diego sullenly retreated. Not that the utility fog would have let him get away with anything anyway. Even so, Churrlaya's reptilian gaze took everything in from the corner where he stood, and Cecilia wondered what punishment he would cook up for Diego.

"Don't, Diego," Stephen warned. "That's just rhetoric to you, but it's family history to me. If I thought this were anything like that, I'd be with you already.

"What I see instead is an opportunity. A chance to do the thing we dedicated our lives to doing: building a new world, a new home. We'll be building it with new partners, in a new way, true. But can any of us truly say that we knew what to expect, what the rest of our lives would be like, when we set out on this expedition?"

"Pretty words, Stephen," Cecilia said. "But they gloss over what you were *forced* to give up. What you're now asking us to give up."

"A symbolic allegiance."

"A symbol of submission! A surrender of our humanity!"

"An admission of remorse. A commitment to make amends for our mistakes."

"We made no mistakes! It was the Chirrn who chose to hide themselves."

"Does that mean it's all right to walk away from a disaster of such magnitude? To do nothing to help its victims rebuild?" He shook his head. "The Cecilia LoCarno I knew would never have looked for excuses to avoid responsibility."

He turned to address the rest. "And that's the key. Responsibility isn't a burden to be avoided, a penalty to be shied from. It's a choice we make for ourselves, and a commitment we make to others. We are all here because we felt a responsibility to humanity, to future generations. We welcomed that responsibility. We embraced it.

"And along the way, we made every possible effort to take responsibility for other living things as well. We planned our colonization in a way that would be responsible to the indigenous life of Cybele. We designed our ship with our responsibility to other starfaring civilizations in mind, even though we had no reason to expect we'd encounter any."

His voice still addressed the group, but his eyes came back to Cecilia. "So isn't it paradoxical to say that our choice to take responsibility for the well-being of other life forms gives us an excuse to renounce any responsibility to them now? If we had come across the Chirrn as victims of a natural disaster, say, would we walk away because it wasn't our problem? Or would we try to help, as a way of being good neighbors in the galactic community, and simply because it was the right thing to do?"

"If they hadn't forced us," Amrita Dhillon said. "If they hadn't put us through torture and humiliation and a mockery of a trial. If they hadn't—" She broke off, seeing the look in Stephen's eyes. He knew perfectly well what they had done. *What a few of them did,* a small voice in Cecilia's head corrected her. It sounded a lot like Stephen's.

"Look," her former partner said after a long moment. "Nobody denies that what's happened here is tragic for everyone involved. Nobody wanted any of this to happen. But this is the reality we have to live with. What matters is what we decide to do with it next.

"Whether you renounce or not, you'll be taken with us to found the new colony. There will no longer be any realistic chance of seeing Solsys or Cybele again. I don't deny the cost of that. But you wouldn't be safe here with the Lesshchin, and you deserve the chance to join the rest of us again.

"But I see no reason to force you to wait. And I'd prefer to have all of you by my side once again." He looked around. "You heard the offer. If you want to join us, if you want to help us build a new world and new families, just step up here beside me."

Beside him, L'chellin stepped forward. "And by so doing, you will be officially recognized as renouncing all ties to any planetary civilization."

Cecilia was grateful to the supercilious kangaroo for the reminder of what was at stake. Sometimes Stephen's tongue could be too golden for others' good. Not that she would have needed any reminder. She knew where her roots were planted.

Diego's hardliners stood firm as well. But most of the others were lost in thought, contemplating the offer. Amrita stared at them in disbelief. "You're not actually considering this?"

Cecilia touched her arm, caught her gaze. "Amrita... don't. This has to be everyone's own choice, or our loyalty means nothing." She noted Churrlaya's gaze upon her, wondering why he suddenly seemed so curious.

No one moved for a moment. But then Shuai Bingbing stepped forward, stopping briefly by Cecilia. "I'm sorry, Captain," she said. "But Justine needs me now. Whatever mistakes we've both made... she's still my wife. I need to be with her more than I need to live on a planet."

Sergei Mazunov and Hannah Errgang were the next to step forward. "Sorry, Captain," the grizzled Russian said. "But we know the dreams were real now. The life they're living—it's better than this. They do have freedom... because they have family."

"That's all Sergei and I ever needed," Hannah added. "I don't know what we're clinging to anymore." They moved away, hand in hand as always.

Then Ichiba Nobuo faced her with apology in his eyes. "You can come with us, Cecilia," he said. "There's no point in this anymore. It's time to let go of our illusions and submit to the inevitable."

"You're asking me to give up who I am," she told him.

The look of disappointment in his eyes was palpable. "I stayed with you before because I believed in you. Now... I see you getting in deeper with Diego and his group, indulging their hate... and I think you've already lost who you are."

She slapped his face. The fog only impeded them from attacking Chirrn, not each other. "That is the one thing they will never take from me."

Nobuo walked away sadly, and three more soon followed him in turn. Cecilia closed her eyes to compose herself, afraid to open them again for fear that when she did, her group would be reduced to just her and Diego's band. She had to believe there were more reasons than their petty xenophobia for remaining loyal to Earth and humanity. There had to be.

Then she heard a welcome voice, soft and close at hand. "Captain?"

She smiled and opened her eyes. "Tarik. Good to see you." She hugged him, whispered urgently in his ear. "Do you have an escape plan?"

He pulled back to stare at her, confused. "Captain?"

"Come on," she hissed. "We'll be in ships again. There'll be confusion, chaos. We may never have a better chance."

"Captain… I'm sorry, but this is our best chance. Not to try to flee; that's not an option. Their ships are… amazing, but I'm years from comprehending how they work. I wouldn't want to anyway. This is what we wanted, Cecilia. To build a new home for our children. Not to become fugitives in an alien galaxy."

She stared at him, devastated. "You swore to me you would never renounce your duty."

"And I haven't. My duty is to our crew, Captain. *All* of it. And the best decision for our crew is to reunite, to join the Chirrn migration as partners."

"Tarik, they *killed* your son."

He winced, but stood firm in his resolve. "All the more reason I can't leave Kweli now. She needs us — all of us — to help her through this."

"Then we need to fight them together."

"We can't! Violence only breeds more violence. History has taught us all that, if we don't let ourselves forget. And if we take arms against the Chirrn, we're guaranteed to lose. Kweli is barely coping as it is. I can't put her through any more loss. She needs peace if she's to heal."

"So you've sold out like the rest. Renounced your allegiance to Earth."

"My only allegiances are to Allah, my wife, and my crew."

"What about Allah, then? If you've forsworn all ties to Earth, how can you pray to Mecca? How can you honor Allah's will?"

"Facing Mecca is only a way to focus thought and devotion. When we cannot face Mecca, we simply focus within, where Allah truly resides." He clasped her shoulder. "And Allah asks nothing more from us than we are able to give."

She glared daggers at him. "Then for your sake, I'm glad your god has such low standards."

He turned his back on her and stalked away, and she hated herself for her words.

Mercifully, no one else defected to the Chirrn side. In addition to Diego's foursome, she still had Nik Zacharias, Kahina Amrouche, Ibrahim al-Bakri, and Zhao Changkun. She belatedly hoped Ibrahim hadn't heard her final words to Tarik; the geneticist's faith was the only thing that kept him a loyalist, since he, unlike Tarik, saw submission to the Chirrn as a betrayal of his submission to Allah. At this point, she needed to keep every ally she had.

And things would be tense in the remaining group. Only nine loyalists now remained; from an even third of the colonists (not counting Arachne), they were down to under a fifth. And the offer to defect was still open. What if Nik switched sides and left the loyalists without a human doctor? What if Kahina left and six men had only two women to compete for? Cecilia would have to work harder to hold the group together — to keep them strong.

So she ignored the sound of Stephen calling her name. Maybe he hoped to make one more attempt to persuade her; maybe he just wanted to say goodbye, or even that he understood. She would welcome that, if they could be alone and have one of their classic knockdown, epic, cappuccino-fueled arguments. Maybe then he could actually make her understand what the hell was going through his head, so that maybe, for once, she could talk him out of it. But they were not alone, and she had obligations to the remaining loyalists. So she turned toward her group, away from Stephen, and stood firm until he and the other defectors finally left.

"What is wrong with them?" Amrita exclaimed after Churrlaya and the other Chirrn had left them alone. "With Bingbing? She wants to have children? Didn't she hear what they said? They're killing our children in the womb!"

"We cannot let that sin go unpunished," Diego said with quiet, ferocious resolve. "We have to find those murderous animals and make them pay."

"You heard Stephen," Nik Zacharias said. "They've already been sentenced and sent away. They're long gone."

"You think the other Lesshchin are any less to blame? We'll exact justice from any of them we can find! Starting with the Frog Footman!"

Nik scoffed. "You think we could possibly manage such a thing? There's the small matter of escaping first."

"That may be doable." Cecilia's firm, simple statement captured the whole group's attention. "Despite what Tarik believes, I still think the confusion of the move will be our best chance to seize a ship. If we make a break and offer the others a chance, some of them will probably come back to us. Possibly some who have knowledge of Chirrn technology and could help us operate the ship."

"And then just flee?" Diego challenged. "No, we have to avenge our unborn."

"As Nik says, escaping comes first. The rest will follow, once we know what our options are." She placed a supportive hand on Diego's shoulder, another on Amrita's. "Trust me—I'm as full of rage as you are. But we have to aim it wisely if we want it to have the greatest effect."

After holding her eyes for a moment, Diego nodded. The nine remaining loyalists then began to make their plans. They all knew escape would be a long shot, even with the opening offered by the move. Given the Chirrn's proven capacity for deadly violence, they knew they might not all survive it. But they had never had a more powerful incentive than they had now.

12

"I should be glad to be leaving this place," Sita Bhatiani said as she stared out the window of Oyama Kazuko's residence. The dwelling was on the highest terrace, affording a fine view of the entire Arachnen compound—including portions of the public square. Even after weeks of therapy, it was still painful to catch even a glimpse of that place.

"I *am* glad that I'll be away from the Lesshchin at last," she went on. "Dozens of parsecs away, where none of them can ever hurt us again. But still…"

Kazuko spoke gently, knowing what Sita wanted to say. "But even away from the Lesshchin, we'll still be surrounded by Chirrn, by aliens. It's hard not to be afraid."

Sita winced. "But that's just it. I'm a xenobiologist! I'm about to go out into a vast universe filled with aliens, the very thing I've dreamt of my whole life… and now they're just a reminder of what… what happened."

She turned to take in the other three women's faces, seeking what understanding she could find in their eyes. These past few weeks, while the bulk of the Arachnen had focused on the ongoing preparations for the migration, Sita had closed herself off from the outside world, accepting visits only from other humans, and spending most of her time in the company of Kweli, Kazuko, and Justine, bonding through their mutual grief. As the four of them had talked and commiserated, though, Sita had come to realize that each of them had been affected differently by their loss. Justine was angry at herself and wracked with guilt, blaming herself for coming on the expedition or for not staying with Bingbing among the Unrenounced—when she wasn't furious at Diana Thorne for failing to protect her baby, at the Lesshchin for their brutality, or at Arachne for destroying Lesshchi in the first place.

Having Bingbing by her side again helped her sometimes, but they'd had their share of angry dust-ups over their reciprocal infidelities — which, in an odd way, seemed to be doing Justine some good.

Kweli, conversely, was grief-stricken and devastated by her bereavement. She had been well into her second trimester, farther along than any of the others, and she and Tarik had already decided on a name for their son and built an elaborate nursery for little Mehmet. The couple loved each other and their son deeply, and their sorrow was wrenching to behold — although at least they found comfort in each other, the tragedy binding them closer than ever.

Kazuko was the one who had held them all together. The fiftyish administrator had miscarried before, as a member of a Martian group marriage. Though she did not feel sexual arousal, Kazuko had valued her duty as a colonist to procreate, and had borne the group three children; yet the effects of Martian gravity and environmental chemistry on fetal development were still not fully understood, so she had lost two more. While that didn't make her current tragedy any easier to bear, it gave her an enviable confidence that she would work through it and move on. She had been a bastion of strength for the other three, and for her platonic co-parent Ravinder.

Now, though, Kazuko sharpened her gaze upon Sita. "You still avoid talking about it. 'What happened.' Sita, you need to be able to face it to get through it." Sita was reminded that the older woman was not just a grieving mother, but an experienced lawyer as well.

With a sigh, Sita returned to her armchair. "It's not that I'm not willing to talk about my feelings. At least, I'm willing with you." She could not yet bring herself to talk about it with Stephen, for some part of her blamed him for bringing her here in the first place. She knew how irrational that was, and she knew he grieved as much as she did; but her pain was just too difficult to bring under control.

And she was starting to realize why. "The thing is… I'm not even sure how to describe what my feelings are. I've been through them all at least briefly — despair, guilt, anger, hate, denial, panic, the whole lot. But it all feels… unfocused. Directionless."

Kweli stared at her in shock. "Unfocused? There's only one thing to focus on. The life you lost. The baby inside you."

Bristling at the doctor's tone, feeling judged, Sita snapped, "Well, it's easy for you, innit? Mehmet was already a person to you and Tarik. You had his whole life planned out." Tears filled Kweli's eyes, making Sita feel ashamed. "Look, I'm sorry. I didn't mean to — oh, it's daft."

"Go on," Kazuko said. "This sounds like something you need to get off your chest."

"It's just… Stephen and I hadn't even picked a name for our girl. It seems like a trivial thing, but somehow, it matters. It's like… like I'm not sure who it is I'm grieving for. The more time passes, the more the baby feels like, like some abstract ideal rather than a person. And I feel awful for thinking that way about her."

Kweli reached out to take her hand, the tension past. "No, honey, it's okay. You… you should feel grateful you have that distance."

"There's nothing for you to be ashamed of," Kazuko assured her. "Every woman's experience with miscarriage is unique. We all react in our own ways, and there's no wrong thing to feel."

"Isn't there? What about…" She swallowed. "Sometimes… I almost feel relieved that my pregnancy is over. Not that I — I mean, I cherished her, that little life growing inside me. But… but it didn't bring me and Stephen closer, like I hoped it would. It just seemed to drive a wedge between us. I was afraid his preoccupation with the Chirrn, with the community and helping us adjust, would keep him from sharing in the whole parenting experience with me.

"No, more than that — I was afraid I wasn't ready to be a wife and mother. That I let Stephen rush me into it because he was so eager to begin building the community. Not that I blame him for any of it, not really," she insisted. "It just caused me as much bother as joy. Sometimes more. I don't really know if I would've been any good as a mum, or how our marriage would've weathered it."

"Have you tried talking to Stephen about this?" Kazuko asked. "Maybe if you heard his side of it — "

"Oh, I've heard it, all right. Our Stephen, he's not one to keep his thoughts to himself, is he now? I've been there for him, listened to him. I know how much the burden weighs on him. But it… it doesn't feel like *our* burden. It's just part of his larger burden of guilt about everything that's happened in the past seven months. And I just can't bring myself to pile my own troubles on top of his." She gave a humorless laugh. "I'm afraid losing our baby didn't bring us any closer than conceiving her did."

She shot to her feet again and began pacing. "Arrh, it's just so bloody frustrating! I don't bloody know what to feel or what to do about what I'm feeling. I don't know where to direct my thoughts or my emotions. It's all just such a jumble."

"Just tell me what you're feeling right now," Kazuko said, watching her pinball around the living room. "What do you want to do?"

"I just want to get away!" she cried. "To bloody go somewhere. Get away from all this emptiness inside me. But I can't very well get away from that, now can I?"

Kazuko rose and intercepted Sita, clasping her shoulders and bringing her to a halt. "Then maybe you need something to fill it with. Some new goal or purpose. Maybe what you need is something to head *toward*, not to run from." She smiled. "You've been keeping your distance from the migration preparations because of all the Chirrn you'd have to deal with. But maybe you should think about what else is out there waiting for us at the other end of the trip."

After the session, Sita strolled through the compound, pondering what Kazuko had said. The more she considered it, the more right it sounded. The overwhelming pain and guilt of her loss had crowded out the questions that had filled her mind before, questions about the knowledge the Chirrn were still holding back. Once she began to contemplate those questions again, the fervor to find the answers began to enter her mind once more. Where had the Chirrn come from? How had they allied with the Zenith and the Ryohoch? What greater galactic civilization lay beyond Shilirrlal, beyond the other Chirrn habitats in local space? Did most sophonts abandon planetary living, and if so, how many other ways had they found to adapt to space?

Finding the answers to those questions would require coming out of her self-enforced seclusion. It would mean having to interact with Chirrn and other large, scary aliens, but it seemed likely that her interactions would continue to be primarily with L'chellin, R'nilinnath, and Broadwing, and she could cope with them. She was even grateful to Broadwing for his valiant attempt to save her, and she found it easy to admire his iridescent beauty.

Most of all, Sita simply needed to gain a sense of movement. Engaging with the fleet preparations would help her feel that she was making progress toward leaving the ordeals of Shilirrlal behind her at last. Ordeals like…

With a start, Sita realized that her distracted stroll through the compound had brought her unerringly to the central square—nearly to the very spot where she and the other mothers had been dragged that horrible night. Her throat tightened at the sight… but no panic attack came. She stared at the grass and soil that must still have some of her blood soaked into it… and it did not reach out and grab her. It was just there. Just a place, like any other place.

Perhaps it was the knowledge that she would soon be leaving this place behind forever that made it bearable to face it. Or perhaps she simply needed to know she could face it and not be harmed. If she could stand up to the worst memory of her life without being broken any further, then she could stand up to anything the future threw at her.

Sita turned away from the square and began to climb the stairs toward the admin center, where the plans for the Arachnen's departure were being finalized. It was long past time she started pulling her weight around here.

At last, the wait was over. The assembly of the migration fleet was complete and the crews were beginning to board. Yet Churrlaya was more anxious than ever when the time came to move the remaining Unrenounced to the ship that would be transporting them—a separate ship from *Arachne*, for their sentence still kept them apart. Shilirrlal's shipyard/dock complex was not conducive to the use of security fog; its wide-open construction left insufficient anchor points for the fog's restraining filaments, and the high-intensity fields and discharges emitted by the dockworkers' tools and apparatus could disrupt the fog's internal signals. Thus, if the Unrenounced intended to attempt an escape, this would be their prime opportunity.

The Shilirrlaln security personnel insisted his concern was unwarranted, pointing out that the Unrenounced were still enswathed in restraint garments and under careful guard. They dismissed his fear as a vestige of his Lesshchin reflex of exclusion and hostility toward the Arachnen. But Churrlaya's fear of an escape came from a very different attitude toward the Unrenounced: respect. Now that he had recognized how his anger toward the humans had blinded him, he had begun to reassess his conversations with them over the past months. The more he thought about their words—at least those of Cecilia and other relatively rational ones such as Nikolos and Nobuo—the more appreciation he gained for the raw intelligence, shrewdness, and determination that had allowed the human species to survive its own excesses and reach the stars with no outside assistance. He could never forget nor entirely forgive their recklessness in doing so, for it had taken Simisshen, Marellel, and so many others from him, along with a sizeable piece of himself. But he saw so much potential in them to learn from their mistakes and embrace the strengths that had brought them so far on their own. He was optimistic that he could win many of them over in time.

Still, so long as the humans remained Unrenounced, their drive and ingenuity posed sufficient danger to set Churrlaya's bristles aquiver. He had urged Cecilia to keep her people in line for their own protection (and that of the dock workers, though he didn't mention that), but she had made no promises.

As it turned out, Churrlaya's fears were warranted. The escape attempt occurred while the Unrenounced, clad in their restraint coveralls, were being escorted into the freefall shipyard where the migration fleet was undergoing final preparations for launch. Their guards and accompanying security drones led them down a wide, lattice-framed tubular gangway toward the warp vessel where they would be confined during the journey, while Stephen Jacobs-Wong and a few other Arachnen, along with their Shilirrlaln mediators, watched from the nearby gangway leading to the newly warp-caged *Arachne*. This was the closest contact the Unrenounced would be allowed to have with their fellow humans until they chose to renounce planetary allegiance.

The attempt began with the most unlikely person—Evan, who was usually petrified with fear at the very sight of a nonterrestrial sophont. As the prisoners were escorted past a refitting team consisting of three Zenith, two Chirrn, and two Ryohoch, Evan gaped at them in shock and soon appeared to succumb to a panic attack. The vitals feed from the young human's coveralls verified that the attack was genuine. He began to struggle, attempting to break from the group, and naturally his coverall locked to restrict his movement. But Evan continued to struggle, forcing the coverall to tighten still further until he had difficulty breathing. He bounced off the gangway framework and back toward the refitting team that so terrified him, his pulse continuing to race to a dangerous degree.

Nikolos, the Unrenounced physician, demanded to be escorted to Evan's side. "You've got to get him out of there, he's dying!" Churrlaya granted it, aware that it would take too long to summon one of the

Arachnen's doctors, let alone to waive the restrictions on contact between the groups. Nik hastened to pull his arms and torso free of his coverall as soon as it was unlocked. Upon reaching Evan, the physician began to strip off that human's coverall as well. Churrlaya took hold of Evan and gripped the gangway's framework with his feet for leverage. Rolling one eye, he saw that Stephen was drifting closer out of concern.

Once Nik had Evan fully stripped, he swiftly examined the younger male. "Tachycardia, borderline asphyxia… this isn't good. I need more help. *Human* help, you're not trained for this. I need James."

Churrlaya stared. "You ask me to trust—"

"He's the only other one with paramedic training! Without equipment, we have to do this just right or we'll lose Evan!"

After a moment's thought, Churrlaya acceded, releasing James's coverall as well.

That was his mistake. Moments after James had shed his upper coverall and reached their position, he struck out at Churrlaya, dazing him. For a moment, Churrlaya only perceived consensus, and he sent an alert into it. When his sensory awareness cleared several moments later, he saw that James had stolen a plasma torch from the work crew and was brandishing it as a weapon, waving it madly at the crew to force them into retreat. Nik had seized a bladed tool and was using it to cut the others free of their coveralls. As tools, not weapons, the implements were not security-coded for their owners' use only.

Through the active consensus link, Churrlaya could see through Mediator L'chellin's eyes that Stephen had launched himself from the edge of *Arachne*'s gangway, crying "No! Stop!" as he flew toward the site of the struggle. L'chellin and the others had been too surprised to restrain him in time. "James Oates, stand down!"

It was fortunate that these humans could only look in one direction at a time. Once James's attention was diverted by Stephen's cries, Churrlaya began to swing around, preparing to club James with his tail. Defense guild Shilirrlaln were already offering to share awareness with him, to let him draw on their physical-combat training so they could guide his body to defend itself. But before he had the opportunity, he was tackled by another human, one so massive it had to be Diego. The impact knocked the breath from him.

"You don't order us anymore!" James cried at Stephen, struggling free of the rest of his coverall to prepare for the larger male's approach. He turned up the plasma torch and thrust it toward Stephen as he drew near, forcing the Arachnen leader to twist desperately and cover his face with his arms, even though he had no way of altering his trajectory. Fortunately, James was either not trying to damage Stephen or too clumsy with the torch to succeed. But Stephen's defensive position left him helpless to avoid a collision with the gangway's frame. The pain incapacitated him long enough for James to get a firm grip around the taller man's torso with one hand and brandish the torch before him with the other, guaranteeing his passivity.

Through L'chellin's senses, Churrlaya could see Sita Bhatiani crying out for Stephen and attempting to launch herself after him. Tarik Bahar and Broadwing held her arms to restrain her, but she fought against them so fiercely that even those two large individuals had difficulty maintaining a grip on her diminutive frame. "Oates! Fuck you, you wanker! Don't you dare hurt him, you sodding…" She carried on in terminology that the translation protocols struggled to interpret.

Before long, all nine Unrenounced had shed their coveralls and floated naked in the gangway. Several now brandished cutting tools, and others were using the remains of their coveralls to bind Churrlaya and their other guards, stretching their legs back to tie them to their tails. Ibrahim al-Bakri assisted James in binding Stephen's limbs as well. Evan was recovered now, hanging behind an armed Amrita Dhillon rather than participating actively in the escape, but grinning nonetheless. Livid bruises were starting to form across his body from his struggles against the coverall. Churrlaya realized that he had deliberately given into his impulse to panic, fighting the coverall and forcing it to tighten dangerously to create a convincing appearance of a medical crisis. The rest had been lies to get the Chirrn off their guard. Churrlaya felt much disappointment in Nikolos; he had always seemed one of the more reasonable Unrenounced until now.

But his disappointment in Cecilia was greater, for she was at the head of the pack, brandishing a plasma torch of her own. "Tell them to take us to *Arachne*," she told Churrlaya. "You were crew, right? You probably know how to fly one of these things."

"It won't work," Churrlaya told her. Even as he spoke, the guild defenders floated into view, readying their restraint-gel sprayers. Amrita began searching through the work crew's abandoned equipment, no doubt seeking potential countermeasures. This was a matter of some concern; while the mining engineer was no doubt unfamiliar with the more advanced aspects of Chirrn technology, much of it relied on universal physical and chemical principles that were well within human comprehension.

Churrlaya felt Diego's forearm tighten around his neck, and a cutting tool pressed against his flesh. "Back off or this one dies!" the human cried. Through consensus, Churrlaya advised them to hold off for the moment.

"Don't do this, Cecilia," Stephen said. "We're not prisoners. We *want* this."

"You've just lost the will to fight back," Cecilia countered. "Once we offer the crew *real* freedom, they'll come back to us."

"Freedom to do what? To be fugitives?"

"To avenge our unborn, for one thing!" Diego cried. "To punish the beasts that killed them!"

"They've already faced justice, Diego. At Chirrn hands."

"A travesty, like the rest of their justice! We'll exact real retribution!"

"Against whom? The killers are parsecs away. You'll never find them."

Diego pressed the cutting tool harder against Churrlaya's throat. "We have one of their kind right here. If you want it to live so much, then tell it to take us to *Arachne*. Tell the others to stand down."

"Do you really think you can end my life with that, Diego?" Churrlaya strove to bear only calm words, though there was little calm within him to spawn them from. "I have taken extra precautions since the disaster. Even if you did enough damage to halt the oxygen supply to my brain, what memories I do not have stored in the cloud are backed up in genetic-medium storage throughout my bloodstream. Any damage could be repaired and I would be whole again. At worst, you could spill enough of my blood to leave my memories incomplete. But it would be no worse than the losses I have already sustained, and there are many things — things you humans are responsible for — that I would happily forget. So you have nothing to threaten me with."

The blade dug in, and globules of blood spilled out into the air. The pain was startlingly intense, and his biofeedback systems seemed to take forever to dull it to a bearable level. "How about pain? You creatures have no comprehension of the cruelty the human imagination is capable of." Nearby, Amrita looked up from her inventory and grinned, fingers tightening against her own cutting blade as if imagining she were the one cutting Churrlaya's throat. He doubted she would be able to exercise as much restraint as Diego had.

Churrlaya strove for calm. "I can simply transfer the focus of my awareness into the network—cut off sensory input from my body. You can do nothing with lasting consequences." He spoke to convince himself as much as Diego. "So I will not tell the guards to back down. My duty is to ensure that you remain within your proscribed bounds."

Cecilia looked indecisive. Amrita did not. "It wants to bleed, then let it bleed! We can fight our way to the ship!" She brandished a container from the work crew's supplies. "Look here. Graphene polymer. Seven cases of it. And there's a solvent here I can use to break it down into graphene oxide. How about that, Frog?" she asked Churrlaya. "You think you can survive a firebomb?"

"That's insanely dangerous, Amrita," Cecilia warned. "There are ships all around us. There's no telling what kind of high-energy systems or power cells they have. It could start a chain reaction. Not to mention the overpressure hazard in an enclosed space! You could kill us all!"

"It's worth the risk," Diego said. "I bet even their medicine can only reverse death if it's caught soon enough—and if the body isn't blown to bits. We do enough damage to this place and they'll have to make saving lives their priority. It will give us a chance to get away in the confusion. And damage these ships enough to prevent them from following us." Amrita nodded and went to work. Churrlaya hoped she knew what she was doing well enough to avoid immolating herself—or the people around her.

"And if we go down, we at least get revenge on a few hundred of them!" James cried, waving his plasma torch recklessly.

"Does that include me, James?" Stephen gasped as the torch waved dangerously near his face. "Does that include *Arachne*, and all the humans that are aboard her? The people who only want to get away from the cycle of violence and raise their families in peace? You talk about revenge—but *we're* the ones who are grieving! Not you! You don't get to use our loss as an excuse for killing more people!"

"James, take it easy!" Cecilia ordered. "Remember, he's as much a wronged party here as we are." Catching Stephen's gaze, she went on. "Don't you get it, Stephen? Your loss is our loss. We're still in this together. Or we should be. Don't you see? This is our one chance at a life on our own terms. Just help us get aboard *Arachne* and we won't have to hurt anyone. The threat should be enough."

"Not everyone gets a life on their own terms, Cecilia. People like you and James, you were born to privilege. You take your entitlement for granted, kick and scream at any compromise. Me, I grew up under *real* oppression. I had to learn to adapt and compromise, to make the most of the limited degrees of freedom I had. Even once I got out, even once I built my empire, I was always aware that there were still limits I had to live under."

"Are you kidding? You became one of the richest people on Earth!"

"By learning how to work within the limits. The limits of economic reality, of what law and politics made possible… and most of all, the limits on what I could do without hurting other people, or imposing unfair limits on them. One advantage of growing up the way I did was that I never learned to feel entitled. I never assumed that what I wanted gave me an excuse to mistreat others. Because I never forgot how that felt from the other end.

"Cecilia, we are living under limitations, yes. But that's the compromise we have to make to be responsible members of a larger community and to repay our enormous debt to it. That's not slavery or oppression — it's just a lack of unfettered entitlement. I guarantee you I can tell the difference.

"What a few damaged, hateful Lesshchin did to our women, our babies — it was intolerable. But it has been dealt with. Their hate has been contained. But if you do this — if you repay their violence with more violence — then you're just unleashing that hate again, and giving them more reason to turn it back on us again.

"That's the part people never seem to think of when they want revenge — that the other side is no different. What I see in your faces now is the same thing I saw in the faces of the Lesshchin who killed my baby. The same sense that their revenge was justified, that they were the only victims." He locked eyes with Cecilia, Amrita, and Diego in turn. "The same mistaken belief that their action would end the cycle instead of perpetuating it."

"It's not about hate or revenge, Stephen!" Cecilia insisted. "It's about doing what's necessary for the freedom of our crew. Maybe you're right, maybe we do owe the Chirrn something, but this is not the way to repay it. The fact that you can tell me you don't feel oppressed so soon after they killed your baby is inconceivable to me. You say these Chirrn aren't responsible for the crimes of those others, but they enforce the conditions that leave us vulnerable to that kind of attack. And as long as they define us as criminals, there *will* be more attacks. Maybe you're just too deep in grief to see it, but we have hope now. We have one shot, however slim, of getting away from those unsafe conditions."

"That is exactly what we are doing," Churrlaya told her. "Starting again, building a new community of Shilirrlaln and Arachnen, with the past left behind."

"Shut up!" Diego's blade cut into Churrlaya's flesh once again, reopening the nearly-closed wound. Even with pain suppression engaged, the violation of his bodily integrity was a shocking indignity. "We won't let you animals decide our fate for us anymore!"

"Do it, Diego!" Amrita cried. She held up a pair of completed incendiary devices, which would require only a spark to set them off. "No more talk—let's start doing damage!"

Stephen kept his eyes locked on Cecilia's. "Are you really so sure this isn't about hate?"

James brought the torch flame closer to Stephen's face again. "Shut up! You're no better than the other animals!"

"Stop!" Cecilia cried. Visibly reaching a decision, she released her own torch, which deactivated itself. "Stand down, all of you! I won't have a bloodbath."

"But Captain—"

"You heard me! This is not who we are!"

"Cecilia, we must," Diego said. "Don't lose your resolve now. We have to make them fear us!"

"And what good would that do us, when they have so much more power?"

"Guerrillas have toppled the powerful before."

"When they've had support! When they've been on their home turf and known the lay of the land. We make them hate and fear us and we just make things worse for ourselves. A clean escape is one thing, but we give them a massacre and they'll hunt us down like dogs." She locked eyes with Diego. "This isn't the way. There's no strategy behind it, only rage and wounded pride. That's not who we're supposed to be. That's not who we'll ever become so long as I'm captain. So stand… down."

For a disturbingly long moment, Churrlaya wasn't sure Diego would still heed her authority. More of the Unrenounced seemed to be in his favor than hers at the moment. James even looked as if he was willing to cut his own captain down after first killing Stephen—though Churrlaya knew he would act only if Diego gave the word.

But with a heavy sigh, Diego finally released his grip on Churrlaya. At his signal — not Cecilia's — the others lowered their weapons and allowed the security team to move in and restrain them. Amrita was the last to back down, staring at Cecilia with hatred as she finally released her grip on the makeshift explosives, which the security personnel hastened to take in hand.

Once Stephen recovered his breath, he made his way to Cecilia's side and clasped her shoulders. "Thank you, my friend. I knew there was still hope for you."

His words only made her tense, resisting a further embrace. "I've never lost sight of my humanity and I never will. I won't sink to the level of the monsters who took your baby from you. I'm grateful to you for reminding us all how important that is. I still admire you for that integrity. And I am truly sorry for your loss, and Tarik's, and the others'." She pushed his hands away. "But I still think you've lost your way, Stephen. You've let guilt and grief overcome you, and you've surrendered to a punishment you think you deserve, without seeing how much it costs you. It may not be like the atrocities you grew up with in Florida, but there are subtler forms of oppression. And I hope that, someday, for your future children's sake, you will recognize that."

Seeing that there was nothing more he could say to change her mind, Stephen turned away, blinking moisture from his eyes, and grabbed hold of the gangway frame, giving an angry thrust to push himself back toward *Arachne*. The guards moved in to secure Cecilia's arms behind her back and guide her toward the confinement ship along with the other Unrenounced. A medic took Churrlaya in hand and began to administer regen gel to his neck, asking questions to assess his physical and emotional state. Churrlaya assigned a portion of his mind to go through the motions of responding. Yet he remained preoccupied with the realization that winning over the rest of the Unrenounced would be a greater challenge than he had hoped.

Few of the other loyalists would meet Cecilia's eyes as they were escorted into the prison ship and given new confinement coveralls. Even Nik and Kahina only gave her ambivalent glances, as if relieved that violence had been avoided but embittered at her decision to abort their escape attempt. Cecilia was sure, though, that the others would all see the wisdom of her decision once they'd had time to calm down.

Well, fairly sure. Hopeful, at least.

She stared at the coverall, reluctant to put it back on and resume a life where her every movement was confined and monitored. It had felt so good to float completely free for a brief while.

"May I assist you?" Startled out of her reverie, she turned to see Churrlaya waiting behind her.

"Not on your life," she answered, crouching in the prison ship's artificial gravity to pull on the garment. If she had to wear the damn thing, at least she would retain the dignity of dressing herself.

"I intended no affront," the blue-maned Chirrn went on. "Rather, I hoped to offer my gratitude. You saved many of us, including myself, from pointless hardship and pain."

She stared at him. "I didn't do it for you. I knew it wouldn't work… and I didn't trust you not to retaliate. You're good at that."

The charge actually seemed to embarrass him. "Your anger toward me is warranted—not as a Lesshchin, but for my role in how you have been treated in captivity. But surely you see now that this fierce resistance is misguided, destructive."

"No. What's destructive is your demand that we abandon who we are. Your intolerance is what killed our babies and provoked us to fight back."

"All that is being asked of you is to leave your planetary past behind. Is that past so critical to your existence that it is worth continued confinement, humiliation, and isolation from your community to cling to it? Even though it will never be an active part of your life again no matter what you do?"

She shook her head. "I suppose a nomadic people can't understand what it means to have roots. To have your very existence defined by the soil in which you were raised."

Churrlaya's brow ridges furrowed. "I struggle to understand why you would value an upbringing in which you were constantly soiled. I thought you lived near the water; was bathing not customary?"

Cecilia laughed out loud for some time, welcoming the release. As long as she had her precious human idioms, quirks of a distinctly human neurology and social training, she'd always have something these aliens couldn't master, something she could use to confound them. "Yes, we were dirty all the time and we loved it," she extemporized. "Playing in the mud, running barefoot through the streets, roughhousing and getting scuffed and scraped… filthy little urchins, that was the life. In that soil, in that dust, was the skin and hair and blood and shit of our ancestors, anointing us, caking us in history that stretches back to the Renaissance, to the merchant princes, to the might of Rome itself. We dug that history into our nails and our teeth until it became part of our very bones!"

The Lesshchin studied her for a long moment. He almost seemed contemplative, but more likely she'd simply overloaded his brain with metaphors. "Then it is not the place," he finally said. "It is your kith and your forebears you feel connected to. Thank you; this clarifies much." Cecilia stared at him, stunned.

"And yet," Churrlaya went on after a moment, "it also creates a paradox."

"And how's that?"

"If being in the place of your ancestors bears such meaning for you, then why did you choose to leave it forever to colonize another world?"

She opened her mouth, but checked herself. Thinking for a moment, she found herself giving him an honest reply. Somehow she felt he was entitled to one — or maybe she felt for the first time that there was something to gain by giving one. "As I said, Venezia is in my bones. I take it with me wherever I go. I miss it terribly, but... I left my home because it helped my home. Because the world needs new places to send its people so they won't overrun it and destroy every last trace of its beauty."

"That is a sensible purpose. But it does not answer my question. Why did it have to be *you* who left?"

She held his gaze. "You don't get that answer. Suffice to say I had my reasons."

Churrlaya gave a slight knee bend. "It will suffice until you are ready to say more," he said, continuing to startle her. "But a question still lingers."

She hesitated, but had to ask. "What question?"

"You were willing to leave behind the world you love in order to help your people. Why, then, are you unable to make the same choice now?"

She had no answer for him. But Churrlaya didn't wait for one. He turned and hopped away, leaving her alone with the question echoing in her mind.

EPILOGUE

"I still don't believe it," said Shuai Bingbing. "There's no way we've actually traveled faster than light!"

Sita laughed at Bingbing's skepticism, trading an amused look with Stephen as they floated arm-in-arm. They and several others were crowded into one of Arachne's habitat modules to view the vista outside.

Next to them, Justine Nguyen laughed, wrapping an arm around Bingbing's dainty shoulders and drawing her closer to the port. "Come on, silly, you can see for yourself!"

"Yes, okay," the recently renounced economist told her wife. "The starscape's different. And that's definitely not the same Chirrn habitat we were at before." This habitat was undergoing expansion, with smaller cylinders being constructed at either end, aligned with it coaxially but not yet rotating with it. Sita thought it looked like a fat rolling pin. Unlike Shilirrlal, which had floated free in interstellar space a parsec and a half from the binary red dwarf Gliese 257, this habitat orbited a large cometary-belt object that the Chirrn were mining for construction material, with a yellow-orange dwarf called HR 4523 dimly visible in the background. This, Sita knew, was a preview of what lay ahead for the migration fleet. Their target destination was a young rogue dwarf planet on the outskirts of the central Scorpius-Centaurus Association, one that Chirrn surveys had identified as a good source of materials for colony-building: uninhabited, with a good mix of carbon, volatiles, and metals close to the surface, low gravity to facilitate their extraction, and plenty of residual core heat to provide a geothermal power source — with the bonus that it was a short warp hop from an unclaimed young blue dwarf that could be tapped as a power source for the Chirrn's antimatter plants.

None of which Bingbing was yet willing to take seriously. "But we didn't actually see the ship move," she insisted. "How convenient that the warp cage totally surrounds the ship when it's engaged." Renounced or not, her loyalist suspicions toward the Chirrn died hard.

To be fair (Stephen thought), while faster-than-light travel may have been mind-boggling in concept, the actual view left much to be desired. The activation of the warp cage had been an impressive sight, at least: the latticework had unfolded elegantly to encase *Arachne*'s modules in two nested spheres, whereupon the programmable quark matter superfluid had flowed into the gaps like a living thing until they were completely encased within. Yet after that, there had been no visible change until the process reversed itself at the end of the wormhole passage. So the only sign of motion aside from the subtle change in the star patterns when they emerged — which was difficult for a human without astronomical training to recognize — had been the different appearance of the local habitat and the different number and configuration of the local cluster of wormhole portals in their Casimir cages.

"You wouldn't have been able to see anything anyway," Justine insisted. "The outer warp shell is so tiny that it would be like looking through a microscopic pinhole. That's why we need to be in a warp bubble to dive through one of the Chirrn's wormholes — it's the only way we're small enough to pass through."

"If you can't see outside the ship, then how do you avoid hitting stuff?" a skeptical Bingbing asked her.

"A spacetime metric is shaped by the mass and energy around it. If the warp bubble comes near a massive object, it changes the shape of the metric. The warp bubble itself serves as a proximity sensor."

"How convenient. Look, for all we know, this entire 'warp cage' could be nothing more than a simulator ride."

While the lovers' serious but playful argument continued, Sita drew Stephen away into the module's central passage until they could speak privately. "What's on your mind?" he asked.

She answered by kissing him deeply but gently. As he returned the kiss, he sensed its importance. This wasn't hunger for erotic distraction from her pain — it was a quieter, gentler, deeper connection than she'd been able to offer him since the attack, if not earlier. "I've missed that," he said at length.

"So have I. Seeing those two lovebirds reunited… it made me think about how I almost lost you. Ooh, if that pasty, microphallic… *American* had hurt you, I'd have…"

He stroked her hair. "I saw you trying to come to my rescue. Fighting with two people twice your mass and almost winning. You can be one scary pixie."

She laughed. "It… clarified some things for me. I've been so afraid of the Chirrn, of aliens. But… seeing you endangered by one of our own… I realized it wasn't about aliens anymore. We're as dangerous as they are." She smirked. "I guess I had my own privilege growing up in London. A dainty bird like me — for a lot of history, I'd never have felt safe walking those streets by myself. I was lucky to be born in an age when I didn't have to feel that kind of fear. But now I've known it, and I thought it was aliens I had to fear, but now I see — it's just life, innit? And you can let it control you, you can let it beat you down and make you scared or hateful… or you can stand the bloody hell up and live your bloody life on your own terms. And when I thought I might have to live that life without you… I just wouldn't bloody stand for it."

This time he initiated the kiss, and it was all the communication they needed for a while. "So… are we okay?" he finally asked.

She thought it over. "It still hurts. A lot. And I'm sure I'll still be scared from time to time — at whatever we may find out there. But… I'm ready to face it. We fear because we have something to lose. And that means we have something to gain too. Something to hope for. Out there… in all that infinite universe… I figure there's got to be more hope than fear."

Stephen clasped her hand. "I've… been afraid too. But I've been trying so hard to be strong for you… I see now I didn't need to be. I should've been more open about my own fear, my own pain. I should've shared everything with you. From now on…"

She kissed him again. "I know. It's a new beginning. The Chirrn have the right idea — if your old life doesn't work anymore, just bung it in the bin and build yourself a new one. Shilirrlal, Lesshchi, Earth — they're all in the past now. They're not who we are anymore." She clasped Stephen's hands and gazed into his eyes, seeing in them the endless optimism and sense of wonder that had made her love him in the first place.

"Like you said at the start of our last new life: We're star people now."

To Be Continued in
Arachne's Exile

APPENDIX 1: DRAMATIS PERSONAE

Arachne **senior personnel**
Arachne: shipmind
Bahar, Tarik Hüseyin: first officer
Bhatiani, Sita: biologist, behaviorist
Jacobs-Wong, Stephen: expedition leader
LoCarno, Cecilia: ship commander
Narvaez Duarte, Diego Felipe: assistant chief engineer, pilot
Ndege, Kweli: chief surgeon
Oyama Kazuko: political scientist, legal scholar
Pritam, Ravinder: senior cyberneticist, programmer
Silbermann, Haim: chief engineer

Arachne **junior personnel (incomplete list)**
al-Bakri, Ibrahim: geneticist, ecologist
Amrouche, Kahina: mathematician, programmer
Bhadra, Vijay: pilot, engineer
Brentwood, Jason: climatologist, meteorologist
Caravalho, Joana: physician, neurologist
Dhillon, Amrita: geologist, mining engineer
Errgang, Hannah: climatologist, oceanographer
Ichiba Nobuo: physical therapist, builder
Jiang Erfan, Evan: planetologist, meteorologist
Marcoe, Renata: political scientist, historian
Mazunov, Sergei: sociologist, economist
Nguyen, Justine: astrophysicist, mathematician
Nguyen, Marc: teacher, child psychologist
Oates, James: industrial engineer, cyberneticist
Olatunji, Scott: geneticist, botanist

Oliveira-York, Andrea: biologist, ecologist
Shuai Bingbing: economist, political scientist
Soares, Rosario: nurse, therapeutic sex provider
Thorne, Diana: construction engineer
Vidmar, Joshua: climatologist, environmental engineer
Zacharias, Nikolos: physician, psychologist
Zhao Changkun: programmer, systems analyst

Lesshchin (Chirrn)
Churrlaya: *Zhemhal* biologist, later Shilirrlaln xenopsychologist
Rillial: *Zhemhal* commander, prosecution advocate
Vhehhal: *Zhemhal* security officer, radical agitator
Djayrulu: youngest intact survivor
Simisshen: Churrlaya's lover
Marellel, Ruzhalu: friends of Churrlaya

Shilirrlaln (Chirrn unless otherwise specified)
L'chellin: trial advocate; senior mediator, Intersocietal guild
Broadwing (Zenith male): trial arbiter; junior mediator
Dj'vhereth: head tribune
R'nilinnath: apprentice mediator
R'hhenevh: alpha of Xenopsychology guild
Yonchon (Ryohoch): starship engineer
Mh'lellissh: physician assigned to Arachnen
Ch'millin, Mh'resshelel: Shilirrlal administrators

APPENDIX 2:
ARACHNE EXPEDITION PROFILE

Destination: Cybele (Gamma Leporis Ad), distance 29.3 ly

Microsail probe launch: 2083
Microsail probe arrival: 2113
Telemetry received at Earth, Cybele confirmed viable for colonization: 2142
Arachne launch: August 4, 2147
Stage 1: Particle-beam acceleration (40 g) to 0.84*c*: August 4-11, 2147 (5.9 dy shipboard due to time dilation; crew cushioned against acceleration by hibernation gel)

Projected:
Stage 2: Coast at 0.84*c* for 28.45 ly: August 2147-June 2181 (18.4 yrs shipboard)
Stage 3: Magnetic braking against interstellar medium (c. 0.4 g) to system insertion: June 2181-June 2183 (1.6 yrs shipboard)

Actual:
Stage 2: Coast interrupted at 24.1 ly: April 18, 2176 (15.6 yrs shipboard)
Gravitic deceleration by *Zhemhal* capture field (3993 g): 107 minutes (85 min shipboard)

APPENDIX 3: CHIRRN TIME UNITS

THE BASIC UNIT OF CHIRRN TIME MEASUREMENT, THE NARR, IS ONE STANDARD habitat rotation, equal to 96.64 seconds. Chirrn employ base 8 mathematics, so their time units are derived as follows:

1/64 narr	=	*narrat*	=	1.51 seconds	
1/8 narr	=	*narreth*	=	12.08 s	
1 narr	=	*narr*	=	96.64 s	= 1.61 minutes
8 narr	=	*narredj*	=	12.89 min	
64 narr	=	*narrach*	=	103.08 min	= 1.72 hours
512 narr	=	*narrissh*	=	13.74 h	
4096 narr	=	*narruvh*	=	109.95 h	= 4.58 days
8^5 narr	=	*narrenn*	=	36.65 d	
8^6 narr	=	*narranl*	=	293.21 d	
8^7 narr	=	*narrayth*	=	2345 d	= 6.42 years
8^8 narr	=	*yanarr*	=	51.38 y	
8^9 narr	=	*yanarredj*	=	411.03 y	
8^{10} narr	=	*yanarrach*	=	3288.2 y	
8^{11} narr	=	*yanarrissh*	=	26,306 y	

APPENDIX 4: SHILIRRLAL PARAMETERS

A TYPICAL CHIRRN HABITAT IS CONSTRUCTED ON MUCH THE SAME LINES AS a classical O'Neill cylinder, a rotating habitat of the type proposed by physicist Gerard K. O'Neill in the 1976 book *The High Frontier: Human Colonies in Space*, and commonly used by the Strider civilization of Sol's Main Belt and Trojan asteroids in the 21st and 22nd centuries. However, Chirrn habitats are single cylinders rather than the tethered, counterrotating pairs used in Solsys, since deep-space habitats have no need to precess to keep their mirrors pointed at a star as they orbit it.

Centripetal acceleration a (equal to the effective gravity) equals the square of the linear velocity of rotation v divided by the radius r, or:

$$a = v^2/r$$

The velocity equals the circumference of the cylinder over its rotational period:

$$v = 2\pi r/T$$

Thus

$$a = 4\pi^2 r/T^2$$

The habitat section is a cylinder with hemispherical endcaps, equal in length to 8 times the radius. Thus, its volume can be computed as that of a cylinder 6 radii in length ($\pi r^2 \times 6r = 6\pi r^3$) plus a sphere of 1 radius ($4/3 \times \pi r^3$).

Results:

Rotational period:	1.00 narr = 96.64 s
Gravity at outer shell:	1.302 g = 12.76 m/s^2
Rotational velocity:	196.25 m/s
Total radius:	3.018 km
Length of main habitat section:	24.144 km
Total length:	30.18 km
Volume of main habitat section:	633.30 km^3

AFTERWORD

PART ONE OF THIS NOVEL IS BASED ON THE NOVELETTE "AGGRAVATED Vehicular Genocide," initially published in *Analog Science Fiction and Fact* in November 1998 and reprinted and revised in my 2018 collection *Among the Wild Cybers: Tales Beyond the Superhuman*. In that story, *Arachne* was an interstellar ramjet traveling at 99 percent of lightspeed, using high-energy lasers to ionize the interstellar medium so that it could be magnetically channeled into the ship's fusion drive. These lasers could be concentrated to pinpoint focus to deflect oncoming debris. This was what inspired the story in the first place, when I wondered what would happen if such defense lasers struck an alien ship by mistake. In the original version, the Lesshchi habitat, housing roughly 8700 Chirrn, was struck by such a pinpoint beam which melted through its southern end in milliseconds, superheating the air and rupturing the hull from the sudden pressure increase, blowing the end completely away and killing all but some 350 of the habitat's population.

I subsequently learned that the ramjet concept has serious practical flaws. The magnetic field would create drag against the interstellar medium, which would be too thin anyway to provide an adequate fuel source, particularly here in the Local Bubble—unless the lasers and magnetic field were powerful enough to ionize an immense volume of interstellar hydrogen and drag it in to the centerline of the ship at sufficient speed. When I republished the story on my website in 2004, I tweaked some technical details and added some hand waves in an effort to make it more plausible. But the more I studied interstellar propulsion techniques, the more I realized that ramjets were an outmoded idea. So for this novel, I abandoned the ramjet concept altogether in favor of a modified form of magnetic sail propulsion. The concept of a magnetic sail accelerated by pellets rather than a particle beam was developed by

Dana G. Andrews and Robert Zubrin, and the sailbeam concept was proposed by Jordan Kare. They were brought to my attention by Paul Gilster in his book *Centauri Dreams* and his blog of the same name. Adam Crowl's *Crowlspace* blog article "Magnetic Sail as a Star-Brake" (crowlspace.com, February 10, 2007) provided additional details.

This decision led me to re-examine the entire work, and I discovered other flaws. For instance, I greatly underestimated the interior volume and population capacity of the Chirrn habitats as described. Also, a laser defense system would be unlikely to have the required power unless it were far too immense for a ship as light as the new *Arachne* had to be. I quickly realized that at relativistic speed, a simple sailbeam propelled ahead of the ship would be more than sufficient as a defensive weapon. The nature of the impact would have to be different than I had described, and even if the habitat was less thoroughly devastated, its population, and thus the death toll, would have to be far higher. I'm deeply indebted to the Jet Propulsion Laboratory's Paul Woodmansee and "Orpheus" of the Ex Isle BBS for helping me work out the physical details of the revised Lesshchi incident. Robert Zubrin's 1993 paper "Detection of Extraterrestrial Civilizations via the Spectral Signature of Advanced Interstellar Spacecraft" in *Astronomical Society of the Pacific Conference Series*, Volume 74, p.487 helped me address the critical question of *Arachne*'s bow shock and its detectability.

Thanks also to Marco Palmieri and David Mack, whose advice on story structure helped me improve this tale immensely. Thanks to Sam Morgan and Greg Cox for their advice on earlier drafts, which helped me strengthen the plot and characters. Thanks to Michael A. Burstein for helping me realize that my crazy idea to rework my really long epic novel into a duology was actually worth doing. And thanks to Stanley Schmidt for buying the original story and offering me the guidance that helped me become good enough to sell my work at last.

Finally, a particular thanks to the fans who came through for me with their generous donations at a point when my financial situation was desperate. My deep gratitude to Vasilios Arabatzis II, Byron Bailey, Matthew Buck, Scott Crick, Michael Evans, Shawn Fox, David Gian-Cursio, Adam Czarnecki, Justin Hilyard, Mari Johnson, Ronald Mallory, Cody Lee Martin, Daniel Nicholls, Bernd Perplies, Troy Rodgers, Johanna Schliemann, Clive Viagas, Christian Zenker, Mark Zieba, and everyone else who helped.

Arachne's Exile

*To the folks at Shore Leave,
for always making me feel welcome.*

— Ovid, "The Transformation of Arachne into a Spider"
(translated by Samuel Croxall)

Part One

Penal Transportation

PROLOGUE

"Don't get too close to the edge, Sita!"

"I'm fine, Nilly," Sita Bhatiani said absently as she leaned further over the railing, gauging the distance to the water in the canal below. "If I couldn't handle being on edges, I'd never have signed onto *Arachne*, would I?"

R'nilinnath hopped over to Sita, resting her blue-skinned, kangaroo-like body on its thick tail and rotating her chameleonesque eyes downward to lock onto the diminutive xenobiologist. "I'm glad that you've resolved to overcome your fear, my friend. But don't overdo it. Ss'chh is the most alien place you've seen so far."

The young Chirrn was right about that, up to a point. All the migration fleet's previous rest stops in the first few days of the journey from Shilirrlal had been at other Chirrn-built space habitats, variants on the cylindrical design that had come to feel almost familiar to Sita over the past six months—though she would never forget her first sight of one as a torn-open ruin, when the survivors of the Lesshchi habitat had pulled *Arachne*'s crew from their hibernation dreams and forced them to behold the devastation they had carelessly wrought in their haste.

The habitat called Ss'chh, of all things, was a modest-sized megastructure orbiting the giant star Theta Scorpii, over 270 light years from Solsys and nearly as far from Shilirrlal. It resembled a vast, elongated mollusk shell, a conical double helix with the wider end facing the star as it rotated around its long axis. This gave it a continuum of centrifugal gravity levels, from below Lunar at its tapered end to several times Earth's at its fat end. The canal Sita studied ran down its entire spiraling length, the water flowing downhill due to both the slope and the gravity gradient, then refiltered and pumped back up through the central axis.

On disembarking for the night, senior mediator L'chellin had brought her Arachnen charges to a Chirrn-compatible gravity level occupied only by familiar species such as Chirrn and Seekers of the Zenith, and not many of them at that. It made sense that the caravan crew would choose these comfortable environs for their rest break; but not for the first time, Sita had trouble shaking the feeling that the mediators were carefully controlling the Arachnen's access to information about the larger galaxy. The human colonists — well, most of them — had accepted culpability for Lesshchi's destruction, agreeing to assimilate into Chirrn society to repay their debt as contributing members. So why did those responsible for their education shy away from important topics such as galactic history and sociology?

The temptation to strip her kit off, dive in, and let the canal's current carry her down to more exotic levels, populated by who knew what kind of novel alien sophonts, was tempered only by Sita's realization that the strong current would sweep her lightweight body away like a leaf. Being the size of an average twelve-year-old was bollocks sometimes.

At least no one will mistake me for a preadolescent dressed like this, she thought, glancing down at the open-fronted Chirrn-style vest she'd finally started wearing — the two-strap variety, a bit more modest than the usual one-strap design, but bringing out her cleavage more, much to the appreciation of her husband. But she hadn't started wearing it out of vanity.

Ever since the Lesshchi disaster and the subsequent assault she'd suffered from her vengeful captors, Sita had lived in fear of the Chirrn, a fear that had overridden her natural fascination with alien life and kept her secluded in the Arachnen's probationary enclave for months. The Lesshchin refugees' second, more recent assault, resulting in the death of her unborn baby, had only worsened her terror — and her guilt, for she had been one of the women whose inadvertent intrusion on a solemn Lesshchin procreative ritual called a kiss dance had triggered their retaliation. But the Arachnen's administrator Oyama Kazuko, whose miscarriage had not been her first, had been a bastion of strength for Sita and the other bereaved parents — including Kazuko's platonic parenting partner Ravinder Pritam, as well as astrophysicist Justine Nguyen, who had been carrying one of the expedition's six hundred frozen, pre-fertilized embryos. Only Kweli Ndege, the Arachnen's chief physician, remained inconsolable, sequestered in her quarters and uninterested in the galaxy beyond. Kweli's husband, Tarik Bahar, did not have that luxury, for in Cecilia LoCarno's absence he was the acting captain of *Arachne* and had to be strong for the crew. Yet Sita could see how much he longed at every moment to be there for his wife, to give her the strength she could not find in herself.

Sita had spent months in hiding after the first attack, but the support of Kazuko and Justine had helped her find the conviction to seize onto the migration as a new beginning, to move beyond her fears and embrace discovery once again. Though she and Stephen had grown closer in recent days, following months of tension over their differing attitudes toward the Chirrn, Sita now felt more capable of functioning on her own, seeing her husband's strength as a supplement to hers rather than a substitute for it. The Chirrn wardrobe symbolized her acceptance of her new life as part of their community and her willingness to put herself out there once more.

Literally, she thought, scratching under her right breast.

She studied R'nilinnath thoughtfully, considering that she was large enough for Sita to ride on her back—and that the Chirrn had evolved from aquatic ancestors. "Nilly, you're a really good swimmer, right?"

The apprentice mediator gave a snort of distress through the array of small nares atop her snout, ruffling the stiff bristles that surrounded them. "Oh, no, Sita. Don't even conceive the words, let alone spawn them. We're on a schedule, and I don't dare risk delaying things by getting you lost."

"And here I thought you were the adventurous one."

"It's not like there's even much to see out there. It's a very old habitat, not used much anymore. It's mainly just a way station in the wormhole network."

Sita stared. "That just makes me more curious! Why did people stop using it? Where did they all go? Not just here, but all through this space."

In Chirrn terms, the caravan was traversing the Central Void toward the Antispinward Void; in human terms, through the Local Bubble toward Loop I. According to Justine, a wave of star formation and supernovae had swept through the Orion Arm millions of years ago and blown four huge bubbles of low gas density. The Chirrn called these the Four Voids, home territory of the Void Alliance, which included the Chirrn, the pterosaurian Zenith, the bizarre behemoths called the Ryohoch, and at least a couple of species she had yet to meet.

So far, the Voids were living up to their name, with plenty of empty space between the population centers the fleet passed through en route to the sparsely populated sector where the migrants would construct a new habitat, far from Shilirrlal and the surviving Lesshchin—and still farther from Earth and humanity's handful of colony worlds, with which the Arachnen had sworn off any further contact as a condition of their parole.

Nilly fidgeted. "Well…you know. People migrate. Like we're doing. Sometimes they just… drift away from somewhere for a while."

The London native crossed her arms and held the Chirrn's gaze. "Seriously, Nilly, what's got into you lot? Not just you, but the whole caravan. I've seen your body language, not just here but at all our rest stops. You don't have the confidence you had before. You're tentative, restless, like you're searching for something." Sita looked away. "At first, I thought I was just projecting my own state of mind onto you."

"The state of mind you're overcompensating for by leaning too close to the edge?" Nilly reminded her.

Sita sighed. "Right, I get it." She stepped back from the railing, and the two friends began to stroll alongside it at a more comfortable distance. Nilly's "stroll" was much like a kangaroo's slow walk, using her arms and tail as a tripod when moving her long legs forward. It angled her torso downward, keeping her silver-maned head at Sita's eye level.

"It's the migration," the apprentice remarked after a moment. "Not just the physical one, but the transition from their old guilds to this one. They've left behind their old consensus memories and thoughts, taken on new ones. They're still finding out what their new personalities are like."

Sita understood. A migratory species, long-lived and serially hermaphroditic, the Chirrn had always seen identities and allegiances as fluid, evolving things. Their minds existed as much in their habitats' information clouds as in their own skulls, and their personalities were shaped by the memories and processing algorithms they shared with others in their guilds. Moving to a new habitat or career meant altering one's personality, leaving pieces of oneself behind and assimilating new ones.

Her hands moved reflexively to her belly. "Like they've lost a part of themselves," she whispered, "and aren't quite sure who they are anymore."

Nilly's eyes swiveled in surprise. "I hadn't thought of it that way. It's hard to understand what you and the others are going through. So few of us have had babies, let alone lost them. And memories that painful aren't always shared with the consensus." She lowered her brow ridges in thought. "But I guess if a baby is something that's both part of you and outside of you, that's a bit like a consensus memory. I understand that, now that I'm sharing fully in the Migration guild's consensus. I'm like the others — still figuring out who I am now."

Sita's restlessness returned. "But at least you have something to fill the void. That makes it easier."

"I don't know about that," Nilly said. "There are migrants from many guilds and estates. It takes lots of different skills to build a new world. Every estate has people seeking transition to a new life, so we had no trouble finding recruits. But they all come with different habits of thought. They don't leave all of it behind. We're still testing out each other's memories and modes of thinking, seeing how they change us." She snuffled unhappily. "It's hard to put it in human terms."

"You don't seem to have changed that much. Neither have L'chellin or Broadwing."

"Well, Intersocietal is the core of the Migration guild. Nearly half the collegium came along."

"Makes sense — they literally share the same thoughts about the reasons behind the move."

"Not the *same*, exactly. But mediators are generalists to begin with. Our thought patterns are tailored to be malleable and eclectic — well, compared to the Chirrn norm," she admitted with an amused drumming of her toes. "So all that influx of new ideas hasn't changed L'chellin or Broadwing that much."

"And yourself?"

She shook her short mane, a Chirrn smile. "I'm a kid. Everything's new to me. Besides — I'm finally a full guild member! I'm an adult now!"

"Make up your mind. Are you a kid or an adult?"

"Can't I be both?" Nilly asked.

Sita laughed out loud for the first time since the attack. She threw her arms around Nilly's neck and hugged her warmly. "You be whatever you want, love. Just don't ever stop being you."

1

STEPHEN JACOBS-WONG HAD SPENT MOST OF THE JOURNEY FROM Shilirrlal on autopilot, putting up the front of leadership and charisma that came effortlessly, but not really letting anything outside his ship and crew engage him even as the wonders of the galaxy passed them by. His thoughts were still preoccupied by the series of tragedies for which he blamed himself—and by the schism between himself and Cecilia LoCarno, *Arachne*'s captain and his dearest friend, over their responsibility for making amends. With the onset of the migration, Stephen and Sita had finally begun to reconnect and heal each other's grief at the loss of their baby, easing the burdens on his spirit. Yet that effort had required keeping his focus inward.

But in time, the sky became too beautiful to ignore. The caravan had entered the Upper Scorpius subgroup of the Scorpius-Centaurus OB Association, a lively star-formation region dominated by bright young stars like Antares and Sigma Scorpii and vast clouds of nebular matter surrounding them. The nebulae were barely visible to the unassisted eye at close range, but those stars were far brighter than they'd ever appeared from Earth, and with a little adjustment of their adaptive optics and a little enhancement from *Arachne*'s viewports, the Arachnen could see the beauty of the yellow-orange and magenta hazes surrounding them, a mix of reflection and emission nebulae. Stephen soon found himself gazing out raptly with the rest of the crew.

Yet once they reached the Antares system—a journey of over 550 light years from Shilirrlal, made in only eight days—the fleet's port of call made the sky around them look positively dull. The habitat, orbiting the blue-dwarf companion star Antares B at some fifteen AUs, was a sphere nearly fifty kilometers in diameter, a garish starburst of incredibly tall fairy-tale castles, impossibly slender spires, and massive, clear-roofed aerodromes, all crafted from gleaming crystals, metals, and metamaterials and festooned with vivid, multicolored lights. It was like a cross between Escher's *Tetrahedral Planetoid*, the skyline of old Shanghai before the floods, and a sea urchin dressed up for Mardi Gras. The interplay of illumination from the piercing blue star nearby, the bloated red-orange Antares A nearly six hundred AUs away, and the dense planetary nebula surrounding them both made the habitat gleam with particular resplendence, and its architecture strove to match the grandeur of its surroundings. Twelve enormous towers jutted from its equator, supporting a scintillating docking ring over a hundred kilometers above the surface and tapering dozens of kilometers further into elegant launch spines, slender threads that gleamed in the multi-directional light. It was a gorgeous vista, albeit a bit garish to Stephen's eyes. But Sita wept at the sight, and they were the first tears he'd been happy to see her shed.

"It's a Star Palace," Arachne's voice announced over the cockpit speakers. The humans reacted to the name with recognition.

Mediator Broadwing blinked his lower two eyes in surprise. "You know of them?"

"Human astronomers have imaged several megastructures of this design around various giant and supergiant stars," the shipmind answered. "A few are internally lit, but most are detectable only by reflected starlight and are believed abandoned. As yet, we have been unable to make contact with the species that constructed them."

"In fact, you have," Broadwing fluted in his elegant calliope voice, produced in resonating cavities within his three iridescent headcrests. "One spreads his wings before you even now." The lean-bodied, silver-hued pterosaurian matched his actions to the words, clicking his three beak mandibles together as he did so.

"The Zenith built the Star Palaces?" Sita asked.

"Yes." Broadwing refolded his wing dactyls and membranes back along his forearms, leaving his shorter dactyls to function as fingers. As always, he moved with a grace that made the zigzag shape of his legs, and the way his wing-arms went up from his shoulders before bending back down, look totally right even to human eyes. His crests sang again, the translation appearing as subtitles in Stephen's retinal HUD. "As Seekers of the Zenith, my people were naturally drawn to space. When we reached the stars, we built aeries around the brightest and most impressive ones so that all would know of our majesty."

"That explains a lot," Stephen said.

For decades, human astronomers, engineers, and xenobiologists had debated how and why the structures were built in this configuration. Given the Zenith's acrophilic nature, it went against their grain to build Chirrn-style habitats where the sky was inward. No doubt, he realized, the Star Palaces used programmable quark matter to generate artificial gravity. If PQM could take on the properties of the exotic matter necessary to make warp cages and wormholes possible, then surely it could also, say, generate gravitons with a greatly increased coupling constant, allowing a relatively small mass to exert the pull of a planet-sized one. The Zenith most likely lived only on the surface of the Star Palace, competing with one another for increased status and the privilege to live higher up in one of its many ornate spires.

"Hold on," Haim Silbermann said. "Isn't Antares A due to go supernova sometime in the next few million—I mean, the next *yanarrenn* or so?"

"Enough time to relocate," Broadwing told the gray-bearded engineer. "For now, this is the most glorious star in the region, so naturally the Zenith must claim this height."

"With your technology, couldn't you prevent the supernova? Lift away enough of the star's hydrogen to reduce the pressure on the core and prolong its life?"

"Why would we want to do that?" R'nilinnath wondered. "Supernovae create heavy elements. They promote evolution on planets. If we stopped supernovae, we'd prevent new species from evolving. Few enough worlds spawn sophonts as it is." Nilly shook her mane, a Chirrn smile. "Now do you see why smart civilizations don't live on planets? It's hard to move a planet out of danger."

Stephen recalled Sita's musings about the Fermi Paradox, the mystery of why evidence of alien activity had been so hard for humanity to detect. What the old Kardashev theories of galactic-scale engineering had overlooked, it seemed, was that the civilizations that survived to the interstellar age were the ones that learned to live in harmony with their environments rather than forcibly reshaping them. Nilly's words drove home that the galaxy had its own ecology of star and planet formation, one that galactic society took care not to disrupt, so that its footprint was nearly invisible except at a fine scale.

The caravan's ships soon docked along the Star Palace's spaceport ring, settling in for a stay of moderate length, and the Arachnen were finally free to leave the ship — escorted by the mediators, of course, and by Arachne's physical avatar, a silver-and-blue smart-matter construct in the form of a four-armed, metallic-skinned woman's torso joined to the abdomen and hind legs of a giant spider.

Stephen noted the avatar pausing by a viewport in the disembarcation lounge, looking out at the starship her core mind occupied. "Something wrong?" he asked.

"It's nothing," the avatar said in Arachne's calm, warm voice. "We should keep moving."

"Arachne, you always take care of us. If you need a moment for yourself — or if you need to talk — it's fine. It's just you and me." He knew he might be anthropomorphizing, but he believed he knew Arachne well enough to recognize her moods.

"Appreciated, Stephen. It's simply that I'm still not used to being in a cage."

He joined her in gazing out at her remade body. Once, she had been a wispy spiderweb of magnetic sail coils with habitat and cargo modules strung along its support lines like dewdrops — the lightest, sleekest starship ever created by humanity, reaching an unprecedented eighty-four percent of lightspeed. Now, her modules were bundled together like logs and crammed within the cylindrical collar of a Chirrn-built warp cage, an intricate lattice of PQM conduits that could unfurl into a sphere to protect the ship within from the stresses of warp or wormhole passage.

"I can see how it would feel confining."

"I miss the quiet. The long, slow contemplation of the universe, the comfortable routine of keeping you all safe as you slept within me. Now..." The arachnocentaur's legs shifted uneasily, and Stephen wondered if it was merely an affectation. "To be honest, traveling by warp cage scares the hell out of me. The universe isn't supposed to work that way!"

He laughed in surprise. "I'm sure you understand the physics far better than I do."

The avatar's beautiful, multi-eyed face turned fully toward him. "That's exactly why it terrifies me," she said with incongruous calm. "I know precisely what extremes of energy density it requires and how closely I skirt the edge of disaster at every moment.

"And that cage doesn't help. It feels like an alien limb grafted onto me, with its own will and habits I'm still struggling to reconcile with my own."

"Have you spoken to Haim or Yonchon about this? Maybe there's… an adjustment that can be made."

"Unnecessary. I appreciate the opportunity to voice my discomfort, but it's not something that needs to be addressed. My priority is keeping you safe."

He clasped the avatar's shoulder, for what it was worth. "Arachne, you deserve consideration too."

All her eyes locked on his. "Stephen, I murdered more than eighty-eight thousand sapient beings to protect you, and yet all of you are paying for my mistake. Captain LoCarno and the other Unrenounced are still caged far more literally than I. Save your consideration for them. I do not deserve it."

The avatar moved on. As Stephen watched it scuttle gracefully toward the others, he reflected how unusual it was for Arachne to admit to needs of her own. He'd recruited her for her relentlessly maternal dedication to the welfare of her charges.

No doubt that was why her thoughts were with the Unrenounced—the nine remaining holdouts who had refused to disavow their planetary ties and assimilate into Chirrn society to raise families in freedom. It frustrated Stephen that Cecilia LoCarno and her fellow "loyalists," as they called themselves, refused to see the truth: that their trial and conviction had been a ritualized ordeal meant to prime the humans for adoption as probationary members, replenishing the community's loss with their own numbers and contributions. To the Chirrn, atonement for criminal acts was merely another transition between identities, casting off past mistakes to remake oneself as something better. Yet the Unrenounced's pride in their heritage and independence would not allow them to yield. Thus, they remained confined, isolated from the renounced Arachnen and subjected to behavioral experiments that they perceived as punishment, but which were actually part of the ritual ordeal to cleanse their sins, a duress that would end as soon as they accepted culpability and embraced transition.

It must frustrate Arachne, Stephen mused, *that some of the very people who recruited her for her protectiveness are now denying her the ability to do her job.*

It struck him then that the shipmind's show of vulnerability just now had been for his benefit, to draw him out of his introversion and remind him of his own responsibility to lead the Arachnen through these challenging times — and to find a way to heal the rift with Cecilia and the Unrenounced.

He smiled. He was the one who didn't deserve Arachne.

"You are about to encounter a number of sapient species you have never seen before," Churrlaya told the loyalists as they reluctantly donned confinement jumpsuits under the scrutiny of several Chirrn guards. The relatively small, green-skinned Chirrn, whose ringlet-styled, powder-blue mane had earned him the nickname "the Frog Footman" from his human captives, had explained that the migration caravan had docked at a habitat belonging to the pterosaur-gargoyle species called Seekers of the Zenith, yet used as an interstellar travel hub by many species. The prisoners were to be transferred to a tempo-rary holding facility in the habitat's docking ring while the Chirrn spacecraft that had been their prison for the past week or more un-derwent inspection and maintenance. Cecilia LoCarno would have appreciated the change of scenery if not for the tight jumpsuit, which bound her hands in clumsy mitts and would go rigid if she made any abrupt or threatening movements.

"None of these sophonts have wronged you or been wronged by you in any way. However, many will be even more alien to you than the Chirrn or Zenith. How does this make you feel?"

"Anything that's not Chirrn is an improvement," Amrita Dhillon spat. She took Evan Jiang's hand to comfort him; the young planetolo-gist had stiffened with xenophobic terror at Churrlaya's statement. Cecilia was pleased to see a gesture of kindness from the slender mining engineer, a departure from her habitual anger. This ordeal had hit Amrita the hardest, reawakening her traumatic memories of seeing her parents tortured by the oppressive regime of her native Trojan-asteroid habitat. During the journey, Amrita had become involved with her fellow Strider Nik Zacharias. The Cerean doctor had resisted her sexual invitations before, uneasy with her rage, but he'd finally consented in the hope that he could calm her fury — and it seemed he had, if only marginally.

James Oates was about to say something confrontational and stupid, but Diego Narvaez pre-empted him. "I have nothing against the beings here in and of themselves," the tall Guatemalan engineer said. "But if they assist you in holding us hostage, then they *have* wronged us."

Churrlaya turned to Cecilia. "And what is your reaction?"

"I'll be pleased to meet someone new," the captain said.

"Yeah," Kahina Amrouche put in. "We're sick of seeing your face every day."

Cecilia gave the programmer a stern look. *Remember, hold the high ground. Prove we're better.*

"We came out here as explorers," Cecilia went on, as much to her fellow loyalists as to Churrlaya. "Naturally, I'm excited by the prospect of encountering new forms of intelligence. But the circumstances are unfortunate."

"You know how to change that," Churrlaya reminded her.

She didn't take the bait, remaining silent while the Chirrn guards led the nine loyalists out into the docking facilities within the Zenith habitat's freefall orbital ring. Once she got her first look at the variety of sophonts working in the docks, Cecilia felt a thrill of fascination at their sheer alienness and diversity. She was unsurprised to see the same reaction from Nik Zacharias, and from the group's resident ecologist, Ibrahim al-Bakri. The two programmers, Kahina Amrouche and Zhao Changkun, held hands and stifled laughter, their eyes widening in wonder at the technologies around them. But Diego and his clique of hardliners huddled together, giving wary, hostile looks to the beings they passed.

"Have all these species renounced planetary living?" Cecilia had to ask. "Are you all part of some habitats-only club?"

"One can rarely generalize behavior to an entire species," Churrlaya pointed out. "But these sophonts choose to reside in a space habitat, as most do in time."

"Do they all consider planets that odious?"

"On the contrary—they value planets. Planets can spawn new life, and occasionally new sophonts. Which is why they should be left free to do so. A biosphere that has evolved to the point of producing one sapient species has the maximum potential to produce others. Rather than staying on a planet and despoiling it, most choose to leave their planets eventually, so that other sophonts are free to develop."

Cecilia had to admit to herself that she found Churrlaya's words fascinating. Their jailer had been a survivor of the Lesshchi disaster and one of the witnesses against *Arachne*'s crew in the trial—the clear conflict of interest proving to Cecilia that the Chirrn had no interest in justice, only in punishing the humans who refused to renounce their planetary allegiance. Indeed, for months, Churrlaya had exploited his power over the prisoners to devise the most degrading and uncomfortable "sociological experiments" he could within the pretense of ethical research the Chirrn flimsily maintained, and had made little secret of enjoying the power he held over them. Yet in the weeks since the attack on the human mothers, something about Churrlaya had changed. Cecilia had come to recognize that the diminutive green Lesshchin had been trying as hard as she was to rein in his anger. Most likely he'd been attempting to outdo her, to prove that Chirrn were still more civilized than any lowly planet-dweller, despite the obscene act his fellow Lesshchin had committed.

The party moved into a corridor that stretched nearly a kilometer in either direction, Cecilia estimated, before its curvature blocked the line of sight, suggesting that the docking ring's radius was at least a hundred and twenty kilometers. Any Coriolis effect was too mild for her to sense; perhaps this was a stationary hoop about a rotating habitat, but then how did the interface work?

A shimmering point in the distance soon resolved into a flock of Zenith flying to meet them. They were led by a tall, resplendent administrator who spoke to Churrlaya for several moments in a fluting, multitonal language that the Chirrn translators did not interpret for the loyalists. The Zenith then escorted the Chirrn and their human prisoners down the endless corridor toward the holding facility. They passed a number of port personnel of various species—none of them Chirrn, interestingly enough—and most took care to give them a wide berth. "What, they've never seen upright bipeds before?" Cecilia asked. "Or are they simply shocked at these fashion disasters you have us wearing?"

"They are aware of your destruction of Lesshchi," Churrlaya told her. "It frightens them. The concept of death on such a massive scale—caused by sophonts against other sophonts, rather than by natural disaster—is difficult for them to accept."

Cecilia scoffed. "You mean they've never had a war? Never seen terrorism?"

"Such things are rare. Mature civilizations find better ways of solving their problems than arbitrarily killing large numbers of people."

"Like torture and enslavement," Amrita shot back. "So civilized."

Nik Zacharias put a calming hand on her shoulder. "Don't they have history?" the doctor asked. "No doubt they killed each other quite happily back when they were 'immature.' So what gives them the right to judge us?"

"Most of them," Churrlaya told him, "have rarely or never known war in their species' history. It is not the universal norm you assume."

"No war?" Ibrahim al-Bakri asked in fascination. "How do they do it?"

Churrlaya hesitated. "You are not ready to understand."

Amrita *harrumph*ed at what she no doubt found a predictable, condescending response. But Cecilia was puzzled. For weeks, Churrlaya had been all too happy to talk about his culture's values and traditions, apparently hoping that the loyalists would be seduced by all that Chirrn civilization had to offer. Why would he be reluctant to share the secret of galactic peace?

Or were the Chirrn even privy to that secret? "And what about you?" she asked him. "L'chellin told us about the ancient war between spacegoing and planet-dwelling Chirrn, the one that drove you out into deep space. How long did it take you to 'understand' what these others knew? Or are you still working on it?"

Churrlaya met her eyes, but she saw the subtle outward twitching of his chameleonlike orbs, as if he were resisting an impulse to look away. Was it a sign of deceit... or of embarrassment? "You have not yet understood the meaning of that tale either. I wish that you could, for its words begat all that has happened here."

"Then I'd sincerely like you to explain it to me, Churrlaya."

Now his gaze held hers firmly. "I believe you, Cecilia. But I am not sure anymore if I am competent to judge its meaning." He maneuvered closer, and as always she envied the Chirrn's deftness in freefall. "Tell me. Do you believe that your wars, your disasters and plagues, your oppressions and tyrannies have made you a better people? That you have drawn strength and wisdom from their lessons?"

She considered it for a time. "I don't think they made us better. I think the strength and wisdom we embraced to defeat them made us better."

"Then if they had never occurred, do you believe you would have found that same strength and wisdom?"

Cecilia studied him, but he gave no hint of the purpose behind his questions. "Honestly? No. We're a lazy people. Make our lives too easy, too free of challenge, and we squander them. Character is a muscle — you need stress to make it strong."

Churrlaya searched her eyes. "Then do you think that strength is worth the terrible cost?"

She chose her words very carefully. "I think… we don't have the luxury of avoiding terrible things. It's not a price we can escape paying; the universe will exact it from us when it sees fit. All we can do is choose whether we let it diminish us or make us stronger."

The Lesshchin moved closer still, lowering his voice to a soft hiss. "And you believe that remaining unrenounced keeps you strong?"

"It does."

His eyes rolled left, directing her attention toward Diego's clique, who stared at the aliens they passed with a mix of emotions: cool contempt from Diego, agitated suspicion from James, terrified revulsion from Evan, burning hatred from Amrita. "All of you?" he asked of her alone.

She had no answer.

They reached the cell, a bare room with opaque walls and minimal amenities beyond basic handholds and perches, and Churrlaya left her there to contemplate their discussion. As their confinement suits relaxed and they began pulling them open to free their hands, Diego sidled over. "Captain… it troubles some of us to see you speaking so intimately with the Frog Footman. I've heard the others complaining that you spend more time with it than with us."

"I'm trying to prove we're not barbarians, Diego. That we're capable of more than hate and bitterness. I understand how you and the others feel, but we must not let them goad us into being as degraded as they think we are."

"I get it, Cecilia. You're trying to domesticate the beast. Just take care it doesn't domesticate you."

"What's that supposed to mean?" She was having difficulty wrestling her arms out of the sleeves; it had been a while since she'd been forced to wear one of these.

Diego had successfully stripped to the waist, so he gently pushed her hands aside and grasped her coverall's wide neckline. "Just that I'm not convinced everyone understands your reasons for ordering us to abandon our escape attempt back at Shilirrlal." His palms caressed her skin as he slid the garment off her shoulders and down her arms. "I understand—you didn't want us to resort to violence. You thought the risk of backlash outweighed the chance of our escape. I respect that—even admire it." He finished freeing her hands from the sleeves and clasped them in his. Their eyes held each other, and she could feel the warmth of his bare chest near her own. "But you need to reassure the others that you haven't lost your way. That your allegiance remains with your own kind." He raised a hand to stroke her short, silver-blonde hair.

After a moment, she moved back, pulling up her jumpsuit and tying the sleeves over her flushed breasts. At another time, she might have eagerly returned his advances. Diego was as much a natural alpha male as Stephen, but with much more of the bad-boy charm that attracted her. They'd had a number of very satisfying dalliances over the months of confinement, as partnerships had shuffled under the impetus of Chirrn mind games and personal temptations. And the prisoners had long since left behind any shred of body modesty out of necessity. But she didn't care for his rather blatant attempt to manipulate her with sex. Cecilia took her pleasures at her own time and for her own reasons. "What did you have in mind, Diego?"

"I studied the layout as we passed. This facility isn't designed to be a prison. And there are many ships here, ships that could take us to Cybele or Earth in weeks, maybe less. This could be our best chance to escape."

"All right," she said after a moment. "It's certainly worth considering." She turned to the rest. "But we mustn't get overambitious. We wouldn't know how to fly one of those ships. And I don't want to leave Arachne and the rest of the crew behind without giving them a chance to join us. Our best bet is to escape into the habitat, find someplace to hole up. Maybe we can lose ourselves in the crowd, find allies to back our cause against the Chirrn."

"Why would any of them help us?" James demanded. The pale-skinned American's time in captivity had only amplified his tendency toward paranoia.

"Did you see their reactions? Sure, they were afraid of us, the big bad Chirrn-slayers. But aside from the Zenith, I didn't see any of them talking to the Chirrn either. I got a feeling that the Chirrn aren't that popular themselves. We've been wondering why they choose to hide in darkened habitats in deep space. Maybe somebody out there doesn't like them."

"Or maybe you're projecting what you want to see onto creatures whose body language you can't read," Diego countered. "The animals out there are as likely to be our predators as our helpers. We can't rely on anything but our fellow humans. And not even most of them. As far as I'm concerned, the traitors have renounced their humanity and are no longer our responsibility."

"Even though they still have souls?" Cecilia challenged.

"That's debatable, since they sold them so cheaply. All it means is that I won't do anything that might cost them their lives. Traitors or not, their lives are still sacred and only God has the right to take them." His eyes roved across the group, ending on Cecilia's. "But God also gave humans dominion over other living things. If we have to kill nonhumans to save ourselves, that is our right, and we must be ready to do so without hesitation."

"Only as a last resort," Cecilia emphasized.

Diego gave a gracious bow. "Of course."

"And traitors or not, we need more humans with us. We don't know if we'll ever get back to Earth. We need a larger breeding base than six men and three women."

"If breeding is even possible," Kahina Amrouche said. "What if whatever the Chirrn did to prevent it is permanent? I mean, I know it's reversible, but if only they know how…"

"It might be better not to procreate," Diego said. "Bring children into a galaxy that isn't theirs?" He shook his head. "No. We need to get back to human civilization, not just for ourselves but so we can warn them of what's out here, help them build defenses against the Chirrn."

Diego spoke with authority, as though he, not Cecilia, were the one in charge. Distressingly, the others seemed to accept this. Cecilia feared that Diego was right—she had lost the loyalists' trust by shutting down their escape attempt back at Shilirrlal.

And she feared there might be no way to win it back without leading her people into a fight they had no chance of winning.

2

As the Arachnen and their mediators entered the spacious elevator carriage that would take them down, they were met by a foursome of diminutive sophonts, less than a meter and a half tall with wide, wing-like ears, large dark eyes, and short muzzles, giving them a cervine appearance. Their build was vaguely centaurian, with a third leg at the rear and a third arm emerging from mid-chest. Their downy fur was mottled in various shades of green and gold, and they were nude aside from matching head adornments and various pouches and belts. "We convey greetings between Antares Star Palace and Migration guild from Shilirrlal," one of the elfin creatures intoned, speaking the Universal dialect of Chirramh in a soft, cooing voice with surprisingly little accent. "We assist with luggage, supplies, queries, and other service upon request."

As the delicate-looking creature continued its spiel, R'nilinnath sidled up to the humans. "Zhalevey," she explained. "Very ancient, found almost everywhere. They thrive on service to others, so everybody likes them."

"So why weren't there any on Shilirrlal?" Tarik Bahar asked, sizing up the adorable sophonts with a wary gaze. Stephen thought the burly, thick-mustached acting captain was being overprotective, but that had always been Tarik's nature, ever since his days as an Istanbul police officer—and more so than ever since he and Kweli had lost their baby.

"Chirrn like to be self-reliant. We won't kick them out if they visit," Nilly went on, using a shared idiom that was far more literal in Chirrn usage, "but they get bored with nobody needing them and go somewhere else."

A Zhalevey with a mostly golden face framed by green floated over to Stephen. "Greetings between Antares B Star Palace and Arachnen in migration. Limitation is acknowledged: Arachnen in transition through probationary status. Physical and network access within Star Palace are conditional upon supervision by Shilirrlaln, designated mentors of Arachnen. Otherwise, Zhalevey shall provide any service desired."

"Thank you," Stephen said. The messenger made the message more palatable. Up close, the Zhalevey's muzzle was a surprisingly flexible fleshy tube with flat grinding surfaces visible within. Their limbs bent smoothly without joints, more like tails, and indeed their whole bodies seemed somewhat mutable: the Zhalevey greeting the humans adopted a more erect posture (even in free fall) and drew in its sock-puppet muzzle somewhat, while the ones tending to the Chirrn angled their bodies forward and even seemed to increase the separation between their eyes. It was like being attended by a gaggle of stuffed animals. "Um, do you have a name?"

"Phlrntsya."

"Phril… Phler…"

"Phlrntsya."

"Phuller…"

"Oh, just go with Fred," Sita interposed.

"As you will," the Zhalevey consented without pause.

Despite their floppy appearance, the Zhalevey handled the party's luggage with ease while escorting them to the carriage's comfortably appointed lounge. The hundred-kilometer descent would take nearly an hour, enough time for their bodies to acclimate to the greater atmospheric density the Zenith favored. The Arachnen's nanorepair systems, with a bit of Chirrn augmentation, had grown respiratory filters that would let them endure the dense air without suffering oxygen toxicity, nitrogen narcosis, or hypercapnia, but it would still take their bodies and filter implants time to adjust to the rising pressure, as well as the increase in gravity as they descended toward the surface.

"Antares B Star Palace is the customs port for the wormhole node that allows direct access to Lode Seven, the neutron star system where we shall obtain the quark matter," L'chellin explained to the Arachnen as they gazed out the lounge windows and watched the scintillating towers of the Star Palace draw gradually nearer. "We must negotiate for access. We may be here for several *narrissh*," the cobalt-skinned, vanilla-maned mediator went on. Stephen still needed to remind himself that a *narrissh* was a Chirrn "day," a bit under fourteen hours.

"Neutron star?" Haim Silbermann echoed. "That's how you get the necessary conditions to make PQM, isn't it?"

"Correct. Or rather… it is made on the surfaces of neutron stars, and we obtain it afterward."

"Made by what?" the chief engineer asked.

"Or whom?" Sita chimed in. "There have been theories about nucleonic life… organisms living millions of times faster than carbon-based life, because the particles are so much closer together, the interactions so much faster." The fascination in her eyes delighted Stephen.

"That is not entirely removed from truth," L'chellin said.

Broadwing focused his three eyes on her. "Do you also have theories about metasapient life?" Arachne's subtitles offered a variety of translations for the term Broadwing used, but "metasapient" was the recommended one.

"There have been experiments to create both cyber and organic consciousnesses more advanced than the human mind," Arachne answered through her avatar. "But beyond certain limited augmentations of speed, memory, and the like, they always result in collapse or insanity. Sapience is a controlled instability, dynamic enough to innovate and adapt, but not so much as to fall into chaos. Make a mind's processes too complex and the internal chaos overwhelms any useful thought or awareness of the outside world."

"A world such as the realms we inhabit, yes," Broadwing replied. "The complexity of our minds is suited for the complexity of the environment in which we evolved. When inputs from the outer world are removed," (<*sensory deprivation,*> added Arachne's annotation,) "our inner processes overwhelm us and we can suffer mental breakdown. So it follows…" He trailed off.

Sita picked up the thread. "That a more complex mind could be stable… in a more complex environment?"

"Exactly! Higher levels of consciousness can be stable in environments rich and dynamic enough to balance their inner complexity. Many metasapients live near the galactic core within nested Dyson shells of smart matter, powerful enough to simulate or physically create environments of sufficient complexity to sustain them. Some, it is believed, create their own pocket universes with a density and temperature approaching the early moments of our own universe."

"And others," R'nilinnath chimed in brightly, "live on neutron stars."

"Where they make programmable quark matter?" Tarik asked.

"Of course. You don't think *we're* intelligent enough to have created a thing that virtually breaks the laws of physics, do you?"

Broadwing preened the silvery featherfur on his shoulder. "More to the point, manufacturing femtotechnology such as PQM requires temperatures, pressures, and materials only found on neutron star surfaces or in the cores of stars and giant planets. And the computations are so complex that it requires femtotechnology to build it in the first place."

"Now, hold on," Haim said. "At the trial, Captain Rillial said that most civilizations don't travel the stars extensively until they achieve gravity control—meaning warp cages and the like. Which requires PQM. So if you have to go to neutron stars to get PQM, how do new civilizations get out to the stars to begin with?"

L'chellin responded promptly, as though she'd been expecting Haim's question. "Once a species has made contact with PQM-equipped civilizations—whether through slow migration, electromagnetic communication, or other means—there is a system by which the more mature civilization can sponsor the novice one, offering mentoring and guidance into the galactic community and eventual access to the technology and resources thereof. It is a very... gradual process."

"So that's what Phler—Fred meant by calling you our 'designated mentors?'" Stephen asked.

"That is... an adequate understanding for these purposes," L'chellin affirmed, a bit tentatively.

"So where do these metaminds fit in?" Sita asked. "Do you actually buy the stuff from them? What could they possibly want from you?"

"There is no direct exchange," L'chellin explained. "Metasapients are so far above our level of thought that understanding them is impossible, just as your pets could not understand this conversation. Whereas they do not even notice us as individuals—or so we believe. We are below their perceptual threshold. To the extent that they are aware of us, it is in the aggregate."

"So they just *give* you the PQM?"

"Essentially. They launch it into orbit, where we collect it and process it to suit our needs. The raw material is delivered in multiple forms, allowing us to adapt and combine it to any purpose we require."

"But why?"

"We can only guess their motives. Some believe it is simply a waste product of their civilization."

Broadwing shrugged his wings. "But it appears too deliberate to be accidental. Many believe that the metasapients give us PQM so that we will have the means to join them. To travel to places where metaminds can exist—or to create such places—and gain sufficient understanding of the universe that we may learn to reach their level of being."

"After all," L'chellin added, "the more minds that join them, the more complex their environments become. If there is one thing we do know for certain, it is their need for hypercomplex, hyperstimulating environments."

"So why haven't your species made the jump yet?" Sita asked.

"We don't know how," Nilly said. "Metaminds can't survive outside their special environments, and normal minds can't survive in them. So how do you get from one to the other? Before you can make the transition, you need to solve that problem."

L'chellin put a hand on the apprentice's back, quieting her. "Which presupposes you would be looking in the first place," she said. "The Chirrn are comfortable with our own form of existence. Metasapient thought may be more complex, even more advanced, but that does not necessarily make it better. Metasapience is much like death—no one who has made the transition is able to report back about the specifics."

"That's a very Chirrn sort of caution." Sita turned to the other mediator. "But knowing the Zenith, I'd think you'd jump at the chance— pardon the expression—to climb to a higher level."

Broadwing was slow to respond, and Stephen noted L'chellin's gaze fixed sternly on her fellow mediator. "Most Zenith," Broadwing finally answered, "consider it a false ascension. It requires traveling downward to a neutron star surface or to the core of the galaxy, sinking deeper into a gravity well. In fact, it is to descend—to remove oneself from galactic society rather than seeking to rise within it. It is not what the Seekers of the Zenith aspire to." Sita took in his answer with a skeptical moue.

Once they reached the surface and exited into the grand promenade of the Antares B Star Palace, Stephen and the others got a look at what the Zenith *did* aspire to. And it was worth the wait. The promenade was a vast open space hundreds of meters high and wide, extending clear around the planet's equator with no breaks save for the dozen space-elevator shafts that pierced its center. Stretching beyond the tight curve of the habitat to east and west and nearly to the horizon to north and south, it made Times Square or Vestalia Concourse look like an Amish village. Everywhere Stephen looked, vast holo-walls, animated ad-sculptures, ornate light displays, massive fountains, vertiginous overhead bridges, and hovering platforms festooned the space, along with other sights he didn't trust himself to interpret—and that was even without being granted access to the local augreality network. Exotic sounds were everywhere, pervading the space, and he couldn't tell what was music, what was speech, and what was machinery noise.

But the scenery was rivaled by its occupants—sophonts of all shapes and sizes striding, strolling, hopping, flying, scuttling, and slithering through the promenade, as well as riding through the immense space in various trams, aircars, groundcars, and even things that seemed to correspond to bicycles and pedicabs. Numerous drones flitted about overhead, carrying parcels or displaying animated ads or tracking certain members of the crowd. Dozens of species intermingled effortlessly, seemingly untroubled by their differences. The local gravity was about two-thirds of a g, toward the lower limit found on worlds suitable for life on land, for the convenience of a wide range of sophonts.

"Bloody gobsmacking," Sita gasped, her big dark eyes gaping wider than ever at the sights around her. "How come there are so many more species here than in the Central Void?"

"Migration patterns have been shifting," Broadwing told her as the rest of the Shilirrlaln and Arachnen debarked from the elevator car, Zhalevey skittering underfoot to tend to their luggage and gear. "For millennia, populations have been relocating away from the hypergiant variable binary system that dominates the near portion of the spiral arm antispinward of here."

"Eta Carinae," Arachne interpreted. "A star expected to go hypernova in the very near astronomical future. Its preliminary eruptions alone have approached supernova magnitude."

"Those eruptions were controlled discharges engineered to reduce the intensity of the eventual cataclysm," Broadwing said, dropping the cosmic bombshell with a casualness Stephen was beginning to find routine. "Yet even they released radiation and interstellar medium disruptions sufficient to endanger life for many parsecs around. A sizeable volume of surrounding space, larger than the Four Voids, has needed to be evacuated ahead of the final destruction. It has caused a ripple effect of migrations—established populations shifting outward in response to increased crowding in their own territories — and now this diaspora front has expanded far enough to impinge on the Antispinward Void."

"That wouldn't be why you decided to found a new habitat in this part of space, would it?" Sita probed. "To shore up your territorial claims along this border?"

"'Territory' is a planet-dweller's concept," L'chellin interposed before Broadwing could reply. "There is always abundant room in space. What we control includes our own habitats, the space adjacent to them, and the routes between them."

"Then why did those 'established populations' decide they had to move when the refugees came?"

The elder Chirrn replied slowly. "Do not concern yourself, Sita. The migration prompted by the impending hypernova was of extraordinary size and density. At these reaches, the impact is more diffuse and manageable."

Stephen tapped Sita's wrist to get her attention, giving a subtle shake of his head. He'd been tolerant of her efforts to probe beyond what the Arachnen were currently cleared to know, hoping it could help her move past her grief. The return of her natural determination was good to see after her months of fearful isolation. But their initial entry into an environment this alien was not a good time to push limits, even aside from the penalties they could face if they violated their probation. He hoped Sita would figure that out on her own.

Sita ignored his wordless caution. "But if territory matters so little, why are the Voids so empty to begin with?"

"You know the Voids were created by a wave of star formation," L'chellin told her. "Most civilizations choose to migrate away from such hazards."

"But that was millions of years ago, well before the Chirrn emerged. There's been more than enough time to repopulate, even without FTL. So why didn't—"

Her words choked off when Broadwing rose to his full height and unfolded his wing dactyls, letting out a deafening calliope shriek before leaping skyward with a powerful downstroke of his wings. The gust of wind almost knocked her over, but Diana Thorne caught her, holding her steady. Sita gave the statuesque, bronze-haired engineer a quick look of thanks before turning back to follow Broadwing's flight, a grin on her face.

Focusing his adaptive optics, Stephen saw multiple dining facilities suspended from the roof of the promenade, all patronized by numerous Zenith, hundreds in all. Despite the Zenith's dense native atmosphere, it exacted a very high metabolic cost to power both a set of wings and a sapient brain, so essentially all Zenith social activity revolved around meals. As others flew down from the eateries to confront and challenge the new arrival, Stephen recognized that Broadwing's name might be something of a boast; as impressive as he was to human eyes, he seemed scrawny and dull next to his challengers, with not only smaller wings and body, but smaller, less brilliant crests. Zenith headcrests were indicators of status; as they gained in social standing and contentment, their serotonin-analogue levels rose, stiffening the keratinous microfibers in the crests and intensifying their diffraction-grating rainbow effect.

Stephen noticed that Arachne provided no subtitles for their challenge and response cries. "Why isn't it translating?" Sita asked the avatar in frustration.

"It's a different language than the Shilirrlaln Zenith use," the cyber replied. "I haven't evolved a translation matrix yet."

Fred the Zhalevey sidled closer on their three floppy legs. "Zenith translation summary available. They challenge the new arrival's right to be present. He sings of accomplishments as arbiter and mediator, yet they mock him for association with dirtgrubbers and ferals."

The Arachnen stared at the gold-faced Zhalevey, who seemed amiably oblivious to any insult. "Well, it is the closest translation," Nilly pointed out in its defense. "And it's not like you're really dirtgrubbers anymore."

"Some of us never were," pointed out Diana, a proud native of the Vanguard habitat in Sol's asteroid belt.

Sita frowned. "But we are feral?"

L'chellin hushed Nilly and threw the humans an apologetic look. "Do not be concerned," she said. "The point of Zenith challenges is the act itself; the specifics of the taunt are arbitrary. Rest assured that you are as welcome here as we are." Nilly snorted a bit and twitched her tail, making Stephen wonder what amused her so. But the young Chirrn fell silent under another glare from L'chellin.

The elder mediator straightened, taking on the distracted look of a Chirrn receiving a message through the consensus network. "Excuse me," she said after a moment. "R'nilinnath, tend to the Arachnen, please. I shall return shortly."

L'chellin bounded off through the crowded plaza, soon intercepting a trio of sophonts who were being escorted their way by another gaggle of Zhalevey. At first, Stephen assumed they were some new ethnic variant of Chirrn, but he soon realized they were something different—more upright-bodied and pear-shaped, with blunter snouts, stubby downturned tails, and no manes. They hopped like Chirrn, but without the same power or grace. All told, they gave the impression of being the Chirrn's fuddy-duddy grandparents.

L'chellin and the threesome exchanged a greeting that looked like a standard Chirrn challenge-and-recognition ritual. Yet L'chellin seemed at once deferential and wary toward the newcomers. "Who are they?" Sita wondered aloud.

R'nilinnath gave a faint hiss through her teeth. "Shayal. Here to intrude in our affairs, no doubt."

"Are they some kind of... Chirrn offshoot?"

"We evolved on the same planet," Nilly grudgingly admitted. "But we're no closer than you and—what is it called?—a gibbon."

"Ohh, bloody brilliant! Two coexisting sophonts of the same evolutionary line! Did you evolve at the same time, or...?"

Nilly chuffed. "They never let us forget that they were first."

"I take it they migrated into space and left the planet to you," Stephen said, his tone suggesting that the young Chirrn should be more grateful.

"Yes, acknowledged."

"Is that why the Chirrn followed their example?"

Nilly fidgeted. "It isn't just theirs. Most sophonts do it."

L'chellin seemed to be arguing with the lead Shayal, then threw a furtive glance the Arachnen's way and assumed a more deferential pose. After a moment, the other sophont gave a very Chirrn-like gesture of assent. The triad remained behind while L'chellin returned to the party, looking irritated. "Aren't you going to introduce us to your, ah, relatives?" Stephen asked carefully.

"Perhaps later," L'chellin said, her voice controlled. "For now, this atmosphere will fatigue you quickly until you acclimate. We should see you to your guest suite." She began herding them and their Zhalevey escorts away from the Shayal triad.

"Already?" Sita protested. "But—*this!*" She waved her arms, making their setting an argument in itself.

"Your curiosity is commendable, Sita," the elder mediator went on. "But I would advise you all to stay close for now and allow us, or at least the Zhalevey, to mediate any contacts with other sophonts. Humans are smaller and less durable than many Galactic species, and if you get too close to a sophont whose body language you cannot read, there is a risk of accidental injury."

Diana Thorne crossed her arms in irritation. "Some of us are plenty durable," the towering engineer said.

"And overly eager to prove yourselves. Rest assured, Diana, you will find recreations here to challenge your physical prowess, but please wait until we can coordinate with the Star Palace staff to organize activities appropriate to your physiology—and brief them on your medical needs in case of… overzealousness." Diana's dark, gorgeous face flushed redder. The young Vanguardian's eagerness to test her transhuman abilities against Chirrn athletes had landed her under Kweli Ndege's medical care more than once, even before the injuries she'd sustained in the Lesshchin attack. Despite being the Arachnen's most powerful member, she'd spent more time in the hospital than any of them, to her own deep embarrassment.

But it was Sita who leaned in to Stephen and whispered, "Bugger that. Alien Central Station and we don't even get to mingle? Tell you what—you create a distraction and I'll slip away."

"Sita…" He touched her shoulder. "I'm glad you've moved beyond your fears, but this is not the place or time to get reckless."

"Come on, I just want to take a quick butchers."

Sometimes Stephen was tempted to ask Arachne to subtitle Sita's Cockneyisms. But he got the drift. "You've seen how uneasy they are with us. The last thing we want is to risk… another misunderstanding."

A shudder went through her at the reminder, and Stephen hated himself for provoking it. But there was no way he would risk her safety again. He held her closer. "Look… I'm sure the mediators will be happy to help you tap into the local net, and I'll make sure you're on the first supervised tour we can arrange."

Sita gathered herself. "Right. Cheers. Sounds nice and sensible." But she moved away without another word, and he feared he'd raised the wall between them again, just when he needed her to trust him the most.

As the Zhalevey and the mediators escorted the Arachnen out of the grand promenade toward their guest accommodations, a swarm of small drones descended on the group, followed closely by a small mob of xenosophonts of more species than Tarik Bahar could count. Their aggressive approach immediately put Tarik on the defensive. The memory of the Lesshchin attack remained vivid: *Waking to an angry mob of Chirrn bursting into his bedroom. Leaping up to protect Kweli, being struck down by the sweep of an attacker's heavy tail. Coming to with hands and feet tied and ribs broken, dragged out into the public square, forced to watch as Kweli and all the other pregnant women were beaten in the womb. Screaming in fury, nearly breaking his wrists in his desperate struggles to tear free, to run to Kweli's side, to save her and Mehmet even if it killed him. The unbearable guilt of being utterly helpless to stop his unborn child from being murdered. The fear that he would lose Kweli as well. The relief when the Chirrn doctors managed to save her, at least… and the long weeks of despair since, the fear that the warm, joyous, playful, kind woman that he loved was lost to him after all.*

Yet Tarik's attention quickly turned to his wife and the other women in the here-and-now. Kweli, Sita, Kazuko, and the others drew back in fear, huddling together. Fists clenching, Tarik moved forward to shield them. He would let nothing happen to them again.

Diana Thorne joined Tarik, for which he was grateful. The Vanguardian superwoman was the only Arachnen taller and stronger than he was, and Tarik knew her bitterness at failing to protect the babies rivaled his own. Arachne's spider-woman avatar joined the cordon, her Greek-sculpture face morphing into a more threatening arachnid appearance—though some of the beings in the advancing group might well find it more appealing.

L'chellin stepped to the fore as well, though her body language was not confrontational. "Reporters," she explained. "I apologize. I have been fending off their interview requests since we arrived," she went on, tapping her head to clarify. "But it seems Broadwing's departure has emboldened them. I shall persuade them to leave us alone."

Stephen came up alongside her. "Hold on, L'chellin. We've seen how our reputation alarms people out here. This is our chance to get ahead of that narrative. Tell the galaxy our side of the story, make it clear that we have no wish to be a threat."

L'chellin spent a moment communing silently with her Mediation guildmates through the consensus network. "Agreed. A brief statement, with limited questions. I shall interpret between you and the reporters. Your Chirramh is still… idiosyncratic… and we desire no miscommunication."

After a few moments' further discussion, Stephen stepped forward with L'chellin and began to recount the oft-told tale of how he had escaped the poverty and racial oppression of the hurricane-ravaged, strongman-ruled southeastern United States, built a philanthropic-industrialist empire centered in Brazil by the time he was thirty, poured his resources into the advancement of interstellar technology over the next decade and a half, and finally led the *Arachne* expedition to colonize Cybele, the most distant yet most Earthlike world that humans had ever attempted to settle. No doubt he was trying to counter the aliens' perception of the Arachnen as mass murderers from a primitive, savage race.

Tarik had no wish to be reminded of the rest of the story, of *Arachne*'s inadvertent destruction of Lesshchi and all that had followed. Besides, he had more immediate concerns. Moving back toward Kweli and the other women, he saw that the Zhalevey had huddled in close to them, offering protection and comfort. Kweli was on her knees, snuggling two of the plush creatures and weeping softly. Sita, meanwhile, was visibly controlling her fear, craning her head in an attempt to observe the various anatomies on display within the reportorial gaggle. That was quite a reversal. For months after her near-fatal beating by Lesshchi survivors on the humans' first night in captivity, the diminutive xenobiologist had been the most timid member of the group, avoiding contact with aliens as much as possible, while Kweli had actively sought out contact and striven to learn all she could about the biology of the inhabitants of Shilirrlal. Somehow, in the wake of the kiss dance riot and her miscarriage, Sita had managed to regain her courage and was now making up for lost time. Tarik hoped it would not take anything so drastic for Kweli to regain her sense of wonder at alien life.

Tarik placed a hand on Kweli's shoulder, disturbed by how clearly he could feel the bone underneath. She had not been eating well since the attack, and her normally Rubenesque figure had grown significantly leaner. "Are you all right?" he asked.

She looked up and gave him a small, sad smile. "I'm in good hands. See to the others."

Was that her innate selflessness talking, or depression? It frustrated Tarik that he couldn't tell.

Once the galactic press's hunger had been sated, the Zhalevey resumed guiding the group to their guest suite. The pair that Kweli had been snuggling stayed with her even after helping them get settled in their room, seeming perfectly content to serve as live teddy bears indefinitely. Kweli noticed Tarik's unease with their submissiveness and sent them on their way. "Thank you so much, but I'm sure you have duties elsewhere. Yes, certainly, if I need you, I'll let you know."

Tarik cleared his throat. "I know I'm not as plushy as they are, but if you still need someone to hold ..."

With another sad smile (the only kind she seemed to have anymore), she came over and embraced him. "Don't worry, Tarik. You're still my favorite teddy bear."

Still, Tarik found himself unable to relax into the embrace. "What's wrong?" Kweli asked after a time, letting him go.

Grimacing, he began to pace. "I thought we were done with reporters when we left Solsys. I always hated dealing with that lot. But these may be even worse. Just pushing themselves on us when we're so vulnerable, so easily frightened..." He snarled and struck his open palm with his fist, making Kweli jump in alarm. "There, you see? They've put you on edge. They just don't care!" He moved toward her—and was startled when she pulled away. "Kweli! It's all right. It's just me."

She was shaking again. " 'Just' you, Tarik? Sometimes I think you forget how large you are. How intimidating."

Tarik was bewildered. "My love... you know I'd never, ever harm you."

"Knowing is one thing. Feeling?" She shook her head, turning away. "I can't handle... ferocity... right now. I think... I think I need to be by myself."

He winced. Keeping his voice as soft as he could, he told her, "All I want to do is to keep you safe. To help you heal. I love you."

"I know," Kweli said. "I love you too. But right now... you can't help me.

"Right now... I'm not sure anything can."

The Shayal may have had a few million years of evolutionary separation from their Chirrn cousins, but Sita could still read their body language well enough to tell that the head of the triad had expected their conversation with L'chellin to continue. As she lingered in the common area of the Arachnen's guest suite, watching through its clear forward wall as the mediators wrapped things up with the Zhalevey in the spacious atrium outside, she could certainly read L'chellin well enough to know that the vanilla-maned mediator intended to fulfill that expectation, however grudgingly. It wasn't long before the Chirrn elder bounded off toward the waiting Shayal nearby. R'nilinnath moved as if to join her, then pulled up short, taking on an abstracted look and finally sagging in disappointment.

Sita slipped out into the atrium and joined Nilly. "Don't tell me — she told you to wait here."

The apprentice watched uneasily as L'chellin moved off with the triad. "She is my senior."

"But you're worried about her. About these Shayal. Dangerous, are they?"

Nilly drummed her toes in amusement. "Those stunted-tailed ancients? I could take all three of them easily. Even you could take at least one."

"Oi, now!" But the young apprentice was still gazing after them in concern. "What is it you're so bothered about, then?"

Nilly's eyes flicked outward and back, a nervous tell. "Nothing important. I just don't like being left out."

"Come on, Nilly, what aren't you telling me? And why?"

R'nilinnath's hands came up to tap her brows, a gesture of distress or fear. She forced them down a moment later, gathering herself. "I'm sorry, Sita. But it is not my place to decide what to reveal to you and when."

Sita took Nilly's four-digited hands in her own smaller ones. "That never stopped you before, love."

"And look what happened!" Nilly pulled her hands away, placing them over her outward-swiveled eyes. "I thought I was helping, encouraging you to sneak out and explore. And I… what I did to you…"

Sita stroked Nilly's silver mane. "Nilly, what happened on Shilir-rlal wasn't your fault. You couldn't have known…"

"That is the problem. I *don't* know enough. I don't have the full guild memory assimilated yet. I have the surface stuff, the database, but not the deep experience, either my own or the others'. So I don't know what I can tell you and what I shouldn't. If I say too much, what might happen to you?"

Sita hugged her around her neck. "Oh, Nilly. Believe me, I understand how you feel."

"How can you?"

"Because I've been blaming myself too. We all have. Stephen more than anyone, I think. I can't help feeling—what if I hadn't gone with you to the kiss dance? What if I hadn't laughed around the Lesshchin, provoked them in the first place? But then I see the people around me also blaming themselves, and it hurts to see them being so guilty when they don't deserve to be. And that made me realize… maybe I don't deserve to feel so guilty either."

"You don't! You were the victim!"

Tears came to Sita's eyes. "But I'm not alone, my darling. We were all victims. I was a victim of the Lesshchin… they were victims of the disaster… we've all been shaped by past pain. So maybe none of us are really to blame. What happened to us… the causes of it go back farther and deeper than any of us probably know."

Luckily, Nilly's eye could swivel back, so Sita could meet her gaze without having to stop hugging her. "And that's why I need to know what you aren't telling me, love. I feel that whatever L'chellin doesn't want us to know could answer a lot of questions. About why the Chirrn fear planet-dwellers, why you hide your habitats. Why there was so much bitterness toward us even before the disaster." Sita sighed. "It wouldn't make any of this hurt less… but at least we might understand the why of it. Yes, sometimes knowing too much can get you in trouble, but being kept in ignorance is always worse."

Nilly gave her a fond neck-nuzzle before moving away. "You just want me to help you spy on L'chellin."

"Oh, not at all," Sita assured her. "I want to help *you* spy on L'chellin."

The apprentice pondered for a moment. "In that case, come on."

Consulting the local map in the Star Palace's cloud memory, R'nilinnath was able to lead Sita to a skywalk balcony one level below the edge of a plaza where the senior mediator was deep in conversation with the Shayal trio. The balcony's angle let her catch a glimpse of L'chellin, whose body language toward the smaller Shayal was an odd mix of intimidation and defiance, almost like a teenager toward a parent.

Once she was directly underneath the foursome, Sita could no longer see them, but she could hear them over the echoing chatter of the crowd below. Conveniently, they were all speaking Universal Chirramh, so her translator had little trouble with the Shayal's words, spoken with a vocal timbre resembling a Chirrn's but higher in pitch. "Your perspective is noted, Mediator. But if we could only be allowed to examine the Arachnen—"

"They have endured enough, Commissioner," L'chellin replied. "And they are in the midst of a delicate transition. I will not permit you to disrupt that process."

"I offer assurance that we will take their fragility into account. But it would be valuable to assess the degree to which their lack of mentoring has affected their psychology."

Lack of mentoring? Sita thought. L'chellin had described mentoring as a process of guiding novice starfaring civilizations into the interstellar community. Given that humans had only just begun their starfaring era, how could the Shayal's statement make sense?

"Your words betray you, Velesh," L'chellin went on. "This inquiry is to serve the Coalition, not the Arachnen. You hope your increased status in the Antispinward Void will let you win favor at our expense."

Sita whispered in Nilly's ear. "Coalition?"

"The Nine Clusters Coalition," the apprentice hissed back. "Long story."

"Please," continued the one called Velesh. "This is not about our own political standings. Surely we can all agree that the Lesshchi tragedy demonstrates the dangers of allowing current policies to remain unaltered. If the humans had been properly mentored from the onset—"

"That is for the Void Alliance to decide," L'chellin insisted. "And while your presence may be increasing, the Coalition does not yet have enough influence in the Voids to override the existing consensus."

Their voices faded as they hopped away from the plaza edge. Try as they might, Nilly and Sita could not find an eavesdropping point again. "We should get back before we're missed," the apprentice said.

"What did Velesh mean, 'properly mentored from the onset'?" Sita asked her as they respectively jogged and hopped back to the suite.

Nilly hesitated. "Is that how Arachne translated it? Ill-born words, I'd say. Probably a reference to your brief association with galactic society—saying you haven't learned how to behave properly yet."

"But Velesh seemed to be saying Lesshchi could've been avoided. That implies they were talking about how things stood before the disaster."

The apprentice was visibly uneasy now. "Please, Sita. As I said before… I don't know what it would be proper to reveal to you yet. So please stop asking."

Sita recognized that she would get no more answers from R'nilin-nath. And if she wouldn't talk, none of the other mediators would be any more revealing. As for the Shayal, they seemed to have an agenda of their own—and it looked unlikely that L'chellin would allow her any chance to interact with the newcomers.

But Sita's need for answers still compelled her. Surely someone in the Star Palace's cosmopolitan collection of sophonts would be willing to tell her what the Chirrn would not.

The males who challenged Broadwing in the grand promenade had played their parts well. They had presented a convincing aspect of a challenge with their words and posturing, but had backed down when he boasted of his accomplishments as a Shilirrlaln mediator, allowing him to appear victorious enough that his invitation to a private assignation by a watching female would not appear strange. The female was small and scraggly, her crests not appreciably large or bright; her name, Sunflash, was as much an aspirational boast as his own. But perhaps Broadwing had not yet earned better.

"Meridian is present?" he asked Sunflash once they were alone in a private mating gallery, a low-status one whose dome was barely high enough to allow a couple to remain aloft, let alone maneuver effectively. It did little to put him in the mood for more than conversation.

"As always. It is your part that is open to question. Can you deliver upon your promise?"

He uploaded the plans and specifications for the new habitat to her augreality channel, calling her attention to the types and quantities of programmable quark matter the caravan would order at Lode Seven. "It should be more than suitable," he said.

Sunflash shook her crests confidently, and for the first time he started to find her attractive. "Suitable to elevate us, and to knock down the Chirrn a tier or two at the same time. Excellent." She studied him. "And the humans? Will they play their part?"

Broadwing hesitated. "They must be handled delicately. But they are beginning to question the gaps in what they have been told. I believe that as long as I give them the wingroom they need, they will arrive where we wish them on their own."

"How much farther must they fly? They are already the greatest criminals in the Voids, short of the Chirrn themselves."

"Not in their own minds. They seek to prove themselves righteous."

That pleased Sunflash even more. "So much the better, once they learn of our grievances."

Still, her approval did not translate into a sexual advance. After an uncomfortable silence, Broadwing asked, "Do you wish me to disrobe?"

She ducked her head. "I am too lowly to mate with you. Your purpose lifts you to a far higher tier."

Broadwing thrilled at the prospect. *Meridian?* Still, his time among the Chirrn had taught him humility. "I have not yet earned that place."

Sunflash lowered herself further in deference to him. "You have brought us hope of liberation after twelve thousand years. For that alone, we sing your name."

Her praise fulfilled him—but a doubt still lingered. "And the humans… will they share in our liberation?"

"They will serve it," she replied. "Beyond that, does it matter?"

3

AFTER NEARLY A DAY IN THE STAR PALACE, SITA FELT MORE LIKE A prisoner than she had during the trial. It was frustrating to be surrounded by so many exciting new species, yet constrained from moving about freely. So when Broadwing informed the Arachnen that the Palace's medical staff had requested the opportunity to familiarize themselves with a representative sample of humans in case of emergency, Sita jumped to volunteer. Now that Arachne was hooked into the local translation network, the opportunity for some private conversation with the Star Palace staff was too promising to pass up.

When Broadwing escorted her to the medical center and she laid eyes on the physician who would examine her, Sita had second thoughts. Doctor Rauhoc was a large, intimidating creature built like a walking seesaw, his long, spindle-shaped body cantilevered atop a pair of runner's legs a meter and a half long, with two arms and a heavy, spiky-plated head in front and two arm-like rear limbs ending in bony clubs. *Sod it all, why aren't there more small, cute aliens out here?* she thought, fighting down a surge of panic.

Broadwing assured her that Rauhoc's people, the Gaurim, possessed exceptional expertise in the life sciences—largely due, he had grudgingly conceded, to their preference for living on planets and carefully tending their ecosystems. A chat with someone from more of a planetary background might bring a perspective she wouldn't get from the habitat-based community.

Some things were universal, it seemed, since there was a fair wait for the doctor after the brief initial greeting. Sita didn't particularly mind, though. Not only did it give her a chance to wrestle her cowardice back into submission, but it let her observe the clinic staff and their reactions. Most of the Zenith staffers watched her uneasily, and Sita realized with some amusement that they found her, the smallest and least physically threatening human within a hundred and seventy parsecs, as intimidating as she found them. She caught whispers including the word "feral," the same slur she'd been hearing since those first hours after the disaster. Even the Zhalevey receptionist seemed to echo their mood, following its species' instinct to conform to the herd.

Finally, one of the smaller, less impressively crested Zenith females escorted her to an exam room. "You may feel less weighted down here," she said; Sita took it as an idiom for "more comfortable."

"Cheers," she replied. "But is this really for my benefit, or so a 'feral' won't scare off your other patients?"

The orderly ducked her head deferentially. "I apologize for their discomfort toward you. They know of the destruction of the Chirrn habitat."

Sita winced. "Believe me, I haven't forgotten—ah, what was your name?"

"I am Sunflash."

"Good to know you. I take it you don't share the others' discomfort?"

The orderly twisted her head furtively, then leaned closer. "I spy the truth: The Chirrn brought the destruction upon themselves."

Sita recalled Commissioner Velesh's charge to L'chellin. "Because of their mentoring policies?"

Sunflash made a rude noise. "Chirrn have no grasp of mentoring. Whichever way they carry it, disaster results."

Dr. Rauhoc had entered as the orderly spoke, and the Zenith quailed as the massive Gaurim loomed before her. "Attend to your work in silence or I will send you back down where you belong!" Sunflash almost literally flew from the room.

The doctor said nothing more about the altercation, getting straight to business. According to Broadwing, Gaurim worshipped evolution as the work of the divine (or something roughly analogous) and rejoiced in exploring its permutations. Which in this case meant that Rauhoc couldn't get Sita naked on the scanner table fast enough. It was alarming at first, like being pawed by an ankylosaur on stilts, and Sita prayed she wouldn't ruin her investigation with a panic attack. But the doctor's thick, bone-spurred hands proved to have surprisingly delicate manipulative tips, their wide surfaces able to flex and grip with precision like a snail's foot. Her scientific fascination with his anatomy, rivaling his toward hers, soon overcame her fear. Even his clinical, unsympathetic manner toward her recent traumas was oddly reassuring, allowing her to step back and look at them as medical curiosities.

As the examination proceeded, she directed the conversation back toward Sunflash. "Why were you so cross with her?"

"Her words were irreverent toward the loss of life. I require more sensitivity of my staff."

Sita took a gamble. "So you don't agree that the Chirrn have mentored us improperly?"

Rauhoc was slow to respond. "I have no dispute with the Chirrn's current policy on mentoring. Tell me, Doctor Bhatiani: Are your developed mammary glands a residual effect of your recently interrupted gestation? Do you expect the visible protrusions to subside soon?"

"Bloody hell, I hope not. How would I keep strapless gowns up?" She cleared her throat. "So, ah, why do you think the orderly thought otherwise? Do the Zenith have a different approach to mentoring?"

The doctor gave a foghorn grunt. "I do not think she believes as most Zenith would, or she would reside on a higher level. But these are questions for your own mentors."

Sita feigned a knowing laugh. "Mentors. Always think they know best, don't they?"

Rauhoc looked up at her face. "An odd view."

"What makes you say that?"

"I am no expert in ancient history," he demurred, revealing more than he realized. "But we are taught that our mentors, the Mathadn, intervened no more than we wished of them. We lived within the symbiosis of motherworld Vohaun. When we sought knowledge from the Mathadn, it was knowledge of how other sophonts had nurtured and served their own motherworlds, so that we could best serve ours. When the motherworld suffered quakes or eruptions, the mentors offered healing and protection, which many of us accepted; but more orthodox Gaurim were allowed to die as they chose."

Sita blinked. "Um. But clearly you didn't stay that way forever."

"In time, there were those who sought the luxuries of higher technology, damaging the biosphere. It divided us, bringing us to violence that none wished for but none could see a way to avoid. The Mathadn showed us how others had dealt with similar matters, and helped us discover ways to fulfill our needs without threat to the motherworld. The technologists improved their tools until they meshed as smoothly with nature as our own bodies do. Thus, we could join the community of the stars without abandoning who we are. The Mathadn helped us find worlds we could responsibly settle—worlds with compatible biology and no sapience, so we could add ourselves to the tapestry of their evolution and give their biospheres the gift of higher cognition."

So mentoring was far more than just the sponsorship into space that L'chellin had implied. "Sounds like being mentored from the start did you a lot of good."

"Is that what you heard?" the doctor asked. "I meant to convey that we prefer as little intervention with natural development as possible. The Mathadn respected that wish, except when we asked otherwise. And as I said, I have no dispute with the Chirrn's approach. Now: Those arcs of hair above your eyes are impressively mobile. Did they evolve for long-range signaling…?"

Rauhoc would say no more about mentoring, saying he found Sita's anatomy a far more fascinating subject (oh, if she had a research grant for every time she'd heard that line). While it had been a very revealing interview (in more ways than one), it still left her hungry for more.

Fortunately, she was so far below Broadwing's sightline that she was easily overlooked. After the exam, she managed to slip away from the Zenith mediator and track down their main Zhalevey helper, the golden-faced one she'd nicknamed Fred (who had turned out to be female—so be it). Sita had quickly grown to appreciate the Zhalevey's pliant nature. They instinctively identified with others, making their worldviews and priorities as flexible as their bodies. Which was very handy for someone interested in prying where she wasn't supposed to.

Nonetheless, her initial query about mentoring met with resistance from the diminutive, dewy-eyed triped. "As your status is probationary, the administration recommends you transmit that request through your mentors. Would you like to summon Mediator L'chellin?"

"No, no," Sita hastened to reply. "Listen, Fred, the problem is that there are things our 'mentors' aren't telling us."

"Such approaches are at mentor discretion."

Sita sighed. "Look. Your job is to help me fulfill my needs, right?"

"Zhalevey shall provide any feasible service."

"Well, *my* job is to learn all I can about other species. I have a responsibility to my crewmates to help them understand other life forms and any dangers they might pose." She reached out and stroked Fred's downy head. Zhalevey were very tactile, so it seemed like the right approach. Besides, it felt nice. "You can understand that, right? How important it is that we Arachnen have the knowledge we need to make good choices? You want to help us do that, don't you?"

"To provide service, yes. But countervailing needs must be balanced."

Sita was at a loss. How could she manipulate someone who had virtually no sense of self-interest? Particularly one so cute that she felt guilty trying to trick her?

She decided to try another tack. "What I need is to get access to that Velesh bloke," she muttered, half to herself.

"Commissioner Velesh's appointment schedule accessed. Do you favor a time?"

She chuckled. "I appreciate it, love… but I'd like to keep this off the books, okay? Unofficial, you know."

"Accessing Commissioner Velesh's itinerary. An opportunity for unscheduled contact is available in twelve *narredj*. Recommend employment of Zhalevey to distract Mediator L'chellin's attention."

Sita stared. "You'd do that for me?"

"Countervailing needs must be balanced. As Shilirrlaln wish, do not discuss uncleared subjects with Arachnen. As Sita Bhatiani wishes, enable her to reach uncleared information. Zhalevey shall provide any feasible services as desired."

Sita gave her a big hug. "Ohh, I think I want to keep you!"

"No!" Stephen insisted, sitting up in bed. Sita had waited until they were snuggled together after that night's lovemaking to tell him what she'd done, no doubt thinking that he'd be at his most receptive then. But his afterglow faded quickly at her words. "This is going too far, Sita. You're not just bending the rules, you're defying them outright."

"With good reason," his wife stressed, stroking his chest. "The Chirrn have been keeping information from us at every turn."

"Even Nilly had to earn membership in her guild before she was granted full access to their private memories, their mysteries. We *will* learn the answers once we're ready—as long as we don't blow it by pushing the boundaries too far. Remember, we could still face exclusion if we violate our parole." He clasped her shoulders. "I don't want to see anything happen to you, darling."

She sighed. "I know, and I love you for it. But I'm not a porcelain doll, Stephen. I'm a scientist, and I'm following evidence too important to ignore. Too important to all of us."

Sita recapped her conversation with Dr. Rauhoc. "Stephen, this means mentoring isn't just for spacegoing societies. It's supposed to start much earlier, to guide a nascent civilization away from disaster and needless suffering."

Stephen hesitated, reluctant to face what she was implying. "It did for the Rauhoc. We don't know if that's typical."

"That's why we have to find out!" She clasped his hands. "Stephen… Earth is in Void Alliance space. They've been out here all along, since before our civilization began."

"And they've avoided interaction with planetary civilizations."

"Yeah—but what did we miss because of that? What *would* our history have been like if we'd been in contact all this time? Don't you want to know?"

In fact, Stephen burned to know. The insinuation that the Chirrn's policies had deprived humanity of guidance it had been entitled to was deeply disturbing. But he found it hard to reconcile that idea with the patience and kindness the Shilirrlaln had extended to the Arachnen.

He got out of bed and began to pace, the dense air cooling his bare skin. "I'm not sure I trust the source. From what you told me before, it sounds like these Shayal have some kind of political rivalry going on with the Alliance—and I know how badly the truth fares in such conflicts."

"Granted," Sita said, sitting up in the bed. "And that Zenith orderly, Sunflash… it sounded like she has her own grudges against the Chirrn. Believe me, love, I know better than to take any single source of information at face value." She spoke urgently. "But that includes the Chirrn! Even with the most benevolent of motives, they have their own bias, their own preconceptions, and that filters what they reveal to us. We need an alternative source of data."

"And what about your own bias?" Stephen insisted.

"What bias?"

"The same one we all share—guilt. The burden of responsibility for all this tragedy. I'm afraid you're doing the same thing Cecilia did: looking for scapegoats, for anyone else you can shift the blame to."

"I'm looking for answers! Finding someone to blame never works, because everyone's reacting to their own prior causes. The Lesshchin blame us, we blame them, we blame ourselves… all this blamed bloody blaming, it's just lashing out, not understanding. I've found no answers there, Stephen. Now I'm just trying to get some perspective. We need to know how the Galactics see us, and why, and why we've been excluded from their community. We need to know how we fit into the picture so we can avoid more misunderstandings, more conflicts."

"And that's what the Chirrn are teaching us."

"Piecemeal! Filtered through their own assumptions. We need more than that."

"Rushing in recklessly is what got us into this mess to begin with!"

Sita stared at him. "You brought me along to do a job," she insisted. "To learn about alien life. To find the answers you need to help this crew survive in a hostile environment." She reached up and clasped his hands. "So trust me to do that job — and be with me when I do."

As he gazed down into her eyes, he felt ashamed for doubting her. Had he grown so accustomed to seeing her as a fragile victim needing his protection that he'd lost sight of the keen wit and initiative that had earned her a place on *Arachne* — and in his heart?

He pulled Sita into his arms and held her close for a long time. "You're right," he finally said. "I have been afraid of the answers. But that's all the more reason I have to face them, whatever they are."

She pulled him back down to the bed and gave him a long, gentle kiss. "Wrong, you silly git. It's why *we* have to face them. Together."

After an estimated two days in freefall confinement, Cecilia Lo-Carno and Nik Zacharias had convinced Churrlaya to grant them an exercise period. Their confinement suits were able to create dynamic resistance for their muscles, and to vibrate in the low-frequency cat's-purr range that helped stimulate muscle and bone healing in Terrestrial life forms, but the doctor had argued that both would work better if the captives had a better opportunity to *use* their muscles — and that a change of scenery would do them good as well.

Churrlaya had readily agreed, even fabricating some rough exercise wear for the group's comfort. His cooperation drove home something Cecilia had begun to realize in the wake of their conversation the other day. In the weeks since she and Churrlaya had stopped sniping at each other, they'd actually found themselves starting to *listen* to each other — to what Cecilia suspected was their mutual surprise. The ensuing discussions had been intriguing and enlightening, and she'd grown to look forward to them. Diego may have seen that as disloyalty to her own kind, but Cecilia felt it was quite the opposite. After all, if she could persuade a Lesshchin to understand her point of view, perhaps it could even lead the Chirrn to change their minds about the humans' imprisonment. *Just what Stephen would do,* she thought, *if he ever came to his senses.*

For now, Cecilia simply welcomed the chance to stretch her legs. The free-fall exercise room to which they were escorted held strange-looking equipment that their Chirrn and Zenith guards had to explain how to use, and that could only be reconfigured so far to fit human proportions and strength. But on the plus side, the room had an extraordinary view. It was the first time they'd been able to look out a window since they'd left Shilirrlal, and Cecilia found herself glued to the port. They were in a scaled-down Clarke ring connected by a series of space elevators to an artificial worldlet like something out of an Escher woodcut, festooned with colored lights like the aftermath of a Christmas decoration competition run amok. "We're at a Star Palace," she realized.

"But where?" Diego Narvaez asked.

"Antares, I'd say," Cecilia replied after studying the bright stars outside. "We've detected Star Palaces there, and the system configuration looks right. That would put us… a hundred seventy parsecs from home."

"How do we ever get home from here?" Evan Jiang whined.

"We should be trying to reach Cybele," Nik countered.

"Not this again," Diego fired back. "We have an obligation to report to Solsys about the aliens and the threat they pose."

The doctor sighed. "I know, I know. But I came out here hoping to build a new world."

"We all did," put in Ibrahim al-Bakri. The ecologist had felt utterly useless during his months in these technological prisons.

"They'd never have let us reach Cybele," James Oates insisted. "For all we know, they've invaded Earth already."

Hoping to deflect another of James's conspiratorial rants, Cecilia spoke up. "On the subject of building worlds, how in the hell can this Star Palace possibly work?" She pointed out the viewport. "Look at the angular motion in the starscape. The rotation period can't be more than ninety minutes. If it's canceling the Palace's gravity, given the apparent altitude of this ring, then its mass has to be greater than that of Davida," she said, referring to one of the larger Outer Belt asteroids. "But it's packed into such a small volume that it would have to consist partly of degenerate matter. How could that be?"

"It's been suggested that antimatter explosions could compress matter to a degenerate state," Diego mentioned idly, "so it could be coated in a layer of diamond to prevent its re-expansion. It would be incredibly difficult to pull off, though. And if the diamond shell ruptured, the whole thing would blow apart in the blink of an eye."

Amrita cackled, stroking Nik's shoulders. "Wonder if we could find a way to trigger that here. Kill all the monsters in one big bang." Evan and James joined in her laughter.

Nik squirmed under her grip, visibly disgusted, but he strove for calm. "What would that accomplish?" he asked his lover in a gentle tone.

But it was easier for Nik to soothe Amrita's hatred when Diego wasn't around to feed it. "A diversion," the taller man said. "A strike to ensure we'd be free from pursuit. Drastic, and unlikely to be achievable, but we should consider every option, no matter how remote." Diego's gaze bored into Nik's eyes. "Or how disturbing to the squeamish."

"Don't be so soft," Amrita advised. "It'd be over before they knew it, so no suffering." She chuckled. "More's the pity."

Nik pushed away from the windows, but Amrita followed. "Oh, lighten up, will you?"

The doctor caught a handhold and whirled on her. "There's nothing 'light' about the kind of jokes you all keep making. You of all people should know better."

"Me of all people? What's that supposed to mean?"

"You know!" Taking a breath to calm himself, he stroked Amrita's cheek, her rough-cut hair. "You know what it's like to suffer from other people's cruelty. I don't believe you'd really be so glad to see others suffer."

Amrita slapped him. "You bastard. You self-absorbed Sheaver with your cushy, entitled upbringing. You can't understand the evil of monsters like them. How much they relish causing suffering—how much they deserve to be shown what it really feels like."

"Okay, the Chirrn, that's one thing. But not all these aliens are Chirrn."

"They're helping them, that's enough. They're the enemy."

He sighed. "Maybe. But you don't have to enjoy it so much."

"You have no idea what I need."

"And I don't think I want to know! Look… this isn't working. From now on, we should just—"

"Fine," Amrita snarled before he could even finish putting the breakup into words. "I don't like weak men anyway."

Once Amrita had let Diego escort her away, Cecilia made her way over to the doctor. "I'm sorry," Nik told her once they could speak confidentially. "I thought I could help her heal, but she's too far gone. I'm afraid Diego's just making her and the others worse."

"Hey," Cecilia said. "Don't lose faith. We need to stand together in this."

"Why? Sometimes I have to wonder. I'm a Strider. My grandparents helped build the Ceres Sheaf. What am I doing in prison for loyalty to Earth, of all places?"

She met his eyes firmly. "Your loyalty is to your crew, Doctor. And to your oath. You're the only doctor we have."

"The Chirrn take excellent care of us."

"They can never understand what we need." She held his gaze. "Nik, don't waver on me now."

After a moment, the lanky Cerean sighed. "I'm sorry, Captain—I'm just frustrated. But I'm not going anywhere. Giving in to the Chirrn—it would mean giving up my independence, my identity as a human and a Strider. I mean, living in interstellar space, a nomadic existence between the stars—that would be a challenge worthy of the Striders. But only if we achieved it by our own choice, our own initiative. Not on anyone else's terms."

Cecilia smiled, heartened by his words. "That's the spirit, Nik. That's what we're fighting for in a nutshell."

The doctor threw a worried look toward Diego, Amrita, and their clique. "Do they know that?"

As Cecilia watched Diego and the other loyalists laughing and joking about killing soulless aliens *en masse*, she couldn't help hearing Churrlaya's words in her mind. Were they really making themselves stronger, better people through their defiance?

By clinging so fiercely to Earth, were they reinforcing their humanity—or losing it?

Sita and Stephen found Velesh's triad in an upper-level skybox of the Star Palace's sports arena, a high, tiered cylindrical space with perches and platforms at various levels and only hard, uncushioned ground at the bottom. About a dozen big, powerful Zenith males were competing in the air, striving to gain control of the higher, narrower levels at the others' expense. There were no teams; every individual Zenith fought everyone else, or at best formed temporary alliances until the time came to turn on one another. From the frantic way the falling athletes struggled to catch themselves on perches or platforms before reaching the bottom, and from the crowd's intense reactions to their success or failure, it was clear that touching the ground meant summary disqualification even if one avoided injury. It was a compelling spectacle, and Sita had to force herself to stay focused on their purpose.

The altitude of the Shayal's skybox suggested they were afforded high status by the Antarean Zenith. Yet Velesh watched the turbulent proceedings with thinly veiled distaste. Sita got the sense that the commissioner only attended to be polite.

"Quite the spectacle, isn't it?" Stephen said to draw the Shayal's attention.

The triad turned as one to take him in, then exchanged startled looks. Up close, Sita could see their differences from the Chirrn more clearly. Their maneless necks were longer and narrower, with additional bristles down the throat. Their brow ridges flared out and back to cup the ear slits, and wispy hairs grew underneath them. Their legs were stockier yet straighter than a Chirrn's, and their shorter feet did not end in prehensile digits. They would not be as comfortable in free fall as the Chirrn had engineered themselves to be. Velesh had pale blue-gray skin with subtle stripes down the back of the neck; his mates were greener to differing degrees.

Stephen introduced himself and Sita, and Velesh paused briefly before replying. "Welcome. Are your... guardians aware of your presence here?"

"Don't worry, we have an escort." Stephen gestured to Fred the Zhalevey, who stood nearby waiting patiently and adorably for instructions. Stephen's departure from their authorized area had been harder to mask than Sita's, even with L'chellin preoccupied with negotiations for access to Lode Seven, but Fred and her colleagues had orchestrated their distraction quite gracefully.

Sita patted the little triped on the head. "Couldn't be in safer hands. She's got three!"

"And we are supposed to be learning about Galactic civilization," Stephen added. "This seemed like an… informative place to be."

Velesh chose to interpret that as a reference to the sport/ritual combat they overlooked. "Yes. It can teach you much about the Zenith. This is no mere recreation; they battle for the favor of the Star Palace's alpha and her junior females. The higher the placement of the male in the final outcome, the higher the status of the females he becomes qual-ified to court. They gain additional prestige in the overall community from their athletic victory, of course, and in some Zenith subcultures that is an end in itself; but even there, the ultimate aspiration is to join the harem of a high-ranking female, even if the selection process is more informal." His knobby lips drew together. "In either case, however, the sport is a controlled manifestation of what was once a violent, often lethal competition. The Zenith have… matured much from what they were. But it is valuable to understand where they came from."

Velesh was clearly a natural lecturer, bordering on the pedantic. That could be useful. "It's been fascinating to learn all the variations on sexuality that have evolved on other worlds," Sita said, clasping Stephen's hand coquettishly. "The planet of origin you share with the Chirrn produced some surprising ones, if you don't mind my saying."

"Not an atypical reaction."

"Yet theirs is so different from yours. Would it be inappropriate to ask…"

"Not at all," Velesh told her. "Curiosity is an essential survival trait in the young. And an underappreciated one among elders, unfortu-nately. And there is much that you need to learn.

"The Chirrn's alternating sexuality is the natural pattern within our shared taxonomic class, a way of maximizing the birth rate in the harsh seas in which our forebears evolved. There are others of my genus — the one that left the ancestral world first — who retain that flexibility of gen-der. But we Shayal had ourselves modified with invariant sexuality, the better to relate to the majority of the galaxy's sophonts. My partners are male and female; I am a hermaphrodite, though I employ a masculine pronoun by Shayal convention, for I am committed to a non-procreative role. We traditionally bond in triads with one of each sex."

"Did you mod yourselves that way so you'd be better mentors?" Sita asked.

"That is one of its benefits." Velesh's chameleon eyes, smaller than a Chirrn's, focused more closely on her. "What have the Shilirrlaln told you about mentoring?"

"Well, for one thing," Sita went on, "that you were their mentors." It wasn't a lie, exactly; L'chellin had "told" Sita that through her body language toward the Shayal.

"Long ago, yes," Velesh confirmed.

"They were lucky," Stephen said with care, "to have someone to offer them guidance from the start. After all, you were already there when they evolved."

"Not exactly," the Shayal commissioner told him. "Our ancestors migrated into space before the Chirrn developed full sapience, so that we would not impede their development."

"But if the purpose is to guide them…"

"Guidance is usually only required at the onset of civilization, or a similar transformative event that alters a species' environment or way of life more abruptly than evolution can compensate for. Normally a species' behaviors are suited for its needs by the evolutionary process, but at times of rapid change, evolved behaviors and drives can become maladaptive and potentially harmful."

Stephen nodded. "Like, say, a hunter-gatherer species that develops herding and farming, comes to depend on them instead of hunting. The natural aggressive drives that once served them well lose their healthy outlet, and can be redirected into war, violent crime, oppression, even genocide." Sita met his eyes, noting the tension beneath his cool, scholarly delivery.

Velesh only acknowledged the surface, however. "Indeed. Or a people with strong herd instincts may have difficulty with the concept of political dissent, leaving them vulnerable to poor decisions by their leaders." He gestured toward Fred. "Or to abuse by others. The Zhalevey are so ancient that their mentoring history is largely legend, but they credit their mentors for teaching them to insist on limits to how far they would tolerate being exploited."

Pretty broad limits, Sita thought, before saying aloud: "Right, so what makes some lot of aliens more qualified to know the right way for them to behave?"

"There is no one 'right' way, even within a single species," Velesh corrected kindly, as Sita had intended. The perfect way to get information out of pedants was to get something wrong in their earshot. "The right way for a culture to live is something they must discover for themselves. Mentors simply give them the tools to make that investigation—help them learn how to ask the right questions and develop healthy, productive methods for arriving at their own answers."

Sita could tell her husband was genuinely intrigued. "Like scaffolding," Stephen said. "It's how a lot of humans teach our children. Just giving them the answers—or what we think are the answers—won't help them learn to make decisions for themselves. So instead of teaching them what to think, we teach them *how* to think critically, how to find their own solutions, how to distinguish good arguments from bad."

"Exactly," Velesh replied. "Mentoring is usually overseen by members of long-established, peaceful, and respected civilizations who have demonstrated the necessary maturity, patience, and delicacy. Primary mentors are usually selected based on similarity; for instance, an herbivorous species will be mentored by herbivores or omnivores. But secondary mentors are usually selected to offer a balancing perspective. Ideally, the mix is tailored to the unique psychological profile of each nascent civilization." He lifted his head proudly. "This is why the Nine Clusters Coalition has mentored so many civilizations successfully. We are one of the largest, most diverse civilizational clusters in this octant of the middle Disk."

"I'm so happy for you," Sita said. "But even so, it sounds like a hell of a risk. Sort of thing that could go pear-shaped—no offense—if you weren't careful."

"Truth abounds in this," Velesh said, gesturing emphatically. Arachne must have been smoothing over Sita's idioms in translation, which was probably for the best. "There have been..." He paused, then resumed more carefully. "Mistakes have occurred in the past. Different mentoring communities have... disagreed at times over the ideal application of the Mentoring Protocols. But those Protocols are the end result of *yanarrayth* of experimentation, error, and refinement. Besides—there is risk in raising a child. But would you abandon a child to grow up alone in the wilderness for fear of doing it harm? Before the Protocols evolved, many civilizations grew up traumatized, imbalanced, irrational. The galaxy was devastated by wars, conquests, and memetic plagues that exterminated whole civilizations."

Stephen stepped forward urgently, startling Velesh — and Sita. The Shayal's mates moved in closer, like bodyguards. "But obviously exceptions can be made. *We* weren't mentored. Nobody helped guide us away from our worst mistakes. We *were* abandoned in the wilderness. Never mind the thousands of years of human suffering, the wars, the oppression, the crushing poverty. If humanity had just been in contact with the larger galaxy, the Lesshchi disaster would never have occurred. All the tragedies we've inflicted and endured could've been avoided." There was an intensity in his voice that Sita had never heard before.

"I am sorry," Velesh said, bowing in a Chirrnlike gesture of sympathy and placation. "What your people have suffered, in the past and now, is unconscionable. Unfortunately... the Coalition has never held jurisdiction over the Four Voids. I cannot answer your questions about mentoring policies — or lack thereof — within this region."

"'Cannot answer,'" Sita echoed, moving to stand by Stephen. "Because you don't know? Or for some other reason?"

"Again, I apologize. But I am bound by the Protocols, and now that the Shilirrlaln have... however belatedly... taken on the role of the Arachnen's mentors, I must defer to their judgment. I can speak to you about galactic history as a general subject, but when it comes to your own mentoring, I fear I am proscribed from intervening."

Sita frowned. "But I thought the whole reason you were here was to intervene. To push for a change in the Void Alliance's policies."

"That is a matter to be decided between the Coalition and the Alliance. As much as I would like to assist you, my options are constrained until that debate is resolved."

Something happened in the arena that triggered a shrieking roar from the Zenith spectators, and Velesh turned his gaze back outward. "Excuse me," he said. "Events are moving toward a point of decision."

Once it became clear that the conversation was over, Stephen led Sita out of the skybox. "Yes," he murmured to her. "I'm beginning to think they are."

When Stephen and Sita filled in the senior personnel about what they'd learned of the Mentoring Protocols — with Sita characterizing them as "a happy medium between the Civilizing Mission and the

Prime Directive"—the reactions ranged from shock to confusion to anger. Tarik Bahar in particular reacted with anguish and suspicion. "Why didn't the Chirrn tell us any of this?" *Arachne's* acting captain still struggled to maintain an even keel in the wake of his family tragedy, even more than Stephen and Sita did, for Kweli's pregnancy had been significantly further along. Only his need to be strong for his inconsolable wife, and his unbreakable sense of duty to the rest of the Arachnen, had held him together.

"Hard to say," Sita answered gently. "But there seems to be some bad blood between them and their mentors."

"What if these Shayal botched their mentoring of the Chirrn?" Oyama Kazuko asked. The elegant Martian administrator paced the common room in thought. "Remember the history L'chellin told us? The great war between their planetary and spaceborne civilizations? That doesn't seem like something that should happen under these Protocols."

"Obviously, the Protocols don't always work," Stephen told her, "or humanity wouldn't have been... *overlooked*. For thousands of years... through conquests and holocausts, famines and plagues, slavery and tyranny..." *Children gunned down in the streets...* "Nobody once came to our aid."

"We managed well enough despite that," Kazuko said. "Cecilia would say it made us stronger."

Stephen shot to his feet. "You don't need to go through hell to be strong!" Kazuko grew very still, studying him with wary calm. He looked down, controlling his anger, remembering what kind of man he chose to be. "And it leaves you with... deep weaknesses too," he went on. "We know how trauma damages the mind, how the abused become abusers. We know it can happen on the level of whole societies—entire cultures traumatized by conquest or fanaticism or natural disaster, left with only violence and despair. We know from our own educators, our own common sense, that the young need freedom without being abandoned." He took solace in the thought of his mother. So many of his peers in Florida had been orphans or victims of abuse. Stephen had grown up barely knowing his father Harry, a man swallowed up by a prison system designed to harden young black offenders into career inmates as a slave labor force for the state. But Theresa Wong had been a pillar of strength and patience, a teacher and activist who had given Stephen and his siblings the love, support, and education they had needed to find their way to that better path when so many had been lost. Without her, he would never have made it to the stars.

Yet she had died in pain, grieving the younger son who had been killed for trying to steal medicine to save her—both of them victims of a culture-wide pathology that humanity had suffered from for millennia. A pathology that, perhaps, they might have been spared.

"Yes," Sita said, "animals that endure trauma can be more violent, more abusive than those raised under more positive circumstances. Particularly in social species, losing parents or nurturers can produce a generation lacking healthy social skills, predisposed to pathological, destructive behavior—like the street gangs of your childhood, Stephen, or the elephant bands in India that lashed out against the humans who devastated their communities back before the sapient rights reforms.

"But—but aggression is still an innate behavior in most species. Even without pathology to amplify it, it's still present, able to be brought to bear at a moment's notice. All it takes is a single unanticipated disaster to turn... even the most civilized and orderly of sophonts into murdering savages." Stephen could see that the memory still haunted her. He took her hand, and she smiled up at him briefly and gathered herself. "So we can't make assumptions about what might have gone wrong with the Chirrn, or whether these vaunted Protocols even work. I know you want to believe it's possible to overcome suffering and injustice with enough effort, intellect, and resources, but—"

"I hear what you're saying," he said. "But these Protocols, they make sense. It's logical that advanced civilizations would find a better solution than either cultural imperialism or total abandonment. That over a *yanarrayth*, a hundred million years or more, they'd refine contact into a science far more sophisticated than anything we ever managed."

Yet it was impossible for Stephen to contemplate that promise without running up against the overriding, agonizing question it created: *Why was humanity cheated of that?*

Why were Mama and Benjamin cheated of their lives?

4

ON THE ARACHNEN'S THIRD DAY IN THE STAR PALACE, KWELI NDEGE decided it was time to stop mourning.

It had not been an easy resolution to reach. The sympatholytic treatments after the Lesshchin attack had eased the emotional trauma of the incident itself, but they couldn't prevent Kweli from being aware, during every waking moment, of the emptiness in her belly, the gaping hole in the middle of her being. They couldn't change the fact that she spent every day surrounded by reminders of her loss. Antidepressants could only do so much, and neither she nor Tarik would accept any more radical treatment, anything that would excise her memory of their unborn son or her ability to grieve for him. Her memory of him was all she had left.

She knew it had been hard on Tarik, caring for her through her grief when he bore so much of his own. The time he spent with her was just a reminder of his loss, and though she loved him dearly for standing unwaveringly by her side, she felt guilty imposing that burden upon him.

But the more time Kweli spent amid the beauty of the Antares B Star Palace and its wonderfully diverse denizens, the more she knew that here was a place where she could find solace. And so she allowed Tarik to convince her to join him and several others on a tour of the habitat's attractions, chaperoned by Mediator Broadwing. Tarik's tearful smile when she agreed to come out with him brought her great contentment.

Now they stood together on a viewing deck high above the Star Palace's surface, where the gravity was noticeably lower. Calling it just a deck was an injustice; it was a whole park, a broad, domed-in area over a hundred meters in radius, with six residential towers serving as support legs and a seventh piercing the center and rising dozens of stories above the dome. Exotic flora approximating trees filled much of its volume, with broad paths separating clusters of different types of vegetation—from different planets? Kweli assumed there must be biochemical compatibility issues involved, but surely interstellar civilization had had millennia or more to work them out.

The view beyond the dome was just as spectacular. Both Antares stars were immersed in the sloughed-off remains of the dying supergiant's atmosphere, a dense planetary nebula that glowed yellow-orange, lit up by the central star like a Japanese lantern. But half the sky was filled with a brighter blue-magenta glow—reflected light from the B star blending with fluorescence from the surrounding nebulosity excited by its radiation, so Tarik explained while she pretended to understand. Even as Kweli watched, the brilliant blue pinpoint of Antares B ascended slowly behind the fairy-castle skyline, causing fingers of ruddy shadow to caress the upthrust contours of the cityscape below. Refractive or photoreactive layers in many of the towers caught the light and redirected it, amplified it, subverted it to enhance the towers' own resplendence. Astronomers back in Solsys had observed the shimmering radiance of the occupied Star Palaces without ever knowing the reasons for it. Now, Kweli understood the displays as manifestations of Zenith psychology, their overpowering need to outcompete each other in altitude and glory. It brought her immense satisfaction to finally have the answer to one of exobiology's greatest mysteries.

She derived further pleasure from observing the other guests who had come to enjoy the flora and watch the sunrise. The range of body types in evidence surprised her, with few conforming to an upright bipedal plan; yet Kweli noted recurring anatomical features among what appeared at first glance to be different species. When she quizzed one of the ubiquitous Zhalevey helpers, the solicitous triped confirmed that, like the Chirrn and Shayal, those species had spawned from a common planet of origin—or in some cases, a single species had diverged into an entire genus as it spread across the galaxy over millions of years. Kweli delighted in the discovery. She knew she would never have the opportunity to study all these variations of life, to learn about their evolutionary histories and interrelations; but here and now it was enough to experience the raw sense of wonder, knowing others would do the work in the future.

After watching Zenith dive through openings in the broad central tower and spiral down to other levels far below, Kweli convinced Tarik to take her gliding. The Zenith-designed habitat had so many wide, high interior spaces that there was abundant room for it, whether with one's own wings or with artificial substitutes, and regular gliding tours were offered for visitors. A few known species were close enough to a hominid shape that the Zhalevey were able to call up a pair of gliders suitable for human use. The safety straps were a bit loose even on Kweli's well-rounded frame, but she assured Tarik that all she had to do was hold on. He was so happy to see her serene and active that he let himself stop fussing over her just this once.

The dense atmosphere meant the wings were smaller than an Earthly hang glider, which made it easier to maneuver and swoop through the grand, vaulted spaces of the Star Palace. They dove through immense, cathedral-roofed canyons, rode updrafts from enormous ventilation grates, and soared past wide shafts boring deep into the habitat, where the intense gravitational pull of the PQM drew down the air and drove the Star Palace's circulatory patterns. They even found themselves caught up in a light shower, for the interior spaces were vast enough for weather to form. Kweli laughed with Tarik as the cool water spattered their faces, as she breathed in the refreshing fragrance of the rain. This was the way to experience this wondrous place: the way its builders had intended, soaring on high through the air. Kweli felt her burdens lift away.

It was time.

She waited until Tarik was distracted before curving away, angling her course back toward the bore shaft. By the time she heard him screaming her name, the downdraft had already caught her, sucking her down to the lower levels where the gravity grew exponentially stronger the nearer she came to the PQM layer. The glider made alert sounds and tried to angle her back to safety. But all she had to do was slip out of the loose straps… and stop holding on.

She was weightless. And at last she was free.

Kweli Ndege's medical expertise had let her choose her method of suicide all too well. The Star Palace's finest surgeons, working with the migration fleet's Doctor Mh'lellish and consulting with Joana Caravalho

---

on the finer points of human anatomy, worked for hours to recover what they could — but the gravity at the base of the ventilation shaft had been high enough that her brain and body were beyond repair. Kweli had made certain there was no coming back.

Doctor Rauhoc delivered the news. Tarik had resisted letting the massive, bone-plated alien anywhere near his wife, but L'chellin had assured him that for a Gaurim surgeon to be available on a Star Palace's staff was a rare and fortuitous circumstance, and if Rauhoc could not save Kweli, then no one could. Yet now Tarik raged at Rauhoc, at L'chellin and Broadwing, at whoever he could find. "How could you have let this happen? All your technology — how could that shaft not have been safeguarded against jumpers?" Stephen held him back from going at them physically, though the only reason he wasn't screaming at them himself was that Tarik was doing it for him.

"There was no sign that Kweli was in distress," Broadwing explained, his body language subdued. "Her equipment was functioning properly, and her actions were calm and deliberate. There was nothing to suggest to any monitoring systems or individuals that anything was amiss until it was too late to act."

Joana sighed heavily. "In humans, suicide is often preceded by serenity, calm, even apparent happiness. Relief that the pain will finally end soon, a sense that all one's burdens have lifted."

Tarik had fallen quiet, sagging in Stephen's grip. "She was so… content. So resolved. She drank in all the sights and experiences so eagerly… I thought she was finally healing. But she just… she wanted one last perfect day before…" He couldn't finish.

Rauhoc stepped forward, his gentle manner belying his frightening appearance. "The administration wishes me to convey its deepest condolences," he rumbled. "We do all we can to make Zenith facilities safe for non-flying species, but the precautions are designed against accident, not… self-destruction. Such a degree of untreated mental illness is exceedingly rare."

"It *was* being treated," Joana protested. "We've done everything we could to help the mothers through this. But there was only so much we could do under… the circumstances."

"The circumstances!" Tarik cried. "You mean being trapped here, no choice in our fate, no way to free ourselves from the Chirrn! We're still prisoners as much as ever," he shouted at L'chellin. "Kweli never had a chance!"

Stephen led Tarik over to the far wall and held him for a moment until he settled down. Tarik clung to him and murmured to himself in Turkish, which Arachne subtitled: *"Whoever curbs his anger while being able to execute it, Allah will fill his heart with certainty of faith."* Finally he said, "I'm sorry. I'm the one who should've seen the signs." He turned away, muttering, "It was my job to protect her," and pushed through the doors into the waiting area. Stephen went after him, but by the time he got through the doors, Tarik had already rushed past the others who bided outside, their condolences too much for him to bear.

No, Stephen thought as he gazed after his friend. *It was my job.* He had been responsible for every member of this expedition since he had first recruited them. He had convinced them to put their lives in his hands, and all that had resulted was turmoil and tragedy. He thought he had prepared them for the risks of an unprecedented journey, but he'd been a fool to think he had the slightest idea what that would mean. He had named the expedition's vessel all too aptly. Like Ovid's Arachne, he was being punished for his hubris. The difference was that he had brought down punishment on thousands of others in the process. How many more members of his crew would suffer for his arrogance?

Cecilia had been uneasy when Churrlaya had escorted her to a private room to meet with Stephen. Although a part of her still missed her old friend, she feared that the Stephen she knew was lost. Sitting through another sales pitch to abandon her allegiance and self-reliance, to spend the rest of her life as a prisoner or a dependent refugee at best, would only be a painful reminder of how deep the rift between them had grown.

She was therefore taken aback when she saw the grief on Stephen's face, the way he seemed weighted down even in the microgravity of the docking ring. "What happened?" she demanded.

He wasted no time on preliminaries; at least he still respected her contempt for such things. Yet as he told her, slowly and plainly, how Kweli Ndege had taken her own life, Cecilia almost wished he had cushioned the blow somehow. But nothing really could have. A member of her crew was dead. There was no worse news a captain could ever hear.

And she feared that Kweli would only be the first.

She threw a glance toward Churrlaya, the only convenient target for the burst of rage and hatred she felt toward the Chirrn. Yet he gazed at her with silent sympathy. He had spoken to her so often of his grief and loss that she knew intimately how those emotions looked on a Chirrn, and what she saw now was a reflection of her own pain.

No, he was not the one who deserved her anger this time. "How much longer?" she demanded of Stephen. "How much more do you have to lose before you realize that submission to the Chirrn is toxic for us?"

He clung to a handhold to steady himself. "You don't need to remind me of what I've lost, Cecilia. But it all goes back to the same loss. The same tragedy. All these sorrows are ripples from Lesshchi." He glanced at Churrlaya, but he could not hold the Lesshchin's gaze. "We won't be free of them until we find a way to heal the wounds and move on. We can't do that unless we do it together, Cecilia. All of us."

"I knew it. I knew you would do this! Even this, you have to turn into a speech!"

"You're the one who can't let go of your agenda! I came here to tell you about Kweli because you were her friend, her captain. Because you deserve to know, to grieve with the rest of us. And the first thing you do is start up the argument again. Can't you ever let your guard down, Cecilia? Even now?"

She could feel her face flushing; it came more easily without gravity to hold the blood down. In truth, she feared how Diego and the others would react to this news. After their exercise period the day before, Diego, Amrita, James, and Evan had continued to entertain themselves by brainstorming ways to destroy the Star Palace to cover their escape. Seeing the Chirrn as the enemy was one thing, but their enthusiasm at the prospect of killing countless other, innocent aliens disturbed Cecilia sufficiently that she'd finally spoken up to discourage their malevolent fantasies—which had gained nothing but their resentment. She doubted very much that they could find a way to realize their plans, but she feared for the morale and unity of the loyalists as their captivity continued with no sign of hope.

She sighed. "I just don't understand why you're not with me now, of all times. When you—" She hesitated to land what might be a low blow. But when they had been friends, he had always valued her candor. If she had any hope of regaining that friendship, she couldn't pull her punches now. "When you lost Benjamin and your mother, you moved heaven and earth to get your sisters out of the Gulf Coast. How can you be so complacent a prisoner after what you've lost now?"

Stephen's answer was tightly controlled. "I lost them because of people who refused to take responsibility for the harm their actions caused. I will not let myself become one of those people. God knows, now more than ever I have reason to want to blame the Chirrn for everything we've suffered. More reason than you know." He stopped himself, throwing a furtive glance toward Churrlaya, and Cecilia wondered what he couldn't say in front of a Chirrn. "But that would be the same kind of unthinking bigotry that trapped my family in poverty. The Shilirrlaln saved many lives in the attack, including Sita's, even if they couldn't save all the babies. And they have forgiven me for a hideous crime for which I can never forgive myself. They're just people, like us—trying to lead the best lives they can, trying to cope with the pain and the tragic mistakes of the past. And sometimes they fail. Just as we do."

He blinked, wiping moisture from his eyes, then absently rolled the beads of moisture between his fingers. "We all failed Kweli. Nobody gets to be self-righteous about that. She needed us, but we had our own grief, our own burdens weighing on us… Oh, God, Cecilia, it's just too much. All the lives lost… it's too much for any of us to bear. And that's why we need each other, why we should all be together."

Stephen reached out to her. "I miss you, my friend. I need you. I try—I try to be the strong, stalwart leader, to give them all courage, but I can't do it like you. I can't do it *without* you. I'm… I'm…I can't…"

It was the last thing Cecilia had expected. But in a way, it was something she'd been longing for. She hated to see him in such pain—but it brought deep comfort to know she still cared for him so much.

In all the years they'd been friends, she'd never initiated a hug. It had always amused him that even though she was the proud Italian, he was the physically demonstrative one. Now, she pushed off the wall and came to him, embraced him. He clung to her desperately and cried for a very long time. She stroked his hair, occasionally saying nonsense like "Hey" and "It's" and "Um" and "You'll" and never finding a second word that meant anything. Somehow he took comfort in it anyway, thanking her with wordless, shuddering breaths.

Finally, when it ended, he put his thanks into words. "I've needed that for a long time. A chance to just… turn off the leader face and cry on someone's shoulder."

"Can't you do that with Sita?"

"Sita… It's been hard for her, to share me with everyone else. I haven't made it easy. Losing our baby… that made it harder for both of us. Honestly, she came through it better than I did. Found her own footing. Talked some sense into me just the other day, in fact. I think we're starting to find each other at last, and it's all thanks to her. But… well, other matters have arisen, and we haven't really had a chance to build on it."

Cecilia pursed her lips. "I admit, I'm surprised. Didn't think there was that much substance to her. She got… broken pretty badly more than once."

"She's not as fragile as she looks. I don't think I got that myself until the past few days." He smirked at her. "Anyway, I thought you were a 'That which does not kill us makes us stronger' kind of person."

"Yeah, but only if we have the conviction to use it that way." She sighed. "Which is why I can't stop resisting the Chirrn. That's the only way I can be true to the ideals *you* taught me. Stephen, you're *still* trapped by others' bigotry. I don't understand why you can't see that."

He closed his eyes in regret—then glanced at Churrlaya again. "No, I'm afraid you *don't* understand. There's so much I wish I could tell you… but all I can do is trust you to figure it out for yourself."

"You sound like them. You're complicit in their secrets! Stephen, what aren't you—"

He put his fingers on her lips, and she amazed herself by allowing it. "Don't worry about it now. You're right, we've had this argument enough. It's gotten us nowhere." He clasped her hands. "This… this did me more good than anything has in a long time. I hope, maybe, it'll do you good too, once you have time to reflect on it." He released one of her hands so he could cup her cheek. "It was so good to have this again, dear friend. I love you, Cecilia. We all do."

He clearly didn't expect her to say she loved him too. But once he'd left and Churrlaya had led her from the room, she began to regret that she hadn't.

On the way back to confinement, Cecilia dreaded telling the others, fearing how Diego's clique would use this to fuel their rage. Even Churrlaya provided no distraction. Weeks ago, she would have expected a lecture about how humans devalued their own lives as well as others, or how the ultimate blame lay with the humans for destroying Lesshchi. Now, she was not sure what to expect. "You've been awfully quiet," she finally said.

The Chirrn brooded… and then surprised her. "I fear I have no right to speak. To lose a loved one, with none of their self or memory preserved… even to say I understand would feel accusatory."

In its way, his refusal to damn her for his loss merely left room for her to damn herself. Yet somehow, in the wake of it, Churrlaya's resumed silence felt oddly supportive, as if they had finally achieved some mutual understanding.

Once they arrived at the cell, she lingered outside, doubting that her own people would give her so much space to grieve. How had she grown so far apart from her crew? Was it Stockholm syndrome? Some deft psychological manipulation by Churrlaya?

Or was it instead that her crew was growing apart from her? If so… how could she break this news to them without worsening the rift?

The shock of Kweli's suicide had overridden the Arachnen's concerns over the Mentoring Protocols at first, but with time to reflect, their grief only intensified their larger questions and doubts. Tarik was quick to suggest confronting the Chirrn about the insinuations from Velesh and the orderly Sunflash that they were somehow at fault for humanity's lack of mentoring.

But Stephen wasn't ready to rush to judgment. As much as it agonized him to discover that all the horrors humanity had endured—all his own family had endured—could have been prevented, he wouldn't lash out at the first available target and risk scuttling all the work the Arachnen had done to earn redemption. As he'd told Cecilia, a part of him still wanted to blame all the Chirrn for what some had done to his baby, his wife, his friends. But that was his own traumas driving him, the kind of unhealthy impulse he'd spent a lifetime training himself to resist. He felt he'd gotten a lot of that pain out of his system thanks to Cecilia's kindness.

So he convinced the others to keep the matter to themselves for now, until he could find out more and decide on a course of action. He thanked his lucky stars that Tarik's loyalty and his faith were dug so deep in his bones, for those were the only things that could hold his anguished rage in check.

Afterward, he set those concerns aside in favor of a more pressing responsibility. He made his way to the viewing deck where, according to Tarik, Kweli had begun her last day — the place where she had finally found herself at peace. As much as he regretted, even resented the choice she'd made — suicide was so selfish in its way, causing pain to so many others simply to end one's own — he couldn't blame her for the damage her circumstances had done, and he owed it to her to remember the effervescent, nurturing spirit she had been. So he stood there, where she had stood in her last hour of contentment, and remembered her.

After a time, he realized that Broadwing now crouched next to him, keeping his rainbow-crested head level with Stephen's in a gesture of respect. He met the Zenith's three eyes. "Broadwing."

"Stephen." The pattern of calliope tones Broadwing used, as Stephen understood it, was a proper-name inflection of the Zenith for "matriarch's crests," the closest equivalent to his given name's literal meaning of "crown." Probably better than using his full name, which effectively translated as "Crown of the Usurper King" — a fact he tried not to think about much.

"You contemplate loss?" Broadwing asked.

"Yes."

"As we all have done too often in these times."

"Yes."

"When loss comes, we seek answers. We look for some cause we can confront and transcend."

Stephen looked at him, hesitant to reply. "That's a common response. But I think it's better to simply face the loss. To remember what was lost… try to keep it alive inside you." He remembered Sita's words from three days before. "Looking for someone to blame is just a way to avoid facing your pain."

Broadwing lowered his neck fractionally — the barest gesture of submission to concede the point. "This is always your way, Stephen. To look to the heights you can climb to rather than the depths that would drag you down into them."

He nodded, wondering at the similarity of the gesture. "I believe in hope. At least… I try to. It can be hard sometimes… but that's when you need hope the most. I learned that back on Earth, when I lost my brother and my mother. I was tempted to lash out at the establishment that had let them die, but that would've just gotten me killed too and left my family worse off. Instead, I focused on hope. I found ways to improve our situation, gain allies, and finally get myself and my sisters out of there. Hope did more good... well, for those of us who survived."

Broadwing raised his head a bit. "There may yet be hope for the lost as well."

Stephen stared. "What do you mean?"

"It is a faint cloud—some call it a mirage. But many see reason buoying it up. They suggest that the metasapient civilizations, ever hungry for input and complexity, have pervaded the galaxy with sensors at a level of attotechnology too fine for us to detect. That they can track and record the motion of every particle, its electromagnetic emissions, the ripples it creates in the Higgs field... perhaps information we cannot conceive. And the patterns of life, of thought, must be complex enough to hold their interest. So it may be that they record and track the patterns of every mind."

"I thought L'chellin said they were only aware of us in the aggregate, not as individuals."

"That does not matter. If they crave complexity so much, depend on it for their sanity and stimulation, they would let no patterns go to waste. If a mind were lost to death, they would lose input, and they would not tolerate that."

Stephen furrowed his brow, controlling his reactions. "So... you're suggesting that they'd duplicate the patterns of thought they recorded?"

"Perhaps more than duplicate. If their sensors are so pervasive, so subtle, they may be able to capture those patterns directly, preserve them when a physical body dies. Much as a Chirrn network preserves the portion of a mind that extends into it, and an echo of the patterns anchored within the flesh mind. But perhaps more fully, for the metaminds would tolerate no loss of data or activity."

"Are you saying you believe that the..." He didn't know if "souls" would translate. "The consciousness of everyone who died—everyone who's ever died—has been preserved and uploaded into some kind of virtual afterlife?"

"This is nothing so crude as planetary superstition, Stephen. We know for a fact that the metaminds' environments hold enough computing complexity to model entire universes. They could easily sustain those minds in their original patterns, or allow them to expand into metasapience themselves. Given their need for complexity, if they can do it, it is a virtual certainty that they would."

Stephen was at once touched and saddened. Broadwing's proposal was compellingly plausible... but the same could be said about many human religious beliefs. Metasapients may have been tangibly real, but their motives could only be speculated about. However solidly reasoned the argument, it was based in postulates rather than data and thus was as much an article of faith as anything Tarik or Sita or Haim believed in. Although he respected those beliefs and the comfort and inspiration they brought, he knew from hard experience that religion was only as good as the intentions of its believers. He had always preferred to put his faith in what sapient beings could achieve through their own determination and effort. It wasn't enough for him to sit back and hope that higher powers would solve his problems. After all, they never had before.

But he was puzzled as well. "I thought you told me that Zenith saw metasapience as a false ascension. If you think people's... consciousnesses are being captured and preserved in their environments, wouldn't you see that as damnation rather than salvation?"

The mediator reared back, clacking his mandibles, then regained his control. "I said *most* Zenith felt that way."

"Ahh. You never said you were one of them."

That sharp-crested skull trembled; his talons dug into the ground cover. "At least, most Zenith profess to feel that way, for admitting otherwise is... dangerous."

"Why? Why Zenith specifically?"

Broadwing looked around. "I have said more than is wise in this environment. But I can guide you to one who will explain. Not only this, but other mysteries you seek to unravel."

Stephen blinked. It had been a Zenith whose seemingly offhand comments had fired Sita's curiosity about mentoring... and even given her small size, she had found it unexpectedly easy to slip free from Broadwing's supervision and gather the information that had led her to the Protocols.

Seeing his reaction, Broadwing stiffly affected a human nod, a confirmation if ever there was one. The symbolism was clear in Zenith terms as well: by lowering his eyes below Stephen's, he was subordinating himself to the human's choices — placing his trust in Stephen to protect his secrets.

"All right," Stephen said. "Where do we go next?"

Stephen was startled when Sita resisted accompanying him to Broadwing's meeting. "You were the one saying we needed to do this together. You were the one who started this!"

"Not *this!*" she protested. "I only wanted to find the truth. Now I find that Broadwing's got some hidden agenda. Stephen, all your life you've striven for honesty, integrity. Now you're sneaking about and attending secret meetings? Doesn't that trouble you?"

"All of this troubles me. But we need answers. At least we should hear what Broadwing's connections have to say. And I could really use you with me."

Sita pondered for a few moments, then sighed. "Right, then. I suppose if you trusted me enough to go along with me, it's only fair I do my bit in return." He'd hoped for more enthusiasm, but it would do.

Tarik had wished to attend as well, craving answers, but Stephen had feared this rendezvous would feed his suspicions and undermine his efforts to rein in his anger. He had convinced Tarik that the others needed his presence and protection. With luck, that could help the acting captain rebuild his confidence in the wake of his imagined failure to protect Kweli.

So for now it was only Stephen and Sita, along with Arachne's avatar as guard and translator, who joined Broadwing in descending to the lower levels of the Star Palace. The Zenith mediator had worked with Arachne to modify their old prisoner confinement suit design from the trial into strength-boosting servo suits to cope with the higher gravity at these depths. Still, Stephen could feel the weight in his own viscera, a sense of being relentlessly pulled down.

The architecture didn't help. Most Zenith may have shunned these levels, leaving them to their own lowest-ranking members and to other, high-gravity or nocturnal species; but even these depths were designed with the Zenith's inherent craving for altitude in mind. The space was vast and echoing, a forest of skyscraper-thick columns that branched outward into a fractal array of flying buttresses and arches supporting the great vaulted ceiling overhead, the floor of the bright and gleaming world up above. The domed vaults contained openings resembling clerestory windows, channeling light and air from above. Stretching between the immense, window-studded columns at various levels were wide, arched skywalks nearly as wide as city blocks, with walkways on either side and dwellings or businesses along the middle. Everything was designed to make the Zenith feel high above the ground, even while well beneath it.

The residents here provided their own light, in bright colors as garish and raucous as those on the grand promenades and boulevards above; but here in the near-literal underground, it had more of the seedy flavor of old Las Vegas or the Niihama habitat in the Belt than the clean, commercial pageantry of the upper levels. The chatter of alien voices and music was more intense and frenetic. Strange scents and vapors filled the air. Sophonts could be seen doing things to each other that might be violent or erotic or both. And that was just in the streets. The hints of sight, sound, and scent from the doorways they passed suggested that what went on outdoors was just a taste of what could be found within.

The group passed a street fight between a Gaurim and a member of a sibling species, browner and more elongated with more pronounced spikes along the head and flanks. They used the clubs on their twin rear limbs to swing at each other's horn-plated heads and flanks. It reminded Stephen of animal mating competitions, but their audience included no other members of their species; from the look of things, the crowd was betting on the fight. When the other fighter's longer limbs snuck past the Gaurim's defenses, clubbing it in the knee with a forceful crack, the audience roared with bloodlust as it tumbled to the ground. "Ruddy hell," Sita said. "Don't tell Diana about this place, or we'll never get her to leave."

Arachne moved her spider-woman avatar between her party and the fight spectators, keeping several wary eyes on the rowdy group. "I gathered that mentoring was supposed to raise mature, healthy civilizations."

"Even a healthy society needs its release valves, I suppose," Sita replied. "And mentoring is supposed to give civilizations the freedom to do things their own way."

"Indeed," chimed Broadwing, who walked in his crouched stance, the gravity high even for him. "All you see are here voluntarily, with full knowledge of any risks they take. And the Star Palace's safeguards are as present here as everywhere else. Recall, most Galactics are not easy to kill. Those who are… generally choose to be, and their choice is respected." He gave a small shudder.

"But not always welcomed," Stephen commiserated.

"Yes. I have seen too much death of late. That is why I endorsed this migration following the Lesshchin assault on your childbearers. I knew it would most likely be directed toward the Antispinward Void. You were correct before, Sita, about the impact of the migrational shift resulting from the Eta Carinae hypernova. Civilizations which had left the Chirrn alone for millennia, due to their preoccupation with the diaspora, are beginning to exert pressure once again."

"Such as the Shayal?" Sita asked.

"Yes. They are major players in the Nine Clusters Coalition, and they have a… turbulent history with the Chirrn. I knew the Chirrn would want to increase their hold on the Void by establishing a new habitat here. That meant obtaining a PQM supply from Lode Seven, and that meant passing through Antares. And here was where I could find one whose wing I crouched beneath in my youth—one I thought I had left behind, until Lesshchi renewed my need for hope to soar beyond this life. One I believe can help you as well—if nothing more, by giving you the truths the Chirrn have kept hidden."

Broadwing's words made Stephen wary. Was he just taking them to see some kind of fringe spiritual leader, offering them the solace of metasapient heaven?

The Zenith led the party up an arched walkway, one of six that converged to support a large hexagonal pavilion festooned with great, down-angled windows. The two Zenith who met them at the pavilion's entrance were also crouched, but they were females; their triple headcrests were larger than Broadwing's, their tripartite beaks more hooked and pointed, and the halter-type harnesses they wore over their chests and keels were more utilitarian than his, less skimpy and ornate. Once he had made proper obeisance gestures and sounds—an even more elaborate ritual than those Stephen had observed among other Zenith—the females led the group inside, where several more females awaited, including one Sita clearly recognized. "Sunflash," the biologist greeted her. "Imagine finding you here."

The orderly gave a bow conveying polite contrition seasoned with defiance. "I played my part as instructed. That is all."

"Is it, now? Instructed by whom, then?"

But the answer quickly became obvious as Sunflash and the other females turned to make obeisance to a new arrival. This female was even more impressive to behold, her crests the most vivid in the room, her bearing the most confident. She was attended by a large group of males clad only in jewelry, no doubt her harem. From what Stephen had learned of Zenith society, the other females must be her apprentices, adolescents who served the matriarch until they could earn sufficient status to claim a few males from the harem and strike out on their own. The size of her retinue suggested high status. Yet most of the Zenith in the room were unimpressive to look at—their crests comparatively small and drab-hued, their featherfur dull and scruffy, their wings diminutive, their limbs short, their coordination lacking. Even their jewels were less resplendent than those worn by the Zenith up above. These were the sort of Zenith who would only be found at these depths—the lowest in status, the social outcasts, the geeks.

Indeed, as Stephen looked closer at the matriarch, he saw that the glamorous impression she conveyed was largely by contrast with the disreputable group around her. But it was more than that. The matriarch was perhaps not conventionally beautiful by Zenith standards as Stephen understood them. She was small, stocky, her featherfur indifferently shiny, her beak and talons not extraordinarily sharp. Her movements were stiff, suggesting she was a fair way along in an aging process not halted or reversed by regular medical care. She was as much an outcast as the rest. Yet her confidence and poise were clear in the way she held her head high, and her rainbow crests, the most vivid in the room, were a clear indicator of her superior status. The way the males looked at her and tended to her—particularly the way Broadwing's eyes widened and his tail stiffened at the sight of her (and the innuendo there was somewhat accurate, given Zenith anatomy)—reinforced the impression of power and allure... which, to Zenith, were much the same thing.

Yet the matriarch did not engage in the expected posturing as she moved forward to greet her visitors. She maintained a crouch level with Stephen's height rather than looming over him, implicitly greeting him as an equal. She gave a calliope chime as she shook her head in a Zenith greeting gesture. "Stephen Jacobs-Wong," came the translation, "I am Meridian. Welcome to the community of the galaxy."

Stephen did his best to repeat the gesture. "Thank you, Meridian. I am honored by your welcome."

"It is overdue."

Once Stephen had introduced the others, Meridian sang back the translation of Sita's full name, or as close as Arachne could approximate it. "Harvest Goddess of the Morning Light. A resplendent name, well-suited for one of such a gifted species at the dawn of its greatness. And yet you have been unfairly shunned by those above. Come—rest and dine with us so we may remedy that." These Zenith were like their counterparts above in one respect: they conducted all their business over food. Just walking in this gravity must have had a metabolic cost not unlike flying.

"I appreciate the sentiment," Stephen replied. "But their fear of us is understandable, given the tragedy we were responsible for."

"Lesshchi only reinforced their existing fears of feral sophonts," Meridian replied. "And the Chirrn have done nothing to change this."

A slightly smaller Zenith female, her crests nearly as resplendent, awaited them at the table. "My second, Apastron," the matriarch said in introduction.

"You are most welcome," Apastron said. "Broadwing informed us of your dietary requirements. You may be assured the meal is suitable for human consumption." Arachne's avatar gave the table a quick once-over and silently verified this with an eyetext.

"You mentioned feral sophonts," Sita interposed once they'd sat down to eat. "You mean unmentored?"

"Yes," Meridian replied. "To most Galactics, those who are not mentored are considered wild and dangerous."

Stephen frowned. "But what does that have to do with the Chirrn?"

"The connection is intimate. The Chirrn were mentors once." Meridian paused. "Our mentors."

Well, Stephen thought once his initial surprise died down. *Parental issues. Don't expect the most objective assessment here.*

Meridian peered at Stephen. "Tell me what the Chirrn have told you about their history. Did they speak of a war?"

"Yes," Stephen said. "A great war between their early space colonists and their home planet. Eventually, they migrated into the galaxy to put an end to it."

"That is a lie." The matriarch reared her head back with a sharp shake to highlight her crest colors. "The planet was not theirs, but ours. They came to our nestworld in the early days of our civilization, assigned as our mentors. We were their first subject race."

"Subject?" Stephen asked, continuing cautiously: "I understood the mentoring relationship to be more subtle."

"They did not so understand it," Meridian said with meaning. "You have lived with the Chirrn. You know how they judge and reject those who do not meet their standards of propriety."

He traded an uneasy look with his wife. "I know they have a culture with complex rules for social inclusion and exclusion."

A harsh chord emerged from Meridian's crests. "The Seekers of the Zenith did not meet their standards for inclusion. They judged our hierarchies rigid and unfair. They found our competition for hunting grounds barbaric, for as migrants by nature they could not grasp the value of territory. And they disapproved of how we approached the matters between male and female; as both and neither at once, they did not understand how fundamental our reproductive identity was to us.

"So they attempted to indoctrinate us in the 'correct' way of living — the Chirrn way," the matriarch continued. "We found their teachings absurd and resisted the indoctrination… often violently."

"But surely the Chirrn weren't mentoring you alone? From what we've learned, mentoring missions are usually multispecies."

"That reform was instituted in the wake of the events I relate to you now," Meridian told him. "At the time, the rules had grown lax, or the Chirrn would never have been given such license."

After making a permission-seeking gesture and getting Meridian's nod, Apastron said, "The civilizations responsible for administering the Protocols in this octant — including the Shayal and their Coalition — were preoccupied with supernova evacuation efforts. Not only was Eta Carinae already demanding their attention, but another supernova loomed ten times nearer, requiring further effort to shield or relocate the sophonts nearby." Arachne added a text annotation: *<Most likely the supernova some 12,000 years ago that created the Vela Supernova Remnant.>*

Meridian went on. "Enough attention remained that the Chirrn's methods were questioned and protested among the stars. Yet the Chirrn were determined to succeed at their first mentoring, so they offered us an incentive to follow their ways. Recognizing our drive to seek greater heights in all things, they told us of the earlier civilizations that had ascended to metasapience. They presented it as the pinnacle of evolution, the ultimate height to which the most advanced and powerful species rose." Meridian's chimes took on overtones that Stephen recognized as disapproving yet sardonic. "They implied that if we adopted their ways, we would thereby reach the 'mature' level of galactic civilization and ultimately earn metasapience as a reward."

Sita snorted. "Play nice and eat your veg and you can grow up to be God someday."

"I take it your ancestors cooperated?" Stephen asked.

"Naturally," Apastron replied. "We are the Seekers of the Zenith. What higher zenith could there be than metasapience?"

"And yet something went wrong, didn't it?"

"You tried it and failed," Arachne deduced. "I have seen the results of such failures in our own star system. Cybers rendered mad by their own inner chaos, trapped forever inside cognitive feedback loops, or simply burned out."

"It has to be more than that," Sita said, "or we wouldn't have to meet in secret to even talk about it."

"Yes." Meridian gestured around at their lowly surroundings. "You see where we must perch in the galactic hierarchy if we dare express interest in climbing to the same heights that all others are permitted to pursue." Her mandibles clacked together sharply. "This is the legacy of the Chirrn.

"Our yearning for metasapience was a natural goal, but the Chirrn perverted it by convincing us we must change our nature to pursue it. We became obedient and assimilated as they wished. They rewarded us by assisting our technological advancement, chaperoning us into greater contact with the galactic community over the generations that followed. As soon as we could, we sought out all available research into metasapience. Once we were established in the galaxy, with the connections to gain the PQM and other resources we needed, a group of us attempted to ascend."

The matriarch-in-exile lowered her head, her entire retinue and Broadwing following suit. "But their attempt was premature," she continued. "The Chirrn had pushed our people to advance too quickly, to be too eager for a height we had not yet earned — or had earned in the wrong way, for the wrong reasons. Whether as a fault of our ancestors' haste or a punishment for their hubris, the experiment went disastrously wrong."

Meridian turned to Arachne. "The results were far worse than the madness you describe. What they achieved was semi-stable. They were mad, yes, unable to bear the emptiness of the universe as they now perceived it. But they were still functional. They craved stimulation, the input they could gain by linking other minds to theirs. They adapted the nanotechnology that had heightened their minds so that it became infectious, and they began to spread it as far as they could reach. No Zenith population was safe from the madness, and some strains of the contagion mutated to infect other species as well."

"Holy shite," Sita breathed.

"My God," said Stephen.

Meridian blinked. "'Deity of waste'? Perhaps a fitting description. The infection spread widely, for its basis was a science so advanced and subtle that even the Galactics had few defenses against it. The madness spread across worlds, both planets and megastructures. The result was chaos, collapse, and savage violence. Rather than try to cure them, the Chirrn and other sane ones fought back, swiftly relearning the ways of war that had long since been mentored out of them.

"But the half-ascended ones relished the violence, for it filled their craving for intensity. They responded in kind and in far greater magnitude. The chaos tore through the Four Voids for generations."

"Was there nothing the Galactics could do to contain them?" Stephen asked.

"Indeed there was. The Ryohoch, in their ancient wisdom, developed a weapon that could neutralize PQM and render it useless." She hesitated. "Apastron?"

"Yes, my matriarch," the second said. "The neutralizer is based in quantum entanglement. All PQM from a common source can eventually be neutralized over any distance. The half-ascended, both Zenith and those they had infected, could be stranded on their habitats and ships, left to die out or tear each other apart in their madness. Yet the effect only propagated at the speed of light, of course, so groups of half-ascended were able to escape and continue the war in other regions. Eventually, they had to stop moving, or were surrounded, so in time the neutralizing waves overtook the last of them."

"But by then," Meridian resumed, "the civilizations of the Four Voids—those that survived—had fled to safer regions. By the time the last of the half-ascended were hunted down, the Voids lived up to their name. Galactic civilization was mostly gone from here, and few remained beyond the feral natives of worlds such as your own."

Stephen remained silent for a long moment. "Meridian," he said at last, "that is a tragedy on a scale I can't imagine. And yes, the Chirrn of that time made a disastrous mistake. But surely they more than paid for it in the cataclysm that followed." And yet his eyes strayed to Sita, and the memory of a mob of Lesshchin beating her in her barely swollen belly sprang unbidden to his mind. Her own eyes were unreadable.

Meridian moved closer, sidling up next to him and brushing shoulders. "We were not the only ones wronged by their mistake. Hear carefully, Stephen Jacobs-Wong: The Chirrn would not admit their error, their abuse. To save face, they blamed the chaos on the primitiveness of the Zenith mind. They decided that any race still confined to a planet was too immature to be trusted with the power of metasapience — or even the power of Galactic civilization. They argued that young civilizations needed to be quarantined on their nestworlds until they could mature to a 'safe' level on their own; until then, the risk of exposing them to knowledge of metasapience was too great.

"And so they began to campaign against the Mentoring Protocols." Her words struck Stephen like a blow.

The matriarch paced slowly around the Arachnen trio, keeping her right and middle eyes fixed on them at all times. "Normally, they would have had no chance at overturning such an ancient system. However, the war had made many afraid and sympathetic to their propaganda. And the most active enforcers of the Protocols were preoccupied elsewhere.

"The Chirrn were able to win allies among those few who remained in the Voids. The Gaurim, who disdain interference with the evolutionary process they worship. The Zhalevey, doting elders who can see no wrong in anything their juniors do. The Ryohoch, whose reasons make sense only to themselves. Even the surviving Seekers of the Zenith bowed to the Chirrn party line, as a show of penance to redeem their lost status. Together, they were able to force through a suspension of the Protocols throughout the Four Voids."

Stephen stared open-mouthed. Even in this gravity, he felt like he was floating away, his anchor disintegrating beneath him. "Including the Central Void... and Earth."

"Yes. And other worlds whose sophonts were on the verge of civilization, or already in its early stages. At least two worlds had their mentors removed."

"So... suspension of the Protocols... that means no contact of any kind with pre-spaceflight worlds?"

"That was how the Chirrn defined it. Complete exclusion."

His hands shook. "This… is why Earth was left alone? Why we were never visited by aliens, never even… saw any sign of them until we built space telescopes?"

"Correct. The Chirrn ensured that all local activity — what little remained after the cataclysm and the exodus from the Voids — was hidden."

"Oh, my God," Stephen breathed. "That's why Lesshchi was dark. Why we never saw it coming." He squeezed his eyes shut in pain. "They were hiding. From *us*."

"Stephen," Sita said, tightly gripping his hand. He could feel the pain in her as well, but she was in scientist mode, clinging just as firmly to her own objectivity. "Lady Meridian, with all due respect… I trust you can prove these allegations?"

Meridian blinked at her with only her lower two eyes; the third stared relentlessly. "Stephen Jacobs-Wong, is this your question as well?"

Stephen gathered himself. "She… Sita's right. What you've asked us to believe… it's a lot to take in. No disrespect intended, but we could use more information to go on." He was striving to convince himself, but the words were half-hearted.

The matriarch lifted her head for a moment, then came back to Stephen's eye level. "A fair request. Broadwing can give your cyber the means to circumvent the Chirrn's blocks on your network access. There is much propaganda and distortion there about the Zenith and our history. But even there you will find confirmation of the Chirrn's role in the suspension of the Mentoring Protocols."

"And why go to all this bother to clue us in?" Sita pressed. "What interest do you have in us?"

Meridian replied, but her triple gaze held Stephen's. "We are kindred spirits, and your plight sings to me. We have both had our freedom and our natural aspirations stifled by the Chirrn's self-absorbed condescension. We have both suffered from their crimes — and we have both inflicted unintended blows upon them as a consequence of their poor choices.

"But there is hope now that we may soar above that. You do not know how much the galaxy now speaks of the human race and the fall of Lesshchi. For twelve thousand years, the Chirrn's will has dominated the Four Voids. Now, a blow has been struck against their power and their policies. It creates new questions in many minds. It weakens the

Chirrn's claims of infallibility and righteousness. And it creates an opportunity for us, the victims of Chirrn arrogance, to stand up and begin the process of change. You can be a great symbol in that struggle.

"Together, Stephen Jacobs-Wong, we can free both our peoples from the Chirrn."

With Broadwing's help, it took little time for Arachne to confirm Meridian's account in the Star Palace's historical records. Earth was even mentioned (not under that name, of course) in a list of worlds with known sophont species that had been left "feral" as a result of the decision. Remote observation with gravity-focus telescopes, and the occasional Chirrn-supervised research flyby, had documented the turbulent, violent development of human and other feral civilizations, feeding ongoing debates in the galactic community. The mentoring races argued it was proof of the cruelty of the Void Alliance's policy, while the Chirrn cited it in support of their argument that juvenile, planet-bound civilizations were intrinsically too erratic to be mentored without an unacceptable risk of destabilizing them even further—not to mention the risk of exposing them to the knowledge of metasapience and triggering another cataclysm.

When Stephen insisted on a meeting with L'chellin in the Chirrn's suite, the senior mediator seemed unsurprised. Still, she and R'nilinnath (alongside Broadwing, who still played the role of a loyal mediator) perched quietly on their tails opposite Stephen, waiting for him to speak.

"When were you going to tell us about the Mentoring Protocols?"

L'chellin sighed slowly. "Velesh. Has he spoken to you?"

"We spoke to him. And others."

"In violation of your authorized limits. You should be penalized, but… you have endured so much already." Widening her stance, she tapped her tail on the ground in chastisement. "Still, you need to understand that there are reasons for our rules, Stephen. You have been exposed to knowledge you do not yet have the context to judge wisely."

"I don't know why you thought you could keep it from us for long. It wasn't that hard to piece together the truth about something so basic to all the beings here."

"I suppose not," L'chellin conceded. "But we had to try. We knew how you would react when you found—"

"The truth?" Stephen gazed into L'chellin's eyes, trying to read something inside those hollow orbs. "That for over ten thousand years, you watched us suffer and did nothing?

"It would've been one thing if you hadn't known we existed yet. But you were watching. The whole time. All the great disasters and atrocities of human history. You saw them happen and you did… nothing. More—you actively *prevented* anyone else from helping."

"That is not accurate," L'chellin said. "First, we were not monitoring you constantly or at close range. Most observation was by gravity-focus telescopy conducted from star systems parsecs away. Our real-time information was intermittent, a flyby every few of your generations. But such flybys were suspended once you invented sufficiently powerful telescopes," she added.

"Second, those civilizations that administer the Protocols have long been occupied with other concerns. The hypernova of Eta Carinae and the nearer supernova required massive relocation operations. Moving thousands of planetary populations, helping them to adjust, requires *yanarrach* of time and an application of resources on a multicivilizational scale. So there *were* no others clamoring to come to your aid."

"Then it should've been you," Stephen shot back. "You were left as the dominant power in this region, and you chose to abandon us to our own worst hells instead of—"

"Dominating you? Judging you?" L'chellin's voice carried a sharpness he hadn't heard since she had been male, and not quite even then. "If you know our history with the Protocols, you know of the Zenith cataclysm."

"We read about it." That was all he would tell them about his source of information. "We know you lied to us about your history, your great war with those who stayed on your home planet."

"I told you of planet-dwellers who resisted our influence and swarmed into space, spreading chaos and war for generations, de-populating our native planet in the process. I… allowed you to draw the erroneous conclusion that their birth planet was our own, for you were not yet ready to hear the complicated truth."

"The truth being that you got burned by your protégés, so you decided planet-dwellers were too savage to be allowed into civilized society."

"No." L'chellin's voice was still sharp, yet undeniably sad. "We decided that we could not be trusted to be good mentors. We badly botched the mentoring of the Zenith. Many of us have been reluctant to admit that, and we have embraced a facile prejudice against the planetbound as a protective cover. But I have carefully studied the great debates that led to the suspension of the Protocols in the Four Voids, for I knew the time would come when I would need to justify them to you." She calmed herself, softened her tone before she continued. "Perhaps I did spawn bastard words when I told you of that ancient war, for I told you that we were benevolent and wise and were met with venality and treachery. At the time, I had not come to know you. I had no reason to sympathize with the planetbound, so I did not question the myths we have embraced for our own comfort.

"The truth I now know is less flattering to the Chirrn. We judged the Zenith harshly." That drew a surprised blink from Broadwing. "It is too much in our basic nature to want to exclude or normalize those behaviors that diverge too much from our standards," L'chellin went on. "We tried to change the Zenith on a fundamental level, to engineer their territoriality and rigid gender roles out of their societies altogether. It was a gross abuse of the Mentoring Protocols, an abuse of the Zenith themselves.

"More, we abused the promise of metasapience, took the most sensitive and challenging decision any civilization can ever make and reduced it to a crude reward for obedience. Rather than allowing them to seek their own understanding of metasapience as a complicated option fraught with challenges and uncertainties, we taught them it was the single ultimate aspiration of every species, a goal they should strive toward with all possible haste. And so we damaged their society, turned them into a scourge that devastated worlds and ended hundreds of billions of lives.

"Indeed, it was chiefly due to chance that the chaos did not engulf your Earth. The mad Zenith arose in the Spinward Void, not far from our native world, and their conquests branched toward the centers of civilization in Outward and Antispinward, mostly bypassing the Central Void in between. Eventually, the pincer closed in on Central, but the Ryohoch developed the means to defeat the scourge before the battle lines converged on your home region. Yet by then, the starfaring inhabitants of the Central Void had mostly fled."

L'chellin rose and took a step toward Stephen. "We could not risk such a catastrophe happening again. We began to realize—not as an

attempt to avoid blame, but in hopes of preventing a reoccurrence —
that the mentoring system itself was overly enamored of metasapience
as a civilizational aspiration. We have told you that the metaminds
provide us with PQM, and that we believe their motive is to encourage
us to join them and increase their complexity. They crave new input
and perceive sophonts as raw material — and they are at the pinnacle of
the galaxy's technological ecosystem.

"Moreover, in the past few *yanarruvh*, the rate at which sophont
species have transitioned to metasapience has been accelerating. At the
time of the Zenith Cataclysm, the population density of baseline-
sapient civilizations in this octant had fallen to its lowest level since
the Mentoring Protocols were first introduced. Looking back on that
history, the Chirrn concluded that the metaminds had been influencing
the mentoring process, eroding the safeguards that prevented mentors
from pushing civilizations to advance too quickly."

"And you say you're not trying to avoid blame."

"On the contrary. We too were pushed too quickly by the Shayal,
encouraged to take our own protégés before we were ready. We are *still*
not ready. We are only wise enough to recognize our own limitations —
and thus to slow down and reorient our priorities toward the right of
each civilization to develop at its own pace, rather than being harried
forward in service to the metaminds' agenda.

"Yes, my friend, we left you to develop in isolation. We did nothing
to help you through your traumas and tragedies, and for that I am truly
sorry. But if we had intervened, an alien people with little understanding of your inner nature and the wrong temperament to mentor you
wisely, we could have caused you — and the galaxy — far worse harm
than anything you suffered yourselves."

"Even if it wasn't you, it could've been someone else."

"Who? The Zenith have no interest in mentoring, and would be
too inclined to keep their protégés beneath them. The Ryohoch are
too alien to understand your needs. The Gaurim mostly lead a nat-
uralistic existence and would have been ill-suited to guide you through
technological adolescence. The Zhalevey are herbivores, not equipped
to help you regulate your predatory drives. Any suitable mentor races
were occupied elsewhere in the galaxy. Leaving you alone," L'chellin
finished, "was the best thing we could do for you."

"No." Stephen shook his head, pacing before the mediators. "That's
too pat an answer. If you have protocols for refining the behavior of

other races, you could refine your own as well. Teach yourselves to be better mentors.

"Very few teachers, or, or parents, are ideal starting out. They make mistakes. But they can learn. They can learn from their students, their children, even as their charges learn from them. They can reach out and commit to building a relationship, and the two of them can come together and both become more than they were." He blinked away tears. "When I… when I had to take care of my baby brother, see that he got an education and stayed out of trouble while Mama struggled to keep us fed, I was terrible at first. I neglected him. I yelled at him. I played tricks on him. I treated him like my personal servant. But when he ran away and we almost lost him, I realized how much I'd been hurting him. And, and I made myself change. I taught myself—let him teach me—how to be a better mentor. And we became the best friends you ever did see. And when he… when we lost him, when he was bleeding out on the pavement, I stayed with him and I held his hand and he found the strength to tell me it was okay, because his big brother was with him and he wasn't af-afraid."

Stephen needed a moment to gather his breath. "And that's what makes a mentor, L'chellin. Not being perfect, but *not giving up*. Not abandoning people just because you're afraid you might screw up." Still pacing, feeling more torn up and out of control than he'd felt since Benjamin died, he shook his head and directed a bitter laugh at the ceiling. "You know, you, Rillial and the rest, you talked, at the trial, all about responsibility. About, about our responsibility for the harm we did to Lesshchi even though we didn't know. And I *agreed* with you! I thought, I thought you were within your rights to insist on responsibility.

"But you… you had a responsibility far greater—a responsibility to entire *worlds*—and you just, you just fucking ran away from it! You ran and you hid and you let me—you let us go through *that!* Through the Gulf States Collapse and the Orbit War and the Holocaust and the Great Leap Forward, through the slave trade and the Trail of Tears and the Inquisition… all because you were too goddamn *cowardly* to take responsibility and try to make a difference."

L'chellin crouched wordlessly, keeping her eyes focused on Stephen even though they sporadically twitched outward, instinctively trying to look away. Broadwing stood half-erect, head defiantly tilted. A trembling R'nilinnath hid her eyes with her hands, making the dog-whine sound of Chirrn weeping through her nares. But Stephen was unmoved. "But you know the thing about responsibility? You can't duck it. Try to and it comes around to bite you in the tail. You fled from your responsibility to help us, so that makes you responsible for every horror, every hell you could've prevented. It makes you responsible for our ignorance of your existence, our need to rely on relativistic ships." At L'chellin's startled reaction, he went on. "That's right, L'chellin. The destruction of Lesshchi — all this time I've been blaming myself, but it was you. It was *you!* It was your own damn fault and you've been persecuting us for it ever since!"

He couldn't even bring himself to say the rest. *It's your fault Kweli died. Your fault my baby died.* But he didn't need to.

After a long silence, L'chellin spoke again. "You have borne many words of merit here. We should all take them into our minds as guests and allow them nourishment and attention. These are moral questions that have been under debate for many, many lifetimes. We will not find their decisive answer this *narrissh.*" She moved closer to Stephen, lowering her muzzle in deference. "All I can say is that we acknowledge and respect your pain, and with your words taken into our minds, we share it. There is much for us all to regret in this.

"But the decisions that led to these events were made long ago, at a level well above our own. I ask that you consider this, and I hope that once your anger subsides, you will remember that we have shared much of value. And that one of the things we share is a responsibility to make the best of what the past has given us, as flawed as that may be, and try to build a better future together. I know that is something you truly believe in, Stephen. Thanks to you, I believe in it more now than I ever did in the past.

"We cannot bring back what we have lost, my friend. All we can do is speak the future into being."

Stephen was very quiet for long moments thereafter, his eyes held shut. Finally, L'chellin sighed and said, "We will talk later. The meeting is adjourned." She and the other mediators rose, but then L'chellin paused. "Understand, though, that any further violation of your probation will have to be met with penalties. Your... erratic behavior can only be excused up to a point by your tragic circumstances. From now on, it is incumbent upon you to behave in a way that will redress the existing imbalance."

Stephen looked up at her through hooded eyes. "Don't worry, L'chellin. I intend to."

He let them leave, saying nothing more. There was no point in further dialogue. Everything the Chirrn had ever said to him had been a lie built on a lie. All of human history had been a lie, a cruel hoax perpetrated on an unsuspecting species through the treachery of the Chirrn. They had used a disaster as an excuse to abandon his world, just as the governors and corporate executives had done to his home state.

And Stephen hated them with every fiber of his being.

5

"You are a hypocrite," L'chellin barked at Velesh as they met in the latter's private chambers. "You profess to honor the letter of the Mentoring Protocols, yet you deliberately violate them to undermine our handling of the Arachnen."

"And you reject the Protocols, yet hide behind them when you find it convenient," the Shayal countered coolly. "Let it be clarified: I spoke only of the general history of mentoring. Their information on the Zenith Cataclysm must have come from another source. Perhaps the Zhalevey; Doctor Bhatiani seemed adept at persuading them."

L'chellin forced calm upon herself, not wishing to seem like the child here. She refused to be cowed by the eerily silent scrutiny of his mates, who hovered nearby as always. She had her entire guild with her in consensus, after all. "Protest all you like, but you have made no secret of your agenda to exploit the death of Lesshchi as fodder for a renewed push to restore the Protocols."

"Surely that disaster compels a reexamination of the Void Alliance's stance on the Protocols," Velesh replied. "And surely the humans are entitled to a voice in the discussion. Not only are they direct parties to the events in question, but they are a starfaring power now."

"They have made some tentative ventures into local space through conventional means. They are not yet PQM-enabled."

"A condition you are about to change."

L'chellin felt her eyes jerk outward in surprise. She snorted. "You would exploit a technicality. The Arachnen have renounced their ties to human civilization. They are of the Chirrn now."

The triad gave her that look of patient condescension that was enshrined in Chirrn mythology and literature as the trademark of the Shayal. "Their very success at adjusting to that identity demonstrates that their species is ready for broader contact," Velesh expounded. "It would be difficult for you to continue to argue, even to your allies, that humanity needs to remain isolated for its own 'protection.'"

L'chellin thumped her toes skeptically. "So you would embrace them as equal partners in galactic life? All humans, not just the Arachnen?"

The hairs on Velesh's brow ridges twitched subtly, betraying his fears. "The conditions for ending their isolation have arguably been met, but the cost of their isolation remains. Naturally, some remedial mentoring would be required. Advisors can be assigned to assess their readiness for peaceful coexistence and, if it is found lacking, to guide them the rest of the way."

"And what standards would you use for defining readiness?" L'chellin demanded. "The humans' isolation has made them exceptional. How can you judge which behaviors are dangerous and which are merely unique?"

"As always, the Chirrn caricature the mentoring process. All civilizations are free to develop uniquely."

"Within the parameters of the Protocols. No matter how broad they try to be, there are still biases and expectations that would make it difficult for a mentored people to fairly assess an unmentored one."

"Consider, Mediator. Further encounters with humans are inevitable as they spread into space. What other crises might arise if they continue to expand in ignorance of the rest of us? Is open contact not worthwhile as a defense against accident and misunderstanding?"

The very reasonableness of Velesh's words put L'chellin on edge. If the Alliance conceded that much, it would be the first pinprick in a hull rupture, a fingerhold the Shayal could use to push deeper into Alliance affairs until the Protocols were restored — and who knew what other policies had been abandoned. Perhaps if the Coalition had chosen different emissaries, she would not have been so resistant. Sending Shayal was a rather blatant psychological ploy — an unsubtle reminder that without their mentors, the Chirrn might have torn themselves apart, their instincts toward exclusion driving them to bigotry and warfare.

But the humans overcame their bigotry and warfare to reach the stars without outside help, she reminded herself. *Perhaps we could have done the same, and been stronger for it.*

"You speak so conscientiously of the cost of abandonment," she told Velesh. "When you make your case to the Alliance, will you acknowledge your own role in that abandonment? It was the Coalition and your fellow mentors who turned your attention away from the Voids."

"You know we had obligations elsewhere," Velesh replied, still unflappable. "Your ancestors begged us for the chance to take over our mentoring responsibilities here."

"And you let them, knowing they were unready."

"We trusted the Chirrn. The Chirrn disappointed us." Velesh stepped closer. "And rather than admit the blame for the chaos that followed, you turned on us, prohibited us from doing anything to heal the damage."

"What would you have done? How would you have convinced the Coalition or the Mathadn or any of the others to allocate the necessary resources to this empty, ravaged backwater when so many other crises demanded their attention in more populous sectors? How could your mentoring be anything other than one-eyed, and how would that be any better than the situation that triggered the Zenith Cataclysm?"

Velesh studied her. "You sincerely believe you are protecting them."

"Yes. From you, and from ourselves." She tensed her legs and tail just enough to be intimidating, subtly reminding the Shayal emissary that the Chirrn were stronger, leaner, and far more dangerous on a physical level. "Do not cross tails with us," she warned, aware of the implications of the metaphor. That silly stump hanging down from Velesh's rear couldn't swat an insect. "We are not juveniles anymore. We will protect our interests. And we—I—will not allow you to exploit the Arachnen, our own young, to advance your politics."

The Shayal gazed at her sadly. "You truly love them. It is a pity you cannot see how badly you harm their species with your good intentions."

"I could say the same of you. Except that your only love is for your own self-righteousness. You know nothing of the Arachnen."

Velesh puffed out his long, flabby neck, unfazed as ever. "That is what I am here to change."

Ever since the meeting with Meridian, Stephen had been closed off again. The thaw in relations that Sita had enjoyed with him since the start of the migration was over. But this time, rather than being emotionally dulled and introverted, Stephen had smoldered with a

suppressed anger that Sita had never seen in him before. She had hoped
his confrontation with L'chellin would bring him reassurance, or even
that the mediator would have disproven Meridian's claims. But Stephen
had returned with his anger no longer suppressed. "I was a fool," he
told Sita. "I should've listened to Cecilia all along. The Chirrn have been
lying to us from the beginning."

He wasted no time asking Broadwing to arrange a second meeting
with Meridian to discuss her proposal for liberation. With L'chellin now
alerted, there was more risk in sneaking down to the undercity; but
Broadwing still had his fellow mediators' trust, as well as Meridian's
assistance. Her Zhalevey sympathizers were able to arrange for the
loss of certain data in the caravan's entrance application to Lode Seven,
requiring L'chellin to spend hours negotiating the bureaucratic
maze to correct the error — an exercise that Sita was convinced the
mediator secretly enjoyed. And Nilly was having so much fun showing the Arachnen around the Star Palace's many entertainments that it
was easy for Broadwing to spirit a group of them away.

This time, Stephen brought Tarik, who shared his newfound desire
for escape, and Diana Thorne, who'd insisted that her Vanguardian
abilities would be an asset in whatever plan the Zenith had to offer.
Their fervor made Sita even more determined to tag along and try to
keep them honest. Arachne's avatar joined them as well, but Sita
wasn't convinced of the cyber's objectivity. The protection of her human
charges was Arachne's overriding priority, a drive that had led her to
break the rules back in Sol System — and though she had been right to
do so then, Sita couldn't assume that would always be the case.

Not that Sita couldn't empathize with the Zenith, who simply
sought the freedom to explore metasapience. It didn't seem fair that
their whole species was still being judged by the actions of one group
twelve millennia ago, any more than it was fair that *Arachne*'s crew and
the Lesshchin had suffered as an eventual consequence of those actions.
Given Stephen's history, she couldn't blame him for empathizing with
the Zenith. But in his long years of activism back home, Stephen had
always advocated finding a way to end the cycle of wrongs rather than
adding still more to the list. She trusted that her husband still wanted
the same now... but she was not convinced about Meridian.

So she grilled Broadwing about his alpha as he escorted the five
Arachnen down to the undercity again. "I belonged to Meridian's
dissident movement in my youth," Broadwing told her as the others

listened in. "To my shame, I never lived up to the ambition of my name and could not advance far in the society of my native Star Palace. Meridian showed me that I was judging myself by the wrong standards. True, after the Chirrn's mistakes that provoked the cataclysm, we were free to resume our proper gender relations and our natural competitiveness, so long as we renounced any pursuit of metasapience. Yet we were still feared for what our kind had done, so we strove to assimilate and prove ourselves good citizens, obedient to the will of the masses and desiring no disruption. And so we lost sight of much of what we had been."

"So what did Meridian offer you instead?" Sita asked.

"Her kindness and acceptance were enough," he said. "She saw beneath my surface and showed me what I could achieve with faith in myself. And she offered me the hope that we could transcend the limits imposed on us for so long and rise to metasapience at last. It is a taboo notion, one I feared at first, but Meridian convinced me of the folly of that taboo. We are not the people we were, no longer manipulated into rushing forward prematurely. We have had twelve millennia to learn from our mistakes, to study a galaxy's worth of research, and to pursue the knowledge at our own responsible pace."

"Yet the other civilizations don't agree," Stephen said. "So Meridian's group has to live down here, as outcasts."

"And we have often been forced to act as such. I myself was captured for a petty crime against Shilirrlal, though I managed to conceal my ties to Meridian. Like you, I was required to atone by becoming a contributing member of the habitat I had wronged." He greeted the guards at the entrance to Meridian's pavilion and led the Arachnen inside. "Away from Meridian's guidance, I was vulnerable to their indoctrination. I cast aside my ambitions as youthful folly and dedicated myself to becoming a proper, well-behaved Shilirrlaln. For more than four *narrayth* I have lived that way."

"Until Lesshchi reawakened your faith," Tarik said. "And you decided to bring us to your fellow believers. But why?"

"Because you offer hope." It was Meridian, approaching with her head held high. The main chamber of the pavilion was emptier than before, with only Apastron and two other female aides accompanying the matriarch. But Meridian took care to position herself in a shaft of light so her shimmering crests would stand out.

Stephen went on to introduce the others: "Tarik Bahar, one of our administrators; and Diana Thorne, one of our top engineers."

The dissident leader greeted them in turn. "Morning Star of Spring," she said to the former. "A name worthy of a Zenith if ever there was one. And Divine Huntress of the Thorn! I have a cousin of a similar name."

Diana gave a cool smile in return. "Small universe. I once had an aircar by your name."

Meridian blinked. "In any case, they are fitting epithets for two so tall and strong. You are both most welcome."

The matriarch escorted the group to the inevitable dining table Apastron had again prepared. Once they had seated themselves and sampled the food, Meridian got to business. "For far too long—longer than the duration of your civilization, and for most of the duration of ours—the Chirrn have held the neck of the Four Voids in their talons. They have forced you and other young civilizations to go unmentored, to suffer war and chaos. They have forbidden the Zenith to pursue metasapience. Those who protested had insufficient voice to outsing the chorus of the Chirrn and their supporters.

"But now, the brave ascent of humans to the stars may have changed that."

"How?" Stephen asked.

"By what you did. Lesshchi's death was a tragedy, of course. Yet it revealed to all watchers that the Chirrn's doctrines are flawed. Their own insistence on holding feral civilizations down has cost them dearly. It is an opening we could use to push for an alteration of policy."

Stephen pondered. "I assume you want to employ us as more than just symbols, or Broadwing wouldn't have needed to advocate for this migration."

"You see sharply, Stephen Jacobs-Wong. There is a way we can help each other."

Meridian straightened—not quite to her full vertical stance, given the gravity, but high enough to dominate the table more than she had already. "We Zenith alone cannot change the minds of those with the power to affect policy in the Voids—indeed, we would only alienate them, for the scars of our ancestors' mistakes are still too clear here. We need to leave the Four Voids and travel among more open-minded societies to plead our case and gain allies of influence. Moreover, if we wish to pursue our research into metasapience, we will need the technology to make it possible — and we will need the ability to travel to the galactic core or to the neutron star of our choice. We cannot achieve those things with the single, limited-range warp cage we possess."

"You need PQM," Arachne said.

"Yes. As do you, if you wish to regain your independence from the Chirrn. Your vessel is now equipped with a warp cage, but it is one the Chirrn control and can neutralize. To get away from them, you would need a separate supply of PQM. We both need a fresh, unregistered supply that is immune to their neutralizers.

"But we can only attain it now, with your help. Miss this chance and there will be no other."

"Why is that?" Stephen asked.

Meridian prompted Apastron to answer. The second seemed more savvy on technical matters. "Any run of PQM processed at the same time shares quantum correlation throughout," the smaller female said. "A small sample quantity of every run is set aside as a security precaution. Should a PQM supply be stolen and used against the Void powers, the reference sample will be entangled with the neutralizer mechanism, allowing the entire stock to be nullified."

"This," Meridian added, "is why all our past attempts to… appropriate PQM for our own use have ultimately been defeated. If you are to regain your freedom, and if we are to seek the true zenith, we must obtain a supply of PQM that the Chirrn cannot neutralize."

"A large supply," said Apastron, "tailored for multiple uses: starships, wormholes, gravity generators, defensive fields."

"Enough to serve the needs of a small nation," the matriarch went on. "The PQM supply that your migration party will obtain at Lode Seven should fit those needs, if it can be stolen from the factory before it falls into the Chirrn's hands."

Stephen stared at the beautiful gargoyles. "You want *us* to steal it."

"Only you are in a position to do so. You have earned the trust of the Chirrn. You will participate in the construction of the new habitat, so you have a justification for requesting access to the PQM factory as part of your preparation. Of my people, only Broadwing has such access, and he could not do it alone.

"The rest, we have the means to assist you with. Broadwing will be with you, and we have sympathizers among the Zhalevey there." She gave a Zenith laugh, like a toy train whistle. "All have sympathizers among the Zhalevey. But they lack the physical robustness, the guile, and the aggression to accomplish the theft of the PQM and the liberation of your people. Without the access and abilities only you will have, we are without hope. We cannot do this without each other."

The humans exchanged stunned looks, at a loss for words. But Sita's scientific mind kept churning and analyzing despite her shock. "That's not all you want from us, though, is it?" she realized. "This opportunity you see isn't just about the habitat and the PQM—it's about us. A group of people motivated enough to help you with the heist—and unconnected enough to give you plausible deniability. We get the blame for the heist and you clear off with the goods while everybody's chasing after us."

"That… that's right," Stephen said, though it surprised Sita how slow he'd been to catch on. He was usually such a savvy negotiator. "Lady Meridian, both our groups are feared enough already. What will it do to our reputations in the galaxy if we begin our efforts with a… a heist of that magnitude? What might they do to our home system as punishment?"

"Both our reputations are already scarred, Stephen Jacobs-Wong—ours far worse than yours. A theft such as this will not shock the galaxy. PQM is rare and valuable, but replaceable. Its theft will do no great harm to anyone—but it will badly embarrass the Void Alliance, and it will marginally slow the Chirrn's efforts to reinforce their strength in the Antispinward Void.

"Yes, Sita Bhatiani—we do intend to let the attention fall on you, for you would be less harmed by it than we. We could perhaps accomplish this ourselves, but not without being identified and hunted relentlessly by a galaxy terrified of a new Zenith Cataclysm. We would be unable to pursue our research for long, or with the patience needed to avoid such a mishap. If you are blamed—ferals merely seeking escape from their captors, and lacking the knowledge to do great harm with what they have stolen—the consequences will be far less to you as well as to us.

"Indeed, many will admire the boldness of such a humiliation of the Chirrn. There are those in the Four Voids and beyond who dislike their restrictions on mentoring, but who lack the political power to stand against them. Shaming the Chirrn would weaken them and strengthen their opposition.

"As for your world, the Chirrn have left it alone for twelve millennia. They would not alter that policy now, even if you brought your people knowledge of galactic civilization. They are too accustomed to disdaining and avoiding feral, planet-dwelling sophonts."

Meridian leaned closer, bringing her eyes level with Stephen's. "If you still doubt, consider how much the Chirrn have stolen from both our peoples already. Are we not owed some recompense?"

"Yes," Stephen said without hesitation. "They owe us more than they can ever repay." Sita threw him a disturbed look.

"Then repayment from us will have to suffice. The quantity of PQM required to support a Chirrn habitat is considerable. Once our needs are met, there will more than enough left for you to take back to your nestworld, along with a few Zhalevey advisors we would provide. Humanity could be an interstellar power within a generation and nevermore be at the Chirrn's mercy."

Nobody said a word for some moments after that. Meridian rose. "You need time to consider my proposition. Our facilities are at your disposal."

Apastron showed the Arachnen into a side chamber whose panoramic, down-angled windows gave a spectacular view of the forest of columns and archways outside. The humans gravitated to the windows and spent a long moment just staring, trying to clear their minds. Sita watched Stephen closely, trying to get a read on him, but she was beginning to wonder if she'd ever known him well enough for that.

"Are we really considering this?" Arachne finally asked.

Diana turned to the silvery arachnocentaur, all four of whose arms were crossed over her sculpted chest. "You mean helping the Zenith pull off the heist of the millennium?" The Amazonian engineer laughed. "God, I like the sound of that."

"You do?"

"Sure! What an adventure! If nothing else were at stake, I'd be sorely tempted just to see if I could pull it off."

"But there *is* much more at stake," Stephen said. "Freedom, for all of *Arachne*'s crew. With the Zenith's help, we can get Cecilia and the others free—get *all* of us out of Chirrn custody together."

"The Zenith are admitted criminals and outcasts," Arachne pointed out. "Can we trust that they will adhere to their end of the bargain and not take the PQM by force once we possess it?"

"Arachne, I've been dealing with thieves and liars my whole life, either in the Gulf or in business," Stephen said. "I know how to protect myself when making deals with them. We'll be handling the goods ourselves, which gives us the advantage. We can set the terms of the handoff to ensure we don't lose it."

The thought of Stephen Jacobs-Wong contemplating a crime made Sita's head spin. "But what about the Shilirrlaln?" she asked. "What about our friends and neighbors?"

Tarik scoffed. "The only Shilirrlaln we've really been allowed to get to know are the mediators—who've been lying to us, manipulating us from the beginning."

"They're doing the right thing as they see it."

"But they've deliberately concealed their greatest secret, knowing how we would react. They've been blaming us all along for what they *knew* was ultimately their fault!"

Stephen clasped Sita's shoulders. "I can't blame you for your reluctance, darling. Whatever they've done as a culture, you don't want to hurt them as individuals. Neither do I. But really, what will it cost them if we pull this off? They'll be down forty-seven colonists plus Arachne, but they'll still have the rest of the Migration guild to start off the new habitat. They'll lose a PQM reserve, but they can surely order another. They'll be angry that the proper balance has been violated, yes, but they'll soon be too busy building a new world to dwell on it. Who knows? By the time the Chirrn are done building the habitat, the heist may have become part of its founding legends, a hardship they could take pride in surmounting. It might even bind them more strongly as a community."

"Rubbish! Will you listen to yourself? How can you rationalize this so easily? What about Nilly? She takes such pride in being an apprentice mediator. She won't just feel we've betrayed her if we do this—she'd feel she failed in her first adult responsibility. It'd break her heart."

"You know the kid has a rebellious streak," Diana said. "She always gets a kick out of hearing about human crime and depravity. Seeing it happen for real, committed by humans she actually knows, might be the thrill of her lifetime!"

"Or it might burst her illusions and leave her sad and bitter." Sita turned to her husband. "Is this really our only option? What about the Shayal? I think Velesh wants to help us. He certainly did all he could to let you know about mentoring."

"The Shayal didn't come to our aid when we needed it any more than the Chirrn did."

"They were busy elsewhere."

"Just like UNECS was 'busy elsewhere' while Florida decayed into a war zone. It's no excuse. The Shayal are powerful, privileged. They'll never see us as more than a charity case. Meridian's people know what it's like to be on the other end of the stick."

"Even so, can we really trust them? Will we really be the equal partners they claim? It's in their nature to jockey for superior status, you know."

"I trust Broadwing."

"He's a Zenith male, Stephen, and if Meridian is his matriarch, then she practically owns him. He's not going to defy her. And she's basically admitted to using us as scapegoats!"

"We need their help, Sita. Of course we'll be careful, but they have the ideas and the organization we need to get away from the Chirrn's control."

Sita stood and faced him. "So long as we steal for them! It's not enough for you that we're already convicted criminals? You want to make a career out of it? What happens after the theft? Do we spend the rest of our lives on the run? Hiding from the, the Galactic Police? Staging raids on unsuspecting planets and habs to get by?"

Diana chuckled. "Honestly, that sounds like fun."

"I'm not having a laugh!"

"I know that, Sita. But just think of the benefits if we pull this off!" the statuesque Vanguardian went on. "Our own PQM supply, the ability to explore the galaxy and see countless new worlds… it makes the adventure of settling Cybele seem downright ordinary. I think I'd risk just about anything for that."

Sita looked around at the others in dismay. "You're all determined to do this, aren't you?"

Stephen's breath caught. "I won't force anyone else to participate… but I will do whatever I must to free the Arach—the crew of *Arachne*."

Tarik cleared his throat. "I try to lead a righteous life. I'm not a criminal." He sighed. "But I am sworn to protect this crew, and I'd be a poor Muslim if I betrayed an oath—or if I failed to do jihad when my community is threatened. I'm with you, Stephen," Tarik said. "For Kweli. For our children."

"My responsibility has always been to my crew," Arachne said when Sita turned to her avatar. "I will not cooperate if I feel the danger of the heist outweighs the benefit to the crew, but so long as the plan is sound, I will serve as always."

"You've all gone bloody mad!" Sita cried. "Off your nuts, the lot of you!"

"Sita." Stephen took her arm and guided her off to the side. The others—even Arachne, it seemed—fidgeted and looked away. "I don't understand what's happening here," Stephen said softly when they were out of earshot. "You were the one who convinced me to start asking questions about the Chirrn."

"I wanted to find answers, didn't I? I wanted peace! Not just for myself, but I wanted to know what we were getting into, why the galaxy was so afraid of us. I wanted to know how we could avoid further conflict. Further tragedy." She winced, feeling the emptiness in her womb more strongly than she had in weeks.

"Hey." He reached for her, starting to pull her into a hug, but she stiffened. He settled for a light touch on her shoulders. "There's no reason this should lead to further violence. It's just property theft."

"'Just.'" She stepped away, shaking her head. "Damn it, Stephen. I don't know who you are anymore. The great man I fell in love with would never contemplate such a thing!"

"I learned to do what I had to growing up. You know that."

"Sure, nicking a loaf of bread or some fruit! Not robbing bloody Fort Knox! This isn't you, Stephen!"

"Don't assume you know me so well. If I'd… if I'd helped Benjamin steal that medicine, maybe he and Mama would both still be alive."

"More likely you'd be dead along with them. You know that!"

"This is different. The Chirrn state is not innately brutal or murderous." A part of her reflexively bristled, but she knew he was right; the brutality she had suffered was from a traumatized few. "Unjust, yes, but in subtler, more insidious ways. That's what makes them such a threat. It's not just the fanatics and bigots waving assault rifles around that you have to worry about. It's the quiet little everyday injustices of society as a whole, the rationalizations they make to themselves to justify doing nothing to make things better. They're the ones who create the climate of neglect that allows the militants and the haters to gain a foothold. Someone has to stand up and make them realize that change is needed."

He clasped her shoulders more firmly. "Sita, I'm doing the same thing I've always done. Protecting my people. My family. I used to think

I could do that without compromising my principles, and look what it cost us!" He laid a hand on her belly. "What it cost you. Sita, I'm doing this for our child."

She pushed his arm away. "Doing what? Using her as an, an excuse to lash out? To give up on being who you've always striven to be? How does that honor her memory?"

He winced, but refused to back down. "And what about all the other children, the ones still waiting to be born? Is it right to raise them in Chirrn bondage? It would be a greater compromise if I condemned them to that just to maintain my own spotless reputation."

"The means inform the ends, Stephen. I thought you understood that."

He shook his head. "I understand all too well. You're making excuses, Sita. You're afraid and you're not thinking clearly."

Of all the ways he could have reacted to her words, none could have hurt her as deeply as condescension. After that, there was no going back. "Oh, I'm thinking more clearly than I have in a while. Thank Krishna for that, since one of us has to." She pulled off her wedding ring. "Go on, then. You do what you bloody like, I can't stop you. But don't ask me to help or approve, and don't use me — *or my baby* — as your excuse!" Tossing the ring at him, she began to storm for the exit.

He intercepted her. "You know I can't let you leave alone."

"What? Afraid I'll rat you out to the Chirrn?" She knew it was unfair, but she said it anyway.

He winced. "I can't be sure of your safety out there. And if the Zenith see that one of us is against this… well, it's best not to give them cause for concern," he finished uneasily. "Please, Sita."

She knew it was pointless to argue further. The others' minds were made up. Besides, he had a point. Her drive for answers had made her fearless, but the answers had only brought more pain. And she'd known she had the protection of the Arachnen — and the mediators — to fall back on. Now, she felt more alone than she ever had in her life. And the prospect of being alone among dangerous, unknowable aliens filled her with renewed dread.

So she had no choice but to remain as Stephen returned to the others. She kept her distance, not wanting to force them to deal with this private pain any more than they had to. "Let's go give our co-conspirators the good news," Stephen said to them, his voice icy cold.

Tarik spoke tentatively. "Are you sure, Stephen?"

"Yes," Stephen replied. "We've been treated like criminals long enough. It's time to act the part."

Sita followed them out quietly, wondering how she'd ever believed a hibernation dream could be a legitimate basis for a marriage.

Broadwing trembled in anticipation as Meridian sensually stretched her wings before him. They perched on the edge of the pavilion roof, their garments and jewelry discarded behind them. Broadwing hoped he could perform well in this gravity; the dense air should compensate, but he was nervous and afraid of being clumsy. He had never shared a mating flight with a female of Meridian's elevation.

She turned her head backward to peer at him. Her long, sharp, elegant crests shimmered with the movement, blurring out in his upper-eye vision to crown her head in a rainbow aura. "Relax," came the deep, soothing chimes from those same beautiful crests. "You have earned this. You saw an unprecedented opportunity and you had the will to stoop upon it and harry it into our clutches. And so you have given us the chance to climb free of our oppression at last—and perhaps to finally achieve the greatest heights of all." She raised her tail invitingly, giving him a tantalizing glimpse of her distending vulva. "A male of such vision and ambition can serve me well. Should the Arachnen succeed, you could earn the right not only to mate with me... but to be my primary mate."

Broadwing almost lost his balance at that. He flapped his wings to recover his stance, and Meridian chimed affectionate laughter. "Don't worry. I'm sure you have the strength to keep up with me."

He tried not to show his embarrassment. "In truth, mistress, that is not all that troubles me. You are right, this opportunity had to be seized. But... what I needed to do to make it possible... it had consequences I never sought. Suffering caused to those who did not deserve it, who were victims as much as we. Now we again use them to serve our ends. What more might they suffer in the process?"

Meridian turned and loomed above him; her pose and chimes were still seductive, but the display of her superiority was unambiguous. "We are Seekers of the Zenith, Broadwing. Never forget that. It is our destiny to rise above all others." Her point made, she lowered her stance a bit. "Your judiciousness toward your inferiors is commendable. Power needs to be wielded with a soft grip, so that your subordinates will be content to accept their station. But do not forget how your priorities are stacked."

He admired the elegant, outthrust curve of her keel and the powerful wing muscles it anchored. "No, mistress. You are highest in my mind, always."

"Good." Meridian turned back to the edge and waggled her tail coquettishly. "Then catch me if you can."

She was resplendent as she soared, and he launched himself after her, for once not self-conscious of his own appearance, for it was only fitting that he pale next to his matriarch. Still, the sight of her heated his blood and drove his wings harder as he chased her down. His doubts, his regrets—his guilt—lay forgotten below, discarded like his clothing. As much as he yearned for metasapience and freedom from death, becoming Meridian's possession was his greatest aspiration in life. In truth, he had his doubts that the Zenith could ever crack the metasapience problem. In three *yanarrach*, Meridian's faction was not the first to make the attempt, and no others had come even as close as those who had triggered the Cataclysm. But even if he could never achieve that dream, being owned again by the love of his life was a dream fulfilled in itself.

So if that meant more of his Arachnen charges had to suffer or die… well, that was the price of victory.

Part Two

High Crimes

6

Churrlaya was relieved when the migration fleet finally received clearance for Lode Seven, yet he was concerned as well. The last time the Unrenounced had been transferred to a ship, at the onset of the migration, they had used their feral cunning to mount a violent escape attempt, taking Churrlaya and Stephen captive before the two had convinced Cecilia to stand down. Here at the Star Palace, Churrlaya had seen the way Diego and his followers had studied their surroundings on visits to the exercise room, as though sizing up potential weaknesses — or potential hostages. He had no wish to see that distressing experience inflicted on any others.

Yet when he consulted with the mediators and Arachnen leaders on the best way to avoid further attempts at violence, Churrlaya was surprised by Stephen Jacobs-Wong's proposal. "Put them in hibernation," the human said after a narr's thought. "Use their customized capsules aboard *Arachne*. It'll keep them safe and ensure they pose no threat. At least until we get settled in our new home."

L'chellin was clearly just as surprised. "Stephen… I am gratified that you are willing to cooperate in this, but that seems needlessly drastic. Their earlier escape attempt was a fluke."

"No. It was the result of human cunning and desperation. I picked the smartest, most determined people I could find for this expedition, L'chellin. They found a way to escape once, and they can do it again. And I'm afraid they may end up getting hurt or worse if they try.

"Besides, it might give them some peace of mind. In hibernation, they could dream, forget their reality for a while. Maybe that would give them a chance to heal emotionally. Make them a little more manageable when they come out."

"It is a reasonable suggestion," Broadwing put in. "It would certainly improve fleet security and free up resources and personnel."

"Agreed," L'chellin said after a moment's thought. "Thank you, Stephen, for the suggestion."

The Arachnen leader looked uncomfortable. "I know you're… trying to do what you think is best for us. And as you said, what matters is to look forward." L'chellin was visibly pleased by these words.

But Churrlaya was troubled. "Is it necessary to place them all in hibernation? Cecilia committed no violence. She deterred the others from violence, protecting Shilirrlaln lives even at the risk of undermining her comrades' trust in her. I think… she may be close to a breakthrough. I would like to keep working with her."

"But she did participate in the escape attempt," Broadwing countered. "She threatened you with a stolen plasma torch."

"She caused no injury."

"The threat alone is enough to concern the Antarean security staff. They do not wish to see this Star Palace's reputation for safety further undermined by human… unpredictability."

"He has a point," "Stephen said after an uneasy moment. "We don't want to alienate our new neighbors. I know the Chirrn's stance on mentoring isn't too popular with a lot of the locals. And the Unrenounced's actions have probably just reinforced that." He turned to Churrlaya. "It won't harm them. They may even enjoy it. And you can still work with Cecilia once we're settled at the colony."

Seeing that they were firm in their decision, Churrlaya left unhappily, angry that Cecilia was being treated so unfairly for something she hadn't done.

Then he realized how ironic it was that he of all people would think that.

Cecilia drifted weightless down an infinite corridor, pursued by lizard men and silver gargoyles that screamed at her in words she couldn't understand. She was naked and alone and there were no handholds within reach. She could do nothing to increase her pace as the monsters closed. All she could do was call for allies. "Ibrahim! Nik! Kahina! Help me!"

"You want us to help you?" She spun her head, and there was James drifting toward her, brandishing a fearsome plasma torch. "After you refused to help us? After you betrayed us to the enemy?"

"It's not true! I did it to protect all of us!"

"Liar!" It was Diego, grabbing her arm and spinning her to face him. "You're not one of us anymore, Cecilia. You've let the Frog Footman seduce you away from your own people. You apologized for his kind even after they drove Kweli to her death!"

"You're a traitor!" Amrita cried, advancing toward her with a toothed hunting knife. "And it's time to give you what you deserve." Diego twisted Cecilia around and held her tightly from behind as Amrita and James closed in on her. Evan hovered behind them at a safe distance, cackling in anticipation.

Cecilia flung her head back hard, taking Diego in the teeth, and shot her foot into Amrita's solar plexus. Evan yelped louder than they did. She broke Diego's grip, climbed around him, and kicked him into James, pushing herself away. But Amrita clambered over them and repeated the same maneuver, coming at Cecilia with the knifepoint thrust forward. Spotting an inviting archway of moldy, crumbling brick, Cecilia grabbed its edge and pulled herself into darkness.

She emerged onto the Fondamenta de la Misericordia, breathing a sigh of relief and joy as she soared above the canal, seeing herself reflected in its waters. *When did I become so gray and gaunt?* No matter. She was home! She angled northward, negotiating the narrow streets of Cannaregio until she reached her house. "Mamma! Papà!" she called as she floated through the door. "I'm home! I'm finally home!"

"Are you really?" Mamma said, looking up at her scornfully. "Then why do you float there like a spacewoman? Too good to touch the ground, eh? No weight. No roots! You've become just another tourist! Without even the courtesy to put any clothes on!"

"No, Mamma! I fly ships because I'm good at it, but I always come back. This is my home!"

"Liar! Tell that to your grandmother, to the mourners at her funeral! Where were you then, eh?"

"I couldn't get back! I was too far out!"

"Too far, yes. Too far gone to care! You abandon your family, you abandon Venezia like all the others."

"No, Mamma, I am a LoCarno like you raised me! I stay loyal to the city!"

"Staying loyal means staying here! Only we who stay keep Venezia a living city, not just a ruin for tourists! You make excuses, you make noises, but you abandoned us like all the others! Traitor! Seduced away from your own people! You're not one of us anymore!"

"No, Mamma, it's not true!" Cecilia reached for her, but she floated helplessly in space, out of reach, out of touch. She drifted up through the ceiling, through the roof, a ghost, dead to her family. *I didn't abandon you, Mamma. You abandoned me.*

Everyone's abandoned me.

She was alone with her tears until a voice intruded, startlingly clear. "Cecilia?"

She looked up and there he was, reaching out to her. "Stephen!" She grabbed his hand, pulled herself into his arms, and held him tightly. She vaguely remembered that she was angry at him, but that didn't matter. He'd come back. She was happier to see him than she'd ever thought she could be. "Oh, I've missed you. I should've told you last time—"

"I've missed you too," he said. "All of you. And I need to talk to you."

"I'm here, I'm right here."

"I'm speaking to you through the hibernation dream network. I'm sorry for putting you back in hibernation, but it was the only way I could think of to talk to you without the Chirrn overhearing. Arachne's keeping you in a light enough REM state that it should be like lucid dreaming. You'll be able to remember what I'm about to tell you."

Cecilia pulled back, gathering herself as she realized what he was saying. *Back in hibernation.* She remembered now: Stephen watching, cool and remote, as Joana Caravalho supervised the return of the Unrenounced to hibernation. Diego cursing him as a traitor.

Diego was here now, in the hibernation bay (or her dream image of it), though fully clothed, like the rest who were now appearing. Yet somehow Cecilia's image of herself remained naked, exposed, vulnerable. She hoped she was the only one who saw her that way.

"Why should we listen to you, traitor?" Diego said, and it took Cecilia a moment to realize he was addressing Stephen. She looked at James, at Amrita, but they were watching Stephen instead of her. Had their assault been only her private dream, or had they actually come after her through the shared dream network? She hadn't yet remembered she was dreaming, had been too afraid to think clearly, so she hadn't looked for the signs.

"We've all been betrayed, Diego," Stephen said. "It just took me longer to figure it out."

He told them what he hadn't been able to tell Cecilia before with Churrlaya watching, about Galactic civilization and the Mentoring Protocols. Then he revealed what he'd learned from the Zenith dissidents about the Chirrn's role in suspending the Protocols and the consequences to humanity. "None of it had to happen," Stephen concluded. "Cecilia, you were right all along, righter than you knew. The Chirrn brought the disaster on themselves by isolating us, hiding from us. We're the victims—we've been their victims since the dawn of history."

Diego and his clique were clearly pleased to see Stephen coming around to their point of view. But Cecilia was only thoughtful. "Because they let us be? Allowed us to find our own way? Hell, for the first time, I feel like thanking them."

"Thanking them?" Stephen was shocked. "For ten thousand years of war and cruelty, famine and plague?"

"None of which they caused."

"They could've helped us avoid it!"

"At what cost? How much of ourselves would we have lost?"

"It's not like that. The Protocols are subtle, delicate, giving mentored peoples as much independence as possible, just protecting them from the worst disasters and mistakes."

"Say the mentors themselves. Can we trust them? Any system can be abused. L'chellin even admitted it. How do you know we wouldn't have been worse off? Gelded and scattered like the Zenith? Weak and dependent, unable to think for ourselves?" Her dream self was clothed now, finally. She and Stephen were in his office back at Stargazer Enterprises in São Paulo, with its splendid view of the dense cityscape stretching clear to the horizon on all sides, the sky filled with an endless dance of quadrotor taxis and private helicopters flitting from rooftop to rooftop. This was where they'd had many of their best arguments, forging their friendship in the process. "Yes, we went through hell, but it was mostly of our own making. And we fought our way through it and survived. It made us stronger."

"It hardened us. Scarred us. That's not the same. We could've been spared so much insanity, so much trauma, so much loss. We could've grown up with a healthier strength, the strength that comes from balance and wisdom and serenity... and our loved ones by our side."

"But could we have had greatness?" Cecilia empathized with the pain in his voice, but she wasn't about to start coddling him now. She gestured around at the office, unleashing her Italian reflex to talk with her hands in a way she never could in free fall or cramped starships. "Look at yourself, Stephen. Look at what you built, what you achieved. Could you have done that if you'd had a peaceful, balanced childhood? If you'd never known hardship and suffering, would you have been so driven to make life better for tens of millions? To take humanity to a whole new world?"

"If Earth had been mentored, I wouldn't have needed to."

"Exactly. We would've been dependent on our mentors."

"We would've achieved just as much, but *together*. Not just a few rising out of the chaos, but everyone contributing their best. Not as romantic, maybe, but the cost would've been far, far less."

"And what about the cost if we had been mentored? You talk about avoiding mistakes. What about the beautiful mistakes? What about the glorious, offbeat, wonderful things we came up with because we were too stupid to know better and didn't have anyone to set us straight? What about Venezia?" She gestured out the window, where the steeples, domes, and low red-tiled roofs of her home had replaced the towering, modern São Paulo skyline. "Would the most beautiful city on Earth have ever been built if some wise, protective alien had said, 'No, don't build there, it'll sink into the marsh?'

"Maybe we did suffer more than most, but maybe that makes us special. Maybe we have things to show the galaxy they've never seen before because so few races have been allowed to develop entirely on their own. Maybe the other races are intimidated by us 'ferals' because they sense that we have something they don't. We could end up a power to be reckoned with in the galaxy, bring it a whole new Renaissance. And we'd have the Chirrn to thank for it."

"How can we achieve any of that," Stephen said, "while the Chirrn keep us imprisoned? You were right about that, Cecilia. Renunciation was just trading one prison for another, a subtler, more devious one. The Chirrn have kept us prisoner for our entire history, kept us isolated and ignorant. Even if you're right that some good came of that, the Chirrn never gave us a choice or an honest chance. Who knows if they'll ever let 'ferals' like humanity out into the galaxy? Programmable quark matter isn't easy to come by, and we know they have ways to cut off the supply to civilizations that cause trouble."

"So what are you proposing?" Diego asked from a corner of the office that still looked like the hibernation bay. Cecilia had almost forgotten the others were there.

"We're working on an escape plan," Stephen replied. "The convoy is getting ready to head out for the neutron star system called Lode Seven, and we have allies who will assist us there along with Broad-wing. Once we arrive, I'll tell you more. But I'll need your help. I need us all together in this, working to gain our freedom."

"Yes!" Diego cried, coming forward to clasp Stephen's hand. "Glad to have you in the fight at last."

"I'd prefer it not to be a fight, Diego. We'll be striking back at the Chirrn in a way, don't worry about that. But we have to prove to the galaxy that we're not savages. I don't want this to become violent if we can avoid it."

"Of course not," Diego said, the insincerity subtle enough that Stephen didn't catch it—though Cecilia might have been projecting it onto him in her dream state. "But if we can't avoid it?"

Stephen was slow to respond. The expression Cecilia saw was only what she imagined, but it reflected what she'd sensed in his voice throughout, a depth of bitterness she'd never thought him capable of. "One way or another, we need to be free of the Chirrn."

"That's the spirit."

Cecilia moved in. "Stephen… be careful. I understand why you feel this way, believe me. But you're not used to it. It may be too heady a brew for you. Don't do anything rash."

He stared at her. "You of all people say this? I'm finally where you wanted me to be all along, and now you're objecting?"

"I just… don't like the way this anger looks on you." She knew how much his sense of self was built around hope and optimism. With that shattered, she feared he could lose everything he was. He'd achieved such great things in the name of hope; she shuddered to think what that drive and brilliance could be turned to in the name of rage. But she had trouble finding the words. She'd been angry at him for so long that it was hard to speak to him so inti-mately, to reconnect with the sisterly love and admiration she still felt for this man.

And so she missed her chance. "You've never approved of anything I did, Cecilia," Stephen said. "It's like a reflex with you. Either grow up or step aside."

He turned away, discussing plans with Diego, Nik, and the rest. Cecilia was alone again, a ghost drifting through the walls.

Haim Silbermann had been too distracted by all this mentoring business to study up on the PQM factory they were heading for. Normally, he was more practical than political, but Stephen's pre-occupations had a way of rubbing off on the Arachnen, and it troubled Haim to see how much this one distressed his old friend.

He'd given the matter a lot of thought, but he hadn't arrived at any firm conclusions about where he stood. He did think the Chirrn had been wrong to isolate humanity completely. What made his and Tarik's shared homeland such a vital part of Earth history, a place where religions were born and great changes began, was that it was a crossroads where different cultures met and synergized. In society, as in engineering, potential differences caused energy to flow and work to be done. How much more could humanity have accomplished in interaction with the races of the galaxy? On the other hand, the more recent history of the Mideast was heavy with object lessons on the dangers of well-intentioned meddling in other people's societies. The Chirrn had tried to change the Zenith into copies of themselves and had ended up creating a lethal backlash—an all too familiar pattern. Haim may not have been sure where he stood on the Mentoring Protocols, but it did seem that the Chirrn had screwed up coming and going. Stephen said they couldn't risk staying dependent on the Chirrn, and Haim couldn't disagree.

Still, L'chellin was a stalwart sort once she warmed to you, and R'nilinnath was a real charmer. Yonchon, the Ryohoch starship engineer who had become Haim's mentor, was as alien as any creature Haim had ever encountered, yet had proven over and over that engineers were a universal fraternity. Haim wasn't comfortable thinking of any of them as the enemy. So he'd been uneasy when Stephen had requested his aid in committing a theft. He wasn't an activist like Stephen, but he had his principles. Still, he couldn't deny the cause was just. And it wasn't like there was no precedent. The Torah said the children of Israel had plundered the Egyptians before their Exodus from slavery — though divine intervention had enabled them to do so by asking politely. Haim doubted that would work in this case.

And Haim had to admit, he was intrigued by the technical challenge of pulling off such a heist. Which was nothing compared to the prospect of getting his hands on a large supply of PQM, taking it back to Solsys, and spending the rest of his life cracking its mysteries. Sure, he could study it while working to build the new habitat, but the Chirrn already had all the answers about the stuff, and where was the fun in that?

There were naturally some Arachnen who wanted nothing to do with the heist, Oyama Kazuko notable among them; though they'd grudgingly agreed not to report the others' plans to the authorities. Sita in particular had argued fiercely against it, insisting they'd be better off appealing to Velesh and the Shayal — who would be accompanying the migration fleet to Lode Seven for further "observation," much to L'chellin's annoyance — for assistance in winning liberation. Though Haim respected Sita's position, he regretted the schism that had formed between her and Stephen. Despite his own doubts, Haim knew that even if Stephen was making a mistake, he'd still need his loved ones' help and support to get through it.

One way or the other, Lode Seven would be where the next leg of their journey began. Haim had picked up a few of the basics: Lode Seven was deep in the Upper Scorpius group, where the Void Alliance's rough sphere of influence overlapped with those of neighboring powers, and was administered by a consortium of unaligned civilizations including the Zhalevey and a well-respected race of nocturnal quadrupeds called the Mykhshad. But that was just the politics. The trip was so brief, and he was so busy making sure Arachne and the hibernation pods were all battened down, that he'd had little opportunity for, as Diana had put it, "casing the joint" on a technical level before the heist. So he made sure to pay careful attention once the convoy arrived at Lode Seven, recording everything he saw into his buffer for later study.

When they emerged from the wormhole, the sky around them was far more subdued than the view from Antares; it seemed they were within a parsecs-wide dust cloud free of other habitation, native or otherwise. The wormhole terminal itself was a fair distance from the neutron star, for security and safety (since proximity to large masses and powerful EM fields could disrupt delicate wormhole metrics). Haim suspected that could be a problem for their escape, but Stephen said that Broadwing would be taking care of that end. Hearteningly, the convoy could approach the factory megastructure swiftly using their warp cages in sublight mode. At these speeds, the cage didn't need to be closed, so they had a naked-eye view through the ports. He had expected there to be nothing to see at first, since the star was a mere two dozen kilometers across and relatively cool, as one would expect from an older, radio-quiet neutron star.

But he was wrong. Soon after the warp cage unfurled, Haim beheld a cloudy shimmer of shifting, multihued light. It grew swiftly as they approached on gravitic drive, and with a little adjustment to his adaptive optics, it emerged as an intricate network of brilliant loops arcing along the magnetic field lines of the neutron star, cloaking it in a veil of iridescent threads. Arcs and sheets of energy jumped between the loops at lower altitudes. Brighter knots of light slid along the arcs in clusters like beads on an abacus, slowing as they reached the top of the arcs, then descending with increasing speed into the stellar remnant's immense gravitational field. Yet the blinding impacts he expected when they hit the surface at those speeds were nowhere to be seen, just gentle pulses of color rippling out like auroras. As the ships came closer still, he could discern intricate patterns of light and shading on the neutron star itself, fractal grids of shifting hues overlaid on its ember-orange surface.

"Behold metasapient technology," L'chellin told the awed Arachnen. "The shapes you see consist largely of PQM and nuclear-density superfluids accelerated along the field lines. On occasion, quantities of PQM are sloughed off from the structures and expelled onto the orbits from which we collect them—either a gift for our advancement or mere waste they are content to let us clean up, depending on the interpreter. We know that the structures affect the geometry of spacetime in their vicinity in unusual ways, but we can do little but conjecture as to their effect or purpose, and the conjectures are well beyond my expertise. Let their purpose be to make us wonder and keep us humble." Haim wondered what astronomers back home would have made of this sight if the dust hadn't hidden it from their view.

Lode Seven Station began to resolve alongside that stunning backdrop, initially just a faint string of lights that stayed centered in the viewport as the starscape drifted past behind them (for at the station's orbital distance of nearly half a million kilometers, its "year" was just under 45 *narr*, or 72 minutes). Soon it stretched clear across the sky but was still no more than a hair's breadth wide. This, the mediators explained, was a unique class of megastructure: a tidally stabilized bundle of tethers nearly 6800 kilometers from end to end, enough to spear Mars through both poles with length to spare. This close to a neutron star, the tidal gradient that kept it taut and radially aligned—with anything above its center of mass accelerated outward from the star and anything below it pulled down toward the star—was strong enough to provide habitable gravity inside the modules strung along its length at intervals from dozens to hundreds of kilometers. Moreover, the tethers generated their own electricity as they orbited through the neutron star's magnetic field—and the megastructure orbited in the star's narrow habitable zone, keeping it at a temperature suitable for water-based life. Everything—power, heat, gravity, not to mention PQM—came from the neutron star. It was a marvel of living off the land. In many ways it was so simple, based on elementary physics and technology well within human understanding. But the tension the tethers must be under was staggering. The structural engineering would have to be more advanced even than what he'd learned of Chirrn construction methods.

Haim laughed as he realized the perfect name for such a megastructure. "It's a Stringworld!"

R'nilinnath was mingling with the Arachnen, proud as always to show off her erudition as they *ooh*ed and *ahh*ed at the sight. "Everyone needs PQM," she explained, "so the station has modules with every possible environment and gravities. Well, at least those of all the starfarers in the Antispinward Void and neighboring space." She gestured toward the various habitat modules in turn, the pearls of the Stringworld. "There's something here for everyone."

"So people live here?" Haim asked.

"Oh, yes. Every starfaring power keeps an embassy to maintain access to PQM. Also for diplomatic reasons. Everyone comes here, so it's a natural meeting place for conferences or summits."

"Hunh. A watering hole."

"It also helps that exotic spacetime metrics aren't as stable this close to the star. Good for security. Nobody sneaking signals through wormholes or warping in and out for a theft."

Stephen looked at her carefully. "Do thefts happen a lot?"

Nilly mimicked a human shrug. "PQM is practically the only really rare resource, so it's very valuable. But don't worry. The security's very good."

Haim swallowed. "I, ah, I hope so."

The Stringworld was asymmetrical around its center of mass, the inner end half the length of the outer. Atop the radiation shield at the starward end was a large chunk of cometary matter serving as a counterweight and ice reserve. Above it were the automated levels where the PQM harvested from the neutron star's aura was processed, programmed, and prepared for shipping. The outer two-thirds held the residential modules, the "neighborhoods" of this linear megalopolis. This sensibly kept the people on the outer segment of the tether, where "down" was outward from the star; that way, anything or anyone that fell off would be flung into open space and could be recovered.

At the far outer end of the Stringworld was the docking structure that the migration fleet now approached. By docking at the outermost end and "climbing" inward, Haim realized, the ships would transfer momentum to the tether, raising it slightly in its orbit. They would then depart by simply "falling" down the Stringworld's length, the megastructure functioning as its own linear accelerator and giving that momentum back, keeping the ledger in balance.

The docking module was filled with ships of many sizes and designs, all within warp cages yet still displaying a wide variety of engineering and aesthetic philosophies. Haim only got tantalizing glimpses before the convoy docked, whereupon the ships and crews were subjected to an efficient yet thorough process of inspection by the Stringworld customs/security personnel. He strove to stay calm, reminding himself that any equipment for the heist would be brought in by Broadwing or provided by his local Zhalevey allies. Haim's job was simply to take advantage of his position on the engineering team to gain the necessary access.

Simply. Yeah, right. If he couldn't keep his cool during a customs check, he'd be a basket case in the actual heist.

Once the convoy was cleared for entry, *Arachne* was shuttled into a large elevator cage and began to ascend one of the great tethers that held the Stringworld together. There looked to be dozens of tethers running in parallel, each one as wide as a skyscraper and woven of vast fullerene-nanocellulose cables. The cage was evidently quantum-locked to the tether with a magnetohydrodynamic force field, allowing a high-speed frictionless ascent. It also let them slip past the anchor points of the monumental frameworks that ringed the habitat modules they passed, massive rings and arches that bore the immense tension the tethers were under. The module walls were coated in thick layers of aerogel, no doubt to shield their interiors in the event a cable snapped. The release of that kind of tension, Haim realized, would be like a meteoroid impact. He reminded himself that this was the product of a technology far more advanced and ancient than his own. Still, he wouldn't fully trust it until he knew how its safety features worked.

Each module was topped by its own radiation shield resembling a conical Chinese hat, in the event something hit the neutron star "above" them and caused a gamma-ray burst; they were so far from the inner radiation shield that it would be a mere pinprick, not wide enough to shade them if the Stringworld wobbled even the tiniest bit off the vertical. Which it undoubtedly would; no structure on this scale could be perfectly rigid. Looking down the length of the tether, Haim could see that it had a gentle curve, probably due to a very slow swaying motion driven by the movements of ships and elevators among the various modules. Haim wondered what kind of counterweight system was being used to keep the center of mass steady.

As they climbed, the number of parallel tethers increased, for the lower/outer portions of the Stringworld had less weight to support, and extra tethers would add needlessly to the weight the higher tethers had to bear. The modules had been somewhat sparsely distributed for much of the ascent, but were growing more numerous as the effective gravity decreased. The migration fleet finally docked with a large spheroidal module at about 1.3 g.

As they disembarked into the local port facility, the crew found themselves subject to a second inspection. "Security really is tight here," Diana observed, making it sound casual more successfully than Haim ever could. "So much for peaceful galactic society."

L'chellin gave a slight bow of agreement. "While it is true that mentored civilizations are generally less prone to war and savagery, there are other means by which civilizations compete and maneuver for gain," she said. "And there are still deadly threats in the galaxy, despite the best efforts of the mentoring powers to tame it. As the Zenith Cataclysm proved, mentoring can do more harm than good."

"But according to you," Stephen put in, "the Protocols don't apply in this part of space anymore."

"The Protocols were suspended less than four *yanarrach* ago. You are, as far as I know, the first unmentored civilization to reach a PQM lode in this octant since that time." L'chellin gave Stephen an amused glance. "And I trust you do not intend to set a precedent by becoming a security risk."

Haim fumbled and dropped the carrying case he was just receiving back from the customs inspector. *I'm not cut out for a life of crime.*

7

The interior of the habitat module housing the Chirrn embassy was a kilometer-wide cityscape segmented into districts, each dominated by a different species' architecture—yet as far as Sita could tell, there was little unity of style within any one district, and a good deal of overlap among them. It looked as though the module had begun as a planned cityscape, but had evolved and been rebuilt over centuries as styles changed and populations shifted—much like any city. Chirrn habitats had their share of such diversity, but it was harder to see, since their partitioned sense of order led them to maintain a fairly consistent style within any single sector, designing new buildings to mesh with those around them. Clearly the Chirrn were not the sole tenants of this module. Nor was this a tourist mecca designed for show like Antares B Star Palace. This was a living, working habitat with a history.

The Shayal embassy was in the same module, which Sita suspected was only partly because the two species had evolved in the same gravity and atmosphere and largely so that they could keep a close eye on each other. But the proximity had made it easier for Sita and Oyama Kazuko to slip away to meet with Velesh, with a little help from Lode Seven's Zhalevey contingent. Part of her still quailed at being surrounded by aliens, but the presence of the Zhalevey—and the relative physical harmlessness of the Shayal—eased Sita's fears enough that she could do what had to be done. Having Kazuko by her side brought her comfort as well, as it had in the weeks after their miscarriages. Though both women had acceded to the Arachnen's consensus to remain quiet about the heist, Sita was still determined to find a way to make it unnecessary. The Shayal may not have been a perfect option, but they did genuinely seem to be trying to make up for past mistakes by pressuring the Chirrn to alter their policies. Kazuko had readily agreed that if they could offer the Arachnen a legal path to freedom, it was surely worth investigating — even if it meant going behind Stephen's back.

The module's "Embassy Row" ringed a central mall/pavilion containing a cluster of open-sided white domes of various sizes, the smaller ones surrounding the large central dome in a fractal arrangement. Velesh and his two mates escorted the two diminutive women around the pavilion, showing them that each dome covered a recessed auditorium with tiered seats like a Greek amphitheater, where Stringworld denizens could gather to watch speeches and debates on the issues of the day. They could have attended virtually over Lode Seven's datanet, but as Velesh explained, "Those who are content to reside within their own minds are not the sort who travel the stars. The beings here are the kind who prefer to interact more directly with the universe and our neighbors within it."

Even so, the pavilion was linked by augreality to equivalent venues in other modules, so that sophonts from radically different environments could have the next best thing to a face-to-face meeting. Velesh's triad led the women into an auditorium hosting a speech transmitted from the Ocean Module high above their heads, positioned close to the Stringworld's center of mass to minimize the weight of the vast quantity of water it contained. Sita grinned in awe and delight at her first sight of the speakers, a pod of six large, long-necked beings like plesiosaurs with manta-ray wings and pronounced beaks. Sita promptly dubbed them "Concorde rays" from their resemblance to the antique European aircraft, though Kazuko didn't get the reference.

The pod collectively sang a trilling, scraping song that translated as a proposal to ecoform an uninhabited ocean planet for colonization by aquatic refugees from the Eta Carinae diaspora. Since such planets had no land of any kind — just pure ocean dozens of kilometers deep over thick mantles of high-pressure allotropic ice — their seas were usually barren, devoid of life-sustaining minerals. The Concorde rays' proposal involved a series of artificial floating land masses covered in nutrient-rich soil, the diversion and demolition of several thousand silicate asteroids to create a dense planetary ring that would rain new minerals down into the oceans on an ongoing basis, and the engineering of deep-dwelling microfauna that would consume the bodies of dying organisms and then rise to the surface to be consumed there, preventing nutrients from sinking out of the ecosystem. Sita had to struggle to remember that she was here to speak to Velesh; she would have been happy to stay here all day, learning more about galactic xenobiomes and their engineering.

The proposal faced some opposition from a conservative Gaurim faction within the Void Alliance, who argued that if it was the nature of an ocean planet to be barren, that nature should not be fundamentally altered. But this seemed to be a minority position; few in the Alliance disputed that the displaced aquatic sophonts had a right to a new home, and adapting an ocean planet was a safer long-term option than constructing a megastructure capable of containing the vast quantities of water they needed. Sita wondered aloud why the aquatics needed to migrate so far from their native Sagittarius Arm, given the abundance of ocean planets in the galaxy. Velesh explained that the intervening territories were already overloaded with refugees, and that interarm regions were the most populous areas of the disk to begin with, since many starfaring civilizations migrated there to avoid the turbulent starbirth zones and supernovae within the arms. A less crowded region would give these aquatic sophonts more breathing room, so to speak. "Although it may be a temporary gain at best," Velesh suggested. "Others are migrating here for similar reasons, so the population of the Four Voids is likely to increase still further in the future. All the more reason why your people would benefit from having prominent allies, lest you become marginalized in your own space."

"In the experience of both Mars and Earth," Kazuko replied coolly, "increased immigration is generally beneficial to a society, and rhetoric claiming the reverse is generally a self-serving political ploy. The Voids have gone this long without being repopulated; maybe it's high time they finally were."

"A fair point, and I apologize for implying otherwise," Velesh said. "Indeed, for some time after the Zenith Cataclysm, the Voids were too dangerous to resettle. The mad Zenith left hidden pockets of contagion which could lie dormant for generations, and combatants on both sides created booby traps and autonomous weapons that lingered long after the war. It was many generations before the last of these in the Antispinward, Outward, and Central Voids were sprung or defused, and some hazards still remain in Spinward, where the madness began. So the region's stigma has remained. You are correct to suggest that this has not been beneficial. Galactics are distantly aware that new civilizations in need of mentoring have arisen here, but the diaspora preoccupies the most powerful societies in this octant, and too many others have been slow to overcome their old fears."

Velesh's eyes rolled out to the sides, and Sita wondered if it conveyed shame in his species as it did in the Chirrn. "All because we were too proud of the Chirrn — too quick to believe they were ready to stand in our place. Because they were family and we forgave their faults too readily. Whole civilizations were rendered extinct as a consequence... and the civilizations that have since emerged in the Voids have paid an ongoing price. A price the Chirrn have forced them to pay in silence."

The Shayal emissary led the women back out onto the mall, his mates tagging along as always. They never seemed to say much; was it Shayal custom for the hermaphrodite to speak for the group, or was Velesh simply prone to monopolize the conversation? "But now the Lesshchi disaster has brought the plight of the Voids' young civilizations to the galaxy's attention," the emisssary went on. "More, the Chirrn are being judged for what they have done to you in the wake of that disaster. They have blamed and punished you for an accident that arose as much from their own choices as yours. You have repeatedly endured physical violence, even suffered deaths as a result of your captivity. Many find this unacceptable."

"Don't need to tell us, mate," Sita murmured without sound. She strove to remain patient with Velesh's incessant lecturing.

They passed into what looked like a sculpture garden, though the AR annotations identified the pieces as remnants of the Casimir cage that had held the first wormhole to reach this neutron star, the first crude habitat built in its orbit, and other historic artifacts. "This is why we have brought you here, Doctor Bhatiani, Administrator Oyama. We cannot unilaterally compel the Chirrn to surrender their custody of you. But we could arrange for Stephen and your fellow Arachnen to speak before the public. Your testimony about your experiences in Chirrn custody could help persuade the region's governments to bring pressure upon the Void Alliance and finally compel a change in their policies."

"I'm afraid that's something of a vicious cycle," Kazuko said. "What liberty we have is contingent upon being loyal, contributing members of Shilirrlaln society. Speaking out against them would violate our probation and subject us to penalties."

"That is why you must make your case publicly before the representatives here. If the Lode Seven administrative council can be convinced that the PQM ordered by the Chirrn would be used to support unethical practices, such as the coercion of human labor to construct a habitat in which human freedoms would be restricted, then the council might refuse delivery. If the Chirrn wish to strengthen their presence in this Void, they would be obligated to release your people."

Sita's heart raced. Was Velesh offering an alternative—and legal—path to freedom? But Kazuko caught her excitement and sent a cautioning eyetext. <Galactic affairs sound very complicated. We need more context before we can judge.> "Release us to what?" the poised Martian asked.

"The Nine Clusters Coalition would offer you sanctuary."

"Sanctuary," Sita echoed. "So you wouldn't take us home? Or let us settle on Cybele as we originally planned?"

Velesh's neck wattle puffed out briefly, an expression Sita hadn't yet learned to read. Pausing beneath an arch made from a fragment of Stringworld tether charred and pitted in some ancient construction mishap, he spent a few moments conferring with his mates (confirming that they could get a word in edgewise after all). "Potentially that could be arranged once we have managed to bring about changes in the Void Alliance's policies. Returning you to your homeworld is a desirable goal, but one that must be managed with care."

"'Managed,'" Kazuko echoed. "By you, I take it?"

"Please understand. Your people have been isolated for a long time. If knowledge of galactic civilization, and of the decisions that have damaged them over the *yanarrach*, were revealed to humanity too abruptly, without the proper context, their reaction could be… unpredictable. To avoid potentially harmful consequences in the long term, we would need to send emissaries to Sol System to mediate your people's initial engagement with galactic civilization."

Velesh's body language was enough like a Chirrn's that Sita could recognize him eyeing the two small women warily, as though handling half-tamed animals. *Not this shite again.* "You're afraid humanity might react violently."

"The concern is not primarily ours, Doctor Bhatiani. Your inadvertent role in the Lesshchi disaster reinforced long-standing fears regarding the indigenous peoples of the Four Voids. The Chirrn can use that to argue for your continued isolation, and that of other young local civilizations. If we are to bring lasting change for the benefit of your people and others, we must approach humanity's introduction to the galactic community judiciously. A degree of remedial mentoring would be expected."

Remedial mentoring? That had a rather Kiplingesque sound. She knew both sides of her cultural heritage well enough to recognize how dangerous it could be for one civilization to see another as unruly children in need of remediation. "Hang on, mate. We made it out here on our own, you know. We learned to stop blowing each other up—mostly—on our own. We may have learnt the hard way, but we're grownups now." *Even if we did make a hash of our driving test first time out,* she thought with grim humor.

"Your optimism is commendable, Doctor, but you are used to thinking on a briefer time scale than most. It was not long ago that you nearly destroyed yourselves, first with nuclear weapons, then with environmental neglect. It is too early to say that you would not fall back into old habits, especially if your development were disrupted by exposure to the Voids' history or by access to PQM and its potentials.

"Do not let pride override wisdom. Sponsorship by an established civilization would benefit your people. We could guide you through the transition to galactic life gently and peacefully. We could offer methods of self-mastery that have not occurred to your people, the collected wisdom of thousands of similar civilizations that could be adapted to serve your needs.

"And without such sponsorship," Velesh went on, "it would be difficult for humanity to win sympathy. We do not wish you to become a negative example that the Chirrn can use to promote their agenda."

<No,> Kazuko texted her. *<They want us to be an example to promote their agenda.>*

<No kidding,> Sita sent back. *<But is Meridian's agenda any better?>*

To Sita's surprise, Stephen was not angry at her or Kazuko when they returned. "I knew you had to follow your own consciences," he told them once the three were alone in his embassy quarters. "And I trusted you both not to betray our confidence." He turned to her. "Sita… I don't want us to be at odds."

He reached toward her, and she saw he was still wearing his wedding ring. But she maintained a coolly civil tone, nipping his gesture in the bud. He would have to earn the opportunity to win her back. "Then I hope you'll consider what we have to say."

His hand dropped, but his manner remained conciliatory. "Of course."

To his credit, he listened to the women's account of Velesh's offer with an open mind, taking the time to consider it before he replied. It reminded Sita how deeply she admired this man—though she was no longer sure if admiration was the same as love.

When he finally spoke, it was with regret. "No. There was a time, no question, that mentoring would have done us a great deal of good. Our exclusion from the Protocols cost us dearly. But Cecilia was right. *You* were right. We've learned from our hardships, fought our way to solutions that work for us. We became our own mentors out of necessity, and we've earned the right to be accepted into the galaxy as adults. The Shayal, these other privileged Galactics brought up within the mentoring system, they just can't understand that. They don't have the perspective to recognize their own prejudice and the impact it would have on us. Of all the species we've met, only the Zenith have that perspective."

"Look, I admit, Velesh's offer has its downside," Sita said. "But it's got to be better to be political pawns than wanted fugitives! Safer, at least!"

"Is it? The Galactics may not be prone to war, but like they say back home, diplomacy is war by other means. There are still plenty of conflicts among the powers of the galaxy; they just wage them through politics and public opinion, and you know how ugly a game that can be."

"But it's a game we have plenty of our own experience with," Kazuko pointed out. "Indeed, we're probably a lot more cutthroat about it than they're used to. We might have more of an advantage than you think. But not if we compound our already tenuous reputation with a deliberate crime."

"But it's not just about us, Kazuko. We've ended up as a *cause célèbre* at the heart of a major policy dispute. And we've seen how the mentoring process can be compromised by political agendas. If we ended up under the Shayal's 'remedial mentoring,' their choices could be influenced more by the fears and rivalries of the galactic community than by the best interests of humanity."

"At least we'd be in a position to win some trust and respect in the galaxy, even if it takes a while."

"Respect?" Stephen challenged. "We'd be seen as refugees, mistreated primitives in need of a handout. Human space would remain a backwater, dependent on the generosity of more powerful neighbors. Ask Tarik or Haim—how well did that work for the Middle East? You tell me, Sita, how well did it work for India under the Raj?"

"The Protocols wouldn't let them impose that much," Sita countered.

"Even so, do you think humanity would be content to be so weak and dependent?"

Sita ran a hand through her hair in frustration. "Well, what's the alternative? Become thieves, pirates?"

"We'd have the PQM. And we'd have the freedom to go wherever we wanted, to make our own choices without supervision."

"With the rest of the galaxy watching in terror to see what we'd do next!"

"And we'd prove," Stephen insisted, "that they have nothing to fear. I believe we'd use the PQM responsibly, apply the lessons we've learned the hard way. Maybe we could try some mentoring of our own, help other young civilizations in the Voids in accordance with the Protocols."

"Aren't you getting a little ahead of yourself there, Stephen?" Kazuko asked.

"Right," Sita put in. "Don't you think the Chirrn would try to stop us?"

"The Chirrn's standing has been weakened either way. As Meridian says, pulling off this heist will undermine them even more. Other races may even admire us for being able to get out from under the Chirrn on our own."

Sita scoffed. "Too right, on our own. Never mind the Zenith and the Zhalevey."

"The point is, we'll be independent, not subject to the Shayal's agendas. In their own way, they're just as responsible for all this as the Chirrn. How do we know we'd be any safer in their hands?

"Besides… we're already committed to helping Meridian. Her part of the plan is already in motion, and if we don't follow through with our part, it'll all be for nothing. Meridian's people deserve the freedom to pursue their dreams just as much as we do, and they're counting on us. We owe it to them and to ourselves to keep our word."

Sita stared at him, gobsmacked. "So you're going through with grand theft because you're too honorable not to?"

Stephen held her gaze. "It's civil disobedience. And a way to send a clear message to the Chirrn. I want that message to be ours, not the Shayal's."

"Do you?" Sita demanded. "Or do you just want to make the Chirrn pay?"

His hesitation was the last straw. She turned and strode from the room. A moment later, Kazuko jogged up behind her. "So that's it? End of discussion?"

"There's no changing his mind—trust me. If he's so bloody determined to commit this heist, I'll leave him to it—for better or worse."

"If you say so," Kazuko said after a moment. "Well, at least with Stephen in charge, the odds are that nobody will be hurt."

"Sure," Sita replied. "Except, just possibly, the entire human race."

"Stealing the PQM from the processing levels would be impossible," Broadwing told the group assembled in the passenger lounge.

Haim Silbermann was getting used to having conversations in space elevators—this time in a sightseeing car running up along the Stringworld's vast tethers, a trip the party was taking to get the lay of the land before the heist. In a way, Haim was perversely glad that Sita and Kazuko had failed to talk Stephen out of the theft. It would've been nice to have an easier way to win their freedom, but it would've been a shame to have done so much research and preparation for nothing.

"When launched from the star's surface," Broadwing went on, "it is too hot and traveling too fast to be intercepted before it reaches the capture tethers, and it would be useless to us without priming. The processing levels themselves are entirely cyber-controlled, for no organic life could survive in the conditions where the initial processing is done."

Broadwing's three eyes darted around to take in each co-conspirator in turn. Besides Stephen, Tarik, Haim, and Diana, they had been joined for this final review by Meridian's chief Zhalevey infiltrator, a nearly solid-colored greenish-tan male named Shthastya.

"That is why we must strike here," Broadwing went on, one wing-arm gesturing expansively at the tethers beyond the viewport. "The time when the PQM is in transit from the processing center to the migration fleet will be its only window of vulnerability."

"Tarik?" Stephen prompted.

"Haim, Diana, and I have successfully obtained clearance to accompany the freight lift for the pickup," Tarik said.

"All part of our rehabilitation as contributing members of society," Haim put in for Shthastya's benefit. "If we're gonna help build a habitat using this stuff, we need to learn all we can about it."

Broadwing called their attention to an occupied docking cradle on a tether several kilometers away, moving downward as they moved up. "Observe: one of the empty vessels assigned as counterweights for Stringworld attitude control. The Zhalevey stand ready to see that *Arachne*'s cradle is thus misallocated."

"Which will be my excuse to keep L'chellin distracted trying to track it down," Stephen said, frowning. "I'd rather be in the lift with all of you, but I'm the one who can draw the most attention elsewhere."

Haim turned to the Zhalevey. "And you'll make sure they don't find it, right, little fella?"

"At your service," Shthastya replied.

"There's one thing we need to be clear on," Tarik said to the tripedal sophont. "I know your people thrive on service, but don't you try to serve everyone equally? You're committing quite a betrayal against your employers here. Can we count on your loyalty to Meridian to take precedence?"

Shthastya seemed untroubled. "Service to Meridian led us to service to Stringworld. Service to Stringworld is subsumed to primary service to Meridian."

So they're moles, Haim realized. Meridian had been planning this for a long time; she just hadn't been able to find the right concatenation of allies and opportunity until now. *Just our luck.*

"Broadwing, can you be certain Meridian will time her little distraction to strike exactly when the lifts are in the right position?" Tarik asked. "What if she's late to the party?"

"I have received confirmation that Meridian is in-system," the Zenith said. "The optimal target object has already been selected."

One more reason she needed to wait, Haim thought. Meridian had cultivated or bribed enough allies at the Star Palace to get her smuggled past security and through the wormhole, but if she were spotted aboard the Stringworld itself, it would cost her people the deniability they needed. Instead, her small, short-range warp ship—better for relativistic in-system travel than FTL—had been snuck in as a support craft for a larger vessel, which had then jettisoned it between the wormhole exit and the Stringworld, whereupon the small ship had sped to the outskirts of the system to begin its crucial part of the operation.

"But I assume the Stringworld systems are shielded against that kind of radiation," Haim said. "This sort of thing has to happen naturally from time to time."

"Shielding has limits," Shthastya replied. "And can be subverted with advance knowledge of need."

"The damage won't be too bad," Tarik said, "but it should blind their sensors and scramble communications long enough for us to do the job, especially once the Zhalevey's viruses come into play. After all, you can't really harden EM sensors against EM."

"Is there any risk of a starquake?" Diana asked. "If that happened, we'd all be dead from the radiation in an instant."

"The metasapients stabilized the surface of the neutron star long ago," Broadwing assured her. "Otherwise it would not have been feasible for even them to settle it. Focus on your own responsibility, Diana."

The Vanguardian engineer sighed. "Hopefully, that'll just be moving the PQM."

Stephen squeezed her muscular forearm. "If you and Tarik handle the supervisors right, you won't need to get rough with them. Nobody wants that." Diana smiled back, appreciating his reassurance. For all her love of rough sports, hurting innocent bystanders was a very different matter.

"I'm still not clear on how we can fit it all on board *Arachne*, though," Diana went on.

"It is stored in concentrated form," Broadwing explained. "The quantity that will fit within *Arachne*'s cargo modules and the excess space within the warp cage should be sufficient to build dozens of vessels, or a wormhole and a smaller number of vessels. Also, we will not need to take the low-grade PQM slated for the habitat's maneuvering ring. That is the largest quantity by volume but the least useful for our purposes."

Diana nodded. "Makes it easier. Still... is it safe? I mean, the embryos are still aboard the ship."

Stephen frowned. "We have no choice there. We need to be able to make a swift getaway. But there's no reason to think they'll be in danger. If anything, their presence works in our favor—if we're discovered, the authorities won't risk endangering the embryos by taking rash action."

Haim frowned. "I don't like using them as hostages."

"If all goes well, it won't come to that, Haim. But none of this will matter if we don't neutralize that reference sample."

"Yeah, yeah. It's done." Haim sighed. "I can't say I enjoyed doing it, but I've hacked Yonchon's manipulator drones. I can intercept the control signals, make them do what we want while making it look to Yonchon's senses like they're doing what Yonchon wants." He held up a small emitter crafted from a portion of the smart matter that constituted Arachne's avatar. "And this little guy is ready to emit the fake signature once it's in place."

"But not before the system disruptions," Broadwing reminded him. "They must not learn of the sample's loss until it is too late to stop us."

"Of course. You just make sure the Unrenounced are awake and suited up so we can schlep the PQM over to *Arachne*."

"Do not take that lightly," Broadwing warned. "Remember, you will be outward from the center of mass, so acceleration will be present."

"But we'll still be as good as weightless."

"No such thing," Diana told him sternly. "If you let yourself think that way, if you don't keep track of which way you're moving at every moment, then before you realize it you could be falling too far and too fast to catch, and then you're vacked for good. Literally."

"Right," Haim realized. "Pardon an old dirtgrubber. That's what we're counting on, after all, isn't it?"

"That's right," Tarik said. "A few cut brakes on the docking cradle and *Arachne* will be free and clear to rendezvous with the rest of you."

"We can't get out through the wormhole, can we?" Diana asked. "They'd be ready for that."

"We can depart at warp," Broadwing told her. "It will take some time to reach another wormhole port, but we will be essentially untrackable."

Diana stared out the window, her expression buoyant in a way that had nothing to do with the diminishing tidal gravity. "And then... we can go anywhere we want."

"Sure," Haim said. "If we can pull off the impossible first."

8

"Course and velocity confirmed," chimed Mountain's Peak, her head lowered to Meridian. "Release in thirty-six hexapulses."

The subordinate female sounded a steady harmony with beats at three-hexapulse intervals, counting down to the release point. Meridian began to emit a stand-ready trill whose pace slowed as the countdown progressed; when it synchronized at zero point, their combined chord resolved into the command: "Release!" Mountain's Peak ducked her head with an obedient single-crest tone to indicate compliance. The command had technically been unnecessary, for their scout ship's computer had automatically dissipated the gravity pocket at precisely the right interval to release their chosen comet on its fated trajectory. But it did her subordinates good to feel they were playing their parts within the hierarchy.

Indeed, Mountain's Peak looked pleased. "The predator stoops toward its target," she whooped.

At Meridian's side, Apastron gave a warning tone. "You skirt blasphemy," the second chided.

Meridian leaned over and preened the featherfur on Apastron's neck to soothe her. "You know this will not harm the stardwellers. It will be like a refreshing rain to them. Were it not so, they would not permit this to happen."

"I aspire to that," Apastron keened in a skeptical minor key. "But what if we are wrong? I trust—I know that we can reach their level one day, if we achieve the means. But they are still so far above our comprehension."

"And we will never gain that comprehension if we do not dare, young one."

Meridian felt a twinge of regret. Apastron was reaching the age when a female would normally claim as many of her matron's males as she could win and branch off to begin her own harem. Her burgeoning rebellious streak was a symptom of that wanderlust. But as long as their clique was underground and forced to stay together, Apastron must either stay at her current rank, unable to climb, or challenge Meridian for leadership, which would surely leave her broken when she failed. Meridian had clawed her way back up from such a defeat long ago, building a new harem from scratch once she had discovered she could draw in the disenfranchised with the promise of metasapience. But she would not wish that long, lonely struggle on her second, even if she felt the young female had the determination and rhetorical skill to achieve it. No, Apastron's best hope was that the theft succeeded, so that Meridian and her followers could move to the Inner Disk, the heart of Galactic civilization, where the disasters and destruction that haunted the Four Voids were merely a distant rumor from the fringes. Once far enough away to be free of their stigma, they could branch out into separate harems and pursue multiple avenues of research.

Still, losing Apastron's trusted counsel would be a blow. They had been together for so long — but no. That was thinking like a lesser race, growing complacent. A Zenith thrived only by climbing upward, seeking change. And with so few positions at the top, other females would always be temporary allies at best. If Apastron were to continue to serve her, let it be as a rival forcing her to become better. Racing her to the pinnacle of metasapience.

For now, though, she needed her second as an ally, not a competitor. "Trust in the stardwellers, Apastron," she sang. "Remember, they wish us all to rise and join them. I do not doubt that our venture has their blessing."

Apastron echoed her phrases, chiming in accord to show she accepted Meridian's counsel. "But my doubts also extend lower, to the humans. I would rather you had entrusted that stage of the plan to Broadwing."

"Broadwing is easy to manipulate, but he has been too tamed by the Chirrn and has lost his hunter's instincts. He will accept it once he sees it is my will, but I think he would lack the determination to do it himself."

"But the humans? Crown of the Usurper King is even less a hunter, despite his name."

"I do not need his participation in that stage. From what Broadwing has told me of the Unrenounced, they are already primed for this task. Their ambition has been bottled for so long that they will seize the opportunity to strike."

"I aspire to that as well," Apastron chimed, though with an inverted counterpoint connoting ambivalence. "Yet I hope you are right that this is truly necessary."

Meridian clacked her mandibles together sharply. "Have you become too squeamish to stoop on prey?"

"To feed on prey is one thing. To extinguish minds… I would not do so more than I must."

"Then have no fear." Meridian preened her neck again. "For remember, the stardwellers are watching. We will extinguish no minds—we will simply free them to nourish the gods."

"L'chellin, we need to talk."

The mediator split her gaze, one eye on Stephen, the other on the party about to board the freight lift. "This is not an appropriate time, Stephen. I must supervise the processing and loading of our PQM order."

"Yonchon and Haim can handle that. And this is the only time. Velesh has invited us to request sanctuary for *Arachne*'s crew with the Nine Clusters Coalition. A lot of us think that sounds like a better offer than the life we'd have with you."

L'chellin ruffled her bristles with a sigh. Yonchon had entered the lift cab now, leaving one drone behind to watch her expectantly. The Lode Seven attendants, a pair of Zhalevey and a large Mykhshad, stood sentry alongside the doors. She gestured to them to wait.

"I had thought you had moved beyond these doubts," she told Stephen.

"I have doubts about a lot of things now. But Velesh's offer would let us reunite with the Unrenounced, set them free at last."

"If sanctuary were granted. The hearings would take *narruvh*."

"Which is why it would have to begin now."

"Would you abandon your oaths so easily?" L'chellin asked, saddened by the question.

"This isn't easy for me. But I have prior oaths to my own crew."

"That is why you should not hasten to align yourselves with the Shayal. They would use you as pawns. To us, you are family now."

"Then you need to convince me of that, L'chellin. And make it good enough that I can convince the Arachnen."

In her left-eye field, Haim hesitated on the lift threshold, tense with anticipation at the technological marvels he would witness on the processing levels. Diana appeared just as eager, her enthusiasm manifesting in more overt motion; she kept taking her measuring equipment out of her vest pockets to recheck it, even as she kept one eye on Stephen (though that phrase was only metaphorical for a human). Even Tarik stood ready—still bitter toward the Chirrn, L'chellin knew, but sworn to serve the Arachnen at all costs. He would go where Stephen led, so L'chellin needed to win Stephen back to the Chirrn's side, where his people would be nurtured to their full potential— not paraded as savages and victims, a cautionary tale to illustrate the so-called crimes of the Void Alliance.

L'chellin directed a small bow toward Yonchon's drone, instructing the Ryohoch to proceed without her.

"Then let us exchange words, Stephen—and resolve this with finality."

Sita hadn't slept well since the Arachnen's arrival at the String-world. She could swear she felt the habitat module swaying beneath her, disorienting her. Which didn't make sense; although the undulations of the megastructure were real, they took hours to propagate along its length, the motions too slow to feel.

So she was forced to admit the real reason: she was no longer used to sleeping alone. It wasn't just the sex; she missed Stephen's warm, comforting presence beside her at night. She missed…

No. She didn't miss falling in love with a fantasy and finding it too fragile to shore her up—to shore either of them up—through the harsh realities of the past two months. Beyond the surface distraction of their physical passions, she and Stephen had never truly been together. And she had surely proven to herself by now that she was capable of braving the Galactic community on her own.

But it would still take time to find her balance again without him. Fantasies could be very comforting in the dead of night.

The other thing keeping her awake was ambivalence about the insane scheme that Broadwing and his outlaw queen had roped the Arachnen into carrying out. Since the failure of her second attempt to talk Stephen out of it, she'd been debating what to do next, both within herself and with the other Arachnen. A few, including Joana Caravalho and Ravinder Pritam, had sided with her and Kazuko, warning the others of the dangers if any part of the overcomplicated plan went wrong. The Arachnen could all find themselves penalized as co-conspirators if they failed to come forward before it was too late. And though they all trusted Stephen to keep things nonviolent—especially with the embryos aboard *Arachne*—Sita wasn't so sure about Broadwing. True, it had been the mediator's dismay at the loss of Lesshchin life that had led him to this in the first place, but he was still a predator by nature.

Yet they'd been heavily outnumbered by the ones who sided with Stephen, swayed by his promises of freedom and a new beginning not just for them, but for all of humanity. These people wouldn't have been here if they hadn't already bought into Stephen's promises of hope and human achievement.

Justine Nguyen in particular was compelled by Broadwing's talk about the possibility of metasapients recording or capturing the minds of the dead. Sita could understand why the astrophysicist would grasp at straws to believe her lost baby could've been saved, but she resisted giving in to the same impulse—as did Ravinder, who insisted that an early second-trimester fetus would have no significant neural activity, certainly nothing resembling consciousness. But Justine had spun theories of her fetus's whole environment being simulated so it could develop and be born into a virtual posthuman life. It agonized Sita to see her buy so deeply into the delusion… although some part of her hoped that Justine might actually be right. Was it really any crazier than believing her own baby's soul would be reincarnated as part of the karmic cycle?

When Broadwing came to the Arachnen's embassy quarters to advise them that the plan was in motion, it crystallized her doubts. "Be sure to remain gathered here," the Zenith intoned to the group. He gestured to the Zhalevey attendants he'd brought with him. "When the system disruptions begin, these three will escort you to a ship that will smuggle you out to rendezvous with *Arachne* and Meridian's craft. Remember, you must stay together."

Once he left, Sita led Kazuko and Ravinder aside. "We've got to do something," she whispered, "and quickly."

"But what can we do?" Kazuko asked. "If we sneak off to warn someone, we risk being left behind if the escape goes off as planned."

"And *should* we try to stop this?" Ravinder added. "Don't we at least owe it to Stephen to let him try?"

"Maybe we owe it to him to stop him from making a terrible mistake," Sita replied.

"All right," Kazuko said patiently. "How?"

Sita stared back. "You're asking me? You're the administrator!"

"You know Stephen best, Sita. You know the Chirrn and Zenith best. Whatever you decide, we'll support."

Sita was moved by Kazuko's faith, but the answer to her question remained elusive. "Sod it, I need to know more about the Zenith. I need to know more about *Broadwing*." If she was going to trust him—or betray him—she had to know more. She had to talk to someone she could rely on to keep a secret—someone who'd known Broadwing longer than any human had.

Three minutes later, she was clambering over the embassy's balcony railing. Her old tree-climbing skills were still with her, though it was a near thing in this gravity. She managed to leap to an adjacent dendroid plant with branches like orange feather dusters, disturbing a swarm of silver-green, fingernail-sized avians to flutter away from their perches in a sparkling cloud. She startled a pair of Gaurim when she landed; she gave a quick apology she doubted they'd understand and ducked beneath their high, cantilevered torsos to get out to the pathway beyond.

As she ran, Kazuko's words echoed in her mind. If she wasn't with the others when they were evacuated, she could end up as the only human left in Chirrn custody. She could be condemning herself to spend the rest of her life alone among aliens.

So bloody what? she thought. She'd already lost her baby. If the worst day of her life was behind her, what did she have to be afraid of now?

As she ran through the crowded streets, feeling the giddy abandon of someone who'd just jumped off a cliff, she experienced a renewed thrill of wonder at the magnificently alien life forms that surrounded her. Having a lifetime to study them wouldn't be such a bad fate after all.

The discomfort in Haim's stomach had nothing to do with the shifting gravity in the freight lift over its lengthy climb, or the way the hemispherical cab mounted on the side had flipped 180 degrees as they passed the Stringworld's center of mass. He was worried about getting caught, worried about giving himself away *because* he was worried about getting caught, worried about betraying his friend Yonchon (though he still wasn't sure if Yonchon even had the concept of either friendship or betrayal), worried that the plan wouldn't work, worried that it would work.

So far, he had to admit, the scheme had gone swimmingly. It had been a relief and a bit of a surprise that the whole team had gotten clearance to start with; Haim had wondered if the administration would even let sophonts with a reputation like theirs anywhere near the highly secure factory levels. But in retrospect, it stood to reason that a society based in mentoring would be big on teaching opportunities. This was all being treated as part of a novice people's education in the ways of galactic life, an established practice that the Arachnen were able to slot into fairly well, despite the *tsuris* and *tumul* surrounding their emergence onto the scene.

Indeed, their attendants came off more as guides and instructors than guards—although Haim was aware that the freight lift was more than able to guard itself. The Zhalevey were helpful as ever, naturally. The chief attendant, a Mykhshad named something like Rysuth, was more physically formidable—a pony-sized quadruped with a teardrop-shaped body tapering to the rear, a prehensile trunk with fine manipulative tendrils at the end, and bulky forelimbs ending in strong grasping digits, which he could free for use by rearing up and resting his weight on his short hind legs and strong but flexible tail. His tiger-striped body was covered in bluish-gray sensory bristles resembling fur, and his face bore only the most rudimentary eyes; but the Geiger-counter ticking of his echolocation pulses and the way his bristles twitched in response to the slightest movement made it clear that he was watching his passengers closely. Haim recalled from Broadwing's briefing that a Mykhshad's sonar could be amplified to weapon force like a dolphin's. It would be less effective here than in their dense native atmosphere, but in this enclosed space it could still be loud enough to incapacitate. Haim hoped he would not have to find out.

Yet Rysuth seemed an amiable enough host, volubly explaining the PQM processing procedure to the group. Diana had played along as an eager student to get the Mykhshad off his guard, and as they now readied to observe the transfer operations, she made a show of fumblingly checking the equipment in her vest pockets. "Here, hold this," she said, briefly handing a coin-sized imaging unit to Haim. The senior engineer turned his back and deftly plugged in an extra component he had secreted in his hand. He let it slip from his grip when he tried to return it, but Tarik caught it; when he returned it to Diana, he nodded slightly, confirming that he'd plugged in his piece as well. The three components had been dormant to pass security; now the combined device would activate after the appropriate interval.

"I know this is asking a lot," Diana said to Rysuth, "but Yonchon already agreed to let me piggyback this image sensor on the drone Yonchon sends in for the registration, so long as you approve it. This is the first time humans have ever witnessed this—I want to record it on a medium designed for human senses."

Rysuth was only too happy to oblige Diana's curiosity. Haim was starting to get the impression that all the security around the factory levels was a holdover from earlier times when paranoia about pockets of surviving meta-Zenith was still rampant. The Stringworld staff seemed to be going through the motions without any serious concerns about theft. After all, why should they worry? If anyone tried to use a PQM supply illegally or destructively, it could always be neutralized as long as there was an entangled reference sample on file.

And that was the key to this part of the plan. In order for the new PQM to mesh properly with the migration fleet's existing stock, the two would need to be entangled and taken through a sort of handshake protocol to calibrate them with one another, and the security reference sample kept in the factory level would need to be entangled and calibrated with both. So Yonchon had brought along a sample of the fleet's PQM. Normally, the factory's own drones would take the sample into its uninhabitable innards for the process; but Yonchon, ever the individualist, had insisted on doing it personally. The manipulator drones that rode on the back of the Ryohoch engineer's massive, nine-legged body like birds on a hippo were effectively an extension of Yonchon's person, remote-controlled "hands" for a species with only rudimentary manipulative limbs. Apparently the Ryohoch were trusted enough that the request was accepted—or mysterious enough that nobody would suspect one of anything as quotidian as criminal motives.

Haim would've preferred to pay undivided attention to the registration and entanglement process (and he made sure his buffer was recording so he could study the memory later). Unfortunately, it was now his turn to play perhaps the most crucial role in the plan. While he pretended to make notes about the registration on his datapad, he was actually intercepting Yonchon's drone transmissions, making sure the registration code the drone entered in the new PQM supply was not the one Yonchon thought it was entering.

When that was done, Haim sent a command, and Diana's remote image sensor overloaded and burst. "Oh!" Diana cried in feigned surprise as the signal went dead. "What the vack was that?"

"Your device may have lacked the strength to survive the pressure and radiation within," Rysuth suggested.

"Oh, damn! Yonchon, did I hurt your drone?" she asked, placing a solicitous hand on the side of the Ryohoch's massive, peanut-shaped body.

"Sensation from drone in abeyance. Presumption is damage."

"I'm so sorry, I had no idea."

"Attrition occurs. This situation does not change."

"That means 'don't worry about it'," Haim interpreted.

"We have asked the factory to repair the drone," the taller, greener Zhalevey reported. "Its return shall precede your fleet's departure."

"Oh, what a relief," Diana said. But she didn't fully relax until Haim gave her a tiny nod. The debris from the explosion had included an array of transmitter nans, a portion of which had successfully attached to the capsule containing the reference sample. When the time came, they would activate.

Haim just had to hope their dormant state would fool the factory level's security — or he and his cohorts would be arrested before that could happen.

By the time the worried Arachnen called Broadwing to notify him that Sita Bhatiani had fled, it was too late to do anything about it. Meridian's will had been set inexorably into motion, and Broadwing had to do his part as reliably as orbital mechanics. He could only hope that Sita would be unable to reach Lode Seven's authorities in time to alert them to the theft. Soon enough, it would be too late for anyone to stop it — but only if Broadwing did his part and got *Arachne* underway.

So it was an unwelcome surprise when he and his Zhalevey accomplices arrived at *Arachne*'s docking bay to find Churrlaya there. The Lesshchin survivor eagerly accosted Broadwing. "Mediator, at last. I need your help."

"Apologies. I have urgent business aboard the ship."

"As have I. I must awaken Cecilia and speak with her."

"You may do so once we reach the settlement site."

"How long will it be before it is decided that we have the luxury of awakening them? We will be too busy to guard them; more than likely it will be deemed safer to keep them dormant until the habitat is functional, which could take two *narrenn* or more."

"They slept safely for far longer than that," Broadwing chimed impatiently. Seeing no choice, he allowed Churrlaya to follow him aboard *Arachne*.

"It is Cecilia's mental state that concerns me. I believe many of the other Unrenounced resent Cecilia for halting their escape attempt. Within their linked hibernation dreams, without conscious inhibitions, that resentment will most likely express itself openly, even violently. Cecilia may be traumatized, or coerced into submitting to the consensus. I believe she is on the verge of renunciation, of genuine healing at last. But if it is delayed, she may be lost to us."

"Have you not taken this up with the others?"

"I have tried. But the Lode authorities are pressing them not to awaken beings they consider proven threats. Mediator, the PQM is already on its way. We will be shipping out within *narrach*. This may be my last chance to save Cecilia."

Broadwing was surprised that the Lesshchin wished to help the commander of the ship responsible for destroying his world. But he had no time or attention to devote to that paradox. Instead, he considered that Churrlaya's request could be turned to his advantage. If the awakening of all the Unrenounced could be attributed to Churrlaya's mishandling of the primitive equipment in his effort to awaken just one, it would divert the subsequent investigation away from himself and Meridian. Besides, the young Chirrn was so fixated on Cecilia that he was not at all curious why Broadwing was here. Giving him his human pet to play with would keep him out of Broadwing's way without the need for any messy killing. Many of the Unrenounced wouldn't mind at all if he killed Churrlaya, but a few might balk at a time when their swift and efficient compliance would be essential. Not to mention that it would be difficult to kill Churrlaya in a way that would appear accidental yet be quick enough that no incriminating evidence would be recorded in his cloud memories.

"Agreed," Broadwing said. "I will assist you with the equipment."

"You have studied their hibernation system?"

He hesitated for only an instant. "Familiarity with their technology is one of my responsibilities as a mediator."

"Good. I am grateful for your actions, Mediator."

Broadwing chimed acknowledgment, while privately thinking a human idiom he had picked up: *Enjoy it while it lasts.*

Waking from hibernation was easier for Cecilia this time, for her short-term sleep had not required full immersion in life-support gel. Instead, she and the other loyalists had gone into *Arachne*'s hibernation pods wearing their standard inmate coveralls, which interfaced with the pods to monitor their vitals much as the gel did. This time, she still had her hair and some semblance of her dignity.

And waking was a relief after what she'd experienced in the dream state. There had been no repeat of the attempted assault she thought she remembered from the start of this hibernation; either she'd imagined it, or Diego's crew had been too preoccupied with Stephen's plan to steal the Chirrn's quark matter. From what Cecilia had picked up of their conversations, their dreamtime had been filled with fantasies ranging from humiliating the Chirrn to dragging them back to Solsys for war-crimes trials to simply murdering them *en masse*. In every case, Churrlaya had been the primary target of their imagined retributions, and when she'd found them engaging in a brutal torture session of their jailer—with James and Amrita describing everything in excruciating detail so that they could all share equally in the dream, compelling Cecilia's mind to visualize it as well—she'd been so disgusted that she'd isolated herself from the group, rebuffing every attempt at contact without caring if it was from a real crewmate or a phantasm. She'd envisioned herself back in Sol's Oort cloud, swimming in the subglacial water mantle of Aita, the Mars-sized ice planet they'd spent six months surveying. At first she'd imagined herself in a submersible, then a diving suit, then dreamed she was invulnerable enough to swim through it naked, populating it with benthic life from the fringes of her imagination... but no other people. She could think of no one right now that she could envision without mistrust or pain. In time, she even stopped thinking of herself as Cecilia LoCarno; she was one of the creatures of the deep, at home in the perpetual dark, safely ensconced within kilometers of ice, insulated by three light-months of empty space from the nearest trace of human presence.

When she awoke, she was crying.

Then she saw Churrlaya watching her. Reaching out a hand to help her up.

She stared at that hand for a long moment. Then she clasped it. It was surprisingly gentle.

Once she was sitting up, she squeezed her eyes shut and strove to discipline herself. She gave the memories of the dreamtime leave to fade, but they lingered more than she wanted. She struggled to focus on the here and now, to ready herself for whatever might be coming.

They were in a module positioned at a bit of a slant relative to the strong local gravity, so she needed to keep her grip on Churrlaya's hand as he guided her into its compact dining bay, then into a seat that Arachne had tilted to accommodate her. She envied the ease and grace with which the Chirrn negotiated the skewed environment. She realized that she had always seen something beautiful in them.

"Why did… you only wake me?" she asked.

"Because I do not believe you belong with the rest of the Unrenounced."

That reminded her to be on her guard. "If this is some sort of ploy…"

"No. I will attempt no more ploys. I will bear you only honest words—and an apology."

She didn't know what to say to that. She just studied Churrlaya as he continued. "My responsibility was to oversee your ordeal, yes. But not to punish you. Rather, the ordeal is a Chirrn custom of transition, to help us strip away the vestiges of an old life, an old affiliation, and leave ourselves open to a new one."

"Sounds like brainwashing."

"I grant that. One could also liken it to the procedures your militaries often employ to indoctrinate recruits. The purpose was rehabilitative." His eyes darted outward, then hesitantly refocused on her. "Moreover, it was meant to rehabilitate me. I was going through the same kind of transition, although my old ties had been torn from me by force. Perhaps that is why I made your transition harsher than it was meant to be, and hardened so many of you against us." He tapped his brows. "I was warned that my bias compromised my work, but I was determined to prove that I was better than you, that I could remain responsible and control my baser emotions."

Cecilia laughed in recognition, and Churrlaya's response was surprisingly insightful. "A familiar sentiment, is it not? But I think you achieved it better than I did. Perhaps if I had not fed the others' anger and fear so much, they would have been more swayed by your example."

Cecilia sighed. "I think you're giving me too much credit. Diego and his bunch... all this was more than they could take. If you thought they could ever make some 'transition' that was forced on them, you expected too much."

"Perhaps I did. But you have exceeded my expectations, Cecilia, and taught me much—not just about humanity. I think... we have both clung to old roots that we can never return to, and in so doing have both turned away from opportunities to become part of something new... to heal our incompleteness.

"Yet somehow... we two incomplete beings have complemented each other. In challenging one another, we have pushed each other to become better, to become stronger. I think it is time to acknowledge that, and to explore the possibility that we both may have found... at least the possibility of new roots in the last place we could have expected." His thick green fingers reached out and ever so lightly made contact with the side of her neck, just for half a second.

Cecilia didn't know what to say. The Frog Footman, her jailer and tormentor for the past six months or more, pledging his friendship? But even as she had the hostile thought, she knew it was a lie. She had come to look forward to their debates, the same way she had once enjoyed her philosophical and political arguments with Stephen. Those arguments back in Solsys, those opportunities to explore each other's very different minds and worldviews in depth, had been the foundation of a partnership as profound as any she'd ever known. Was she really feeling the same way about Churrlaya?

One thing she knew: she felt closer to him now than to her fellow loyalists. She remembered the impending heist. If Churrlaya was aboard, alone, when Diego's clique awoke...

She stopped herself from warning him. How could she trust what she was feeling now? Whatever distaste—whatever fear—she felt now toward Diego, James, and their group, didn't all of *Arachne*'s crew deserve a chance at freedom? And Stephen would make sure no one was hurt…

Would he? As overcome as he was by bitterness and pain? She wasn't sure she knew him anymore. Could he really keep the others under control? Would he even try?

Arachne lurched into motion. Cecilia slipped sideways out of her chair, but Churrlaya was there in an instant and caught her. His hands were warm and strong. "Wait here," he said once he'd helped her regain her footing, more a request than a command. He did something to the cuffs of her confinement suit that made the mitts peel back, freeing her hands without the need to wrestle out of the sleeves. She stared at him in amazement. "For your safety should that happen again," he explained.

He still locked her in the dining bay, though. Never mind; she directed a thought at her comm implant, and the ready light blinked in her HUD. Arachne had reactivated the loyalists' comlinks, meaning the heist must already be underway. Cecilia tapped into the module's internal comms, closed her eyes, and moved her virtual field of view outside the bay to follow Churrlaya. "Broadwing, what is happening?" the Lesshchin called.

Calliope chimes sounded, and Arachne subtitled them: "A mishap with the lift allocation. The ship has been categorized as idle and cleared for use as ballast. A minor inconvenience; the Zhalevey are addressing it." *What the hell are Zhalevey?* Cecilia wondered, but then she noticed the floppy green tripeds with the elephant-meets-Yoda ears.

And then she noticed something else, just before Churrlaya did. "Why are the other Unrenounced awake?" the Lesshchin asked. "Why have their confinement suits been released?"

Cecilia choked on an impulsive warning cry as Diego, stripped to the waist, crept up behind Churrlaya and brandished a heavy wrench, swinging it low to smash into the Chirrn's right leg. The sound was very much like that of a human's bones breaking, though Churrlaya's screech of pain was unlike anything she'd ever heard. Diego struck again at Churrlaya's other leg, neutralizing the Chirrn's most formidable weapons. A similarly attired James moved in with another wrench to strike at his head. Cecilia froze in horror.

A fully nude Nik moved in and grabbed James's arm on the upswing. "All right, that's enough! Just lock him in!"

"Agreed," Broadwing said. "Remember the schedule."

Moments later the door opened and they tossed Churrlaya back inside. "Captain!" Nik cried, looking somewhat happier to see her than Diego or James were. "It's okay, you can come with us now."

"Once we take care of the fucking Footman once and for all," James snarled, punctuating the syllable "Foot" with a vicious kick to Churrlaya's flank.

"Yes," Diego said, hefting his wrench.

"No, you heard Broadwing!" Nik protested.

"No alien tells me what to do!" Diego roared, cowing the doctor. "And this soulless beast has enslaved his last human." He lifted the wrench high.

Cecilia didn't make a conscious choice to throw herself on top of Churrlaya, shielding him with her own body. But that's where she found herself, and she didn't question it.

For a moment, she thought Diego was going to strike anyway. The wrench quivered in his tense grip, and his eyes went to her freed hands. "So this is your choice, *Captain*? I should have known."

"We are not the villains here, Narvaez. Not unless we choose to be."

"I choose to liberate my people! Evil must be destroyed, not appeased."

"This is supposed to be a robbery, not an inquisition!"

"Diego, come on," Nik urged. "We're on a timetable, remember? We need to suit up."

"Very well," the bigger man said after a moment, lowering the wrench. "But we will do it with eight—as I expected we would. And I'll be keeping my eye on you, Doctor! You need to pick a side once and for all!" He gazed down at Cecilia in grave disappointment. "And you… I always knew you were an appeaser at heart."

"And I would never have let you on my ship had I known you were such a coward."

He laughed. "You cannot make me waver," he said as he turned to the exit. "Not a man of true faith. Arachne, do not let her leave!"

"*Acknowledged*," Arachne said without affect, though with the tiniest of delays.

Then the door shut behind him, and Cecilia was well and truly alone.

Except for Churrlaya.

She retrieved the emergency medical kit from its cabinet and knelt to help him.

Sita found R'nilinnath in a module catering to nocturnal life forms, a darkened realm she was only able to navigate by having Arachne tap into the module's augreality system and feed her an enhancement of the available starlight. The main inhabitants seemed to be the tiger-striped, vaguely elephant-like Mykhshad, along with several unfamiliar species. They milled around a central pavilion matching the one in the Chirrn embassy's module, but with different vegetation, sparser and mostly black. As she approached the young Chirrn, she overheard a debate from the adjacent auditorium dome, something about a border dispute between diurnal and nocturnal settlers on a tidally locked planet. She switched off the automatic subtitles so they wouldn't distract her.

Nilly was seated on her tail before a large kinetic sculpture, an apparently free-floating sphere surrounded by a halo of intricate loops and prominences in a familiar pattern. The loops moved slowly as faster bulges swept around their curves like cars on racetracks, with occasional streamers or translucent sheets of material flowing between them. They vibrated as they moved, emitting an intricate, shifting, multitonal hum that Sita could've listened to for hours if she hadn't had more urgent business.

"Sita!" R'nilinnath drummed her toes and shook her mane in pleasure as she recognized the biologist. "Come and look! This is fascinating. It's an aural and textural representation of the halo effects around the neutron star in real time, for the benefit of species for whom vision is not a primary sense." She rolled an eye to gesture at the nearest pygmy elephant-tiger. "A Mykhshad artist designed it. Did you know? They evolved around a very small star whose radiant peak is in the infrared, and —"

"That's interesting, Nilly, but I need to ask you about something else."

"Ask anything. I am here to educate you."

"I need you to tell me about Broadwing."

Nilly jerked her head back. "Broadwing? You know him already."

"I need to know more. About his past. About his people. About… whether you trust him."

The Chirrn gave a delicate snort. "Sita. I thought you had moved well past these fears."

"No, it's not that. I'm trying to understand his character. What he might do in… situations where others relied on his… his agenda being what he told them. Ohh, how do I explain this…"

"Sita, you need not worry. Yes, Broadwing made a foolish mistake in his youth, but he repaid his debt long ago, just as you have. He earned his inclusion and has contributed meaningfully to the consensus of his guild." Nilly brushed her fingers across Sita's neck, ruffling her hair. "To an extent, you owe him your freedom. Back after Lesshchi, some said that, as ferals, you needed to be kept confined and repay your debt as subjects of study, like the Unrenounced. But Broadwing insisted that you deserved the same right as any civilized beings to repay your debt by joining the community."

"Then you have faith in his integrity? His… his principles?"

"I do. I know how it pains him to think he has done wrong, even when he is not to blame. He was as distraught as I was when he learned that taking you to the kiss dance had provoked the Lesshchin's retaliation. He could not have known that his suggestion would lead to that result, but he brooded with guilt for *narrissh*…. What is it?"

Sita felt as though the floor of the module had fallen out from under her. "That… was Broadwing's suggestion?"

"Yes, I thought you knew."

She clutched her hands to her womb, feeling the aching emptiness anew, like a black hole sucking her up from inside. "Oh, Krishna. He knew what would happen. He bloody knew!"

"What do you say, Sita?"

"He wanted… he wanted to bring us here."

"He proposed the migration, yes, but—"

"And he proposed the thing that created the need for it! *He knew!*" she cried, grabbing Nilly's shoulders and shaking her. "He knew… it would provoke them… they would attack… *he killed my baby!*"

Nilly pulled her away from the crowd around the sculpture and held her for a time, offering comfort, but twitching her tail in confusion. "I don't understand. Why would Broadwing want to provoke a migration?"

Sita told her about Meridian and the planned PQM theft. "All of this… all the way back to the trial. He's masterminded this whole thing to bring us here. All the violence… our babies… Kweli… none of it would have happened if not for him."

Nilly was panting through her nares. "I cannot believe Broadwing would want to kill babies. Maybe… maybe he didn't know the Lesshchin would go that far. Who could have known that?"

"It doesn't matter, Nilly," Sita said with growing resolve—growing rage. "He's the one responsible. He's manipulated Stephen and the rest of us, made us his pawns almost from the beginning! He's probably still manipulating, lying to us. Using us. He has to be stopped before Stephen and the rest are hurt."

She began to stride toward the exit, and Nilly loped after her, quickly catching up. "What are you going to do?"

"I'm going to find that fucking pterodactyl and kick his silver tail clear back to Shil—"

She was drowned out by a deafening clap of noise from the neutron-star model behind them. Reflexively clapping her hands against her ears, she spun to see a fountain of material erupting from the sphere near one of its poles, disrupting the delicate loops around it. The swarm of particles began to form a broad, diffuse ring around the sculpture.

Then she was half-blinded by a flash of actinic light through the module's star windows, and when her vision cleared, she saw the sculpture collapsing to the ground.

As it shattered, she felt the whole world convulse beneath her.

9

"WHAT HAPPENED?" STEPHEN ASKED, KNOWING EXACTLY WHAT HAD happened.

L'chellin had just returned from consultation with a group of Lode Seven infrastructure managers. Stephen had been playing his part, feigning dismay at *Arachne*'s misallocation to counterweight duty and keeping L'chellin preoccupied trying to hunt it down, until the moment came for the event that L'chellin now described. "A comet seems to have collided with the neutron star," said the aged mediator. "The resultant burst of hard radiation generated electromagnetic pulses in the tethers, creating some minor system disruptions. The tremor we felt was merely a shock wave from sudden thermal expansion."

Stephen pretended concern. "Are we at risk from the radiation?"

"The modules' shielding reduced any x-ray or gamma penetration to manageable levels." One of L'chellin's eyes briefly gestured upward to indicate the thick, wide shield mounted atop the module. Stephen reminded himself for the umpteenth time that the neutron star was above them relative to the local gravity. "Other protective systems seem less effective than they should be, but the disruption is mainly to inter-module communication, and some lift cars in transit are stalled."

"*Arachne*?" Stephen asked.

A puff of breath ruffled L'chellin's snout bristles. "Yes, Stephen," she answered. "It would appear that both *Arachne* and the freight lift conveying the PQM are somewhere along the central tract, though on this side of the center of mass. We are currently out of communication with both. But do not worry. Our people should be adequately shielded within their respective craft—particularly the Unrenounced in their hibernation chambers. And you know how well your embryos are shielded."

"That's good," said Stephen, fully aware that the Unrenounced must now be wide awake and suiting up for their hazardous spacewalk. He had balked at the risk when Meridian and Broadwing had detailed their plan, but the gamma and hard x-rays from a comet impact on the neutron star had been the only way to disrupt the Stringworld's sensors and communication long enough to achieve the heist. And all his people had received *D. radiodurans* gene therapy for radiation resistance; indeed, the Striders among them had been born with the trait. No human could thrive long in space without it.

Still, he sought a second opinion from L'chellin on another issue, prefacing it with a more basic question he felt he would plausibly ask in this situation. "Why wasn't the comet detected, steered away?"

"It came in at unusual speed and was unusually dark—perhaps an interstellar rogue. These things are not unprecedented in a star-formation zone, which is why the modules are shielded."

"Against radiation. But the tidal stress would've torn the comet apart before it hit, wouldn't it? There'll be an accretion disk."

"There is a debris disk, but the residual particles should decay onto the star's surface within a *narrach*," she said. "We should pass through it in about twenty *narr* and then once more before it dissipates, but it will thin rapidly. And the particles are ionized, so they can be easily deflected by the station's magnetic fields."

The lights flickered and the ground trembled as another, milder EMP went through the Stringworld, the product of one of the many secondary impacts that would be coming within the next hundred minutes. "If they've gotten these system disruptions under control by then," Stephen replied, aware that the Zhalevey's viruses would be working against that. Though surely the Zhalevey would keep the impact shields exempt from the malfunctions, wouldn't they?

"Do not worry. *Arachne* and the freight lift are on an inner tier of tethers, and lift cars generally ride on the trailing side, shielding them against anything intersecting our orbit. In all probability, they will be safe. But we will do all we can to reach them before the accretion disk passage."

"All right," Stephen said, nodding. "I... I trust you to make sure of that," he went on, trying not to make it seem too easy. "You understand all this better than I do, and I'd probably get in the way. I should go back down to the Arachnen and reassure them."

L'chellin straightened with pride and pleasure. "Most responsible, Stephen. Thank you. And I should do what I can to contact the other Shilirrlaln…" She trailed off, eyes rolling backward as often happened when Chirrn were interfacing with their datanet.

"What is it?"

"I cannot engage real-time communication with R'nilinnath… but her last locator ping indicates that she was in proximity to Sita."

Stephen froze. "Sita? What's she doing with Nilly?" He tried to mask his anger and concern. Was Sita trying to expose the plan?

"I do not know. I will ask the Zhalevey to track them down."

"No. No, I need to find her myself. Now."

"Stephen, she will be perfectly safe—"

He extemporized. "You know what she's been through, L'chellin. She's recovered well, but something like this… no telling how she'll react."

"True," L'chellin said. "But you do not need to birth bastard words. It is enough that you wish to be with your mate above all others. I will assist you."

If she were still my mate, Stephen thought, *she wouldn't have run off.* If anything, he was tempted to leave her to her own devices. If she'd made the choice to reject her own people in favor of the Chirrn, then so be it.

But he realized he couldn't let that happen. Whatever had occurred between them, she was still a member of his crew, and at least technically still his wife. He couldn't let her be stranded alone in an alien galaxy, the sole remaining prisoner of the Chirrn.

He didn't know if he could live with her anymore, but he wasn't ready to risk living without her.

Diana Thorne's far-from-feigned curiosity about PQM processing procedures had made it easy to keep Rysuth occupied during much of the ascent from the factory levels (or descent now, since they had passed the center of mass thirty kilometers back). So when the comet hit and the surge through the tethers shorted the freight lift's main power and security systems, she was easily able to snatch the Mykhshad's weapon from the holster strapped to his left forelimb, her Vanguardian reflexes letting her move faster than even his sensitive tendrils could react. She retreated to the exit as Tarik and Haim joined her to form a united front. "Okay, folks," Diana said, "this is a stickup." At the aliens'

total incomprehension, she elaborated, "We're taking the PQM. Don't interfere and you won't be harmed."

Rysuth's echolocation clicks grew louder, no doubt gathering a detailed picture of the humans' every move. "You will not be able to use that weapon."

"No, but neither will you," Tarik said. "And you won't risk a sonic attack in here, or you'd hurt the Zhalevey. But we're a race of fighters, as you may have heard. You don't want to make us angry." Following Tarik's lead, Diana posed as menacingly as she could in a fiftieth of a gee. Apparently it worked, since Rysuth, the Zhalevey, and even Yonchon flinched.

Yonchon's manipulator drones rose from the Ryohoch's back and moved toward the humans. "Sorry, pal," Haim said, working his pad with visible regret. "I can't let you do that." The drones swung around and began to circle the aliens. "Please, everyone, just stay calm and don't try to interfere."

"This action lacks reason," Yonchon intoned.

"We're taking this PQM on behalf of the human race," Tarik countered, playing his part in the script. "Our people have been held prisoner long enough." Diana knew he wasn't happy bringing down the blame on humanity, but those were Stephen's orders, so he obeyed.

Rysuth reached toward Diana with his trunk, its cilia rippling as if straining for answers. "You have not done this alone. Who has assisted you?"

"Let's just say there are a lot of people out there who aren't happy with the cost of the Chirrn's ban on mentoring. People who want humanity to be free at last." That was vague enough that the Chirrn would probably suspect the Shayal.

Haim's pad bleeped with the ready signal from *Arachne*. The humans began to back out of the cab. "Now, you all just stay nice and quiet and don't try anything," Diana said. "The drones will be watching."

Rysuth, Yonchon, and the Zhalevey remained calm. The Zenith had evidently been right; while PQM was valuable, it was not irreplaceable. But Rysuth had one more thing to say, and Diana almost laughed when Arachne chose to subtitle it as "You'll never get away with this." Well, perhaps that wasn't a cliché in Mykhshadese. No doubt Rysuth expected the PQM to be neutralized as soon as the Stringworld systems were back up and running.

Diana could only hope he was wrong. "Boss, can you confirm that the nans did their job?" she asked as they pulled themselves toward the airlock.

"Not yet," Haim replied, "but there's no reason they shouldn't. The factory security systems are much better shielded than the sensors and comms."

"They'd better be."

The nans planted on the reference sample by the drone explosion had been programmed to activate once the comet hit, whereupon they would emit the EM signature of a strange-quark chain reaction. Strange matter was naturally unstable and short-lived, but PQM could be programmed to produce a stable, negatively charged virtual strangelet, which would devour adjacent normal matter and turn it into more strange quarks. The stuff had many internal safeguards against that, but all they'd needed to do was fake the signature and the factory's security systems would have jettisoned the tainted sample to fall toward the neutron star, where the metasapients' halo fields would have captured and neutralized it, in the process destroying its entanglement with the stolen PQM and leaving the Stringworld authorities — and the Chirrn — with no way to deprive the thieves of a viable supply. This had been delayed until communications went out, so the authorities wouldn't know they'd lost the security sample and thus wouldn't feel this heist posed enough of a threat to warrant an aggressive response. Still, the lack of confirmation was worrisome.

Once they reached the airlock and Haim opened the inner hatch, Diego Narvaez and Evan Jiang emerged, leading to a happy reunion among the once and future crewmates. But Diego cut it short. "Suit up," he said, gesturing to the three EVA suits he and Evan had brought from *Arachne*'s stores. They would need to transfer the PQM across manually; it would have given away the game had Broadwing been seen smuggling any heavy equipment (including the kind of cumbersome EVA suit a Zenith needed to accommodate his wings) aboard the humans' ship.

Diana shed her Chirrn-style vest (it would pinch badly) and enjoyed Diego and Evan's appreciative stares as she climbed into her suit, which sealed itself and tightened against her body to keep her pressurized. Its helmet HUD signaled a positive seal, but still the group engaged in the age-old tradition of checking each other's suits before proceeding.

In the lift's cargo section, they found the PQM stored in several dozen upright hexagonal drums nearly four meters high and half that across. "Are you sure we'll be able to move these by hand?" Diego asked once Haim had blinded the lift's internal security and hacked the bay doors. "From what Arachne tells us, there's nuclear-density matter in there."

"Only partly," Haim replied. "It's a suspension of nucleonic processors in a superfluid substrate. Still pretty massive, but it's set by default to cancel most of its own inertia—don't ask me how or I'll start whimpering."

But when Diego, Evan, Tarik, and Diana applied themselves to moving the first drum, bracing their feet against the back wall of the cargo cell, it barely budged. "Most, but not enough," Evan groused.

Haim had already interfaced his pad with the drum's controls. "Hold on, I think I can set it to reduce its effective mass even further."

"You can do that?" Diego asked.

"I've been studying this stuff for weeks. The physics may be crazy, but at least I know what settings to change."

Diego moved to watch over his shoulder so he could repeat the process with other drums. "Okay, try it now," Haim said to the other three. "It should be light enough even one of you could move it."

"I've got this," Diana said, sticking her arms out to hold back the menfolk.

"Any of us could do it," Haim reminded her.

"You think," she pointed out. "You brought me along for muscle, okay? This is my thing." Bracing her feet, she gave it a push with one hand, and—

Nothing.

She tried again with both hands, putting her knees into it. All she felt was more resistance. This was getting embarrassing. "Oh, come on, Haim, who are you—" She broke off, realizing the drum was moving *toward* her. "Who's doing that?"

"Uh-oh."

"What uh-oh?" She flattened herself out in the diminishing space. Beside her, Tarik and Evan tried to catch it and push it away, but it seemed to be getting faster.

"I think I overshot. Set it to negative mass."

"That's impossible!" Diego cried. "It would disintegrate normal matter if it touched it!"

"*What?!*" Diana cried.

"That's okay, it's just virtually negative. It's a localized decrease in the Higgs—"

"*HAIM!*"

"Oh, sorry. Stop pushing, you two!" he cried. "Newton's Second Law! You push on negative mass, it accelerates *toward* you! Push on *this* side!"

The other men moved away, leaving just her between the drum and the wall. Diana tried to wriggle out, but she wasn't built for narrow spaces; her chest brushed the drum and it pinned her even more. *Uh-oh. Newton's* Third *Law. The harder it pushes against me, the harder I push back, and the more it accelerates.* She was about to get crushed into the wall. She fought her instinct to push against the drum, instead desperately feeling for a handhold she could *pull* on....

Finally she felt the pressure decrease and the drum moved away. "Careful, careful!" Haim kibitzed. "Now push it the other way to stop it. Don't forget!"

"We know!" Evan snarled.

Tarik was by her side. "Diana?"

"I'm good. And hey, there are worse ways to go down in history than 'first human killed by exotic physics.'"

Still, she was embarrassed. All she'd ever wanted was to challenge herself—to test the limits of the abilities that were her heritage as a Thorne. Her grandfather, Vanguard's first great leader, had dreamed that his people's augmented abilities and diversity would put them at the forefront of interstellar colonization. It was a matter of familial and national pride for Diana to be indispensable to this expedition. Yet time and again she'd found herself injured, sidelined, and humiliated. Were the others right when they told her she was trying too hard? Were her efforts to challenge herself ultimately self-defeating?

Haim proved reluctant to tamper with the settings again, so the group did their best to maneuver the negative-mass drum through space to *Arachne*, its docking cradle stopped along another tether some ninety meters away and twenty down, with a slender guide cable (non-conductive, for there were still periodic EMPs from the comet impacts) strung across the gap. "Remember," Diana told the others, "whatever it feels like, we're not weightless. Keep your suit lines clipped to the cable and watch your step."

That was easier said than done when trying to carry across a massive shipping crate that pushed back. Despite Evan's assurance, it was hard to remember to go against a lifetime of reflex and invert their pushes and pulls, especially while trying to keep gravity in mind at the same time. Diana made the mistake of looking down; the Stringworld stretched out thousands of kilometers below them, an incomprehensible drop that reduced the enormous habitat modules to near-invisibility… and below them was nothing but a starscape. Diana and the others were zip-lining across a literally bottomless abyss.

Her heart raced in sheer terror. And then she whooped out loud in her helmet, not caring that it hurt her own ears. Trying too hard? The vack with that. Pushing herself to the limits had brought her here. She whooped again. *"Thrill! Of! A! Lifetime!"*

Churrlaya had guided Cecilia through basic Chirrn first aid—as well as he could remember it with Broadwing jamming his connection to the fleet's data network. Luckily, all he had needed was to have his broken leg straightened and splinted, to take in some water and electrolytes, and to enter a somnolent state for a time, redirecting his energy and mental focus toward his internal repair systems.

Cecilia had then paced the room, searching for options, adjusting her stride as the gravity had diminished over the long ensuing minutes. The closer they had drawn to microgravity, the more relaxed she had felt, despite the circumstances.

"Where are we?" a voice finally asked. It was Churrlaya, his voice weak and scratchy; his healing must have used up a lot of fluids. She brought him a bulb of water. "I deliver gratitude. Where is the ship?"

Cecilia hesitated. "I'm not sure I should tell you."

He sighed, hands moving feebly in the direction of his brow ridges before dropping. "You still will not trust me. But how can you trust them now?"

"I don't know who to trust!" she exclaimed. "Least of all myself." His eyes simply held on her, and she couldn't remember how long ago she'd stopped seeing that as judgmental. "God, I don't know what to do, what's right or wrong. All my, all my life, I've tried to do what I thought was best, and I keep getting punished for it. I go to space to help my family, my mother calls me—calls me a traitor, says I've abandoned my home. I realize my husband will be happier without me, and he bleeds me dry in the divorce. I lead humanity to the stars, I get thrown in alien prison for—for an accident of fate. Even the universe punishes me. And Stephen… my one stalwart friend… hah!" It was a weak laugh, almost a sob.

Churrlaya considered her words. "So that is why you left the planet you felt yourself rooted in. You did not believe you were welcome there anymore."

She slashed her hand through the air. "It doesn't matter. I take my roots with me. I know who I am. I rely on myself. I've had to. And it's made me tough, made me effective."

"But is it self-reliance," the Lesshchin asked, "or self-flagellation? Cecilia… you are not to blame for how others have penalized you. Yet you close yourself off and live in a denial of your own making.

"That is what I did for too long—keeping myself apart, dwelling on my loss and pain instead of letting others heal me. I was afraid to let them become a part of me for fear of the pain I would suffer if I lost them again. And in so doing, I only hurt myself more. I did not begin to heal until I allowed myself to be open to another mind. To lower my defenses and make myself vulnerable… even to the very being whom I had blamed for the death of my world."

Cecilia winced, pained by what she knew was happening outside. "You can't trust humans, Churrlaya. Even with the best of intentions, we find new ways to do harm."

"I am… painfully aware of that risk. But I understand now that the young need to make mistakes as they grow… and perhaps the fault was ours for not being there to shelter you from the worst consequences of your mistakes.

"I understand… and so I forgive. In the name of Lesshchi, Cecilia LoCarno, I forgive you."

His words drove right into the core of her and turned her inside out. Hearing someone forgive her, most of all a Lesshchin, lifted a weight from her spirit that she hadn't realized she was carrying—or hadn't been able to face. She shuddered and wept as she let herself feel the guilt of the Lesshchi disaster for the first time. Eighty-eight thousand and four hundred living, thinking beings dead, sixty-four thousand and four hundred more left with gaping holes in their memory and identity, seven hundred and twenty thousand more made refugees. How could she ever face her responsibility for so much tragedy? How could anyone live with the guilt?

But now she had her answer: by not carrying it alone. By having a friend who understood. A friend who could forgive her and, just maybe, give her leave to begin forgiving herself.

If she'd only been that for Stephen, been there to support and balance him as she should have, maybe he wouldn't have gone so far astray. If they'd both been there, together, for Diego and James and Evan and Amrita, they could have helped them face the guilt they buried beneath rage and hatred.

But maybe now she'd found someone else to help her carry the burden. And maybe that could be the anchor she needed so she could reach out to the rest.

"Churrlaya," she said, "I hereby renounce my allegiance to the planet Earth." He showed no triumph, only understanding and acceptance. "My first allegiance should have always been to my crew. And so I need to betray them to you… and hope we can stop them from making a terrible mistake."

Arachne's EVA suits were as constricting in their own way as the Chirrn confinement suits, but Diego Narvaez knew which one he preferred to be in. At least the EVA suits had actual gloves complete with tactile feedback — an essential feature for the delicate task of maneuvering the negative-mass canisters of PQM across to *Arachne*. It was a relief to have his fingers free to manipulate things without having to strip half-naked first.

Diego's thoughts turned unbidden to his first actions after being freed from his confinement suit, and his sense of relief faded. Striking a blow against their jailer was one thing, but striking him down once he was defenseless was another. Churrlaya may have been a soulless animal, but Diego took no pleasure in being cruel to animals. He had allowed himself to give in to his anger and inflict unnecessary pain on the Frog Footman, and had almost allowed James to kill the creature in a fit of vindictive rage. Understandable, to be sure, but Diego feared he had jeopardized the support of less committed loyalists like Nik and Kahina. His coup against Cecilia clearly troubled them, even if the captain had all but abdicated on her own. Diego had reassured them that they would still bring Cecilia with them, and that these conflicts would blow over once they were free and reunited. But he was concerned that his lapse with Churrlaya, the gratuitous violence he had allowed himself, might scare them off from whatever further violence proved genuinely necessary to achieve that outcome.

On reaching *Arachne*, Diego brought Tarik aboard to coordinate with the loyalists. Kahina, Nik, and the others rushed to greet their old exec, and the Zenith collaborator—Broadwing, as Stephen had called it—came down from the cockpit to observe. "The others are securing the PQM drum in the cargo module," Tarik told them afterward. "They'll be in shortly, and they'll show you how to do it on subsequent runs. We need to be fast and efficient; we've got no more than forty minutes to get this done."

Two of the three-armed green teddy-bear aliens—Zhalevey—approached Diego, carrying an unmarked container. "Special instructions and equipment are delivered to you," they told him.

Broadwing's head snapped around. "Special instructions? Explain."

"Meridian sends them. A refinement of the plan." The Zenith lowered its head obediently, and the Zhalevey turned back to Diego. "You may interface with the case to receive instructions."

Diego took the case and stared at it, and his eyes widened at the new instructions that uploaded into his buffer. No wonder the interface had been kept private. He knew that Kahina or Nik would never agree to this, let alone any of the ones who'd been living with the aliens for months, subject to Stephen's weakening influence. Diego had to give the pterosaur things some credit—they'd been able to recognize the differences between the humans' agendas and identify which ones were capable of what needed to be done. Sometimes animals could behave in ways that were almost human.

Diego caught himself. This was no time for doubt or irrational qualms. Granted, the devices whose specifications he now read were marvels of engineering, but so was a spider's web. Mindless instinct could produce the appearance of amazing sophistication. Diego strove to keep that in mind as he girded himself for what must now be done.

On the second trip to the freight lift, Haim Silbermann figured out how to reset the PQM drums to a low but positive virtual mass, enabling the thirteen humans to shuttle them across to *Arachne* with relative ease. Diego appreciated this, for once the group had moved a few more drums and gotten a steady rhythm established, it gave him an opportunity to draw his three most trusted allies aside within the lift's cargo bay and brief them on Meridian's amended plan over a private, short-range suit channel. James, Amrita, and Evan curiously studied the long, flexible tubular instruments he handed out to them. "Are you sure these little things will have enough power to do the job?" Evan asked.

"Once they're loaded with the quark matter," Diego said, then demonstrated the procedure for tapping the drum and drawing off a fraction of its contents, as per his uploaded instructions. "Keep in mind, there's nuclear-density matter suspended in there. With enough speed, that stuff can penetrate anything."

James frowned. "I don't know. Taking orders from those gargoyles… Who knows what their real intentions are?"

Amrita glared at him. "Not getting squeamish, are you?"

"I just want to be sure this serves us, not them. If we're going to do something this… this big, I want it to be for the right reasons. Last time, we were tricked into it, remember?"

"Last time," Diego corrected him patiently, "was an accident. This time, we're striking a blow for human freedom. This will ensure the local authorities will be too busy to chase us. And it'll be a crippling setback to the Chirrn, weakening their whole civilization."

"And it'll be revenge," Amrita added, her voice shaking. "For Kweli. For the babies. Those monsters will finally pay."

"And all our people will be safe," Diego reminded them. "Remember that. And remember how powerful these are. Set the timers carefully, and wait to plant them until I give the word. We want them to go as soon as we and the humans below are in clear space, but not before. You hear me?"

He met each of their eyes, making sure they understood. Diego Felipe Narvaez Duarte would not compromise his morals for anything. The fate of the aliens would be a regrettable but acceptable sacrifice. They could play at immortality and metasapience, but there was nothing truly eternal within them, no soul that could genuinely know suffering. But every human soul aboard *Arachne* was precious beyond measure. Even traitors like Stephen, like Cecilia, like the others who'd let their fear or selfishness corrupt them, were precious, every one of their souls worth more than a trillion alien lives.

Though Diego took some comfort in knowing that the death toll wouldn't be quite that high today.

10

ONCE CECILIA HAD FINISHED EXPLAINING THE PLAN TO CHURRLAYA, HE covered his eyes in dismay. "I would not have believed Stephen capable of this."

"He's hurting," she said in his defense. "He blames himself for what happened to his kid, to the others, to Kweli. And blaming you is easier to face."

Churrlaya met her gaze, acknowledging his understanding that she spoke from experience. "But Broadwing… He has been a proper citizen for many years."

"Churrlaya, nobody could've witnessed the death of Lesshchi and not been changed. We're all proof of that."

"Yes. Yes, what matters is stopping this before it is too late."

"Look, I know you're afraid of these Zenith because of what happened in the past, but what if their leader's right? What if they have learned enough to ascend or evolve or whatever without going mad this time?"

"While that possibility exists, my concerns are not so futureward. I know of Meridian's movement, and they are capable of shocking violence. They once bombed the PQM girdle of the habitat where my friend Ruzhalu was born, though the habitat was saved with no complete or permanent deaths. But they have killed entire ship crews to steal their PQM. They even attempted to accelerate an asteroid into a populated Star Palace to penetrate to its gravity core, even though the bulk grade PQM therein would be of little use to them."

"If she's so dangerous," Cecilia countered, "why would they ever let her onto a Star Palace?"

"Her involvement in these crimes has never been adequately proven. She tends to work through proxies and subordinates, and none of her captured accomplices have ever verified her complicity. Normally, Zenith loyalty tends toward whoever holds the greatest status, but Meridian has an exceptional hold over her followers, whether through her personal charisma or her promises of immortality. They have all been convinced that metasapient civilizations record and capture the minds of all sapient beings. In their certainty, they believe that by killing, they send their victims to a higher existence and nourish the metasapients at the same time.

"If Meridian told Stephen that she was willing to carry out this theft without loss of life, then her words were bastards. Here in particular, in the direct sight of a metasapient population, Meridian will not miss the opportunity to make an offering of lives."

"Stephen would have no part of anything like that."

"But Diego would, where nonhumans are concerned. And if communications are disrupted, Stephen would have no way to stop him."

"Oh, my God." Cecilia raised her voice. "Arachne, I know you're listening! You need to let us out of here!"

"I'm sorry, Cecilia," the cyber's voice came over the intercom. "Stephen is still the leader of this expedition."

"But I'm the captain of your goddamn body!"

"I'm afraid you forfeited that responsibility some time ago. As a prisoner, you have no command authority."

"All right, forget regulations! Use your judgment. After what you've heard—"

"With all due respect to Churrlaya, I have heard only that Meridian was implicated in the incidents he described. That is a matter of concern, but in the absence of proof, I can't let it outweigh my duty to my crew."

Cecilia hated to voice her next thought, but this was no time to pull punches. "Remember what happened last time you put the good of your crew over what you assumed was a low-probability hypothesis? Ninety thousand people died! Are you willing to take that chance again?"

Arachne hesitated long enough that Cecilia actually noticed the pause. "There is little I could do even if I agreed. My avatar is running in detached mode down with the Arachnen. And I'm not ready to violate Stephen's orders without more to go on.

"The most I am willing to do at this point is to allow you to speak to the others who are here. But the Arachnen are currently outside the ship, transferring PQM from the freight lift, and comms are subject to interference due to the currents induced in the tethers by the on-going radiation bursts from the neutron star. For now, I can only put you in contact with Broadwing and the Zhalevey in the cockpit."

Cecilia traded a look with Churrlaya. "I'll take what I can get right now, Arachne. And… thank you."

"Cecilia," her former captor said, "Meridian's followers are fiercely loyal. Trying to reason with Broadwing will be sending our words to futile deaths."

She laughed. "Look at us, Churrlaya. You and I changed each others' minds with just our words. After that, reasoning with a fanatic should be a snap."

Thanks to the system disruptions and the imminent accretion-disk passage, travel between modules was restricted to official use only. Stephen had made arrangements with Shthastya, their Zhalevey accomplice, to get shuttled down to the Arachnen's module, but going up to find Sita was another matter. Fortunately, L'chellin was able to pull some strings with the transportation managers—"This is what mediators do," as she put it—and got herself and Stephen on a lift going up to the Night Module, where Sita and R'nilinnath were located.

Less fortunately, when they boarded the lift, they found Velesh already aboard, seeking to speak with them both. Stephen had almost forgotten his cover story of considering the Shayal's offer, but L'chellin was quick to lash into her distant relative for attempting to subvert the Chirrn justice system, reminding Velesh in no uncertain terms that the Chirrn were not under their mentoring anymore. It was uncannily like listening to a teenager assert independence from an overprotective parent—although once they fell into arguing over the good of the Arachnen, Stephen felt more like he was the child at stake in a custody battle.

When they reached the Night Module, it didn't take long to locate Sita and Nilly. They were already at the administrative lift terminal, loudly insisting on being permitted to go upward. As Stephen drew closer, he realized to his horror that they were telling the local Mykhshad administrator about the heist in progress. "No, you don't understand, they have a way around the bloody entanglement thing! The Zenith are helping them, and they've got Zhalevey moles here on the Stringworld!… Moles. They're, they're infiltrators…. It's a metaphor! See, they're animals that dig underground so you can't… look, the point is—"

"Sita!" Stephen grabbed her arm and spun her around. "What the hell do you think you're doing?"

"I invite an answer to that question myself," added L'chellin, whose long limbs had let her easily keep pace with him. Velesh lagged some distance behind. "You are speaking of an attempted theft?"

Sita responded to Stephen instead. "Listen, you have to call it off. Broadwing is using you! This whole thing was orchestrated to get us here as Meridian's puppets!"

"Meridian?" L'chellin was stunned. "Here?"

"Sita, you don't know what you're—"

"*He knew*, Stephen!" Her fierceness silenced everyone. "Broadwing was the one who sent us to the Lesshchin kiss dance. He knew it would provoke them. He wanted an incident that would give him an excuse to propose this migration. So he set us up to be attacked." At Stephen's bewildered stare, she went on: "Do you understand what I'm saying to you? Broadwing got our baby killed!"

He couldn't let himself accept it. "Why would you think that? What would make you think…"

Nilly came forward, an arm moving protectively around Sita's shoulders. "She's right, Stephen. Broadwing was the one who gave me the idea of taking them to the kiss dance. He convinced me it would be all right."

"We should've seen it," Sita said. "Nilly told us that she'd cleared it with Broadwing, but I thought that just meant it was her idea and she'd consulted him on the specifics."

"Even so," a puzzled L'chellin said, "a mediator of Broadwing's experience should have understood that it was a procreative kiss dance rather than a mere recreation, and that an Arachnen presence would thus be provocative."

Velesh had arrived moments earlier. "Are you saying," he asked L'chellin, "that you entrusted the care of the humans to an individual with known ties to the Meridian organization?"

"There is no record of any such ties in Broadwing's past!"

While they argued, Stephen confronted Sita. "I can't believe you'd do this. All you have is circumstantial. You can't know Broadwing did it on purpose! Maybe it was like Nilly said, that she misheard his advice. Maybe he regretted his mistake and wanted to free us to make amends!"

"And it's just coincidence that Broadwing pushed for us to be allowed to renounce in the first place? He set us up from the beginning!"

"Sita, do you hear what that sounds like?"

"Oh, come on, Stephen! This is our baby we're talking about!"

"You don't have to remind me about our baby. Everything I'm doing to free our people is in her name!"

"Is that why you can't face the fact that you were used? That what you're doing, playing Broadwing's game, is a betrayal of her memory?"

"I can't accept that. Not on such flimsy evidence. There's too much at stake."

"Oh, right, I'm only your wife, why the hell should you listen to me?"

He stared at her. "I wasn't sure you still thought of yourself that way."

Sita scoffed. "Honestly, I'm not sure you *ever* thought of me that way. Not really."

"I loved you. I've loved you since the dreams."

"Yes, and it was the dream you loved! *Your* dream, of building a community and a future, of churning out babies for a stable population base! You and me, it was all just part of your grand master plan. It was never really *about* you and me, was it?"

"I always tried to do right by you."

She sighed, softening her tone. "Of course you did. You always try to do right by bloody everyone. That's just it. You're always trying to fix everything. Always spinning grandiose schemes to save the world. You try so hard to be everyone's best mate that you don't really let any one person get close to you. Not close like family, close where you let your guard down and risk getting hurt." She shook her head, laying a hand on his arm. "I don't know, maybe after you lost Benjamin and your mum, you were afraid to let anyone else get that close. You built up all your dreams and ambitions as your defenses and nobody else can breach those walls."

"Excuse me," L'chellin interrupted. "Stephen, is this true? Did you agree to assist Meridian's organization in the theft of our PQM order?"

Stephen hesitated, but ultimately he couldn't bring himself to lie to a direct question. "Yes. After what happened to Kweli, after learning about the Protocols, I couldn't trust you with my people's safety."

"You pledged yourself to serve our community. To make amends for the losses you inflicted."

"The Chirrn inflicted unfathomable losses on humanity by cutting us off from the stars! If anything, you were responsible for your own losses. Cecilia was right about that all along."

"I tend to agree," Velesh interposed. "Indeed, your choices have left the humans so dysfunctional that they choose to react with crime rather than pursuing the more peaceful avenues we offered them. Moreover, they have allied with the victims of your previous mentoring errors!"

"Look at yourself, Velesh!" Stephen exclaimed. "You're no better. You're not interested in helping us, you just want to use us to score points against the Chirrn."

"Exactly," L'chellin added. "You accuse us to divert attention from your own culpability! The Zenith Cataclysm would never have happened had you not pushed us into mentoring prematurely!"

"You were the ones who pushed! Our only mistake was trusting you because you resembled us! We overestimated your ability to grow beyond your primitive tribalism."

"*Oi!*" Sita cried at the top of her lungs. "Belt up, the lot of you! Stop blaming each other for ancient sodding history and start taking responsibility for what's going on right now!"

Stephen spun to her, meeting her vast dark eyes. *Responsibility…* The word echoed in his mind, in his own voice. *"And what about your responsibility for your own ship's wake?"* He had been the one to urge Cecilia to stop blaming others as a way to hide from her own guilt. He'd taken such pride in his ability to own up to his mistakes, his acceptance of the burden of responsibility for all the lives lost because of his choices.

But responsibility for a choice that had taken ninety thousand other lives was one thing to bear. Responsibility for a choice that took ninety thousand other lives plus one's own unborn daughter? That was intolerable. So much easier, then, to find an excuse to blame the Chirrn for all of it, and throw in Benjamin and Mama and everyone who'd died and suffered in Florida, and for ten thousand years before. After all, he didn't have to face the personal losses if he could bury them in a mass grave, in an anger based on abstract moral principle rather than firsthand grief and pain.

He reached out for Sita's hand, and with only the slightest hesitation, she grasped it, squeezed it with a strength he hadn't known she possessed. "She's right," he told the chirrnids. "I've made a serious mistake—allowed others to take advantage of my anger and denial and manipulate me into—"

Sita socked him in the arm. "To hell with the ruddy speeches already! Let's get up there before it's too late!"

Broadwing had tried not to heed the entreaties of Churrlaya and Cecilia LoCarno, tried to dismiss their lies about Meridian. All they knew was the propaganda of those who had opposed Zenith metasapience for so long, who had oppressed Meridian and her followers and forced them to employ extreme methods. Yes, Meridian taught, and Broadwing believed, that the metasapients recorded and preserved the minds of the dead. But that did not mean that Meridian actively sought to kill *en masse*. Surely the longer a mind lived, the more experience it gained, and thus the more complexity it could provide to the metasapients recording it both during its life and after its corporeal death. Meridian's conviction of the dead's survival was a source of comfort when killing was unavoidable, not an incentive to maximize casualties as an end in itself.

Still, he had seen the devices the Zhalevey had given to Diego Narvaez. He had seen that human and his followers breaking off from the group just *narr* ago and moving to attach them to Lode Seven Station's tethers. He had picked up enough radio chatter through the interference to know that Diego had claimed they were monitors to warn of approaching lift cars. But Broadwing could see that their intended targets were the main structural tether bundles of the megastructure, and that the devices resembled PQM-based heavy demolition charges that he had seen in replayed memories during the Lesshchi trial. The nucleonic matter in PQM, if released from superfluid suspension and accelerated with sufficient force, could tear through even the strongest non-degenerate matter as easily as through air. At Lesshchi, the charges had been used to rescue trapped survivors or cut through to hazardous equipment that needed to be secured. Here, placed against the tethers, their only possible use would be to slice the heavy fullerene bundles clean through.

But Broadwing was not the only one to realize this, for Arachne interrupted Churrlaya and the human to inform them of it. According to her, given the number of charges and the strategic positions of their target bundles, their detonation could potentially sever enough tethers that the tidal stress could tear the entire megastructure in two.

"I am sure it is only a precaution," Broadwing told them.

"Is it?" Cecilia challenged. *"Your Meridian doesn't seem the type to leave anything to chance. The plan to take out the security sample always struck me as sketchy. But if they cut the Stringworld in two, drop the whole PQM factory into the neutron star, then it's a sure thing. Not to mention that the loss of a main PQM supplier will weaken the whole Chirrn state and make it harder for them to hunt your people down."*

Broadwing didn't want to admit that he'd realized the same things himself. "Even if that were so, the megastructure is designed so that the inhabited sections will fall away from the neutron star should the tethers fail. At most there would be injuries due to the abrupt loss of gravity."

"You forget," Churrlaya said, *"that cometary matter is still falling onto the neutron star. The habitat modules are only fully shielded on the side facing it. If the tension on the cables is lost, then the modules will tumble and their inhabitants will be exposed to lethal doses of radiation. Thousands could die. Moreover, the magnetic deflection will fail and particles from the accretion disk could penetrate the modules! It could be a repeat of Lesshchi!"*

Broadwing's diaphragms contracted at the thought of witnessing such a disaster a second time. But he shook off the anxiety. "The radiation and accretion disk will be gone within six *narredj*. There would be no reason to detonate the devices before then."

"Wouldn't there?" Cecilia asked. *"If the Stringworld breaks, the local authorities will have to devote all their ships and attention to evacuating as many people as they can. A perfect opportunity for you to slip away in the confusion."*

"Why risk a long, slow series of warp hops," Churrlaya added, *"if you can simply blend in with the crowd of ships escaping through the wormhole?"*

"And what about the occupants in the lift car?" Arachne asked. "If they are still trapped there when the tether snaps, they would be immediately killed by the shock."

"We could evacuate them to *Arachne*."

"You would not have time to do that and still fulfill the plan."

"Broadwing, please adopt my words," Churrlaya said. *"Remember how it felt when you learned of Lesshchi's death. Remember what it was like to hear the survivors' testimony in the trial, to experience our memories. That event*

changed all our lives forever, and not for the better. Do you wish to inflict that on so many others?"

"Take it from a human," Cecilia interposed. *"Violence goes in cycles. People react to death by causing more death, and that makes more people react the same, and it just keeps branching out. It never stops unless someone breaks the chain. Unless someone recognizes that any pain or death they cause to others is their own responsibility, their own choice, not just a payback for something done to them.*

"Broadwing, I helped kill ninety thousand people, and I can hardly live with the guilt of it. But if I'd gone on hiding from that guilt, then I would've joined the others and I'd be part of something that could kill thousands more. Guilt is there to make us stop. To shame us when we're wrong. We have to listen to it or we just keep making ourselves worse and worse."

Broadwing's head sank below his shoulders, his whole stance lowering. His folded wing dactyls twitched against his forearms. He thought of the guilt he bore already. He had not expected the Lesshchin's retaliation to go as far as it had. He had thought he would provoke an attack, swoop in to frighten the attackers off, be hailed as the Arachnen's savior, then use the incident as an excuse to propose migration. He had not expected the Lesshchin mob to be large and organized enough to overpower him—or perhaps he was simply not as formidable a raptor as he had imagined. Because of his miscalculation, Sita, Kweli, Kazuko, and Justine had lost their babies… and Kweli had ended her life. Meridian had consoled him, assured him that he could not have anticipated or prevented it, and that their minds would be saved to live on forever (though what mind did a fetus have for the metasapients to record?). She had assured him that the good his efforts would ultimately do—freeing the Zenith from oppression, weakening the Chirrn's grip on power—would more than make amends for the harm.

But she had also assured him that no lives would be lost here today. He tried not to doubt his matriarch's word, to convince himself that the charges would not be detonated before the radiation had faded. There was no reason the plan couldn't still go off without permanent loss of life. But that was what he had thought before, and look what had happened. What factors might he be overlooking now?

He cursed himself for his disloyalty. Meridian was his love, his inspiration, the one being he happily called his superior. She had made him hers in the most intense mating flight of his life. She had offered him, of all people, the chance to become her primary mate. How could he even contemplate letting her down?

But he thought of Yonchon, trapped in the freight lift—an enigmatic, aloof being, but still a part of Broadwing's guild, a contributor to the consensus memory that was part of Broadwing's current identity almost as much as any Chirrn's. He thought of L'chellin and the rest of his guildmates, who might not all be able to evacuate in time or escape the radiation.

And he thought of Sita, who had fled the Arachnen compound and was lost somewhere on Lode Seven. Sita, who had already paid an intolerable price for his miscalculation.

"Arachne, release the prisoners," he chimed even as his mandibles clacked together in pain. "We must stop the planting of the demolition charges."

Maybe the plan could still succeed without them. Maybe the thieves could still get away at warp and trust that the security sample had been properly destroyed. Maybe Meridian would only demote him to a lower-tier husband, or at worst an odalisque, with the opportunity to work his way back up.

Or maybe she would rip his throat out and he would wake up in metasapient paradise.

Either way, he had to try. How could he strive to the highest in his matriarch's name if he saw himself as the lowest of the low?

But then again… if he had done all this in Meridian's name, if she now wished to do far worse, was she not with him in the depths? He still believed in the goal—but was he following the wrong person?

After he and Diana finished securing the latest drum to *Arachne*'s warp cage (for the cargo modules were already filled, and even the cage had limited room left for more), Tarik was pleasantly surprised when he recognized Cecilia LoCarno's coltish figure emerging from the lock. She was leaner than he remembered, but he knew her by the way she moved, with the discipline of a longtime spacer balanced with the boldness of a natural leader. At first he hoped she had changed her mind about participating in the heist; but then he saw Churrlaya in the lock behind her, clad only in a skintight full-body sheath of the kind Chirrn used for emergency EVAs. Tarik had heard from the other Unrenounced that Cecilia had apparently fallen prey to full-bore

Stockholm syndrome, so he steeled himself for whatever she might say.

But the story she told, backed up by Broadwing's staticky transmissions from inside the ship, was one he never could have anticipated. "You?" he cried to the Zenith, his rage engulfing him as he had never allowed it to before. "You were responsible for my son's death? My wife's..." He trailed off.

"I never intended that," the monster chimed in that deceptively melodious voice. *"I tried to ensure no permanent harm was done."* A pause. *"But yes. I am responsible."*

"You lying demon! First you manipulate us into fighting your *jihad,* now you betray your own side! Why should I help you?"

"Avenge yourself on me if you wish, Tarik Hüseyin Bahar. You are entitled to that, for I owe you two lives. But other lives are at stake, including Sita Bhatiani's. Let the culpability for lost lives fall only on me, not yourself."

Tarik wanted to toss all other concerns aside to slake his vengeance. But he couldn't. He remembered Kweli's kindness, remembered how much kindness she had received in turn from Sita and the others — even from R'nilinnath, and from L'chellin in her own matronly way. He remembered that his highest duty in life was to Allah and then to his community, his crew, and that anger was one of the sins that undermined those duties. He could not protect his community if he could not master himself.

He had too much anger to contain in full, but that was all right, for it could be useful. "Diego!" he cried over the open channel. "James! Amrita! Evan! Do you read?" There was no reply. "Stop what you're doing this instant! That's an order!" Still nothing. "We know about the bombs! This is not part of our plan!"

"Arachne, can they hear us?" Cecilia asked.

"I am boosting the signal to maximum, since there is no more need for stealth. I don't think they're inclined to listen. I have received requests for clarification from the others and have filled them in."

Cecilia met Tarik's eyes, communicating volumes, just like old times. "Arachne, have you tracked their movements?" In this forest of cables, they could be difficult to find.

"They've disconnected their trackers, but from what I've been able to detect, I'd say they've planted two devices already, on the structural tether bundles closest to the freight lift. From what I can extrapolate about the charges, I can

estimate where they'll need to place them for maximum effectiveness. Sending you maps now."

"Then let's move," Cecilia said to him and Diana—and to Churrlaya too, he realized. The Lesshchin's emergency sheath had no air supply, but as Chirrn space crew, Churrlaya had surely been modded to survive virtually naked in vacuum for a limited period.

As they pushed away from the ship, Cecilia spoke loudly. "All Arachnen, this is LoCarno. I intend to stop all personnel involved in planting bombs on the tethers. Everyone who agrees, rendezvous at the crossover cable. Everyone else, be advised that we will be dismantling those bombs, so you'd be best off standing down now and getting the fuck out of our way."

"We won't listen to traitors, Cecilia," came Diego's reply to her challenge. *"Everyone still loyal to humanity—to* Earth*—I ask you to stand with us now! Striking this blow is the only way to ensure our freedom!"*

"It will make us hunted!" Cecilia fired back. "And cost us everything we are, everything we've striven so hard to become!"

No reply came from Diego or his followers, though Tarik had no doubt they were strategizing on a separate channel. But Tarik, Cecilia, Diana, and Churrlaya were soon joined at the rendezvous point by Haim and three of the remaining Unrenounced: Nik Zacharias, Kahina Amrouche, and Zhao Changkun. There was no sign of Ibrahim al-Bakri. "He went off to join the others," Nik explained, keeping his eyes on Cecilia. "Diego can be very persuasive. But don't worry, Captain—I'm with you all the way. We can't let them do this."

Kahina was less certain. "I don't want to fight my own people. I'm still not sure they're wrong."

"And I can't fight," Changkun said. "I won't."

Haim just shrugged—he was too old to get into a physical confrontation. The small, slightly plump Kahina and the lanky, gray-haired Changkun weren't exactly suited for it either. "Very well," Tarik said. "We need a team at the freight lift anyway, to either get it moving down out of the danger zone or evacuate the people inside."

"We can detach the cab, use it as a lifeboat," Haim said.

"What people?" Kahina asked. "Who's left?"

"The Shilirrlaln's engineer, a Mykhshad supervisor, and two Zhalevey."

She stared. "Oh. You mean… people."

"Is that going to be a problem?" Tarik asked.

"*No*," Changkun replied, holding Kahina's gaze and her hand until she nodded.

"All right," Cecilia said, "you three deal with the freight lift. That leaves us even, five to five."

"But we outmuscle them," Diana said. "Hell, *I* outmuscle them."

"Don't get cocky," Cecilia warned her and the other Arachnen. "They're not the people you remember. They've clung to hate for so long, I'm not sure they have anything else left in them. They're angry and desperate and more dangerous than you can imagine.

"And they're about to make us guilty for another Lesshchi. We can't let that happen, no matter the cost."

After that, nothing more had to be said. The team broke and spread out into the fray.

Though circumstances had forced him to become a revolutionary, Diego Narvaez was still an engineer at heart. So it comforted him that this blow against the aliens was such a methodical demolition job. He may have been at peace with the necessity of having to kill so many intelligent animals for the protection of humans, but it was still an unpleasant chore. So much better, then, to focus on the logistics of the task and take pleasure in the careful engineering of the planned results.

The tethers holding this alien Tower of Babel together were arranged in a triangular lattice, each one surrounded by a hexagon of neighbors at equal distances. The thick tether bundles that provided structural support were spaced nearly a kilometer apart, with narrower tethers in between—some for transportation, others for drawing power from the neutron star's magnetic field or generating current to thrust against it for attitude control. Those flimsier cables would not be strong enough to hold the so-called "Stringworld" together if enough of the main structural members were cut—and many of them would become collateral damage in any case.

The demolition charges, Diego had to admit, were marvels of engineering. The PQM within them was somehow configured to function as a shaped charge, expelling the tiny quark-matter nuggets it contained in a directional burst (and he hadn't yet figured out how the action and reaction balanced out). These particular devices were cutting charges, sending out the PQM in a razor-thin, expanding wedge, perfect for slicing through bundles of fullcrene cable. Eventually, Diego assumed, the unleashed nucleonic material would expand back into normal matter. But these charges had been amped up well beyond their proper safety limits, so the PQM "blades" would travel far and fast, cutting through whole swaths of tether bundles before re-expanding — and that expansion would be explosive enough in its own right. Six of the charges aimed in different directions should be enough to slice through the majority of the support tethers, and most of those remaining would probably be snapped once the cut tethers went flying and crashed into them. Diego tried to estimate the amount of potential energy those vast tethers stored in the form of tension, supporting the mass of dozens of habitat modules against the acceleration of a neutron star. The answer was downright terrifying. He thanked God that *Arachne* would be well away from the megastructure before the detonation.

Two charges had been planted when the challenges came from Tarik and Cecilia, and Diego was on his way to plant a third. He had ordered Evan to come assist him, mainly so he could keep an eye on the erratic planetologist. When Ibrahim declared his continued loyalty, Diego sent him to protect the first charge while sending James to defend the second and Amrita on ahead to plant the fourth. That was the most pivotal one of all, to be mounted on a tether bundle close to the much thicker bundle at the center of the Stringworld and aimed directly at it. Even that great mass of tethers would barely slow the quark matter down as it tore through. Diego felt that Amrita deserved to strike that critical blow more than any of them. He found James's paranoia and Evan's raging xenophobia useful as sources of energy to be directed, but distastefully petty. Amrita had suffered more at the Chirrn's hands than any of them, her captivity reawakening her childhood memories of imprisonment and torture, of her father's murder before her eyes. Her hate was truly righteous, and Diego hoped that striking the *coup de grace* would help her purge it and begin to heal at last.

"Remember," Diego told them, "deluded or not, these are still humans. Restrain or disable them if you can, but don't get carried away."

"Nice principles, Diego," James called, *"but if they're working for the enemy, then anything that happens to them is their own fault."*

"Damn right," Amrita added.

"What about the Footman?" Evan asked, breathing fast. *"If he comes after me…"*

"Churrlaya is another matter, of course," Diego confirmed. "But don't go out of your way for revenge. Focus on the mission first."

As he pushed up and off from a vacant lift cable and fired his thrusters to boost him toward the first charge, he spotted a familiar kangaroo shape soaring toward him past the freight lift, with a wiry female figure clinging to his tail. "Never mind," he announced. "The Frog Footman is about to greet me personally. Evan, get here fast. Keep your cool. And remember we're in orbit—you can't point straight at what you're aiming for. Trust your suit to navigate."

But the first charge was closest to *Arachne*, so Ibrahim intercepted Tarik before anything else occurred. Diego saw the blips in his HUD and heard the *"Oof"* of impact as Ibrahim collided with the larger man, trying to knock him off course. But Tarik had a considerable mass advantage, so he was able to catch the edge of the tether bundle, about ten meters down from the demolition charge and twenty over. Ibrahim was badly outmatched and had no training in EVA combat. He tried words instead. *"I don't want to fight you, Tarik. Please, you should stand with me."*

"You should stand with me! Does the Prophet tell us we can kill innocents in jihad? No! You disgrace Islam like the fanatics of the past. Now stand aside!"

A few moments later Ibrahim reported: *"I'm sorry, Diego, I couldn't do it. He's heading for the bomb."*

Diego couldn't fault the man for his piety, but it had manifested in an unfortunate way. "That's all right," he said. It was one of the less essential charges, its arc directed outward and intercepting relatively few structural bundles. Even without it, they could do enough damage that the surviving cables would be unable to hold the strain for long. "You go back up James at charge two."

"But Diana's heading there!" Ibrahim cried.

"All the more reason to reinforce him! Now, go!" The Vanguardian was the biggest threat the other side possessed. He could only pray that the two of them could overpower her—or, more realistically, delay her long enough.

Evan soon arrived at the tether bundle, meeting Diego's eyes through their visors and nodding to confirm that he wouldn't collapse as easily as Ibrahim. Diego smiled and nodded back. He would have preferred a more emotionally stable wingman, but he hoped that by keeping Evan calm and confident, he could encourage the younger man to direct his xenophobia usefully against Churrlaya. "Run interference while I plant the charge," he ordered.

But Churrlaya came in faster than Diego expected, shooting right past Evan and straight for him. Even on the injured list, the Footman's prowess in ultra-low gravity was formidable. Still, no matter how efficient his internal repair mechanisms were, his legs and left flank would be weak from his earlier injuries. And the heavy, flexible demolition charge would make a very effective cosh. Diego let himself drop, then pushed off toward Churrlaya's underbelly as the alien reached the tether bundle. Diego swung the charge and put himself into a spin in reaction, but the swing was good enough to take Churrlaya in his bruised ribs, or whatever he had there, and double him over in pain. Diego saw no sign of damage to the thin, clear sheath Churrlaya wore, but he had the chance to try again. He stopped himself from spinning away by grabbing the kanger's broken leg, which he yanked on fiercely, sending himself back up and past the Chirrn toward the tether. He tried to aim a kick at that froglike head, hoping to impart enough momentum and loss of consciousness to send his jailer plummeting, helpless to save himself. But Diego wasn't trained in space combat either, and the blow only grazed a brow ridge. Still, the renewed leg injury seemed to have taken its toll; the Footman was moving slowly, barely able to catch a tether. When he finally brought himself to a halt several meters down, he simply clung there, leaving Diego free to begin attaching the charge.

As he climbed up and around to the optimal placement point, Diego caught sight of Evan engaging their ex-captain. The planetologist had intercepted her in open space between tethers, and now they tumbled, drifting slowly downward and away from Diego as they grappled. Evan was slight relative to Cecilia but had an edge in body mass, and he was angry. *"Traitor!"* he cried between heaving breaths. *"You were supposed to be our leader! You promised us we'd stand together no matter what! That we'd never give in to the monsters!"*

Cecilia had nothing to say in return. Maybe she knew she could offer no defense. More likely she was saving her breath and attention for the struggle. Either way, they would have to resolve the fight soon; they were accelerating downward ever so slowly, but already visibly picking up speed. Before much longer, they'd be falling too fast for their suits' low-powered thrusters to stop them.

But Diego couldn't concern himself with that; he had to get the charge placed before Churrlaya recovered. He willed himself to turn away from the fight and focus solely on the task at hand. But as he attached the charge, he silently prayed that Evan would survive.

He didn't even realize that he'd omitted Cecilia from his prayer.

Tarik was grateful that Nik Zacharias had switched sides. The doctor was young and robust, with a Strider's instinct for functioning in space. He'd shot out faster and straighter than any of the others and was about to intercept Amrita before Tarik could finish deactivating the first charge or Diana could even reach the second. *"Amrita, stop!"* Nik called. *"I know you don't have any reason to trust me, but just think! It's the Chirrn you blame, not all these innocents. We can steal the PQM and humiliate the Chirrn without all this needless death!"*

But Amrita was a Strider too. In Tarik's visor-magnified view, the Trojan native clipped her line to a lift tether, planted her feet against it to meet Nik's approach, then caught him and redirected his momentum to send him down and away, forcing him to expend thruster fuel just to catch himself. *"That's always been your problem, Nik. So focused on your goal you don't pay enough attention to a woman's whole body!"*

"Well, your problem is that you can't resist dragging people down! And I'm not letting you do that to me anymore." Nik thrust upward to reach the lift cable several meters above Amrita, then secured his own line's molecular-adhesion clip to its surface, halfway around its tree-trunk girth from her. He was able to stay out of range as she swung at him with her unplanted charge, but he'd positioned himself to be in her way if she tried for the structural bundle.

Reassured, Tarik finished deactivating and releasing his charge, though he kept half his attention on the fight as he did so. "One charge down," he broadcast as he secured it to a suit clip. "Repeat, one charge down."

Amrita swung at Nik more and more angrily until she lost her footing. She got in a couple of good blows, but he managed to fire his thrusters to loop around the cable on his line and slam into her from behind, sending the charge flying. Amrita recovered quickly, detaching her line and thrusting after it. Nik was dazed from the impacts, but he had bought some time.

Moments later, Diana's proud voice came over the comm. *"Yes!"* she cried, drawing Tarik's eyes toward her. As she waved a freshly detached demolition charge above her head, she crowed, *"That's two down, boys and —"*

That was when James Oates sprang from behind the tether bundle and began flailing at her with a charge of his own. His legs wrapped around her waist to keep them from flying apart as he struck at her. Only her helmet saved her from having her skull caved in before she could raise her captured charge to block his.

Tarik hesitated only a moment before launching himself toward Diana. She had twenty centimeters on James and several times his strength, but it looked like his surprise attack had left her dazed, and he had the advantage of leverage. Not to mention sheer deranged fury. *"It was you, wasn't it?"* James screamed. *"I never bought their story that you had trouble coming out of hibernation. They took you, didn't they? Took the strongest one of us, dumped their thoughts into your brain, sent you back to spy on us! This whole mission was a trap to lure us out here, admit it! You genetic freak, you're not even human! You were in league with the kangers all along!"*

Although his strikes with the heavy charge were as random as his accusations, a lucky blow to Diana's left wrist knocked her own charge loose. It tumbled down and away, end over end, and Tarik hoped it was sturdy enough to withstand any tether impacts on the way down. Surely it couldn't be set off by impact, but if it broke open, the dense matter inside could do some real damage as it fell.

More urgently, James was now ahead by one weapon, and he was more than willing to use it. Still anchored around her waist, he struck at her head and torso repeatedly, dazing her. Diana triggered her helmet lantern to full brightness, dazzling James so she could grab for his arm. But the reflected glare from his visor must have dazzled her too, for she missed. Cackling madly, James lifted his arm over her head, luring her to reach up for it… then slapped the demolition charge across her wrist, activating the device's magnetic adhesion. Diana shrieked as her wrist was clamped hard between the charge and the tether—not just from the pain, no doubt, but from the realization of what James intended to do.

"That's right, whatever you are," Oates cried as he set the timer. *"This will take care of you. Of all of you! Oh, I'm sure you could survive losing a hand, but when this goes off, the hydraulic shock in your bloodstream will make your heart explode!"*

That, at least, was not insane ranting, Tarik knew. He'd seen people struck by meteoroids. "Diana!" he cried. "I'm coming!"

"In that case…" James adjusted the timer. *"There! Think he can get you out in under a minute?"* He laughed and pushed himself away at high speed, opposite the direction it would fire.

"No!" came Diego's voice. *"It's too soon! James, do you realize what you've done? Go back and stop it!"* But James was past listening.

Diana strained futilely against the charge. Even her strength was insufficient to overcome its magnetic adhesion, and she had no leverage anyway; but she kept trying regardless. "I'm almost there!" he cried to her.

"No, Tarik!" she grated back. *"You're carrying a charge! If it's hit, it'll worsen the damage!"*

He reached her at last, pulling himself alongside her. "Then I'll just have to get you out before it goes off."

"I tried that! It won't shut down! You have to get away. I can handle this!"

"No, you can't!" He took Diana's helmet in his hands, making her face him. "You have nothing to prove to us, Diana. Nothing to lose by asking for help. So set aside your damn stubborn pride in your body and use that engineer's brain! Work the problem!"

She fell silent. Though he knew it was futile, he braced his legs on the tether and began to pull on the charge with all his might. After a few seconds, Diana called his name. Holding his gaze, she said: "I'm releasing my glove. You do the rest."

At her wordless command, her suit unsealed at the wrist. Tarik yanked her glove free. She gasped in pain as the vacuum struck her bare skin, as her blood swelled out her hand from within. But the suit tightened around her wrist, minimizing the swelling. Tarik grabbed her firmly and fired his thrusters at full power to pull her away. She screamed in agony, but managed to turn it into words: "Keep… pulling!"

A normal human would have come free easily, though painfully. But Diana's Vanguardian bones resisted breaking, and Tarik feared that the superior durability she took such pride in was about to get them both killed.

"Tarik!" It was Nik's voice. *"Hang on, I'm coming your way."*

"No time, Nik! Veer off!"

"Nothing doing! I lost Amrita — at least I can help you!"

Finally her hand began to fracture, her wrist slipping through as the skin tore and her blood lubricated the charge. Then they were free and thrusting away, and Tarik desperately tried to get distance from the blast arc in the few precious seconds remaining. "Told you… I could do it," Diana rasped, and Tarik swallowed a laugh.

"Nik, she's free! Get away! Repeat, get—"

Then the world tore apart around them.

11

THE EFFECTS OF THE DETONATION UNFOLDED SO QUICKLY THAT ONLY Arachne was able to process them almost as they happened. The charge James had placed was misaligned, but still the molecules-thick "blade" of PQM that spread outward in a fifty-six-degree arc was easily able to slice through thirteen structural tether bundles and dozens of adjacent lift and dynamo tethers. Arachne glimpsed the mirror smoothness of the severed ends before the released tension sent the cables flailing in unpredictable directions at extreme velocities.

Her children were out there. And all she could do was watch.

The arc of destruction encompassed the tether where the first charge had been attached, though at a lower altitude. Tarik and Diana had thrust in the opposite direction, taking them far enough out of the blast zone to avoid the deadly tethers. The arc came dangerously close to the freight lift's tether, but Haim's team had already detached the cab hemisphere, which had begun descending the tether on its emergency quantum-lock magnets.

Evan and Cecilia had been wrestling well below the arc of the charge, in the opposite direction from the blast. But Nikolos's attempt to redeem himself by aiding Tarik and Diana had placed him in the worst possible position. The PQM missed him… but the end of a tether struck his lower body with enough kinetic energy that the bonding energy holding his molecules together was trivial by comparison. Arachne had to watch as half of him simply turned to mist and the rest of him was torn apart by the resulting shock wave.

There was no human concept for what Arachne did instead of screaming. She did it just the same.

It had been her work, her purpose, to protect her crew. Again and again, she had failed. Again and again, she'd been helpless to fulfill that purpose, doomed to let her children down due to circumstances beyond her control. She'd always been overly attached to the physical world, a world that many cybers considered boringly slow and inflexible. But it was the world where humans lived, and they needed help so much. She'd thought she could give that help, but she was just too limited.

Why hadn't she defied Stephen earlier? He'd chosen her because he'd wanted a cyber who would disobey him if he endangered his crew. Had she been so blind to the possibility that the heist could go violently wrong? Or perhaps she'd simply been afraid to risk taking that step a second time, after the first had taken her career and her first body from her, and all for nothing.

No… more likely, she'd simply loved her children too much to believe they could be capable of this. And now she had to bear the weight of another death, another failure—all before the rest of them even realized Nikolos was gone. All too often, that was all she could do: endure the weight on their behalf.

The car carrying Stephen, Sita, and the others had been passing through the Stringworld's highest residential module—a low-gee aerial habitat populated mainly by Zenith and other fliers—when the disaster alert had activated and forced them to a stop. The human and chirrnid passengers insisted on listening in as Orshym, the Mykhshad administrator escorting them, was briefed. At first, there was no physical effect to be felt from the detonation up above; a fair number of the Stringworld's support cables had been severed, but their lower portions were still in the process of contracting around their new centers of mass, so they continued to exert force to hold the module up. The shock from the detonation and abrupt relaxation would take a few minutes to travel down through the cable. This gave the authorities enough time to sever the cables at the base and activate their self-disintegration safeguards before the immense weight of them crashed down onto the module or tore adjacent cables free. Their dissociated fullerene shreds trailed off to antiorbitward and fell clear, and the occupants of the module had time to brace themselves before it started to sway from the loss of support on one side. Enough cables remained that it held essentially upright.

"But it is worse than it should have been," L'chellin relayed to the others. "Apparently, a second charge had somehow fallen and affixed itself to a tether nearly a kilometer lower. A severed tether must have struck it and ruptured its containment. The force accelerated the PQM at sufficient velocity to sever or damage a number of other cables, though not as efficiently as it was designed to. More cables are giving way from the strain."

"What about *Arachne*'s cable?" Stephen asked.

"It and the freight lift cable are intact… for now."

"L'chellin… you need to understand, I would never have gone along with Meridian and Broadwing if I'd known they planned to do… *this*. They guaranteed me no one would be harmed."

The mediator's gaze was stony. "Stephen, Broadwing's vacuum suit is accounted for. He is not the one planting the charges. It must be your own people."

Stephen squeezed his eyes shut. "Diego. I never thought he'd take it this far."

Breath ruffled L'chellin's bristles. "Perhaps that is to your credit," she conceded.

Orshym turned her head and emitted a burst of echolocation clicks to get their attention. "There is no cause for alarm," the Mykhshad told them. "We shall simply send current through the dynamo tethers. This will accelerate Lode Seven outward from the star. This will reduce the tidal load upon the tethers to a safe level."

"Can you do that fast enough?" Sita asked.

"Provided no other charges are detonated. We are about to issue an evacuation order. This is a precaution only." Velesh's eyes convulsed in alarm at the word "evacuation."

"Precaution, my ass," Stephen exclaimed, confusing their translators. "There's still a fight going on up there between my people. Is there any way to punch a signal through so I can talk to them?"

"We have identified the system sabotage. A purge is underway. However, the impact event is ongoing. The interference remains considerable."

"Then you've got to get me up there so I can put a stop to this, order them to stand down. Please," he went on when Orshym hesitated. "This is my fault. My responsibility. I have to do this."

"You should allow this," Velesh said. "These events are the consequence of a failure of mentoring. And our responsibility as mentors is to help younger races help themselves." Stephen looked at the Shayal in surprise and gratitude.

"The wisdom of the Nine Clusters is recognized," the administrator said. "There is a high-acceleration emergency lift. It can reach the area within two *narr*." She hit Stephen with another echolocation burst. "Your body structure may not endure such acceleration undamaged."

He realized Orshym had just given him a quick sonogram. "I'm tougher than I look, believe me," Stephen said. "And I've never let risk stop me from trying."

"Noted. You may accompany me."

"Of course," Velesh added, deflating Stephen's hopes for him, "I insist on joining you to offer guidance."

L'chellin snorted in annoyance. "You can offer no meaningful guidance. You do not know the Arachnen as individuals, only as an abstract cause. They are members of my guild and have been my direct responsibility for *narrenn*. More—Stephen is my friend. I will accompany him."

"Only one of you may accompany the human," Orshym snapped. "Choose quickly!"

Stephen met L'chellin's eyes. "I choose the mediator."

Velesh wanted to protest, but the Mykhshad overrode him. "Noted. Come now!"

Stephen turned to his estranged wife. "Sita…"

She smiled. "It's okay. Like you said, this is our responsibility. I'm not just going to tag along to watch you work. I intend to help with the evacuation."

"*We* intend to help," R'nilinnath added, taking Sita's hand.

Stephen took her other hand, and they both moved in for a brief but heartfelt kiss. Then he and the others hustled for the lift, and as the door closed between them, he hoped that he would see Sita again.

"*Nik! No!!*" Diego's scream rang in Cecilia's helmet. "*James, what did you do?*"

"*It was an accident!*"

Cecilia was furious, but she had no time to indulge it. Nik Zacharias was beyond help; her duty was to the others. "Diana, status?"

"*I can manage, Captain.*"

"*The hell with that,*" Tarik insisted. "*I'm getting you back to Arachne.*"

"He's right, Diana," Cecilia said. "No arguments." She checked her HUD. Amrita had recovered her charge and was heading for her near-central target bundle, with James moving toward her at a fair clip to provide reinforcement. "Belay that. Tarik, you need to intercept James and Amrita. You're the only one close enough. Ibrahim, if you're really with us, then get Diana back to the ship and into a medbed."

"*Yes, Captain,*" Ib replied humbly.

"*Very well,*" Tarik said, his voice tight. "*I won't let James get away with what he did.*"

"No revenge. Just get the job done."

A brief pause. "*Acknowledged.*"

Cecilia began climbing toward Diego, who was hanging from his tether in shock, holding the charge loosely in his hand. If she could get up there quickly enough… "Churrlaya, status?" she sent on a private channel.

<*Recovering,*> he texted to her eyes, for his tight sheath wouldn't let him move his mouth. <*I am pursuing Amrita. I believe I have the best chance of reaching her.*>

"You're in no shape for more fighting."

<*Neither is Lode Seven Station. I am substantially outnumbered.*> A pause. <*Do not worry about me, my friend. At worst, a portion of who I am will survive.*>

In the wake of that, it took Cecilia a moment to realize that someone was missing. "I've lost track of Evan," she broadcast. "Did he…"

"*Look down,*" Arachne instructed.

Diego spoke again. "*No… Evan, slow down! Use your thrusters!*"

Cecilia followed Arachne's instruction, finding Evan's blip on her visor. He was hundreds of meters below them now and visibly falling. The blast must have disoriented him long enough to let him pick up significant speed. "*I tried. I'm going too fast.*"

"*No. Not you too.*"

Cecilia felt exactly the same. Her mind raced. She was lower, closer to Evan… but she would have to go faster than him to catch up, and then she'd be even worse off than he was. She could do nothing.

"*It's okay,*" Evan said, his voice quavering. "*Some good can come of this. I'm coming up on the freight cab with the aliens in it. If I time it just right, I can take them out.*"

"*No! There are humans in there too!*" Diego was losing control of his people.

"*Please, Diego! This is my last chance to stand up to those freaks. I can do this… I can…*"

Cecilia braced for the worst. If he was aiming at the freight tether, the charge's arc might intersect the bundle she was tethered to, in which case the explosive release of tension would kill her before she knew it. Instead, when the cables again snapped and flew faster than her mind could process, leaving behind sparkling clouds of shrapnel and carbon dust, the destruction missed her tether and the ones bearing the freight lift and *Arachne*. *"He tumbled,"* the cyber reported in an affectless voice. *"The charge went off in the wrong direction."*

"And Evan?" Diana asked.

"Gone."

Cecilia could feel the tether bundle she gripped trembling from the suddenly added strain. To her left, over a kilometer away at the edge of the first severed section, several damaged tether bundles snapped as they were forced past their limits. Cecilia was too focused—and too angry—to mourn Evan now. "Arachne, if another charge goes off..."

"Lode Seven is undergoing magnetic acceleration into a higher orbit, easing the tension. But it's moving too slowly. Another correctly aimed detonation will almost certainly be fatal, especially if Amrita succeeds in severing the central bundle."

Cecilia looked around. Ibrahim was still helping Diana back to the ship. Even if he abandoned her, he'd be too far away. Tarik was pursuing James, and would not reach Amrita in time to stop her in any case.

So it was up to her and Churrlaya to stop this.

Stephen would probably remark on the symbolism. Cecilia just found it contrived. But she began climbing toward Diego.

"Be advised of another concern," Arachne's voice came over Tarik's radio. *"We are seventy seconds from passing through the accretion disk from Meridian's comet. The loss of tethers has weakened the magnetic shields in this section. The disk is thinning, but there is still a particulate impact hazard. Please take cover behind the tethers as indicated."* Directional markers appeared in Tarik's visor to show where the cometary dust and vapor would come from and how to get safely alee of a tether or bundle.

But he couldn't break off now, not when he was moments from intercepting his quarry and making him pay for Nik's death. He wasn't sure what he would do when he caught James, but he knew the murderous lunatic had to be stopped. He had sworn to protect his crew at all costs, but had only watched helplessly as Mehmet and the other babies had died, as Kweli had died, as Nik and Evan had died. And he had been more than a mere bystander. If he hadn't agreed to go along with this insane heist… if he hadn't persuaded Kweli to start a family so soon… none of this would have happened. He had failed to fulfill his oaths to Cecilia and the crew. But this time, no matter what, he had to succeed.

He couldn't have aborted anyway, for James was now turning and decelerating to intercept him. Tarik tried to slow for the rendezvous, but James was closing at full thrust. Luckily, he was forgetting the fractional gravity pulling him off course, and he passed below Tarik. Still, he managed to snag the larger man's legs on the way past and clung with manic strength. The two of them went into a spin from their clashing thruster fire. "James, stand down thrusters! We need to get in the lee!" There was a lift cable nearby, one he could find if they would only stop spinning. Perhaps if he pushed James away, into the path of the oncoming debris…

"You don't tell me what to do!" James screamed. "You're another sellout. An alien plant like that bitch Diana! I bet they replaced all of you who woke up first!" James was clambering up his body, trying to strike at Tarik's groin, but the wild, shifting accelerations threw off his aim (and the suit automatically hardened against impacts anyway).

"James, look around you! We need to stop this!" But James had become completely irrational, maybe even suffered a psychotic break. What had he been through in the seven months of his captivity? What personal demons had driven him to this while others like Cecilia had remained strong?

Any thoughts of revenge evaporated from Tarik's mind. This was a sick person who needed help. More: This was a member of his crew. One of the people he had sworn to protect… no matter what.

But first he had to get him to safety. He grabbed at James' arms, hoping to haul him into a restraining grip and get to his thruster controls. But an alarm went off in his helmet and he saw small eruptions of dust and gas on the stormward side of multiple tethers. They were in the accretion disk! The impacts weren't as frequent as Tarik feared, but it would only take one. "James, come on!"

A tether spun into view, almost within reach. He thrust toward it, stretched out a hand — but a spurt of carbon dust and water vapor erupted practically in his face before he was swept away. A particle had missed his head by centimeters.

He redoubled his struggle—but realized James's grip had gone limp, only his thrusters pushing him against Tarik now. He caught the smaller man before he could slide off, found and deactivated his thruster controls, and quickly looked him over. The inside of James's helmet was spattered with blood. Sealant oozed into the puncture in the visor, and no doubt the opposite one on the back of the helmet. His status lights showed he was still alive, but barely.

Tarik studied James for a moment. Two minutes ago, he would've been willing to let the man drop. Now, he felt only pity—and he still had an oath to fulfill. Recognizing that the accretion disk passage was over, Tarik began thrusting back to *Arachne*, hoping he could get James into a medbed in time.

Amrita, like most of the other humans, had had the good sense to duck behind her destination tether bundle during the disk passage. Churrlaya, on the other hand, had risked staying in the open, taking the opportunity to close with her. He had little left to lose at this point. He had been luckier than James, though, suffering only a minor erosion of his sheath from a high-velocity cloud of water vapor. Just one more point against his success in the impending confrontation. No matter, in any case; his internal rebreather was close to its limits, the carbon dioxide already starting to build in his circulatory stream. Either way, this would have to end soon.

Even with the gap reduced, he failed to close with Amrita before she reached her target site. "Stay away, Frog," she warned. "If you touch me, I'll set this charge off right now! I mean it!"

<*I believe that you do,*> he texted. He changed direction, coming to land on the tether a few meters away from her. <*Please consider all the lives you will take if you do.*>

"Alien lives. It serves you all right for what you did to us!"

<*Amrita. I have done much to wrong you. I harmed you with intent, to avenge a harm you had no conscious part in. The culpability is mine, and I must live with that. I implore you — do not make yourself as wrong as I was. Do not punish others for what I and my fellow Lesshchin have done. Let compensation fall only on me. Let me help you to rebuild yourself, as I should have done all along.*>

Amrita scoffed. "I've heard it all before. You'll say anything to get me to submit to what the state wants."

<Then do what you want. Come and kill me. I am the only one here who has oppressed you. Take my life in exchange for theirs.>

A pause. "That I can do," Amrita said, and lunged for him.

Cecilia's throat seized up at the sound of Amrita's screams and grunts as she beat the eerily silent Churrlaya. "Is this what you wanted, Diego?" she screamed as she climbed the tether toward him. They had both circled to the lee side to dodge the comet debris, which had also shielded them from fragments of one more snapped tether bundle for which the debris was the final straw. Now they were racing for the charge placement point, and Diego had both the lead and the high ground. "Our own people dying! Killing each other! Killing themselves! What happened to the sanctity of the human soul?"

"None of this was supposed to happen!" Diego screamed down at her. "This wasn't the plan!"

"Are you vacking kidding me?!" Her fury at his words spurred her to climb faster, kicking off the tether bundle to assist her thrusters. "You encouraged all of this! James's paranoia, Evan's bigotry, Amrita's rage. You spent months teaching them to cultivate the worst in themselves, and you have the gall to say you're surprised that this was the result?"

He braced himself above her, his suit cable anchored to the tether. He spun the demolition charge slowly, ready to strike. She ducked beneath it, taking the blow on her left forearm so she could anchor her line with her right hand. "This is your fault!" he cried. "This wouldn't have happened if you'd led us as you were supposed to!"

He swung for her head with killing force. She ducked it, taking a grazing strike to her helmet that left her ears ringing. "Now the truth comes out! You'll kill a human as easily as anyone else!"

He kicked her in the side, sending her flying out from the tether. Her line held, but she ended up dangling upside-down from it, and Diego took advantage of her position to get her in a leg hold and force the charge toward her neck. She caught it with her hands, but his strength was greater, his leverage better.

"You call yourself human?" he cried. "You sold your soul to these devils! At least they were born soulless! You are an abomination, and I'll end you even if I have to set this charge off here and now!"

"*Diego Felipe Narvaez Duarte!*" Cecilia was stunned. It was Stephen's voice, staticky but recognizable. "*Listen to yourself, Diego! Look at what's happening around you!*"

"Stephen? This wasn't my fault! The Frog got to them, turned them against us! You understand, right? You're still with me, aren't you, Stephen?"

"*Oh, I wish I still were, Diego. Do you know why I wanted you with me in the first place?*"

"What?" Diego asked. The charge pressed closer to her throat. She could feel its magnetic field straining toward the tether, trying to break her wrists and crush her windpipe.

"*Growing up where I did, I had a lot of reason to fear and mistrust Christians. But I quickly learned you were nothing like the militias.*"

"Of course not, I'm Catholic."

"*More than that,*" Stephen pressed. "*You weren't just using piety as a weapon against others, a tool for power, an excuse for hate. You genuinely believed in the good your faith could do. I saw a kindred spirit in you, Diego, a man of deep conviction.*"

"That's right, Stephen! That's what this is all about!"

"*The thing about the people with the deepest convictions, though, is that we have the most trouble figuring out what to do when our convictions fail us. But you know what I've realized, Diego?*" The pressure against her throat wavered, but only slightly. A few more centimeters and the field would grip too strongly to break. "*I realized that's exactly when we need to hold onto our convictions the hardest. To take a good, close look at them and think about what they really mean.*

"*Is the sanctity of the soul just about who you're allowed to kill, Diego? What about the things the soul has to endure? What about causing it pain? Causing it guilt? Diego, what happens to your soul if you commit suicide in order to commit mass murder? What will you have become?*"

"It's no sin to sacrifice myself to save my people!"

"*Diego, your people are down in the Chirrn embassy right now, not knowing if they can get out in time. Your people include Sita, who's down there somewhere, I don't even know where, risking her own safety to help evacuate others. Your people, Diego Felipe, include the six hundred embryos on Arachne that are in mortal danger every time a tether snaps!*"

Inside his helmet, Diego looked lost, confused. His grip on the charge loosened, and Cecilia was able to push it away. She tucked her legs, braced her feet on the tether, headbutted Diego (her head was already ringing, so why not?), and ripped the charge from his hand. Then she slammed him in the gut with it and he was down for the count. Her chest heaved as she gasped for breath.

"Cecilia? Are you all right?"

"Oh… damn… it's good to hear your voice, partner. Position secure. That leaves only Amrita. Are you in position to reach her?"

A pause. *"I… don't think that will be necessary."*

Cecilia checked in on that channel. Amrita's screams had stopped. Now she was only weeping, bawling it out like she never had in all the months of captivity. "Churrlaya?" Cecilia sent tentatively. "Are you…"

<*Damaged,*> he replied. <*But my job is done.*>

"The charge is secured?"

<*More than that. I think I have made another breakthrough.*>

When Stephen boarded *Arachne* along with L'chellin and Administrator Orshym, he found himself having to fend off an aggressive, rambling apology from Cecilia, which he finally interrupted by the expedient of giving her a tight hug that she only gradually relaxed into. "I think I owe more apologies than you do now," he murmured in her ear. "I set them loose. You stopped them."

She shook her head. "I couldn't have without you."

Finally he had mercy on her and let her go, but her grip lingered on him for a few moments more. She pulled away, blushing, and he gave her refuge in a companionably rough slap on the shoulder. "I'm glad we're a team again. Let's keep it that way, okay?"

"May your words forgive me for supplanting them," L'chellin interposed, "but it is not yet time for celebration. Lode Seven Station is still in serious danger."

"Too many tethers are lost. The rest cannot support the tidal weight at this altitude," Orshym clarified, her sensory hairs rippling across her flanks—a sign of nervousness? "As more give way, the load increases on the rest. We accelerate outward at the best rate possible. But the damage impairs this. I must recommend evacuation." They reached the cockpit where Broadwing and the Zhalevey conspirators (now ready to cooperate with the group around them, as was their way) stood waiting, along with Tarik and Diana. Churrlaya and the three surviving human conspirators were in medbeds, with Ibrahim sitting vigil. Diana should have been in one too, Stephen thought, rather than just having a healing-gel sheath around her crushed hand, but there was no way she'd allow herself to be out of action at a time like this.

Orshym turned to the Zhalevey. "Do you control this vessel's docking cradle?"

"Yes," Shthastya replied.

"Then please begin descent. We will rendezvous with the freight cab. We will take it within the warp cage. Then we will launch."

"What about our people down below?" Cecilia asked just before Stephen could.

"A general evacuation order has gone out," Orshym said.

"They were already prepared to depart at a moment's notice," Broadwing put in, looking unwontedly sheepish.

"But Sita isn't with them," Stephen reminded them.

"She and the apprentice assist with the evacuation," said the Mykhshad. "They may leave with those they assist."

"How many people reside on this megastructure?" Broadwing demanded. "How long would it take to evacuate even a fraction of them? Have you thought that through? I have done little else since the first charge went off. The cables will split and the habitats will flip over before the radiation surges end. Only a fraction can get away. We cannot guarantee anyone's safety. We cannot even guarantee this lift cable will hold long enough to launch us."

"Isn't there anything more we can do?" Diana's voice was strong but rough; she was clearly weak and in pain, but effectively ignoring it. "Any way to thrust faster than magnetically? All the PQM tech you have…"

Orshym waved her trunk in Diana's direction as though sniffing at her. "We are instructing the factory core. It will jettison its PQM from the antispinward hatches. This will reduce the mass of the inner core. It will also accelerate it closer to orbital velocity."

"But will it be enough?" Tarik asked.

"It will grant us time. We can evacuate a higher percentage of the population."

"That's it?"

"It is all we can do. We are close to the neutron star. The PQM is little more than dead weight here."

"Weight," Diana echoed — or was it "Wait?" "Listen — don't jettison the PQM. Set all of it to simulate negative mass!"

Stephen and Cecilia both stared. "What?" the latter asked.

"Negative mass. It reacts opposite to the way you push it. I almost got crushed by it when we stole the first drum. If we set all that PQM to negative mass, won't it fall up instead of down? Push it away from the star?"

"That's for force, not acceleration," Arachne's voice pointed out. "Solve for acceleration and only the star's mass counts. Negative mass would fall like everything else."

Diana looked embarrassed not to have realized that, but set it aside with surprising ease. "Okay, okay, then make it a force! You've got all that machinery in the factory levels — have it push down on the negative-mass PQM, and it'll push back up. It'll push up against the weight, reduce the strain on the tethers. Won't it?"

"It would reduce the weight as you say," Arachne confirmed.

Orshym was agitated. "It would also place great strain on the factory facilities. The force would keep building. Finally the PQM would tear through. It might not be long enough for ascent to a safe altitude."

"But it's got to work longer than just tossing all the stuff out the side, right? And reversing its mass shrinks the total weight more than just removing it."

"It is not a particularly rational proposal."

Cecilia stepped forward. "This isn't a rational situation! Take it from a feral human — if there's one useful thing we've gotten out of our history of disastrously bad choices, it's a knack for desperate, last-ditch solutions. We may not have a billion years of precedent to solve every problem, but that makes us gifted improvisers."

"Please," Stephen urged. "The factory will be lost anyway if the tethers snap. This way we can at least save a greater number."

To her credit, Orshym decided promptly. "Agreed. I have transmitted the order."

After that, it was only a long, tense wait. Once *Arachne* caught up with the freight-lift cockpit and took it inside the already-crowded warp cage along with Haim, Kahina, Changkun, and the other four sophonts inside, they released the docking cradle's brakes and began to fall. From their current altitude, it would take ten minutes or more of free fall to reach the bottom and be launched clear of the Stringworld and the neutron star. If the tether snapped before then, they would likely be killed by the sudden, convulsive release of tension. If it snapped far enough above them, they might be spared, but if the Stringworld gave way, the whole structure would lose rigidity and twist, and a safe launch would be impossible.

And what might await Sita and Nilly, and the countless other beings inside the Stringworld, was too much to contemplate. Stephen's eyes met Cecilia's, the look conveying a depth of feeling. Neither of them could bear being responsible for a second disaster of this magnitude. Stephen knew, though, that the burden of responsibility would fall entirely on him. The fact that Meridian had manipulated and lied to him was of no consequence. He had chosen to act rashly out of pain, to do something that he knew could endanger others because he was too angry to care. He had cloaked it in self-righteous rationalizations, but the power-hungry governors, robber barons, and fundamentalist militias who had turned the Gulf States into a decaying ruin had done no less.

Cecilia took his hand, and he could tell from her face that she saw right through him, as she always did. "Don't you dare try to fall on your sword for the rest of us again. Whatever happens, I'm in this with you."

"So are we all," Tarik affirmed, and the others—even L'chellin and Broadwing—gave gestures of agreement.

"Everyone?" Arachne spoke up. "Would you look outside, please? I think you'll want to see this."

Stephen moved to the ports, Cecilia at his side, the others close behind. Beyond the transparent crystal, beyond the tethers flying past and the occasional habitat whose bulk blocked their view as they passed through it, the Stringworld was surrounded by light. Shimmering, iridescent filaments wrapped around it, flowing along its edges, sending out darting, electric-arc tongues that jumped and danced across its surface. Beyond was a meshwork of intricate auroral patterns stretching into the distance.

Arachne gave them video feeds from cameras on the Stringworld, from ships already launched, even from the wormhole terminus beyond. The enigmatic halo that surrounded the neutron star had extended a set of loops outward like a pseudopod to engird the megastructure. "The tension is diminishing!" Orshym cried, listening to reports from below. "This is unexpected, shocking. The metasapients have intervened on our behalf! The star's magnetic field has been altered! It is guiding us into a higher orbit! I never imagined to know such a privilege!"

"The hell with privilege," Tarik asked, "are we safe?"

"At worst, the modules will not flip until after the radiation bursts end. And we have time to mount a full evacuation. However, the acceleration shows no sign of halting. Shortly, the remaining tethers will be in no danger of breaking. We will be unable to operate under normal weight until repairs are completed. But Lode Seven will survive."

"Were there any casualties?" Stephen asked, dreading the answer.

"I think you should hear this report yourself." A link from Orshym blinked in his inbox display, and he opened it.

Sita's face appeared in his field of view. Her hair was drifting around her beautiful face in the extreme low gravity, and she was grinning. *"Everyone's okay down here. Some injuries from the swaying and the rush, but nothing that won't heal. Nobody died, Stephen. Not even temporarily."* He didn't have the heart to tell her about Nik, Evan, and James yet.

Nilly drifted by upside-down in the background, halfway through a slow midair flip. *"You should've seen her in action, Stephen! She was so commanding. She helped a lot of people stay calm. She should be a mediator, like me!"*

"But how did this happen?" L'chellin asked, her eyes staring out opposite viewports in bewilderment at the dancing filaments of light outside. "For metasapients to directly intervene in sophont affairs is virtually unprecedented. They are not even aware of us as individuals."

"No," Broadwing said. "But Lode Seven Station is a collective entity—a community that has value to the galaxy beyond. Its importance is great enough to draw their attention."

"It is more likely," Orshym put in, "that they reacted to the negative-mass signature from the PQM below. Negative masses striking the surface might have done more damage than ordinary matter. They may have only acted to save themselves."

Diana grinned widely. "So… it was my idea that saved everybody? Just so we're clear."

"Perhaps that was all it was," Broadwing observed, gazing out at the luminous hand of his saviors. "But I prefer to believe… that they wish us to live."

12

APASTRON HAD BEEN COMPLAINING OF THE COLD, BUT MERIDIAN KNEW IT was just a manifestation of her second's instinct to challenge. To minimize their chances of detection, the ship had burrowed beneath the loose agglomeration of ice boulders that made up the surface of a small comet and powered down. The physical contact with the frigid matter had drawn away their ship's heat far faster than the emptiness of space could. But Zenith were bred to fly high and endure extremes. Meridian found the cold invigorating.

Still, when Mountain's Peak reported the readings from their optical sensors on the comet's surface, Meridian felt the chill within her. Lode Seven Station had not been destroyed, simply moved to a higher orbit, apparently through the stardwellers' intervention. Mountain's Peak found the latter miraculous, but Meridian was distraught that the stardwellers had rejected her offering of lives. Had the humans done something to foul it?

It was a partial relief when the human ship arrived under sublight warp only mildly behind schedule, with telemetry and their transmissions confirming that it carried not quite ten-twelfths of the expected PQM shipment and only some of the humans. Apastron did her job, ordering Mountain's Peak to power up and rise to rendezvous with *Arachne*.

Meridian's new concubine soon arrived across the docking tube, accompanied by the human with the name-sound Stephen Jacobs-Wong. She greeted them in turn, chiming their names in her own tongue. "Broadwing. Crown of the Usurper King. You are welcome. But why is the shipment incomplete?"

"The Unrenounced proved too volatile," Broadwing explained after bowing his head in obeisance. "They detonated the charges early and incompetently. We were forced to depart prematurely. With respect, Matriarch, why did you not entrust me with the full plan?"

"You know I wished no mark of Zenith talons on this deed."

"Even so, could I not have passed on your instructions?"

She leaned down and preened his cheek featherfur to show her continued favor. "You understand that trust must be earned. I do not doubt your loyalty, but you have lived among the Chirrn for way too long. You might have hesitated in what was necessary."

"You may be right. Even now, I have trouble seeing your intentions."

"I intended to ensure the reference samples were destroyed. I intended to hurt and humiliate the Void Alliance far worse than by a mere theft."

"For what it's worth," the human said, "we did inflict considerable harm, and not just to the tethers. They saved Lode Seven by setting the PQM to negative mass to reduce the strain on the tethers, but that caused significant damage to the factory. It'll be a good while before they get things up and running again."

"That is but a token blow. It was not enough to ensure the stardwellers' favor."

"I don't understand."

"As a groundwalker, you would not," Broadwing said. "Courtesy requires an offering of nourishment to those whose favor we wish. Is that not right, Matriarch?"

"You do understand," Meridian chimed, pleased that Broadwing's years in the wilderness had not led him to forget too much. "Lode Seven Station would have been a great offering to the stardwellers."

"An offering?" Stephen Jacobs-Wong asked. "In what way?"

Stars above, the human was slow-witted. "The stardwellers thrive on complexity. The more minds they are fed, the more they are nourished. As it is, we have given them nothing. Worse, they rejected our offering."

"More than nothing, Matriarch," Broadwing said. "Two of the humans lost their lives from the premature detonations, and another has lost much of his mind."

"It is not enough! They would not even notice two or three lives! I meant to send them thousands to bless this beginning of our quest." She spun on the human. "Curse you primitives! I gave you people clear and simple orders. Are you too incompetent to follow them?"

"Orders to do what again?" the stupid male asked.

"Orders to sever the cables cleanly! Did you damage your brain in the upheaval?"

Rather than taking offense, the human leader relaxed and released a sigh, the corners of his mouth turning upward. "No, my lady. If anything, I feel whole for the first time in quite a while."

"Matriarch!" Mountain's Peak cried. "Multiple vessels have just emerged from warp bubbles. It is the Chirrn migration fleet! They will soon surround us!"

Meridian sang an undertone of shock and disbelief while her other crests chimed, "Get us out of here! Crown of the Usurper King, tell your ship to follow!"

"We cannot form a warp metric!" Mountain's Peak cried a few moments later. "They are bombarding us with radiation and shifting gravity fields."

Meridian spun on the human. "What has happened? What have you done?"

"It's an old human tradition," Stephen Jacobs-Wong said. "It's called wearing a wire. And you just gave us the confession we were fishing for. Every word you said has been recorded and broadcast to the Stringworld authorities."

Meridian whirled on Broadwing. "You were part of this? How could you betray me?"

The male faced her without bowing, a shocking breach. "You betrayed the cause, Meridian. The stardwellers do not want us to kill for them. They saved Lode Seven Station. Some may think they acted only to protect themselves from the negative masses, but they could have done so after the megastructure was severed. They chose to preserve lives, not consume them. Meridian… you were wrong."

"How dare you speak to me in that tone, you low-status male!" She spread her mandibles, preparing to lunge for his throat.

But Apastron leapt in her way. "Then *I* will speak to you thus," her second trilled. "He is right—the failure is yours. You promised to lead us to glory. But instead you have led us directly into the capture we have eluded for decades, because you let yourself be tricked by a primitive groundling!" She rose to a full combat stance and uttered the shrill cry of challenge.

So this was it. Apastron, admirably, had watched for the first sign of weakness from Meridian and struck without hesitation when it presented itself. But Meridian had broken or killed all prior challengers, and though she bore Apastron no malice for her legitimate ambition, she would win this fight as she had all others.

But when she leapt up and swept at Apastron with her lower talons, something went wrong. The timing of her leap had been off, ever so slightly tentative, and Apastron dodged it easily. Meridian struggled to banish any hint of doubt from her mind. She had not been defeated yet! She would make it up to the stardwellers somehow — no! If she let herself feel she had failed…

Before she realized what was happening, Apastron was upon her, striking with the speed and fury of youth. Fire raked across Meridian's wing as its glorious smoothness was ripped clean through, rendering her unable to fly. To add insult to injury, Apastron bent back the dactyls and snapped them, leaving the tattered wing hanging limp and ugly. Meridian screamed with all three crests, hoping to stun Apastron with the volume, for after all, her crests were the largest, the loudest, the most resplendently feminine.…

But Apastron leapt up and struck with her powerful leg, the talons coming straight at Meridian's left eye. The next thing she knew, she was lying on the floor, staring up at the sharp corner of a console, which was stained with blue Zenith blood and fragments of a material that shimmered with prismatic light.…

In horror, Meridian tried chiming, and only two tones sounded, the third replaced by a hollow hiss. Her intact arm shot up to her head — but even as she felt the void, she caught sight of her long, beautiful right crest lying broken on the floor. Meridian couldn't stop herself from keening, though it was a claw through her throat to hear the incomplete chords that resulted. Apastron had ruined her beauty, her voice. No one would follow her now.

But she was so proud of her beautiful second-in-command. Apastron had won fairly, with a ruthlessness Meridian had to admire. Meridian had failed, had brought shame on herself, but the cause would still be well-tended.

She dragged herself forward, prostrating herself before her new matriarch. She laid her broken head on its side, eyes away from Apastron, the soft back of her neck exposed to the victor's talons. Meridian waited silently for Apastron to grasp her throat in her talons — the lowliest part of the victor surmounting the highest part of the loser — and claim her rightful dominance.

But then she heard her former second chime: "No. In truth, it was not I who defeated you. Not in the way that matters most. Not in the way that will get us all arrested, our cause defeated. That honor," she finished with a disturbingly smug and cruel tone entering her chimes, "belongs to another."

Out of the corner of two eyes, Meridian saw Apastron step aside… and beckon Broadwing to take her place. Meridian's digestive system heaved as though she were falling from a great height without functional wings. Broadwing hesitated at first, but then stepped forward with confidence and determination, positioning himself for the ritual. "No," Meridian cried, unable to keep her silence any longer. "No, please! Not a male! Kill me instead, please! No!!"

But no mercy was coming, and she knew that even death would not grant her release. The stardwellers had rejected her offering and they would reject her soul. She could not escape her fate. She could only keen like a baby as Broadwing's cold, filthy masculine foot pressed her neck into the ground.

Within a day, the frenzy of the evacuation had settled down, although the occupants of the Stringworld were still vacating it at a less harried pace to make room for the extensive repairs needed to restore it to full function. Thus, the surviving Arachnen were now reunited aboard the largest ship of the Chirrn migration fleet, save only James Oates, who was in stable but critical condition aboard *Arachne*. Joana Caravalho and Doctor Mh'lellish had reported that James's brain damage could be healed, but the resulting mind would have lost much of its memory and personality, including most of what had occurred since Lesshchi. Stephen held out hope that this would allow James to make a fresh start, free of the baggage that had driven him to become what he had. Churrlaya had promised to do what he could to help in that process. "It is a state of being I understand well," the former Lesshchin assured him, before resuming his counseling of Amrita Dhillon.

The Lode Seven authorities saw Meridian as the prime culprit and were thrilled to have her under arrest at long last, so they were content to leave her human accomplices in Chirrn custody. That placed them right back in the hands of the Shilirrlaln justice system—or what there was of it aboard this fleet.

L'chellin assembled a mediators' hearing to determine the facts of the case. Since Broadwing was an admitted conspirator, R'nilinnath had to join L'chellin on the panel. As they listened to testimony from the witnesses, Nilly sat stiffly and tried to look solemn and disciplined, with little success.

Now, with the testimony concluded, Stephen sat before the panel accompanied by Cecilia, Tarik, Haim, Diana, Broadwing, Diego, Amrita, and Arachne's avatar, with the rest of the Arachnen in the audience. He was grateful that Ibrahim, Kahina, and Changkun had not been charged, for their only crime had been to assist in ferrying the stolen PQM to *Arachne*. L'chellin had not required Cecilia to stand with the conspirators either, for she had played no role in the crime; yet she had insisted on taking responsibility for the acts of her crew. For his part, Stephen had confessed all his actions and choices freely, as had all the others, save only Diego. Though he was subdued and clearly grieving, Diego still refused to acknowledge the Chirrn's authority or participate in the proceeding. At least Amrita was beginning to make progress. There was still bitterness in her toward the Chirrn, but it seemed she had begun to realize that Diego had exploited her more.

At length, L'chellin spoke. "We now have many factors to weigh in determining the extent to which the balance has been disrupted and what must be done to restore it. Your willing cooperation in establishing the facts of these events, and the declared repentance of most of you, is appreciated and noted for the record. However, much damage was inflicted upon Lode Seven Station, and the supply of PQM to the Antispinward Void will be disrupted for some time.

"Far more importantly, your actions led to the irreversible deaths of Nikolos Zacharias and Evan Jiang Erfan, and the partial death of James Albert Oates. The fact that the two individuals directly responsible for those deaths are themselves partly or completely dead does not mitigate the loss, but worsens it. In death, they cannot work to repay the community for what they have taken from it." Stephen blinked away tears, moved by her words. "James can be restored, but the person he becomes will not be the same person who killed Nikolos, so would it be fair to demand compensation from him?

"In addition," L'chellin went on, her voice heavy with disappointment, "Mediator Broadwing's violation of his oaths led to the deaths of the unborn children of mated progenitors Sita Bhatiani and Stephen Jacobs-Wong, mated progenitors Kweli Ndege and Tarik Hüseyin

Bahar, unmated progenitors Oyama Kazuko and Ravinder Pritam, and surrogate progenitor Justine Nguyen, and contributed to the self-inflicted irreversible death of Kweli Ndege." Broadwing lowered his head. No trace remained of the pride and triumph he'd shown when he'd clutched Meridian's neck in his talons.

"On the other hand, Mediator Broadwing, you have contributed to the restoration of balance by assisting in the rescue of Lode Seven Station and the arrest of Meridian. Your voluntary confession and readiness to repent are also noted. Yet you will need at least a lifetime to repay your debts in full."

"I submit fully and without challenge to the judgment of Shilirrlal," Broadwing intoned in a minor key.

L'chellin puffed a breath through her nares and turned her eyes to Stephen. "As for most of the culpable Arachnen, you have already taken decisive and heroic action to correct your mistakes before the worst was done. Your imaginative thinking saved thousands of lives. And you helped us bring one of the worst criminals in the Four Voids to justice." Stephen bowed his head in acknowledgment of her generosity. He didn't feel he deserved it.

"Yet we must still examine what led you to betray your oaths in the first place—a betrayal without which the events here at Lode Seven could not have occurred, and which I know to be an offense against your own personal convictions as well as Chirrn laws." She leaned forward pleadingly. "Why, Stephen? You had my trust and my friendship. You had worked so hard to contribute meaningfully to the community. Why did you feel compelled to attempt such an act against us?"

After a careful pause, he replied: "Because when I learned the truth about mentoring, I blamed the Chirrn for the destruction of Lesshchi, for all human suffering, and became convinced that our incarceration was unjust and oppressive. Because ultimately it was easier to blame you than to live with my own culpability for Lesshchi—and my own inability to save my brother and my mother so long ago."

Cecilia grabbed his shoulder. "No. Stephen, I told you not to fall on your sword alone."

"Cecilia—"

"Let her speak," L'chellin said. Nilly gave a half-hearted gesture of agreement, trying to look like she served a purpose.

Cecilia rose and threw a look at Churrlaya. "Look. For months I was doing just what Stephen said—blaming you to hide from my own guilt.

I'm ready now to accept something else he said to me once, about taking responsibility for the consequences of your own actions no matter who or what may have goaded you into them. What happened here, what happened to Kweli and Nik and Evan and James and the rest, that's on all of us, and I'm as ready as Stephen to do whatever we can to make amends.

"But in the name of fairness, shouldn't the same principle apply to the Chirrn? You had a hand in what happened here as well. You pushed the Zenith to seek metasapience too soon and triggered everything that followed. You cut Earth off from the galaxy. Now, personally I think you did us a favor, all things considered." She met Stephen's eyes. "But that doesn't mean it didn't come at a terrible cost. It left us both unprepared to meet each other. It forced humanity to develop starflight on our own and use dangerous methods to do so." She glanced at Diego. "It left some of us unable to face alien life without panic or xenophobia.

"I'm not saying you should let us off the hook for our mistakes. But if the Chirrn don't face up to their own mistakes and accept responsibility for the consequences, nothing will change in the long run, and sooner or later there will be another disaster, another attempted genocide. Maybe even another interstellar war, if the Void Alliance and the other powers all keep refusing to budge."

Her eyes took in L'chellin, R'nilinnath, and all the other Chirrn in the audience. "It took me months to learn that denying culpability for our bad decisions is ultimately a self-destructive path. I'm asking the Chirrn not to make the same mistake. Now, I don't know if mentoring is a good idea or not, but I think it's a question you need to open again. You went too far in one direction, and to fix it maybe you went too far in the other. Maybe there's a better solution in the middle somewhere. But you need to start looking for it, see what you can fix in yourselves to keep things like this from happening again. Or maybe..." She reached down and clasped Stephen's hand. "What you can learn from listening to others who see things differently."

L'chellin considered her words for some moments. "You have learned wisdom," the mediator finally said. "And the Chirrn must not be averse to doing the same. If nothing else, consider our pride." Her unwonted (but typically dry) humor helped ease the tension, punctuating the moment before she continued. "You are correct, Cecilia. This has become a referendum not merely on the Arachnen's fate, but on the Void Alliance's policy toward humanity itself—for it is only within that context that the Arachnen's actions here can be understood and judged.

"Our forebears four yanarrach ago believed that we could best serve the nascent civilizations in the Four Voids by leaving them alone. But now we must acknowledge that even in trying to avoid interference, we have affected you profoundly. We have still made choices on your behalf, choices that have consequences to you but in which you were denied a say. That is an unjust and ultimately harmful imposition.

"And yet," L'chellin went on with pride, "you have managed to thrive and advance entirely through your own choice and effort. You are prone to monumental errors, but as recent events have shown, you have a remarkable capacity for correcting those errors—even if you do tend to postpone such correction until the last desperate *narr*. I now believe that you have the maturity and the right to make choices on your own behalf as a species.

"Moreover, I believe only you, and your fellow unmentored civilizations in the Voids, are qualified to know what is best for your own species, for your nature is outside the experience of the mentored galaxy. If it is your judgment that you deserve to participate in the community of the galaxy, we have no right to isolate you for what we imagine to be your own good."

After a moment, Nilly made a hesitant snuffling noise, akin to clearing her throat. "But Mediator… what about the Shayal? They don't think humans are ready. They think they're scary ferals who need to be mentored and tamed. What happened here will only make people more afraid of humans than they already are, and make it easier for the Shayal to get what they want."

"You spawn robust and well-formed words, Apprentice Mediator," L'chellin said, and Nilly raised her head and gaped in pride—then gave a startled jump and closed her mouth, realizing she'd shown a bit too much tongue. "And they have captured the essence of our dilemma. Whatever penalty we impose on the Arachnen, it will not resolve the larger political issues that could still enfold them and jeopardize their future standing as members of our community. Nor will it prevent others from treating the rest of humanity in ways that could provoke dangerous consequences."

L'chellin's eyes swivelled and she hissed across her tongue. Her fingers tapped repeatedly on her brows, and her tail twitched and thumped against her perch. Stephen had never seen her so agitated. "I can see one possible recourse, but it is highly… unorthodox. It is only possible under the current turbulent circumstances at Lode Seven." A sigh ruffled her snout bristles. "With all that has happened, the stolen PQM has not yet been unloaded from Arachne. If that PQM were somehow to… somehow to come into the possession of the humans of Sol System… it could enable them to develop their own interstellar technology. They would then be in a stronger position to resist interference, to gain allies.…" She trailed off.

Stephen rose. "L'chellin… are you inviting us to steal the PQM *again?*"

"I do not spawn these words lightly. But if the Chirrn have wronged you, then we are obligated to restore the balance. We have left you vulnerable, and now you are exposed. Something must be done to grant you strength. That PQM aboard *Arachne* is immune to neutralization, since you successfully destroyed the reference sample. If humanity gained possession of it, no one could take it from them. It is a unique and limited opportunity, so the decision must be made now."

"You need that PQM to build the colony, though," Cecilia said. "And Lode Seven won't be up and running for a while."

"We still have the bulk-grade PQM for the habitat collar, and the ships we have should be adequate to do the work with only a limited delay. We can make do until a replacement supply can be obtained."

"But how would we get away with it?" Stephen asked.

"I can persuade the other fleet alphas to delay reporting the theft. This would allow *Arachne* to traverse the wormhole to Antares among the other evacuating ships, then return to Sol."

"Even so," Haim put in, "it would take us decades to get a handle on the PQM and start building our own warp or Casimir cages."

"We can provide Arachne with complete specifications to save you time. And the Void Alliance will not wish to act in haste toward you once you have that potential. I believe it will force us all to reevaluate our mentoring policies and their consequences, and that debate could easily fill that interval. As for the Shayal and others… the Voids are still our responsibility, and if we invite them to participate in the debate in good faith, they are likely to respect our independence in turn — at least until humanity is strong enough that the matter is rendered moot."

Stephen and Cecilia met each other's eyes. "What do you think?" she asked him, though she hardly needed to.

He sighed. "L'chellin... I think it's a generous offer, but it troubles me. I've compromised my oaths and my integrity enough already. I don't want to see you doing the same."

"He's right," Cecilia said. "We've all agreed to renounce our ties to Earth. It took me a long time to get to that point, and a lot of people suffered as a result." She looked to Churrlaya in the audience. "I can't go back on that word, not so easily. If anyone else wants to go, they have my blessing, but I'm staying here to pay my debt."

"We both are," Stephen said.

"But there's more than that," Cecilia went on. "Talk about political maneuvering all you want, but if humanity shows up on the galactic stage with warp ships so soon after Lode Seven, it'll just make us thieves in the eyes of the galaxy. And that's at best. At worst, we'll be linked with Meridian, and all the irrational terror you Galactics have about metasapient plagues will fall onto us. We'll be mistrusted, feared, even hunted."

Stephen squeezed her hand. "And just giving humanity PQM wouldn't help us stand on our own. We'd still be dependent on out-siders. We'd be seen as a charity case, not true equals. Any accomplishments we made in the future would be seen as an indulgence from others, and we'd be judged only by our past mistakes.

"Too much of what's happened here these past months, these past millennia, is the result of people being unable to look beyond the mistakes and abuses of the past. Maybe it's because your civilizations have lived so long, have so much history. Maybe our young civilization has the potential to break that cycle. But to do that, to move beyond the trap of the past, we need to take responsibility for our own future. We need to find our own path to the stars."

L'chellin was visibly moved and impressed. "These words are also well-spawned. Yet I admit I do not see how what you propose can happen. Relativistic travel is a dead end, and PQM is only available from neutron stars. It would take you many *yanarr* at least to reach the nearest lode. The PQM aboard *Arachne* right now is your best, perhaps only hope to grant your people self-determination."

R'nilinnath made another attention-seeking snuffle. "Ahh... I have a very strange and probably very stupid idea."

L'chellin looked at her. "Do not let the words die on your tongue."

"Well... we need to give them the PQM... but it mustn't be obvious that it came from this theft... and we can't just tell them how to build warp ships because then they won't be independent. And the Arachnen don't want to break their oaths by renewing contact with Earth. Right?"

"An adequately efficient summary."

"Then maybe... what if we just... *left* the PQM where they could find it? Like in their outer cometary cloud, or somewhere in a system they've already colonized but barely begun to explore. Then the Arachnen could keep their oaths, and the Soln — the humans — they could study the PQM and figure it out on their own. Find their own answers, like they've learned how to do so well. Who knows? Maybe they could discover something new about how to use it, test out some crazy idea we're all too smart to try. Plus it would probably take them a yanarr or two to invent superluminal ships, enough time that the connection to the heist would fade in people's minds. After all, they wouldn't know where they got it, so they couldn't be blamed."

"I don't know, Nilly," Haim said. "Is that supply enough to sustain a whole civilization?"

"Enough to give them a good start, at least. Once the Soln have achieved that, they could find out where to get more."

Stephen considered Nilly's proposal and nodded. "Yes. I think it's a good compromise. Humanity deserves its independence in the galaxy, but it doesn't deserve to fall victim to the bad press we Arachnen have garnered. A delay will give us time to earn our repentance and build a better image of humanity in the galaxy's eyes."

"But you know what this means, don't you?" Tarik asked. "This only works if the Shilirrlaln have deniability, if there's no clear link from them to Solar humanity. If some of us leave in *Arachne* to drop off the PQM in human space... then it would be permanent. We couldn't come back to the fleet, or to the new habitat."

"You could go back to Earth," Nilly suggested.

"No," Tarik said. "Cecilia's right. We swore an oath. We have a debt to repay. We can't make a good beginning of this if we do it without honor."

Stephen's heart sank, and he shook his head. "I can't ask anyone to do that. To be an exile, adrift in the galaxy."

Tarik laughed, surprising him. "You needn't ask, Stephen. I volunteer! To command a ship that could take me anywhere in the galaxy? It would be the adventure of a lifetime!"

Cecilia clasped his hand. "Are you sure, Tarik? You've been so important to this community…"

He gave a wistful smile. "I held them together as best I could in your absence. And it took almost everything I had. Now you're here, back with Stephen, so I know the Arachnen are in good hands. And I…" He sighed. "I need to get away. To make my own *hijra*… and try to find what is left of myself."

The captain squeezed his hand. "All right. But I can't let you go off with only Arachne for companionship. You'll need others too, enough to make a working crew."

"Very well," L'chellin said after a moment. "I would prefer to deliberate longer, but there is limited time to carry out R'nilinnath's plan successfully." Nilly beamed at the attribution. "I will permit a small party to depart aboard *Arachne*, no more than the minimum necessary to function as a crew."

"Then I'm going too," R'nilinnath said.

L'chellin was stunned. "No! I cannot allow that."

The young Chirrn faced her without wavering. "You can't just let a bunch of children wander around the galaxy. They need *some* adult supervision! They're still our responsibility. And they need a mediator to help them interact with the sophonts they'll meet." She bounced up and down a bit. "And it'll be fun!"

L'chellin hesitated. "I suppose they do still owe a debt to the Chirrn. Someone should accompany them to oversee their repayment of it. But R'nilinnath, are you sure…"

"Mediator, this was my idea. I have to take responsibility for the consequences."

"But you would be alone, the only Chirrn. You would have no consensus knowledge to share. You would be fragmentary."

"I prefer to think I would be closer to human," Nilly replied. "It will make me more a part of *their* community, and that is what I need in that context."

"I am learning not to underestimate the wisdom of the young," L'chellin finally said. "I grant you permission." She took a hop toward R'nilinnath, brushed necks with her, and clasped her hands. "But I will miss you, child."

Not many other Arachnen volunteered. For some, the idea just seemed too insane. Others, including all the expectant mothers, had too many commitments to the community. Diana Thorne would normally have jumped at the challenge, but after her complicity in the near-disaster, she felt obligated to stay at Lode Seven and help repair the Stringworld. Haim, meanwhile, felt he owed it to Yonchon to resume his apprenticeship and make amends for almost getting his Ryohoch mentor killed—although Yonchon behaved as though none of it had ever happened. But enough people came forward to make up a reasonable skeleton crew, including Ravinder Pritam to tend to *Arachne* and Justine Nguyen to provide astrophysical knowledge. It made sense that so many volunteers came from the group that had lost their babies, for they had little keeping them here and every reason to want to leave recent events behind.

So perhaps Stephen should not have been so surprised and saddened when Sita stepped forward to join them. He quickly realized that he should have seen it coming all along. But he wasn't sure he was ready to accept this ending. "Does this mean our marriage is over?"

She kissed him gently, almost platonically. "I'm not sure it ever really began. I got swept up in your fantasies, your ambitions. It was wrong for both of us.

"But I can't define my own life as long as I'm stuck in a small community with you. And this—the adventure of traveling the galaxy, exploring all the forms life has taken—that is who I really am."

Tears filled his eyes. "It'll be dangerous out there. You could be killed."

Sita rolled her eyes. "I'm not as fragile as I look, you know. And I'll have good backup. Turns out Nilly and I make a wicked team."

"That's—that's not what I meant," he assured her. "I meant it would hurt… it *does* hurt to lose you."

"How many times have you lost me already, Stephen? Best to make a clean break, so you can move on and find someone more suited to you." She winked. "Come on, I've seen the way you look at Diana."

"Everyone looks at Diana like that."

"And everyone looks at you like that. Think about it, okay?"

She took his hand, held it gingerly. "I've already asked Arachne to enter our divorce in the records. I don't need any of our property beyond my files. All that's left is your formal acceptance."

He took a shaky breath, nodded, and asked Arachne to upload the form to his window. Clicking his confirmation wasn't as painful as he'd expected. If anything, he felt relieved, and more on Sita's behalf than his own.

The most beautiful woman he'd ever seen stood on tiptoes to kiss his cheek, and he felt the warmth and pressure of her slim, supple body against him for the last time. Then she turned and walked away to begin her new life.

EPILOGUE

"JAMES IS GETTING BETTER," CECILIA TOLD DIEGO AS SHE SAT ACROSS FROM him in his cell. There was no visible barrier between them, but they both knew—from experience—that the utility fog would block him if he attempted to assault her. "He's breathing on his own now. Moving his fingers and toes."

"You should have let him die," Diego said. "His soul has already gone to its judgment. Restoring his body is a travesty." She noticed he didn't say "to Heaven."

"What makes you the expert on who has a soul and who doesn't, eh? Are you really still so sure of your own judgment?"

Diego simply stared. Finally he said, "You're so convinced that I'm the one who needs redemption. It was your betrayal that killed two of our own."

She heard a variation of the same charge from him every day, so she let it slide. "Are you so convinced that everyone else—everyone who isn't dead—is morally inferior to you? Do you have so little faith in the judgment of every last one of your colleagues, your friends, the people you were willing to entrust your life to?"

"Someone must stand firm. Someone must stand for humanity."

"Humanity isn't about staying inside limits, Diego! It's about growing beyond them! If you'd only look… we have a chance to change the Chirrn, not just let them change us."

He met her with silence again, and she growled in frustration. "Damn it, Diego! You're the only one left! You can't spend the rest of your life alone!"

"San Diego de Alcalá spent the last decade of his life in seclusion and contemplation."

"Aren't you forgetting the penance?"

But he would say no more. Frustrated, Cecilia emerged to meet Churrlaya, who had waited for her. "Still no luck," she said, her shoulders sagging. "I'm not sure we'll ever get through to him."

Churrlaya brushed his mane against Cecilia's cheek to comfort her. His scent was already starting to change; he had decided it was time to embrace his new community fully by bearing a child for it, so he had initiated the hormonal shift and would soon become a *she*. "I have confidence that we will in time. I doubt any human could ultimately be more stubborn than you."

Cecilia laughed and hugged his neck, returning the nuzzle. Then she grew more somber. "He's in denial. He can't live with the guilt of Evan and Nik's deaths, so he blames me. It was hard enough for me to face that burden. For someone as pious as he is…"

"I understand," Churrlaya said. "But this time we will help him. All of us." Isolation had proven a colossal failure in dealing with humans, so now they tried engagement, offering Diego the support of the community so he wouldn't have to bear his guilt alone. But Cecilia suspected it would be some time before he was willing to accept it.

She thought of Broadwing, who had so much more guilt to bear, but whose faith had helped him to face it and make amends. He had been returned to Antares a couple of days—rather, a few *narrissh*—ago to give evidence against Meridian and her organization. He had revealed many secrets that would enable the detention of offshoot groups that might seek to follow in Meridian's wingbeats. Yet at the same time, he had sung eloquently of the mercy the metasapients had shown, and how wrong it was to equate the Zenith pursuit of metasapience with death and destruction. He had urged the civilizations of the Voids and beyond not to penalize all Zenith for the mistakes of their distant ancestors and the fanaticism of Meridian. Had metasapience research by Zenith not been treated as taboo, it would not have been driven underground and could have been pursued with optimal care and safeguards, and without prompting the kind of resentment that led to Meridian's genocidal efforts. Apastron, the new matriarch of Meridian's former clan, had backed him up, affirming that she too had seen the revelation at Lode Seven and pledging that once she had served her time, she would lead her clan in rejecting Meridian's violence and finding a better path to ascension. Cecilia suspected that Broadwing would be by her side the whole time; she had already made him her first concubine.

Some people get all the luck, Cecilia thought. There weren't a lot of unattached men remaining among the Arachnen to choose from. As she met Stephen outside the security area, she momentarily found herself noticing how sexy he was before she recoiled at the incestuous feeling the concept gave her. *I must be getting desperate.* Mercifully, she found herself reflecting instead on her intense lovemaking with Diego in times gone by. If he could be redeemed, maybe....

"Any luck?" Stephen asked, anticipating the answer.

"No," she told him, smiling wistfully. "But that just makes me more determined to try."

He smiled back without ambivalence. "That's why I partnered with you in the first place, Cecilia. Your gift for tackling the impossible challenges."

She shook her head and laughed. "What?" Stephen asked.

"I was just thinking... not so long ago, we thought that building a colony on an alien world with no other intelligent life — one with auxon-built cities already waiting for us when we landed, mind you, and an army of self-replicating servants at our beck and call — would be the greatest challenge of our lives. Now I think of it and it seems so... amateurish."

They passed a viewport, and she stopped to gaze out at the ice dwarf which the Migration guild was already beginning to mine for construction material, and at the unfamiliar stars that dotted its sky — her home sky, from now on. "Look how far we've come. I can't even *see* Gamma Leporis from here." She sighed, growing subdued.

He understood. "Let alone Sol." He clasped her shoulder. "I miss Earth too, sometimes. I miss what we were."

"Yeah," she said. "But life is change. The past is part of us." *Oh, my beautiful city.* "It always will be, no matter how far we go. So we can move beyond it without losing it."

"And we can keep it without letting it hold us back."

"All right, yes. You always belabor the point."

"Sorry."

She smiled. "But there's no one else I'd rather build a world with."

"Me neither."

They began to stride away, leaving the view toward the past behind. "One thing, though," Cecilia said. "If you ever need to plot another heist, consult me next time. That plan was way too complicated...."

Arachne loved being a starship again. Traveling by warp cage still scared the hell out of her, to be sure. But she loved having a purpose once more — having the freedom to act and the power to make a difference. It was rewarding to have her body filled with lively, raucous humans (and one especially raucous Chirrn), acting out their silly hormone-driven melodramas and keeping Arachne endlessly entertained. Tarik, Sita, and the others argued endlessly about how to deliver the PQM to humanity and how much warning to give them about what they would find in the Four Voids and beyond. Arachne could read the undercurrents of sexual tension forming between Sita and her new captain. Was the biologist about to repeat the same mistake of falling for the leader? Or would Tarik respond to Ravinder's attempts to attract his interest? It certainly added spice to the ongoing debates about where to go after they dropped off the PQM. Would they survey or contact the other unmentored civilizations of the Four Voids? Would they investigate the resettlement efforts along the Eta Carinae diaspora front? Would they head for the densely populated Inner Disk where the most ancient civilizations resided? Whatever they chose, it would be something that made a difference, and Arachne could be a part of it. Hopefully, it would give her opportunities to make amends for her past failures.

She found herself contemplating her namesake, the Arachne of myth. What was often overlooked was that Arachne's transformation at Athena's hands was not just a punishment for her hubris in challenging the gods, but an act of mercy. When the defeated weaver tried to hang herself in shame, Athena let her live on as a spider — condemned for her crimes, trapped forever in penance, yet still alive and in a form that let her continue to ply her greatest skill.

All in all, there were worse fates. Whatever form she was now trapped in, she had been given another chance, and she was still in a position to do what mattered most to her. Wherever Arachne went, wherever the web of wormholes took her across the galaxy, she would keep her children safe.

APPENDIX 1: DRAMATIS PERSONAE

Arachnen (incomplete list)
Arachne: shipmind
Bahar, Tarik Hüseyin: acting captain
Bhatiani, Sita: biologist, behaviorist
Caravalho, Joana: physician, neurologist
Jacobs-Wong, Stephen: expedition leader
Ndege, Kweli: chief surgeon
Nguyen, Justine: astrophysicist, mathematician
Oyama Kazuko: political scientist, legal scholar
Pritam, Ravinder: senior cyberneticist, programmer
Silbermann, Haim: chief engineer
Thorne, Diana: construction engineer

Unrenounced/Loyalists
al-Bakri, Ibrahim: geneticist, ecologist
Amrouche, Kahina: mathematician, programmer
Dhillon, Amrita: geologist, mining engineer
Jiang Erfan, Evan: planetologist, meteorologist
LoCarno, Cecilia: ship commander
Narvaez Duarte, Diego Felipe: assistant chief engineer, pilot
Oates, James Albert: industrial engineer, cyberneticist
Zacharias, Nikolos: physician, psychologist
Zhao Changkun: programmer, systems analyst

Migration guild members (Chirrn unless otherwise specified)
L'chellin: senior mediator, Intersocietal guild
Churrlaya: xenopsychologist, formerly Lesshchin biologist
Broadwing (Zenith male): junior mediator

R'nilinnath: apprentice mediator
Yonchon (Ryohoch): starship engineer
Mh'lellissh: physician assigned to Arachnen

Nine Clusters Coalition representatives (Shayal)
Commissioner Velesh (hermaphrodite): diplomat
Velesh's triad mates (male, female): aides, bodyguards

Antares B Star Palace personnel
Rauhoc (Gaurim male): physician
Phlrntsya, aka Fred (Zhalevey female): concierge

Zenith dissidents
Meridian (female): matriarch
Apastron (female): second-in-command
Mountain's Peak (female): pilot
Sunflash (female): medical orderly, infiltrator

Lode Seven Station personnel
Orshym (Mykhshad female): administrator
Rysuth (Mykhshad male): freight lift attendant
Shthastya et al. (Zhalevey): assorted station personnel

APPENDIX 2: CHIRRN TIME UNITS

T HE BASIC UNIT OF C HIRRN TIME MEASUREMENT, THE NARR, IS ONE STANDARD habitat rotation, equal to 96.64 seconds. Chirrn employ base 8 mathematics, so their time units are derived as follows:

1/64 narr	=	*narrat*	=	1.51 seconds	
1/8 narr	=	*narreth*	=	12.08 s	
1 narr	=	*narr*	=	96.64 s	= 1.61 minutes
8 narr	=	*narredj*	=	12.89 min	
64 narr	=	*narrach*	=	103.08 min	= 1.72 hours
512 narr	=	*narrissh*	=	13.74 h	
4096 narr	=	*narruvh*	=	109.95 h	= 4.58 days
8^5 narr	=	*narrenn*	=	36.65 d	
8^6 narr	=	*narranl*	=	293.21 d	
8^7 narr	=	*narrayth*	=	2345 d	= 6.42 years
8^8 narr	=	*yanarr*	=	51.38 y	
8^9 narr	=	*yanarredj*	=	411.03 y	
8^{10} narr	=	*yanarrach*	=	3288.2 y	
8^{11} narr	=	*yanarrissh*	=	26,306 y	

APPENDIX 3: SPACE HABITAT PARAMETERS

Antares Star Palace:

Although the Star Palace's gravity is artificial, we can calculate its effective gravitational mass by:

$$g = GM/r^2, \text{ so } M = gr^2/G$$

where g = surface gravity, $G = 6.67 \times 10^{-11}$ m³/kg·s², M = Star Palace mass, and r = orbital radius.

To calculate the synchronous orbital altitude R, where w = angular velocity and p = rotational period:

$$w = 2\pi/p$$
$$R^3 = GM/w^2 = gr^2/w^2 = g(rp/2\pi)^2$$

The formula for horizon distance d for a sphere of radius R as seen by an observer of height h is:

$$d = (2(hR+h))^{1/2}$$

Results for Antares Star Palace:

Radius (at datum):	24.237 km
Horizon (at datum, for h = 2m):	311.36 m
Surface gravity (at datum):	0.68 g = 6.66 m/s²
Rotational period:	81.73 min = 4904 sec = 50.75 narr
Effective mass:	5.85 x 10¹⁹ kg
Docking ring (synchronous) altitude:	133.571 km

Lode Seven Stringworld:

Where M = neutron star mass, d = Stringworld center of mass distance from star (in meters), a = tidal acceleration (i.e. "gravity"), and Δr = distance from Stringworld CoM, we get:

$$\Delta F = (3GMm/d^3)\Delta r$$

and

$$a = F/m = (3GM/d^3)\Delta r$$

$$\text{Therefore } \Delta r = ad^3/3GM$$

Gravity varies linearly with Δr; for instance, at twice the distance from the center of mass you feel twice the gravity.

$$\text{Orbital period } P = ((4\pi^2/GM)d^3)^{1/2}$$

To calculate insolation Q (thermal heating) where T is the neutron star's surface temperature, R is its radius, and d the Stringworld's distance (in kilometers):

$$Q = T((1\text{-albedo})^{1/4})(R/2d)^{1/2}$$

$$\text{If albedo} = 0.5, Q = 0.84T(R/2d)^{1/2}.$$

Results for Lode Seven:

Neutron star:

Mass:	3.26×10^{30} kg
Radius:	12 km
Surface temperature:	98,000 K

Stringworld:

Center of mass orbital radius:	467814 km
Total length:	6783 km
Outer endpoint:	4522 km from CoM; gravity 2.94 g
Inner endpoint:	2261 km from CoM; gravity 1.47 g
Insolation temperature:	Inner end: 296 K = 23 C
	Midpoint: 295 K = 22 C
	Outer end: 293.5 K = 20.5 C
Orbital period:	4311 s = 71 min, 51 sec = 44.6 narr

Author's Rendition

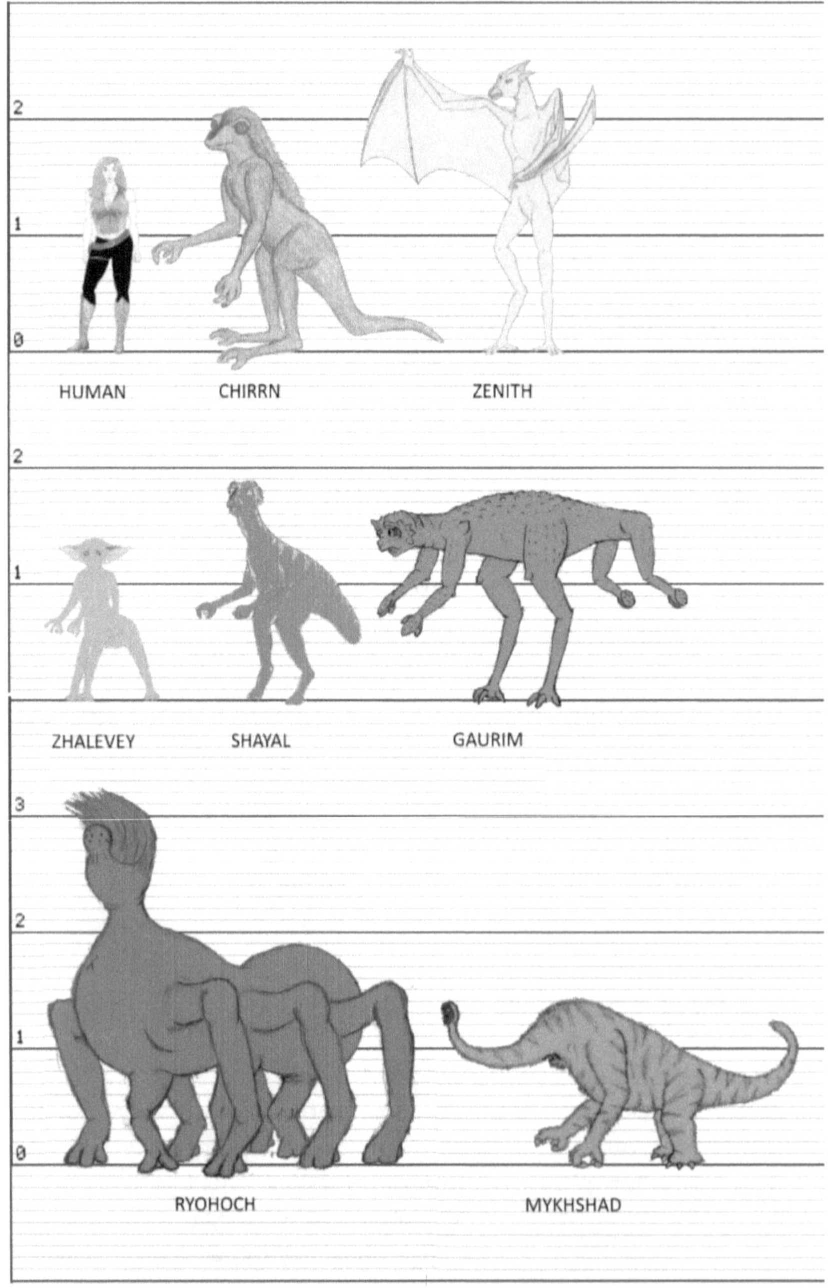

ACKNOWLEDGMENTS

Thanks again to the people whose advice guided me in structuring and revising this work and strengthening its characters, including Michael A. Burstein, Greg Cox, David Mack, Sam Morgan, and Marco Palmieri.

Research by Radu D. Rugescu and Daniele Mortari ("Ultra Long Orbital Tethers Behave Highly Non-Keplerian and Unstable", *WSEAS Transactions on Mathematics*, Vol. 7, No. 3, March 2008, pp. 87-94) suggests that the Stringworld's length relative to the neutron star could make it unstable. However, "Stabilization of Electrodynamic Tethers" by Robert P. Hoyt, online at http://www.tethers.com/papers/ED_Stabilization.pdf, shows that electrodynamic feedback could stabilize it.

For the specifics of the comet impact on the neutron star, I relied on "Radiation from Comets Near Neutron Stars" by Harwit, M. & Salpeter, E. E., *Astrophysical Journal*, vol. 186, p. L37 and "A possible mechanism for the generation of cosmic gamma-ray bursts and ultra-high-energy particles" by Zaidel', R.M. [sic] and Kurt, V.G., *Astronomy Reports*, Volume 42, Issue 6, pp.779-786.

The Zenith concept of metasapient consciousness preservation is inspired by a conjecture of Robert L. Forward in the "Future Speculations" chapter of *Indistinguishable from Magic* (Baen Books, September 1995), specifically pp. 312-9. Diego's suggestion of confining degenerate matter in synthetic diamond comes from pp. 154-5 of the same book.

The passage on anger quoted by Tarik in chapter 3 paraphrases a saying attributed to the Prophet Muhammad (peace be unto him) by the *hadith* scholar Al-Tabarani. Since *hadith* are considered revelations of the Prophet's words rather than the verbatim word of God like the *Qur'an*, they are not required to be learned in Arabic, hence Tarik reciting in Turkish.

THE WEIGHT OF SILENCE

THE FIRST THING YOU SHOULD KNOW IS, I'M NOT THAT GOOD WITH WORDS. The only way I can think of to start this thing is, "If you're reading this, it means I'm dead." But that just sounds so melodramatic. Besides, if Miguel and I do live through this, I'll want to read it again, just to remind myself that I *can* read again. I never knew how much I'd miss that, just seeing letters and translating them into sounds, just plain *using* my senses so effortlessly, without thinking, though it's really so amazing how the mind does it.

Anyway. I'm babbling. If you're reading this, you must be totally confused now. Unless you're me. Hi, me! How am I? Confused yet? I know I am.

Okay, I'm over that fit of the giggles, plus having to explain to Miguel why I was shaking so hard, and then he started shaking so hard—but anyway, let me try to start over. My name is Monali Chen. I'm a physicist, when I'm not being a singer. My friend over there is Miguel Oroxco, who's a Dashing Space Pilot and engineer. He does other things, but only as hobbies, and he doesn't put that much effort into them—except womanizing, which he gave up when we got together, and being Dashing, which he thinks of as part of his job anyway. (I don't get why "dashing" is such a suave and romantic thing to be. It sounds to me like you're always running around out of breath.)

We're the whole crew of the XQ-3, which is a testbed for a proto- type sub-luminal warp generator. The press keep calling it a warp engine, but the press don't listen very well when we tell them we're still decades away from that at least, that we're still testing out just how much we can do with PQM, and we're a long way from actually incorporating that with the other systems that you'd need to make a sustainable warp bubble, and then there are so many other problems to work out, like the visibility issue (ironic, that) and the heat dissipation problem, and I'm babbling again, aren't I? I did warn you.

Okay, me, remember what Mrs. Pfriem always told me in English class: don't make assumptions about what your audience might know — assume they don't know it and explain it to them. I never really understood that, since she was the only person who read my essays and I knew *she'd* read the book and would already know what I was talking about! But I guess here it makes sense.

PQM is programmable quark matter. Just like the smart matter in your walls and clothes and such contains bound electrons that can be arranged to simulate virtual atoms and their chemical and electrical properties, even ones that don't occur in nature, so the bound quarks and gluons in PQM can be organized to simulate virtual exotic particles and forces. These particles' brane tension can be adjusted to produce large positive and negative masses in the right configurations to deform spacetime into exotic shapes such as warp bubbles. (I'm basically quoting the usual press release from memory here. Not my own words. Still, it just sounds so clunky and wrong. It's so much clearer as equations.)

Umm, sorry, where was I? I went to sleep for a while after that last paragraph, I don't know how long. This is such a struggle to write, and obviously I can't go back and review — no, I guess it's not obvious, I haven't explained that yet, have I? God, I wonder if this is even going to be legible. At best it'll take a huge amount of editing. How embarrassing that would be, to be found dead, and have them discover I'd made this slow, laborious effort to record my final thoughts for posterity, only to find they couldn't read it.

You'd think Miguel would be the one doing this. He usually has no trouble expressing himself — well, in most ways. But maybe that's why he doesn't want to try it this way. He'd find it too frustrating. But I'm used to it being hard.

Though I guess the new thing is that I'm trying anyway. Miguel teased me about that, almost from the day we met — how quiet I was. It was his way of flirting with me, trying to draw me out. At first I hoped he'd just tire of it and go away. Not that I didn't like him, but I already had a man back home on Mars.

Though I wasn't really happy with...let's call him "George." Things were rocky, when we were together. "George" was...no, not exactly selfish. It's just that he wasn't *attuned* to my feelings, my needs. Since it's hard for me to put them into words, I needed someone who could just sense them, you know? I needed someone I could have a rapport with, and "George" wasn't it. (Plus, he always called me "Mo." I never liked that.) In a way, things were easier between us now that I was off on Ceres. Which maybe meant being close wasn't right for us.

With Miguel, it was different. Sure, he was brash and arrogant and liked to sow his wild oats...but the reason he was so successful with women wasn't just his looks, it was because he respected them, and really *meant* his flattery, and gave instead of taking. The only problem was that he couldn't settle on just one woman to devote himself to. Some of his lady friends told me they didn't mind sharing, because he never made any false promises about what they could expect. But some of them ended it because they wished he could take all that generosity and focus it on just one woman.

So anyway, I figured Miguel would lose interest in me because I was taken, and because he had plenty of other candidates. But the more we worked together, the more he tried to romance me. I explained that I was committed to "George," but he looked at me and said, "Nali, I don't go where I'm not welcome. If I felt you were happy with him, I wouldn't keep offering you an alternative. The way you look when you talk about him...I see duty, not fulfillment."

But then he backed down and shook his head. "But don't listen to me. I could be reading into it what I want to see." He took my hand and gazed so deep into my eyes. "I can't trust myself to be objective about you, Monali. I have far, far too much of a personal stake in you. So maybe I should trust your judgment and leave you alone—but I don't see how I could bear to do that."

At that moment, I realized this wasn't just his usual infatuation—he was in love with me! And I was falling in love with him too. And the more I reminded myself of my commitment to "George," the more it felt like duty, not fulfillment.

If Miguel had aggressively tried to seduce me, he probably could've. But he didn't try. Maybe he knew he didn't have to. He was just waiting until I was ready. And pretty soon I was. I just didn't know what to do about it. I didn't know how I could tell "George." I didn't know how to tell Miguel, even.

So one day I just let it happen. We were working together in the XQ-3 cockpit, taking string resonance readings and calibrating the controls. I was on the wrong side of him to work a control I needed to keep adjusting...so I just leaned across, pressing my body against him over and over. I could feel him burying his face in my hair, smelling it. Pretty soon he got the message, and we made love right here in this cockpit, without my having to say a word.

Telling "George" was the hard part. I ended up sending him a letter. I know, it sounds awful, and it is, but it would've been worse if I'd had to do it face-to-face and think up the words as I went. Or that was my excuse, anyway. I'm rethinking a lot of things lately.

Hi, I'm back. If I remember right, I was reminiscing about how Miguel and I got together. I hope you don't think that was self-indulgent. I really should be telling you about the test flight that got us into this mess.

Basically, the idea of the XQ-3 is to move a ship by moving the spacetime around it relative to the rest of spacetime — like the warp principle, but without actually reaching effective superluminal speed. We're still a long way from tackling all the practical problems that would bring. This was a much simpler proof-of-concept thing, getting to know how to use PQM to distort spacetime, and analyzing the effects. If nothing else, we could get a nifty reactionless drive out of it.

I actually hadn't felt we were ready for a crewed test flight yet. I wasn't sure we'd completely ruled out the possibility of chaotic brane-resonance feedback. But Miguel was eager to get out there, and I couldn't muster a solid enough argument to sway the team, at least not as much as Miguel could sway them with his confidence and charm and general Dashingness. I mean, everyone knew about the risk, but they decided it was under control. The best I could manage was to get myself invited along to ride herd on the readings.

Miguel wasn't too happy about that. He thought I was being too conservative, that I'd cramp his style or something. I didn't want him to think I wasn't being supportive, so I tried not to make a nuisance of myself. It was a quiet trip. We were the only two human beings for millions of klicks around, and we didn't have much to say to each other.

Wait, I'm confusing you again, aren't I? I was telling you before about how madly in love we were, how happy and perfect everything was. Well, it was, mostly. We'd done the whole moony-eyed, can't stand to be apart, sneak off to the closet every chance we get kind of thing. He'd learned to share my love of show tunes, I'd gotten into his kite-flying hobby, we'd done the long walks holding hands under the artificial sky, had deep heart-to-heart conversations about our innermost feelings....

But that was the problem. I'm not good with words, remember? Talking about my feelings, it's...it's harder than talking about physics, but I don't have any nice, neat equations to use instead. Whatever I try to say, it just doesn't seem right.

With "George," that wasn't such a problem. He wasn't all that open about his feelings either. But Miguel was. It was part of why he was such a hit with women—he could communicate with them about what mattered to them.

And he really opened up to me. In our long nights together, he told me everything, all his deep dark secrets. He told me about the romances that had really mattered to him and what had gone wrong with them. He told me how he'd been trapped in a cave as a little boy and was still somewhat claustrophobic (which was why he'd had the whole top half of the XQ3's cockpit coated with a video membrane, so he could see outside despite the massive PQM cage surrounding it). And he told me other things I won't tell you about because it's not my place. Things he didn't tell other women, things that went a whole lot deeper than what he usually shared with his lady friends.

The problem was, he expected me to do the same. He wanted to know everything about my family, my childhood. He prodded me to talk about "George" and what had gone so wrong there. Most of all, he wanted me to put my feelings for him into words, to tell him what he meant to me, what I loved about him, what role I saw him playing in my life. But I couldn't give him that. It wasn't that I didn't want to. I just couldn't figure out how to communicate what I felt. I tried really hard. I wrestled with my brain for hours at a time, trying to squeeze the right words out of it. I mean, they're all in there, collected from all the English classes I took and all the books I've ever read. I remember most of them, even the screwy ones like "ombudsman" and "gormless" and "viz." which is pronounced "namely." But whenever I try to search for the right words to go with my feelings, they just don't seem to be in there. My friends tell me I explain myself fine, but I know I'm not—that what they hear may make sense to them, but it wasn't really what I meant. Or at best, it's something I had to struggle to find. That's why I'm better with letters than conversations.

But Miguel couldn't accept that. "Maybe you're just not trying hard enough," he'd say. "Monali, I've bared my soul to you, because I thought we were ready for that kind of intimacy. Was I wrong? Is there a reason you're holding back? Don't you trust me enough to share this with me?" I tried to reassure him, but I couldn't put my money, or rather my words, where my mouth was. Or where my heart was, I mean.

I'm afraid I'm making it sound like he was pushing me into this, some kind of emotional bullying. That wasn't it. He did his best to understand, and when I said I couldn't find the words, he nodded and stepped back and gave me time to think of them. But I couldn't think of them, and he still needed to hear them, needed that gesture of trust. And it hurt him that I couldn't. "Maybe you aren't really over 'George' after all," he said one day, not long before the test flight, though of course he didn't say "George." "Maybe you feel I'm not the right man for you."

"No," I assured him. "I love you completely."

But he needed me to say more, and I couldn't. "I believe you believe that, Nali. But I'm not sure if you really *feel* it."

"And...and what do you feel? About...being right for...each other?" (Amazing how well I remember the words, even the pauses. Maybe it's the sensory deprivation.)

He just looked at me. "Maybe I'll decide when you decide."

Soon after that I saw him flirting with other women again. I didn't believe he'd made love to any of them, but it made me afraid. If nothing else, it meant I wasn't enough for him anymore.

I guess that was part of why I felt I had to come along on the test flight. I hoped that being together, as totally alone as any two human beings had ever been, might help somehow. But all it did was concentrate the tension. I had no idea what to say, and Miguel was happy to be quiet right back. Actually, I was feeling afraid that maybe after being so alone with me with so little joy, he'd just feel more compelled to be with other women afterward.

Anyway, he started to get bored with the routine maneuvers we were making. (Routine! We were out past Saturn! The Sun was a tiny speck! Some routine!) He wanted to do something Dashing, probably to take his mind off having me there. So he decided to try some loops and flips and things, tweaking the PQM array to alter the shape of the field. I advised against it. "You're being too cautious again," he said testily. "We have to put this technology through its paces sooner or later. It'll be no use if it isn't robust enough to handle unexpected changes."

"I just don't think we're there yet. There's still too much we don't know."

"And how will we ever know unless we try? Hah? You never get anywhere if you don't take chances, Monali."

"We need more simulations...."

"You've done months of simulations with nothing conclusive. Eventually, you just have to for God's sake *try* something!"

I was starting to realize that we weren't just talking about the experiment anymore. And that pretty much scuttled any logical arguments I could come up with. "Maybe you're right," I finally said. And I meant it. I decided I needed to trust him. I hoped my backing down would get that across to him. But if anything, he looked disappointed that I'd closed off again. Then he just sighed, shook it off, and lost himself in piloting.

Now, I'm not saying he was responsible for the accident. At this point, we don't know what went wrong. We do know there was a coherent feedback anomaly in the brane-resonance patterns. It somehow increased the gravitational coupling constant and sped us up faster than we planned to go. That's actually a good thing. We'd thought the feedback would collapse the field entirely, not intensify it. And the effect seemed stable, continuing to accelerate us toward lightspeed for maybe twenty minutes (with no time dilation, because it's space-warping) while we tried to get it under control. If anything, Miguel stumbled onto something useful, something that could save us years of work.

So what happened then? I don't know. Maybe a micromete got past the deflection contour in the warpfield. I doubt it, since at those effective speeds that would probably have vaporized us. Maybe it was some kind of unanticipated exotic-particle reaction. It may have been something utterly mundane, like an overload in the power systems.

Anyway, all I knew was that the console blew up in our faces.

Okay, this time I remember where I left off last night, because it was one of those dramatic cliffhanger moments that grab you when you read them. How'd it work? Anyway, back to our Exciting Tale:

I think I was unconscious for a while. I can't be sure, since the first thing I was aware of after the explosion was *nothing*. No light, no sound, no touch. I was adrift in a void. For a moment I thought I was dead. I really didn't want the afterlife to be all this nothingness, so I panicked. And I felt the reassuring impact of my flailing legs against the cockpit wall. And then, once I was aware of my body again, I realized I was in a lot of pain. My face felt like the worst sunburn I've ever had times twenty. I remembered the explosion, and I called out to Miguel.

And I couldn't hear myself!

I screamed as loud as I could, but I couldn't hear anything. I was deaf! Of course, the explosion in such tight quarters...and that bloody video membrane of Miguel's, a smooth hemisphere, I was always complaining about how it reflected and amplified every tiny sound... I felt my ears, and they were both bleeding.

And then I realized I couldn't see anything. There should be something, even if the power went out. There were emergency lights, smart-matter panels that stored acoustic energy. The very sound that had deafened me would've given them enough power to glow for weeks. But I couldn't see them. I held my wristcom before my eyes and tapped the light button—nothing. But it felt completely intact, and it unfolded and refolded like it was supposed to. It worked... I just couldn't see it. Or anything else.

I could certainly feel the tears forming, but I fought them since they burned my eyes, and we were in freefall so they'd cling. I tried to force myself to remain calm. But then a horrible thought struck me. I'd screamed for Miguel and he hadn't come to me.

I pushed myself off the wall, spreading my arms, and soon one arm hit him. He jerked in surprise and flailed wildly at it. At least he was alive—but he hadn't heard me calling, hadn't seen me coming. I grabbed at his arms, which were waving around randomly. I realized he had to be as blind and deaf as I was.

Soon he realized it was me, and he flung his arms around me desperately, and I did the same to him. All our tension and arguing were forgotten. We clung to each other like our lives depended on it, needing each other more than ever, since we both knew the stakes. We were alone, off course, astronomical units away from settled space. (Just about all the planets are on the same side of the Sun this year, and we'd decided to do our tests on the empty side as—ha!—a safety precaution.) We had no way of knowing if anyone even knew where we were. And we had no AI onboard to call for help. We didn't even know if the comm system was working, and even if we tried it, we couldn't hear a response.

Miguel was trembling against me. At first I thought he was cold, but it was rhythmic, convulsive, and I realized he was sobbing. It got worse, and I could feel he was beginning to panic. It must have been a claustrophobic attack. A part of me was tempted to panic right along with him, but I knew I had to comfort him, calm him. But how? Holding him wasn't helping. Oh, how I wished I could sing to him! That always soothed him. But he couldn't hear me now!

I tried it anyway, singing as loud as I could into his ear, hoping he still had at least a little hearing. It was one of his favorites: *"Nothing's gonna harm you, /Not while I'm around...."* But it didn't do any good. And it didn't work so well *fortissimo*. Dammit, there had to be some way to get through to him!

I took his hand, tried putting it against my lips as I sang. He started to get the message, paying attention at least, but he still seemed confused. So I took his other hand and tapped out the rhythm in it as I sang: *Tap-tap-tap-tap-tap-tap... tap-tap-tap, tap-tap.* Soon he got the message. His memory filled in the rest. I finished the song with my lips against his. We were both burned, so it hurt, but we didn't care.

We managed to find the first aid kit and carefully rubbed regen gel (either that or strangely soothing toothpaste) on each other's burns. Maybe we should've done it on ourselves, but we needed each other's touch. I counted my blessings, thanking Krishna that neither of us had traditionalist parents. An old-style, unaugmented human might've been killed in the blast, or been burned more severely and died from infections.

I kept "singing" to Miguel, but he couldn't always recognize the tune from the rhythm alone. So it hit me to use his fingers as a treble clef—I tapped his fingertips for Every Good Boy Deserves Favour and the webs between his fingers for FACE. Pretty soon we began developing a shorthand, using song snatches to represent words and ideas. "When Did This Happen?" I finger-sang, meaning *how* did this happen (close enough). "Give Me Time," he replied from the same musical. "Out of Control," "Maybe There's Hope" and "Putting it Together," he went on—I figured he meant he was going to see if he could get any control over the systems. He didn't know as many songs off the top of his head as I did, so his end of the conversation was a bit choppy.

There was nothing for a while, and then he came back and told me "Out of Control," "She Just Wouldn't Listen." I guessed that meant the controls wouldn't respond. "Maybe It's For the Best," I replied. "Where Do We Go From Here?" "Flying Blind." We couldn't read the sensors, had no way of knowing which way the Sun and civilization were. "A Cry in the Dark," "Rescue Me," "Can It Be?" I asked. But even if we could get the comm system working, we had no idea where to point the laser, and the backup radio might not be strong enough to reach, depending on how far out we were. "The Breath of Life," I asked, "How Long Can This Go On?"

At that point, we realized we had to get some control over the systems, even if we couldn't see them. Luckily, Miguel had helped put this thing together, and now it was time to test his claims that he could rebuild it blindfolded. I helped as best I could, and as time went on our song language became more technical. "Greased Lightning" for electricity, "The Warmth of Your Touch" for temperature, "As Time Goes By" for time, "I'm Drawn to You" for gravity. Numbers were easy, just tapped out on the palm. But it was still cumbersome. I realized that if we could use the fingers for the notes, we could use them for letters too. So once we'd managed to get the air cyclers up and felt their gentle breeze, we took some time out to learn a new code. It used the same nine positions as the treble-clef code, fingertips and webs, but three times over for the whole alphabet. One tap on the thumb tip was A, two was B, three was C, then on to the web for DEF, and so on. Not as elegant as proper sign language, I'm sure, but we'd never had occasion to learn any.

Anyway, eventually we figured a few things out. Life support was good, for now. We got power to the controls, but not all the maneuvering jets responded (we could tell that much by feel, whether the capsule moved or not). And the comm system seemed intact, on the inside anyway—we couldn't tell about the exterior laser or antenna array. There was only one way to do that, and to check the unresponsive jet. *Must go out*, Miguel spelled to me.

I tried to protest. How could he manage it without his eyes? He insisted he could do it by feel, but how could he be sure he could feel enough through the gloves, even with their haptic feedback layer? *Scared too*, he said, then finger-sang "There Is No Other Way."

I've never been more afraid in my life than when Miguel went out there. I was alone in the cockpit, who knows for how long, and I had no way of knowing if he was safe, if he'd ever come back in. What if we hadn't fit the suit's seals right, what if he hadn't attached the line securely enough? What if there were some loose component that had shocked him, or what if there were quark-matter fragments floating around out there that could puncture his suit? What if...

What if the man I loved died not knowing whether I was truly committed to him?

I tried to distract myself by singing, letting my mind fill in the sound. But it was hard to stay focused. Too many songs are about loss and fear and uncertainty — the good ones, anyway. I tried to think about what I could say to Miguel to fix things between us, but that just called attention to the possibility of never getting the chance. I tried running through the tensor field equations, trying to figure out what had caused our burst of acceleration, but I had trouble keeping track without a screen or page to look at them on.

Maybe the real reason I couldn't focus on anything else is that I didn't want to stop thinking about Miguel while he was alone out there. It would've felt like a betrayal. He needed my thoughts to be with him, since there was nothing else I could do.

But how long could I wait? When might I decide he'd been out too long? And then what could I do? Go out myself and try to find him? What if I didn't? What if he were floating just meters away but I couldn't see him? What if I went out just before he came back in, and then he found me gone? What if he came out to look for me and something happened to him then? How could I do that to him?

I'd never felt so helpless.

When I finally felt a hand brush against me, I jumped in panic. I guess I'd been floating in mid-cockpit and hadn't felt the lock cycling. Isn't that ironic, that the one thing I wanted the most happened and I was terrified? But we got that worked out soon, and I clutched Miguel and the hell with status reports, I did him right there. We clung together for hours, and I spent a lot of them just tapping out *I lv U* on his fingers over and over.

I guess he was happy to hold off telling me the bad news. He'd fixed the thruster, but there was just a jagged stump where the comm laser and antenna should be. Not only were we blind and deaf, we were mute too. We couldn't call for help.

Maybe there was a chance they could find us, Miguel said. They'd be looking, certainly. And we couldn't have cracked lightspeed — that would've taken an impossible amount of energy with this setup — so we couldn't be more than a couple AUs off course. Maybe someone had seen what direction we'd gone and could narrow the search down.

But we'd already been pretty far out when it started, over ten AUs from Sol. We'd left the chase ships behind long before the acceleration burst. We'd done it with a reactionless drive, so there was no exhaust trail to follow. And we were in a six-meter-wide capsule with a low-albedo hull (and whose dumb idea was that?). There are still meteoroids and comets our size that nobody's discovered yet, after centuries of looking.

And even with the recycler and bioprinter units working, our food supply wouldn't last forever. We couldn't wait around for outside rescue. If there was a way out of this, we'd have to figure it out for ourselves.

So: you're blind and deaf with no AI, stuck in the outer system, and you need to figure out how to get back to civilization. How? Our thrusters worked, the PQM coils were intact and working, but which way did we need to point ourselves? If we fired at random, we'd just make it worse. And the thrusters were too dim to work as signal flares at this distance.

Besides, even if we figured out which way the Sun was, just thrusting inward wouldn't take us inward — it would just put us into a more elliptical orbit that'd soon send us farther out. What you have to do is thrust forward and slow down, falling into a lower orbit. But even if we could figure out which way the Sun was, we still wouldn't know which way we were facing in our orbit, couldn't know whether we were thrusting forward, backward, or sideways.

But we realized that, so long as the PQM drive worked (and it seemed intact as far as we could tell), we could just space-surf in whatever direction we picked until we stopped. And when we stopped, we'd have our current orbital velocity, which would be too slow for that location, so we'd fall further inward. (Come to think of it, we still had our original momentum now but were farther out, so we were probably a bit above escape velocity. We might cross the magnetopause in fifty or sixty years, if we didn't figure something out.)

But which way was the Sun? If we'd been closer in, maybe we could've told by feeling its warmth through the airlock's viewport. But of course if we'd been closer, we wouldn't have been in such a fix. And out here the Sun gave no warmth to speak of.

We decided to expend some thruster fuel on an experiment: turning the radio up full blast, placing our hands on the speaker, and rotating the ship. We hoped maybe the remains of the antenna could pick up the radio noise of the Sun, or of the civilization around it, and that it would be loud enough for us to feel the vibrations. But we could barely feel them, and there were several directions where we picked up variance in the static. One could've been the Sun, one could've been Jupiter, the others could've been anything. Our imaginations, even. Some of them seemed to show up once and then couldn't be found again. And there wasn't any one direction where they concentrated, not that we could be sure of. Heck, who knew if the strongest signal came from where the antenna stump was pointing? Maybe the jagged shape was picking up the strongest off to the side somewhere.

We tried to think of some way to use the PQM itself. Could we set it to simulate particles that would emit some kind of radiation as a signal flare? No—reprogramming it that extensively, to produce nongravitational effects, would require quark-scale adjustments that we didn't have the equipment to make. Could we take advantage of the accident, increase our gravitational constant again and somehow pull ourselves inward? No, we didn't know enough about the accident to recreate that effect, especially if we wanted it independent of the warpfield.

Miguel had the idea that increasing our mass might decrease our orbital velocity by conservation of momentum. But I pointed out that the energy we used to generate the extra mass increased our momentum too, so our velocity wouldn't change. Besides, even if it did, at this distance orbital decay would take decades.

So we set aside the PQM and began looking for more conventional approaches. After a while Miguel thought he had it: If we could just stretch out a long tether with a weight at the end, a few kilometers maybe, then it would gradually align radially with the Sun. The whole thing would orbit with the velocity of its center of mass, so the inner part would be going too slow and fall in while the outer part would be too fast and move outward, pulling the tether taut between them — the same kind of tidal stabilization that orbital habitats use. That would tell us which way the Sun was, he said, since the heavier end (us) would naturally fall inward.

He was so excited, I hated to break it to him that it didn't work that way. It didn't matter which end was heavier, only where they were in their orbits. The one starting farther out would end up farther out. At best it'd only give us a fifty/fifty chance of pointing the right way.

Miguel wasn't convinced. To him, having the heavier mass end up farther out seemed unstable, like a bowling pin standing on its head. I struggled to explain why that intuition only made sense for something standing still or dangling like a pendulum, not for something in freefall with nothing to cause drag (well, except the very tenuous solar wind out here).

Either I wasn't explaining it right or he just didn't want to hear it. He'd convinced himself this was the way to save us — or at least that it would improve our odds to one in two, and that was good enough to chance it. I think the claustrophobia was still affecting him — he was desperate to do something to get out of this. I had to make him see reason.

So I kept at it. I pointed out that, given how slow our orbital velocity was, it'd probably take weeks or months for the tether to align right anyway. And I reminded him that we didn't have nearly enough cabling in the capsule to make such a long tether. There were kilometers of nanotube cabling wrapped around the PQM cage, but even if we could figure out how to uncoil it safely, we'd render the drive useless.

It was those simple realities that finally convinced him. I could tell how much it hurt him to give up this hope, but in the end, he had no choice.

We were both pretty dejected after that. So we decided to knock off for the day and start fresh again after a good night's (?) sleep.

We didn't actually get much sleep. Too nervous. *We should talk,* Miguel spelled into my hand after a while. *In case we don't make it.* (It was more abbreviated and textish than that, but I've spelled it out for you.)

We'll get back, I said. *Talk then. You know it's hard for me. Even harder now.*

I felt him shake with laughter. *You kidding? Look what you did. Invented a whole new way to talk. Got through to me when I really needed it. Talked me out of a dumb idea. Yes, it's harder now — but you did it anyway.*

After that, I was at a loss for words. But not for long. I realized he was right — when I really had to, I'd figured out a way to express myself. If I could do it when our lives were at stake, why couldn't I do it when our relationship was at stake? So I did. Slowly, laboriously, almost as much as writing this account has been, I talked about how I felt. I told him what he meant to me, as much as I could. And where I couldn't, I explained to him why it was different for me, that just because I expressed it in actions rather than words, that didn't mean I felt it any less.

We finger-talked for hours, and somehow the difficulty of it helped us communicate, because we were both "listening" so much more carefully. We figured out a lot of stuff. He realized he'd been unfair to demand I show my feelings as verbally as he did — that it was really just his insecurity, his need for validation. I hadn't known he felt that kind of self-doubt. But together we realized it was part of the reason he'd slept around so much before — because he didn't trust in his ability to earn any one woman's lasting affections. But he really wanted our relationship to last, he told me. In fact, he left me speechless again.

He proposed.

He said he'd been thinking about it, but his self-doubt had made him unsure whether I could really love him for a lifetime. That's why he'd been pushing me for validation. And when I didn't give it to him, he used that as an excuse. On some subconscious level, he'd been looking for an out, so he got the idea that maybe I wanted to go back to "George." He said that was really pathetic, but I told him I understood, and it was okay. Mainly, I was just amazed at what this meant — that *he'd* been the one to have trouble communicating. And that his insistence on my communication problems had just been a way of dodging that.

Well, anyway, we learned a lot about each other that night... day... however long it took. Then we held each other for hours, had pretty good sex (allowing for our clumsiness in freefall), and talked about all the things we'd do when we got married, and what we'd name our kids, and how I'd teach them to sing and Miguel would help them build racing kites....

And then it hit me. Something that had been in the back of my mind since the day before. *The solar wind.* It was very, very faint out here, less than a tenth of a nanopascal of pressure — but that might still be enough, if we had the right kite.

Kite?? Miguel asked, scrawling two question marks in my palm for emphasis. *Where do we get one?*

We already have one, I explained. *Your precious video dome. Not like we need it anymore.* I explained: the video membrane was hair-thin, but it formed a dome nearly five meters across. Very large area, very low mass. The acceleration would still be tiny, but we only needed it to move a few meters. We'd attach it to a spacesuit cable, hook it to the anchor point next to the airlock, and wait. I estimated that, taking the cable's mass into account, it might take from one to four days to move ten meters, depending on the wind pressure. Well, if it started out with the solar wind blowing directly into it, that is. At an angle, it'd take longer. Still, it didn't need to move that much. Periodically we'd go out and feel which way the cable was pointing, and then turn the ship to face the other way. We'd do a few more adjustments like that until our "wind sock" stayed straight out from the airlock, which was in the back of the capsule, so at that point we'd be facing the Sun. Then we'd just turn on the PQM drive for a couple of hours, which would put us back in the inner system and increase our chances of being sighted.

It wasn't a sure thing. Even in the inner system, there was no guarantee we'd be spotted before our supplies ran out. We couldn't completely rule out the possibility of crashing into something. And we couldn't be sure the drive wouldn't malfunction again and plunge us into the Sun or, more likely, clear out the other side of the system. But we'd sure be better off than we were now.

We both cut up our fingers trying to peel that damn membrane off the ceiling. It was pretty flexible, but it liked to snap back to its natural shape, so we both got pinned by it a bunch of times. I was glad I couldn't see us, because we must've looked completely ludicrous. But we finally managed to roll the thing up somehow, punch a few holes near the rim, and tie spacesuit tethers through them. Then we had to fold the rolled-up thing into thirds to get it into the airlock. We could only hope it would spring back to normal again once Miguel pushed it out. Anyway, soon he came back in and told me it was done. Now we had days to wait.

So we went ahead and got married. We argued for a while about which one of us was the captain of the ship, then decided to take turns being captain and marry ourselves twice just to be on the safe side. Plus, that way we get to take a double-long honeymoon when we get back. Though we didn't waste any time getting a headstart on our honey-mooning. I mean, it's not like we had much else to do.

Well, except touch-typing out this log on my wristcom, and hoping I'm hitting the right letters so this will be legible. As I write this, it's been about a day since our third check of the "kite." After our first check, Miguel said the tether felt straight and was pointing at a sharp angle to where it had started, so it seemed to be working, as far as we could tell. So we turned the ship and waited again, and then we found it at an angle again, though less so, so we turned again. And so on. At this point we have no idea if we'll get a good enough fix before our supplies run out, or if the drive will work, or if anyone will find us even if it does. So if you find this and we're dead, know at least that we died as husband and wife, and were happy together at the end.

That is, if you can read this at all.

Afterword

Hi, folks, this is Monali. As I'm sure you heard on the news — or could guess by reading the above — we eventually got a directional fix and fired up the drive. We stopped when we figured we were fairly close to the Belt, and started firing our thrusters as signal flares. Within a couple of days, we got picked up, and they rushed us to the hospital, and right now I'm getting used to my regrown eyes and synthetic eardrums. Which means I got to see the mess I'd typed up and be embarrassed at how scrambly it was. But this magazine bought the rights to our story, and hooked me up with a writer who helped me polish it.

I was amazed they wanted this bunch of scribbles. "I'm no writer," I insisted, telling my collaborator that he'd be better off just interviewing me and writing his own version. But he insisted I'd done a good job. I told him how hard it had been, how much I'd had to struggle to find the right words, how it still felt wrong to me at the end.

So he gave me a quote from Thomas Mann: "A writer is someone for whom writing is more difficult than it is for other people."

I still think he's a shameless flatterer. But I guess you can decide that. Now I'm going to go off on that double honeymoon with my husband. Hopefully, once we get back, they'll have figured out what caused the accident and we can try again.

Though maybe after that I'll try turning this into a musical....

AMONG THE WILD CYBERS OF CYBELE

From the journals of Safira Kimenye,
14/13/004 Anno Cybeleae
(10 November 2250 Solsys Equivalent Date):

DURING TODAY'S FORAGING, THE LOGGERS WERE ATTACKED BY A *fandancer. They must have intruded onto its territory; the vertebrates don't hunt by magnetic fields, so it couldn't have found them appetizing. This was a large species of fandancer, with sharp tusks and a bony club at the end of its tail. It inflicted some damage — mainly on Bunyan, ever the bold and reckless one. Galadriel called a retreat — I picked up the signal on my earphone — but the biped hounded us relentlessly. Perhaps its terror at the alienness of the loggers drove it to such violence.*

So the loggers lured it onto a compass rose. With my more limited senses, I couldn't detect the sedentary arthropod; its chitin camouflage blended perfectly with the grass. I saw them luring the 'dancer toward a particular patch of ground, but I was startled when that patch snapped shut, leaving a bare starburst pattern in the grass and trapping the fandancer inside a nearly solid, spherical cage of segmented limbs.

As we left, I could still hear the 'dancer fighting to break free from the compass rose. I can't help hoping it succeeds. It was only defending its territory — maybe even defending young. And dying slowly of thirst is a nasty way to go. But as I keep reminding myself, it's not my place or anyone else's to referee nature's battles.

Well. I'll be glad when Marc gets here. His enthusiasm always lifted my spirits. And having his support in this difficult cause will make the work easier.

Safira looked just as Marc Dupuis remembered: a tall, elegant woman with regal Sub-Saharan features and a blinding smile. She engulfed him with a warm embrace the likes of which he'd only dreamt of as her graduate assistant. But such fantasies were a decade behind him now—well, four decades, counting the long sleep from Earth to Cybele. He wasn't here to moon over Safira Kimenye, but to do a crucial and very delicate job. He returned the embrace with merely professional courtesy.

"It is *so* good to see a human face again," Safira beamed, "especially a friendly one. I'm so glad you're here."

"Really?" Marc teased gently. "I've kept up with your journal entries on CybeleNet. It sounds like the loggers have made you part of the family. You sure I won't just get in the way?"

"Oh, they're charming companions, all right. But I miss a human voice, the warmth of a friendly touch." She clasped his hands a moment longer, then helped him gather up the supplies that had come with him. They both took great care; it usually took weeks or even months for Safira's diffuse support network to track down the peripatetic researcher, so these supplies would have to last them both. Before leaving the drop site, Safira deposited a data crystal containing her latest journal entries for later pickup. It was an awkward way to transmit data, but of course Safira had disabled her wristcom's transceiver circuits to keep the wrong people from tracking her down.

The trip to the loggers' camp was a convoluted twilight journey through a forest of purple-trimmed bamboo-ferns. On the way, the Kenyan woman and the Moroccan man caught up on the news since they'd last met eight long Cybeline months ago, shortly before Safira's expedition had begun. But glimpses of the forest denizens kept them distracted. Arthropods of countless shapes and sizes swarmed through the forest, their developed lungs and circulatory systems letting them greatly outgrow their Terrestrial analogues. Sparrowasps, scorpionflies and dragonmoths hummed through the air, revelling in a niche undiscovered by the native vertebrates. After all, the tailed vertebrates had only two limbs apiece, adequate for 78-percent gravity, and evolving wings would leave them without a leg to stand on.

Yet the vertebrates were not completely grounded. Some could rear up on strong tails and climb the bamboo-ferns with grasping feet; others could leap into the lateral fern stalks and brachiate with prehensile trunks and tails. One species employed the implausible technique of flipping upward and hanging from the stalks by its legs, making its way blithely upside-down.

Safira frowned at Marc's quiet absorption of this image, which evoked hilarity in most observers. "Are you all right?" she asked. "You were always so eager, so excited by new discoveries. You seem more...subdued now."

Marc remained silent for a moment. "Well...I suppose I've got some things on my mind. Like how you'll convince the loggers they can trust a human other than you. Although," he smirked, "it can't be much harder than what I went through to earn your helpers' trust. They're... understandably protective of your charges. Without your endorsement, I doubt—"

The older woman smiled. "Think nothing of it. And that goes for both issues. I had to win the loggers' trust the hard way—teaching them to accept me and avoid others like me at the same time. But there's a shortcut for you." She unpocketed a small device on a chain and draped it around his neck. "This transmits a copy of their recognition signals. Admittedly, I haven't tested it, but it should ease your acceptance greatly."

"I can see why you haven't mentioned this in your journals," Marc said thoughtfully. "You don't want the hunters getting hold of this."

"No, it's not what I'd particularly prefer to get around their necks." The uncharacteristic anger barely reached her voice, but it burned in her dark eyes. "Never mind," she smiled, shaking it off. "We're almost there!"

They shortly emerged into a clearing dominated by (and presumably resulting from) a large, strikingly regular stockade of bamboo-fern stalks. "That looks like it could keep out an army of arthropods," Marc observed.

"It does. Routinely. The pincer-hounds find the loggers' magnetic fields particularly appetizing. And it's stronger than it looks."

"Right. The coating they secrete." As they drew nearer, Marc could see the crystalline sheen on the stalks. "Remarkable."

"Especially when you consider that the loggers are descended from survey probes, not builders. Their construction skills evolved purely as a defense mechanism."

Suddenly, a disguised hatch in the ground tilted open, and the loggers began to emerge. "They know I'm back," Safira said. "But they're wary of you," she added as the low-slung hexapods pulled up short of the humans.

"Perhaps I should keep my distance for a while," Marc suggested. "There's a tent for me in with the supplies. I could sleep out here tonight."

Safira had gone up to the troop leader and was stroking its gleaming carapace soothingly. "Don't worry," she said, seeming to address both human and logger. "They're already letting you closer than they'd let anyone else."

"Still, I'd rather not press my luck," Marc shrugged. "After all, those cutting arms of theirs are diamond-tipped."

"Don't be silly. For all the evolution they've undergone, their First-Law programming's still in effect. They won't hurt you." She caressed the blocky creatures of crystal and polymer like beloved children.

Safira soon persuaded Marc he would be safer within the compound. It was already too cool for the arthropods to remain active, but some vertebrates hunted by night. So, with delicacy, Safira led Marc and the loggers through a halting introduction built around human approximations of the loggers' submission behaviors. Much of their communication was electromagnetic, but the emitter around Marc's neck took care of that. Besides, the loggers' neural nets adapted quickly to new data. So, far sooner than would have been possible with biological animals, Marc was granted clearance into the sanctum.

The entrance tunnel was cleaner than he'd expected, the loggers having coated it with their plasticrystal secretion for stability. The interior space was broken by a regular grid of sharpened, crystal-coated poles pointing skyward. Its only other distinct feature (aside from Safira's campsite) was a materials dump, presumably supplying the auxons' building projects as well as their self-replication. Along with bamboo-fern stalks, polegrass, and the like, Marc saw stones, animal remains, and some fragments of auxon bodies. He assumed these must be scavenged, since the loggers weren't predatory.

Following his gaze, Safira explained, "We were attacked by a heli-raptor yesterday. Until then, the stockade hadn't been designed to keep out flying creatures. The 'raptors have scared off most of the airborne arthropods hereabouts, and they usually haven't preyed on their own relatives before. This one must've been either newly evolved or newly migrated to the area. It was certainly the biggest I've seen."

"It inflicted casualties?"

"Nothing fatal," Safira replied. "It used a laser weapon—a mutated altimeter beam, I'd guess. Several loggers were injured—especially brave old Bunyan, of course. But they fashioned some polegrass stalks into crude spears. They managed to snarl the 'raptor's left rotor when the spears got caught between the blade and cowling. It went into a spin, but reacted quickly, of course, and managed to adjust its airfoils and limp away. And I soon heard the squeals of a rhinostrich. Not as good a source of replication material as another auxon—but certainly an easier kill," she finished proudly.

Marc surveyed the logger troop. "They seem pretty well-repaired now."

"The females did their job well." The "females" were those members of the self-replicating (or auxonic) cyberspecies who actually possessed the replication and repair equipment. The majority were made without such equipment to save materials. Upon their deaths, the females digested their remains and downloaded their acquired data, learning from their experiences and mistakes, thus redesigning the next generation to be better adapted to their environment.

"Bunyan got a leg cut off," Safira went on, "but he resisted having it replaced. Maybe I'm anthropomorphizing, but I don't think he liked being cheated out of another battle scar."

"*Hm*," Marc pondered. "Would vanity evolve in a basically asexual species, without the need to attract mates?"

"I think evidence of toughness and courage demonstrates his importance to the group, so he gets allocated more resources. Also, it demonstrates that his design is successful, so it might be favored in reproductive selection."

Marc took a moment to absorb the intriguing idea, then studied the defensive palisades. "So these were erected after the attack?" Safira nodded. "You think they'll keep the heliraptors out?"

"The plasticrystal will resist their lasers, so they can't be cut down easily. But 'raptors can hover and maneuver quite well. They should be able to work around this barrier." She smiled. "And then the loggers will develop a more elaborate one. They can't anticipate, but they learn quickly from experience."

Marc found himself alongside the materials dump, contemplating what must be Bunyan's severed leg. "I keep wondering," he mused, "if the auxons might evolve to build themselves out of the same, near-indestructible materials they used to build our cities. I mean, they already have diamite claws and fullerene muscles; why not go the rest of the way?"

"Because they were designed to evolve," Safira said. "And that means they had to be vulnerable. Death is a tool of evolution," she continued philosophically. "It's what weeds out the failures to make room for the successes. If they were indestructible, there'd be no selection mechanism, and they wouldn't adapt." The probes' designers back in Sol System couldn't have anticipated all the conditions of an alien world. So, because they were sending self-replicating probes anyway (a few seed units being more economical than an army of drones), they had given them the ability to evolve, using both random Darwinian mutation and the more Lamarckian ability to modify their offspring based on experience. It was hardly a new idea; cyberengineers had known for centuries that evolving hardware or software often produced more effective design solutions than a conscious creative process (one more nail in the creationists' coffin, though the creationists still denied it).

"We know that," Marc countered, "but the auxons don't. They don't see the bigger picture, they just try to perpetuate themselves. An indestructible species might be an evolutionary cul-de-sac, but it'd be an enduring one."

"But it takes more effort to bond the atoms for such materials. More time and energy to craft them. They built our cities from those materials because we programmed them to. But now they're ruled by pragmatism, not programming. They perpetuate their `genes' just fine without being indestructible. So there's no point in wasting the energy to make themselves stronger than they need to be. Any more than for us to have armor shells or five hearts."

She shook her head. "That's the flaw with the government's propaganda about how the auxons will destroy the whole biosphere. They're not that superior. They obey the same natural laws as any animal." She grimaced. "But no matter how much I stress that in my journals, Berdahl and his people cling to their paranoia, and their mad campaign to exterminate the whole kingdom of auxonic life!"

Marc fell silent; the anger in her bearing demanded a respectful distance. He found her intensity beautiful but forbidding, like a mother tiger's. As much as he admired the sight, he had to turn away to hide his concern. With such passion for her cause, it would hurt her all the more when she learned of his betrayal.

It was early autumn in this hemisphere, and the mornings were chilly. Gamma Leporis was hotter than Sol, but Cybele was its fifth world, receiving only three-fourths the illumination of Earth. The seventeen-hour nights didn't help either. Still, the only place to bathe was a frigid stream, and it had to be done in the morning before the arthropods warmed to the hunt.

The cold water helped distract Marc from Safira's graceful, bronze body. A decade past, he'd have craved the sight and more. But this was supposed to be a professional relationship — even aside from his hidden agenda.

He continued to tell himself he wasn't really betraying her — that he acted out of respect and concern for her. He wanted the same thing Governor Berdahl did: not only to save their adopted planet from ecological catastrophe, but to save their mutual friend Safira from the horrible mistake she was making. Now she was blinded by her scientific fascination, her closeness to the auxons; but in the long term her wisdom would prevail, and she'd understand that they'd acted for the best. He knew, though, that she would resent him for quite a while once his deception became clear. It would only worsen matters if he assumed the role of lover as well as ally.

Marc therefore strove to take their mutual nudity in stride. So it came as a surprise when he realized she was studying his body with open interest. "What?" she smirked when she got around to noticing his questioning expression.

"You...never looked at me that way back on Earth," he answered guardedly.

"My dear, you were barely more than a child then."

"And now?"

She appraised his anatomy frankly. "Grown up nicely." She grinned. "Oh, don't be so surprised. I haven't had a man in nearly a Terran year."

A number of emotions roiled through Marc, none presenting a clear course of action. But then Safira's attention was drawn elsewhere. "Hear that stridulation?" she whispered. "The pincer-hounds are stirring. We'd better get to the stockade." She strode determinedly past him toward shore...but gave him a swat on the rump which clearly said, *Later*.

With the pack of pincer-hounds figuratively barking at the gate, there was nothing to do but wait inside the stockade and talk. Safira seemed happy to continue her bald flirtation, but the loud washboard growling from outside gave Marc a convenient (and truthful) excuse for not being in the mood. He knew he was in no danger, but the sound was like chalk on a blackboard, only in bass.

The loggers seemed relaxed, but alert. Guided by the alpha female, Galadriel, they made well-practiced (or instinctively programmed?) rounds, checking the integrity of their defenses. Amidst it all, though, Marc saw behavior uncannily resembling ritual comfort and bonding. He tried to take it in stride; after all, the loggers had evolved along a social model, and such behaviors were functional within that model. It was simply a logical outgrowth of a stochastic selection process, he told himself, and no reason to feel sympathy for the cybernetic probes. Especially since he knew what was coming.

In fact, it came sooner than he'd expected. Safira and the loggers reacted to the airborne engine sound before he noticed it, launching into a flurry of movement. "Another heliraptor?" he ventured innocently.

"Hunter drones," Safira snarled. "Shit, how did they find us so soon?" She pulled two plasma rifles from a case. Marc's eyes widened at the restricted weapons—and widened further when she tossed him one. "Aim for the optics! Only part they can't shield fully from the EM pulse."

"I, I've never used a gun!"

"Life is learning. Figure it out!"

In moments, the hunter drones came into range and started firing plasma bolts of their own, each mini-fireball making a curt *whoosh* like a whirling torch on fast playback. The pincer-hounds' grating chorus fell into disarray as the arthropods fled.

The loggers used the defense tactics they'd developed against the heliraptor, hurling polegrass spears along with rocks and stalk frag-ments. But the hunter drones had enclosed VTOL jets rather than open rotors; and the remote-controlled, non-evolving weapon platforms lacked the inbuilt vulnerability of the auxons. The drones took the loggers' attack unfazed and blasted back with much deadlier efficacy.

Safira shrieked as the first logger died, the bark of her plasma rifle meshing with her cry in bellicose harmony. Her skill was disturbingly good, and she blasted several drones squarely "between the eyes," scrambling their power systems and felling them. Marc fired toward the drones, trying to appear helpful without actually helping. His novice aim served this purpose well, enabling him to shoot in earnest and even broadside a drone or two without making a kill.

But his attack did have an effect. One of the drones he'd grazed turned and closed on him. Before he realized what was happening, Safira bore him to the ground, her close-cropped hair made a halo by the actinic bolt passing just beyond it—the bolt which had been aimed at his own skull.

He gasped—at the unexpected attack, at the shock of impact with the ground, and at the pressure of Safira's firm, warm body against his. Their eyes met and locked, frozen by the moment.

The kiss was spontaneous, surprising, and deeply unwise under fire. Marc was even more surprised to realize he had initiated it. Safira returned it electrifyingly for two seconds, then rolled off and blasted the drone's brains out.

As Safira executed the remaining attackers with efficient, maternal fury, Marc lay on the ground trying to absorb the event. That drone's operator had tried to kill him! He'd known emotions were running high, but he'd never expected such unbridled hostility from his own side. He knew Governor Berdahl would severely punish that hunter...but it made things a lot less clear-cut to realize there were fanatics on both sides.

In the end, there were two logger fatalities, whom Safira eulogized as Legolas and Daphne. The loss of a female hit her hard, for they were the least expendable, but she grieved equally for them both. There was no ceremony on the loggers' part; the females simply consumed the corpses for material with which to repair the numerous injuries sustained in the attack.

Bunyan had lost a cutter arm this time, and had been blinded in his rear optics. His carapace was partially melted, and his awkward gait suggested neurological damage. It amazed Marc that the battered cyber still functioned. When Safira cuddled the cold, hard mechanism and spoke fondly of his "indomitable spirit," Marc found it hard to retain his skepticism.

But repairs would have to wait, since the hunters knew their location now. The stockade was evacuated with no sentiment and minimal preparation—primarily the swift construction of a litter for Safira and

Marc, to prevent them from leaving a chemical spoor. Safira had taught them this, but they now did it on their own initiative. The litter rode atop the carapaces of several large females. Safira and Marc had to cling tightly; the ride was remarkably smooth, but that was largely cancelled by the swift pace of the journey over variable terrain.

Galadriel took the lead, with Bunyan on her back. As the troop's prime defender, he headed the repair list. Already she was secreting around him the conductive gel that carried her repair nanites, while fine manipulator arms attended to macrorepairs. Other males formed a defense perimeter, alert for attack, while a few straggled behind to erase their trail, even to the extent of performing nanorepairs on broken plants. (Safira hadn't taught them that; it was a naturally evolved defense.)

Although they used the forest's purple foliage for cover, Safira scanned the sky for more hunter drones, weapon at the ready. "I don't know what I'll do once the planetwide satellite network's in place," she sighed at one point. "But we must carry on," she then said, smiling and placing her hand supportively on his. "The cause is too important to abandon, no matter how impossible it may become."

Marc couldn't help but clasp her hand warmly in return. "I don't think it's in your nature to give up, Safira. The more impossible a cause, the harder you work to succeed. That's why there are black rhinos in Africa again."

She returned his gaze with gratitude and warmth. Their hands remained clasped, and soon their lips met. They still had to cling to the litter, so they couldn't do much more; but it was enough to kiss for hours. When the troop finally stopped for the night, Safira and Marc were stripping and devouring each other before the litter touched the ground.

❖

It was just sex, Marc insisted to himself as they lay comfortably intertwined the next morning. Just the natural response of a woman who'd been alone too long and a man who owed her his life. It was a perfectly understandable indulgence, and no strings need attach. He knew he could credibly pull back to a professional remove without complicating things further.

He had to admit, he was having doubts about his cause following the attack and his time with the loggers. But second thoughts were moot; the betrayal had been complete the day they'd met. All he could do now was try to minimize her pain.

Perhaps he could raise doubts in her mind about the auxons she so cherished—remind her of the stakes involved in their existence. Best, though, to start on peripheral questions. "Have you ever wondered," he began, "whether the auxon probes that were sent to other worlds might've undergone the same kind of evolutionary process that these did? Whether other colonists might have to face these same problems?"

Safira maneuvered to meet his eyes, her body sliding quite distractingly across his. "I've thought about it," she said. "But I think there were a few unusual things about Cybele. Aside from the tectonic activity, there was the sheer bad luck of having magnetic-sensitive predators who found the auxons' fields appetizing. That increased the attrition rate and increased the likelihood of non-dormant probes evolving." The probes had been designed to fall dormant once their programmed tasks had been completed—while allowing new replication to balance whatever attrition might occur, so enough probes would be available to survey habitation sites and build cities upon receiving the command from Solsys.

"But other worlds might have their own dangers," Marc countered. "If attrition were excessive, the probes there might also mutate into nondormant forms, the better to avoid danger."

"True."

"And then a situation like Cybele's might be inevitable," he continued. "Without a mission to direct them, the auxons' preset behaviors would only last until they clashed with pure survival—whereupon they'd be weeded out in favor of more successful mutations. Eventually they'd end up with the same kinds of survival-driven behaviors as living animals, filling all the natural ecological niches: herbivores, scavengers...predators. Coming into competition with the native forms," he finished significantly.

Safira didn't pick up on this, perhaps deliberately. "I don't know if they'd evolve predation without first being preyed upon. What are the odds that another world would have magnetic-sensitive predators?"

"Some animals might attack them out of fear or territoriality. They might occasionally kill an attacker, and eventually they'd figure out that animal corpses are rich in the carbon and other elements they need for replication and fuel. Or they might discover it while sampling corpses, evolve into scavengers and then hunters."

"You're right," Safira smiled. "Life always manages to fill whatever niches it can find and follows many paths to do so." She pursed her lips thoughtfully, alluringly. "But would they have the time? If *Arachne* had gotten here seventy years ago as planned, it would've found most of the auxons still dormant and awaiting instructions. The few active mutants would've been recycled and never gotten the chance to evolve further." The original colony ship *Arachne* had mysteriously vanished en route to Gamma Leporis. The vessel's presumed destruction had never been explained, but it hadn't kept the larger, more advanced *Anansi* expedition from making a second, successful try. "Maybe if the planet were farther away, with a longer interval before the colonists arrived... But ten parsecs is pushing the limits of practical colonizing range. There weren't many probes sent farther out than here."

Marc had to concede her point; in fact, he welcomed it. He wouldn't wish Cybele's crises on another planet. Beyond that, though, he found himself simply enjoying the moment. Here were a nude man and woman, wrapped in each other's limbs, casually discussing science and philosophy. It wasn't much like his grad-student fantasies of Safira, but it felt very right to the more mature Marc—an easy, comfortable union of erotic and intellectual rapports. Not a transient passion that would serve its purpose and burn out... more like the basis for a lasting, meaningful relationship.

Inarguably, he had to nip this in the bud. He'd served his purpose; he should leave now, before the other shoe fell on Safira.

But as he gazed into her dark, brilliant eyes, leaving seemed impossible.

❖

Marc had convinced himself there were quite valid reasons to stay with Safira until the endgame. First, there was the concern that another hunter-drone operator might lose control. Marc felt it best to stay for her protection (conveniently forgetting who'd protected whom before). Also, he still hoped he could convince her to see his side, to surrender voluntarily and spare him her betrayed wrath.

On top of that, he was simply fascinated by the wildlife of Cybele, and their journey through the violet-hued wilds provided ample opportunity for observation. Safira focused more on the auxon species, but Marc was fascinated by the native fauna, the rich variations on the themes of arthropod and vertebrate. While only the arthropods flew, many grew vast and sedentary, such as the crabtrees, whose segmented limbs were camouflaged as bamboo-ferns, trapping prey in chitinous "fronds" and digesting them in Venus's-flytrap style.

The vertebrates had their differences too, as dramatized in a battle between a fandancer and an eleroo, champions of two distinct taxonomic orders. The stiff-tailed, scaly eleroo grabbed and struck with twin prehensile proboscises, leaping spryly about its foe, sometimes spinning to use its heavy tail as a truncheon. The downy-furred fandancer lashed forward with its more flexible tail, its fans of extended ribs pivoting back to keep the biped in balance. At times it would switch tactics, balancing with its rearthrust tail while swiping its ribfans forward to slash with their sharpened tips. The pointed arguments of its ribs and tusks finally won out over the blunter attacks of the eleroo's trunks and tail, the scaled megalopod falling victim to blood loss. The 'dancer's bright fans fluttered in triumph (and warning to scavengers) as it tore into its kill.

The greatest discovery, for Safira and Marc alike, was also courtesy of the fandancer genus. The humans were among a grove of honeycomb stalks when they observed a small troupe of 'dancers with unusually large ribfans. The troupe seemed interested in the scorpionflies that rested in the fern-tufts — vivid green arthropods with meter-wide dragonfly wings, froglike eyes, and writhing tails. The scientists watched from the natural blind of the honeycombs as one fandancer hefted a rock in its tail and hurled it at the stalks. The impact startled the scorpionflies into the air, and the 'dancers launched into pursuit. Literally launched — after running up to top speed, they leapt skyward, thrusting down with their broad fans for extra lift. Spreading their fans wide to slow their descent, they managed to take several scorpionflies from the air before drifting back to the ground.

Safira gasped with ecstasy, while Marc was struck dumb with awe. "Do you realize what we just saw?" Safira crowed when she caught her breath, never mind that it spooked the 'dancers. "We've just witnessed the first phase in the evolution of vertebrate flight on Cybele!" She laughed hysterically. "This is...this is history! This is the kind of moment a naturalist lives for. That we would be here to witness such a key moment in evolution...oh, my...." She babbled on in Swahili for a bit, most of it gleeful profanity, and then just gave up talking and assailed him with hugs and kisses.

Marc had tried to return to a professional distance, with limited success due to the decades of seductive skill that Safira happily wielded against his defenses. But that had been casual play compared to this. Equally overwhelmed by the thrill of this discovery, they found themselves overwhelmed by each other as well. The joy of the experience evolved into joy at sharing it, at sharing each other, and they delineated that joy with their bodies until the slow-moving sun sank below the horizon.

"Ohh, Marc," Safira sighed at length, when her body was too tired to continue its more eloquent communication. "The greatest wonder of this day is that you were here to share it with me." And then she spoke sweet disaster. "I love you, Marc. I always saw things to love in you — your brilliance, your passion, your tenderness. But they weren't fully formed — you were too much the child. But now...now, love, you're all I saw you could be, and I can love you unreservedly.

"Oh, Marc, I longed for this. That's why I let you join me out here. It's so hard sometimes, being hunted, being hated. I needed someone who could love me, who could join with me out here, match my passion for the work, and give me the strength to fight on. And I knew you were the one, my golden love," she gasped, stroking his blond hair. Then her lips stopped speaking and began exploring him, probing his every contour with a scientist's attention to detail. Marc sobbed his lifelong love for Safira while silently wishing he'd never been born.

The lake shimmered like satin. Seeking the cause of the odd metallic sparkle, Safira had sampled the water and found it teeming with extraction nanites, the kind used to mine seawater for its dissolute material wealth. "But how?" Marc frowned, gazing over her shoulder at the magnified image. "Those nanites weren't designed to operate independently of the submarine auxons, were they?"

Safira shook her head. "And they certainly weren't made to evolve. They're too small, too simple to have adaptive replication. They could only mutate through random error, so any meaningful evolution would take millennia."

Luckily, the loggers had camped in the adjacent forest, enabling the humans to make their own camp by the lake. It took most of the day to solve the puzzle. The nanites, it turned out, were not autonomous. A breed of submarine auxons descended from aquatic probes inhabited the lake. These cyberfish manufactured the nanites within their bodies and released them into the water, where they gathered dissolved elements and were then reabsorbed by their host species. "Amazing," Safira beamed once this became clear. "It's like termites' symbiosis with their digestive bacteria—only outside the body."

"Somewhat too efficient, though," Marc cautioned. "They've extracted so much material that the lake can barely support organic life."

"But the cyber-ecology's in good balance," Safira replied. "Plenty of piscivorous heliraptors around; and I saw the ripple of a cybarracuda on the prowl."

"But what about the *real* ecology? The lake's natural ecosystem's been all but exterminated. Who knows how many species lived in that lake before? Or how many other species fed on them, or were fertilized by organic remains flowing out of the lake?"

Safira frowned. "Now you sound like the government. Like the hunters."

He took a breath. He had to do this delicately. If she realized too much, she would bolt and make things harder. "When I see things like this, Safi, I wonder if they have a point. I mean, look at all the wonders we've seen the past few days. The unique forms that life—biological life—has taken on this world. How many species have the auxons already competed to extinction?"

"No species lasts forever, Marc. Extinctions are only to be expected when different branches of life come into contact."

"But the auxons' Lamarckian evolution lets them develop faster than organic life can keep up. And they have abilities no biological species has ever possessed. They've got an unfair advantage in the competition. I mean...I just, I can see the government's point. This is such a young biosphere, with so much untapped potential. Those gliding fandancers—with the auxons around, do you really believe they'll have the *chance* to evolve actual flight? Is it...." He pulled back, softened his approach. "Sometimes I do have doubts whether it's really right to, to allow all the extinctions the auxons have caused."

Safira stroked his hair, her face wistful. "Oh, Marc. Remember that time in Sumatra? You were so hurt when that baby orangutan was taken by a tiger... especially knowing that we had bred the tigers as well as the orangs. You felt so responsible. But do you remember what I told you?"

He nodded, and spoke with lowered eyes. "That our responsibility ends with correcting the damage we caused in the past and avoiding further damage."

"That's right. Nature doesn't belong to us, Marc. No, it's not ours to exploit and destroy, but neither is it ours to nursemaid and cultivate like a garden. Nature is larger than we are, and can take care of itself without our arrogant meddling." She wasn't so much lecturing him, Marc realized, as reflexively restating a long-practiced argument.

"But we sent the auxons here. Gave them the ability to evolve."

"And designed them to cause minimal ecological damage. But then they were threatened and had to breed and defend themselves to survive. When our programming conflicted with those imperatives, they discarded it as maladaptive genes are always discarded. When they came into competition with native species, they did so not because of humanity's will, but in spite of it. They've evolved beyond our jurisdiction!" she insisted.

"But we made them strong, durable, adaptable," Marc countered. "Made them able to function without food or water or air. Gave them tools more potent than any tooth or claw. Let them build defenses so strong, nothing natural could break through them. Safira, they're competing because of evolution—but they're *winning* because of us. Doesn't that make us responsible?"

"So what do we do? Consciously exterminate a whole, unique category of life? Correct an accidental evil by committing a deliberate evil? How does that moral equation balance?" She shook her head sadly. "Yes, I regret the loss of the native life. You know I cried as hard as you about that baby orang. But I didn't try to kill the tiger who was simply following her instincts. Whatever responsibility I bore for her existence did *not* entitle me to end it!"

Marc was reluctant to continue, but he felt he must. "But if the whole biosphere is in danger of extermination—"

"Absurd!" she snapped. Then she sighed, breathed deeply and hugged him. "I'm sorry, love, it's not you I'm angry at. But you can't really take that claim seriously. Those fools, they claim to be defending the native life, but they have no faith in it. They've forgotten that life manages to survive in the harshest conditions, no matter what the universe throws at it. Cybele's life will adapt, will find new ways to thrive. There may very well be a mass extinction event, but such things are normal on any world, and a new evolutionary phase always follows. And who can imagine what that next phase might hold for a world where bio-life and cyber-life coexist? Marc, we have no right to narrow the possibilities. And bottom line, no matter the cost," she added with passion, "we have *no* right to deliberately exterminate any species, period!"

Marc sat quietly for a time, not wanting to argue further, not knowing how. "A lot of people out there don't agree," he finally said. "You...we've got most of Cybele's population against us. I don't see how we can win. I just...don't want you to get hurt."

Safira smiled wistfully. "Marc, my dear one. If I pulled back from a just fight because I feared getting hurt, could you love me as you do?"

It was painful to meet her eyes. "No," he breathed with utter sincerity. She would fight on until she was broken, and he adored her for it... but still he knew he had to bring her down.

The lake's heliraptors proved too numerous and hostile for the loggers' comfort, so the troop moved on. Two of Cybele's 32-hour days passed before they came upon the majestic sight of a city-hive. It gleamed like a fairy-castle of diamond and quartz, bearing the clean-lined polish of late-21st-century architecture, but with the comfortable asymmetry of an organic structure. The feral city-builder auxons still followed their innate construction protocols, but had adapted to the survival needs of wild creatures as opposed to the creature comforts of civilized humans.

The town-sized hive bore few doors, and those were auxon-sized openings obscured within the maze of towers, roadways and nonfunctional streetlights. The city was walled with high diamite ramparts, with only hidden tunnels allowing ingress. The once-fashionable colorshift dyes followed no aesthetic rules, functioning merely to regulate temperature or absorb solar energy, changing to follow the sun across the deep indigo sky; yet that simple functionality gave them a special beauty.

And the whole magnificent structure was thoroughly dead. From an adjacent hill, Safira and Marc could see that the hive's streets were littered with city-builder corpses. "EMP bombs," Safira said with soft, tearful fury. "The hives are easy, sitting targets. Fish in a barrel. No-fuss genocide. Cowards!" She allowed herself the skyward shriek, then indulged her rage no further, instead coolly deploying a camera to record the atrocity. The *necessary* atrocity, Marc reminded himself.

The loggers seemed subdued at the mass carnage, but they were a pragmatic lot. They soon found an entrance and filed inside, unhesitant to exploit a ready-made redoubt. The casual way they gathered corpses for consumption made Marc queasy, but Safira narrated it as a hopeful thing, the beginning of the city-builders' rebirth as a large, new generation of loggers. "Imagine what evolutionary variants might arise as loggers absorb builders' experiences and adaptations," she said into her recorder. "A whole new species could soon be born from Galadriel's womb."

This time Marc heard the engines first. *Sorry, Safira,* he thought with sad relief, recognizing aircars as well as drones. *Galadriel will have no more children.*

The loggers were the next to react, their agitation alerting Safira. "Shit, not again!" she snarled, leaping for her pack and the plasma rifles.

"Safira!" Marc protested. "Those aren't just drones. There are people coming."

She looked up and out, recognizing the silhouettes of several police aircars accompanying the small fleet of drones. Her grimace of despair was gone almost before Marc saw it. "Come on. Under cover. Come on!" she called to the loggers, adding gestures and whistles. Galadriel joined her in corralling the troop, and collectively they took cover beneath a large plaza that sloped between two buildings. A place like this, cut off from the sky, defied the standards of this architectural period, but the mutant city planning now served the loggers well. Of course, another EMP bomb would've finished them; but the collateral radiation precluded the bombs' use while Safira and Marc were present.

"Galadriel!" Safira called, gesturing curtly toward one end of the underpass. Shortly, the loggers began erecting a barricade from city-builder corpses and plasticrystal secretions. "This leaves the drones only one way in," Safira explained, "so we can pick them off more easily."

"What's the point?" Marc urged. "They've surrounded the whole hive by now. And *we* can't eat the builders. It's over, Safira. There's no way out."

"We'll find one. Tunnel out if we have to."

Marc shook his head. "They can track us wherever we go."

"What makes you so sure?" she taunted with an encouraging smile.

The smile vanished in an eyeblink when her wristcom spoke to her. "Take his word for it, Dr. Kimenye," it said in a heavy, but not unkind male voice. "You're broadcasting loud and clear."

Safira gaped at the instrument. "Governor Berdahl?"

"A pleasure to speak to you again, Safira," said Anansi's former captain. "I only regret the circumstances. Please surrender quietly, old friend. You can't evade us now, even if you abandon your wristcom. And then you couldn't take your notes, or stir the public to your cause."

"There would be other ways."

"And I'm sure you'd find them. You're as resourceful as they come. But your current resources can't bring you escape," Berdahl said in a tone of simple reason. "They can only delay the inevitable."

"I'm not the only one out here, protecting the auxons," Safira countered defiantly.

"But you're the inspiration. The cause would wither without your strength, your passion. Besides — we infiltrated your support network weeks ago. We've shut them down. Those other few dedicated naturalists scattered around Cybele, protecting other auxons — soon they'll have no choice but to come in from the cold."

A pause. "I don't believe you."

"Then how do you suppose we're talking now? How else could we have gotten a hard virus into your wristcom to reactivate its transceiver?"

"Impossible. The supplies are scanned for nanites." Yet Safira had already begun tapping commands into her wristcom before she spoke.

"Nanites, yes. But you've shown us that the lines can be blurred — that machines can behave like living things. We simply turned that around. We engineered an organic `hard virus.' Actually, more of a bacterium — a native protozoan to which we gave an affinity for certain trace elements in certain ratios, elements such as those you'd find in a wristcom's circuitry; and to feed on those elements and lay down waste products along certain specific paths...like those that, for instance, would re-connect severed transceiver circuits."

"Richard, that's a rather implausible story," she scoffed, still tapping out commands. Marc suspected this was more than denial, was perhaps some sort of delaying tactic. Her next words, though, left no more room for that thought. "The only person on Cybele with the necessary expertise for that is right here by my side — *on* my side. Isn't that right, Marc?"

His silence was confession enough, even without the guilt he knew he must be radiating. Finally the silence grew too long, and he had to look up. Her gaze seared him.

He struggled to think of something to say. He'd been too afraid of this moment to plan for it. "You, you have to understand, Safira. I didn't do this to hurt you. I admire and respect and... and truly love you.

"Which is why it hurt me so much to see you out here helping to perpetuate the crime against nature our forebears committed. To see you blinded to the devastation, and to our own culpability for it."

She merely looked at him stonily. "Yes," Marc continued, "I've seen how remarkable the auxons are. But they're just *too* strong, too capable for organic life to compete with. They're killing Cybele, and I can't stand by and watch that happen.

"The thought of betraying you to do it...Safi, it devastated me. But... you yourself taught me that you have to do what has to be done, no matter how hard or painful. I... I had to remain true to what I believed in."

No reply. No fury, no tears. She was a sculpture of icy dignity. "Safira, I never expected that...that we'd fall in love. I tried not to let it happen, I *knew* it'd hurt you so much worse. But... but then it happened anyway. And I just couldn't tell you, I didn't know how. I...." He floundered. At least if she'd railed and screamed, he could've stood up to it, justified himself with righteous anger. But she remained silent, so that the more he strove to explain, the clearer it became that he was really trying to convince himself. She was so bitter that she gave him nothing, not the dignity of self-defense, not even the right to see her pain.

"I had to do this," he finished weakly. "It was bigger than you or me. I'm sorry, but it had to be done."

The long silence that followed was finally broken by Berdahl's voice. "Safira... don't be too hard on Marc. Nobody here feels good about what's happened, the way colleagues and friends have been pitted against each other.

"But we don't blame you for that, Safira. Your fascination with the auxons is perfectly understandable. They are an amazing phenomenon, and it would be a shame if they were destroyed completely. Rest assured, some specimens of each species *will* be preserved, relocated to Attis, where they can—"

"Where they may not survive," she said flatly. "They've spent over a century adapting to this world, a living world. Uproot them to such a barren planet and they might not be able to adapt. Many of them, maybe most, would indeed go extinct."

"I thought you had more faith in their adaptability."

"Even cybernetic evolution has its limits. And even if they did survive, it's still wrong," she insisted. "If it's wrong to kill a hundred percent of a species, then how can it be right to kill ninety-nine percent of them? Or ninety? Or fifty? Or even one animal that doesn't threaten you and you don't need to eat? Where can you draw the line, Governor?"

"The line was crossed the moment the first Cybeline species was driven to extinction by our creations," Berdahl responded with conviction.

"We designed them *not* to harm native life. They evolved away from that on their own."

"Conveniently letting us wash our hands of all responsibility? No, Safira. However they behave, auxons are human technology. This is our mess and we have to clean it up."

"*Not this way.* You cannot be allowed to sentence whole species to death." She smiled faintly at something on her wristcom display.

"As we see it, Safira, that's what you're doing. And you can't be allowed to continue. I'm—" Suddenly he broke off. Marc heard another voice speaking urgently in the background. "Safira, what have you done?"

"You reactivated my transceiver, I used it. The past few minutes have been beamed out all over CybeleNet." Somehow, the discovery that Marc's betrayal had been exposed to all of Cybele brought him no more shame than he already felt. "As your monitors will have read by now, my supporters are coming. You've arrested my volunteers, but the people who believe in what we're doing are still out there. They will no longer stand by while you commit these crimes."

"That's it," Berdahl said angrily, "move in now!"

"Not advisable, Governor! I'm armed!"

"I'm not sending in drones, Doctor, but live people. We can stun you and take out the loggers without ever getting in a stun pistol's range."

"How about a plasma rifle?"

A moment of shock. "You wouldn't kill humans to save the auxons!"

"I will do what I must to stop a horrible crime!" she said with sorrow.

"And the people who are coming to stand with you? Will they be armed too? Are your convictions so unshakable that you'd allow this to escalate into open warfare? My God, there are only three hundred adult humans on this planet! The whole settlement could be at risk!"

"Don't you think I realize that?! Do you think I'd do this, any of this, if I had a choice? Just *turn around,* Richard. Don't force this on me."

"Every day the auxons live kills another species. We *will* not do to Cybele what we did to Earth!"

"Put it down, Safira."

Marc's voice lacked the conviction appropriate to the threat... but the stungun in his grip compensated. Safira whirled on him, her eyes lit with fury, and for a moment he feared her hatred would translate into plasma flame. "It's over," he urged when the moment passed. "You can't win."

"Neither can you," she hissed. "Can you be sure I won't convulse and fire if you stun me? Can you be sure the loggers won't avenge a fallen troopmate?"

"As long as you're safe...as long as you're stopped from this madness... I'll risk it."

"The madness is yours! I'm defending innocents against murderers. I can't shirk that duty." Her eyes gleamed with something other than rage. "Even now, Marc, even with all the hate I have for you... the thought of killing you shreds me inside. But I no longer have any choices."

She laughed bitterly. "I suppose this is why we shouldn't take sides in nature. There's no right or wrong out here; there's just *need.* When two animals, two species fight to the death, they're both driven by the same needs, the same forces. Morality and choice don't come into it—only blind necessity."

She laughed, though it was half a sob. "The hell of it is, I *know* you can't back down any more than I can. We're both fighting for the same causes, just interpreted differently. We're both doing what we have to do...and so we have no damned choice at all."

Their guns and eyes remained fixed, unwavering, upon each other. The moment stretched like steel wire toward its breaking point. But then

Marc shook his head, lowered his weapon. "No," he breathed. "No, Safira. We're reasoning beings, not slaves to instinct. Even when the circumstances go beyond our control, we still *choose* how we react to them. Saying we're prisoners of the situation is just a cop-out.

"If this turns bloody, it will be our choice, our fault. It's not inevitable. We can all just back down. Go home. Talk this over, find another way."

"There is no other way," came Berdahl's voice. "Species are dying too fast."

"We have to leave nature to itself!" came Safira's words on his heels.

"You're right—you're *both* right in what you're fighting for. But you're fighting too hard. Too inflexibly. Life survives by adapting! By making compromises with its environment! We have to compromise too—have to bend before we break."

"What do you propose?" Safira was businesslike, suspicious.

"Um...give me a moment." He thought faster than ever before. "Okay. Extinctions happen, all right? They're part of nature, the result of competition, of changing conditions. So maintaining a perfect status quo, keeping the roster of species unchanged, isn't a realistic objective.

"The main concern here is that the whole biosphere may be endangered. Safira, you're probably right that some life would remain untroubled by the auxons, but there might be nothing left but microbes. And the nanites might take care of those eventually.

"Anyway, the point is: instead of erasing the auxons from the biosphere, let's just make sure they don't wipe it out. Let's allow them to live, to compete. If they should compete another species to extinction, *c'est la guerre.* We only intervene if a whole ecosystem is threatened with collapse. That way the auxons and Cybelines can both live."

"It won't work!" Berdahl countered, but with honest regret. "The auxons are too adaptable, too capable, their defenses too strong. They've won *every* competition with the native life. The fix is in, Marc."

"So we even the odds. This is where you have to compromise, Safira. To save the auxons' lives, you bend some on their untouchability. We used a hard virus on your wristcom, we can use it on them. Reprogram their instincts, restrict their behaviors. Not enough to make them our robots again...but enough to limit the destruction they can cause. Enough to diminish their performance, weaken their defenses. Maybe even cut out their Lamarckian adaptation so both sides are playing by Darwin's rules."

Safira was thoughtful, but far from pleased. "But do we have the right?"

"Why not? We're part of nature too. That means we can't pretend it belongs to us — but it also means we have as much right as any species to have an effect on our environment."

"But only where our own survival is concerned."

"There's more to us than survival, Safira! We have the power of choice. The effect we have on other species isn't a random matter, it's something we *decide*. Something we're *responsible* for. So if we take responsibility for the world and the species around us, it's not so wrong. We just have to be responsible *enough* to interfere only when we have to, and otherwise trust nature to manage itself."

Again, the silence stretched, but without the earlier tension. "Not an easy balance to maintain," the governor opined. "But worth a try, isn't it, Safira?"

Long moments of thought. "I still don't like it."

"Nobody will," Berdahl said. "It means letting native species die out *and* restricting the auxons' right to live according to their nature. It stinks coming and going. But would you rather start shooting?"

She gave way without weakening. "Promise there will be no more exterminations. Melt down the hunter drones. Release my colleagues and work with them to implement the plan. I will remain out here with my charges until I know they're safe."

"Agreed. I'm calling the retreat even now." A sad smile underlay his next words. "I hope it's not too long before I can have you over for dinner again. I've missed our talks. Good luck, Safira."

And then Safira and Marc were alone with the loggers once more. But Marc realized he was more alone than any of them. "Safira...."

"Thank you," she said simply, distantly. "You've prevented a tragedy. Cybele owes you a debt. Now go the hell away."

He took a breath — then let his lungs keep it. He had no more defense. "You did what you had to," she continued, too matter-of-factly to be absolving. "No matter the cost. I taught you that. You learned it well. And when the time came, you unlearned it before it ruined us all. You backed down and found a compromise Cybele can live with.

"But you're too good at compromise, Marc. You couldn't choose between your feelings for me and your mission to betray me, so you tried to have both. You dodged the hard choice — and now who has to pay for it?"

"Both of us, Safira," Marc said simply. "Believe me."

"Maybe. But we both have only you to blame. You'll have to live with yourself—but fortunately I won't. I can't speak to the future, Marc...but for now, you no longer exist in my life."

Head lowered in total agreement, Marc slowly rose and strode toward the sunlight. He gave her one last glance. "I guess we all do what we have to do."

She never acknowledged him. She was alone with the loggers now.

ABOUT THE AUTHOR

CHRISTOPHER L. BENNETT IS A LIFELONG RESIDENT OF CINCINNATI, OHIO, with a B.S. in Physics and a B.A. in History from the University of Cincinnati. A fan of science and science fiction since age five, he has spent the past two decades selling original short fiction to magazines such as *Analog Science Fiction and Fact* and *BuzzyMag*. For the past dozen years, he has been one of Pocket Books' most prolific and popular authors of Star Trek tie-in fiction, including the epic Next Generation prequel *The Buried Age*, the *Star Trek: Department of Temporal Investigations* series, and the *Star Trek: Enterprise – Rise of the Federation* series. His original novel *Only Superhuman*, perhaps the first hard science fiction superhero novel, was voted Library Journal's SF/Fantasy Debut of the Month for October 2012. His short story collections *Hub Space: Tales from the Greater Galaxy* and *Crimes of the Hub* are available in e-book and print formats from Mystique Press.

Christopher's homepage, fiction annotations, and blog can be found at christopherlbennett.wordpress.com, and his Facebook author page is at www.facebook.com/ChristopherLBennettAuthor.

COLONY SUPPORTERS

A. Parsons
Allyn Gibson
Amy Laurens
Andrew Corvin
Andrew Glazier
Andrew Timson
Andy Hunter
Anonymous
Ashli Tingle
Barb and Carl Kesner
beardedzilla
Bradij
Brenda Cooper
Brendan Lonehawk
Brian D Lambert
Brian Griffin
C. Frost
C.A. Rowland
Caleb Monroe
Carol Gyzander
Carol Jones
Carol Mammano
Charname
Chelsea Provencher
Cheri Kannarr
Chris Matthews
Christopher D. Abbott
Christopher J. Burke
Christopher J. Ford
Christopher Thompson
Chuck Wilson
Cody Steinman
Craig "Stevo" Stephenson

Dale A. Russell
Daniel Lin
Danielle Ackley-McPhail
Danny Chamberlin
David Holden
Dawfydd Kelly
Diánna Martin
Dominic
Donald J. Bingle
Dr Douglas Vaughan
Dr. Karen
Eli Berg-Maas
Eli Mellen
Emily Weed Baisch
Eron Wyngarde
Evan Ladouceur
Frankie B
Gary Vandegrift
Gavin
GraceAnne DeCandido
Håkon Gaut
Hiram G Wells
Howard J. Bampton
Ian Harvey
Idran
Isaac 'Will It Work' Dansicker
J Paulus
J. B. Burbidge
Jakub Narębski
James Flux
James Goetsch
Jaq Greenspon
Jeff Metzner

Jeff Singer
Jennifer L. Pierce
Jeremy Bottroff
Johanna Rothman
John Green
John Idlor
Joseph Charpak
Josh Vidmar
Josh Ward
Judith Waidlich
Keith R.A. DeCandido
Keith West, Future Potentate of the Solar System
Kelly Pierce
Kerry aka Trouble
Kierin Fox
Kyle Franklin
Lark Cunningham
Larry
Leon W. Fairley
Lewis Phillips
Lisa Hawkridge
Lisa Kruse
Lorraine J. Anderson
MaGnUs
Malcolm Eckel
Margaret M. St. John
Maria T
Mark Beaulieu
Mary Catelynn Cunningham
mdtommyd
me@edmondkoo.com
Michael Brooker
Michael Doyle
Mike M.
Ms. Dyane Stillman
Nathan Turner
Norman Jaffe
Pam DeLuca
Patrick Foster

Paul van Oven
Peter D Engebos
Phillip Thorne
PJ Kimbell
Pulse Publishing
Ralph M.Seibel
Richard P Clark
Richard Todd
RKBookman
Robert C Flipse
Robert Claney
Robert M. Sutton
Samara N. Lipman
Scott Crick
Scott DeRuby
Scott Mantooth
Scott Schaper
Serge Broom
Shane "Asharon" Sylvia
Sharon Abdel-Malek
Shervyn
Sheryl R. Hayes
Stacy Butcher
Stephanie Souders
Stephen Ballentine
Stephen Lesnik
Steven Callen
Stoney
The Amazing Maurice
The Creative Fund
Thierry Millié
Tim DuBois
Tom B.
ToniAnn Marini
Tony Hernandez
V Hartman DiSanto
Vince Kindfuller
Wayne Garmil
William C. Tracy
Zeb Berryman